PENGUIN CLASSICS

FYODOR MIKHAILOVICH DOSTOYEVSKY was born in Moscow in 1821, the second of a physician's seven children. His mother died in 1837 and his father was murdered a little over two years later. When he left his private boarding school in Moscow he studied from 1838 to 1843 at the Military Engineering College in St Petersburg, graduating with officer's rank. His first story to be published, 'Poor Folk' (1846), had a great success. In 1849 he was arrested and sentenced to death for participating in the 'Petrashevsky circle'; he was reprieved at the last moment but sentenced to penal servitude, and until 1854 he lived in a convict prison at Omsk, Siberia. Out of this experience he wrote *Memoirs from the House of the Dead* (1861). In 1861 he began the review *Vremya* with his brother; in 1862 and 1863 he went abroad where he strengthened his anti-European outlook, met Mlle Suslova who was the model for many of his heroines, and gave way to his passion for gambling. During the following years he fell deeply into debt. In 1867 he married Anna Grigoryevna Snitkina (his second wife) and she helped to rescue him from his financial morass. They lived abroad for four years, then in 1873 he was invited to edit *Grazhdanin*, to which he contributed his *Author's Diary*. From 1876 the latter was issued separately and had a great circulation. In 1880 he delivered his famous address at the unveiling of Pushkin's memorial in Moscow; he died six months later in 1881. Most of his important works were written after 1864: *Notes from the Underground* (1864), *Crime and Punishment* (1865–6), *The Gambler* (1866), *The Idiot* (1869), *The Devils* (1871), and *The Brothers Karamazov* (1880).

•

DAVID MAGARSHACK was born in Riga, Russia, and educated at a Russian secondary school. He came to England in 1920 and was naturalized in 1931. After graduating in English literature and language at University College, London, he worked in Fleet Street and published a number of novels. For the Penguin Classics he translated Dostoyevsky's *Crime and Punishment*, *The Idiot*, *The Devils*, and *The Brothers Karamazov*; *Dead Souls* by Gogol; *Oblomov* by Goncharov; and *Lady with Lapdog and Other Tales* by Chekhov. He also wrote biographies of Chekhov, Dostoyevsky, Gogol, Pushkin, Turgenev and Stanislavsky; and he is the author of *Chekhov the Dramatist*, a critical study of Chekhov's plays, and a study of Stanislavsky's system of acting. His last books to be published before his death were *The Real Chekhov* and a translation of Chekhov's *Four Plays*.

THE IDIOT

FYODOR
DOSTOYEVSKY

TRANSLATED
WITH AN INTRODUCTION BY
DAVID MAGARSHACK

PENGUIN BOOKS

PENGUIN BOOKS

Published by the Penguin Group
Penguin Books Ltd, 27 Wrights Lane, London W8 5TZ, England
Penguin Books USA Inc., 375 Hudson Street, New York, New York 10014, USA
Penguin Books Australia Ltd, Ringwood, Victoria, Australia
Penguin Books Canada Ltd, 10 Alcorn Avenue, Toronto, Ontario, Canada M4V 3B2
Penguin Books (NZ) Ltd, 182–190 Wairau Road, Auckland 10, New Zealand

Penguin Books Ltd, Registered Offices: Harmondsworth, Middlesex, England

This translation first published 1955
29 30

Printed in England by Clays Ltd, St Ives plc
Filmset in Monophoto Ehrhardt

List of Contents

Translator's Introduction

The Idiot *was the first of Dostoyevsky's masterpieces to be written abroad. Dostoyevsky left Russia to escape from his creditors, who threatened to have him imprisoned for debt, in April 1867, a month after his second marriage to his young stenographer, Anna Snitkin, and he did not return till 8 July 1871. He began working on the first draft of the novel in the autumn of 1867 and he finished it in January 1869. During that period he lived for a short time in Berlin, for two months in Dresden, for six weeks in Baden-Baden (where he met and quarrelled with Turgenev), for eight months, from September 1867 to June 1868, in Geneva, for three months, from June to September, in Vevey, for three months in Milan, and for seven months, from the end of November to July 1869, in Florence.*

It was while on his way to Geneva that he saw Hans Holbein's painting of Christ taken from the cross at the Basel museum. The picture, which he describes in The Idiot, *made a tremendous impression on him. 'He stood for twenty minutes before the picture without moving,' his wife recalls in her reminiscences. 'On his agitated face there was the frightened expression I often noticed on it during the first moments of his epileptic fits. He had no fit at the time, but he could never forget the sensation he had experienced in the Basel museum in 1867: the figure of Christ taken from the cross, whose body already showed signs of decomposition, haunted him like a horrible nightmare. In his notes to* The Idiot *and in the novel itself he returns again and again to this theme.'*

Dostoyevsky's position after his flight from Russia was a desperate one. He had borrowed 3,000 roubles from Mikhail Katkov, editor of The Russian Herald, *as an advance on his projected novel, and lost the money at the roulette tables. He borrowed another 1,000 roubles and lost them, too, and had to write desperate letters to his few remaining friends in Russia begging them to help him out with small loans. His passion for gambling did not leave him even when he had settled in Switzerland and when he was expecting the birth of his first child. In November 1867 he went to Saxon-les Bains, where he again lost all he had at the roulette tables. 'Now,' he wrote to his wife from Saxon-les-Bains, 'the novel, the novel alone can save us, and if only you knew how much I rely on it! Be* sure that I shall achieve my aim and be worthy of your respect. Never, never shall I gamble again! The same thing happened to me in 1865. I could not have been in a more desperate position than I was then and yet my work saved me. I shall start on my work with love and hope, and you will see how different things will be two years hence.'

But it was not only his financial position that was so desperate. His illness, too, was wearing him down. His epileptic fits occurred at short intervals all through this period. 'As soon as I arrived in Geneva,' he wrote to the poet Apollon Maykov, 'my fits began. And what fits! Every ten days a fit, and it took me five days to recover from it. ... I ought to sit down to work in earnest,' he wrote to the same correspondent in another letter, 'and yet my fits incapacitate me completely, and after every attack I cannot collect my thoughts for four days. ... What's going to happen to us, I don't know. And yet the novel is my only salvation. There is no other way; it is a *sine qua non*. And how can it be good when all my faculties are utterly shattered by my illness? I have still my imagination, and it isn't a bad one at that; I tested it on my novel the other day. But my memory seems to have gone!' His fits kept recurring even after he had left Switzerland for Italy. And it was not only his memory that suffered after each attack; he was also overwhelmed by 'a feeling of terrible guilt' just as though he had committed 'some dreadful crime'. But his feeling before the onset of the fit (as he described it in *The Idiot*) seemed to compensate him for its terrible aftermath. 'For a few moments before the fit,' he wrote to the critic Nikolai Strakhov, 'I experience a feeling of happiness such as it is quite impossible to imagine in a normal state and which other people have no idea of. I feel entirely in harmony with myself and the whole world, and this feeling is so strong and so delightful that for a few seconds of such bliss one would gladly give up ten years of one's life, if not one's whole life.'

His epileptic fits became less frequent with the improvement in the weather but, unfortunately, the weather in Geneva that autumn and winter was particularly bad. Nor did Dostoyevsky take to the Swiss. He found them 'dishonest, vile, incredibly stupid, and intellectually backward'. He had left Russia a fugitive and almost an outcast 'with death in his heart', as he confided to Maykov. He had renounced his liberal ideas and was regarded as an apostate by all his former friends, while his new conservative allies were still suspicious of him and the authorities still regarded him as a dangerous person and censored his private correspondence. 'How can a patriot who has cleared himself and has declared his allegiance to them to the point of betraying his former convictions, a man who worships the Emperor – how can such a man,' he wrote to

Maykov from Vevey on 2 August 1868, 'bear being suspected of relations with some wretched Poles or with The Bell?* *How do they expect me to serve them? They have missed hundreds of guilty men in Russia, but they still suspect Dostoyevsky!' His 'betrayal' of his former political convictions was quite naturally accompanied by his loss of all faith in 'the moral influence of Europe', and it is no wonder that, driven to desperation by poverty and illness, everything he saw abroad exasperated and depressed him. Then he suffered another cruel blow: his first child, his baby daughter Sophia, died of pneumonia in May 1868. 'She was beginning to know me, to love me, and to smile every time I came near her,' he wrote to Maykov from Geneva. 'When I sang songs to her in my ridiculous voice, she loved to listen to them. She did not cry or pucker up her face when I kissed her; she stopped crying when I went up to her. And now as a consolation they tell me that I am going to have more children. And where is Sophia? Where is that little personality for whom I honestly declare I should have accepted a martyr's death to bring her back to life? ...'*

Harassed by financial worries, his nerves shattered by illness and by grief, it is no wonder Dostoyevsky found his work on The Idiot *almost beyond his strength. 'After all this,' he complained to Maykov, 'they demand from me a work of pure art and poetry, without strain, without tearing passions, and point to Turgenev and Goncharov. Let them remember under what conditions I do my work. ...'*

On the other hand, it is no less true that Dostoyevsky's method of writing seemed to demand a condition of continuous mental strain, a condition of constant over-excitement and tearing rage. Unlike Turgenev, who always took character for his point of departure and who never sat down to write any of his novels before he had worked out a detailed plan of its development, Dostoyevksy first began with the main idea of his novel and never had a carefully-worked-out plan of it or its characters. The Idiot *can serve as an excellent illustration of this painful method of composing a creative work. At the very beginning of his work on the novel, Dostoyevsky wrote to Maykov: 'For a long time I have been tormented by an idea, but I was afraid to make a novel of it because it was such a very difficult one and I was not ready for it, though it is a tempting one and I like it very much. The idea is the representation of a perfect man. Nothing in my opinion can be more difficult, especially nowadays. ... I caught fleeting glimpses of this idea before, but that is not enough. It is only my desperate condition that forced me to take up this immature idea: perhaps it will develop under my pen. This is unpardonable.'*

During his work on the first draft of The Idiot, *Dostoyevsky prepared*

* *The revolutionary periodical published by Alexander Herzen in London.*

eight different versions, in some of which the 'idiot' belonged to a different family and became involved in all sorts of melodramatic adventures before he achieved 'perfection'. In the end, having already written the first part of the novel (which originally was to be in eight parts), he scrapped it and began writing quite a different novel. 'And now,' he wrote on 13 January 1868, to his niece, Sofia Ivanov, to whom he subsequently dedicated the novel, 'just before I was going to send off the novel to Moscow, I decided to scrap it because I did not like it any longer (and if I did not like it any longer, I could not possibly write it well). ... Then about three weeks ago (on 18 December N.S.), I began writing a new novel and worked on it day and night. I wrote the first part in 23 days and have just sent it off. The second part, which I am sitting down to write to-day, I shall finish in a month (I have worked like this all my life).'

To Maykov he wrote at the same time: 'I spent the whole summer and autumn trying to put together various ideas (some of them highly diverting ones), but a certain experience made me feel in good time the falseness, the difficulty, or the immaturity of some idea. At last I chose one of them and sat down to work. I wrote a lot, but on 4 December I scrapped it all. I assure you it would have turned out to be a mediocre novel and I got sick and tired of it just because it was mediocre and not positively good. I did not want that. Well, what else could I have done?'

Dostoyevsky had undertaken to have the first part of his novel ready for publication in the December issue of The Russian Herald, *and as he had been getting more and more advances from Katkov all the time, he felt that he had to keep to the deadline. He carried out his undertaking by finishing most of the first part in three weeks and, thanks to the difference of about a fortnight between the Old and the New Styles, he just made it. It was published in the January number of* The Russian Herald.

What, then, was the genesis of the novel? Fortunately, Dostoyevsky's notes have been preserved, and one can thus obtain a good idea of the first eight original versions of the novel and the main themes and characters that eventually evolved from them. It becomes clear from these versions that Dostoyevsky was at first trying to present the 'perfect man' in the process of evolution and not, as in the final version, as the embodiment of the Christian ideal of the 'perfect man'. He had already decided on the title of the novel, but at first the problem whether to make his hero a 'real' idiot, that is to say, a man who has suffered and is again liable to suffer from complete 'idiocy' or lunacy, or one who merely is maliciously declared to be an idiot, seemed at first to have seriously hampered the development of the plot.

The first version deals with three different families: the chief family, consisting of a bankrupt landowner, his wife, his two sons, the first de-

scribed as 'Handsome' and the second as an 'idiot', his daughter Masha, and his adopted daughter Mignon; then there was the family of the landowner's brother (a rich man), referred to as 'uncle', and his son; and, finally, the family of Masha's fiancé, an army officer, including his father, mother, and sister (an old maid), and his cousin, described as the 'Heroine', who was engaged to a senator. Here is the synopsis of this first version of the novel as it appears from Dostoyevsky's notes:

'The idiot – got his reputation as an idiot from his mother who hates him – epilepsy and nervous attacks – falls in love with the cousin of his sister's fiancé – twenty-four – she flirts with him – drives him to distraction – on one of these occasions rapes Mignon – sets fire to the house – burns a finger at Heroine's behest. The idiot has powerful passions, a burning need for love, excessive pride, wishes to master and conquer himself out of pride. Finds delight in self-abasement. People who don't know him laugh at him, but those who know him begin to fear him. He has good handwriting – spends three months at an office. His whole idiocy is the invention of his mother, so that when his uncle made inquiries about it, they all began to wonder whether he was an idiot or not and to their amazement could not understand where the notion had arisen from and how it had become generally accepted. ... Mignon [the first sketch of Nastasya Filippovna] is the daughter of a landowner – she attempts to hang herself but is cut down in time – she kisses the hands and feet of the Heroine – her feet in order to hate her more intensely – hot-tempered and envious – kill her and she won't ask you for forgiveness, but trembles like a coward (nervous) – she would strangle herself rather than beg for bread and would refuse to accept it even if it were offered her – naïve in her desires – would like to revenge herself on everyone, be smothered in gold – great friends with the idiot – slavishly attached to him, but they are equals – worships him – when Handsome wanted to have her she almost killed him – she took it for mockery though she is in love with Handsome – but when the idiot raped her, she offered no resistance (without love) and did not even refer to it later – so it passed off between them, neither the one nor the other mentioning it. Mignon tells the idiot all her dreams – terribly clever and notices everything. The idiot becomes uncle's clerk – his handwriting – the uncle is amazed. The idiot, seeing off the Heroine, starts kissing her – she does not complain of him, but begins flirting – Do you love me very much? – he burnt his finger and the same evening raped Mignon. The idiot is driven out – he and Mignon wander about the streets of Petersburg – his father stole the money, not the idiot – the idiot takes a flat for Mignon – the uncle realizes that the idiot, whom he wanted to thrash, is far deeper and higher than he. Mignon tells the uncle that after revenging herself on everybody she would commit suicide – the

uncle marries the Heroine. Chief characteristic of the idiot: self-mastery from pride (not from morality) and a frenzied desire to solve his own problems – so far only attempts: in this way he might have committed monstrous crimes, but love saves him – he is filled with profoundest compassion and forgives mistakes (that happened already when he forgave his father – his father's death) – instead attains high moral perfection through his development and heroic self-renunciation. Mignon finally goes mad – or: the Heroine abducts the idiot on the eve of her marriage – the uncle leaves his fortune to the idiot and Mignon – they give it to Handsome and Heroine and go away feeling higher and prouder for it.'

As can be seen, this first version already contains several of the themes of the final version: the idiot is an epileptic and is subject to nervous attacks, his excellent handwriting, his attachment to two women, his unexpected inheritance, the incident of the theft of money, Mignon's madness, and the flight of the heroine on the eve of her marriage. The non-Russian name of Nastasya Filippovna's prototype is rather puzzling and it may well be, as the editor of Dostoyevsky's notes suggests, that Dostoyevsky had in mind the heroine of Goethe's novel Wilhelm Meister's Lehrjahre, *although it is questionable whether he wished to create a Russian counterpart of Goethe's romantic heroine; it seems more likely that what he had in mind was to depict Mignon shorn of her romantic aura.*

The second version still adheres to the same scheme of the three separate families, but in it Dostoyevsky makes the heroine marry the idiot. As in the first version, the heroine runs away on the day of her marriage. 'The heroine to the idiot: Take me away – a mad elopement – all the time she is in hysterics – cries and laughs [this Dostoyevsky retained in the final version] – her marriage to the idiot – but after marrying him, she is filled with disgust and terror – uncle's marriage to Mignon.'

This alternative plan Dostoyevsky at once rejected for 'a new and last plan'. The chief and cardinal change in the third version concerns the first emergence of the two generals and their families. The first family consists of a retired general (General Ivolgin of the final version), his mother and wife, his son, still described as Handsome, his second son – the idiot, his daughter Masha, and – here Dostoyevsky again introduced a cardinal change – no longer Mignon, but a governess by the name of Olga Umetsky.

In his novels Dostoyevsky frequently includes the most topical and sensational crimes that occurred in Russia at the time. The story the prince tells Rogozhin about a murder by a peasant of his friend 'for a silver watch' was lifted by Dostoyevsky from a Russian paper he read in a Geneva café. The same happened with the incident concerning Olga Umetsky, a fifteen-year-old girl, who had been cruelly treated by her parents and who, in revenge, set fire to three houses. The trial of Olga Umetsky and her parents caused a sensation throughout Russia and Dostoyevsky was keenly interested in it and, especially, in the character of the young girl. The trial, incidentally, took place in a district town of the province of Tula, and Umetsky's estate was in the Myshkin district of the same province, and that is probably where Dostoyevsky got the surname of his hero.

Dostoyevsky immediately made Olga Umetsky one of the chief characters of his projected novel. The third version still keeps the two other families of the first two versions, namely, the uncle and his son, though the latter takes no part in the plot, and Masha's fiancé, now an engineer, his father, and the Heroine. In addition, there is the other family of the general, his wife, their two sons, and their daughter, aged twenty-five, and another family of a rich widow and her daughter, who is in love with Handsome.

The new version is summarized by Dostoyevsky as follows: 'The general's family in Petersburg – the general's old mother who worships him – pompous and featherbrained wife (she is still flirting and dressing up), not without character, nor without good qualities [the first sketch of Mrs Yepanchin?] – two sons: Handsome and the idiot – their daughter Masha and Olga Umetsky, a governess – lawsuit on the outcome of which the fortune of the family depends.' The other general is a 'Lieutenant-General' and he and his wife are 'persons who consider themselves to be people of consequence'. They have two sons, 'the elder one shows promise and the younger one is a murderer', and a daughter, aged twenty-five. The uncle, the brother of the first general, 'is treated with condescension by the general's family, but they accept a loan of 100,000 roubles from him all the same'. The idiot gets involved in some scandalous story (a theft). 'At first the idiot is accused, but Handsome is the guilty one – they sacrifice the idiot. The idiot is secretly in love with the Heroine – burns his finger – kisses her feet. They lose their lawsuit. The Heroine runs away with the idiot on the day of her marriage out of spite and during an attack of nerves. Olga Umetsky enters the general's family with the idea of revenging herself on her family, but afterwards she hates them and prepares to revenge herself on the general's family who wish to marry her off to the idiot.'

At this point Dostoyevsky suddenly decided to use Iago as the prototype for the idiot: 'The idiot's character to be based on Iago, but he ends divinely. He maligned everybody, intrigued against everybody, got the money, took the bride, but renounces everything.'

This version, too, however, is at once abandoned and a fourth plan is sketched out. According to this, the second general and his family, whose place in the novel Dostoyevsky had not apparently had time to consider, is entirely eliminated. The idiot, too, is removed from the first general's family and becomes the son of the rich and despised uncle. (Dostoyevsky could not make up his mind whether he was to be the uncle's stepson, his legitimate son, or his illegitimate son.) The characters of the fourth version, therefore, include: the general and his wife, this time a young woman, his son Handsome, another son, a daughter by his first marriage, the Heroine, who is a governess, and Olga Umetsky. The uncle's family consists of the uncle himself, his elder son, and the idiot. In addition, a new family is introduced, consisting of Sofia Fyodorovna, an aunt (the idiot's mother?), her husband, daughter, and little son. The general's daughter, no longer referred to as Masha, is still engaged to the engineer, whose father is a legless major. He has a mother and four sisters. The notes on this version are rather scanty: 'Always frigid, the idiot suddenly frightens the heroine by the strength of his passion – his passion is steel-like, a cold razor, utterly insane – but when he falls in love in earnest and realizes what being in love means, he rejects the heroine and sends her back to his brother – he is really in love, though, but conceals it – burnt his finger and frightened her terribly.'

In the fifth version the idiot again becomes the son of the general. His elder brother, however, is no longer described as Handsome, but as Ganya (the first mention of the name). The heroine of this version is still a governess or an adopted daughter. In addition, the family includes Olga Umetsky and two little sons, Lyova and Kostya. The main theme of the novel, Dostoyevsky notes, is 'the struggle of love with hatred'. This version also contains the first characterization of Ganya as a 'homogeneous character'. It would appear from this version that Dostoyevsky harked back to the first version by making the idiot rape Olga Umetsky, with whom he burns down a house.

In the sixth version Dostoyevsky again places the idiot in the uncle's family, as the uncle's son. In this version the idiot is married, and it includes the idiot's mother, another son, and the idiot's aunt, still kept as his prospective mother should Dostoyevsky decide to make him illegitimate. In addition, there is the general's family, consisting of his wife, his son Ganya, a daughter Anna, and the heroine, who, according to one of the notes, appears to be a princess. There are, finally, the Umetskys, including Vladimir Umetsky, the father, his son, an engineer, Olga Umetsky, and two more sons, Lyova and a nameless one who is consumptive (the first appearance of Ippolit). The idiot appears in this version for the first time as a 'real' idiot and is sent to Switzerland for a cure. In Switzerland he leads 'a dark and melancholy' life. He reads a lot and is actuated by envy and spite. The idiot and his brother meet in a railway carriage (just as the idiot and Rogozhin do in the novel) on the former's return to Russia. 'The idiot tells the son how he has acquired his reputation as an idiot: he was ill as a child and was brought up by the Umetskys who always wrote that he was an idiot and obtained money from his father under the pretext of paying doctors' bills. He was made drunk and married off to his present wife, but later it appears that he married his wife from pity. He spent two years in Switzerland. Afterwards it is discovered that he possesses a document proving his legitimacy, but he keeps torturing his uncle by pretending that he is his illegitimate son.'

Here again Dostoyevsky goes on to define the main idea of the novel. 'The main and fundamental idea of the novel,' he writes in his notes, 'is that the idiot is so morbidly proud that he can't help considering himself a god, and yet at the same time he respects himself so little that he can't help despising himself violently. He feels that his wish to revenge himself blindly on everyone is base, and yet he does it – he commits all sorts of wicked acts and revenges himself – he feels that there is no reason why he should not revenge himself on people because he is just like anyone else and he should therefore rest content, but since because of his boundless vanity and at the same time his passion for truth he demands more from everyone, all this is not enough for him – he has absorbed all these poisons and principles, which become part of his nature, from his environment and his upbringing. A man who has always been humiliated and insulted usually possesses infinite generosity and love, but he does not possess them and, therefore, he commits acts of wickedness against, and revenges himself on, those he would have liked to love and for whom he would have gladly shed his blood. Instead of useful activity – wrong doing. His hopes for the future: I shall become a banker, a King of the Jews, and I shall trample them all underfoot and keep them in chains – either to lord it over everyone like a tyrant or die for everyone on the cross – that is the only thing that I think a man of my nature is capable of, for I do not want to drag out a useless existence till I am old and worn out. He is obsessed with the desire to do something heroic so as to distinguish himself and become higher than anyone else. He rapes Olga Umetsky. It appears that Olga Umetsky has always loved him and always sacrificed herself for him and his wife. This coarse rape was the greatest happiness and death for her. His wife dies – signs of poisoning – I killed her, the idiot declares, but it is Olga Umetsky who is guilty. He still insists: I killed her. Uncle leaves him most of his fortune and only a small part of it to his other son, but the idiot refuses it in favour of his brother. In Switzerland: I often read the gospels there and Renan's works. Story of the Holbein painting at Basel. The idiot loves Olga Umetsky – a strange and childish friendship between them. Already as a child he thought: I shall be higher than everyone. A Christian and at the same time he does not believe in God: dichotomy of a deep character. N.B. tongue in mirror. The most important question: how can the personality of the idiot express the idea more interestingly, more romantically, and more palpably – as a legitimate or an illegitimate son? He is ill and in a state of frenzy. The heroine suddenly comes to him before her wedding in her wedding dress. Death of his wife: It is I who killed her. Byronic despair. ...'

In the seventh version Dostoyevsky got rid of some of his characters of the earlier versions, including the idiot's wife, but still kept the uncle (who is supposed to be the brother of the general's first wife) and his son, as well as Vladimir Umetsky and his daughter Olga. In this version the general has only two sons, Ganya and the idiot, who is a son by a former marriage. 'The idiot is a fire-raiser at the beginning. The heroine lives in their house. I am wicked. He takes her away on her wedding day. The uncle intervenes and sends him abroad. When he returns from abroad, he finds that they are all poor – lost their lawsuit – he supports his family and they all hate him. The heroine falls in love with Ganya. Suddenly the idiot inherits 300,000 roubles. They all leave him. Ganya is an ideally beautiful character. The heroine does not forgive the idiot for raping her and poisons herself. The idiot with the children. Their first conversation: And we thought you were so dull. The character of the idiot must be depicted in a masterly fashion.'

Finally, in the eighth version the uncle and his family are eliminated, leaving only the general's family, consisting of the general, his wife, the idiot, Ganya, Varya (her first appearance), the adopted daughter, two more sons, Kolya (his first appearance), and the aunt; and the Umetsky family, including Vladimir Umetsky, his wife, Olga, Ustinya, and Nastya (the first appearance of Nastasya Filippovna under her own name).

'Nastya,' Dostoyevsky writes in his notes, 'is twenty-three – she wants to kill her seducer – her character is violent, relentless, furious, mad. The idiot's face – an eccentric – possesses queer propensities – quiet (sometimes never utters a word – suddenly begins reading to them all about their future blessedness) – the idiot is nineteen, soon twenty – at first an outcast – since childhood has a passion for children. The idiot and the woman who gives birth to a child. When he returns to Russia everyone laughs at him. The children are particularly struck by the fact that he delivered the woman's child. The main thing: his attitude to children. Very delicate health. N.B. An incident where the idiot reveals his true character: the idiot is in the province of Saratov when her seducer abandons Nastya – the idiot takes her to his house – she gives birth to a child which he delivers, and so on. Hurt and furious at having been abandoned, she swears and laughs at him, and afterwards grovels at his feet – finally

falls in love with him, but when he offers to marry her, she runs away (I am violent, I do not ask forgiveness, I am vile) – he believes he is just as she pretended he was when she laughed at him – she is surprised at his simplicity and meekness: Teach me –– But you are ill now –– Never mind, teach me, yes, yes! I want to be taught! And she tells him, trembling as in a fever, how she is going to revenge herself: I am vile, I am wicked, I do not recognize truth, I am done for. All the education she has, she got from the idiot. She goes back to the Umetskys who seize and beat her. The son [*Ganya?*] *rescues her and takes her to Petersburg (that is all he does) and falls in love with her. She treats him with derision and leaves him – then she really falls in love with the son and decides to go to a brothel –says to the idiot: I worship you in place of God, but it is him I love. Runs to the son with all her shame (stormy scenes from the idiot: yes, yes, it is so! – and suddenly runs to drown herself) and so on – darling sweetheart – she is passionate. N.B. It was the idiot's Christianity that first impressed her greatly.*

'*Change of plan: Ganya is twenty – he is the son of the second wife. The general had long ago squandered his fortune. The idiot is the son of the first wife – he is rich – just got his fortune. The general proposes to Umetsky that he should marry Ustinya Alexeyevna, the widow of an army lieutenant, a mettlesome lady, educated, depraved – lives with Captain Pavlenko and with Trotsky who keeps her – Pavlenko and Ustinya fleece Trotsky – Ustinya is twenty-seven – she takes Nastya to Petersburg to place her in a brothel, but instead Nastya takes in washing. ...*'

Having gone so far, Dostoyevsky began to write the first part of the novel (which he destroyed on 18 December). His notes for that part run as follows: '*The idiot lived in the country at the Umetskys', why no one seems to know. The fact is that he lived with the Umetskys before, as he needed rest and country air. His stepmother never could stand him (he lived at home till the age of ten, though), because he is her stepson, rich, and an idiot. Then, because his father was an army general and had to live in different parts of the country, he was left with the Umetskys in the country. He grew up with their elder son and daughters. Then he was sent to Switzerland at the age of nineteen and spent four years there. On his return to Russia, he went straight to the Umetskys (his father was serving somewhere in the province of Simbirsk) and hired a room (for the children), but the children are taken away. Vladimir Umetsky maltreats his wife and his daughter, etc. On the other hand, the general's family: mother, daughter, Ganya, Kolya, Yasha, Nina(?). She* [*Ustinya? Nastya?*] *gave Trotsky a slap in the face in public. N.B. Nephew (son) – face of former idiot – tirade about the King of the Jews – Varya with him – her dream to save him. ...*'

It can be seen that the different developments of the plan of his novel did not take Dostoyevsky very far. It is true that he had at last decided to make his hero a real idiot, that is to say, a man who had suffered from a mental illness since childhood (*as the prince tells Rogozhin at the end of the first part of the novel*), *but the idea of showing his gradual transformation into 'the perfect man' did not work out at all, chiefly, it would seem, because Dostoyevsky tried to involve him too intimately in a family relationship with the other characters of the novel. The solution of the problem must have come to him suddenly. In the notes of the last version he had scribbled the phrase: 'The idiot is a prince!' He had therefore made up his mind to sever the prince's connexion with the other characters of the novel, which of course entailed a drastic revision of all he had so far done.*

'I began painfully to think out a new plot of a novel,' Dostoyevsky wrote to Maykov. 'I thought from 4 December to 18 December inclusive. On the average I made six different plans (no less) daily. My head was turned into a windmill. How I did not go mad, I don't understand. At last on 18 December I sat down to write a new novel and on 5 January I already sent off five chapters of the first part to Moscow. ... Yesterday, 11 January, I sent off two more chapters.' He finished the first part in February. 'The finale [of the first part, i.e. the description of Nastasya Filippovna's birthday party],' Dostoyevsky wrote to Maykov on 1 March, 'I wrote by inspiration and it cost me two epileptic fits one after another.'

In the final version of the first part, therefore, Dostoyevsky returned to one of his original conceptions of two generals and their families, but he relegated the general's family, to which the idiot had at first been related either as a son or as a nephew, to a secondary place in the novel as General Ivolgin, his wife Nina, his two sons Ganya (who was also given a minor part, which involved a complete change of character) and Kolya, and his daughter Varya, and gave one of the prominent places in the novel to the entirely new family of the Yepanchins, one of whose daughters, Aglaya, was to take the place of the original 'heroine' of the first versions. Nastasya Filippovna's character had already been more or less worked out as an amalgam of Mignon, Olga Umetsky, and Nastya. There was also Nastasya Filippovna's seducer Totsky (originally Trotsky). He further introduced the completely new characters of Rogozhin, Lebedev, and Ippolit.

But Dostoyevsky was not out of the wood yet. The second part was giving him great trouble. He had to send it to Moscow by 1 April, but on 2 April he wrote to Maykov: 'Imagine it: the whole of the last month I have not written a single line. Lord, what is going to happen to me?' And on 21 April he wrote to the same correspondent: 'I am working but I can't get anything right. I am just tearing up pages. I'm in a state of terrible depression. I fear nothing will come of it. The day before yesterday I had a violent fit. But yesterday I did manage to write something in a condition that was indistinguishable from insanity. I don't seem to get anything right.'

His notes reveal a complete confusion of ideas. The prince becomes engaged to Aglaya, who continues to hold him up to derision and to tell him that she hates him. On the day of their marriage, Aglaya changes her mind and runs off with a count. Then he wonders whether he should not marry the prince to Aglaya after all: 'N.B. Does he marry her or not? – that is the question.' Then Rogozhin falls in love with Aglaya! Nastasya Filippovna runs away to Rogozhin and spends three days with him in debauchery. She has run off after agreeing to marry the prince (as in the final version). Next Aglaya visits Nastasya Filippovna and tells her that 'it is contemptible of her to play the part of Mary Magdalene, that it is like committing hara-kiri, that she ought to end her life in a brothel.' In the end she offers her arsenic. Nastasya Filippovna tells her that she is already a princess, but when she goes back to the prince (as his wife?), she behaves in a depraved manner and, finally, decides to poison herself. The prince forgives everybody – Ganya (who has been intriguing against him), Rogozhin and Aglaya. He is busy founding a club and schools for children.

On 10 March Dostoyevsky tried another version. Nastasya Filippovna has run away from Rogozhin. She feels that she is very much in love with the prince, but considers herself unworthy of him. She would like to become a washerwoman, but is more inclined to go to a brothel. Here Dostoyevsky thought of arranging another meeting between her and Aglaya, who advises her to go to a brothel. Aglaya tells Nastasya Filippovna that she is marrying the prince because he is rich, but Nastasya Filippovna guesses by certain inflexions in her voice and her strange behaviour that she herself is in love with the prince. After leaving Aglaya, Nastasya Filippovna 'gives herself up to a life of debauchery – the general again – she incites Ganya and Rogozhin to ruin Aglaya – Nastasya Filippovna's fury and jealousy – her death in a brothel (description)'.

No wonder Dostoyevsky was in despair and was tearing up pages as soon as he wrote them. On the same day he jotted down this characteristic of the idiot (again altered later on): 'The main feature of the prince's character: a feeling of oppression, fright, humility, meekness, and utter conviction that he is an idiot. N.B. His opinion of the world: he forgives everything, sees the causes of everything, cannot understand unpardonable sin and excuses everything – considers himself lower and worse than any-

body – sees through people – absolutely convinced that everyone thinks he is an idiot – only in children does he find his companions – (Am I an idiot or not?) – Aglaya persuaded him (before) that he was an idiot (this she did on purpose: Aglaya expects protests and gibes and sees only meekness).' Dostoyevsky again brings in the incident of the burning of the finger as proof of love, but this time it is Ganya and not the idiot who does it in front of Aglaya. 'Ganya's attitude to Aglaya: as soon as Ganya recovers from his faint, he at once thinks: What will Aglaya say? (Tries to convince someone rather unsuccessfully that he had proposed to Nastasya Filippovna because he was in despair over being rejected by Aglaya). ... N.B. N.B. Finis is that Aglaya becomes reconciled with Nastasya Filippovna and Ganya strangles Aglaya.'

'The idiot', he wrote on the following day, 'does not consider himself capable of an act of heroism but longs for it. By saving Nastasya Filippovna and looking after her, he merely acts in accordance with his feeling of spontaneous Christian love.' He then wonders whether he should not start the second part with Ganya. He writes: 'As the idiot's marriage to Nastasya Filippovna is a coup de théâtre, she ought not to be brought on before the scene with Aglaya.' Next day he notes that there are three kinds of love in the novel: (1) Rogozhin – love based on passion; (2) Ganya – love out of vanity; and (3) the prince – Christian love. He also notes that the idiot's chief social conviction is that the economic teaching about the uselessness of an individual act of charity is an absurdity and that, on the contrary, everything depends on individual endeavour. On 13 March he comes back to the idea of a meeting between Aglaya and Nastasya Filippovna, during which Aglaya offers her arsenic. He also wonders whether he should not marry off Nastasya Filippovna to Rogozhin: 'She marries Rogozhin – has a terrible life with him – is beaten by him – scenes of jealousy, reproaches, and desperate love. Rogozhin kills her. Zhdanov fluid. [In the novel Rogozhin does beat her 'black and blue' in Moscow and, finally, of course, he does kill her and puts Zhdanov disinfectant round her body.] After Nastasya Filippovna's death the prince marries Aglaya and then dies.' On 15 March Dostoyevsky wrote: 'Must write less diffusely. Must make it all very polished, sympathetic (brief and to the point) and entertaining.' On 16 March he thought of the incident of Pavlishchev's son. He tries another variation with Ganya: after burning his finger, Ganya feels drawn back to the prince and 'in the end shoots himself'. On 17 March he again reminds himself to write more briefly and keep to the bare facts. On 20 March he toys with the idea of describing the prince's work for the children and his foundation of a children's club, but decides against it. (In the novel the fact that the prince wanted to found schools is merely mentioned in the episode with Pavlishchev's son.)

On 21 March he is still uncertain how to make his readers like the idiot. 'If,' he writes, 'Don Quixote and Pickwick, as positive characters, are sympathetic to the reader and come off, it is because they are funny. If the hero of my novel, the prince, is not funny, he possesses another sympathetic characteristic, namely, he is innocent!' He once more returns to the theme of the children and the children's club, and wonders whether he could not make the children play an active part in the relationship between the prince, Aglaya, and Nastasya Filippovna, and even (he puts a N.B.) make Rogozhin confess his crime through the influence of the children. On 1 April he writes: 'Meekness is the most powerful force that exists in the world.' On 8 April he at last seems to get the scene between Aglaya and Nastasya Filippovna in the right perspective: 'Scene of the meeting between Aglaya and Nastasya Filippovna. Insults her. Nastasya Filippovna in a frenzy. "So I shall marry the prince!" The prince agrees. They are engaged. The prince looks ridiculous. How he gets out of being laughed at. She runs away on the day of the wedding and marries Rogozhin(?). The prince and his activities. Aglaya a convert. Rogozhin kills Nastasya Filippovna.' At last on 10 April he gets the character of the prince fully into focus: 'N.B. The prince – Christ,' a statement which he repeats a few times. On the same day he makes up his mind about another important fact in the development of the novel: 'N.B. The prince is in love with Aglaya.' He goes on: 'The main problem is the character of the idiot. This must be developed. That is the idea of the novel. How Russia is reflected. ... Revealing the prince gradually in action will be enough, but! – this requires a good plot. To make the hero's character as charming as possible, one has to invent a sphere of action for him.'

He next turns to Lebedev's character. 'Lebedev', he writes, 'is a highly gifted personality. He is loyal, he weeps and prays and cheats the prince and laughs at him. ... Lebedev's profound remarks. An immature philosopher. Drunkenness.'

On 15 April he decides to make the prince write a letter to Aglaya and have Kolya deliver it. He introduces Prince Sh. (Shcherbakov) as Aglaya's fiancé, then on the same day decides that he is to be Adelaida's fiancé (as in the novel). He then jots down another version of the events following the murder of Nastasya Filippovna, according to which Aglaya takes the idiot abroad, but on 22 April decides to change it all again. On 28 April he jots down the cryptic remark: Shakespeare (a harking back to the Iago theme?), and decides on a new twist in the plot (later abandoned): 'Nastasya Filippovna marries Rogozhin. She intervenes to bring about the prince's marriage to Aglaya. Aglaya is hurt. Sees that prince tries to calm Nastasya Filippovna. Aglaya is jealous and Nastasya Filippovna is jealous. Aglaya marries the prince. She arouses Rogozhin's jealousy. The prince's admonishments. Rogozhin kills Nastasya Filippovna. Aglaya dies. The prince is with her.' On the same day he invents 'the scandalous scene' at the bandstand.

It is interesting that no mention is made in the notes of Rogozhin's attempt to kill the prince. By the end of May, however, he has already sent off the first five chapters of the second part, including the prince's meeting with Rogozhin and Rogozhin's attempt to kill him at the hotel. On 4 June he wrote to Maykov: 'All this time I literally worked day and night in spite of my fits. But, alas, I notice with despair that for some reason I am not able to work as quickly as I did a short while ago and before that. I crawl like a crab, and then I begin to count the sheets – three and a half or four in a whole month. This is terrible, and I don't know what will happen to me.' However, he managed to send off three more chapters, ending with the episode of Pavlishchev's son, for publication in the June number and the four final chapters of the second part for publication in the July number of The Russian Herald.

Writing from Vevey to Maykov on 22 June, Dostoyevsky declared that in the episode of Pavlishchev's son he had tried to present 'an episode of our modern positivists from the extremist section of our younger generation. I know,' he went on, 'that I have written it correctly (for I wrote it from experience; no one but me ever had those experiences or observed them) and I knew that they would all abuse me and say, This is absurd, naïve and silly, and untrue.'

He was now occupied with the working out of the characters of Radomsky and Ippolit. So far as Radomsky is concerned, it is obvious from his resignation from the army and his rather mysterious appearance in mufti and the rumours about his own and his uncle's affairs that Dostoyevsky first conceived him as a rather melodramatic character who comes to a bad end. This becomes at once evident from his notes, according to which Radomsky is 'a real aristocrat, a brilliant character, but without ideals, who commits suicide out of vanity'. His vanity, Dostoyevsky explains in another note, is of the Lacenaire* type. He would have liked, Dostoyevsky explains, to be a bon viveur (like his uncle), but he was too educated a man. Neither did he want to become a 'Gogol landowner'. He marries Lebedev's daughter Vera 'to have a bit of fun at her expense' and because the prince comes to his rescue and saves him from the debtors' jail by giving him 400,000 roubles (in the novel the prince only inherits a little over 100,000 roubles). 'He accepts the money from pride, but that maddens

* Pierre François Lacenaire, thief and murderer, was executed at the age of thirty-six in Paris on 9 January 1836. When arrested, he betrayed his accomplices and tried to father his crimes on them. After his death, a volume of his memoirs and poetry created a stir in Paris society. His melodramatic attitudinizings as an enemy of society fascinated Dostoyevsky.

him all the more, and he shoots himself. He had long been in the hands of creditors,' Dostoyevsky adds, 'and that is why he resigned his commission.' This was obviously what Dostoyevsky planned at first, but after the publication of the second part (in May, June, and July 1868), he completely altered his plan and, as appears from the fourth part and the Conclusion, made Radomsky into a positive character, leaving him his fortune and hinting at the possibility of his romantic marriage to Vera Lebedev.

Before sitting down to write the third part, Dostoyevsky told Maykov that he was 'disgusted' with the novel, and this feeling of disgust can be understood if one takes into account the fact that although he had tried all sorts of solutions of the complex problems of a novel of such psychological depth, he was not as yet clear in his mind what to do with his characters. The idea that the characters take such a hold of the author that they write themselves obviously does not apply to Dostoyevsky. 'I have done my best to carry on with the work,' he wrote to Maykov in the same letter, 'but I couldn't: my soul is sick. Now I shall make a last effort to write the third part. If I improve the novel, I shall improve myself. If not, I am lost.' However, he finished the first three chapters in time for publication in the August number, three more chapters in the September number, and the four last chapters in the October number of The Russian Herald. *'What worries me so much,' he wrote to Maykov, 'is that if I wrote a novel in one year and then spent three months in copying and revising it, I should have got quite a different result – I can vouch for that. Now I can see it clearly.'*

But there was still the fourth part to write, and he still was not sure how to end the novel. He had hoped to finish it in a month, but now he despaired of ever being able to finish it. He felt that the whole idea of The Idiot *had foundered. 'Even if it has or will have any merit,' he wrote to Maykov, 'the effect it will create will be small.' But at last he got his ending.* He jotted it down in his notes: 'Rogozhin and the prince over the dead body. Finale. Not bad.' He wrote to Maykov on 23 December from Milan: 'I believe I wrote to you that I got stuck with the ending of* The Idiot *and would not be able to finish it in time for the December number. I informed Katkov of this* mea culpa *quite frankly, that is, that he would have to publish the end of the novel next year as a supplement to his journal. Now I have suddenly changed my mind. I have*

* *The similarity between the endings of* The Idiot *and of* Othello *– both bedroom scenes in which a young woman is killed by a jealous lover – is more than coincidental. At the end of his notes, Dostoyevsky again refers twice to* Othello, *which shows how much Shakespeare's tragedy was in his mind at the time of the writing of* The Idiot, *and it is more than likely that* Othello *suggested his ending to him.*

decided to finish everything, *the fourth part as well as the conclusion, in time for the December number of the present year, but on condition that it is published later than usual. ... From to-day I shall have to write seven printed sheets in four weeks. I suddenly realized that I shall be able to do so without spoiling the novel too much. But what remains has already been written down roughly and I know every word by heart. If there are readers of* The Idiot, *they will perhaps be a little astonished by the unexpected ending. On the whole, the ending is one of my most successful ones, I mean, simply as an ending. I am not speaking of the merits of the novel as a whole. ...'*

An important point that concerns not only The Idiot *but all the other of Dostoyevsky's great novels, and indeed the whole conception of reality in a work of art, is discussed by Dostoyevsky in a letter to Strakhov from Florence on 10 March, written shortly after the publication of the novel. Already in his notes, Dostoyevsky was worried by the 'fantastic' elements in his story, that is to say, by the question whether his readers and critics might not consider certain characters and events in it as incredible. What was truth? he asked himself. What was reality? 'Reality', he wrote in his notes, 'is the most important thing of all. It is true,' he goes on, 'that my conception of reality may be different from the conception of other people. Perhaps in the idiot man is more real. However,' he concludes, 'I agree that I might be told: All this is so, you are right, but you were not able to bring it off, you were not able to justify your facts, you are a bad artist. Well, this, of course, is quite a different matter.'*

In his letter to Strakhov, however, Dostoyevsky does attempt to justify his 'facts' and at the same time to define 'reality' from the point of view of the artist. 'During the last six weeks', he writes, 'I have been busy finishing The Idiot. ... *I have my own idea of reality in art; and what most people will call almost fantastic and an exception sometimes constitutes for me the very essence of reality. The ordinariness of events and the conventional view of them is not realism in my opinion but, indeed, the very opposite of it. In every newspaper you find accounts of the most real facts which are also the most strange and most complex. To our writers they appear fantastic and they do not even bother about them, and yet they are reality because they are* facts. *Who is there to notice, explain, and describe them? They happen every minute and every day and they are not an* exception. ... *Is not my fantastic "Idiot" reality and the most ordinary reality at that? Why, it is just now that such characters ought to exist among our uprooted classes of society, classes which actually become fantastic in real life. But it is no use talking about it! There is a lot in my novel that is hastily written and diffuse, and that I have failed to bring out properly. It is not my novel but my idea that I stand up for. There is a great deal in my novel that I am dissatisfied with. But, then, I am its father.'*

There can be no doubt that in The Idiot *Dostoyevsky has successfully attempted to present the ideal of a Christian. But, unlike Christian in* The Pilgrim's Progress, *he endows his hero with real and not allegorical traits of character and places him in a real and not an allegorical and fantastic world. But in placing the 'idiot' in a real world, Dostoyevsky has also provided a crushing criticism of this world and, particularly, of the Russian ruling class of his time. Indeed, the whole novel is a bitter attack upon the Russian aristocracy. The prince's appeal to 'the princes' at the end of the seventh chapter of the fourth part of the novel is a warning as well as a prophecy. To ask them to be servants so as to become masters may be held to show his total incapacity to gauge the true nature and ambition of a class which he realized was doomed to extinction; but it also showed his great wisdom. He saw further than the politicians who laughed at him and, strange to say, he even saw further than his own creator; for Dostoyevsky put into his mouth ideas which reflected his own unbalanced views rather than the views of his ideal hero.*

D.M.

PART ONE

I

At about nine o'clock in the morning at the end of November, during a thaw, the Warsaw train was approaching Petersburg at full speed. It was so damp and foggy that it was a long time before it grew light, and even then it was difficult to distinguish out of the carriage windows anything a few yards to the right and left of the railway track. Among the passengers there were some who were returning from abroad; but it was the third-class compartments that were crowded most of all, chiefly with small business men who had boarded the train at the last stop. As usual, everyone was tired, everyone looked weary after a night's journey, everyone was chilled to the marrow, and everyone's face was pale and yellow, the colour of the fog.

Two passengers had found themselves sitting opposite each other by the window of one of the third-class compartments since daybreak – both of them young men, both travelling light, both far from fashionably dressed, both of a rather striking appearance, and, finally, both anxious to start a conversation with one another. Had they known what was so extraordinary about them at this moment, they would no doubt have been surprised that chance should have so strangely placed them opposite each other in a third-class compartment of the Warsaw–Petersburg train. One of them was a short man of about twenty-seven with curly hair that was almost black and a pair of tiny, but fiery, grey eyes. His nose was broad and flat and he had high cheekbones; his thin lips were continually curled into a sort of insolent, sarcastic, and even malicious smile, but his forehead was high and well-shaped and did a great deal to atone for the far from prepossessing features of the lower part of his face. The most striking thing about his face was its deathly pallor, which, in spite of his rather sturdy build, gave the young man a look of utter exhaustion and, at the same time, of something agonizingly passionate, which seemed to be out of keeping with his coarse and insolent smile and his surly and self-satisfied expression. He was warmly dressed in a large lamb's-wool-lined black overcoat and had not felt the cold during the night, while his fellow-passenger had experienced all the delights of a damp Russian November night for which he was obviously quite unprepared. He wore a fairly large, thick cloak with an enormous hood, the sort of thing travellers often wear during the winter months in a distant foreign country, in Switzerland or, for instance, in northern Italy without, needless to say, having to bargain for such long stretches of country as those between Eydkuhnen and Petersburg. But what was appropriate and in every way satisfactory in Italy turned out to be not altogether suitable in Russia. The owner of the cloak with the hood was also a young man of about twenty-six or twenty-seven, slightly above medium height, with very thick, fair hair, hollow cheeks, and a thin pointed and almost white little beard. His eyes were large, blue, and piercing, and there was something gentle but heavy in their look, something of that strange expression which makes people realize at the first glance that they are dealing with an epileptic. The young man's face, however, was pleasant, sensitive, and lean, though colourless and, at this particular moment, blue with cold. A meagre bundle of old, faded silk material, which apparently contained all his belongings, dangled from his hands. He wore thick-soled shoes and gaiters – all of it quite un-Russian. His dark-haired fellow-passenger in the lamb's-wool-lined coat scrutinized it all, partly because he had nothing else to do, and, at last, asked with that callous grin with which people sometimes so casually and unceremoniously express their pleasure at the misfortunes of their fellow-men:

'Chilly?'

And he hunched up his shoulders.

'Very,' his fellow-passenger replied with the utmost readiness; 'and, mind you, this is only a thaw. What would it be like in a frost, I wonder? I never thought it would be so cold at home. Afraid I'm no longer used to it.'

'Not from abroad, are you?'

'Yes, from Switzerland.'

'Whew! Good Lord!'

The dark-haired man whistled and burst out laughing.

They entered into conversation. The readiness of the fair-haired young man in the Swiss cloak to answer all the questions of his swarthy fellow-passenger was quite remarkable and showed not the slightest suspicion of how scornful, irrelevant, and frivolous some of them were. In answering them, he incidentally disclosed the fact that he really had been away a long time from Russia – over four years – that he had been sent abroad for reasons of health, because of some strange nervous disease, something in the nature of epilepsy or St

Vitus's dance, some kind of convulsive spasms and twitchings. The swarthy young man grinned several times as he listened to him, and he laughed outright when, in answer to the question whether he had been cured, the fair-haired man replied that he had not.

'I see!' the swarthy young man observed sarcastically. 'I can just imagine how much money you must have wasted on those fellows, and here we still believe in them.'

'You're absolutely right!' a shabbily dressed man, who was sitting beside them, intervened in the conversation (he was a man of about forty, of strong build, with a red nose and pimply face, and looked like a low-grade civil servant who had grown case-hardened in the service). 'You're absolutely right, sir. All they do is to bleed us Russians dry without giving us anything in return!'

'Oh, but you're quite wrong in my case,' the Swiss patient exclaimed in a gentle and conciliatory tone of voice. 'Naturally, I'm not in a position to argue with you, because there are so many things I don't know, but my doctor paid for my fares out of his own pocket. He shared his last penny with me, and he's kept me at his own expense for nearly two years in Switzerland.'

'Why?' asked the swarthy young man. 'Wasn't there no one to pay for you?'

'I'm afraid not. You see, Mr Pavlishchev, who'd been paying my fees there, died two years ago. I wrote afterwards to Mrs Yepanchin, a distant relative of mine who lives in Petersburg, but I've had no reply. So that's why I've come back.'

'Where to?'

'You mean where am I going to stay? Well, as a matter of fact, I have no idea. Somewhere, I suppose.'

'Not made up your mind yet, have you?'

And both his questioners burst out laughing again.

'And I expect that little bundle of yours is all you've got in the world?' the swarthy man asked.

'I wouldn't mind betting you've hit the nail on the head, sir,' the red-nosed civil servant interposed, with a highly satisfied air, 'and that the gentleman hasn't any luggage in the van either, though, mind you, poverty is no crime, sir – a fact that must be pointed out.'

It appeared that it was so indeed: the fair-haired young man at once admitted it with quite extraordinary promptitude.

'Your small bundle, sir, is not without its significance, for all that,' the civil servant went on after they had laughed to their hearts' content (oddly enough, the owner of the bundle, looking at them, began at last laughing himself, which increased their mirth), 'and though I don't mind betting that it isn't stuffed with rolls of gold coins, either French, or German, or even Dutch – a fact, sir, that can be deduced from the gaiters investing your foreign shoes – I'm sure that if we were to add to your small bundle, say, a relation of the social position of a Mrs Yepanchin, the wife of a general, it, too, would appear in a somewhat different light, always provided, of course, that Mrs Yepanchin is a relation of yours and that you're not making it up through – er – absence of mind, which is not at all uncommon with people because – well, shall we say, because of an excess of imagination.'

'You've got it right again,' the young man exclaimed, 'for really I have nearly made a mistake. I mean, she's hardly what you'd call a relation, so that, as a matter of fact, I wasn't at all surprised at receiving no answer from her. Indeed, I quite expected it.'

'Wasted your money on the postage, you did, I'm very much afraid, sir. But – er – at any rate, you're simple-hearted and frank, and that, indeed, is highly commendable! H'm – I know General Yepanchin quite well, of course. I mean, because you see, sir, everyone in town knows him. And I also used to know the late Mr Pavlishchev, who kept you in Switzerland, sir – if, that is, it is Nikolai Andreyevich Pavlishchev, for there were two cousins of that name. One of them still lives in the Crimea. As for the late Mr Pavlishchev, he was a very worthy man, a man with most excellent connexions. Owned four thousand serfs in his day. Yes, sir.'

'That's right, his name was Nikolai Andreyevich Pavlishchev,' said the young man and, having replied, he looked intently and searchingly at Mr Know-all.

These know-alls are sometimes – indeed, quite often – found in a certain class of society. They know everything, and all the restless inquisitiveness of their minds and all their faculties are bent irresistibly in one direction, no doubt because they lack more important and vital interests and opinions, as a modern thinker would put it. The words 'They know everything', however, must be understood to cover a rather limited field, namely, at what government department a certain man is employed, who are his friends and acquaintances, what he is worth, what province he was governor of, who his wife is, how big a dowry she brought him, who are his first and second cousins, etc. etc. – everything of that sort. These know-alls mostly walk about in shabby old clothes and their salaries do not exceed seventeen roubles a month. The people whose most intimate secrets they know would, of course, have been hard put to it to imagine what their motives might be, and yet many of them are positively consoled by this knowledge, amounting almost to an exact science, and they derive their self-respect and even their highest spiritual satisfaction from it. It is, indeed, a fascinating science. I have known scholars, men of letters, poets, and politicians who sought and found in this science their peace of mind and the realization of their highest ambitions, and who even owe their careers exclusively to it.

During the whole of this conversation the swarthy young man kept yawning, looking aimlessly out of the window, and waiting impatiently for the end of the journey. He seemed preoccupied – a little too preoccupied, somehow, almost perturbed – and, indeed, behaved rather strangely: sometimes he seemed to be listening without hearing, looking without seeing, and laughing without often quite knowing or remembering what he was laughing at.

'Excuse me, sir,' the pimply gentleman suddenly addressed the fair-haired young man with the small bundle, 'whom have I the honour – –'

'Prince Leo Nikolayevich Myshkin,' the young man replied with perfect and prompt readiness.

'Prince Myshkin? Leo Nikolayevich?' the civil servant repeated wonderingly. 'I'm afraid I don't know it, sir. Indeed, I've never heard of it. I don't mean the name, of course. It's an historic name, sir. You'll find it in Karamzin's history. Quite certain to. I'm speaking of you personally, sir. I'm afraid no Myshkins are to be found anywhere nowadays. You never hear of them even.'

'Why, of course not!' the prince replied at once. 'There are no more Prince Myshkins left now except me. I believe I'm the last one. As for our fathers and grandfathers, some of them were only peasant freeholders. My father, though, was a second lieutenant in the army. He'd been a cadet at a military college. But I've no idea how Mrs Yepanchin came to be a Princess Myshkin – the last of her kind, too, I suppose.'

'Ha, ha, ha!' the civil servant tittered. 'The last of her kind! Ha, ha! How beautifully you put it!'

The swarthy man grinned, too. The fair-haired one was a little surprised at having made a joke, though it was rather a feeble one.

'You know, I said it without thinking,' he explained at last, looking surprised.

'Why, of course, sir, of course!' the civil servant assented gaily.

'Done a lot of studying, too, with that professor of yours, haven't you, Prince?' the swarthy man asked suddenly.

'Yes, I have.'

'And I never studied nothing.'

'Oh, I too only studied a little,' added the prince, almost apologetically. 'Because of my illness it was found impossible to teach me systematically.'

'Know the Rogozhins?' the swarthy man asked quickly.

'No, I'm afraid I don't know them at all. You see, I know very few people in Russia. Are you a Rogozhin?'

'Yes, I'm Parfyon Rogozhin.'

'Parfyon?' the civil servant began, looking more self-important than ever. 'Aren't you one of those Rogozhins --'

'Yes, yes, one of those, one of those,' the swarthy man interrupted him quickly and impatiently, without, however, turning to the pimply civil servant, but speaking from the very beginning only to the prince.

'You are? But how is it possible?' the civil servant exclaimed, almost thrown into a stupor with astonishment, his eyes nearly starting out of his head and his whole face assuming a reverential, obsequious, and, indeed, frightened expression. 'Do you mean, sir, you're the son of Semyon Parfyonovich Rogozhin, member of the hereditary order of citizenship, who passed away a month ago and left a fortune of two and a half million roubles in ready money?'

'And how the hell do you know he left two and a half million roubles in ready money?' the swarthy young man interrupted, without vouchsafing even to glance at the civil servant. 'Look at him!' he winked at the prince, motioning towards the civil servant. 'And what, I ask you, do they hope to get by falling over themselves? But it's quite true my dad's died and I'm returning from Pskov a month after with hardly a decent pair of boots to my feet. Sent me nothing, they didn't, neither that scoundrel of a brother of mine, nor my mother – no money and not a line to say what's happened. Just as if I was a dog! Been lying ill with fever in Pskov for a whole month, I have!'

'And now you'll be getting a cool million all at once – that at least, O Lord!' the civil servant exclaimed, throwing up his hands.

'What has it got to do with him; tell me, please,' Rogozhin said, motioning irritably and angrily towards the civil servant again. 'Why, you wouldn't get a penny from me even if you walked upside down in front of me.'

'And I shall, sir; I shall walk upside down!'

'You will, will you? But, mind, I won't give you nothing, not a damn thing, even if you danced round me for a whole week!'

'I don't ask for anything! Serves me right. Don't you give me anything! And I shall dance round you. Leave my wife and my little ones, and dance round you. Must give honour where honour's due.'

'Oh, to hell with you!' exclaimed the swarthy man, looking disgusted. 'Five weeks ago,' he addressed the prince, 'I ran away from my dad, with a small bundle, like yours, to my aunt in Pskov. I fell ill of a fever there and took to my bed, and he died while I was away. Died of a stroke, he did. May his soul rest in peace, but he nearly killed me that time; he did and all. Believe me, Prince; I swear it's true. If I hadn't run away then, he'd have done me in for certain.'

'I suppose you must have done something to make him angry, didn't you?' asked the prince, examining the millionaire in the lambskin coat with a special sort of curiosity.

But though there might have been something remarkable in the mere fact of a million and in being left an inheritance, it was something else that astonished and interested the prince; besides, Rogozhin himself for some reason seemed to be rather anxious to engage the prince in conversation, though his desire to talk to someone was a physical rather than a moral necessity; it seemed, somehow, to have arisen more out of his preoccupations than out of his simplicity of soul, to be the result of his agitation and need to look at someone and go on talking about something. He seemed still to be in a fever or, at least, running a temperature. As for the civil servant, he was hanging on Rogozhin's words, not daring to breathe, catching at each word and weighing it as though he were searching for a diamond.

'Angry? I should think so; and with good reason!' cried Rogozhin. 'But it was that brother of mine who got my goat. Mother's all right. She's an old woman. Reads the lives of the saints, sits with her old women, and what my brother says goes. And why didn't he let me know in good time? Aye, why not, indeed? Mind you, it's quite true I was lying unconscious just then. Besides, he did send a telegram. He did that. But, you see, the telegram arrived at my aunt's, who's been a widow for thirty years and spends all her time, from morning till night, with holy fools. She isn't a nun – she's worse than that. So she got scared of the telegram and took it to the police station without bothering to open it. It's still there, for all I know. It was Konyov, a friend of mine, who came to my rescue. Sent me a full account of everything, he did. That brother of mine cut off the tassels from my dad's coffin at night; solid gold they was. No use wasting them, he thinks; cost a fortune, they does. Why, damn him, I could send him to Siberia for that, so help me, for it's sacrilege, it is! Hey, there, you old scarecrow,' he turned to the civil servant. 'It's sacrilege, ain't it? By law, I mean?'

'Sacrilege! sacrilege!' the civil servant assented at once.

'You could send a man to Siberia for that, couldn't you?'

'You could, sir. To Siberia. Straight to Siberia.'

'They still think I'm ill,' Rogozhin went on. 'But I stole out of the house without breathing a word, ill as I was, got into the train, and – here I am: open up the gates, brother dear! He was always telling tales to my dad about me; I know that. But, of course, it's quite true I got my dad's back up because of Nastasya Filippovna. I did that all right. Got myself into a proper mess, I did.'

'Because of Nastasya Filippovna?' the civil servant asked obsequiously, as though wondering about something.

'Why, you know nothing about her!' Rogozhin cried impatiently.

'Don't I?' the civil servant replied triumphantly.

'Do you now? Why, there are hundreds of Nastasya Filippovnas. And what a cheeky beggar you are, let me tell you! I knew,' he went on, addressing the prince, 'that some cheeky wretch like that would immediately fasten on to me like a leech!'

'Well, sir, perhaps I know, perhaps I do,' the civil servant said, shaking with excitement. 'Lebedev knows! You, sir, are pleased to reproach me, but what if I can prove it to you? You see, sir, it's the very same Nastasya Filippovna who was the cause of your being chastised by your father with a stick. Miss Barashkov, aye, that's her surname, and she is, one might say, a well-born lady, too, also a princess of a kind, and she's been associating with a certain Afanasy Ivanovich Totsky, and only with him, a landowner and a very wealthy man, a director of all sorts of companies and, on that account, a great friend of General Yepanchin's.'

'Oho, so that's the sort of chap you are!' Rogozhin exclaimed, genuinely surprised at last. 'Well, I'm damned, he really does know!'

'I know everything! Lebedev knows everything! Why, sir, I spent two months driving about with Alexander Likhachov, after his father's death, too; and I know everything – all the ins and outs, I mean. In fact, things went so far that he wouldn't budge an inch without Lebedev. I'm afraid he's in the debtor's jail now, but before he was put away I had every opportunity of knowing Armance and Coralie and Princess Patsky and Nastasya Filippovna; and there isn't much, sir, I didn't have the opportunity of knowing.'

'Nastasya Filippovna?' Rogozhin cried, staring at him angrily, with pale and trembling lips. 'Why, was she and Likhachov – –'

'There was nothing between them! N-nothing at all! Absolutely nothing!' the civil servant said quickly, recollecting himself at once. 'I mean, Likhachov couldn't get what he wanted for love or money. No, sir, it wasn't the same as with Armance. It was no one but Totsky. In the evening she would be in her box at the Bolshoy or the French

Theatre, and, I daresay, the gentlemen officers might have been telling all sorts of tales about her, but even they could prove nothing. All they could say was, "See that lady there? She's the notorious Nastasya Filippovna," and as for the rest – nothing! For there was nothing to tell.'

'That's just how it is,' Rogozhin confirmed gloomily, frowning. 'Zalyozhnev said the same to me at the time. You see, Prince, I was just running across Nevsky Avenue in my dad's long, three-year-old overcoat when she came out of a shop and got into her carriage. I was struck all of a heap there and then, I was. Then I met Zalyozhnev – he's as unlike me as can be, goes about like a hairdresser's assistant, an eye-glass in his eye, and at my dad's house we walks about in tarred boots, and all we have for dinner is thin cabbage soup. Well, so he says to me, she ain't your sort, he says. She's a princess, he says, and her name's Nastasya Filippovna, and her surname's Barashkov, and she lives with Totsky, he says, and Totsky don't know how to get rid of her now, because, he says, he's getting on – fifty-five he is, if a day – and he wants to marry one of the greatest beauties in town. It was then he gave me the idea. You can see Nastasya Filippovna, he says, to-day at the ballet at the Bolshoy Theatre, where she'll be in her own box at the side of the stalls. Well, it wasn't so simple a matter for me to go to the ballet, I can tell you, for if my dad found out he'd make short work of me! He'd kill me for sure. However, I managed to nip down there for an hour in secret and see Nastasya Filippovna again. That night I didn't sleep a wink. Next morning my dad gave me two five-per-cent government bonds. Go and sell them, he says to me, and take seven thousand five hundred roubles to Andreyev's office and bring the rest back to me. Mind, he says, don't stop anywhere on the way. Bring me back the money. I'll be waiting for you, he says. Well, I sold the bonds, got the money, but I never went near Andreyev's office. Instead, I went straight to the English shop and bought a pair of ear-rings with a diamond the size of a nut in each of them. Cost me four hundred roubles more than I had on me, but I gave them my name and they trusted me all right. So off I went to Zalyozhnev with the ear-rings. I told him what I had done and I says to him, Come along to Nastasya Filippovna's, old man. So off we went. How we got there I don't know. I could see nothing on the way and couldn't remember nothing afterwards. We went straight into her drawing-room. She came out to us herself. At the time, you see, I didn't let on who I was. So Zalyozhnev, he says, Will you, he says, accept this from Rogozhin in memory of his meeting you yesterday? Please accept it, he says. So she undid the parcel, had a look at the ear-rings, and smiled. Will you thank your friend Mr Rogozhin, she says, for his kind attention? And she bowed to us and went out. God, why didn't I die there on the spot? For, you see, if I went there it was only because I thought to myself, I won't come back alive, anyway! But what made me really mad was that swine Zalyozhnev taking all the credit to himself. I'm a short fellow, as you see, dressed like a tramp, and I stood there staring at her without opening my mouth. I was that ashamed, and he was dressed like a dummy in a shop window, his hair oiled and waved, rosy cheeks, check tie, bowing and scraping, damn him, and I'm sure she took him for me. Well, I says to him as we was going out, don't you go getting any ideas in your head, I says, or else -- He laughed. What I'd like to know, he says, is what you're going to tell your dad now? To tell the truth, I'd half a mind to throw myself into the river without going home first, but I thought to myself, It's all one, anyways, and I went back home like I was damned.'

'Dear me,' the civil servant exclaimed, grimacing and positively shuddering. 'You see, sir' – he turned to the prince – 'his late father used to make a man's life a hell on earth for ten roubles, let alone for ten thousand.'

'A hell on earth!' Rogozhin repeated. 'What do you know about it? Well,' he went on, addressing the prince, 'he got to know all about it at once. Besides, Zalyozhnev told everyone he met the whole story. So my dad took me to an upstairs room, locked the door, and started laying about me with his stick for a whole hour. This, he says to me, is only a foretaste, for I'll be coming back, he says, to bid you good-night. Well, what do you think he did? He went straight to Nastasya Filippovna's, the old fellow did, bowed down to the ground to her, besought her, and wept. So at last she went out, fetched the box, and flung it in his face. Here are your ear-rings, she says, you old grey-beard. They're ten times more precious to me now, she says, seeing as how Parfyon got them at so great a danger to himself. Give my regards to Parfyon, she says, and thank him for me. Well, meanwhile I borrowed twenty roubles from Sergey Protushin, with my mother's blessing, and left by train for Pskov and arrived there in a fever. The old girls started muttering prayers over me, and me sitting there drunk. Then off I went from pub to pub and spent all the money I had on drinks, and afterwards lay dead drunk in the street all night. By the morning I was in a raging fever, and during the night the dogs had worried me. How I came to I don't know.'

'Well, well,' the civil servant tittered, rubbing his hands, 'Nastasya Filippovna will be singing a different tune now! Who cares about those ear-rings now, sir? We shall make it up to her with such ear-rings now – –'

'If I hear you say another word about Nastasya Filippovna,' cried Rogozhin, seizing him fiercely by the arm, 'I'll thrash you within an inch of your life, though you used to drive about with Likhachov!'

'If you thrash me, you won't spurn me! Thrash me, and you shall have me. By thrashing me, you shall have put your seal on me. ... Ah, here we are!'

They were, in fact, entering the station. Although Rogozhin said that he had left Pskov in secret, several men were waiting for him. They shouted and waved their caps at him.

'Good Lord, Zalyozhnev's here too!' Rogozhin muttered, looking at them with a triumphant and what appeared to be almost a malicious smile, and he suddenly turned to the prince. 'Prince,' he said, 'I'm sure I don't know why I've taken a fancy to you. Maybe it's because I've met you at such a time, but then' (he pointed to Lebedev) 'I met him too, and I've taken no fancy to him. Come and see me, Prince. I'll get those silly old gaiters off you. I'll put a fine marten fur-coat on you, get a fine frock-coat made for you, a white waistcoat, or any you like; I'll stuff your pockets with money and – we'll go and pay a call on Nastasya Filippovna! Will you come or not?'

'Do as he says, Prince!' Lebedev broke in in an impressive and solemn tone of voice. 'Don't miss such a chance! Don't miss it!'

'I'll come with the greatest of pleasure,' the prince said, getting up and holding out his hand courteously to Rogozhin, 'and I thank you very much for liking me. I daresay I may even come to-day, if I can manage it. For I tell you frankly I'd taken a great fancy to you myself, especially when you were telling me about those diamond ear-rings. I liked you before that too, though you have such a gloomy face. Thank you also for the clothes and the fur-coat you've promised me, for I'm afraid I shall need some clothes and a fur-coat soon. And I've scarcely any money on me at all now.'

'You shall have money – you shall have it to-night; come!'

'You shall have money, you shall have money,' the civil servant echoed. 'By the evening and before the going down of the sun you shall have it.'

'And are you fond of the ladies, Prince? Tell me in good time.'

'Me? N-n-no! You see, I – – Perhaps you don't know, but, you see, I've been ill since I was a child and I have no knowledge at all of women.'

'Well,' Rogozhin cried, 'if that is so, then you are a regular holy fool, Prince, and such as you God loves.'

'And such the Lord loveth,' the civil servant echoed.

'You'd better come along with me, you dirty little copying clerk,' said Rogozhin to Lebedev, and they all got out of the carriage.

Lebedev ended up by getting what he wanted. The noisy crowd soon disappeared in the direction of Voznessensky Avenue. The prince had to turn towards Liteyny Avenue. It was damp and wet. The prince asked his way of passers-by: he had about two miles to go before he reached his destination, and he decided to take a cab.

2

General Yepanchin lived in his own house, not very far from Liteyny Avenue, towards the Church of the Transfiguration. Besides this (most excellent) house, five sixths of which was let, the general owned another huge house in Sadovaya Street, which also brought him in a large income. In addition to these two houses, he had a big and highly profitable estate within a mile or two of Petersburg, as well as a factory of some kind in the Petersburg district. Many years earlier, as everyone knew, the general had dabbled in government monopolies. Now he enjoyed considerable influence as a shareholder in a number of sound joint-stock companies. He was reputed to be a very rich man, a man who led a very active business life and was well connected socially. He had succeeded in making himself quite indispensable in certain quarters, including the ministry in which he served. And yet it was also a well-known fact that Ivan Fyodorovich Yepanchin was a man of no education and the son of a private in the army; the last circumstance, no doubt, could only redound to his credit, but, though an intelligent man, the general was not without some small and entirely pardonable weaknesses, and he disliked allusions to certain subjects. But there could be no doubt that he was an intelligent and clever man. So, for instance, he made a point of never pushing himself forward where it was wiser to keep in the background, and indeed many people valued him just for his self-effacing disposition, just because he always knew his place. But if only those judges of character had had an inkling of what was sometimes passing in the heart of General Yepanchin who knew his place so well! Though he did possess practical experience of life and some quite remarkable abilities, he liked to show off as a man who would rather carry out someone else's ideas than have a mind of his own, a man who was 'loyal without cringing' and – true to the spirit of the age – one who was a hundred per cent Russian, and a warm-hearted Russian to boot. He was involved in a number of rather amusing incidents in this connexion, but the general never lost heart, not even during the most amusing of these incidents. Besides, he was lucky, even at cards, and he played for very high stakes, quite deliberately refusing to conceal this supposedly little weakness of his, which came in so useful to him on numerous occasions, and displaying it for the whole world to see. He moved in very mixed company, but always, of course, among 'men of substance'. Everything, however, was still before him, he had plenty of time, and everything was bound to turn up sooner or later. The general, besides, was, as the saying goes, in the prime of life – that is, fifty-six, and not a day older, which under any circumstances is the most flourishing age in a man's life, the age at which *real* life can be rightly said to begin. His excellent health, his fine complexion, his sound though discoloured teeth, his stocky, solid figure, his preoccupied air in the morning at the department, his gay face in the evening at cards or at the count's – everything contributed to his present and future success and strewed roses in his path.

The general was the head of a flourishing family. It is true it was no longer all roses there, but, on the other hand, there was a great deal there, too, on which his fondest hopes and chief aims had long been earnestly and eagerly concentrated. And indeed what aim in life can be more important or more sacred than a father's? What is one to cling to if not to one's family? The general's family consisted of his wife and his three grown-up daughters. The general had been married a long time. While still a lieutenant he married a girl who was almost of the same age as he, who had neither education nor beauty, and who brought him a dowry of only fifty serfs, who, it is true, formed the basis of his future fortune. But the general never afterwards complained about his early marriage, never spoke of it slightingly as the result of an infatuation of his imprudent youth, and he respected his wife so much, and was sometimes so much afraid of her, that he could be said even to love her. The general's wife was a Princess Myshkin by birth, of a very ancient but by no means brilliant family, and she was extremely proud of her birth. A certain influential personage, one of those patrons whose patronage costs them nothing, agreed to take an interest in the marriage of the young princess. He opened the gate for the young officer and pushed him in, though indeed the young man did not need pushing – a mere look would have been sufficient: it would not have been wasted! On the whole, husband and wife spent their long married life happily together. While she was still a very young woman, the general's wife, as a born princess and the last of her family and, perhaps, too, because of her personal qualities, succeeded in finding a few influential ladies who took an interest in her. Later on, as her husband grew wealthy and acquired a high position in the service, she even began to feel at home in those exalted circles.

During those last years the general's three daughters – Alexandra, Adelaida, and Aglaya – had grown up. It is true they were only Yepanchins, but on their mother's side they belonged to a princely family, with no small dowries, with a father who in time might attain to a very high position, and – what was rather important – all three were remarkably good looking, including the eldest, Alexandra, who was already twenty-five years old. The second was twenty-three, and the youngest, Aglaya, was only just twenty. The youngest was, indeed, a great beauty, and was beginning to attract much attention in high society. But that, too, was not all: all three were distinguished by their education, cleverness, and talent. They were known to be extremely fond of each other and to be always ready to stand up for each other. It was even rumoured that the two elder sisters had made some sacrifices for the sake of the company of their youngest sister – the idol of the whole household. In society they not only disliked showing off, but were perhaps a little too modest. No one could accuse them of arrogance or superciliousness, and yet everyone was aware that they were proud and knew their own value. The eldest one was a musician, and the second one was quite an outstanding artist, but hardly anyone had known anything about it for many years, and it had become generally known only quite recently, and that, too, by sheer accident. In short, people said many nice things about them. But there were also people who were ill disposed towards them. These spoke in horrified tones of the large number of books they had read. They were in no hurry to get married; though they set store by belonging to a certain social circle, they did not think too much of it. That was all the more remarkable as everyone knew their father's attitude to life, his character, and his aims and ambitions.

It was about eleven o'clock when the prince rang the bell at the general's flat. The general lived on the second floor and occupied a flat that was rather modest, though in accordance with his social position. The door was opened by a liveried footman, and the prince had to spend a long time explaining who he was and the purpose of his visit to the man, who from the very first looked suspiciously at him and his bundle. At last, on his repeated and most precise declaration that he really was Prince Myshkin and that he had to see the general on most urgent business, the puzzled servant took him to a small ante-room, leading from the entrance hall to the reception-room next to the general's study, and handed him over to another servant, who was on duty every morning in the reception-room and announced visitors to the general. He was a man of over forty, wore a frock-coat, and had a preoccupied air. He was the general's personal attendant, and therefore had a high opinion of his own importance.

'Will you please wait in the reception-room, sir, and leave your bundle here,' he said, sitting down unhurriedly and importantly in his arm-chair and looking with stern astonishment at the prince, who had sat down beside him on a chair with his bundle in his hand.

'If you don't mind,' said the prince, 'I'd rather wait here with you. What am I going to do there alone by myself?'

'I'm sorry, sir, but I'm afraid you can't possibly stay in the ante-room, because you are a visitor, or, in other words, a guest. Do you want to see the general himself, sir?'

The servant, apparently unable to reconcile himself to the idea of having to admit such a visitor, decided to repeat his question.

'Yes, I have some business – –' the prince began.

'I'm not asking you what your business is, sir. My duty is only to announce you. And I'm very sorry, sir, but I cannot announce you without the secretary's permission.'

The suspiciousness of the man seemed to increase more and more: the prince was too unlike the usual run of daily visitors, and though the general received all sorts of visitors almost every day at a certain hour, especially on business, the servant, though used to it and in spite of the wide nature of his instructions, was very doubtful: he felt that he had to have the secretary's authorization before he announced the prince.

'Have you really come – er – from abroad, sir?' he asked almost involuntarily, and – stopped short in confusion; what he wanted perhaps to ask was: 'Are you really Prince Myshkin?'

'Yes, I've come straight from the station. I think what you wanted to ask me was whether I was really Prince Myshkin, but did not ask it out of politeness.'

'H'm,' the astonished servant grunted.

'I assure you I haven't told you a lie, and you won't have to answer for me. And as for my being dressed like this and carrying a bundle, there's nothing surprising about it, for, you see, my circumstances are not exactly bright at the moment.'

'H'm. ... You see, sir, that's not what's worrying me. It is my duty to announce you, and I expect the secretary will interview you, and providing you're not -- Aye, that's just the trouble, sir, providing -- Begging you pardon, sir, you haven't come to ask the general for money, have you?'

'Oh no, not at all. You need not worry about that. My business is of quite a different nature.'

'I'm very sorry, sir. I asked because of your appearance. Will you, please, wait for the secretary. The general is engaged with the colonel at the moment. The secretary will be here presently – the secretary of the company, sir.'

'Well, if I have to wait for some time I'd like to ask if you could tell me where I could have a smoke? I've got a pipe and tobacco.'

'Smoke, sir?' the servant asked, giving him a look of scornful bewilderment, as though unable to believe his ears. 'Smoke? No, sir, you can't possibly smoke here. Why, sir, I wonder you're not ashamed even to think of it. Dear me, this is a queer business and no mistake.'

'Oh, not in this room, of course. I realize I can't smoke here. I'd have gone anywhere else you'd have shown me, for I'm used to smoking, and I haven't had a smoke for three hours. However, just as you like. There's a saying, you know, when in Rome --'

'Well, how am I going to announce a gentleman like you, sir?' the valet muttered in spite of himself. 'To begin with, you oughtn't to be sitting here at all, but in the reception-room, because you're almost a visitor, sir, or, in other words, a guest, and I shall be held responsible for that. You're not intending to live with us, are you, sir?'

'No, I don't think so. Even if they were to ask me, I shouldn't stay. I've just come to make the general's acquaintance – that's all!'

'Make the general's acquaintance, did you say, sir?' the valet asked with surprise and redoubled suspiciousness. 'Why then did you say at first that you had come on business?'

'Well, hardly on business! That is, if you like, I have a certain business, but that's only to ask for advice. I've come here chiefly to introduce myself because I'm Prince Myshkin, and Mrs Yepanchin is a Princess Myshkin, the last of them, and except for her and myself there are no more Myshkins left.'

'You're not a relation, too, are you, sir?' asked the servant with a start, looking almost frightened.

'Well, no, not quite. But, then, if I were to stretch a point, we are of course relations, but so distant that it's hardly worth taking into account. I wrote a letter to Mrs Yepanchin from abroad, but she did not reply. Still, I thought it only right to get in touch with her on my return. I'm telling you all this now so as to remove all doubts from your mind, for I can see that you are still worried. Just announce me as Prince Myshkin, and the announcement itself will explain the reason of my visit. If I'm received, well and good; if not, it's perhaps just as well. But I don't think they can refuse to receive me: Mrs Yepanchin will of course want to see the last and only representative of her family, and, as I have been reliably informed about her, she is very proud of her descent.'

It would seem that the prince's conversation was ordinary enough, but the more ordinary it became, the more absurd it sounded in the present case, and the experienced valet could not help feeling that what was quite appropriate between one man and another was utterly inappropriate between a visitor and a *servant*. And as servants are much more intelligent than their masters assume them to be, it occurred to the valet that there were only two possible explanations: either the prince was some sort of a cadger and had certainly come to ask the general for money, or the prince was just a simpleton and had no sense of personal dignity, for an intelligent prince with a sense of dignity would not be sitting in an ante-room discussing his private affairs with a servant. In either case, would he not have to answer for him?

'All the same, sir,' he said as insistently as possible, 'you ought really to wait in the reception-room.'

'Why,' the prince remarked with a gay laugh, 'if I had been waiting there I shouldn't have been able to explain it all to you, should I? So that you'd still be worried at the sight of my cloak and my bundle. And now you need not perhaps wait for the secretary, but can go and announce me yourself.'

'I'm very sorry, sir, but I can't possibly announce a visitor like you without the secretary, particularly as the general himself gave me precise orders this morning not to disturb him for anybody while the colonel was with him, and Mr Ivolgin goes in without any announcement!'

'You mean, the civil servant?'

'Mr Ivolgin, sir? No, sir. He is employed by the company. Won't you put your bundle down just here, sir?'

'Thank you, I shall put it there, if you don't mind. I was thinking of doing so myself. And I may as well take off my cloak, mayn't I?'

'Why, yes, sir. You can't very well go into the general's study in your cloak, can you?'

The prince got up, hurriedly took off his cloak, and remained in a fairly decent, well-cut, though rather threadbare, jacket. He wore a steel watch-chain across his waistcoat. On the end of the watch-chain was a silver Geneva watch.

Although the prince was a simpleton – the servant had made up his mind about *that* – it seemed nevertheless improper to the general's valet to continue his conversation with a visitor, in spite of the fact that for some reason he could not help liking the prince – after his own fashion, of course. But looked at from a different point of view, the prince aroused in him a feeling of most violent indignation.

'And when does Mrs Yepanchin receive visitors?' asked the prince, resuming his seat.

'That, sir, has nothing to do with me. She receives visitors at different times, all according as to who they may be. Her dressmaker would be admitted as early as eleven o'clock. Mr Ivolgin, Gavrila Ardalionovich, too, is admitted earlier than anybody else. She even sees him at early lunch.'

'It's much warmer here in your rooms than it is abroad in winter,' observed the prince. 'But it's much warmer in the streets there than it is here. A Russian who is not used to their way of life finds it almost impossible to live in their houses in winter.'

'Don't they heat them?'

'Yes, they do, but their houses are differently built – I mean, their stoves and windows.'

'I see, sir. Have you been away long, sir?'

'Four years. But I stayed almost in the same place all the time. In the country.'

'I daresay everything here must seem very strange to you, sir.'

'Yes, that's also true. You know, I can't help feeling surprised at not having forgotten my Russian. Here I am talking to you now, and all the time I cannot help thinking that I'm not talking so badly after all. That's perhaps why I talk such a lot. Ever since yesterday I've just wanted to go on talking Russian.'

'H'm – yes! Did you live in Petersburg before, sir?' (However much he tried, he found it impossible not to keep up so polite and courteous a conversation.)

'In Petersburg? No, hardly at all, except when I happened to pass through. I had no idea what was going on here before, and now I'm told there are so many new things happening that those who did know what was going on have to learn everything afresh. People here are talking a lot about the new criminal courts.'

'Aye, the courts. It's quite true, sir, the new courts are – well, courts, sir. And what about them foreign courts, sir? Are their laws fairer than ours?'

'I don't know. I've heard much that's good about ours. Then again we have no capital punishment.'

'Do they execute people there?'

'Yes, they do. I saw it in France, in Lyons. Dr Schneider took me with him there.'

'Do they hang them there?'

'No. In France they always cut their heads off.'

'Well, sir, do they scream?'

'Good heavens, no! It only takes an instant. The man is laid down, then a sort of broad knife falls down on an engine – they call it a guillotine. It comes down heavily, with tremendous force. In less than a second the head is cut off. It's the preliminaries that are so awful. When they read out the death sentence, get the man ready for execution, pinion him, take him up the scaffold – that's what's so horrible! People all crowd round, even women, though they don't like women to look on.'

'It's not their business.'

'Why, of course not! Such agony! The criminal was a middle-aged man, intelligent, fearless, strong – Legros was his name. Well, believe it or not, I tell you he wept when he walked up the scaffold. White as a sheet, he was. Is such a thing possible? Isn't it horrible? Whoever heard of anyone crying for fear? I never thought that a grown-up man, not a child, could cry for fear, a man who never cried before, a man of forty-five. What do you think is going on in such a man's soul at the time? Think of the mental anguish he suffers. It's an outrage on the soul, that's what it is! It is written, Thou shalt not kill. Does that mean that because he has killed we must kill him? No, that's wrong. It is a month since I saw it, and I can still see it as though it were happening before my eyes. I've dreamt of it half a dozen times.'

The prince grew animated as he spoke; a faint flush suffused his pale face, although he spoke as quietly as ever. The servant watched him with sympathetic interest, as though he could not bring himself to take his eyes off him; he, too, was probably a man with imagination, with a capacity for reasoning.

'It's a good thing, sir,' he observed, 'that there is not much suffering when the head flies off.'

'Do you know,' cried the prince, 'you've just made that observation and lots of people are of the same opinion as you, and the engine, the guillotine, was invented for that very reason. But at the time the idea occurred to me – what if it is even worse? You may think such an idea absurd and ridiculous, but if you have some imagination you can't help getting such ideas. Just think: take, for instance, torture: you get suffering, wounds, bodily agony, all of which distracts the mind from mental suffering, for up to the very moment of your death you are only tormented by your wounds. Yet the chief and the worst pain is perhaps not inflicted by wounds, but by your certain knowledge that in an hour, in ten minutes, in half a minute, now, this moment your soul will fly out of your body, and that you will be a human being no longer, and that that's certain – the main thing is that it is *certain*. Just when you lay your head under the knife and you hear the swish of the knife as it slides down over your head – it is just that fraction of a second that is the most awful of all. Do you realize that it is not only my imagination, but that many people have said the same? I am so convinced of it that I will tell you frankly what I think. To kill for murder is an immeasurably greater evil than the crime itself. Murder by legal process is immeasurably more dreadful than murder by a brigand. A man who is murdered by brigands is killed at night in a forest or somewhere else, and up to the last moment he still hopes that he will be saved. There have been instances when a man whose throat had already been cut, was still hoping, or running away or begging for his life to be spared. But here all this last hope, which makes it ten times easier to die, is taken away *for certain*; here you have been sentenced to death, and the whole terrible agony lies in the fact that you will most certainly not escape, and there is no agony greater than that. Take a soldier and put him in front of a cannon in battle and fire at him and he will still hope, but read the same soldier his death sentence *for certain*, and he will go mad or burst out crying. Who says that human nature is capable of bearing this without madness? Why this cruel, hideous, unnecessary, and useless mockery? Possibly there are men who have sentences of death read out to them and have been given time to go through this torture, and have then been told, You can go now, you've been reprieved. Such men could perhaps tell us. It was of agony like this and of such horror that Christ spoke. No, you can't treat a man like that!'

Although the footman could not have put it all in the same words as the prince, he did of course grasp the most important point of it, if not everything, and indeed it was evident from the look on his face that he was deeply moved.

'I daresay you could have your smoke, sir,' he said, 'if you want it badly, only you will have to be quick about it. For what if the general suddenly asked for you and you were not here? You see that door there under the stairs, don't you? Well, as you go through the door, you'll see a small room on the right. You can have your smoke there, only please open the little window, because we don't allow this sort of thing here.'

But the prince had no time to go and have his smoke. A young man with papers in his hands suddenly came into the ante-room. The footman began to help him off with his fur-coat. The young man glanced at the prince out of the corner of his eye.

'This gentleman, sir,' the footman began confidentially and almost familiarly, 'says he is Prince Myshkin and a relation of the mistress's. He has just arrived by train from abroad with that small bundle in his hand, but – –'

The prince did not catch the rest of the sentence because the footman started whispering. The young man listened attentively, looking at the prince with great interest. At last he stopped listening and approached the prince hurriedly.

'Are you Prince Myshkin?' he asked with the utmost politeness and amiability.

He was a very good-looking young man, also about twenty-eight, slender, fair-haired, of medium height, with a small imperial, and an intelligent and very handsome face. Only his smile, for all its amiability, was somewhat too exquisite, revealing a row of altogether too dazzling and even teeth; and in spite of all his gaiety and apparent good nature, the look in his eyes was a little too intent and searching.

'I expect when he is alone he doesn't look like that at all and, quite possibly, he never laughs,' the prince could not help reflecting.

The prince explained in a few words all he could, almost in the same words as he had told the footman and before that Rogozhin. In the meantime the young man seemed to recall something.

'Wasn't it you,' he asked, 'who sent a letter a year ago, or not quite so long ago, to Mrs Yepanchin, from Switzerland?'

'Yes.'

'In that case they know about you here and most certainly remember you. You want to see the general? I'll announce you presently. He'll be free in a minute. Only – er – you ought really to be waiting in the reception-room, you know. Why is this gentleman here?' he asked the footman sternly.

'I told you, sir, he preferred it.'

At that moment the door of the study was opened and an army officer with a brief-case under his arm came out, talking loudly and taking his leave.

'Are you there, Ganya?' cried a voice from the study. 'Come in, please!'

Ganya nodded to the prince and went hastily into the study.

Two minutes later the door was opened again and Ganya's cheerful and affable voice called:

'Please come in, Prince!'

3

General Ivan Fyodorovich Yepanchin stood in the middle of his study and looked with great interest at the prince as he entered the room. He even advanced two steps towards him. The prince went up to him and introduced himself.

'Very pleased to meet you,' said the general. 'What can I do for you?'

'I have no urgent business of any kind, sir. My object in calling on you was simply to make your acquaintance. I'm sorry to disturb you. I'm afraid I don't know your visiting hours and what your other arrangements are. But I've only just come from the station myself. I've just arrived from Switzerland.'

The general smiled faintly, but thought it over quickly and checked himself, then he thought again, screwed up his eyes, once more looked his visitor up and down from head to foot, then motioned him to a chair and, sitting down himself at a somewhat oblique angle towards him, waited impatiently for him to begin. Ganya was standing at the other end of the study by the bureau, sorting out papers.

'I'm afraid I've not much time for making acquaintances,' said the general, 'but as you have no doubt some reason for wishing to see me, I – –'

'I felt sure,' the prince interrupted, 'you'd think I had some special reason for my visit. But I assure you, sir, I have no personal reason at all except the pleasure of making your acquaintance.'

'It is of course a great pleasure for me too, but people can't spend all their time in amusing themselves. Sometimes, you know, they have to attend to their business affairs. Besides, I'm afraid I haven't been able to discover so far anything – er – in common between us, I mean, any – er – reason – er – –'

'Oh, there's no reason at all and we naturally have very little in common. For the fact that I'm Prince Myshkin and that Mrs Yepanchin belongs to the same family as I is most certainly no reason. I quite understand that. All the same, that's really why I've come. You see, sir, I haven't been in Russia for over four years and I really can hardly say that I ever left it, for when I did leave it I was scarcely in my right mind. I knew nothing then, and I know even less now. I'm in need of good, kind people. In fact, I have some business I'd like someone to advise me about, but I don't know where to turn to. While still in Berlin, I thought: they're almost my relations, so why not start with them? Perhaps we may be of some use to each other – they to me and I to them, if, that is, they are good people. And from what I've heard you are good people.'

'Thank you very much, sir,' replied the general, looking rather surprised. 'May I ask where you're staying?'

'I'm not staying anywhere as yet.'

'So you've come to see me straight from the station, have you? And – with your luggage?'

'Well, sir, all my luggage consists of a small bundle with a change of clothes and nothing more. I usually carry it in my hand. I shall have plenty of time in the evening to engage a room at a hotel.'

'Oh, so you do intend to engage a room in a hotel, do you?'

'Why, of course.'

'Well, from what you said I was almost afraid that you'd come straight here to stay with us.'

'I should never have done that without an invitation from you. And I don't mind telling you that I shouldn't have stayed even at your invitation, not for any particular reason, but just because – it's not in my character.'

'Well, in that case it's a good thing I haven't invited and am not inviting you to stay. And may I add, Prince, I mean, just to remove all misunderstandings at once, that having agreed just now that there couldn't be any question of any relationship between us – though of course I should have been extremely flattered – therefore – –'

'You mean, therefore I'd better get up and go, don't you?' said the prince with rather a gay laugh, half rising to go, in spite of his unmistakably straitened circumstances. 'And really, General, though I've had no practical experience of your customs, nor of the way people live here, I had an idea that this was how our interview would end. Well, perhaps it's for the best. I never got a reply to my letter either. Well, good-bye, and I'm sorry to have troubled you.'

The prince's expression was so good-natured at this moment and his smile was so free from the slightest suspicion of any concealed unfriendly feeling that the general suddenly stopped short and, somehow, looked at his visitor in quite a different way; the change in his expression took place almost in an instant.

'Look here, Prince,' he said almost in a different voice, 'I really don't know you at all and I suppose Mrs Yepanchin may like to have a look at a person bearing the same name as she. Stay a little longer, if you like, and if you can spare the time.'

'Oh, I can spare the time, sir,' said the prince, at once putting his soft, round hat on the table. 'My time is entirely my own. I confess I had hoped that Mrs Yepanchin would perhaps remember that I had written to her. While waiting outside just now, your servant suspected me of coming to ask you for money. I noticed it, and I expect you must have given him strict orders about that. I assure you I haven't come for that, but really to become acquainted with people. But I'm afraid I have disturbed you, and that does worry me.'

'Well, Prince,' the general said with a cheerful smile, 'if you really are the sort of person you seem to be, then I daresay it will be a pleasure to make your acquaintance. Only, you see, I'm a busy man and I'll have to sit down presently and sign some papers, then I'll be going to see his excellency, and after that to the department, so pleased as I am to see people, I mean, good people, I – – But I'm sure you've been brought up so well that – –And how old are you, Prince?'

'Twenty-six.'

'Oh! I thought you were much younger!'

'Yes, I'm told I do look much younger than my age. And you needn't worry, sir; I shall soon learn how not to disturb you, for I dislike disturbing people myself. And, besides, I can't help feeling that we appear to be so different in every way – I mean, because of all sorts of reasons, that we can't perhaps have many things in common, though, you know, I don't think it's quite true, because very often it only seems that people haven't anything in common, while, in fact, they have – I mean it's just because people are lazy that they are apt to divide themselves into different groups just by looking at one another and can't find any common interests. ... I'm not boring you, am I? You seem to – –'

'Just one thing more: have you any means at all? Or do you perhaps intend to take up some sort of work? I'm sorry I'm so – –'

'Good heavens, sir, I fully appreciate and understand your question. For the time being I have no means at all, nor have I any occupation, either, though I'd like to have one. The money I have had was not mine. Dr Schneider, the professor who taught and treated me in Switzerland, gave me enough money for the journey and not a penny more, so that now, for instance, I've only got a few coppers left. It is true I have a certain business matter to attend to and I'd like some advice, but – –'

'Tell me, please, how do you intend to live meanwhile and what exactly are your plans?' interrupted the general.

'I'd like to get some sort of work.'

'Oh, but you are a philosopher, I see! But – er – have you any special aptitude for anything, any talent, I mean, anything you can earn a living by? I'm sorry – –'

'Oh, don't apologize. No, sir, I don't think I have any talent, or any special aptitude for anything. Why, quite the contrary; for, you see, sir, I'm an invalid and I've never had any regular education. As for earning a living, I think – –'

But the general interrupted him again, and again started questioning him. The prince told him what has been told already. It appeared that the general had heard of Pavlishchev and had even known him personally. Why Pavlishchev had been so interested in his education, the prince could not explain – however, it was probably simply because he had been an old friend of his father's. The prince had lost his parents while still a small child and spent all his life in the country, as his health demanded country air. Pavlishchev had put him in charge of some old ladies, relations of his; first a governess had been engaged for him, then a tutor. He declared, however, that, though he remembered everything, there was not much he could explain satisfactorily because there were many things he could not account for. His frequent fits had made almost an idiot of him (the prince actually used the word 'idiot'). Finally he said that one day in Berlin Pavlishchev had met Professor Schneider, a Swiss doctor who specialized in those particular diseases and who had a clinic in Switzerland in the canton of Valais, where he treated patients suffering from idiocy and insanity according to his own methods, consisting of a cold-water cure and exercises, teaching them all sorts of subjects at the same time and, generally, attending to their spiritual development; that Pavlishchev had sent him to Switzerland to Schneider about five years ago and had died suddenly two years ago without making any provision for him; that Schneider had kept him for two more years until the end of his treatment; that he had not cured him, but had helped him a great deal; and that, finally, at his own request and because of a certain unforeseen circumstance, he had sent him now to Russia.

The general was greatly surprised.

'And,' he asked, 'have you no one in Russia, absolutely no one?'

'No, sir, I have no one at the moment, but I hope – besides, I've received a letter – –'

'At least,' the general interrupted, having missed the prince's remark about the letter, 'you have had some education, and your illness, I suppose, will not prevent your taking some easy job in an office, will it?'

'Oh, I'm sure it won't. And, as a matter of fact, I'd be very glad to get some job, for I'd like to see what I can do myself. I have been studying for the last four years continuously, though not quite regularly, but according to Dr Schneider's special system. And I've managed to read a large number of Russian books during that time.'

'Russian books? Then I suppose you must have a pretty good knowledge of Russian and can write it without mistakes, can't you?'

'Oh, yes, sir. Very much so.'

'Excellent. And what about your handwriting?'

'My handwriting is very good. Indeed, I've quite a talent for that. I'm quite a calligraphist. Please,' the prince said warmly, 'let me write something for you as a specimen.'

'Do; it is rather important. And, you know, I appreciate your willingness, Prince. You are very nice, I must say.'

'You've got such wonderful writing materials, sir – so many pencils and pens, and such fine thick paper. ... And what a fine study you have. I know that landscape – it's a view in Switzerland. I'm sure the artist painted it from nature, and I'm sure I've seen the place – it's in the canton of Uri. ...'

'Very likely, though it was bought here. Ganya, give the prince some paper. Now, here are your pens and paper – here, on this table, please. What's that?' the general said, addressing Ganya, who had in the meantime taken out and handed him a large photograph from his brief-case. 'Why, it's Nastasya Filippovna! Did she send it to you herself? Did she?' he asked Ganya excitedly and with great interest.

'Yes, sir. She gave it to me herself when I went to offer my congratulations. I've been asking her for it for a long time. I don't know whether it wasn't meant as a hint at my going to see her empty-handed, without a present, on such a day,' Ganya added with an unpleasant smile.

'I'm sure it wasn't,' the general said with conviction. 'What a funny way of looking at things you have, to be sure! It would never occur to her to hint at – and she isn't a mercenary woman at all. Besides, what sort of present could you make her? Why, you'd have to spend thousands on it! Your portrait, perhaps? By the way, she hasn't asked you for your portrait yet, has she?'

'No, not yet, sir. Perhaps she'll never ask for it. You haven't forgotten to-night's party, have you, sir? You're one of those who have been specially invited.'

'Of course, I haven't forgotten, and I shall be there. I should say so – her birthday – her twenty-fifth birthday! Well – yes. ... You know, Ganya, I think I'd better let you into a secret – prepare yourself. She promised Mr Totsky and me that she'd make known her final decision at the party to-night: to be or not to be! So mind you are prepared!'

Ganya suddenly looked so upset that he even turned slightly pale.

'Are you sure she said that?' he asked, and there seemed to be a catch in his voice.

'She gave us her word the day before yesterday. We both begged her so much that we forced her to give in. But she did ask us not to tell you until to-night.'

The general scrutinized Ganya intently. He obviously did not like Ganya's discomfiture.

'I should like you to remember, sir,' Ganya said, hesitantly and looking troubled, 'that she granted me absolute freedom of choice right up to the time when she made up her mind herself. And even then I have the last word – –'

'But, my dear fellow, haven't you – haven't you – –' stammered the general, looking suddenly alarmed.

'Oh, I haven't decided anything.'

'But, good Lord, man, think what you're doing to us!'

'But I haven't refused, have I? I'm afraid I can't have expressed myself properly. ...'

'Refused, indeed!' the general said with vexation. 'You see, my dear fellow, it's no longer a question of your *not* refusing, but of your willingness, of the pleasure and the happiness with which you will receive her consent. How are things at home?'

'At home? Oh, at home what I say is law. Only father is playing the fool as usual, but then he's been behaving utterly disgracefully for some time. I no longer speak to him, but I keep a tight rein on him and, as a matter of fact, but for mother I'd have turned him out of the house long ago. Mother, of course, is always crying; my sister is in a temper, but I told them at last that I'm jolly well going to do what I like and that it was my wish that at home they did as I told them. At least, I made it perfectly clear to my sister in my mother's presence.'

'Well, my dear fellow,' the general said, musingly, with a slight shrug of his shoulders and a perplexed movement of his hands, 'I simply can't understand it. Your mother, when she came to see me the other day – you remember? – kept moaning and groaning. What's the matter? I asked. Well, it seems that they look upon it as a *dishonour*. But what sort of dishonour is it, may I ask? Who can reproach Nastasya Filippovna with anything? What can anyone say against her? Not, surely, that she has been living with Totsky? Why, that is simply nonsense, especially if certain facts are taken into consideration! You wouldn't let your daughters associate with her, she says. Well, really! Who would have thought your mother would say a thing like that; I mean, how can she fail to understand – –'

'Her own position?' Ganya prompted the embarrassed general. 'She does understand it, sir. You mustn't be angry with her. Anyway, I gave her a good talking to at the time. I told her to mind her own business. Still, the fact remains that everything has so far been quiet at home because the final word has not yet been said, but the storm is bound to break. If it is spoken to-night, it will all come out.'

The prince heard all this conversation while sitting in a corner of the room writing his calligraphic specimen. He finished, went up to the table, and presented his page.

'So this is Nastasya Filippovna!' he said, looking at the portrait attentively and curiously. 'She's wonderfully beautiful!' he added at once, warmly.

The portrait was indeed of an extraordinarily beautiful woman. She was photographed in a black silk dress of an extremely simple and elegant cut; her hair, which appeared to be a dark brown colour, was done up in a simple, homely style; her eyes were dark and deep, her forehead was pensive; her expression was passionate and, as it were, haughty. She was rather thin in the face and, perhaps, pale, too.

Ganya and the general looked at the prince in astonishment.

'What did you say? Nastasya Filippovna? Do you already know Nastasya Filippovna too?' asked the general.

'Yes,' replied the prince. 'I've only been twenty-four hours in Russia and I already know a beautiful woman like that,' and he told them of his meeting with Rogozhin and repeated all Rogozhin had told him.

'There's another piece of news for you!' the general exclaimed again in alarm, after having listened attentively to the prince's story. He looked searchingly at Ganya.

'I expect it's just a bit of silly nonsense,' Ganya muttered, looking a little put out, too. 'A rich merchant's son on the spree. I've heard something about him before.'

'I, too, have heard of him, my dear fellow,' the general put in. 'Nastasya Filippovna told me the whole story after the incident with the ear-rings. But now it's quite a different matter. We are quite likely dealing with millions here and – passion, a disgraceful passion, no doubt, but passion for all that, and we all know what such gentlemen are capable of when infatuated! H'm, I only hope there won't be a scandalous scene!' the general concluded thoughtfully.

'You're not afraid of his millions, are you, sir?' Ganya asked with a grin.

'You're not, of course!'

'What was your impression, Prince?' asked Ganya suddenly, addressing the prince. 'Is he a serious person or just a rowdy fellow? What do you think?'

There was something peculiar taking place in Ganya when he asked that question. It was as though he were struck by some new and peculiar idea, which blazed up impatiently in his eyes. The general, who was genuinely and frankly ill at ease, also glanced at the prince, but without expecting much from his reply.

'I don't know how to tell you,' replied the prince. 'Only I did feel that there was a good deal of passion in him, a sort of morbid passion. And he seemed to be quite ill, too. I shouldn't be at all surprised if he had to take to his bed in a day or two, especially if he starts drinking.'

'Oh? So that's what you thought?' the general said, clutching at the idea.

'Yes.'

'Yet scandalous incidents of that kind may well happen not only in a day or two, but also before this evening, and indeed, something might happen even today,' Ganya said, grinning at the general.

'Well, of course, it might and, if it does, everything will depend on any crazy idea that might enter her head on the spur of the moment.'

'And you know what she is sometimes like, don't you?'

'What do you mean by that?' the general, thoroughly roused by now, cried angrily. 'Look here, Ganya,' he went on, 'don't for heaven's sake contradict her much today and try to – well – to be as nice to her as you can. Well, what are you grinning at me like that for? Look here, I think I may as well take this opportunity of asking you what we are doing all this for. I want you to understand that so far as my personal interest in this matter is concerned, I have long given up worrying about it. In one way or another, I shall settle it to my advantage. Totsky has made up his mind irrevocably, which means that I have nothing to worry about, either. So that if I happen to want anything now, it is entirely for your benefit. You can judge for yourself – or don't you trust me? Besides, you're – you're an intelligent chap and – er – I have been counting on you, and in the present case that – that – –'

'– is the chief thing,' Ganya finished the sentence, coming to the rescue of the embarrassed general again, and his lips distended into a most sarcastic smile, which he no longer attempted to conceal.

He stared straight at the general with feverish eyes, as though anxious that he should read there all that was in his mind. The general turned purple with rage.

'Yes, intelligence is the chief thing!' he agreed, looking sharply at Ganya. 'What a funny chap you are, to be sure! You really seem to be glad of that absurd merchant fellow, I notice, as a way out for yourself. But it is just here that you ought to have applied your intelligence from the start. It is just here that you should have understood and – er – dealt honestly and fairly with both sides, or else – er – warned us beforehand so as not to compromise others, particularly as you had plenty of time for it, and, indeed, there's still plenty of time even now' (the general raised his eyebrows significantly), 'in spite of the fact that there are only a few hours left. Do you understand? Do you? Are you willing or aren't you? If you aren't, say so, and – and welcome! No one is stopping you, sir, no one is trying to drag you into a trap by force, if, that is, you really see a trap here.'

'I am willing,' Ganya said in an undertone, but in a firm voice, dropping his eyes and lapsing into a gloomy silence.

The general was satisfied. He had lost his temper, but he was evidently sorry he had gone too far. Turning to the prince, he suddenly seemed to have been struck by the disagreeable thought that the prince had been there and could not help hearing what was said. But he was instantly reassured: one glance at the prince was enough to feel entirely reassured.

'Oho!' cried the general, examining the specimen of handwriting presented by the prince. 'Why, that's real calligraphy! And of an uncommon type too! Have a look, Ganya! There's real talent for you!'

On the thick sheet of vellum the prince had written in medieval Russian characters 'The humble Abbot Pafnuty hath put his hand hereto.'

'This,' the prince explained with great pleasure and animation, 'is the exact signature of the Abbot Pafnuty, copied from a fourteenth-century manuscript. They used to sign their names beautifully, all those old abbots and bishops of ours, and sometimes with what taste, with what care! Haven't you really got a copy of Pogodin's edition, General? And here I've written in a different script: it's the large round French script of the last century; some letters were written quite differently; it's the writing of the market-place, the writing of public scribes, faithfully copied from their samples (I had one myself). You will admit that it is not without its good points. Look at these round *a*'s and *d*'s. I have adapted the French characters to Russian lettering, which is very difficult, but it turned out very satisfactorily. Here is another beautiful original script – this sentence here: "Zeal conquers everything." That's a Russian script used by scribes or, if you like, by military scribes. That's how official documents to important personages are written, also a round script, an excellent *black* script, but with remarkable taste. A calligraphist would have frowned upon those flourishes or rather those attempts at flourishes, those unfinished tails – you see them – but look, on the whole they have a character of their own and, indeed, you can see the very soul of the military scribe peeping out of them: a desire to throw caution to the winds and give full play to one's talent, but the military collar is drawn tightly round the neck, and you can observe how discipline has fashioned the handwriting, too – it's lovely! I was struck by a specimen like that lately – I came across it by chance, and in Switzerland, of all places! Well, and this is a simple, ordinary English script: elegance can go no further, it's all so perfectly exquisite – it's like a string of beads or pearls – it can't be improved on; but here is a variation of it, and again a French one – I got it from a French commercial traveller: it is the same as the English lettering, but the thick strokes are a trifle thicker than in the English, with the result that the relationship between light and shade is destroyed. And observe that, too: the oval has been changed, it is a tiny bit rounder and, furthermore, the flourish is allowed, and a flourish is a most dangerous thing! A flourish requires extraordinary taste, but if it is successful, if the right relationship is found, such lettering is quite incomparable, so much so that one could fall in love with it.'

'Oho!' the general laughed. 'So that's the kind of refinements you go in for, is it? Why, my dear fellow, you're not just a calligraphist – you're an artist! Eh, Ganya?'

'Wonderful,' said Ganya, 'and he fully realizes his vocation, too,' he added, laughing sarcastically.

'You may laugh, but there's a career in it,' said the general. 'Do you know, Prince, what personage we'll have you write official documents to? Why, one could offer you thirty roubles a month from the start. However, it's already half past twelve,' he concluded, glancing at the clock. 'To business, Prince, for I'm in a hurry and I may not see you again to-day. Sit down for a minute. I have already explained that I cannot receive you very often, but I should like very much to be of a little assistance to you, a little, of course, I mean, in the most essentials, and as for the rest, you'll have to do as you please. I'll find you a job in the office, not a very exacting one, but it will require accuracy. Now as to your more immediate plans. In the house, that is, in the family of Mr Ivolgin, this young friend of mine, with whom

I'd like you to become acquainted, his mother and sister have set aside two or three furnished rooms which they let with board and attendance to highly recommended lodgers. I'm sure Mrs Ivolgin will accept my recommendation. You, Prince, will find it more than convenient, because you won't be on your own but, as it were, in the bosom of a family, for I don't think you ought to be left alone at first in such a capital city as Petersburg. Ganya's mother and sister are ladies for whom I have the utmost respect. Nina Alexandrovna, Ganya's mother, is the wife of Ardalion Alexandrovich, a retired general, a former colleague of mine when I served in the army, but with whom, for certain reasons, I regret to say, I'm no longer on speaking terms, which does not prevent me, however, from feeling a certain respect for him. I'm telling you all this, Prince, because I want you to understand that I am recommending you personally and, therefore, in a way vouching for you. The terms are extremely moderate and I hope your salary will soon be quite sufficient to meet them. It is true, a man needs pocket money, however little, but I know you won't be angry with me, Prince, if I tell you that you'd be better off without any pocket money, and indeed without any money in your pocket. I'm telling you this merely from my first impression of you. But as your purse is quite empty now, let me offer you these twenty-five roubles, to begin with. We shall, of course, settle it later, and if you are such a sincere and nice person as you appear to be, there can be no difficulties between us in this matter, either. As for my taking such an interest in you, I have a certain object in view, which I shall let you know in good time. You see, I'm perfectly frank with you. I hope, Ganya, you've nothing against the prince's finding accommodation in your flat, have you?'

'Oh, quite the contrary, sir! Mother, too, will be very glad,' Ganya declared courteously and obligingly.

'I believe you've only one room let. That fellow – what's his name? – Fer – Fer – –'

'Ferdyshchenko.'

'Oh yes – I must say I don't like that Ferdyshchenko of yours – a sort of low buffoon. And I can't understand why Nastasya Filippovna encourages him so. Is he really a relation of hers?'

'Oh no, sir, that's only a joke. They are not even distantly related.'

'Well, to blazes with him! Well, Prince, are you satisfied or not?'

'Thank you, General, you've been very kind to me, especially as I haven't even asked you for anything. I'm saying this not out of pride. I really didn't know where I was going to spend the night. It is true Rogozhin invited me to stay with him.'

'Rogozhin? No, take my fatherly or, if you prefer it, friendly advice and forget Mr Rogozhin. I should, in fact, advise you to stick to the family which you are about to enter.'

'As you are so kind, sir,' the prince began, 'there is just one matter I'd like to ask you about. I have been informed that – –'

'I'm sorry,' the general interrupted, 'I haven't a minute to spare now. I'll go and tell Mrs Yepanchin about you. If she wishes to see you now – and I shall indeed do my best that she should – I'd advise you to take advantage of the opportunity and get her to like you, for she could be very useful to you. You're of the same family, too. But if she doesn't wish to, it just cannot be helped – another time, perhaps. And you, Ganya, look through these accounts in the meantime – Fedoseyev and I could make nothing of them. We mustn't forget to include them.'

The general went out, and the prince did not manage to tell him about the business, which he had tried in vain to discuss for the fourth time. Ganya lit a cigarette and offered one to the prince. The prince accepted it, but refrained from talking, not wishing to interfere with Ganya's work. Ganya barely glanced at the figures which the general had indicated to him. He was preoccupied. The prince could not help feeling that Ganya's smile, expression, and thoughtfulness became even more painful when they were left alone. Suddenly he went up to the prince, who was at that moment bending over the portrait of Nastasya Filippovna examining it carefully.

'So you like a woman like that, do you, Prince?' he said suddenly, looking piercingly at him, as though there were some urgent reason for his question.

'A remarkable face!' replied the prince. 'And I'm sure her life has not been an ordinary one. Her face looks cheerful, but she has suffered a lot, hasn't she? Her eyes show it and her cheekbones, those two points under her eyes. It's a proud face, a terribly proud face, but what I can't tell is whether she is kind-hearted or not. Oh, if she were! That would make everything right for her!'

'But would *you* marry such a woman?' Ganya went on, without taking his feverishly burning eyes off him.

'I can't marry anyone,' said the prince. 'I'm a sick man.'

'And would Rogozhin marry her? What do you think?'

'Well, there's no difficulty about marrying a person: one could do it any time. He might marry her to-morrow and, perhaps, murder her a week later.'

No sooner had he uttered those words than Ganya gave so violent a start that the prince almost cried out.

'What's the matter?' he said, seizing him by the arm.

'His excellency, sir, requests your presence in her excellency's apartments,' announced the footman, appearing at the door.

The prince followed the footman.

4

The three Yepanchin daughters were tall and healthy girls, in the first bloom of youth, with magnificent shoulders, powerful chests, and strong, almost masculine arms; being so strong and healthy, they, of course, sometimes liked to have a good meal, which fact they had no desire to conceal. Their mother, Lisaveta Prokofyevna, sometimes looked askance at the frankness of their appetites; but as certain of her opinions, in spite of the outward show of respect with which they were accepted by her daughters, had in effect long ceased to exercise their original and indisputable authority over them, so much so indeed that the firmly established harmonious conclave of the three girls invariably began to prevail, Mrs Yepanchin found it more convenient to preserve her own dignity by giving in to them without any arguments. It is true that the good lady's temperament very often got the better of her and refused to submit to the dictates of reason; Mrs Yepanchin was growing more capricious and impatient every year; indeed, she was becoming quite an eccentric person, but as her submissive and well-trained husband was always near at hand, she usually vented all her accumulated spleen on him, and then harmony was again restored in the household and everything went on as well as could be expected.

Mrs Yepanchin, though, never lost her appetite herself, and at half past twelve she usually partook with her daughters of the substantial lunch which was almost indistinguishable from a dinner. The girls had a cup of coffee earlier, punctually at ten o'clock, in bed, as soon as they woke up. They had grown to like this regime, and it had become a regular rule with them. At half past twelve the table was laid in the little dining-room, near their mother's apartments, and, if time allowed, the general himself was sometimes present at this intimate family luncheon party. Besides tea, coffee, cheese, honey, butter, special fritters, one of Mrs Yepanchin's favourite dishes, cutlets, and so on, strong hot soup was also served. On the particular morning on which our story begins, the whole family gathered in the dining-room in expectation of the general, who promised to put in an appearance at half past twelve. If he had been even a minute late, he would have been sent for at once; but he arrived punctually. As he went up to his wife to wish her good morning and kiss her hand, he noticed this time a rather peculiar expression on her face. And though he had had a presentiment the night before that it would be so owing to a certain 'episode' (as he usually put it), and was already worried about it as he fell asleep, he could not help feeling apprehensive again. His daughters went up to kiss him; although they were not angry with him, there was still something peculiar about them too. It is true that owing to certain circumstances the general had become a little too suspicious, but as he was both an experienced and clever father and husband, he at once took appropriate measures.

It will perhaps help to make our narrative a little clearer if we make a little digression here to give a more direct and exact account of the relationships between the members of General Yepanchin's family and the circumstances in which we find them at the beginning of our story. We have already said that the general, though not a man of great education, but, on the contrary, as he described himself, a 'self-taught man', was an experienced husband and intelligent father. He had, incidentally, made it a rule not to hurry his daughters into marriage, that is to say, not to keep constantly nagging and worrying them by his fatherly loving care and anxiety for their happiness, as happens again and again even in the most intelligent families suffering from a surfeit of grown up daughters. He even succeeded in persuading his wife to accept his 'system', though it was a difficult business altogether, difficult because it was so unnatural; but the general's arguments were extremely impressive, being based on palpable facts. Besides, given complete freedom to decide for themselves, girls of marriageable age would quite naturally be forced to come to their senses at last, and then things would start moving fast, for they would set to work with a will, casting aside their capriciousness and forgetting to be so difficult to please. All that would be left to their parents to do would be to keep a watchful eye on them, without letting them suspect it, of course, so as to prevent any undesirable choice or unnatural aberration, and then, seizing the most opportune moment, do their utmost to assist the successful issue of the business by their influence. Last but not least, the very fact that their fortune and social position were growing every year in geometrical progression meant that the longer they waited the more their daughters gained even as prospective brides. But among all these incontestable facts, another fact confronted the fond parents: their eldest daughter Alexandra suddenly and almost quite unexpectedly (as always happens) reached the age of twenty-five. Almost at the same time Afanasy Ivanovich Totsky, a gentleman who moved in the highest society, with the highest social connexions and of immense wealth, once again expressed his long-cherished desire to marry. He was a man of fifty-five, of a refined character and quite extraordinarily artistic tastes. He wanted to make a good marriage; he was an exceedingly fine judge of female beauty. As he had been for some time on most friendly terms with General Yepanchin, especially strengthened by their partnership in some financial enterprises, he communicated his intention to him under the guise of asking for his friendly advice and guidance: would a proposal of marriage to one of the general's daughters be accepted or not? A great change was quite obviously about to take place in General Yepanchin's placid and happy family life.

The most beautiful girl in the family was, as has already been said, the youngest daughter, Aglaya. But even Totsky, a man of quite exceptional egoism, realized that he stood no chance there and that Aglaya was not for him. Perhaps the somewhat blind love and the uncommonly warm friendship of the sisters exaggerated the position, but Aglaya's future, as they had most sincerely decided among themselves, was not to be an ordinary one, but an embodiment of the ideal of heaven on earth. Aglaya's future husband was to be a model of perfection and a paragon of all virtues, not to mention his great wealth. The sisters had even agreed among themselves, and that without wasting many words, about the necessity of sacrificing, if need be, their own interests in favour of Aglaya; her dowry was to be colossal and something quite out of the ordinary. The parents knew of this agreement between the two elder sisters, and that was why, when Totsky asked for advice, they had hardly any doubts that one of the elder sisters would most certainly not refuse to set the seal on their expectations, particularly as Totsky would make no difficulties about the dowry. The general, with his singular knowledge of the world, immediately appreciated Totsky's proposal very highly. As, owing to certain circumstances, Totsky himself had for the time being to exercise extreme caution in minding his steps and was merely exploring the ground, the parents presented the whole thing to their daughters just as a remote possibility. In reply they received, if not quite a definite, then at least a reassuring statement that their eldest daughter Alexandra might not refuse him. She was a good-natured and sensible girl, easy to get on with, though rather strong-minded; she might very well have married Totsky quite willingly, and if she gave her word, she would have kept it honourably. She was not fond of high life and, far from causing trouble and violent upheavals, she might indeed be expected to sweeten and soothe her husband's life. She was very pretty, though not in a showy way. What better wife could Totsky wish?

All the same, the matter was proceeding very slowly. Totsky and the general had mutually agreed in a friendly way to avoid for the time being taking any formal and irrevocable step. The parents had not even begun to discuss the subject openly with their daughters; there were indeed even certain signs of a rift in the lute: Mrs Yepanchin, the mother, seemed for some reason to be dissatisfied, and that was a very serious matter. There was one disconcerting circumstance, a certain complicated and tiresome affair, which might ruin the whole business completely.

The complicated and tiresome 'affair', as Totsky himself expressed it, had begun a long time before, about eighteen years before. Next to one of Totsky's wealthiest estates in one of the central provinces of Russia was the estate of a poverty-stricken landowner. This man was remarkable for his persistent and quite absurd run of bad luck. He was a retired army officer of good family – much better than Totsky's, in fact – a certain Philip Alexandrovich Barashkov. Burdened with debts and mortgages, he at last succeeded, after working very hard, almost like a peasant, in getting his small estate into a more or less satisfactory condition. The least success raised his spirits inordinately. Encouraged and radiant with hope, he went for a few days to the small district town to see one of his chief creditors and, if possible, come to a final agreement with him. On the third day after his arrival in the town, the bailiff of his village appeared on horseback with his beard singed and his cheek burnt and told him that his 'country seat' had burnt down the day before, at noon, his wife had perished in the flames, but that his children were unhurt. This surprise was too much even for Barashkov, inured as he was to the 'blows of fortune': he went mad, and died of brain-fever a month later. The burnt property, with its poverty-stricken peasants, was sold to pay his debts. Totsky, in the generosity of his heart, undertook to bring up and educate Barashkov's daughters, two girls of six and seven. They were brought up together with the children of Totsky's estate agent, a retired civil servant with a large family, and a German to boot. Soon only one girl, Nastasya, remained, the younger one having died of whooping-cough. Totsky, who was living abroad at the time, soon forgot all about them. Five years later, on his return to Russia, it occurred to him that he might as well look in on his estate while on his way elsewhere, and he suddenly noticed in the family of his German agent a lovely child, a girl of about twelve, playful, charming, and intelligent, who promised to become an extraordinarily beautiful young woman; so far as that was concerned, Totsky was an unerring judge. On that occasion he spent only a few days on his estate, but he had time to make all the necessary arrangements; there was a great change in the girl's education: a highly respectable and well-educated Swiss governess, who was experienced in the higher education of young ladies and who taught other subjects besides French, was engaged. She took up her residence in the agent's house, and the scope of little Nastasya's education was considerably enlarged. Exactly four years later this education came to an end; the governess left, and a lady, whose estate was near to one of Totsky's estates in another and more remote province, arrived to fetch Nastasya, on his instructions and by his authority, and took her away to live with her. On her small estate, too, there was a small, newly built wooden house. It was exquisitely furnished, and the little village on the estate, as though on purpose, was called 'Eden'. The lady brought Nastasya straight to this quiet little house, and as she, a childless widow, lived herself only about a mile away, she installed herself in the house with her. An old housekeeper and an experienced young maid were soon there to wait on Nastasya. In the house she found musical instruments, an exquisite library of novels for young ladies, pictures, prints, pencils, paints and brushes, a wonderful Italian greyhound, and a fortnight later Mr Totsky himself put in an appearance. ... Since then he seemed to have grown particularly fond of this remote little village in the heart of the steppes, visited it every summer, stayed there for two or even three months, and so passed a fairly long time – about four years – peacefully and happily, in tasteful and elegant surroundings.

It so happened that one day at the beginning of winter, four months after Totsky's visit to 'Eden' (he had spent only a fortnight there on that occasion) a rumour was spread, or rather a rumour reached Nastasya, that Totsky was going to be married in Petersburg to a rich and beautiful society woman – in short, that he was making a sensible and brilliant match. The rumour turned out afterwards not to be correct in all particulars: the marriage was at the time merely being planned, and the whole thing was still very vague, but since then a great change had come into Nastasya's life, all the same. She suddenly showed unusual determination and displayed quite unexpected strength of character. Without wasting any time, she left her little house in the country and suddenly arrived in Petersburg all alone, and went straight to see Totsky. Totsky was amazed, and tried to speak to her, but he suddenly discovered, almost from his first word, that he had to change completely his language, the inflexion of his voice, the subjects of the agreeable and refined conversations he had hitherto employed with such great success, and his logic – everything, everything, everything! Quite a different woman was sitting before him, a woman who was not at all like the girl he had known and had left in the village of 'Eden' only the previous July.

This new woman appeared, in the first place, to know and understand quite an extraordinary lot – so much, indeed, that one could not help marvelling where she had picked up such knowledge and where she could have acquired such precise ideas. (Not from her young lady's library, surely?) What was more, she had a pretty good understanding of legal matters and a positive knowledge, if not of the world, at least of how certain matters are arranged in the world; secondly, her character was quite different from what he had known, that is to say, there was not a trace left of her former timidity and schoolgirlish uncertainty, which had been sometimes so delightful in its unaffected playfulness and sometimes so melancholy and pensive, astonished, mistrustful, tearful, and restless.

Oh no! it was quite a surprising and unusual creature who laughed at him and taunted him with her bitter and sarcastic words, who told him to his face that she had never felt anything but the deepest contempt for him – nauseating contempt which she had felt immediately after her first shock. This new woman declared that she did not care in the least if he married at once anyone he liked, but that she had come to prevent this marriage, and to prevent it out of spite, simply because she chose to do so, and that therefore it must be so – 'if only to have a good laugh at you, darling, for now, at last, I too want to laugh'.

This, at least, was what she said; she did not perhaps tell him all she had in mind. But while this new Nastasya Filippovna laughed and told him all this, Totsky considered the situation and tried as best he could to bring his somewhat scattered wits into some kind of order. This deliberation took him some time; he considered the matter from every angle and tried to make up his mind for almost a fortnight, but by the end of the fortnight he had taken his decision. The fact was that Totsky was at that time almost fifty, and he was an extremely sedate man with set habits. His position in the world and society had long been established on the most firm foundations. He loved and prized himself, his peace and comfort more than anything in the world, as indeed was fit and proper for a highly respectable gentleman. Nothing was to be allowed to destroy or in any way to interfere with what it had taken him all his life to build up and what had assumed so splendid a form. On the other hand, his experience and deep insight into things told Totsky very quickly that he was dealing with quite an exceptional woman, a woman who not only threatened to do something, but would most certaintly do it, and, what was even more important, would most certainly stick at nothing, particularly as she did not care for anything in the world, so that it was quite impossible to buy her off. There was evidently something else here, some storm of the heart and mind, something in the nature of romantic indignation, goodness only knows why and against whom, a sort of insatiable feeling of contempt that was completely unaccountable – in short, something highly ridiculous and inadmissible in good society, something that a decent man could only regard as a damned nuisance. No doubt, a man of Totsky's wealth and social position could easily rid himself of any unpleasantness by some quite innocent little act of knavery. On the other hand, it was no less evident that Nastasya Filippovna was hardly in a position to do any harm, in the legal sense, for instance; she could not even create any considerable public scandal, because it would always be so easy to clip her wings. But all that was true only if Nastasya Filippovna decided to act as any woman would act in such circumstances, without departing too eccentrically from the accepted rules. It was here that Totsky's sound judgement stood him in good stead: he saw quite clearly that Nastasya realized perfectly well that legally she could do absolutely nothing against him, but that there was something else in her mind and in – her flashing eyes. Caring for nothing, and least of all for herself (it required a great deal of insight and intelligence for him to realize at that moment that she had long ceased to care for herself, and for a sceptic and cynical man of the world like him to believe in the seriousness of that feeling), Nastasya Filippovna was quite capable of ruining herself, irrevocably and horribly, by running the risk of being sent to Siberia to serve a sentence for murder, so long as she could vent her spite on a man for whom she had such an inhuman aversion. Totsky never concealed the fact that he was a bit of a coward or, to put it more flatteringly, that he was highly discreet. If, for instance, he had known for certain that he would be killed at his wedding in church, or that something of the kind would happen – something that was considered extremely indecent, ridiculous, and disagreeable in society – he would of course have been frightened, but not so much of being killed or seriously wounded or of someone spitting in his face in public, and so on, as of such a thing happening to him in a form so unnatural and unpleasant. And that was just what Nastasya

Filippovna had in mind, though so far she had kept silent about it; he knew that she had studied and understood him thoroughly, and hence knew how to hurt him most. And as his marriage was really still very much in the air, Totsky made a virtue of necessity and capitulated to Nastasya Filippovna.

There was another thing that helped him to take this decision: it was difficult to imagine how unlike this new Nastasya Filippovna was to the one he knew before. Before she had been only a very pretty girl, but now – Totsky could not forgive himself for having failed to see for four years how beautiful she was. It is true that the sudden and inward change that takes place in the attitude of two people towards each other also means a great deal. He remembered, though, that before, too, there were moments when, for instance, strange thoughts occurred to him as he looked at those eyes; he seemed to feel the presence of some deep and mysterious darkness in them. Her eyes looked at him as though they were asking a riddle. During the last two years he had often wondered at the change in Nastasya Filippovna's complexion; there were times when she became terribly pale and, strange to say, looked even prettier for it. Totsky, who, like all gentlemen who have had their fling in their day, at first could not help feeling contempt for the inexperienced girl he had got so cheaply, was more recently beginning to wonder whether he had not made a mistake. He had, in any case, made up his mind as long ago as last spring to give her a good dowry and marry her off to some sensible and decent fellow employed in a government office in another province. (Oh, how horribly and maliciously Nastasya Filippovna laughed at this idea now!) But fascinated by the entirely new woman he saw now, Totsky wondered whether he could not again exploit her. He decided to install Nastasya Filippovna in Petersburg and surround her with luxury and comfort. If he could not get one thing, he might as well try another. He might show off Nastasya Filippovna and even brag about her in certain circles. And Totsky was so very proud of his reputation in that particular line.

Five years of this kind of Petersburg life passed and, of course, quite a number of things had become abundantly clear in that time. Totsky's position was not a happy one; the worst thing was that, having once shown what a coward he was, he could never again feel at peace with himself. He was afraid and did not know himself what he was afraid of: he was simply afraid of Nastasya Filippovna. For some time, during the first two years, he began to suspect that Nastasya Filippovna wanted to marry him, but said nothing about it because of her extraordinary vanity and was waiting determinedly for him to propose to her. It was a preposterous idea, but Totsky had become suspicious: he frowned and brooded unhappily. To his great and (such is the heart of man!) somewhat unpleasant surprise, he became convinced by a certain occurrence that even if he had proposed to her, he would not have been accepted. For a long time he could not understand it. It seemed to him that there was only one possible explanation, namely, that the pride of that 'humiliated and fantastic woman' had reached such a pitch of frenzy that she would much rather express her contempt for him by a refusal than regularize her position and achieve a state of unrivalled magnificence. The worst of it was that Nastasya Filippovna had got the better of him so disastrously. Neither did money make any impression on her, however large the sum, and though she accepted the comforts he offered her, she lived very modestly and had scarcely saved up anything during those five years. Totsky tried a very cunning stratagem to break his chains: imperceptibly and skilfully he began to tempt her with cleverly contrived assistance by putting in her way all sorts of ideal inducements, but these personified ideals, such as princes, hussar officers, secretaries of embassies, poets, novelists, even socialists made no impression whatever on Nastasya Filippovna, as though her heart was made of stone and her feelings had dried up and withered for ever. She lived a somewhat withdrawn life: she read, even studied, and was fond of music. She had few acquaintances; she mostly associated with poor and rather ridiculous women, the wives of low-grade civil servants, she knew one or two actresses, some old ladies, she was very fond of the large family of some respectable schoolmaster, and she too was very much liked by that family and always found a warm welcome there. Quite often four or five friends – no more – came to see her in the evening. Totsky called on her frequently and regularly. More recently, and not without some difficulty, General Yepanchin made her acquaintance. At the same time a young civil servant, Ferdyshchenko by name – a very coarse, lewd fellow, who was fond of drink and prided himself on his wit – made her acquaintance without any difficulty whatever. Another of her acquaintances was a rather strange young man, Ptitsyn by name, a modest, neat, and foppish fellow, who had risen from poverty and become a moneylender. Finally, Gavrila Ivolgin, too, was introduced to her. ... The upshot of it was that Nastasya Filippovna gained a strange reputation: everyone knew that she was a beautiful woman, but that was all; no one could boast of his success with her and no one had anything to tell of her. Such a reputation, coupled with her education, her elegant manners, and her wit – all this convinced Totsky that the plan he had devised for her would work. It was at this point that General Yepanchin began to play such an important and active part in this affair.

When Totsky had so courteously asked the general for his advice in respect of one of his daughters, he at once, like a true gentleman, made a full and candid confession. He admitted that he had made up his mind *to stop at nothing* to regain his freedom; that he would not feel happy even if Nastasya Filippovna herself assured him that she would leave him in peace in future; that mere words were not enough for him, that he wanted the fullest possible guarantees. They came to an agreement and decided to act together. It was their intention to try the gentlest measures first and, as it were, touch only upon 'the most honourable chords of her heart'. They paid a call on Nastasya Filippovna together, and Totsky began straight by telling her of the unbearable agony of his position; he blamed himself for everything and told her frankly that he could feel no remorse for having seduced her because he was an inveterate sensualist and was not responsible for his actions, but that now he wished to get married and that it was for her to decide whether that eminently desirable society marriage should take place or not – in short, he put all his hopes on her generous heart. Then General Yepanchin, in his capacity as father, began to speak, and he talked sensibly, avoiding all sentimentality and merely mentioning the fact that he fully recognized her right to decide Mr Totsky's fate. He very cleverly showed off his own humility by pointing out that the fate of his eldest daughter, and possibly of his two other daughters, now depended on her decision. To Nastasya Filippovna's question what exactly they would like her to do, Totsky confessed with the same disarming frankness that he had been so intimidated five years before that it was quite impossible for him to feel at ease even now until Nastasya Filippovna was herself married to someone. He added at once that such a request would of course have been quite absurd on his part if he had not some foundation for it. He had observed and, indeed, knew for a fact that a young man of good birth and from a highly respectable family, to wit, Mr Gavrila Ivolgin, whom she knew and received at her house, had long been passionately in love with her and would, of course, give his life for the mere hope of winning her favour. Mr Ivolgin had quite frankly told him, Totsky, about it himself long ago, in a friendly way, and General Yepanchin, who was interested in the young man's future, had long known about it too. As a matter of fact, if he, Totsky, was not mistaken, Nastasya Filippovna had herself long been aware of the young man's love and, indeed, he could not help feeling that she did not entirely disapprove of it. Of course, he was the last man in the world to speak of it, but if Nastasya Filippovna would only concede that, apart from his selfish desire to make arrangements for his own future, he, Totsky, had some thought for her good, she would have realized how strange and, indeed, how deeply grieved he felt to see how lonely she was: that what she was suffering from was a general depression of spirits and an utter disbelief in the chance of a new life, which might dawn for her so beautifully in love and a family of her own and which might thus give her a new aim in life; that if she went on as she was doing she might ruin her talents, which were perhaps of the most brilliant kind, and lapse into brooding and melancholy – that, in short, she was suffering from a kind of romantic spell which was unworthy of her common sense and her generous heart. Having repeated once more that he found it harder than anyone else to speak of it, he concluded by expressing the hope that Nastasya Filippovna would not reject with contempt his sincere wish to provide for her future by offering her a sum of seventy-five thousand roubles. He added in explanation that he had anyway left her that sum in his will – in short, that it was not at all a question of any compensation, and that, after all, why should she not allow and excuse in him a human desire to do something to ease his conscience, and so on and so forth, the sort of thing one usually says in such circumstances on a subject like this. Totsky spoke eloquently and at great length, adding, as it were, in passing, the highly interesting information that it was the first time he had ever mentioned the seventy-five thousand roubles, and that even General Yepanchin knew nothing about it – that, in fact, *nobody* did.

Nastasya Filippovna's reply astonished the two friends.

Not only was there no trace of her former sarcasm, her former hostility and hatred, her former laughter, the very recollection of which sent a shiver down Totsky's spine, but, on the contrary, she actually seemed glad of the opportunity of speaking to someone frankly and in a friendly way. She confessed that she had long wished herself to ask for friendly advice and that it was only her pride that had prevented her, but now that the ice was broken, nothing could be better. First with a sad smile and then with a gay and playful laugh, she admitted that there could be no more any question of a repetition of any stormy scenes; that for some time her views on things had undergone a certain change, and that though there was no change in her heart, she had had to accept many facts in view of what had happened; what was done could not be undone, that it was no use crying over spilt milk, and that, indeed, she thought it rather strange that Mr Totsky should still be so afraid. At this point she turned to

General Yepanchin and told him, with an air of the profoundest respect, that she had long since heard a great deal about his daughters and could not help feeling a profound and genuine respect for them. The very thought that she could in any way be of some service to them would make her proud and happy. It was quite true that she felt depressed and bored, so very bored; Mr Totsky had divined her dearest thoughts: she wished she could start her life all over again, for she realized that she had to find a new aim in life, if not in love, then in a family of her own, but she was sorry she could tell them hardly anything about Mr Ivolgin. She thought it was true that he loved her; she could not help feeling that she, too, might care for him if only she could be sure of the firmness of his attachment; but he was very young, though admittedly sincere. That being so, she found it hard to make up her mind. Still, what she liked best about him was that he was working and supporting his family by his own unaided efforts. She understood that he was an energetic and proud man and that he was eager to make a career, to make his way in the world. She also understood that his mother, Mrs Ivolgin, was an excellent and highly estimable woman, that his sister Varya was a most remarkable and energetic girl. She had heard a great deal about her from Ptitsyn. She had heard that they were putting up cheerfully with their misfortunes, and she would very much like to make their acquaintance, but she was not sure whether they would welcome her in their family. On the whole, she would not like to say anything against the possibility of such a marriage, but she would like to think it over carefully; she would prefer not to be hurried. As for the seventy-five thousand roubles, she thought there was really no need for Mr Totsky to feel so embarrassed in speaking about it. She knew the value of money and would, of course, accept it. She thanked Mr Totsky for his delicacy in not mentioning the matter even to the general, let alone to Mr Ivolgin, but she saw no reason why the latter should not know about it beforehand. She did not see why she should be ashamed of accepting this money on entering their family. In any case, she did not intend to ask anyone's forgiveness for anything and she wished people to know that. She would not marry Mr Ivolgin until she was quite certain that neither he nor his family harboured any secret thoughts about her. In any case, she did not think she was to blame for anything, and she thought it would be better if Mr Ivolgin knew the conditions under which she had been living in Petersburg during the last five years, what her relations with Mr Totsky had been, and whether she had saved up a lot of money. If, finally, she accepted so large a sum of money now, it was not as payment for her loss of virtue, for which she was not responsible, but merely as a compensation for her ruined life.

She became so worked up and irritable in explaining all this (which was quite natural, however) that General Yepanchin was highly gratified and considered the matter settled; but Totsky, having been once so thoroughly intimidated, did not quite believe her even now, and was for a long time afraid that there might be a snake lurking beneath the flowers. But the negotiations had been started, and the point on which the whole scheme of the two friends turned, namely, the possibility that Nastasya Filippovna might be attracted to Ganya, gradually began to assume a clearer and more definite form, so that even Totsky at times began to believe in the possibility of success. Meanwhile Nastasya Filippovna had talked the matter over with Ganya. She said very little, as though the subject was too painful for her modesty, but she recognized and approved of his love, though she made it perfectly clear to him that she had no intention of committing herself to anything, that till their wedding day (if there were to be any wedding) she reserved to herself the right to say no up to the last moment, and that she conceded absolutely the same right to him. Soon Ganya learnt positively through an obliging friend that Nastasya Filippovna already knew all the details of his family's hostility to the marriage and to her personally, which were disclosed by the scenes at home. She had not mentioned it to him herself, though he was expecting it daily. There was a lot more that could be told of the incidents and circumstances arising out of this proposed match and the negotiations in connexion with it, but we have run ahead already, particularly as some of these circumstances took the form of rather vague rumours. For instance, Totsky is said to have been told by someone that Nastasya Filippovna had entered into some sort of secret and unspecified relations with the Misses Yepanchin – a highly improbable story. But he did believe another rumour and feared it like a nightmare: he was told for a fact that Nastasya Filippovna was perfectly aware that Ganya was marrying her only for her money; that he had a wicked, rapacious, impatient, envious, and quite inordinately selfish nature; that though at first he had been passionately set on a conquest over her, he grew to hate her like poison the moment the two friends decided to exploit the passion both of them were beginning to feel for one another to their advantage and to buy Ganya by selling him Nastasya Filippovna as his lawful wife. Passion and hatred seemed to be strangely mingled in his heart, and though after painful hesitations he had given his consent to marry the 'fallen' woman, he swore in his heart to wreak his vengeance upon her and 'wipe the floor with her' afterwards, as he was said to have put it himself. Nastasya Filippovna seemed to have known all this and to be hatching some plan in secret. Totsky got into such a panic that he even stopped confiding his anxieties to Yepanchin, but there were moments when he, like the weakling he was, most decidedly plucked up courage and regained his high spirits: he had plucked up courage, for instance, when Nastasya Filippovna at last promised the two friends to give them her final decision on the evening of her birthday. On the other hand, the most extraordinary and quite incredible rumour concerning the most estimable General Yepanchin himself appeared to be, alas, all too true.

At the first glance the whole thing seemed utterly preposterous. It was difficult to believe that General Yepanchin, a venerable old gentleman of high intelligence and a practical knowledge of the world, and so on, should have become infatuated with Nastasya Filippovna himself, and indeed to such a degree that this whim of his was almost indistinguishable from passion. What exactly he was hoping for is difficult to imagine; perhaps he counted even on Ganya's co-operation. Totsky suspected the existence of some tacit agreement, founded on their thorough understanding of each other, between the general and Ganya. It is of course a well-known fact that a man who allows himself to be carried away by passion, especially if he is getting on in years, becomes totally blind and is ready to see hope where there is none; what is more, he loses his reason and acts like a foolish child, however intelligent he may be. It was known that the general was going to give Nastasya Filippovna for her birthday present a wonderful string of pearls, costing an enormous sum, and that he had shown a great interest in this present, although he was aware that Nastasya Filippovna was not a mercenary woman. On the day of Nastasya Filippovna's birthday he was in a state of great agitation, although he concealed his feelings very cleverly. It was of this string of pearls that Mrs Yepanchin had heard. It is true that Mrs Yepanchin had long since got wind of her husband's infidelities and, indeed, had grown to some extent used to them, but it was obviously quite impossible for her to overlook such an incident: the rumour of the pearls interested her very greatly. The general had discovered that in good time; they had had words about it on the previous day and he felt that a most thorough-going inquiry into the matter was imminent and dreaded it. That was why he was so anxious not to have lunch in the bosom of his family on the morning on which we began our story. Before the arrival of the prince he made up his mind to excuse himself on the plea of urgent business in order to get out of it. By 'getting out' of something the general sometimes meant simply getting out of the house. He wanted to gain this day at least and, above all, the evening, without any unpleasantness. And suddenly the prince had turned up so opportunely. 'As though the good Lord has sent him,' the general thought as he entered his wife's drawing-room.

5

Mrs Yepanchin was very proud of her descent. It was therefore a great shock to her to learn, suddenly and without due preparation, that the last representative of her family, Prince Myshkin, of whom she had heard something already, was nothing but a wretched idiot and practically a beggar, and was ready to accept charity. The general was anxious to create an effect in order to engage her interest at once and, by turning her attention in another direction, avoid the question of the pearls under the cover of this sensational piece of news.

In moments of crisis Mrs Yepanchin's eyes would pop out of her head and she would look vacantly before her, leaning back in her chair slightly without uttering a word. She was a tall, spare woman, of the same age as her husband, with still thick, dark hair, turning very grey, a somewhat aquiline nose, hollow, sallow cheeks, and thin, sunken lips. She had a high but narrow forehead, and rather large grey eyes, which sometimes had a most unexpected expression. A long time ago she had been so vain as to imagine that her eyes were extraordinarily effective – a conviction that nothing could shake.

'Receive him? You say I'm to receive him now, this minute?' Mrs Yepanchin cried, staring with bulging eyes at General Yepanchin, who stood fidgeting before her.

'Oh, there's no need to stand on ceremony so far as that is concerned,' the general hastened to explain, 'if only you wish to see him, my dear. He's quite a child; such a pathetic-looking fellow, too. He seems to have some kind of nervous fits. He has just arrived from Switzerland, straight from the station. He's strangely dressed, like a German, and, besides, he hasn't a penny, literally not a penny. Poor chap, he's almost crying. I gave him twenty-five roubles and I'd like to find him some small job as a clerk in our office. And,' he turned to his daughters, 'I'd like you to offer him some food, because I can't help feeling that he must be hungry, too.'

'You surprise me,' Mrs Yepanchin went on as before. 'Hungry and fits. What sort of fits?'

'Oh, they don't occur so often, and, besides, he's almost like a child. An educated child, though. As a matter of fact,' he addressed his daughters again, 'I'd like to ask you to put him through an examination. You see, it would be a good thing to know what he is capable of.'

'An ex-amin-ation?' Mrs Yepanchin drawled in profound astonishment, staring open-eyed at her husband and her daughters in turn.

'Oh, my dear, don't put such a construction on – er – – However, just as you like. I was thinking of being kind to him and introducing him to you, for it is almost an act of charity, isn't it?'

'Introduce him to us? From Switzerland?'

'Switzerland has nothing to do with it. However, as I said before, just as you like. I proposed it first of all because he is of your family and, perhaps, even a relation of yours, and, secondly, because he has nowhere to go. I must say I thought you might be a little interested to see him, for, after all, he is a member of our family.'

'Of course, Mother,' Alexandra, the eldest daughter, said, 'if we needn't stand on ceremony with him. Besides, he must be hungry after the journey, so why shouldn't we give him a meal, if he hasn't anywhere else to go?'

'And, besides, he's a perfect child and one could have a game of blind man's buff with him.'

'Blind man's buff? What do you mean?'

'Oh, do stop pretending, Mother,' Aglaya interrupted in vexation.

The second daughter, Adelaida, who was quick to see the funny side of everything, could not control herself and burst out laughing.

'Send for him, Father,' Aglaya decided. 'Mother gives her permission.'

The general rang and told the footman to call the prince.

'But only on condition he has a napkin tied round his neck when he sits down at table,' Mrs Yepanchin declared. 'Call Fyodor or Mavra – to stand behind his chair and look after him when he eats. Is he at least quiet during his fits? He doesn't wave his arms about, does he?'

'Why, on the contrary, he's very well-bred and his manners are excellent. He's a bit too simple at times. ... Ah, here he is himself. Let me introduce him to you, my dear. Prince Myshkin, the last of his family, a namesake of yours and perhaps a relation, too. Be kind to him and make him feel at home. Lunch will be served presently, Prince, and you must do us the honour – er – I'm sorry, I must be off, I'm late – –'

'We know where you're off to,' Mrs Yepanchin said impressively.

'Yes, yes, I'm in a hurry, my dear; I'm late! and don't forget to show him your albums, my dears. Let him write something there for you. His handwriting is quite extraordinarily good! A talent, a real talent! You should have seen how he wrote out in old lettering: "The Abbot Pafnuty hath put his hand hereto". Well, good-bye!'

'Pafnuty? The Abbot? Wait, wait a minute. Where are you off to? Who is this Pafnuty?' Mrs Yepanchin cried with persistent annoyance and almost in alarm after her escaping husband.

'Yes, yes, my dear, there was an abbot of that name in the old days. I'm afraid I've to run off to see the count; he's been waiting for me for hours and, the worst of it is, he made the appointment himself. Good-bye, Prince!'

The general left the room hurriedly.

'I know what count he's going to see!' Mrs Yepanchin said sharply and turned her eyes irritably to the prince. 'What was I going to say?' she began petulantly and peevishly, trying to remember. 'What was it? Oh, yes. What abbot?'

'Mother,' Alexandra began, and Aglaya even stamped her foot.

'Don't interfere with me, my dear,' Mrs Yepanchin rapped out. 'I want to know too. Sit down here, Prince, in this arm-chair, opposite me – no, here – move nearer to the light – in the sun, so that I may see you. Well now, what abbot?'

'The Abbot Pafnuty,' the prince replied, attentively and seriously.

'Pafnuty? That's interesting. Well, what about him?'

Mrs Yepanchin put her questions impatiently, rapidly, and sharply, without taking her eyes off the prince, and when the prince replied, she nodded her head at every word.

'The Abbot Pafnuty of the fourteenth century, madam,' the prince began, 'was the head of a monastery on the Volga in what is now our province of Kostroma. He was famous for his holy life. He used to visit the Tartar headquarters, helped in the management of public affairs, and signed a certain document. I've seen a copy of that signature. I liked the handwriting and I learnt to copy it. When the general wanted to see my handwriting so as to find me a job, I wrote several sentences in different letterings, and one of them was, "The Abbot Pafnuty hath put his hand hereto", which I wrote in the Abbot Pafnuty's own handwriting. The general liked it very much, and that's why he spoke of it just now.'

'Aglaya,' said Mrs Yepanchin, 'please remember: Pafnuty. Better write it down, or I'm sure to forget. But I thought it would be something more interesting. Where's that signature?'

'I think it is still on the table in the general's study.'

'Send someone to fetch it.'

'I could write it again for you if you like.'

'Why, of course, Mother,' said Alexandra, 'we'd better have lunch now. We're famished.'

'Very well,' Mrs Yepanchin agreed. 'Come along, Prince. Are you very hungry?'

'Yes, I'm afraid I am feeling rather hungry now, and I'm very grateful to you.'

'I'm glad you're polite, and I see you're not at all such an – er – eccentric as you were described. Come along. Sit here, please, opposite me,' she fussed, making the prince sit down when they went into the dining-room. 'I want to be able to see you. Alexandra, Adelaida, look after the prince. He isn't really such – er – an invalid, is he? Perhaps he needn't have the napkin. You don't have a napkin tied round your neck at meal-times, do you, Prince?'

'I believe I did when I was a boy of seven, but now I usually have my napkin in my knees at meal-times.'

'Quite right. And your fits?'

'My fits?' the prince said, looking a little surprised. 'I don't have fits very often nowadays. Still I don't know. I'm told the climate here may be bad for me.'

'He speaks well,' Mrs Yepanchin observed, addressing her daughters and continuing to nod her head at every word the prince uttered. 'I didn't expect it. It seems, then, that it was all stuff and nonsense. As usual. Help yourself, Prince, and tell me where were you born and where were you brought up. I want to know everything. You interest me very much.'

The prince thanked her, and, while eating with great appetite, began telling them what he had already repeated several times that morning. Mrs Yepanchin looked more and more pleased. Her daughters, too, listened very attentively. They discussed their relationship, and it seemed that the prince knew his family tree pretty well; but however hard they tried, they could find scarcely any connexion between the prince and Mrs Yepanchin. Among their grandfathers and grandmothers there seemed to have been some kind of distant relationship. Mrs Yepanchin was particularly pleased with this dry subject, for she hardly ever managed to discuss her pedigree, however much she desired to do so. She got up from the table looking very animated.

'Let's go to our sitting-room,' she said. 'Our coffee will be served there. We have such a common sitting-room,' she said, addressing the prince and leading him there. 'It's really my small sitting-room, where we all meet when we are by ourselves, and each of us does her own work. Alexandra, my eldest daughter here, plays the piano or reads or sews; Adelaida paints landscapes and portraits (and never finishes anything), and Aglaya just sits. I'm afraid I'm not much good at things, either: can't get anything right. Well, here we are. Sit down here by the fire, Prince, and tell us something. I should like to know how you tell a story. I want to be absolutely certain, and when I see old Princess Belokonsky, I shall tell her all about you. I want them all to take an interest in you. Well, go on, please.'

'But, Mother,' Adelaida observed, 'that's a very strange way of asking someone to tell a story.'

Adelaida had in the meantime adjusted her easel, picked up her brushes and palette and started copying a landscape she had already begun from an engraving. Alexandra and Aglaya sat down together on a small sofa and, folding their arms, prepared to listen to the conversation. The prince noticed that he had become the centre of special attention.

'If I were ordered to tell a story like that,' Aglaya observed, 'I'd refuse to say anything.'

'Why not? What's so strange about it? Why shouldn't he tell us something? He's not dumb, is he? I want to know whether he can tell a story. Well, anything you like, please. Tell us how you liked Switzerland – your first impression of it. Mark my words,' – she turned to her daughters – 'he'll start at once and do it very well.'

'My first impression,' the prince began, 'was a strong one.'

'There, you see,' the impatient Mrs Yepanchin broke in, turning to her daughters, 'he's begun.'

'Do let him speak, Mother,' said Alexandra, stopping her. 'This prince,' she whispered to Aglaya, 'is probably a great rogue and not an idiot at all.'

'I'm sure you're right,' Aglaya replied. 'I saw it at once. And I think it's mean of him to play a part. Does he really think he'll gain anything by it?'

'My first impression was a very strong one,' the prince repeated. 'On my way from Russia, passing through many German towns, I just looked about me in silence and, I remember, I never asked any questions. That was after a long series of violent and painful attacks of my illness, and I always relapsed into a state of complete stupor when my illness became worse and I had several attacks on the same day. I lost my memory and, though I was fully conscious, the logical sequence of my thoughts seemed to be broken. I could not follow the course of events consecutively for more than two or three days. That's how it seems to me. But when my attacks abated, I became well and strong again, just as I am now. I remember I felt terribly sad. I even felt like crying; I was in a state of constant wonder and anxiety. The thing that affected me most was the thought that everything around me was *foreign*. I realized that. The fact that it was foreign depressed me terribly. I completely recovered from this depression, I remember, one evening at Basel, on reaching Switzerland, and the thing that roused me was the braying of a donkey in the market-place. I was quite extraordinarily struck with the donkey, and for some reason very pleased with it, and at once everything in my head seemed to clear up.'

'A donkey?' Mrs Yepanchin observed. 'That's strange. Still,' she went on, looking angrily at her laughing daughters, 'there's nothing strange about it. I shouldn't be surprised if one of us fell in love with a donkey. It happened in mythology. Go on, Prince.'

'Ever since I've been awfully fond of donkeys. I feel a sort of affection for them. I began making inquiries about them, for I'd never seen them before, and came almost at once to the conclusion that it was a most useful animal – hardworking, strong, patient, cheap, and long-suffering. And because of that donkey I suddenly acquired a liking for the whole of Switzerland, so that my former feeling of sadness was gone completely. ...'

'All this is very strange, but I think you'd better leave the donkey and pass on to something else. Why do you go on laughing, Aglaya? And you, too, Adelaida? The prince told the story about the donkey excellently. He saw it himself, and what have you seen? You've never been abroad!'

'I've seen a donkey, Mother,' said Adelaida.

'And I've heard one,' Aglaya said.

The three girls laughed again. The prince laughed with them.

'It's too bad of you,' Mrs Yepanchin observed. 'You must forgive them, Prince. They are good girls. I'm always quarrelling with them, but I love them. They're scatter-brained, thoughtless, crazy.'

'Why?' laughed the prince. 'In their place I shouldn't have missed such an opportunity, either. But I'm all for the donkey, in spite of everything. A donkey is a good-natured and useful creature.'

'And are you good-natured, Prince?' asked Mrs Yepanchin. 'I'm asking it out of curiosity.'

They all laughed again.

'That wretched donkey again!' cried Mrs Yepanchin. 'I wasn't thinking of it at all. I assure you, Prince, I never thought of – –'

'Hinting? Oh, I believe you implicitly!'

And the prince went on laughing.

'It's very nice of you to laugh,' said Mrs Yepanchin. 'I can see you are a very good-natured young man.'

'I'm not always,' replied the prince.

'But I am,' Mrs Yepanchin put in unexpectedly. 'And, if you like, I'm always good-natured, and that's my only fault, for one mustn't always be good-natured. I'm often angry with these girls, and especially with my husband, but the trouble is that I'm most good-natured when I'm angry. I was angry just before you came in and I pretended that I didn't and couldn't understand anything. I am like that sometimes – just like a child. Aglaya taught me a lesson. Thank you, Aglaya. But it's all nonsense. I'm not so silly as I seem and as my dear daughters would like to pretend I am. I have a will of my own and I'm not easily put to shame. I'm saying this without malice, though. Come here, Aglaya, give me a kiss – there – that'll do,' she observed when Aglaya had kissed her with feeling on the lips and on the hand. 'Go on, Prince. Perhaps you'll remember something more interesting than your donkey.'

'I must say I still don't understand how one can tell a story straight away like that,' Adelaida observed. 'I'm sure I could never do it.'

'But the prince could because he is extremely clever, at least ten times, and perhaps twelve times, cleverer than you. I hope you'll realize it after this. Prove it to them, Prince. Go on, please. There's really no need to harp on the donkey any more. Now, what did you see abroad besides the donkey?'

'It was clever about the donkey too,' observed Alexandra. 'The prince spoke very interestingly about his illness and how the shock of seeing the donkey made him like everything around him. I've always been interested to know how people go mad and then recover again. Especially when it happens suddenly.'

'Yes, yes!' Mrs Yepanchin cried excitedly. 'I can see that you, too, are sometimes very clever, dear. Well, stop laughing, please! I believe you were speaking of Swiss scenery, Prince – well?'

'We arrived at Lucerne and I was taken to the lake. I felt how beautiful it was, but it made me feel awfully depressed,' said the prince.

'Why?' asked Alexandra.

'I don't know. I always feel perturbed and depressed when I look at such a beautiful scene for the first time – it makes me feel happy and restless at the same time. But, of course, I was still ill just then.'

'Oh, but I'd like to see it very much,' said Adelaida. 'I can't understand why we don't go abroad. I haven't been able to find a subject for a picture for two years: "The East and the South have long since been painted. ..." Do find me a subject for a picture, Prince.'

'I'm afraid I know nothing about it. It seems to me that all you have to do is to look and paint.'

'But I don't know how to look.'

'Why are you talking in riddles? Can't understand a word!' Mrs Yepanchin interrupted. 'What do you mean you don't know how to look? You have a pair of eyes, haven't you? Well, look with them! If you don't know how to look here, you won't know how to look abroad. You'd better tell us, Prince, how you looked at things yourself.'

'Yes, that will be much nicer,' added Adelaida. 'I'm sure the prince has learnt how to look at things abroad.'

'I don't know. All I did was to improve my health there. I don't know whether or not I learnt to look at things. I was very happy there most of the time, though.'

'Happy?' Aglaya cried. 'Do you know how to be happy? In that case how can you say you didn't learn how to look at things? I daresay you could teach us.'

'Please do,' Adelaida laughed.

'I can't teach you anything,' said the prince, laughing too. 'I spent almost all my time abroad in the same Swiss village. I very rarely went for short trips in the country. What could I teach you? At first I was just not bored. Soon I began to get better; then every day became precious to me, more and more precious as time went on, so that I began to notice it. I went to bed feeling very contented and I got up feeling happier still. But why it was so, it is very hard to say.'

'So you didn't want to go anywhere?' Alexandra asked. 'You felt no urge to go?'

'At first – at the very beginning, I mean – I did, and it made me feel very restless. All the time I was thinking how I was going to carry on. I wanted to find out what sort of future I could expect. At certain moments I was especially restless. You know there are such moments, particularly in solitude. There was a waterfall there, a small one; it fell from high up in the mountain and in such a thin thread, almost perpendicularly – white, splashing, and foaming. It fell from a great height, but it seemed quite near; it was a third of a mile away, but it seemed only fifty yards. I liked to listen to its sound at night; it was at those moments that I sometimes became very restless. This also happened to me at noon when I went for a walk in the mountains, stood half-way up the mountain-side, with huge, old, resinous pines all round me; high up on the top of a precipitous cliff there were the ruins of an old medieval castle; our little village was far, far below, hardly visible; the sun shone brightly, the sky was blue, and everything around was terribly still. ... It was there that I seemed to hear some mysterious call to go somewhere, and I could not help feeling that if I went straight on and on, and kept going for a long, long time, I should reach the line where sky and earth met and find the key to the whole mystery there and at once discover a new life, a life a thousand times more splendid and more tumultuous than ours. I dreamed of a great city as big as Naples, full of palaces, noise, uproar, life. ... But, then, what didn't I dream of? And afterwards I could not help feeling that one might find an immense life in prison too.'

'Your last highly laudable reflection I read in my school book when I was twelve,' said Aglaya.

'That's all philosophy,' observed Adelaida. 'You're a philosopher and you've come to instruct us.'

'Perhaps you are right,' said the prince with a smile. 'I daresay I really am a philosopher, and, who knows, perhaps I really have the intention of instructing people. ... Yes, that may very well be so – indeed, it may.'

'And your philosophy,' Aglaya put in again, 'is exactly like Eulampe Nikolayevna's, a civil servant's widow who comes to see us, a sort of sponger. All she cares for in life is cheapness – to live as cheaply as possible – all she talks about is pennies, and yet she has money, you know; she's an awful rogue. It's the same with your immense life in prison, and, perhaps, also with your four years of happiness in the little village for which you have given up your city of Naples, and at a profit, too, it seems, though of a few pennies only.'

'I agree,' said the prince, 'that there may be more than one opinion about life in prison. I heard the story of a man who spent twelve years in prison. He was one of my professor's patients. He had fits, he was sometimes very restless and wept, and once he even tried to commit suicide. His life in prison had been very sad, I assure you, but not by any means trivial. His only friends were a spider and a little tree that grew under his window. ... But I'd better tell you of another meeting I had with a man last year. There was a strange incident in his life, strange because it so rarely happens. This man had once been taken, together with others, to a place of execution where a sentence of death was read out to him. He was to be shot for a political crime. Twenty minutes later his reprieve was read out to him, another penalty for his crime being substituted. Yet the interval between the two sentences – twenty minutes or, at least, a quarter of an hour – he passed in the absolute certainty that in a few minutes he would be dead. I very much liked to listen to him when he used to recall his impressions of those moments, and I questioned him several times about it. He remembered everything with the most extraordinary distinctness, and he used to say that he would never forget anything he had been through during those minutes. Three posts were dug into the ground about twenty paces from the scaffold, which was surrounded by a crowd of people and soldiers, for there were several criminals. The first three were led to the posts and tied to them; the death vestments (long, white smocks) were put on them, and white caps were drawn over their eyes so that they should not see the rifles; next a company of several soldiers was drawn up against each post. My friend was the eighth on the list and his would therefore be the third turn to be marched to the posts. The priest went to each of them with the cross. It seemed to him then that he had only five more minutes to live. He told me that those five minutes were like an eternity to him, riches beyond the dreams of avarice; he felt that during those five minutes he would live through so many lives that it was quite unnecessary for him to think of the last moment, so that he had plenty of time to make all sorts of arrangements: he calculated the exact time he needed to take leave of his comrades, and decided that he could do that in two minutes, then he would spend another two minutes in thinking of himself for the last time, and, finally, one minute for a last look round. He remembered very well that he had decided to do all this and that he had divided up the time in exactly that way. He was dying at twenty-seven, a strong and healthy man; taking leave of his comrades, he remembered asking one of them quite an irrelevant question and being very interested indeed in his answer. Then, after he had bidden farewell to his comrades, came the two minutes he had set aside for thinking of himself; he knew beforehand what he would think about. He just wanted to imagine, as vividly and as quickly as possible, how it could be that now, at this moment, he was there and alive and in three minutes he would merely be *something* – someone or something – but what? And where? All that he thought he would be able to decide in those two minutes! There was a church not far off, its gilt roof shining in the bright sunshine. He remembered staring with awful intensity at that roof and the sunbeams flashing from it; he could not tear his eyes off those rays of light: those rays seemed to him to be his new nature, and he felt that in three minutes he would somehow merge with them. ... The uncertainty and the feeling of disgust with that new thing which was bound to come any minute were dreadful; but he said that the thing that was most unbearable to him at the time was the constant thought, "What if I had not had to die! What if I could return to life – oh, what an eternity! And all that would be mine! I should turn every minute into an age, I should lose nothing, I should count every minute separately and waste none!" He said that this reflection finally filled him with such bitterness that he prayed to be shot as quickly as possible.'

The prince fell silent suddenly: they all expected him to go on and draw some conclusion.

'Have you finished?' Aglaya asked.

'I beg your pardon? Oh, yes,' said the prince, emerging from his momentary reverie.

'But why did you tell us this?'

'Oh, I don't know – I just remembered it – I – er – I thought it might do as a subject for conversation – –'

'You're very abrupt, Prince,' Alexandra observed. 'I expect what you wished to say was that it was impossible to put a price on any moment of our life, and that five minutes were sometimes more precious than all the riches in the world. All this is very laudable, but tell me what about that friend of yours who told you all those terrible things – his sentence was altered, wasn't it? – which means that he was granted that "eternity of life". Well, what did he do with that wealth afterwards? Did he count every minute separately?'

'Oh, no, he told me himself – I asked him about it – he didn't live like that at all, and he wasted many, many minutes.'

'Well, let that be a lesson to you. It seems it's impossible actually to live "counting every minute separately". Whatever the reason, it's impossible.'

'Yes, whatever the reason, it's impossible,' the prince repeated. 'I thought so myself. And yet I somehow can't believe it. ...'

'You think, then, that you'll live more wisely than everyone else, do you?' asked Aglaya.

'Yes, I have thought so sometimes.'

'And you still think so, don't you?'

'Yes – I do,' the prince replied, looking as before at Aglaya with a gentle and rather timid smile, but he immediately laughed again and looked gaily at her.

'Modest, aren't you?' said Aglaya, looking almost irritated.

'But how brave you are! You're laughing, but I was so struck by that man's story that I dreamt about it afterwards, I mean, of those five minutes. ...'

He looked round at his listeners again, gravely and searchingly.

'You're not angry with me for anything?' he asked suddenly, as though in embarrassment, but looking them straight in the face.

'Whatever for?' the three girls cried in surprise.

'Why, because I seem to be lecturing you all the time.'

They all laughed.

'If you are angry, then please don't be,' he said. 'I know perfectly well myself that I've lived less than other people and that I know less of life than anyone. I'm afraid I talk rather strangely sometimes. ...' and he was overcome with confusion.

'If, as you say, you were happy, you must have lived more and not less than other people, so why do you play the hypocrite and apologize?' Aglaya began severely and captiously. 'And please do not worry about lecturing us. You have nothing to be so superior about. With your quietism one might live happily for a hundred years. Whether one showed you an execution or a little finger, you'd be quite sure to draw highly laudable conclusions from either, and remain happy and contented, too. To live like that is easy.'

'Why are you so cross? I can't understand you,' cried Mrs Yepanchin, who had been observing their faces for some time. 'And I can't understand what you are talking about, either. What little finger and what's all this nonsense? The prince talks beautifully, though a little sadly. Why do you discourage him? When he began he was laughing, and now he looks quite glum.'

'Never mind, Mother. But it's a pity you didn't see an execution, Prince. I'd have liked to ask you something.'

'I have seen an execution,' replied the prince.

'You have?' cried Aglaya. 'I might have guessed it! That puts the finishing touch to everything. If you've seen it, then how can you say that you've been living happily all the time? Well, didn't I tell you the truth?'

'But do they execute people in your village?' asked Adelaida.

'I saw it at Lyons. I went there with Schneider. He took me. I got there just in time for the execution.'

'Well, did you like it very much? Was there much that was edifying? Was it instructive?' Aglaya asked.

'I didn't like it at all, and I was rather ill afterwards, but I must confess that I looked as though rooted to the spot. Couldn't take my eyes off it.'

'I couldn't have taken my eyes off it, either,' said Aglaya.

'They don't like women to go and look at it there. They even write in the papers about such women.'

'Which means that if they don't consider it fit for women, they admit (and therefore justify it) that it is fit for men. I congratulate them on their logic. And, of course, you're of the same opinion.'

'Tell us about the execution,' Adelaida interrupted.

'I'm sorry I don't feel like it now,' the prince said, looking embarrassed and almost frowning.

'You almost seem to grudge telling us about it,' Aglaya taunted him.

'No, you see, I've just been telling someone about that execution.'

'Who were you telling it to?'

'Your footman, while waiting in the entrance hall.'

'Which footman?' they all asked in one voice.

'The one who sits in the entrance hall. He has greyish hair and a reddish face. I sat in the entrance hall waiting to see General Yepanchin.'

'That's strange,' Mrs Yepanchin observed.

'The prince is a democrat,' Aglaya snapped. 'Well, if you told Alexey about it, you can't possibly refuse to tell us.'

'I'm dying to hear it,' Adelaida repeated.

'You see,' the prince said, turning to her and speaking rather animatedly (he seemed to get rather animated very quickly and unsuspectingly), 'just now when you asked me for a subject for a picture it occurred to me to tell you to paint the face of a condemned man a minute before the fall of the guillotine blade, when he is still standing on the scaffold and before he lies down on the plank.'

'The face? Only the face?' Adelaida asked. 'That would be a strange subject. And what sort of picture would it make?'

'I don't know, but why not?' the prince insisted warmly. 'I saw a picture like that at Basel not long ago. I'd be glad to tell you about it – some day, perhaps – it impressed me very much.'

'You shall certainly tell us about the Basel picture some other time,' said Adelaida, 'but now I'd like you to explain to me the picture of this execution. Can you tell me as you imagine it to yourself? How is one to draw this face? Just a face? What sort of a face is it?'

'It's exactly one minute before death,' the prince began quite readily, carried away by his memories and apparently forgetting everything else in an instant – 'the moment he has mounted the ladder and stepped on the scaffold. Just then he glanced in my direction. I looked at his face and understood everything. But how am I to tell you about it? I'd be awfully glad if you or someone else would paint it – awfully! You most of all! I thought at the time that such a picture would do a lot of good. You see, you must show everything that happened before – everything, everything. He has been in prison, waiting for his execution for a week at least; he had been counting on the usual red-tape, on the paper with his sentence having to be forwarded somewhere and coming back only after a week. But for some reason the usual procedure was cut short. At five o'clock in the morning he was asleep. It was at the end of October; at five o'clock it was still cold and dark. The governor of the prison came in quietly with the guard and touched him gently on the shoulder. He sat up, leaning on his elbow, and saw the light. "What's the matter?" "The execution will take place at ten o'clock." He was still too sleepy to believe it. He began arguing that the paper with his sentence would not be ready for a week, but when he was wide awake he stopped arguing and fell silent – so I have heard it told. Then he said: "All the same, it's very hard that it should be so sudden," and fell silent again, and wouldn't say another word. The next three or four hours were spent on the usual things: the priest, the breakfast at which he was given wine, coffee, and boiled beef. (Isn't that a mockery? Just think how cruel it is, and yet, on the other hand, these innocent people do it out of pure kindness of heart and are convinced that it's an act of humanity.) Then he was dressed for execution (do you know what the dressing of a condemned criminal is like?), and at last they took him through the town to the scaffold. I cannot help thinking that while he was being driven through the town he must have felt that he had still an eternity to live. I think he must have thought on the way, "I've still a long, long time; there are still three streets more to live. As soon as I pass through this, there will be that one, and then that one with the bakery on the right – oh, it'll be ages before we get to the bakery!" All round him there were crowds of people yelling, shouting, ten thousand faces, ten thousand eyes – and all this had to be endured, and, worst of all, the thought: "There are ten thousand of them, and none of them is being executed, but I'm going to be executed!" Well, all this is just the preliminaries. A ladder leads up to the scaffold, and it was just in front of the ladder that he suddenly burst into tears – a strong and brave man like him – a very wicked man, he was, I was told. The priest was with him all the time, drove with him in the cart, and never stopped talking to him; but I don't think he heard a word of what the priest said, and even if he tried to listen, he would not understand more than a couple of words. That's how it must have been. At last he began going up the ladder: his legs were tied and he could only take very small steps. The priest, who must have been an intelligent man, stopped talking, but kept giving him the cross to kiss. At the foot of the ladder he was very pale, but when he reached the top and stood on the scaffold, he suddenly grew as white as a sheet of paper, a sheet of white note-paper. His legs must have grown weak and wooden and he must have felt sick too – as though something were choking him and that gave him a sort of tickling sensation in the throat – did you ever experience that feeling in moments of terror, when your reason remains unaffected, but it has no power left? I can't help feeling that, for instance, in a moment of unavoidable destruction, if a house is collapsing on top of you, you are suddenly overcome by a desire to sit down, close your eyes and wait – come what may! ... At that very moment, when this weakness was beginning, the priest quickly, with a sort of rapid movement, silently put the cross to his lips, such a little cross, a square silver one – and kept it to his lips every minute. And every time the cross touched his lips, he opened his eyes and his legs moved on. He kissed the cross greedily, he seemed to be in a hurry to kiss it, as though he were eager not to forget to take something with him in case of need, but I doubt if he was conscious of any religious feeling at the time. And so it went on till he reached the plank. ... It is odd that people seldom faint at those last moments. On the contrary, the brain, tremendously alive and active, must, I suppose, be working hard, hard, hard, like an engine going at full speed. I imagine all sorts of thoughts – all unfinished and absurd too, perhaps, quite irrelevant thoughts – must be constantly throbbing through his brain: "That man is looking at me – he has a wart on his forehead – one of the buttons on the executioner's coat is rusty. ..." and all the time he knows everything and remembers everything; there is one point which one can never forget, and one can't faint, and everything goes round and round it, round that point. And to think that this goes on to the last fraction of a second when his head already lies on the block and he waits, and he – *knows*, and suddenly he hears the iron come slithering down over his head! He must certainly hear that! If I were lying there, I'd listen for it on purpose and I'd hear it. There is only perhaps one tenth part of a second left, but one would certainly hear it. And, imagine, there are still some people who maintain that when the head is cut off, it knows for a second perhaps that it has been cut off – what a thought! And what if it knows for five seconds? ... Paint the scaffold so that only the last step can be distinctly and clearly seen in the foreground; the condemned man stepping on it: his head, his face is as white as paper, the priest is holding up the cross, the man greedily puts out his blue lips and looks and – *knows everything*. The cross and the head – that is the picture, the priest's face, the faces of the executioner and his two assistants, and a few faces and eyes below – all this can be painted as a background. That's the kind of picture.'

The prince paused and looked at them all.

'That, of course, isn't much like quietism,' said Alexandra to herself.

'Well, and now tell us how you were in love,' said Adelaida.

The prince looked at her in surprise.

'Listen,' Adelaida went on, speaking rapidly, as though she were in a hurry, 'you've still to tell us about the Basel picture, but now I'd like to hear how you were in love. Don't deny it, you were! Besides, the moment you begin telling something you stop being a philosopher.'

'As soon as you have finished your story,' Aglaya observed suddenly, 'you seem to be ashamed of what you've said. Why is that?'

'This is just silly,' Mrs Yepanchin snapped, looking indignantly at Aglaya.

'It's not clever,' Alexandra agreed.

'Don't believe her, Prince,' Mrs Yepanchin said, addressing him. 'She does it on purpose out of some sort of spite. She hasn't been brought up as badly as that. Don't think there's anything wrong because they're teasing you. I expect they are up to something, but I can see that they like you already. I can read their faces.'

'I can read their faces too,' said the prince, with particular emphasis on his words.

'What do you mean?' Adelaida asked curiously.

'What do you know about our faces?' the other two sisters exclaimed, also eager to know what he meant.

But the prince was silent and grave. They all waited for his answer.

'I'll tell you afterwards,' he said quietly and gravely.

'You're just trying to arouse our curiosity,' cried Aglaya. 'And what solemnity!'

'All right,' Adelaida said, again speaking very rapidly, 'if you are such an expert on faces, you must certainly have been in love. I was right, then. Tell us, please!'

'I have not been in love,' the prince replied as quietly and gravely as before. 'I – was happy in a different way.'

'How? In what way?'

'Very well, I'll tell you,' said the prince, as though deep in thought.

6

'You are all looking at me now with such curiosity,' began the prince, 'that if I didn't satisfy it, you would probably be angry with me. No, I'm not joking,' he added quickly with a smile. 'There were always children there, and I spent all my time with the children, only with the children. They were the children of the village where I lived, a whole gang of them, who went to the local school. I did not teach them, oh no, they had their own schoolteacher for that – Jules Thibaut.

I suppose I did teach them in a way, but I was simply with them mostly, and I spent all my four years there like that. I did not want anything else. I used to tell them everything. I concealed nothing from them. All their parents and relations got angry with me because in the end the children could not get on without me, and were always flocking round me, so that at last the schoolmaster became my worst enemy. I made many enemies there and all because of the children. Even Schneider remonstrated with me. And what were they so afraid of? A child can be told everything – everything! I've always been struck by the fact that grown-ups, fathers and mothers, know their children so little. One must never conceal anything from children on the pretext that they are little and it is too early for them to know things. What a lamentable and unfortunate idea! And how quick children are to notice that their fathers consider them to be too little to understand, while they understand everything. Grown-up people do not realize that a child can give extremely good advice even about the most difficult matters. Why, when that pretty little bird looks at you so happily and confidingly, you can't help feeling ashamed to deceive it. I call them little birds because there is nothing better than a bird in the world. But, as a matter of fact, everyone in the village was angry with me, chiefly because of a certain incident ... while Thibaut was simply jealous of me. At first he just shook his head and wondered how it was that the children understood everything I told them and hardly ever understood him, and then he began laughing at me when I told him that neither he nor I would teach them anything, but that they were most likely to teach us. And how could he be jealous of me and tell discreditable stories about me when he spent his life with children himself! It is through children that the soul is cured. ... There was one patient in Schneider's clinic, a very unhappy man. His was such a terrible misfortune that I doubt if there can be anything like it. He had been sent there to be treated for insanity. In my opinion, he was not insane, but was greatly distressed – that was all that was the matter with him. And if only you knew what our children meant to him in the end. ... But I'd better tell you about that patient another time; I'll tell you now how it all began. At first the children did not like me. I was so big, I am always so clumsy; I know I am ugly, too. And there was, of course, also the fact that I was a foreigner. At first the children laughed at me, and then, when they saw me kiss Marie, they even began throwing stones at me. And I only kissed her once. ... No, don't laugh,' the prince hastened to check the smile of his listeners, 'it was not a question of love at all. If only you knew what an unhappy creature she was, you'd be sorry for her as I was.

She lived in our village. Her mother was an old woman. One of the two windows of their ramshackle little house was set apart by permission of the village authorities, and from it the old woman was allowed to sell laces, thread, tobacco, and soap, all for a pittance, and that was what they lived on. She was an invalid; her legs were all swollen, so that she always stayed in the same place. Marie was her daughter, a girl of twenty, weak and thin; she had contracted consumption long before, but she kept going from house to house doing heavy work as a daily – scrubbing floors, doing the washing, sweeping out yards, looking after the cattle. A French commercial traveller, who was passing through the village, seduced her and took her away, but a week later he deserted her and went off, leaving her stranded. She returned home, begging on the way, all bespattered and in rags, with her shoes all in holes. She had walked for a week, had spent the nights in the fields, and caught a bad cold. Her feet were covered in sores, her hands were chapped and swollen. But then she had never been a beauty before; only her eyes were gentle, kind, and innocent. She was terribly taciturn. One day – it happened long before – she suddenly burst into song when she was at work, and I remember how surprised everyone was and how they all laughed: "Marie was singing! What did you say? Marie was singing!" She was terribly put out and was silent for ever after. In those days people were still very kind to her, but when she came back ill and bedraggled, no one felt any pity for her! How cruel people are in a case like that! What distressing ideas they have! Her mother was the first to welcome her spitefully and with contempt: "You have disgraced me now!" She was the first to expose her to public contumely: when the news of Marie's return spread through the village, everyone ran to have a look at her, and almost the whole village gathered in the old woman's cottage – old men, children, women, girls, all – a scrambling, eager crowd. Marie was lying on the ground at the old woman's feet, hungry and in rags, and she was crying. When they all crowded into the cottage, she buried her face in her dishevelled hair and lay huddled up face downwards on the floor. They all looked at her as if she had been something too vile to be regarded with anything but profound disgust. The old men blamed and scolded her, the young people laughed, the women scolded her, blamed her, looked upon her with contempt as though she had been some loathsome spider. Her mother allowed it all, sitting there nodding her head and approving. The mother was very ill at the time and almost dying; two months later she did die. She knew she was dying, and yet up to the very day of her death she made no attempt to be reconciled to her daughter. She did not speak to her, she turned her out to sleep in the passage, and gave her hardly anything to eat. She had to bathe her bad legs in hot water, and Marie bathed her legs every day and nursed her. She accepted all her services in silence and never said a kind word to her. Marie put up with everything, and afterwards, when I made her acquaintance, I noticed that she accepted it all without protest and, indeed, regarded herself as the lowest creature in the world. When the old woman took to her bed at last, the old women of the village took turns in nursing her, as is their custom. Then they stopped giving food to Marie altogether, and in the village everyone drove her away and no one would even give her work as before. They all seemed to spit on her, and the men no longer looked on her as a woman, and they all said such horrible things to her. Sometimes, though very rarely, when the men got drunk on a Sunday, they amused themselves by throwing coppers on the ground for her to pick up. Marie picked them up without uttering a word. She had begun to cough and spit blood by that time. At last her rags became so tattered and torn that she was ashamed to show herself in the village. She had gone barefoot ever since she came back. It was just then that the children in particular, the whole gang of them – there were over forty schoolchildren – began teasing her and even pelting her with mud. She had asked the cowherd to let her look after his cows, but the cowherd drove her away. Then she began to go away with the herd for the whole day without his permission. As she was very useful to the cowherd and he realized it, he no longer drove her away, and sometimes even gave her the remnants of his dinner, bread and cheese. He thought it a great kindness on his part. When her mother died, the pastor was not ashamed to hold Marie up to public shame and derision in church. Marie was standing behind the coffin, in her rags, weeping. A large crowd of people had come to watch her weeping and walking behind the coffin; it was then that the pastor – he was still a young man and his whole ambition was to become a great preacher – turned to all the people and, pointing to Marie, said: "It is this girl who was the cause of this worthy woman's death." (It was not true, for the old woman had been ill for two years.) "Here she stands before you and dare not look up because she has been marked by the finger of God. Look at her, barefoot and in rags, a living warning to those who lose their virtue! Who is she? She is her daughter!" And all in this vein. And, just think of it, this infamy pleased almost everyone, but – here something extraordinary happened. The children took her part because by that time the children were all already on my side and had begun to love Marie. This is how it happened. I wanted to do something for Marie. What I should have done was to give her some money, but I never had a penny while I was there. I had a little diamond pin and I sold it to a pedlar who went from village to village buying and selling old clothes. He gave me eight francs for it, though it was certainly worth forty. I tried hard to meet Marie alone. At last we met by a hedge outside the village, on a by-path leading up to the mountain, behind a tree. There I gave her the eight francs and I told her to take good care of them because I should have no more. Then I kissed her and said that she wasn't to think that I had any evil intentions, and that I kissed her not because I was in love with her but because I was very sorry for her, and that I had never, from the very beginning, thought of her as guilty, but only as a poor, unhappy girl. I was very anxious to comfort her and to assure her that there was no reason why she should consider herself beneath everyone, but I don't think she understood me. I saw that at once, though she scarcely uttered a word all the time and stood before me with downcast eyes and looked dreadfully ashamed of herself. When I had finished, she kissed my hand, and I at once took her hand, intending to kiss it, but she snatched it away quickly. It was just then that the children saw us, a whole crowd of them. I found out later that they had been secretly keeping watch on me for a long time. They began whistling, clapping their hands and laughing, and Marie ran away. I tried to talk to them, but they started throwing stones at me. Everyone knew about it the same day – the whole village. Again they all came down on her: they began to dislike her more than ever. I even heard that they wanted to take her before the magistrate for punishment, but, thank God, it didn't come to that. But the children would not let her alone. They teased her more than ever and threw mud at her. When they chased her, she ran away from them; when she, with her weak chest, stopped, panting for breath, they were still after her, shouting and cursing and swearing at her. Once I even had a fight with them. Then I began to talk to them; I talked to them every day as much as I could. Sometimes they stopped and listened to me, though they still abused me. I told them how unhappy Marie was, and soon they stopped abusing me and began to walk away in silence. Little by little, we began talking together. I concealed nothing from them. I told them everything. They listened with great interest and soon they began to feel sorry for Marie. Some of them began greeting her affectionately when they met her. It is their custom when meeting – whether friends or strangers – to bow and say, "Good-morning". I can imagine how astonished Marie was. One day two little girls got some food and took it to her. They gave it to her, then came back and told me about it. They told me Marie had burst into tears and that now they loved her very much. Soon all of them began to love her, and at the same time they suddenly began loving me too. They started paying me regular visits and always begged me to tell them stories. I think I must have told them well because they liked listening to me very much. Afterwards I studied and read just to be able to have something to tell them, and for the remaining three years I used to tell them stories. When later on everybody, including Schneider, blamed me for speaking to them like grown-up people and for not concealing anything from them, I told them that it was a shame to tell them lies, that they knew everything anyhow, however much you concealed it from them, and that they might learn it in a nasty way, while they wouldn't do so from me: one has only to remember one's own childhood. But they did not agree. ...

'I kissed Marie a fortnight before her mother died; but when the pastor preached his sermon, the children already were all on my side. I at once told them of the pastor's action and explained it to them. They were all angry with him, and some of them were so disgusted that they threw stones and broke his windows. I stopped them, for that was wrong. But everyone in the village got to know about it at once, and it was then that they started accusing me of corrupting the children. Soon they got to know that the children loved Marie and they were terribly alarmed; but Marie was happy. The children were forbidden to meet her, but they ran out secretly to the herd, nearly half a mile from the village, to see her. They brought her presents, and some of them simply ran to hug and kiss her and say, "*Je vous aime, Marie!*" and then ran back as fast as they could. Marie nearly went mad with such unexpected happiness: she had never thought it possible in her wildest dreams; she felt ashamed and she was overjoyed. But what the children liked doing most, especially the girls, was running to tell her that I loved her and talked a lot to them about her. They told her that I told them all about it and that they loved her now and were sorry for her and that they would always be like that. Then they would run to tell me that they had just seen Marie and that Marie sent me her regards. In the evenings I used to walk to the waterfall; there was a place there which was completely hidden from the village and surrounded by poplars. It was there that they came to see me in the evenings, some of them even by stealth. I think that they took tremendous pleasure in my love for Marie, and it was in this alone that I deceived them during the whole of the time I spent in their village. I did not undeceive them by telling them that I did not love Marie, that is to say, that I was not in love with her, but that I was merely very sorry for her; I could see that they'd much rather have it as they imagined it themselves, and that was why I kept silent and pretended that they had guessed right. And how delicate and tender their little hearts were! They could not reconcile themselves to the idea that while their good Léon loved Marie so much, she should be so badly dressed and be without shoes. Well, so they got her shoes, stockings, linen, and even some sort of dress. How they managed to do it, I don't know. The whole gang must have clubbed together to make it possible. When I questioned them, they only laughed happily, and the girls clapped their hands and kissed me. I too sometimes went to see Marie in secret. By that time she had become very ill and could hardly walk; at last she gave up working for the cowman altogether, but went out with the cattle each morning all the same. She used to sit apart. There was a ledge on one sheer, almost vertical, rock there. She used to sit down on the stone, leaning against the rock, out of sight of everybody, and sit there motionless all day, from early morning till it was time for the cattle to go home. She was already so weakened by consumption that she mostly sat with her eyes closed and head leaning against the rock, dozing and breathing heavily. Her face was as thin as a skeleton's, and the sweat stood out on her brow and temples. That was how I always found her. I used to go for a short time and I, too, did not want to be seen. As soon as I appeared, Marie would give a start, open her eyes, and begin kissing my hands. I no longer tried to take them away because it made her happy. All the time I sat with her she trembled and cried. It is true that sometimes she tried to speak, but it was difficult to understand her. She seemed beside herself with excitement and delight. Sometimes the children came with me. When they did so, they generally stood a little way off to keep guard over us against someone or something, and that pleased them exceedingly. When we went away, Marie was again left alone, sitting motionless as before, with her eyes closed and her head leaning against the rock; perhaps she was dreaming of something. One morning she could no longer go out with the herd and remained at home in her deserted house. The children got to know of it at once, and almost all of them came to see her that day; she lay in bed, all alone. For two days she was nursed by the children, who ran in to her by turns, but afterwards, when it became known in the village that Marie was really dying, the old women went to sit with her and never again left her alone. I believe the villagers had begun to pity Marie, at least they no longer interfered with the children and did not scold them as before. Marie was drowsy all the time, her sleep was restless: she coughed dreadfully. The old women drove the children away, but they kept running under the window, sometimes only for a moment, just to say, "*Bonjour, notre bonne Marie.*" As soon as she caught sight of them or heard them, she grew all animated and, without paying attention to the old women, tried to raise herself on her elbow and nodded to them and thanked them. They brought her presents as before, but she scarcely ate anything. I assure you it was because of them that she died almost happy. Because of them she forgot her bitter troubles; it was as though she had received forgiveness from them, for to the very end she considered herself a great sinner. Like birds, they fluttered their wings against her window, calling to her every morning: "*Nous t'aimons, Marie.*" She died very soon. I thought she would live much longer. The day before her death, at sunset, I went to see her. I think she recognized me, and I pressed her hand for the last time: how her hand had wasted away! Next morning they came and told me that Marie was dead. The children could not be restrained any more now: they smothered her coffin in flowers and laid a wreath on her head. In the church the pastor no longer reviled the dead girl. There were not many people at her funeral, anyway; only a few put in an appearance out of curiosity. But when the coffin had to be carried out, the children rushed forward all at once to carry it out themselves. As they could not do it alone, they helped to carry it, running after the coffin and weeping. Marie's grave has been reverently kept by the children: they bring flowers to it every year and they have planted roses all round it. But ever since that funeral all the villagers began to persecute me because of the children. The pastor and the schoolmaster were the chief instigators. The children were strictly forbidden even to meet me, and Schneider undertook to see that I kept away from them. But we did see each other all the same, communicating by signs from a distance. They used to send me little notes. In time it all blew over, but while my persecution lasted it was very nice: my friendship with the children grew stronger than ever because of it. In the last year I was almost reconciled with Thibaut and the pastor. Schneider kept talking and arguing with me a great deal about my harmful "system" with children. My system! As though I ever had one. At last Schneider said something to me that struck me as rather strange – it was just before I left. He told me that he had come to the firm conclusion that I was a complete child myself, a real child, in fact, that it was only in face and figure that I was like a grown-up person, but in development, in soul and character and, perhaps, also in intelligence I was not grown-up, and I would stay like that even if I lived to be sixty. I laughed very much. Of course, he was wrong, for what sort of a child am I? But in one respect he was quite right: I don't really like to be with grown-up people – I noticed it a long time ago – and I don't like it because I don't know how to behave with them. Whatever they say to me, however kind they are to me, I somehow feel depressed in their company and I'm awfully glad when I can get away to my companions, and my companions have always been children. But this is not because I am a child myself; it is simply because I always felt drawn to the society of children. When at the very beginning of my life in the village, at the time when I used to go brooding in the mountains, I sometimes, on my solitary walks, especially at midday, came across all that noisy gang of children running home from school, with their satchels and slates, shouting, laughing, and playing games, my soul went out to them at once. I don't know, but every time I met them I was overcome by an exceedingly powerful sensation of happiness. I stood still and laughed happily as I looked at their little legs, flashing by and always racing along, at the boys and girls running together, at their laughter and tears (for on their way home from school many of them managed to have a fight, cry, make it up and start another game), and I forgot all about my depression. Later on, all through the last three years I spent in the village, I simply could not understand how and why people are sad and dejected. I devoted all my life to them. I never expected to leave the village and it never occurred to me that I might ever go back to Russia. I thought I would always stay there. But I realized at last that Schneider could not afford to keep me; and then something turned up, something so important apparently that Schneider himself was anxious for me to go at once and wrote to say that I was coming. I'm going to find out what it is and take advice. Perhaps my life will be completely changed, but that does not matter: it is of no importance. What does matter is that my life is already changed. I left a great deal there – too much. It is all gone. As I sat in the train, I thought: "Now I'm going among people; I may not know anything, but a new life has begun for me." I made up my mind to do my duty honestly and resolutely. I may find it painful and dull to be among people. To begin with, I decided to be frank and courteous with everybody; no one can expect more than that from me. Perhaps even here they will regard me as a child – it can't be helped! For some reason everyone regards me as an idiot, too, and it is quite true that I was so ill at one time that I really was almost an idiot. But what sort of an idiot am I now when I know myself that people take me for an idiot? As I come into a room, I think: "They look upon me as an idiot, but I am intelligent for all that and they don't seem to realize it." I often think like that. It was only in Berlin, when I received several letters from the village children, which they had already managed to write to me, that I realized how much I loved them. It was very painful getting that first letter! How sorry they were to see me go! "*Léon s'en va! Léon s'en va pour toujours!*" We met every evening as before at the waterfall and always talked of how we should part. Sometimes we were as happy as before; it was only when we parted company at night that they started hugging me warmly, which never happened before. Some of them came to see me in secret; one at a time, to kiss and hug me alone and not in the presence of the others. When the time came for me to leave, all of them – the whole crowd of them – saw me off to the station. The railway station was about a mile from the village. They did their best not to cry, but some of them could not restrain themselves and they cried aloud, especially the girls. We were in a hurry not to miss the train, but one or another of them would suddenly rush up to me, throw his little arms round me, and kiss me, and stop the whole crowd only to do that; though we were in a hurry, we all stopped and waited for him to say good-bye. When I had taken my seat in the carriage and the train started, they all shouted "Good-bye!" and stayed on the platform until the train was out of sight. I, too, kept looking at them. ... Listen, when I came in here a short while ago and looked at your dear faces – I am always scrutinizing people's faces now – and heard your first words, I felt happy for the first time since then. I couldn't help thinking that perhaps I am lucky, for, you see, I know you don't often meet people to whom you take a liking at once, but I met you almost as soon as I left the train. I know very well that one ought to feel ashamed to talk of one's feelings to everyone, but I'm talking to you and I don't feel ashamed. I am an unsociable person, and quite possibly I won't come to see you again for a long time. But please don't think badly of me for saying this; I didn't say it because I do not value your friendship. And please don't think that I have taken offence at something, either. You asked me about your faces and what I noticed in them. I'll tell you that with pleasure. You, Miss Adelaida, have a happy face, the most sympathetic face of the three. Besides your being very good-looking, one can't help saying to oneself when one looks at you, "She has the face of a kind sister." You approach one simply and gaily, but you are quick to know a man's heart. That's what I think of your face. You, Miss Alexandra, have also a very sweet and beautiful face, but perhaps you have some secret sorrow. You have, I'm sure, the kindest heart – but you are not gay. There's something special about your face which reminds me of Holbein's Madonna in Dresden. Well, so much for your face. Am I good at guessing? You said I was yourselves. But your face, Mrs Yepanchin,' he said, turning suddenly to Mrs Yepanchin, 'your face tells me – and I am not conjecturing but I say so with absolute confidence – that you are a perfect child in everything, oh, in everything, in everything good and in everything bad, in spite of your age. You're not angry with me for saying so, are you? You know what I think of children, don't you? And don't think that I've spoken so candidly about your faces now because I'm simple-minded. Oh no, not at all! Perhaps I, too, have something in mind.'

7

When the prince ceased speaking, they all looked gaily at him, even Aglaya, but especially Mrs Yepanchin.

'Well, so they have put you through your examination!' she cried. 'Well, my dear young ladies, you thought of patronizing him like some poor little fellow, but he hardly deigned to choose you for his friends, and that, too, with the reservation that he wouldn't come to see you very often. So it is we who've been made to look foolish, and most of all your father, and I'm glad of it. Bravo, Prince; my husband told us to put you through an examination, and we have! And what you said about my face is perfectly true: I am a child and I know it. I knew that long before you told me. You put it in a nutshell. I think your character is exactly like mine, and I'm very glad of it – like two drops of water. Except, of course, that you're a man and I'm a woman and have never been to Switzerland. That's all the difference.'

'Don't be in such a hurry, Mother,' cried Aglaya. 'The prince says that he has something in his mind in making his confession and that he was not speaking without some hidden motive.'

'Yes, yes,' the others laughed.

'Don't make fun of him, my dears. He is perhaps shrewder than all the three of you put together. You'll see. But why didn't you say anything about Aglaya, Prince? Aglaya is waiting and so am I.'

'I'm afraid I can't possibly say anything now. I'll tell you later.'

'Why not? You can't help noticing her, can you?'

'No, you can't. You're extraordinarily beautiful, Miss Aglaya. You're so pretty that one is afraid to look at you.'

'Is that all? And what about her qualities?' Mrs Yepanchin insisted.

'It is difficult to pass judgement on beauty. I'm afraid I am not ready yet. Beauty is a riddle.'

'That means that you've set Aglaya a riddle,' said Adelaida. 'Guess it, Aglaya! But she is beautiful, Prince, isn't she?'

'Extremely!' the prince replied warmly, looking entranced at Aglaya. 'Almost as beautiful as Nastasya Filippovna, except that her face is quite different!'

They all looked at one another in astonishment.

'As who?' Mrs Yepanchin drawled. 'As Nastasya Filippovna? Where did you see Nastasya Filippovna? What Nastasya Filippovna?'

'Mr Ivolgin was showing her portrait to General Yepanchin just now.'

'Oh? Did he bring her portrait to my husband?'

'To show it to him, ma'am. Nastasya Filippovna gave it to Mr Ivolgin to-day, and he brought it to show.'

'I want to see it!' Mrs Yepanchin cried excitedly. 'Where's the portrait? If she's given it to him, he must have it, and he's still, of course, in the study! He always comes to work on Wednesdays, and he never leaves before four o'clock. Call Mr Ivolgin at once! No, I'm not exactly dying to see him. Do me a favour, my dear Prince, go to the study, take the portrait from him, and bring it here. Tell him we want to see it. Please!'

'He's nice, but a little bit too simple,' said Adelaida after the prince had gone.

'Yes, a bit too much,' Alexandra agreed. 'I'm afraid it makes him a little ridiculous.'

Neither seemed to be saying all she thought.

'He got out of it very well though – about our faces, I mean,' said Aglaya. 'He flattered you all, even Mother!'

'Don't be so clever, please,' cried Mrs Yepanchin. 'It was not he who flattered me. It is I who am flattered.'

'You think he was trying to get out of it?' asked Adelaida.

'I don't think he's as simple as all that.'

'There she goes!' Mrs Yepanchin cried angrily. 'I think you're more ridiculous than he is. He is simple, but he's got his wits about him, in the best sense of the word, of course. Just like me.'

'It was wrong of me to have mentioned the portrait,' the prince reflected on his way to the study, feeling a little guilty. 'But – perhaps it wasn't so wrong to have mentioned it, after all. ...'

A strange, though still rather vague, idea was beginning to take shape in his head.

Ganya was still sitting in the study, engrossed in his papers. He did not apparently draw his salary from the joint-stock company for nothing. He was awfully embarrassed when the prince asked him for the portrait and told him how the ladies in the drawing-room had come to know about it.

'Oh dear, and why did you have to blab about it?' he cried in angry vexation. 'You don't know anything. ... Idiot!' he muttered to himself.

'I'm awfully sorry. I did it without thinking, I'm afraid. It just slipped out. You see, I said that Miss Aglaya was as beautiful as Nastasya Filippovna.'

Ganya asked him to tell him exactly what had happened. The prince told him. Ganya looked at him sarcastically again.

'You've got that Nastasya Filippovna on the brain,' he muttered, and, stopping short, sank into thought. He was evidently very upset. The prince reminded him of the portrait.

'Look here, Prince,' Ganya said suddenly, as though struck by a sudden idea, 'I'd like to ask you a great favour, but I honestly don't know – –'

He looked embarrassed and stopped short. He seemed to be making up his mind about something and struggling with himself. The prince waited in silence. Ganya scrutinized him again with intent and searching eyes.

'Prince,' he began, 'they are, I believe – er – a little angry with me in there – er – because of some strange and – er – absurd incident for which I – er – am not responsible – well – er – oh, it doesn't really matter. You see, because they're a little angry with me, I have for some time been rather reluctant to go in without being asked. But now I simply must speak to Miss Aglaya. I have written a few words just in case I'm not able to see her' (a small folded note suddenly materialized in his hand), 'and I don't know how to give it to her. Would you, Prince, mind very much if I were to ask you to give it to her at once, but to her alone, so that no one should see it – do you understand? It isn't such a terrible secret, there's nothing compromising there, but – er – will you do it?'

'I don't think I quite like it,' replied the prince.

'Oh, Prince, but it's a matter of life and death to me,' Ganya began entreating him. 'You see, she may answer. ... Believe me, I shouldn't have asked you if it weren't so vitally important. ... Who else can I send it by? It's very important – frightfully important to me. ...'

Ganya was terribly afraid that the prince would not consent, and he gazed into his eyes with timid entreaty.

'All right, I'll deliver it.'

'But, please, make sure no one notices it,' Ganya besought him, overjoyed. 'And, look here, Prince, I can rely on your word of honour, can't I?'

'I won't show it to anyone,' said the prince.

'The note isn't sealed, but --' Ganya, who was too excited to realize what he was saying, paused in confusion.

'Oh, I won't read it,' the prince said quite simply and, taking the portrait, walked out of the room.

Left alone, Ganya clutched his head.

'One word from her and I – and I really might break it off! ...'

He was so excited and so anxious for a reply to his note that he could not sit down to his papers again, and began pacing the room from one corner to another.

The prince went back deep in thought. He was troubled by his commission and he was troubled by the thought of a letter from Ganya to Aglaya. But two rooms before the drawing-room he suddenly stopped, as though remembering something, looked round cautiously, and, going up to the window nearer the light, began looking at Nastasya Filippovna's portrait.

He seemed anxious to solve some mystery that was hidden in that face and that had struck him before. The impression it had made on him had scarcely left him, and he seemed to be in a hurry to verify it. He was even more struck now by the extraordinary beauty of her face and by something else in it. There was a sort of immense pride and scorn, almost hatred, in that face, and, at the same time, also something trusting, something wonderfully good-natured; this striking contrast seemed almost to arouse in him a feeling of compassion as he looked at it. That dazzling beauty was quite unbearable – the beauty of that pale face, those almost hollow cheeks and burning eyes – a strange beauty! The prince gazed at it for a minute, then, suddenly remembering where he was, looked round nervously, quickly put the portrait to his lips and kissed it. When a minute later he entered the drawing-room, his face was perfectly composed. But as he entered the dining-room (separated by one room from the drawing-room), he almost ran into Aglaya, who was coming out. She was alone.

'Mr Ivolgin asked me to give you this,' said the prince, handing her the note.

Aglaya stopped, took the note, and looked rather strangely at the prince. There was not the slightest embarrassment in her look, except perhaps a certain surprise, and that, too, seemed to refer only to the prince. Aglaya seemed to demand an explanation from him – how he had got himself mixed up in this affair with Ganya – and she was demanding it from him calmly and disdainfully. They stood facing each other like that for a few moments; at last a sort of ironic look seemed to come into her face; she smiled faintly and walked past him.

Mrs Yepanchin examined Nastasya Filippovna's portrait for some time in silence, slightly scornfully, holding it at arm's length in a way that was calculated to make an effect.

'Yes,' she said at last, 'she's good-looking – very good-looking. I've seen her twice, only at a distance. So it's this kind of beauty you admire, is it?' she said, turning to the prince.

'Yes, I do,' the prince replied with some effort.

'Do you mean this kind especially?'

'Yes, especially.'

'Why?'

'Because, you see, there is so much suffering in that face,' the prince said, as though involuntarily, as though speaking to himself and not in answer to her question.

'I daresay you're talking nonsense,' Mrs Yepanchin declared firmly, throwing down the portrait on the table with a haughty gesture.

Alexandra picked it up. Adelaida went up to her and the two began to examine it. At that moment Aglaya came back into the drawing-room.

'What power!' Adelaida cried suddenly, looking eagerly over her sister's shoulder at the portrait.

'Where? What power?' Mrs Yepanchin asked sharply.

'Such beauty is power,' Adelaida said warmly. 'With such beauty one can turn the world upside down.'

She walked away thoughtfully to her easel. Aglaya cast only a cursory glance at the portrait, screwed up her eyes, pushed out her lower lip, walked away, and sat down a little distance away with folded arms.

Mrs Yepanchin rang the bell.

'Ask Mr Ivolgin to come in, please,' she said to the servant who answered it. 'He is in the study.'

'Mother!' Alexandra exclaimed significantly.

'I just want to say two words to him and that's all!' Mrs Yepanchin rapped out sharply, cutting short any objections. She was evidently irritated. 'You see, Prince, we've all got secrets here now – nothing but secrets! It seems to be expected of us, a sort of etiquette – silly! And in a matter, mind, which demands the greatest frankness, clarity, and honesty. Marriages are being arranged – I don't like these marriages. ...'

'Mother, what are you saying?' Alexandra again hastened to stop her.

'What does it matter to you, dear daughter? Do you like them? I don't mind the prince hearing it, for we are friends. He and I are anyway. God is looking out for men, good men, of course. He doesn't want the wicked and the fickle, especially the fickle, who make up their minds to do one thing one day, and say something else another. Do you understand, madam? You see, Prince, they say I'm eccentric, but I know how to distinguish between two kinds of people. For the heart is the great thing; the rest is nothing. Of course, one must have brains, too – perhaps brains is the most important thing really. Don't smile, Aglaya. I am not contradicting myself: a fool with a heart and without brains is the same sort of unhappy fool as one with brains and no heart. It's an old truth. I am a fool with a heart and no brains, and you're a fool with brains and no heart. We are both unhappy. We are both suffering.'

'What are you so unhappy about, Mother?' Adelaida, who seemed to be the only one of the whole company who had not lost her good humour, could not resist asking.

'First of all, because of my learned daughters,' Mrs Yepanchin snapped, 'and as that alone is quite sufficient, I needn't go into any other reasons. We've had plenty of talk. We shall see how you two (I don't count Aglaya) will solve your problems with your brains and your talk and, whether you, madam, will be happy with your fine gentleman? Ah,' she exclaimed, seeing Ganya enter the room, 'here comes another matrimonial alliance. How do you do?' she said in reply to Ganya's bow, without asking him to sit down. 'Are you about to contract a marriage?'

'Marriage? What do you mean? What marriage?' murmured the dumbfounded Ganya. He was overcome with confusion.

'Are you getting married, I ask you, if you prefer that expression?'

'N-no -- Me? – no,' Ganya lied, his whole face colouring with shame.

He threw a quick glance at Aglaya, who was sitting apart from the others, and quickly looked away again.

Aglaya looked intently, coldly, and calmly at him, without taking her eyes off him, watching his confusion.

'No? Did you say no?' the inexorable Mrs Yepanchin questioned him persistently. 'Very well, I shall remember that to-day, on Wednesday morning, you said "No" in answer to my question. It is Wednesday to-day, isn't it?'

'I think so, Mother,' replied Adelaida.

'They never know the day of the week. What date is it?'

'The twenty-seventh,' replied Ganya.

'The twenty-seventh? That's just as well for a certain business I have to settle with someone. Good-bye, sir. I believe you're very busy, and it's time for me to dress and go out. Take your portrait and give my regards to your unhappy mother. Good-bye, my dear Prince. Come and see us often, and I'll make a point of calling on the old Princess Belokonsky and telling her about you. And listen, my dear. I believe God brought you to Petersburg from Switzerland just for my sake. I daresay you will have all sorts of things to attend to, but it was chiefly for my sake. That was God's intention, I do believe. Au revoir, my dears. Alexandra, I'd like to see you before I go, dear.'

Mrs Yepanchin went out. Ganya, completely deflated, confused, and furious, took the portrait from the table and turned to the prince with a twisted smile.

'Prince, I'm going home now. If you haven't changed your mind about living with us, you can come along with me, for you don't even know our address.'

'Wait a minute, Prince,' said Aglaya, rising suddenly from her arm-chair. 'You must write something in my album. Father said you were a calligraphist. I'll bring it you at once.'

And she went out.

'Good-bye, Prince; I'm afraid I must be going, too,' said Adelaida.

She pressed the prince's hand warmly, smiled graciously and cordially at him, and went out. She did not look at Ganya.

'It's all your fault,' Ganya snarled, flinging himself upon the prince as soon as everyone had gone. 'It was you who blabbed to them about my getting married,' he muttered in a rapid undertone, his face working furiously and his eyes flashing angrily. 'You're a shameless blabber, sir!'

'I assure you, you're mistaken,' the prince replied calmly and courteously. 'I didn't even know you were getting married.'

'You heard General Yepanchin say this morning that everything would be settled to-night at Nastasya Filippovna's and you told them that. You are lying! Who else could have told them? Damn it, who could have told them except you? Didn't the old woman as good as hint as much to me?'

'You ought to know best who told them, if you think she hinted at it to you. I didn't say a word about it.'

'Did you give my note? Any answer?' Ganya interrupted him with feverish impatience.

But at that moment Aglaya came back and the prince had no time to answer.

'Here it is, Prince,' said Aglaya, putting her album on the table. 'Choose a page and write something for me. Here's a pen, a new one, too. You don't mind a steel one, do you? I understand calligraphists never use steel pens.'

Talking to the prince, she did not seem to notice Ganya's presence. But while the prince was trying out his pen, looking for a page and preparing to write, Ganya went up to the fireplace where Aglaya was standing on the prince's right hand and whispered almost in her ear in a shaking, broken voice:

'One word – one word only from you – and I am – saved.'

The prince turned round quickly and looked at them both. There was despair in Ganya's face; it was as though he had uttered those words without thinking, on a sudden impulse. Aglaya looked at him for a few seconds with the same expression of calm surprise as she had looked at the prince, and this calm surprise of hers, this bewilderment, as though she were utterly at a loss to understand what was said to her, appeared to be a hundred times more terrible to Ganya at this moment than the most withering contempt.

'What shall I write?' asked the prince.

'I'll dictate it to you,' said Aglaya, turning to him. 'Are you ready? Write, please: "I don't bargain." Now put the date, please. Show me.'

The prince handed her the album.

'Excellent! You've written it marvellously. You've a wonderful handwriting! Thank you. Good-bye, Prince. Wait a minute,' she added, as though recollecting something. 'Come along with me, I want to give you something to remember me by.'

The prince followed her, but as soon as they entered the dining-room, Aglaya stopped.

'Read this,' she said, giving him Ganya's note.

The prince took the note and looked at her in bewilderment.

'You see, I know you haven't read it and that you couldn't possibly be that man's confidant. Read it. I want you to read it.'

The note had evidently been written in a hurry.

'To-day my fate will be decided, you know how. To-day I shall have to give my word irrevocably. I have no right to ask for your sympathy; I dare not have any hopes, but once you uttered one word, only one word, and that word lightened the darkness of my life and has been a beacon for me ever since. Speak one more such word now – and you will save me from ruin! Only say to me: "Break off everything", and I will break everything off to-day. Oh, what will it cost you to say that! That word I only beg as a sign of your sympathy and compassion for me – and only that, *only that!* And nothing more, *nothing!* I dare not cherish any hope because I am *unworthy* of it. But after that word from you I shall put up with my poverty again and I shall gladly endure my desperate situation. I shall take up the fight, I shall be glad of it, I shall rise up again with renewed strength.

'Let me have that word of sympathy (*only* sympathy, I swear!). Do not be angry with the impertinence of a man in despair, a drowning man, for daring to make a last effort to save himself from ruin. G. I.'

'This man assures me,' Aglaya said sharply, after the prince had finished reading the note, 'that the words: *break it all off* will not compromise me and will not commit me to anything, and, as you see, he gives me a written undertaking of it himself in this note. Observe how naïvely he hastened to underline certain words and how crudely his secret thought shows through it. He knows, though, that if he had broken it all off – if he did it himself, alone, without waiting for any word from me and without even saying anything to me about it, without hoping for anything from me – I should have changed my feelings towards him and, perhaps, have become his friend. He knows it for a fact! But he has a sordid soul: he knows and yet cannot make up his mind; he knows and he is asking for an undertaking in spite of it. He is incapable of making up his mind and taking one on trust. In exchange for the hundred thousand he wants me not to deprive him of the hope of marrying me. As for the word I am supposed to have given him, which he mentions in his note and which he claims to have brought light into his life, it is an impudent lie. I was sorry for him only once. But he is shameless and insolent: he immediately got the idea that there was hope for him. I realized it at once. After that he began trying to catch me out, and he is still at it. But enough. Please take this note and return it to him. I mean as soon as you have left the house, of course, not before.'

'But what shall I tell him?'

'Nothing, of course. That is the best answer. So you are going to live at his house, are you?'

'Your father himself advised me to stay there,' said the prince.

'In that case, be on your guard with him. I warn you, he will never forgive you for giving him back his note.'

Aglaya pressed his hand lightly and went out of the room. She frowned and looked grave. She did not even smile when she nodded to him at parting.

'I shall only be a minute. Let me get my bundle and we will go,' the prince said to Ganya.

Ganya stamped his foot with impatience. His face turned purple with fury. At last both went out into the street, the prince with his bundle in his hands.

'The answer? The answer?' Ganya cried, pouncing upon him. 'What did she say to you? Did you give her the letter?'

The prince gave him the note without saying a word. Ganya was stunned.

'What's that? My note?' he cried. 'You never gave it to her! Oh, I should have known! Oh, damn it. Now it's clear why she didn't understand anything! But how, how, how could you have failed to give it to her! Oh, damnation!'

'I'm sorry, but, you see, I did manage to give her your note at once, almost as soon as you'd given it me and exactly as you asked me to. I've got it now because Miss Aglaya has just given it back to me.'

'When? When?'

'When I finished writing in her album, and she asked me to follow her to the other room. You heard her, didn't you? We went into the dining-room, she gave me the note, asked me to read it, and told me to return it to you.'

'To r-read it?' Ganya shouted almost at the top of his voice. 'To read it? Did you read it?'

And he again stood still, horror-stricken, in the middle of the pavement, so amazed that he forgot to close his mouth.

'Yes, I did. Just a moment ago.'

'And she gave it you to read herself – herself? Herself?'

'Yes, I assure you, I shouldn't have read it without her permission.'

'Impossible! She couldn't have told you to read it. You're lying! You read it yourself!' Ganya cried after a minute's silence.

'I'm speaking the truth,' replied the prince in the same imperturbable tone of voice, 'and, believe me, I am very sorry that this should have upset you so much.'

'But, you wretch, didn't she say something to you at the time? She must have made some answer?'

'Yes, of course.'

'Well, tell me, tell me, damn it!'

And Ganya stamped his right foot, encased in a galosh, twice on the pavement.

'As soon as I'd finished reading it, she told me that you were trying to catch her, that you would like to compromise her so that you might obtain a promise from her and, relying on her promise, break your other promise without running the risk of losing a hundred thousand. That, if you had done so without bargaining with her and without asking her for any guarantee beforehand, she might have become your friend. That's all, I think. No, there's something more. When, after taking your note, I asked her what was her answer, she said that no answer was the best answer. I think that was what she said. I'm sorry if I've forgotten her exact words. I'm telling you as I understood it.'

Ganya was overcome by ungovernable rage and his fury burst out without restraint.

'Oh, so that's how it is, is it?' he snarled. 'So she's throwing my notes out of the window, is she? Oh, she won't bargain, won't she? Very well, then I will! We shall see! I've lots of things up my sleeve – we shall see! I'll make her do what I want yet.'

His face was working, he grew pale, he shook his fist. They walked several yards like this. He did not pay any attention to the prince, and behaved as if he were alone in his room, for he regarded him as a man of no consequence whatever. But suddenly an idea occurred to him and he recollected himself.

'But how,' he suddenly addressed the prince, 'how is it that you ("an idiot!" he added to himself) were taken into her confidence two hours after meeting her for the first time? How is that?'

Envy was the only torment he had not experienced till then, and now it stung him to the heart.

'I'm afraid I can't explain that,' replied the prince.

'It was not to make you a present of her confidence that she called you out into the dining-room, was it? She was going to give you something, wasn't she?' he asked, looking malignantly at the prince.

'Yes, I think that's what it was.'

'But why, damn it? What did you do in the drawing-room? What made them like you? Look here,' he said excitedly (his mind at that moment seemed to be in such ferment that he was unable to collect his wits), 'look here, can't you possibly remember exactly what you were talking about there? I mean, every word you said from the very beginning. Didn't you notice anything? Can't you remember?'

'Why, of course I can,' replied the prince. 'At the very beginning, when I went in and made their acquaintance, we began talking about Switzerland.'

'Oh, to hell with Switzerland!'

'Then we talked of capital punishment. ...'

'Capital punishment?'

'Yes, in connexion with something or other – then I told them how I spent three years in a Swiss village, and the story of a poor village girl. ...'

'Oh, to hell with your village girl! Go on,' Ganya urged him on, wild with impatience.

'Then how Schneider told me his opinion of my character and made me – –'

'To blazes with Schneider and damn his opinions! Go on!'

'Then, apropos of something, I began to talk of faces, or rather, of the expression of faces, and I said that Miss Aglaya was almost as beautiful as Nastasya Filippovna. It was then, I'm afraid, that I mentioned the portrait.'

'But you didn't tell them what you heard in the study this morning, did you? Did you?'

'I tell you again, I didn't!'

'But how the devil – oh, I see! Did Aglaya show my note to the old woman?'

'I assure you most definitely that she did not. I was there all the time, and, besides, she hadn't the time to.'

'Well, perhaps you didn't notice it. Oh, the damned idiot!' he cried, completely beside himself. 'He can't even tell anything properly.'

Having begun to swear and meeting with no resistance, Ganya gradually lost all restraint, as is always the case with certain people. A little more and he would perhaps have gone even further, so furious was he. But it was his fury that blinded him; he would otherwise have noticed long ago that this 'idiot' whom he treated so disgracefully could see through things a little too quickly sometimes and was capable of giving an excellent account of them. But suddenly something quite unexpected happened.

'I must tell you, Mr Ivolgin,' the prince said suddenly, 'that it is perfectly true that at one time I was so ill that I really was almost an idiot; but I have made a complete recovery since then and, I'm afraid, I find it rather unpleasant when people call me an idiot to my face. I'm quite ready to excuse you in view of your disappointment, but I must point out that, giving way to your disappointment, you have abused me twice already. I must say I don't like it at all, particularly as in your case it's happened so suddenly after so short an acquaintance. So, as we are just now standing at the crossroads, don't you think we'd better part company? You go home to the right and I'll go to the left. I've got twenty-five roubles, and I'm sure I shall be able to find some furnished rooms.'

Ganya was terribly embarrassed, and even blushed with shame at having been caught out so unexpectedly.

'I'm terribly sorry, Prince,' he cried warmly, suddenly changing his offensive tone for one of extreme courtesy. 'Do forgive me, for God's sake! You see what trouble I'm in. You scarcely know anything, but if you knew all, I'm sure you would forgive me a little. Though, of course, I don't deserve to be forgiven. ...'

'Oh, I don't require such profuse apologies,' the prince hastened to answer. 'I quite see how unpleasant it must be for you and that's why you're so abusive. Well, let's go to your house. I'll come with pleasure. ...'

'No,' Ganya thought to himself, glancing angrily at the prince as they walked along, 'it is impossible to let him go like that now. The scoundrel wormed everything out of me and then suddenly removed his mask. ... There's something behind it. Well, we shall see! Everything will be cleared up – everything, everything! And to-day!'

They had by now reached the house.

8

Ganya's flat was on the third floor. It was reached by a very clean, light, spacious staircase, and consisted of six or seven large and small rooms – very ordinary rooms, in fact, though rather beyond the means of a clerk with a family, even if he did earn two thousand roubles a year. But they had intended letting some of the rooms to boarders, and it had been taken by Ganya and his family not more than two months before, to Ganya's intense annoyance, at the insistent demand of his mother and sister, who wished to be of some use, too, in contributing their bit to the family's income. Ganya scowled and called taking boarders disgraceful; because of it he seemed to be ashamed to be in society where he was accustomed to appear as a young man with a brilliant future before him. All these concessions to necessity and all this annoying feeling of being cramped in his own home hurt him deeply. For some time now he had begun to be intensely and quite disproportionately irritated over every trifle, and if he still consented to give in and put up with it for a time, it was only because he had made up his mind to change it all drastically before very long. And yet the very change, the very course he had decided to adopt, was no easy problem – a problem, indeed, the solution of which threatened to be more troublesome and painful than all that he had gone through before.

The flat was divided by a passage which led straight out of the entrance hall. On one side of the passage were the three rooms which were to be let for 'specially recommended' lodgers; on the same side of the passage, at the very end of it, next to the kitchen, was a fourth room, smaller than the others, which was occupied by General Ivolgin, the father of the family, who slept on a wide sofa and who was obliged to go out of the flat through the kitchen and by the back stairs. The same room was shared by Kolya, Ganya's brother, a schoolboy of thirteen. He too had to live in these cramped conditions, study and sleep on another very old, narrow, and small sofa with a torn cover and, above all, look after his father, who was more and more in need of such attention. The prince was given the middle one of the three rooms; the first, on the right, was occupied by Ferdyshchenko, and the third, on the left, was still vacant. But Ganya first of all conducted the prince to the other half, occupied by his family. This half consisted of a large drawing-room, which, whenever required, became a dining-room, a smaller drawing-room, which was a drawing-room only in the morning, becoming Ganya's study and bedroom in the evening, and finally, of a small third room, the door of which was always closed; this was the bedroom of Ganya's mother and sister. In short, the whole place was very cramped. Ganya merely gritted his teeth; though he wished to be respectful to his mother, it was at once apparent that he was the tyrant of the family.

Mrs Ivolgin was not alone in the drawing-room; her daughter Varya was with her. Both were busy knitting and talking to a visitor, Ivan Petrovich Ptitsyn. Mrs Ivolgin seemed to be about fifty; she had a thin, haggard face with dark rings under her eyes. She looked ill and a little mournful, but her face and expression were rather pleasant; at the first word she uttered one could see that she was of a serious disposition, had true dignity, and possessed firmness and resolution of character. She wore a very modest dark dress, just like an old lady, but her manner, her conversation, and everything about her showed that she had been used to spend her time in better surroundings.

Ganya's sister Varya was a girl of twenty-three, of medium height, rather thin. Her face was not beautiful, but it was one that possessed the secret of pleasing without beauty and of inspiring true passion. She was very like her mother and was dressed almost like her, being completely indifferent to smart clothes. The expression of her grey eyes could occasionally be very gay and affectionate, if it had not more often been serious and thoughtful, too much so sometimes, especially of late. Her face, too, expressed firmness and resolution, but one could not help feeling that her firmness could be much more energetic and enterprising than her mother's. Varya was rather apt to fly into a temper, and her brother was quite often very much afraid of her temper. Their present visitor, Ivan Ptitsyn, was also afraid of it. He was quite a young man, in his late twenties, modestly, but elegantly, dressed, with pleasant but somehow much too sedate manners. His little dark-brown beard showed that he was not a civil servant. He knew how to conduct an intelligent and interesting conversation, but he was more often silent. He made a pleasant impression on the whole. He was quite obviously not indifferent to Varya and he did not conceal his feelings. Varya treated him in a friendly way, but she still delayed answering certain questions, and even did not like them; however, Ptitsyn was not unduly discouraged. Mrs Ivolgin was very nice to him, and more recently she had begun to confide in him a great deal. It was generally known, though, that he was chiefly occupied in making a fortune by lending money at a very high rate of interest and on more or less good security. He was a great friend of Ganya's.

After an abrupt, though circumstantial introduction by Ganya (who greeted his mother very drily, did not greet his sister at all, and immediately took Ptitsyn out of the room), Mrs Ivolgin said a few kind words to the prince and asked Kolya, who looked in at the door, to show him to the middle room. Kolya was a boy with a cheerful and rather charming face and a confiding and simple manner.

'Where's your luggage?' he asked as he led the prince into his room.

'I've only a small bundle. I left it in the passage.'

'I'll bring it you presently. We have only a cook and a maid, so I help too. Varya looks after everything and gets cross. Ganya says you've just arrived from Switzerland.'

'Yes.'

'Is it nice in Switzerland?'

'Very.'

'Mountains?'

'Yes.'

'I'll bring you your bundle now.'

Varya came in.

'Our maid will make your bed directly. Have you a trunk?'

'No, just a bundle. Your brother has gone to fetch it. It's in the hall.'

'There's no bundle there except this little one,' said Kolya, coming back into the room. 'Where did you put it?'

'Why, that's the only one I have,' the prince answered, taking his bundle.

'Oh! And I was wondering whether it had been carried off by Ferdyshchenko.'

'Don't talk nonsense,' said Varya sternly.

She spoke very drily to the prince, too, and was only just civil to him.

'I say, dear sister,' said Kolya, 'you can treat me a little more affectionately, you know. I'm not Ptitsyn.'

'You should still be whipped, Kolya, you're so stupid. Please ask the maid for everything you want. Dinner is at half-past four. You can have it with us, if you like, or you can have it in your room. Come along, Kolya; you're in the way.'

'Come on, you big bully!'

At the door they met Ganya coming in.

'Is father at home?' Ganya asked Kolya, and, receiving an affirmative answer, whispered something in Kolya's ear.

Kolya nodded and followed Varya out of the room.

'Just one word, Prince. There's something I forgot to tell you with all that – business. I'd like you to do me a favour, if it's not too much to ask. Please don't say anything here about what has passed between Aglaya and me, or about what you'll find here *there*. For, you see, there's plenty of disgusting things happening here too. To hell with it, though. ... But to-day, at any rate, do your best to restrain yourself.'

'I assure you I talk much less than you think,' said the prince, somewhat annoyed at Ganya's reproaches.

Their relations were quite obviously becoming more and more strained.

'Well, I don't know, you've already given me a lot of trouble to-day. In short, I beg you not to.'

'I should also like to point out to you, sir, that I wasn't bound in any way, so that there was no reason in the world why I shouldn't have mentioned the portrait. You didn't ask me not to.'

'Dear me, what a horrible room,' Ganya observed, looking round with a disdainful air. 'Dark and the windows looking out into the yard. I'm sorry to say you've certainly come here at the wrong time. Well, it's none of my business. I'm not the landlord here.'

Ptitsyn looked in and called Ganya, who left the room hurriedly, though there was something else he wanted to say, but he was evidently embarrassed and seemed to be ashamed to begin; he made his unflattering remark about the room, too, as though he were ill at ease.

The prince had barely had time to wash and make himself a little presentable, when the door opened again and a new person looked in. This was a gentleman of about thirty, rather tall and broad-shouldered, with a huge curly ginger head. His face was red and fleshy, his lips thick, his nose broad and flat, his eyes, which were tiny and lost in fat, seemed to be winking all the time. Taken as a whole, he gave the impression of something rather insolent. His clothes were rather dirty.

First he opened the door just enough to thrust his head through. The protruding head looked round the room for about five seconds, then the door began to open slowly, and the whole figure of the man was outlined in the doorway. The visitor still did not come in, but, screwing up his eyes, continued to scrutinize the prince from the threshold. At last, closing the door behind him, he came near, sat down on a chair, seized the prince's hand firmly, and made him sit down on the divan facing him.

'Ferdyshchenko,' he said, looking intently and interrogatively at the prince's face.

'What about it?' the prince replied, almost laughing.

'A lodger,' Ferdyshchenko said again, looking at him as before.

'Do you want to make my acquaintance?'

'Oh dear,' the visitor said, ruffling up his hair and sighing, and he began to stare at the opposite corner. 'Got any money?' he asked suddenly, turning to the prince.

'A little.'

'How much?'

'Twenty-five roubles.'

'Show me.'

The prince took out his twenty-five rouble note from his waistcoat pocket and gave it to Ferdyshchenko, who unfolded it, looked at it, turned it over, and then held it up to the light.

'Funny,' he said as though wonderingly; 'why should they turn brown? These twenty-five-rouble notes do turn terribly brown sometimes, while others fade. Take it.'

The prince took his note back. Ferdyshchenko got up from his chair.

'I just came to warn you, in the first place, not to lend me money, because I'm quite sure to ask you to.'

'Very well.'

'Do you intend paying here?'

'I do.'

'Well, I don't. Thank you, sir. My room is the first door on the right – did you see it? Do not bother to call on me too often. I'll be coming to see you, don't worry. Seen the general?'

'No.'

'Heard him?'

'Of course not.'

'Well, you will see him and hear him. Why, he even tries to borrow money from me. *Avis au lecteur*. Good-bye. Is it possible to live with such a surname as Ferdyshchenko? What do you think?'

'Why not?'

'Good-bye.'

And he went to the door. The prince found out later that this gentleman apparently considered it his duty to take everyone by surprise by his high spirits and originality, but somehow it never seemed quite to come off. On some people, indeed, he made a rather unfavourable impression, which grieved him greatly, but he still went on trying. In the doorway, however, he succeeded in rallying his drooping spirits by colliding with another gentleman who was just coming in; after letting this new visitor, who was unknown to the prince, into the room, he winked warningly several times behind his back, and so managed to make an effective exit after all.

The new gentleman was a very tall and rather corpulent man of fifty-five or more, with a fleshy, bloated, purplish-red face, set off by thick grey side-whiskers and moustache, and large, rather protruding eyes. His figure would have been quite distinguished, if there had not been something decayed, seedy, and even soiled about it. He was dressed in an old threadbare frock-coat, with elbows almost in holes, and his linen, too, was dirty – one could see at once that he was at home here. At close quarters he reeked a little of vodka, but his manner was rather showy, a bit studied, and with an obvious desire to impress people by its dignity. The gentleman approached the prince without hurry, took his hand silently and with an affable smile, and, holding it for some time in his, peered into his face as though recognizing familiar features.

'It's he – it's he!' he said softly, but triumphantly. 'His living image! I heard them repeating a dear and familiar name and it brought back long-forgotten memories to me. Prince Myshkin?'

'Yes, sir.'

'General Ivolgin – retired and unhappy, sir. Your name and patronymic, may I ask?'

'Leo Nikolayevich.'

'Yes, yes! The son of my friend and companion of my childhood, if I may say so, Nikolai Petrovich!'

'My father's name was Nikolai Lvovich.'

'Lvovich,' the general corrected himself, but without haste and with complete assurance, as though he had never forgotten it, but had merely made a slip of the tongue inadvertently.

He sat down and, taking the prince's hand again, made him sit down beside him.

'I used to carry you in my arms.'

'Did you?' the prince asked. 'My father died twenty years ago.'

'Yes, twenty years and three months ago. We went to school together. I went straight into the army – –'

'Why, my father was in the army too: a second lieutenant in the Vassilyevsky regiment.'

'In the Belomirsky regiment, sir. He was transferred to the Belomirsky regiment shortly before he died. I was at his bedside and gave him my blessing before he died. Your dear mother – –'

The general paused, as though overcome by his sad memories.

'Why, she, too, died six months later from a chill,' said the prince.

'Not from a chill, sir. Not from a chill – you can take my word for that, sir. I was there and I went to her funeral. She died of grief for her prince, sir, and not of a chill. Yes, sir. I remember the princess very well! Ah, youth! Why, sir, the prince and I, childhood friends the two of us, nearly became each other's murderers because of her.'

The prince began to listen a little incredulously.

'I was passionately in love with your dear mother, sir, when she was still betrothed – betrothed to my friend. The prince noticed it and was deeply shocked. He came to me before seven o'clock in the morning and woke me up. I was dumbfounded, sir, but I dressed. Neither of us spoke. I saw it all. He took two pistols out of his pocket. Across a handkerchief, sir. No witnesses. What did we want witnesses for when in five minutes we would be sending each other into eternity? Well, sir, we loaded, stretched out the handkerchief, put the pistols to each other's hearts, and looked at each other. Suddenly tears gushed from the eyes of both of us. Our hands trembled. Both – both at once! Well, sir, we naturally fell upon each other's necks, vying with one another in generosity. The prince shouted, "She's yours!" I shouted, "She's yours!" In short – in short – you – er – you have come to live with us?'

'Yes, sir, for a short time, perhaps,' said the prince, as though a little uncertain.

'Prince, Mummy wants to see you,' cried Kolya, looking in at the door.

The prince rose to go, but the general put his right hand on his shoulder and made him sit down again on the sofa in a very affable manner.

'I want to warn you as a true friend of your father's,' said the general. 'As you can see for yourself, I am the victim of a tragic catastrophe, but without a trial, sir. Without a trial! My wife, sir, is a rare woman. My daughter Varya is a rare daughter! Circumstances compel us to let rooms – a dreadful come-down for us – for me, sir, who had been offered the post of governor-general! But we are always glad to have you, sir. And yet, sir, and yet there's a tragedy in my house.'

The prince looked at him interrogatively and with great curiosity.

'A marriage is being arranged, sir. A rare marriage. A marriage between a woman of doubtful reputation and a young man who might have become a Court Chamberlain. This woman is to be brought into my house where my daughter and my wife are! But as long as there is breath in my body, sir, she shall not enter it! I will lie down on the threshold and let her step over my dead body! I hardly speak to Ganya now. Indeed, I avoid meeting him. I warn you beforehand, sir – but I suppose as you will be living with us, you'll see it, anyway. You, sir, are the son of an old friend of mine, and I have the right to hope – –'

'Prince, will you kindly come into the drawing-room,' Mrs Ivolgin called him, appearing in the doorway herself.

'Fancy, my dear,' cried the general, 'it appears that I dandled the prince in my arms!'

Mrs Ivolgin looked reproachfully at the general and searchingly at the prince, but did not utter a word. The prince followed her, but no sooner did they go into the drawing-room and sit down and no sooner did Mrs Ivolgin begin telling the prince something in a hurried undertone, than the general himself made his appearance. Mrs Ivolgin fell silent at once and bent over her knitting with unconcealed annoyance. The general quite likely noticed her annoyance, but it made no difference to his high good humour.

'The son of my friend,' he cried, addressing Mrs Ivolgin. 'And so unexpectedly! I had long given up thinking about it. But, my dear, don't you remember Nikolai Lvovich? You met him in – Tver?'

'I don't remember Nikolai Lvovich. Was he your father?' she asked the prince.

'Yes, but I believe he died in Yelisavetgrad and not in Tver,' the prince observed timidly to the general. 'Pavlishchev told me – –'

'In Tver,' the general insisted. 'He was transferred to Tver just before he died and even before he contracted his last illness. You were too little to remember his transference or the journey. I daresay Pavlishchev may have been mistaken, though he was a most excellent man.'

'Did you know Pavlishchev too?'

'A wonderful fellow, but I was there at the time. I gave him my blessing on his deathbed.'

'My father died awaiting trial,' the prince observed again, 'though I could never find out what he was accused of. He died in hospital.'

'Oh, it was all about the case of private Kolpakov, and he would quite certainly have been acquitted.'

'Would he? Are you sure?' the prince asked with great interest.

'Of course he would!' cried the general. 'The court broke up without coming to a decision. The whole case was absurd! Indeed, I'll go as far as to say that it was a real mystery! Senior Lieutenant Larionov, the C.O. of the company, died. The prince was appointed commanding officer for a time. Very good. Private Kolpakov committed a theft – stole some boot leather from a comrade, sold it, and spent the money on drink. Very good. The prince – in the presence, mark you, of the sergeant and the corporal – gave him a good dressing down and threatened to have him birched. Very good. Kolpakov went back to the barracks, lay down on his bunk, and died a quarter of an hour later. Excellent. But, you see, the whole thing was quite unexpected, almost impossible, in fact. Anyway, Kolpakov was buried. The prince sent in his report and Kolpakov's name was removed from the lists. Well, what could be better? But exactly six months later, at a brigade review, private Kolpakov, as though nothing had happened, turned up in the third company of the second battalion of the Novozemlyansk infantry regiment of the same brigade and the same division.'

'Good Lord!' cried the prince, beside himself with astonishment.

'It isn't so, I'm afraid; it's a mistake,' Mrs Ivolgin said, turning suddenly to the prince and giving him an almost anguished look. '*Mon mari se trompe.*'

'Well, my dear, *se trompe* is easily said, but how do you explain a case like that? Everyone was baffled. I was the first to say *qu'on se trompe*. But, unfortunately, I was an eye-witness of the whole affair and a member of the commission of inquiry. All the confrontations showed that this was the very same private Kolpakov who, six months earlier, had been buried with the usual military honours and the beating of drums. It is indeed, sir, a most unusual case – almost an impossible one, I admit, but – –'

'Father, your dinner is served,' Varya announced, entering the room.

'Oh, that's excellent, excellent! I am rather hungry. ... But it's, one might say, a psychological case, sir – yes, a – –'

'Your soup will be cold again,' Varya said impatiently.

'Coming, coming,' muttered the general, as he went out of the room. 'And in spite of all inquiries,' he could be heard saying in the passage.

'If you stay with us,' said Mrs Ivolgin to the prince, 'you'll have to excuse my husband for many things, I'm afraid. You see, he dines by himself too. You must admit we all have our shortcomings and our – little peculiarities. Some even more than others, I mean, more than those who are regarded as eccentric by most people. One thing I must ask, you, Prince: if my husband should at any time approach you about the rent, you must tell him that you've already paid me. I mean, everything you give the general will, of course, be deducted from your bill, but I ask you to do this for me so that we don't get into a muddle over our account. What is it, Varya?'

Varya had come back into the room, and she handed her mother Nastasya Filippovna's portrait in silence. Mrs Ivolgin gave a start and examined it for some time, first, it seemed, fearfully, and then with an overwhelming feeling of bitterness. At last she looked questioningly at her daughter.

'A present to him to-day from her,' said Varya. 'Everything is to be settled this evening.'

'This evening!' Mrs Ivolgin repeated softly, as though in despair. 'Well, there can be no more any doubt about it, then, and no hope, either. She announced her decision by her portrait. He didn't show it to you himself, did he?' she added in surprise.

'You know we've hardly said a word to each other for a whole month. Ptitsyn told me everything. I found the portrait in his room. It was lying on the floor near the table. I picked it up.'

'Prince,' Mrs Ivolgin said, turning suddenly to the prince. 'I wanted to ask you (that's really why I asked you to come here) how long you've known my son. I believe he said that you'd only arrived to-day from somewhere.'

The prince gave a short account of himself, leaving out the greater part. Mrs Ivolgin and Varya heard him out in silence.

'I'm not trying to find anything out about my son in questioning you,' Mrs Ivolgin observed. 'Please don't misunderstand me. If there's anything he doesn't want to tell me himself, I don't want to ferret it out behind his back. I'm saying this simply because both when you were here and when you had gone out Ganya said in reply to my questions that you knew everything and that I needn't stand on ceremony with you. Now, what does it mean? I mean, I should like to know to what extent – –'

At this point Ganya and Ptitsyn suddenly came in. Mrs Ivolgin fell silent at once. The prince remained sitting on the chair beside her, and Varya moved to the other side of the room. Nastasya Filippovna's portrait remained lying on Mrs Ivolgin's work-table, in the most conspicuous place, straight in front of her. Catching sight of it, Ganya frowned, snatched it up from the table with vexation, and threw it down on his writing-desk at the other end of the room.

'Is it to be to-day, Ganya?' Mrs Ivolgin asked suddenly.

'Is what to be to-day?' Ganya said with a start, and all at once pounced on the prince. 'Oh, I see, it's you, is it? Why, good God, is it a sort of disease with you? Can't you keep quiet? Can't your Lordship understand once and for all – –'

'I'm to blame for it, Ganya, and no one else,' Ptitsyn interrupted him.

Ganya looked inquiringly at him.

'You see,' Ptitsyn murmured, 'it is much better this way, Ganya, particularly as, so far as you are concerned, the thing is settled.'

He moved away and, sitting down at the table, took a piece of paper covered with writing out of his pocket and began examining it carefully. Ganya stood sullenly, waiting uneasily for a family scene. It never even occurred to him to apologize to the prince.

'If everything is settled,' said Mrs Ivolgin, 'then Mr Ptitsyn is, of course, right. Please don't scowl, Ganya, and don't lose your temper. I'm not going to ask you anything you don't want to tell me yourself, and I assure you I'm completely resigned. Please, don't worry.'

She said it without stopping her work and, it seemed, perfectly calmly. Ganya looked surprised, but he was careful not to say anything, and he looked at his mother, waiting for her to express herself more clearly. He had suffered too much already from family scenes. Mrs Ivolgin noticed this cautiousness and added with a bitter smile:

'You're still doubtful and you don't believe me. You needn't worry. So far as I'm concerned, at any rate, there will be no more tears and no more entreaties. All I want is for you to be happy, and you know that. I'm resigned to my fate, but my heart will always be with you, whether we remain together or whether we part. Of course, I only answer for myself. You can't expect the same from your sister. ...'

'Oh, her again!' cried Ganya, looking sarcastically and with hatred at his sister. 'Mother, I swear to you again that I shall keep my word, and that so long as I am here – so long as I live, no one shall ever dare to show any disrespect to you. I shall insist that anyone who crosses our threshold shall show the utmost respect to you – whoever it may be.'

Ganya was so relieved that he gazed almost propitiatingly, almost tenderly at his mother.

'I was never afraid for myself. You know that, Ganya. I was never worried and anxious for myself all this time. I am told to-day everything will be settled. What will be settled?'

'She promised to say at her house this evening whether she consents or not,' replied Ganya.

'For almost three weeks we've tried not to speak of it, and it has been better so. But now, when everything is settled, I should like to ask you how she could give you her consent and even make you a present of her portrait when you don't love her. How can you hope to deceive such a – such a – –'

'Experienced woman, you mean?'

'No, that's not what I was going to say. How could you have taken her in so completely?'

There was a sudden note of intense irritation in her last question. Ganya thought for a moment and, without attempting to conceal his derision, said:

'You've allowed yourself to be carried away by your feelings, Mother. Again you just couldn't restrain yourself. That's how it always starts. A spark followed by a conflagration. You said there were going to be no interrogations and no reproaches, and now they've begun already! Let's leave well alone. Please let's. You meant well, at any rate. I shall never abandon you. Not for anything in the world. Anyone else would have run away from such a sister at least – look how she is staring at me now! Let this be the last of our squabbles! I was already congratulating myself. ... And how do you know that I'm deceiving Nastasya Filippovna? As for Varya, let her please herself and – enough of that. Yes, we've certainly had quite enough of it now!'

Ganya was getting more and more excited with every word he uttered, and he kept pacing the room aimlessly. Such conversations immediately became a sore point with every member of the family.

'I've said that if she comes here I shall go at once, and I shall keep my word,' said Varya.

'Out of obstinacy!' cried Ganya. 'You don't get married out of obstinacy too! What are you snorting at me for? I don't care a damn, sister dear! You can carry out your threat at once, if you like. I'm sick and tired of you. Dear me, so you've decided to leave us at last, Prince, have you?' he shouted at the prince as he saw him get up from his place.

The note of irritation in Ganya's voice had reached that pitch when a man is almost glad to let himself go and give himself up to it without restraint and almost with ever increasing delight, regardless of any consequences. The prince turned round at the door to say something in reply, but realizing from the exasperated expression on Ganya's face that another drop would fill the cup to overflowing, he turned and went out in silence. A few minutes later he became aware, from the voices in the drawing-room, that in his absence the conversation had become even noisier and more outspoken.

He went through the large drawing-room into the hall on the way to the passage and from there to his room. Passing close by the front door he heard someone outside trying vainly to ring the bell. But something seemed to have gone wrong with it, for it only shook a little without making a sound. The prince unbolted the door, opened it, and – stepped back in amazement, startled out of his wits. Nastasya Filippovna stood before him. He recognized her at once from her portrait. Her eyes flashed with annoyance when she saw him. She walked quickly into the hall, pushing him out of the way with her shoulder, and said angrily, as she flung off her fur-coat:

'If you're too lazy to mend the bell, you might at least wait in the hall when people knock. There, now he's gone and dropped my coat, the oaf!'

Her fur-coat was indeed lying on the floor. Without waiting for the prince to help her off with it, Nastasya Filippovna had flung it at him herself from behind without looking, but the prince was not quick enough to catch it.

'They ought to sack you. Go along and announce me.'

The prince wanted to say something, but he was thrown into such confusion that he could not utter a word and, carrying the coat which he had picked up from the floor, walked towards the drawing-room.

'Well, now he's taking my coat with him! What are you carrying my coat for? Ha, ha, ha! Why, you're not mad, are you?'

The prince came back and stared at her speechlessly. When she laughed, he grinned too, but he still could not utter a word. At first, when he opened the door to her, he was pale, now the blood suddenly rushed to his face.

'Oh, you idiot!' Nastasya Filippovna cried indignantly, stamping her foot. 'Where are you going now? Who are you going to announce?'

'Nastasya Filippovna,' murmured the prince.

'How do you know me?' she asked him quickly. 'I've never seen you before. Go, announce me. ... What's all that shouting?'

'They're quarrelling,' the prince replied and went to the drawing-room.

He went in at a rather critical moment. Mrs Ivolgin was on the point of forgetting entirely that she was 'resigned to everything', but, then, she was defending Varya. Ptitsyn, too, was standing beside Varya, having left his pencilled note. Varya was not exactly intimidated, either (she was not the timid sort), but her brother's rudeness was becoming every moment more discourteous and more unbearable. On such occasions she usually stopped talking and only stared ironically and in silence at her brother. This trick, as she knew, could drive Ganya to distraction. It was at that moment that the prince stepped into the room and announced:

'Nastasya Filippovna!'

9

There was dead silence in the room; all looked at the prince as though they didn't understand him – or did not want to understand him. Ganya was numb with horror.

The arrival of Nastasya Filippovna, especially at this juncture, was the strangest and most painful surprise for everyone. The very fact that she had paid a call on them for the first time was enough; till then she had carried herself so haughtily that in talking to Ganya she never even expressed the wish to be introduced to his family, and of late had not even mentioned them, just as though they never existed. Though Ganya was rather pleased that so painful a topic should be put off indefinitely, he made up his mind to add her haughtiness to the account he was determined to settle with her afterwards. In any case, what he expected from her was biting and sarcastic remarks about his family and not a visit to his house; he knew for a fact that she was aware of all that was going on in his home in connexion with his engagement and what his family thought of her. Her visit *now*, after the present of her portrait and on her birthday, on the day on which she had promised to give him her final answer, was almost equivalent to the answer itself.

The bewilderment with which they all gazed at the prince did not last long: Nastasya Filippovna herself appeared in the doorway and again, as she entered the room, slightly pushed the prince aside.

'At last I've managed to get in – why do you tie up the bell?' she said gaily, giving her hand to Ganya, who rushed to meet her. 'Why do you look so upset? Do introduce me, please. ...'

Ganya, completely disconcerted, introduced her first to Varya, and, before shaking hands, the two women exchanged strange glances. Nastasya Filippovna, though, laughed and concealed her feelings by her assumed gaiety; but Varya had no wish to conceal her feelings and looked at her with grim intensity; not even the ghost of a smile, which was after all demanded by ordinary courtesy, appeared on her face. Ganya was horrified; it was too late and quite useless to ask her to change her attitude, and he threw such a menacing look at her that its malignity made her realize what that moment meant to her brother. It was only then, it seemed, that she decided to give in to him and smiled faintly at Nastasya Filippovna. (They were still very attached to each other as a family.) Mrs Ivolgin mended matters a little. Ganya, thrown into utter confusion by now, introduced her after his sister, and even took her up to Nastasya Filippovna first. But no sooner did Mrs Ivolgin begin to say how 'very pleased' she was to meet her, than Nastasya Filippovna turned suddenly to Ganya and, sitting down (without waiting to be asked) on the small sofa in the corner by the window, cried:

'Where's your study? And – er – where are your lodgers? You do take in lodgers, don't you?'

Ganya blushed crimson and was about to say something when Nastasya Filippovna added at once:

'Where do you keep your lodgers here? You haven't even got a study. Do tell me,' she asked, turning suddenly to Mrs Ivolgin, 'does it pay?'

'It's rather troublesome,' Mrs Ivolgin replied. 'Of course, it ought to pay. But we've only just – –'

'How funny you look! Oh, dear, how funny you look at this moment!' Nastasya Filippovna cried laughingly, without listening.

After a few moments of her laughter, Ganya's face certainly became very distorted: his stupefaction, his comic, cowardly confusion was suddenly gone, but he turned terribly pale, his lips were twisted convulsively, he stared viciously and in silence at the face of his visitor who went on laughing.

There was another observer of the scene who, too, had not yet recovered from his stupor at the sight of Nastasya Filippovna. Though he stood 'like a post' in the same place at the door of the drawing-room, he was quick to notice Ganya's pallor and the maleficent change in his face. This observer was the prince. Almost in dismay, he involuntarily stepped forward.

'Have a drink of water,' he whispered to Ganya, 'and don't look like that.'

It was quite evident that he had said it without any ulterior motive or any special intention, on the spur of the moment; but his words produced an extraordinary effect. All Ganya's spite seemed suddenly to be turned against the prince: he seized him by the shoulder and looked at him in silence, vindictively and with hatred, as though unable to utter a word. A general commotion ensued. Mrs Ivolgin even gave a little scream. Ptitsyn stepped forward in alarm, Kolya and Ferdyshchenko, who appeared in the doorway, stopped in amazement, and Varya alone looked on frowningly, though watching the scene intently. She did not sit down, but stood beside her mother with her arms folded across her bosom.

But Ganya recollected himself immediately, almost as soon as he stretched out his hand to seize the prince, and burst into nervous laughter. He recovered his self-possession completely.

'Why, Prince, you're not a doctor, are you?' he cried, trying to sound as good-natured and gay as possible. 'He quite frightened me. Let me introduce him to you, Nastasya Filippovna. A most admirable fellow, though I've only known him since the morning.'

Nastasya Filippovna looked bewildered at the prince.

'A prince? Is he a prince? Fancy that, and I took him for a footman just now and sent him in to announce me! Ha, ha, ha!'

'Never mind, never mind!' Ferdyshchenko put in, going up to her quickly and relieved that they had begun to laugh. 'Never mind. *Se non è vero* – –'

'Why, I nearly scolded you, Prince. I am sorry. Ferdyshchenko, how do you happen to be here at this hour? I didn't expect to meet you here, at any rate. Who? What prince? Myshkin?' she repeated her question, addressing Ganya, who had by now introduced him, though he still kept holding him by the shoulder.

'Our lodger,' Ganya repeated.

It was evident that the prince was being presented to her as a sort of curiosity (who had come in very useful to them as an escape from a false situation) and almost thrown at her head; the prince even distinctly caught the word 'idiot' whispered behind him, probably by Ferdyshchenko, as an explanation for Nastasya Filippovna.

'Tell me, why didn't you disabuse me just now when I made such – er – such a dreadful mistake about you?' Nastasya Filippovna went on, examining the prince from head to foot in a most unceremonious fashion.

She was waiting impatiently for his answer, as though perfectly certain that his answer would be so stupid that she would not be able to refrain from laughing.

'I was surprised at seeing you so suddenly,' the prince murmured.

'But how did you know it was I? Where have you seen me before?

But, really, it does seem as though I had seen him before! And do you mind telling me why you were so dumbfounded just now? What is there so dumbfounding about me?'

'Come on, old man, speak up!' Ferdyshchenko went on playing the fool. 'Come on, man! Good Lord, the things I'd say in answer to such a question! Come on! Dear me, what a lubberly fellow you are, Prince, to be sure!'

'Why, I, too, would have said lots of things in your place,' the prince laughed, turning to Ferdyshchenko. 'This morning,' he went on, addressing Nastasya Filippovna, 'I was very struck by your portrait. Then I spoke about you with the Yepanchins and – early this morning in the train, before I arrived in Petersburg, Parfyon Rogozhin told me a lot about you. ... And at the very moment that I opened the door to you, I was thinking about you, too, and there you stood before me!'

'And how did you recognize me?'

'From the portrait and – –'

'And?'

'And also because I imagined you to be like that. ... I, too, seemed to have seen you somewhere.'

'Where? Where?'

'I seem to have seen your eyes somewhere – but that's impossible! I'm afraid I – you see, I've never been here before. Perhaps in a dream. ...'

'Stout fellow, Prince!' Ferdyshchenko cried. 'No, sir, I was wrong: I take back my *se non è vero*. Still, still,' he added regretfully, 'he says it all in his innocence!'

The prince uttered his few sentences in a faltering voice, pausing and taking breath now and again. Everything about him betrayed great agitation. Nastasya Filippovna looked at him with interest, but she no longer laughed. At this moment a new loud voice was suddenly heard behind the group, which crowded round the prince and Nastasya Filippovna, and, as it were, divided it into two separate parts. General Ivolgin, the father of the family himself, stood before Nastasya Filippovna. He wore an evening coat and a clean shirt-front; his moustache was dyed.

That was too much for Ganya. Vain and conceited to a fastidious and morbid degree; always during the past two months looking for something to hold on to, something that would show him to be a decent and honourable man; feeling that he was still inexperienced in his chosen career and might for all he knew be a failure; in despair making up his mind at last to behave at home, where he was a despot, with the utmost insolence, but not daring to do so before Nastasya Filippovna, who kept him in suspense till the last moment and ruthlessly persisted in having the upper hand of him: 'the impatient beggar', as he had been told Nastasya Filippovna had called him; having sworn by all that he held dear to make her pay for it all afterwards and, at the same time, occasionally indulging in childish dreams of establishing himself on a sound financial basis and reconciling the warring parties – he had now to drain this dreadful cup to the dregs and, most of all, at such a moment! One more undreamt-of but, for a vain man, most horrible torture – the agony of blushing for his family, in his own house, had fallen to his lot. 'But, good Lord, is the reward worth it?' flashed through Ganya's mind at that moment.

What was happening now had for the past two months been his nightmare, sending an icy chill down his spine and making him burn with shame: at last the meeting between his father and Nastasya Filippovna had taken place. Sometimes, in a fit of self-exasperation, he had tried to imagine the general at his wedding, but he had never been able to complete the agonizing picture and quickly gave up the attempt. Perhaps he exaggerated the calamity too much, but that is always the case with vain people. During those two months he had had time to examine the situation thoroughly and to make up his mind, and he decided to keep his father in his place, somehow or other, for a time at least, and get him out of Petersburg by hook or by crook, whether his mother agreed to it or not. Ten minutes earlier he was so astonished and dumbfounded at the entrance of Nastasya Filippovna that he completely forgot the possibility of his father's appearance on the scene and took no steps to prevent it. And now the general was there, in front of them all, having, besides, got himself up solemnly for the occasion in an evening coat at the very moment when Nastasya Filippovna was only looking for an excuse 'to heap ridicule upon him and his family'. (He was quite convinced of that.) Indeed, what else did her present visit mean, if not that? Had she come to make friends with his mother and sister, or to insult them in his house? But from the attitude of both parties there could no longer be any doubt about it: his mother and sister, thoroughly humiliated, were sitting at the other end of the room, and Nastasya Filippovna seemed to have forgotten that they were in the same room as she. ... And if she behaved like that, she had her own reason for it!

Ferdyshchenko took hold of the general and led him up to Nastasya Filippovna.

'Ardalion Alexandrovich Ivolgin,' said the general with dignity, bowing and smiling, 'an unhappy old soldier and the father of a family which is happy in the hope of including such a ravishing – –'

He did not finish, for Ferdyshchenko quickly pushed a chair up from behind and the general, a little weak on his legs so soon after dinner, sank or rather collapsed into it, which, however, did not disconcert him in the least. He seated himself comfortably directly opposite Nastasya Filippovna and, with a pleasant smirk, slowly and impressively raised her fingers to his lips. It was extremely difficult to disconcert the general. Except for a certain slovenliness, his appearance was rather genteel. He had often moved in very good society, and he had been ostracized from it only a year or two before. Since then he had been indulging unrestrainedly in some of his weaknesses, but he still retained his accomplished and agreeable manners. Nastasya Filippovna seemed very glad to see the general, whom she only knew from hearsay.

'I hear my son – –' began General Ivolgin.

'Yes, your son! You're a fine father, too! Why do you never come and see me? Do you hide yourself away or does your son hide you? I should have thought you of all people could come and see me without compromising anyone!'

'The children of the nineteenth century and their parents – –' the general began again.

'Nastasya Filippovna, will you please excuse the general for a moment,' Mrs Ivolgin said in a loud voice. 'Someone is asking for him.'

'Excuse him? Why, I've heard so much about him and I've been wanting to see him for so long! And what business can he have? He's retired, isn't he? You won't leave me, General, will you? You won't go away?'

'I promise you he'll come and see you, but now he needs rest.'

'Why, General, I'm told you need rest!' cried Nastasya Filippovna, with a displeased and querulous mien, as though she were a frivolous and silly woman who was being deprived of a toy.

The general did his best to make himself look more foolish than ever.

'My dear, my dear,' he cried reproachfully, turning to his wife solemnly and laying his hand on his heart.

'Won't you come away, Mother?' Varya asked loudly.

'No, Varya, I'm going to stay to the end.'

Nastasya Filippovna must have heard the question and the answer, but it seemed only to increase her high spirits. She at once overwhelmed the general with more questions, and five minutes later the general was in a most triumphant frame of mind and was holding forth amid the loud laughter of the company.

Kolya pulled the prince by his coat-tails.

'Can't you get him out of here, somehow? Can't you, please?' There were tears of indignation in the poor boy's eyes. 'Oh, damn Ganya!' he muttered to himself.

'Why, of course, I used to be a great friend of General Yepanchin's,' the general held forth enthusiastically in reply to Nastasya Filippovna's questions. 'He, I, and the late Prince Leo Nikolayevich Myshkin, whose son I have embraced to-day after twenty years' separation, we were three inseparables, a regular cavalcade, so to speak: Athos, Porthos, and Aramis. But, alas, one is in his grave, struck down by slander and a bullet, another stands before you, still putting up a fight against slander and bullets --'

'Bullets!' cried Nastasya Filippovna.

'They are here, in my chest, ma'am. I received them at the siege of Kars, and I feel them in bad weather. In every other respect I live like a philosopher. I go about, take walks, play draughts in my café, like a retired business-man, and read the *Indépendance*. But, I'm sorry to say, I've nothing more to do with Yepanchin, our Porthos, since the affair with the lap-dog on the railway two years ago.'

'A lap-dog? Why, what was that?' Nastasya Filippovna asked with great interest. 'With a lap-dog? Let me see, and on the railway, too!' she exclaimed, as though trying to remember something.

'Oh, it was a stupid affair, ma'am. Not worth repeating. It was all because of Princess Belokonsky's governess, Mrs Schmidt; but, really, ma'am, it's not worth repeating.'

'No, no,' Nastasya Filippovna cried gaily. 'You simply must tell me!'

'And I haven't heard it, either,' observed Ferdyshchenko. '*C'est du nouveau*.'

'Ardalion Alexandrovich!' Mrs Ivolgin cried again, imploringly.

'Daddy, someone wants to see you!' cried Kolya.

'Oh, it's a stupid affair and can be told in a few words,' began the general complacently. 'Two years ago – yes, just about, soon after the opening of the new railway, I had to go somewhere on some highly important business in connexion with my resignation from the service (I was already in mufti at the time). I took a first-class ticket, got into the train, sat down, and began to smoke. I mean, I went on smoking. I had lighted my cigar before. I was alone in the compartment. Smoking, you know, is not prohibited, but it isn't allowed, either. Sort of half allowed, as usual. Depends on the smoker, you know.

The window was down. All of a sudden, just before the whistle, two ladies with a lap-dog got in and sat down just opposite me. They were late. One of them was very smartly dressed in light blue, the other one, more modestly, in black silk and a cape. Not at all bad-looking, either of them. Had a disdainful air, though. Spoke English. Well, of course, I just took no notice. Went on smoking. I mean I did wonder a little, but I went on smoking. Dash it all, the window was open and I was blowing the smoke out of it. The dog was lying on the light-blue lady's lap. A little thing, no bigger than my fist, black with white little paws – quite a curiosity. Had a silver collar on with a motto on it. I took no notice, though I must say the ladies seemed a bit resentful. At my cigar, of course. One of them glared at me through her lorgnette. A tortoise-shell one. But I took no notice, for, dash it all, they said nothing to me! If they'd said anything, warned me, asked me – I mean, damn it, there's such a thing as speech! But they said nothing. Suddenly, without the slightest warning, mind you, without as much as a by your leave, just as though she had gone out of her mind, the light blue one snatched the cigar out of my hand and flung it out of the window. The train was flying along. I just stared at her like – like a half-wit. A wild woman, I mean, as though she had just emerged from a wild state – rather plump, though, stout, tall, a blonde with red cheeks (too red, if you know what I mean). Glaring at me with flashing eyes. Without saying a word, I just bent over, and with perfect courtesy, with the most perfect courtesy, indeed I might say with the most refined courtesy, I got hold of that lap-dog with two fingers, picked it up delicately by the neck, and slung it out of the window after my cigar! All the poor thing did was to let out a yelp. The train went flying on. ...'

'You monster!' cried Nastasya Filippovna, clapping her hands like a little girl.

'Bravo, bravo!' cried Ferdyshchenko.

Ptitsyn, too, grinned, though he had been highly displeased by the appearance of the general. Kolya laughed and shouted, 'Bravo!'

'And I was right, damn it, I was absolutely right!' the triumphant general went on, warmly. 'For, you see, if cigars are prohibited in a railway carriage, dogs are much more so.'

'Bravo, Daddy!' Kolya cried enthusiastically. 'Splendid! I'd most certainly have done the same!'

'And what did the lady do?' asked Nastasya Filippovna impatiently.

'The lady? Well, ma'am, that's where the whole unpleasantness arose,' the general continued, frowning. 'Without saying a word and without any warning whatsoever, she slapped me on the cheek! Yes, ma'am, a wild woman. Yes, just as though she had emerged from a wild state of nature!'

'And you?'

The general dropped his eyes, raised his eyebrows, shrugged his shoulders, pursed his lips, spread his hands, paused, and suddenly said:

'I lost my head!'

'Did you hit her hard? Hard?'

'No, dash it, not very hard. There was a scene, but I didn't hit her hard. Brushed her aside, but only just to brush her aside. But there was the devil to pay, all the same. You see, the light-blue lady turned out to be the governess or some sort of family friend of Princess Belokonsky, and the one in the black dress was Princess Belokonsky's eldest daughter. An old maid of five-and-thirty. And you know, of course, what great friends Mrs Yepanchin is with the Belokonsky family. All the princesses fainted, tears, mourning for the pet lap-dog, shrieks from the six princesses, shrieks from the Englishwoman – bedlam! Of course, I went to apologize, expressed my regrets, wrote a letter. But they refused to receive me or my letter. Quarrelled with the Yepanchins, ostracized, banished!'

'But, please, General, how is it possible?' Nastasya Filippovna asked suddenly. 'Five or six days ago I read in *Indépendance* – I am a regular reader of *Indépendance* – exactly the same story. But absolutely the same! It happened on one of the Rhine railways, in a carriage, between a Frenchman and an Englishwoman. The cigar was snatched away in exactly the same way, the lap-dog was thrown out of the window in the same way, and it ended in the same way, too. Even her dress was light blue!'

The general blushed terribly. Kolya, too, blushed and clutched his head in his hands. Ptitsyn turned quickly away. Ferdyshchenko alone went on laughing as before. There is no need to speak of Ganya: he stood still all the time, going through unbearable torment in silence.

'I assure you, ma'am,' muttered the general, 'exactly the same thing happened to me too.'

'Daddy really had an unpleasant scene with Mrs Schmidt, the Belokonskys' governess,' Kolya cried; 'I remember it.'

'Oh? Exactly the same thing? One and the same incident at the opposite ends of Europe and exactly the same in every detail, even to the light-blue dress?' Nastasya Filippovna persisted pitilessly. 'I'll send you the *Indépendance Belge*!'

'But please observe, ma'am,' the general still persisted, 'it happened to me two years earlier. ...'

'Oh, well, in that case!'

Nastasya Filippovna laughed as though she were in hysterics.

'Father, please come out for a moment,' Ganya said in a shaking, harassed voice, seizing his father mechanically by the shoulder. 'I have something to tell you.'

His eyes blazed with deadly hatred.

At that moment there was a very loud ring at the front door – so loud, indeed, that it was a wonder the bell was not torn off. It was the prelude to a most extraordinary visit. Kolya ran to open the door.

10

The entrance hall suddenly became full of noise and people; from the drawing-room it seemed as though several men had come in and that more were still coming in. Several voices spoke and shouted simultaneously; there was also shouting and talking on the stairs, as the front door had apparently not been closed. It seemed to be a most peculiar visit. They all exchanged glances; Ganya rushed into the large drawing-room, but several men had already entered it.

'Oh, there's Judas!' a voice, which the prince recognized at once, cried. 'Hullo, Ganya, you dirty dog!'

'Yes, it's him all right!' another voice said.

There was no longer any doubt in the prince's mind: one voice belonged to Rogozhin and the other to Lebedev.

Ganya stood as though stunned in the doorway and gazed at them in silence, without doing anything to prevent ten or twelve people from coming in one after another in the wake of Parfyon Rogozhin. It was a very diverse company, distinguished not only by its diversity but also by its perversity. Some of them walked in, just as they were in the street, without bothering to take off their overcoats or fur-coats. None of them, however, was completely drunk, but all of them certainly had had a drop too much. They all seemed to be in need of each other's support to enter, for none of them had sufficient courage to enter alone: they all appeared to be pushing each other in. Even Rogozhin walked circumspectly at the head of the crowd, and he looked gloomily and irritably preoccupied. The rest were only the chorus, or rather the gang of his supporters. Besides Lebedev, there was Zalyozhnev, who threw off his overcoat in the entrance hall and came in jauntily and flauntingly with his hair waved, and two or three more gentlemen like him, all of them evidently well-to-do merchants' sons. One man in a semi-military greatcoat; a very fat little man, who kept laughing continuously; a huge man over six feet tall, also very fat, but extremely morose and taciturn, who evidently had great faith in his fists. There was a medical student; there was a little cringing Pole. Two ladies looked in at the door, but did not venture to come in. Kolya slammed the door in their faces and shot the bolt.

'Hullo, Ganya, you dirty dog!' Rogozhin repeated on reaching the drawing-room, stopping in the doorway before Ganya. 'Didn't expect to see Parfyon Rogozhin, did you?'

But at that moment he caught sight of Nastasya Filippovna, who sat facing him in the doorway. It had clearly never occurred to him that he might meet her there, for the sight of her produced an extraordinary impression upon him; he turned so pale that his lips went blue.

'So it's true,' he said quietly as though to himself, looking utterly confounded. 'That's the end! Well,' he snarled suddenly, looking at Ganya in a towering rage, 'I'll make you pay for this! Oh – damn!'

He seemed to be short of breath and he could scarcely speak. He moved mechanically into the drawing-room, but as he crossed the threshold he suddenly caught sight of Mrs Ivolgin and Varya, and stopped dead, looking a little embarrassed in spite of his agitation. After him came Lebedev, who followed him about like a shadow and was already very drunk indeed, then the student, the gentleman with the enormous fists, Zalyozhnev, who bowed right and left, and, finally, the fat little man squeezed through the door. The presence of the ladies still restrained them all a little and apparently rather hampered them – only at the *beginning*, of course, till they found the first excuse to start shouting and to *begin*. ... After that no ladies in the world would have hampered them.

'Good Lord, you're here too, Prince?' Rogozhin said absent-mindedly, only a little surprised at meeting the prince. 'Still in your silly gaiters? Ugh!' he sighed, forgetting all about the prince and directing his gaze again at Nastasya Filippovna, still drawn nearer and nearer to her, as though by a magnet.

Nastasya Fillipovna, too, looked at the visitors with uneasy curiosity.

Ganya recollected himself at last.

'But, look here, what in the name of goodness does it all mean?' he said loudly, looking sternly at the new-comers and addressing himself chiefly to Rogozhin. 'You've not barged into a stable, gentlemen. My mother and sister are here. ...'

'We can see it's your mother and sister,' Rogozhin muttered through his teeth.

'Yes, sir, it's your mother and sister all right,' Lebedev echoed, feeling called upon to support the statement.

The gentleman with the fists, evidently thinking that the time had come to start the row, began to growl.

'But hang it all,' Ganya cried, exploding suddenly and raising his voice somewhat excessively, 'first I must ask you to step into the large drawing-room, and then I should like to know --'

'He don't know!' Rogozhin said with a malignant grin, without moving from his place. 'Don't you know Rogozhin?'

'Well, yes, I did meet you somewhere, but --'

'How do you like that? He did meet me somewhere, he says. Why, only three months ago I lost two hundred roubles to you. My dad's money it was, too. The old man died without knowing anything about it. It was you who dragged me into it, and Knif cheated. Don't know me, eh? Ptitsyn was there and saw it all. Why, if I was to show you three roubles, if I was to take them out of my pocket right now, you'd crawl on all fours after them, you would, as far as Vassilyevsky Island – that's the kind of fellow you are! That's the way you're made! Why do you think I've come here now? To buy you for cash, that's why! Never mind the boots I'm wearing. I have pots of money, I have. Yes, sir, pots of money. Enough to buy the whole damned lot of you if I like. I can buy you all – the whole damned lot!' he cried, getting more and more excited and, seemingly, more and more drunk. 'Oh, to hell with it!' he shouted. 'Nastasya Filippovna, don't throw me out. Tell me one thing: are you going to marry him or not?'

Rogozhin asked his question like a man in despair, addressing himself to her as though she were some deity, but with the recklessness of a man sentenced to death who has nothing more to lose. He waited for her answer in deadly anguish.

Nastasya Filippovna looked him up and down haughtily and ironically, but after casting a glance at Mrs Ivolgin and Varya and looking at Ganya, she changed her tone.

'Of course not! What are you talking about? And what do you mean by asking me such a question?' she replied quietly and seriously, but apparently with some surprise.

'No? No!!' cried Rogozhin, almost beside himself with joy. 'So it's no, is it? And they told me – oh well, they told me, Nastasya Filippovna, that you was engaged to Ganya! To him! To that fellow! Why, it's impossible! I told them that – all of 'em! Why, I can buy the whole of him, bag and baggage, for a hundred roubles, and if I gave him a thousand, well, three thousand, to stand aside, he'd run off on the day of the wedding, he would, and leave his bride to me! Isn't that so, Ganya, you dirty dog? You'd take three thousand, wouldn't you? Here, take 'em! I've come to get your receipt for it. I said I'd buy you off, and I will buy you off!'

'Get out of here, you're drunk!' Ganya cried, blushing and turning pale by turns.

His outburst was followed by an explosion of several voices: the whole of Rogozhin's gang had long been waiting for the first challenge. Lebedev was whispering something very earnestly in Rogozhin's ear.

'Right-o, civil servant,' replied Rogozhin, 'right-o, you drunken sot, you! Oh, to hell with it! Nastasya Filippovna,' he cried, looking at her like a maniac, hardly daring to speak and suddenly emboldened to the point of arrogance, 'here's eighteen thousand!' And he flung on the table before her a roll of notes wrapped in a piece of white paper and tied across with string. 'There! And – and there's more to come!'

'No, no, no!' Lebedev again whispered to him, with a terribly frightened look.

It was clear that it was the magnitude of the sum that had frightened him and that he had suggested to try a much smaller one.

'No, sir, you're just a fool in this kind of business,' Rogozhin said. 'You don't know who you're dealing with. Well,' he recollected himself, suddenly startled by Nastasya Filippovna's flashing eyes, 'it seems I'm a fool like you. Oh, I've gone and made a mess of it by listening to you,' he added with deep regret.

Glancing at Rogozhin's downcast countenance, Nastasya Filippovna suddenly burst out laughing.

'Eighteen thousand for me? One can see you're just a yokel, my lad,' she added suddenly, with insolent familiarity, getting up from the sofa as though she were about to leave.

Ganya watched the scene with a sinking heart.

'Well, forty thousand, then, forty, not eighteen!' cried Rogozhin. 'Ptitsyn and Biskup promised to let me have forty thousand by seven o'clock. Forty thousand – paid on the nail!'

The scene was becoming more and more disgusting, but Nastasya Filippovna went on laughing and did not go, as though she were deliberately prolonging it. Mrs Ivolgin and Varya also got up and waited fearfully and in silence to see what would come of it. Varya's eyes were flashing, but the whole scene had a very painful effect on Mrs Ivolgin; she was trembling and seemed to be on the point of fainting.

'All right, if that's not enough, then – a hundred thousand. I'll let you have a hundred thousand to-day! Ptitsyn, there's a good chap, you'll make a packet on it!'

'You're mad!' Ptitsyn whispered, going up to him quickly and seizing him by the arm. 'You're drunk. They'll send for the police. Can't you see where you are?'

'He is drunk,' said Nastasya Filippovna, as though taunting him, 'and he's talking a lot of nonsense!'

'I'm not! I tell you the money'll be there! It'll be there in the evening. Ptitsyn, you dirty moneylender, get it for me! Take whatever you like, but get me the hundred thousand before the evening. I promise you won't be sorry!' cried Rogozhin, working himself up into a frenzy.

'What's all this?' General Ivolgin suddenly cried in a menacing voice, getting angry and walking up to Rogozhin.

The suddenness of the old man's outburst after his long silence made it very comic. Some of Rogozhin's friends laughed.

'Hullo, hullo!' Rogozhin laughed. 'Come with us, old fellow; we'll make you drunk!'

'That's just mean!' exclaimed Kolya, crying with shame and vexation.

'Isn't there anyone here who'll take this shameless creature away?' Varya cried suddenly, trembling with rage.

'It's me they call a shameless creature!' Nastasya Filippovna parried with disdainful gaiety. 'And like a fool I came here to invite them to my party to-night! That's how your dear sister treats me, Mr Ivolgin!'

For several moments Ganya stood as if thunderstruck by his sister's outburst, but seeing that Nastasya Filippovna was really going this time, he pounced on Varya like a madman and seized her by the hand.

'What have you done?' he cried, looking at her as though wishing to reduce her to ashes on the spot.

He was quite beside himself and did not know what he was doing.

'What have I done? Where are you dragging me to? You're not going to ask me to apologize to her, are you, for insulting your mother and for having come here to disgrace your family, you low-down wretch?' Varya cried again exultantly, looking defiantly at her brother.

For a few moments they stood like that, facing each other. Ganya still clasped her hand in his. Varya tried to pull it away with all her might, but, unable to restrain herself any longer and beside herself, she suddenly spat in her brother's face.

'What a girl!' cried Nastasya Filippovna. 'Bravo, Ptitsyn; I congratulate you!'

Ganya felt dizzy and, completely forgetting himself, he aimed a blow at his sister with all his strength. He would have struck her in the face, if another hand had not suddenly caught hold of his. The prince stood between him and his sister.

'There, that'll do,' he said insistently, but also trembling all over, as though from a violent shock.

'Damn you,' Ganya roared, letting go of his sister's hand, 'you're not always going to stand in my way, are you?' And, mad with fury, he gave the prince a resounding slap in the face.

'Oh,' Kolya cried, horrified, 'oh, my God!'

Exclamations could be heard on all sides. The prince turned pale. He looked Ganya straight in the face with strange, reproachful eyes; his lips quivered as he tried to say something; they were twisted into a strange and completely incongruous smile.

'Oh, well, I don't mind you striking me, but I shan't let you touch her!' he said quietly at last, but, suddenly, he could no longer control himself and, leaving Ganya, covered his face with his hands and, walking to a corner of the room, stood with his face to the wall, and said in a faltering voice:

'Oh, how you'll be ashamed of what you've done!'

Ganya did indeed stand there looking utterly crushed. Kolya rushed up to the prince and began embracing and kissing him. Rogozhin, Varya, Ptitsyn, Mrs Ivolgin, and even the old general, all crowded round him.

'Never mind, never mind!' murmured the prince in all directions with the same incongruous smile.

'He'll be sorry for this!' Rogozhin cried. 'You'll be ashamed, Ganya, of having insulted such a – sheep!' (He could not find another word.) 'Prince, my dear fellow, leave them. Send them all to the devil. Come along with me. You'll see how much Rogozhin loves you!'

Nastasya Filippovna, too, was greatly astonished at Ganya's action and the prince's answer. Her usually pale and pensive face, which had all along been so out of keeping with her seemingly affected laughter, was now evidently stirred by a new emotion; yet she did not seem to wish to betray it, and seemed to do her best to preserve her sarcastic expression.

'I do think I've seen his face somewhere,' she said quite seriously, suddenly remembering the question she had asked him.

'And aren't you ashamed of yourself?' cried the prince suddenly with deep, heartfelt reproach. 'You're not the woman you pretend to be. Why, it isn't possible!'

Nastasya Filippovna looked surprised. She smiled, but seemed to be concealing something behind her smile. She was a little embarrassed and, glancing at Ganya, went out of the room. But before she reached the entrance hall, she suddenly returned, went up to Mrs Ivolgin, took her hand, and raised it to her lips.

'He was right, I'm not really like that,' she whispered rapidly and fervidly, flushing all over, and, turning round again, walked out so quickly this time that no one had time to realize what she had come back for. All they saw was that she whispered something to Mrs Ivolgin and seemed to have kissed her hand. But Varya heard and saw everything, and she followed her with surprise out of the room.

Ganya recollected himself and rushed to see Nastasya Filippovna off, but she had already gone. He caught her up on the stairs.

'Don't see me off,' she shouted to him. 'Good-bye till the evening. You must come, do you hear?'

He came back, looking confused and thoughtful; a heavy perplexity lay on his heart, much heavier than before. And there was the prince, too. ... He was so preoccupied with his thoughts that he scarcely noticed Rogozhin's crowd thronging past him and pushing him back against the door as they followed Rogozhin hastily out of the flat. They were all talking loudly about something. Rogozhin himself walked with Ptitsyn, talking earnestly about something important and seemingly very urgent.

'You've lost, Ganya, old fellow!' he shouted as they walked past him.

Ganya gazed after them uneasily.

11

The prince left the drawing-room and shut himself up in his room. Kolya ran in at once and tried to console him. The poor boy seemed unable to keep away from him now.

'It's a good thing you've gone,' he said. 'There's going to be a bigger row than ever there now. Every day it's been like this, and it all started because of that Nastasya Filippovna.'

'I'm afraid you've got all sorts of problems here, Kolya,' observed the prince. 'Very painful problems.'

'Yes, very painful problems. But it's no use talking about us. It's all our own fault. I've a great friend who is much more unfortunate. Would you like to meet him?'

'Yes, very much. Is he a schoolfellow of yours?'

'Yes, sir. I mean he's almost like a schoolfellow. I'll tell you all about it later. But what do you think of Nastasya Filippovna? She's beautiful, isn't she? You see, I've never met her before, though I did try to. She quite bowled me over. I'd have forgiven Ganya everything, if he wanted to marry her for love. But he's after her money – that's the trouble.'

'I'm afraid I don't like your brother at all.'

'I should think not! How could you after -- But, you know, I can't stand all those silly ideas. I mean, if some madman or some fool or some scoundrel slaps a man's face in a fit of madness, that man is supposed to be dishonoured for life, and he can't wipe it out except with blood or if the other man begs his forgiveness on his knees. I think it's absurd and tyrannical. Lermontov's play *The Masquerade* is based on that and – it's silly, in my opinion. What I mean is it's not natural. But, then, he wrote it when he was almost a child.'

'I liked your sister very much.'

'The way she spat in Ganya's face! She's a brave one, Varya is! But you didn't spit at him, and I'm sure it wasn't for want of courage. But here she is herself – speak of the devil. ... I knew she'd come. She's a nice girl, though she has her faults.'

'You've no business here,' Varya said, pouncing on Kolya. 'Go to Father. He isn't being a nuisance, Prince, is he?'

'Not at all, on the contrary.'

'Now she's started on me! That's what I don't like about her. And, by the way, I thought Father would be quite sure to go off with Rogozhin. I expect he must be feeling very sorry now. I'd better go and see how he is,' Kolya added, going out.

'Thank God, I've got Mother away without any more trouble, and put her to bed. Ganya is terribly worried and very depressed – and not without reason! What a lesson! I've come to thank you again, Prince, and to ask you whether you knew Nastasya Filippovna before.'

'No, I didn't.'

'What then made you tell her to her face that she was not "like that"? I believe you are right. It seems she really isn't like that. I can't make her out, though! Of course she came here with the idea of insulting us – that's clear. I've heard many strange things about her before. But if she came to invite us to her party, how could she behave like that to Mother? Ptitsyn knows her well and he says that he could not make her out to-day. And the way she talked to Rogozhin! It's impossible for anyone with self-respect to talk like that in the house of her -- Mother is also very worried about you.'

'Oh, that's nothing!' said the prince, dismissing it with a wave of the hand.

'And how she obeyed you --'

'You mean?'

'You told her she ought to be ashamed of herself and she suddenly became quite a different person. You have an influence over her, Prince,' added Varya with a faint smile.

The door opened and, quite unexpectedly, Ganya came in. He never hesitated even when he saw Varya. For a moment he stood in the doorway and then went up resolutely to the prince.

'Prince, I've behaved like a cad,' he said suddenly with deep emotion. 'Forgive me, my dear fellow.'

There was an expression of great pain in his face. The prince looked at him with surprise and did not reply immediately.

'Please forgive me,' Ganya persisted impatiently. 'Forgive me, please! Well, if you like, I'll kiss your hand!'

The prince was deeply touched and, in silence, put both his arms round Ganya. They kissed each other with great sincerity.

'I never thought you were like that,' the prince said at last, drawing a deep breath. 'I – I thought you were – incapable --'

'Of saying I am sorry? And what made me think this morning that you were an idiot? You notice things other people never notice. One could have a real talk to you, though, perhaps, one had better not.'

'Here's someone else you should apologize to,' said the prince, pointing to Varya.

'No, sir. They're all my enemies. You may be sure, Prince, I've tried over and over again, but here you won't find true forgiveness!' Ganya cried warmly, and he turned away from Varya.

'Yes, I will forgive you,' Varya said suddenly.

'And will you go to Nastasya Filippovna's this evening?'

'I will, if you want me to, only do you really think it's possible for me to go there now?'

'But she isn't at all like that. You see the sort of riddles she poses. It's all tricks!' – and Ganya laughed spitefully.

'I know myself that she's not like that – that she likes to play tricks, and what tricks! Besides, Ganya, do you realize what she must take you for? She may have kissed Mother's hand – it may be one of her tricks, but she did laugh at you for all that, didn't she? It isn't worth seventy-five thousand, it really isn't, dear! You're still capable of honourable feelings and that's why I'm telling you this. Please, don't go there, either! Take care! It can't possibly end well!'

Having said this, Varya left the room in a state of great agitation.

'They're all like that!' said Ganya, with a laugh. 'And don't they realize that I know that myself? Why, I know a damn sight more than they do.'

Saying this, Ganya sat down on the sofa, evidently intending to prolong his visit.

'If you know it yourself,' the prince said timidly, 'how can you have chosen all this agony, knowing that it really isn't worth seventy-five thousand roubles?'

'I wasn't talking about that,' muttered Ganya. 'By the way, I'm rather anxious to know your opinion – so you don't think this "agony" is worth seventy-five thousand, do you?'

'I don't think it is.'

'Well, of course. And is such a marriage shameful?'

'Very.'

'Well, I want you to know, then, that I'm going to marry her and that I'm most certainly going to do it now. This morning I was still hesitating, but now no longer! Don't say anything. I know what you're going to say.'

'I was not going to say that at all. What surprises me is that you should be so sure of it.'

'Sure of what? Of what?'

'Why, that Nastasya Filippovna is quite certain to marry you and that the whole thing is already settled, and, secondly, if she does marry you, that the seventy-five thousand will be safe in your pocket. But, I'm sorry, there's, of course, quite a lot I know nothing about.'

Ganya made a quick movement towards the prince.

'Of course you don't know everything,' he said. 'And why else do you think would I assume such a burden?'

'I don't know, but it happens again and again. People marry for money, and the money remains with the wife.'

'No, sir, it won't happen with us. You see, here there are – there are certain circumstances – –' Ganya murmured, pondering uneasily. 'As for her answer, I don't think there can be any doubt,' he added quickly. 'What makes you think she will refuse me?'

'I don't know anything about it except what I've seen. Miss Varya, too, said just now – –'

'Oh, they are talking like that because they don't know what to say. She was laughing at Rogozhin. You may be sure of that. I saw it. That was obvious. This morning it frightened me, but now I see through it. Or perhaps you think so because of the way she behaved to Mother, Father, and Varya?'

'And to you.'

'Perhaps, but that's just a woman's way of getting her own back. Nothing more. She's a terribly irritable, touchy, and vain woman. Just like some civil servant who has not received his promotion. She wanted to show off and to show her contempt for them and – well, for me, too, I suppose. That's true, I don't deny it. But she will marry me all the same. You have no idea the sort of tricks human vanity is capable of. She, you see, thinks I'm a rotter because I'm marrying her, another man's mistress, so openly for her money, but she doesn't realize that another man would have cheated her in a more rotten fashion; he would have followed her about spouting liberal and progressive ideas, dragging in the woman question, so that in the end she would have been completely in his power. He would have made the conceited fool believe (and so easily, too!) that he married her only because of her noble heart and her misfortune, while he really would have married her for her money alone. I'm not liked because I don't want to play a double game, though I ought to. But what is she doing herself? Isn't it just the same? Why, then, does she despise me in that case? Why does she get up to all those tricks? Why? Because I refuse to give in and because I show some pride. Oh, well, we shall see!'

'Surely you couldn't have loved her till this happened, could you?'

'I did love her at first. Well, never mind that. There are women who are only good for mistresses and nothing else. I don't say that she's been my mistress. If she wants to live quietly, I shall live quietly; but if she shows fight, I'll leave her at once and take the money with me. I don't want to be made to look ridiculous. Above all, I don't want to be made to look ridiculous!'

'I can't help feeling,' the prince observed cautiously, 'that Nastasya Filippovna is clever. Why should she walk into a trap when she can see the agony it will mean to her? She could marry someone else, couldn't she? That's what I can't understand.'

'Ah, but, you see, she has her reasons for that! You don't know everything, Prince. You see – besides, she's convinced that I'm madly in love with her. I swear, she is, and, you know, I strongly suspect that she loves me too, in her own way, of course. You know the saying: "Whom he loveth, he chasteneth". She will treat me like dirt all her life (and perhaps that's what she wants) and she'll love me in her own way all the same; she's preparing herself for that, that's the sort of character she has. She is a typically Russian woman, I tell you.

Well, I, too, am preparing a little surprise for her. The scene with Varya just now was an accident, but it's to my advantage: she has seen and convinced herself of my devotion and my readiness to break all my ties for her. Which means that I'm no fool, either; you can be sure of that. By the way, you don't think I'm a chatterbox, do you? Perhaps, my dear Prince, I'm really making a mistake in confiding in you. But just because you're the first honourable man I've come across, I've pounced upon you – and, please, don't take "pounced upon you" literally. You're not angry for what happened just now, are you? It is perhaps the first time in two years that I've spoken my mind freely. There are terribly few honest people about: there's none more honest than Ptitsyn. You're not laughing, are you? Scoundrels love honest men – didn't you know that? And I am – but in what way am I a scoundrel? Tell me frankly. Why do they all follow her example in calling me a scoundrel? And, you know, I follow their example and hers and call myself a scoundrel too! That's what's so rotten, really rotten.'

'I shall never think of you as a scoundrel again,' said the prince. 'Just now I thought you were a really wicked man, and suddenly you have given me so pleasant a surprise – it's a lesson to me not to judge without experience. Now I can see that one ought not to think of you as a wicked man, nor as a very depraved one. In my opinion, you're simply a very ordinary man, the most ordinary man that could be, only perhaps very weak and not at all original.'

Ganya smiled sarcastically to himself, but said nothing. Seeing that his opinion displeased Ganya, the prince felt embarrassed and was silent, too.

'Has Father asked you for money?' Ganya asked suddenly.

'No.'

'He will, but don't you give him any. You know, he used to be quite a decent fellow once. I remember it well. He used to be received by nice people. And how quickly they all degenerate, these elderly decent people! The moment their circumstances change, there's nothing left of their former selves, they just disappear into thin air! He never used to tell such lies before, I assure you: before he was just a little over-enthusiastic and – that's what it has all come to now! Of course, drink is at the bottom of it all. Do you know that he keeps a mistress? Now, he's not just an innocent little liar. I can't understand how my mother can stand it so long. Has he told you about the siege of Kars? Or how his grey trace-horse began talking? That's how far it's gone.'

And Ganya suddenly roared with laughter.

'What are you looking at me like that for?' he asked the prince.

'Well, I'm surprised you laughed like that. You can still laugh like a child, you know. A short while ago you came in to make your peace with me and said, "If you like I'll kiss your hand" – it's exactly how children would make it up. Which means that you're still capable of talking and feeling like that. And then you suddenly start reading a whole lecture about all that horror and those seventy-five thousand. Really, it all seems somehow absurd and impossible.'

'And what conclusion do you draw from it?'

'Well, I'm wondering whether you're not perhaps acting a little too thoughtlessly and whether you ought not to consider it carefully first. Miss Varya is perhaps right.'

'Oh, morality! That I'm still a boy, I know myself,' Ganya interrupted warmly, 'and that is amply proved by my discussing these things with you. It isn't entirely from mercenary motives that I'm embarking on this horror,' he went on, letting the cat out of the bag like a young man whose vanity is stung. 'If I were impelled only by mercenary motives, I should most certainly have come a cropper, for I'm still far from strong in mind and character. No, sir, I'm driven by my passion and inclination, for the goal I'm aiming at is a very important one. I suppose you think that as soon as I get the seventy-five thousand, I shall immediately buy myself a carriage and pair. No, sir. I shall go on wearing the old coat I've worn for three years and drop all my club acquaintances. We have very few people with perseverance, though all of us are usurers at heart, and I want to persevere. The main thing is to hold on to the bitter end – that's the whole problem! When Ptitsyn was seventeen he slept in the street and sold pen-knives – he began with a few pennies, now he is worth sixty thousand, but the things he had to do to get it! Well, I'm going to skip it all and start straight off with some capital. In fifteen years people will say, "There goes Ivolgin, the King of the Jews!" You tell me I am not an original person. Observe, my dear Prince, that to a man of our age and race there can be nothing more offensive than to be told that he is not original, that his character is weak, that he has no special talents and that he is just an ordinary person. You did not even deign to consider me a good scoundrel and, you know, I felt like tearing you to pieces for that just now! You offended me more than Yepanchin, who thinks (and that, mind you, in the simplicity of his heart, without wasting any words and without holding out any inducements) that I'm capable of selling my wife to him! That, my dear sir, has been driving me mad for a long time, but I want money. Having made a fortune, I shall – mark you – become a highly original person. The most disgusting and hateful thing about money is that it even endows people with talent. And it will do so till the end of the world. You'll say it's all rather childish and, perhaps, even romantic. Well, what about it? I shall be all the merrier for it and I shall do it all the same. I shall carry it through and I shall persevere. *Rira bien qui rira le dernier!* Why does Yepanchin insult me like that? Out of spite? Never, sir! Simply because I'm too insignificant. But, my dear sir, just let me – – However, that's enough. It's time I was off. Kolya has poked his head in twice already: he's calling you to dinner. And I'm going out. I shall come in and have a chat with you sometimes. You'll be all right here: now they'll treat you as one of the family. Mind, don't give me away. I think we shall either be friends or enemies. And what do you think, Prince, if I had kissed your hand (as I sincerely offered to do), would that have made me your enemy afterwards?'

'I'm quite sure it would, only not for ever. You wouldn't have been able to keep it up and you would have forgiven me,' the prince laughingly decided after thinking it over.

'Oho, I can see I'll have to be more careful with you. Damn it, you've put a drop of venom in that, too! But who knows? Perhaps you are an enemy of mine. By the way – ha, ha, ha! – I forgot to ask you. Was I right in imagining that you liked Nastasya Filippovna very much yourself, or wasn't I?'

'Yes – I like her.'

'Are you in love with her?'

'N-no.'

'Why, you're blushing all over and you look unhappy. All right, all right, I won't laugh. Good-bye. But, you know she's a virtuous woman – can you believe it? You think she's living with that man – Totsky? Not a bit of it! Not for a long time. And did you notice how awfully awkward she was and how embarrassed she was at times to-day? Yes, indeed. It's people like her who love to dominate others. Well, good-bye!'

Ganya went out in a good humour and much more at his ease than he had been when he came in. The prince remained motionless for ten minutes, sunk in thought.

Kolya again thrust his head in at the door.

'I don't want any dinner, Kolya; I had a good lunch at the Yepanchins'.'

Kolya came into the room and gave the prince a note. It was from the general – folded and sealed. It was clear from Kolya's face how he hated giving him it. The prince read it, got up, and took his hat.

'It's only a few yards from here,' said Kolya, looking very embarrassed. 'He's sitting there now over a bottle. How he got them to give him credit, I can't understand. Please, Prince, don't say anything to them here afterwards about my giving you the note. I've sworn a thousand times not to pass on such notes, but I'm sorry for him. And, please, do not be afraid to hurt his feelings: give him a few pennies and that'll satisfy him.'

'As a matter of fact, Kolya, I was thinking of it myself. I have to see your father in connexion with – a certain business. Come along.'

12

Kolya took the prince not far away to a café with a billiard-room near Liteyny Avenue. The café was on the ground-floor and one walked into it straight from the street. General Ivolgin had installed himself in a little room to the right of the entrance, like an old habitué, with a bottle in front of him on a little table and, to be sure, with the *Indépendance Belge* in his hands. He was expecting the prince; as soon as he saw him, he put down the newspaper and embarked on a long and heated explanation, of which the prince, however, could understand very little, for the general was already almost drunk.

'I haven't got ten roubles,' the prince interrupted him, 'but here's a twenty-five-rouble note. Change it and let me have fifteen back, for otherwise I shall be left without a penny.'

'Oh, thank you, sir, and you may be sure I'll do so at once. ...'

'I have, besides, come to you with a request, General. You've never been to Nastasya Filippovna's, have you?'

'Me? Not been there? Are you saying this to me? Why, my dear fellow, I've been there several times, several times!' cried the general in an access of triumphant and self-satisfied irony. 'But I stopped going there myself, for I did not want to encourage an improper alliance. You've seen for yourself, sir, you were a witness this afternoon: I did all a father could do, a meek and indulgent father. But now, sir, a different kind of father is about to appear on the scene and then we shall see, sir, whether an honourable old soldier, sir, will scotch this intrigue or whether a shameless whore will force her way into a most honourable family.'

'Well, and I was going to ask you whether as an old friend you could introduce me to Nastasya Filippovna this evening. I simply have to be there to-night. I have some business, but I don't know how to go there. I was introduced to-day, but I was not invited, and she has a party there this evening. I am quite ready to disregard certain conventions, I don't even mind being laughed at, if only I can get in.'

'Why, my dear young friend, you've hit on my idea entirely – entirely,' cried the general enthusiastically. 'I didn't ask you to come here for this trifle,' he went on, taking the money, however, and putting it in his pocket, 'I asked you to come here to invite you to join me in a campaign against Nastasya Filippovna. General Ivolgin and Prince Myshkin! How will that strike her? As for myself, I shall, on the pretext of a courtesy call on her birthday, announce my will at last – not directly. Indirectly, of course. But it will be just as good as though done directly. Ganya will then see for himself what he has to do: whether to choose between his father, an honourable gentleman and – so to speak – and so on, or – – But what will be, will be! Your idea is a capital one, sir. At nine o'clock we will start. We've plenty of time, sir.'

'Where does she live?'

'A long way from here, near the Bolshoy Theatre, at Mrs Mytovtsov's house, almost in the square, on the first floor. ... There won't be many people there, though it is her name-day, and they will be going early. ...'

It was very late in the evening; the prince still sat listening and waiting for the general, who began an inexhaustible number of anecdotes and never finished a single one. On the prince's arrival he asked for another bottle and only finished it an hour later; then he asked for a third and finished it too. It may be assumed that the general had by that time managed to tell almost the whole story of his life. At last the prince got up and said that he could wait no longer. The general emptied the last dregs out of the bottle, got up, and went out of the room, walking very unsteadily. The prince was in despair. He could not understand how he could have been taken in so foolishly. As a matter of fact, he never really was taken in. He had counted on the general simply because there was no other way of getting to Nastasya Filippovna's, even at the cost of some scandalous scene, though he did not reckon on anything very scandalous. The general turned out to be very drunk and exceedingly eloquent. He spoke without pausing, with great feeling and with tearful emotion. His main theme was that everything was going to rack and ruin because of the bad behaviour of all the members of his family and that it was high time to put a stop to it. They reached Liteyny Avenue at last. It was still thawing.

A warm, damp, oppressive wind went whistling up and down the streets, carriages splashed through the mud, the horses' hoofs struck the cobbles in the road with a ringing sound. The people on the pavement slouched along in wet and dejected crowds with here and there a drunken man among them.

'Do you see those lighted first-floor windows?' the general asked. 'That's where all my comrades live, and I, who have seen more active service and suffered more hardships than any of them, have to walk on foot to the Bolshoy Theatre, to the house of a woman of doubtful reputation! A man who has thirteen bullets in his chest – you don't believe me, do you? And yet it was entirely on my account, sir, that Pirogov telegraphed to Paris and left besieged Sebastopol for a time, and Nelaton, the Paris court doctor, obtained a safe-conduct in the name of science and came to examine me in Sebastopol. The highest authorities know about it. "Oh, that's the Ivolgin who has thirteen bullets in him!" That's how they speak of me. Do you see that house, Prince? An old comrade of mine, General Sokolovich, lives there on the first floor with his large and most respectable family. That house, sir, as well as three houses in Nevsky Avenue and two in Morskaya Street, make up my present circle of acquaintances, my personal acquaintances, I mean. My wife resigned herself to circumstances long ago. But I still go on remembering the past and – er – so to speak, relax in the cultured society of my old comrades and subordinates who still worship me. This General Sokolovich (I haven't been to see him for some time, I'm afraid, and I haven't seen Anna Fyodorovna, either) – you know, my dear prince, when you don't receive visitors, you willy-nilly stop visiting people yourself. And yet – h'm – I don't think you believe me. ... Still, why shouldn't I introduce the son of my best friend and childhood companion into this delightful home? General Ivolgin and Prince Myshkin! You will see a simply ravishing girl, my dear sir, and not only one but two and even three, all ornaments of this capital city of ours and of society: beauty, education, modern ideas, the woman question, poetry – all united in a happy and diversified combination, to say nothing of a dowry of at least eighty thousand roubles in hard cash for each of them, which never comes amiss, sir, notwithstanding all the woman and social questions – in short, sir, not only must I introduce you, but I consider it my duty to do so. General Ivolgin and Prince Myshkin! Yes, sir. It will cause a sensation!'

'At once? Now? But you've forgotten – –' the prince began.

'I've forgotten nothing, sir. Come along! This way – up this magnificent staircase. I'm surprised there's no porter, but I suppose it's a holiday and the porter has gone off. They haven't sacked the drunken lout yet. This Sokolovich is indebted to me, and to me alone, for all the happiness of his life and army career, but – here we are, sir.'

The prince offered no objection to the visit, and meekly followed the general to avoid irritating him, in the firm hope that General Sokolovich and his whole family would gradually fade away like a mirage and prove to be non-existent, so that they could quietly go downstairs again. But, to his horror, he was beginning to lose this hope: the general led him up the stairs like a man who really had friends living there, every moment adding more biographical and topographical details with mathematical exactitude. At last, when they had mounted to the first floor and stopped on the right before the door of a luxurious flat and the general was about to ring the bell, the prince made up his mind to escape, but one strange circumstance stopped him for a moment.

'You've made a mistake, General,' he said. 'The name on the door is Kulakov and you were going to see Sokolovich.'

'Kulakov – Kulakov proves nothing. This is Sokolovich's flat, and I'm ringing at Sokolovich's door. To hell with Kulakov. Ah, there's someone coming!'

The door was, in fact, opened. A footman looked out and announced that there was no one at home.

'What a pity, what a pity; just my luck!' General Ivolgin repeated several times with profound regret. 'Please tell them, my good man, that General Ivolgin and Prince Myshkin wished to pay their respects in person and greatly, greatly regret – –'

At this moment another person looked out of the door of one of the rooms, a housekeeper apparently, or perhaps a governess, a woman of about forty in a dark dress. Hearing the names of General Ivolgin and Prince Myshkin, she approached inquisitively and mistrustfully.

'Maria Alexandrovna is not at home,' she said, staring hard at the general. 'She has gone to her mother's with the young lady, Alexandra Mikhaylovna.'

'So Alexandra Mikhaylovna's out with them, too! Good Lord, what bad luck! Would you believe it, madam? I've always such bad luck! Will you be so good as to give them my best regards and remember me to Alexandra Mikhaylovna – in short, madam, give them all my best wishes for what they wished for themselves last Thursday evening while listening to Chopin's Ballade. They'll remember – my cordial wishes! General Ivolgin and Prince Myshkin!'

'I won't forget, sir,' said the woman, looking less suspicious as she took her leave of them.

As they went downstairs, the general continued with undiminished warmth to express his regret that they had not found them at home and that the prince had missed making such a charming acquaintance.

'Do you know, my dear sir, I'm a bit of a poet at heart – have you noticed that? However – however, it seems we did call at the wrong place,' he suddenly concluded quite unexpectedly. 'The Sokolovich's, I have just remembered, live in another house, and I believe they're in Moscow now. Yes, I'm afraid I have made a little mistake, but – it doesn't matter.'

'All I want to know, sir,' the prince observed dejectedly, 'is whether I can rely on you at all, or had I better go alone.'

'Rely on me, sir? Go alone? But why should you, sir, when this is a matter of vital importance to me on which so much of the future of my family depends! No, my young friend, you don't know Ivolgin well enough. To say "Ivolgin" is to say "a rock". You can rely on Ivolgin as on a rock, that's what they used to say in the squadron in which I began my service. Only I'm afraid I shall have to call for a minute on the way at the house which for several years now has been my refuge from my trials and tribulations. ...'

'You want to go home?'

'No, sir, I want to go and see Mrs Terentyev, the widow of Captain Terentyev, one of my subordinate officers and – er – I might say, a friend of mine. There, at Mrs Terentyev's, I'm refreshed in spirit, and it is there that I bring all my worldly cares and family troubles. And as to-day I have a particularly heavy load on my mind, I – –'

'I'm afraid,' murmured the prince, 'I've behaved very stupidly in troubling you this evening, sir. Besides, you're – good-bye!'

'But, my young friend, I cannot, I really cannot let you go,' cried the general. 'A widow, a mother of a family, whose feelings strike a chord in my heart. A visit to her is merely a matter of five minutes. I practically live there. I'll have a wash, make myself a little presentable, and then we'll take a cab and be off to the Bolshoy Theatre. I'm afraid I shall need you all the evening. It's there, in that house – here we are. Ah, Kolya, you're here already? Is Marfa Borisovna at home, or have you only just come?'

'Oh, no,' replied Kolya, who had run into them at the gateway, 'I've been here a long time with Ippolit. He is worse. He was in bed this morning. I've just been to a shop for some playing-cards. Marfa Borisovna is expecting you. Only, Daddy, you're in an awful state!' Kolya concluded, staring at the way the general walked and stood. 'Oh well, come along!'

The meeting with Kolya induced the prince to accompany the general to Mrs Terentyev's, but only for one minute. The prince needed

Kolya, but he made up his mind to leave the general behind anyway, and he could not forgive himself for having taken it into his head to rely on him. It took them a long time to climb to the fourth floor and by the back stairs, too.

'Do you want to introduce the prince?' Kolya asked on the way.

'Yes, my boy, to introduce him – General Ivolgin and Prince Myshkin, but how – how is Marfa Borisovna?'

'Well, Daddy, I really don't think you ought to go! She'll eat you alive! You haven't been here for two days and she is expecting the money. Why did you promise her money? You're always like that! Now you'll jolly well have to get out of it as best you can!'

On the fourth floor they stopped before a low door. The general quailed visibly and kept pushing the prince in front of him.

'I think I'll stay here,' he muttered. 'I want to give her a surprise.'

Kolya went in first. A woman of forty, heavily made up, in slippers and a short, fur-lined jacket, her hair plaited in pigtails, peered out of the door and the general's surprise immediately fell flat.

'There he is,' she screamed as soon as she caught sight of him, 'the base, wicked man! I knew it in my heart!'

'Come in – it's all right,' the general muttered to the prince, still smiling innocently.

But it was not all right. No sooner had they passed through the low dark passage into a narrow sitting-room, furnished with half a dozen wicker chairs and two card-tables, than Mrs Terentyev went on in what must have been her customary nagging voice:

'Aren't you ashamed, aren't you ashamed of yourself, you cruel, inhuman wretch, you tyrant of my family, you inhuman monster, you? You've robbed me of everything, sucked me dry, and you're still dissatisfied! How much longer am I to put up with you, you, you shameless and dishonest man!'

'Marfa Borisovna – this – er – is Prince Myshkin,' stammered the quailing and abashed general. 'General Ivolgin and Prince Myshkin!'

'Would you believe it,' Mrs Terentyev suddenly addressed the prince, 'would you believe it, this shameless man has not spared my orphan children! He robbed me of everything, carried everything off, sold and pawned everything, left us nothing. What am I to do with your I.O.U.s, you cunning, unscrupulous wretch? Answer me, you cunning rogue, answer me, you grasping villain! How am I to feed my orphan children? Look at him – drunk and scarcely able to stand on his feet! Oh, what have I done to bring down the Lord's wrath upon me? Answer me, you base, disgraceful hypocrite!'

But the general had other things in his mind.

'Marfa Borisovna, twenty-five roubles – it's all I can – thanks to this generous friend of mine! Prince, I was cruelly mistaken! Such – such is life, and now I'm sorry I'm very weak,' the general went on, standing in the middle of the room and bowing in all directions. 'I am weak, sir. I'm sorry. Darling Lena, a pillow – my dear!'

Lena, an eight-year-old girl, at once ran for a pillow and put it on the hard ragged sofa, covered with American cloth. The general sat down on it, intending to say much more, but the moment he touched the sofa, he fell on his side, turned his face to the wall, and sank into the sleep of the just. Mrs Terentyev mournfully and ceremoniously motioned the prince to a chair at one of the card-tables. She sat down opposite, leaned her right cheek on her hand and, looking at the prince, began sighing. Three small children, two girls and a boy, of whom little Lena was the eldest, went up to the table, put their hands on it, and also began gazing intently at the prince. Kolya appeared from the next room.

'I'm very glad I have met you here, Kolya,' the prince said to him. 'I wonder if you can help me. You see, I must be at Nastasya Filippovna's. I asked your father to take me there, but he is asleep, as you see. Will you please take me there, for I don't know the streets or the way. I've got her address, though: near the Bolshoy Theatre, Mrs Mytovtsov's house.'

'Nastasya Filippovna? Why, she never lived near the Bolshoy Theatre, and Father has never been at her place, if you really want to know. Funny you should have expected anything of him. She lives near Vladimirskaya Street, at the Five Corners. That's much nearer here. Do you want to go at once? It's half past nine now. All right, I'll take you there.'

The prince and Kolya went out at once. Alas, the prince had no money to pay for a cab and they had to walk.

'I wanted to introduce you to Ippolit,' said Kolya. 'He's the eldest son of this captain's widow in the fur-lined jacket. He was in the other room. He's ill and has been in bed all day. But he is such a strange chap. He's terribly sensitive, and I couldn't help feeling that he would be ashamed to see you because you came at such a moment. You see, I don't feel as ashamed as he because, after all, it's my father, but it is his mother. It makes all the difference, you know, because it's not discreditable for a man to be in such a position. But, I suppose, it's just a prejudice that men are more privileged in a case of this sort. Ippolit is an excellent fellow, but he is a slave to certain prejudices.'

'Did you say he had consumption?'

'Yes, I think it would be best if he were to die soon. I should certainly wish to be dead if I were in his place. He's sorry for his brother and sisters – the little ones you saw. If it were possible, I mean if we had money, he and I would have taken a flat and disowned our families. This is our dream. And, you know, when I told him just now about your affair with my brother, he flew into a rage and said that anyone who did not challenge the man who had slapped his face to a duel was a scoundrel. But he's awfully irritable. I've stopped arguing with him. So Nastasya Filippovna invited you to her party, did she?'

'Well, that's the trouble, you see. She didn't.'

'But then, how can you go there?' cried Kolya, stopping dead in the middle of the pavement. 'And – in such clothes, too. It's her birthday party, you know.'

'I'm afraid I really don't know how I shall go in. If they let me in, all right; if not, then my business has failed. As for my clothes, I'm afraid that can't be helped.'

'You have some business, then? Or are you only going just *pour passer le temps* in "society"?'

'No – as a matter of fact – I mean, I have some business – I'm afraid I can't explain it, but – –'

'I don't care what your business is – it's your affair. The thing that interests me is that you're not going to a party because you want to be in the charming society of trollops, generals, and usurers. If you did, I'd have laughed at you and despised you. I'm sorry, Prince, but I should. There are very few honest people here, so few that there is nobody one can entirely respect. You can't help looking down upon them, but they all demand to be respected, Varya especially. And have you noticed, Prince, that in our age everyone is a sordid adventurer! And that is particularly true of Russia, of our dear motherland. And how it all happened, I don't understand. Everything seemed to be built on such solid foundations, but what is it like now? Everyone is talking about it. Everywhere they are writing about it. Making exposures. Everyone in Russia is making exposures. Parents are the first to go back on their word and are ashamed of their old morals themselves. In Moscow, for instance, a father tried to persuade his son *to stop at nothing* to get money. It was reported in the papers. Look at my general. Well, what has become of him? And yet, you know, I can't help feeling that my general is an honest man. I'm sure he is! It's only his disorderly life and drink – I'm sure it is! I can't help feeling sorry for him – I'm only afraid to say so, for everyone will be laughing at me – but I'm sorry for him. And what good is there in these intelligent people? They're all money-grubbers, every one of them! Ippolit justifies usury. He says it is necessary – economic crises, booms, and slumps – damn 'em! It makes me angry to hear him talk like that, but then he is so bitter. You could hardly believe it, but his mother, Mrs Terentyev, gets money from the general and lends it at high interest – could anything be more shameful? And do you know that Mother – I mean my mother – helps Ippolit with money, clothes, and everything, and the children, too, through Ippolit, because their own mother neglects them. And Varya does the same.'

'Well, there you are! You say that there are no honest people and that all are money-grubbers; but here you have strong-minded people – your mother and Varya. Is it not a sign of moral strength to help people in such circumstances?'

'That beastly Varya does it out of vanity and because she wants to show off, so as not to lag behind Mother, and – well – Mother really is – I respect her for that. Yes, I respect this sort of thing and I think it right. Even Ippolit feels it, and he is terribly embittered. At first he laughed, and said it was ignoble of my mother to act like that, but now he begins to feel it sometimes. I see! So you call it strength? I shall make a note of that. Ganya doesn't know about it, or he would have called it connivance.'

'So Ganya doesn't know? It seems to me Ganya doesn't know a great deal,' the prince, who had been thinking of something else, blurted out.

'You know, Prince, I like you very much. I can't forget what happened this afternoon.'

'I like you very much too, Kolya.'

'Listen, how do you intend to live here? I shall soon get a job and shall be earning some money. Let's live together, you, Ippolit, and I, the three of us together. Let's take a flat, and then the general will be able to come and see us.'

'I'd love to do that. Anyhow, we shall see. I'm afraid I'm very – very much upset now. What? Are we there already? This house – what a magnificent entrance hall! And a porter! Well, Kolya, I don't know what will come of it, I'm sure.'

The prince stood still, looking completely lost.

'You'll tell me all about it to-morrow! Don't be too much afraid. I do hope everything will be all right, for I share your opinions in everything, Prince. Good-bye. I'm going back to tell Ippolit about it. I'm quite sure you'll be received. She's an awfully original woman. Go up those stairs to the first floor. The porter will show you.'

13

As he ascended the stairs, the prince was greatly troubled in his mind and he did his best to cheer himself up: 'The worst that can happen,' he thought, 'is that they won't receive me and will think badly of me, or that, perhaps, they will receive me and start laughing in my face. ... Oh, who cares?' And, as a matter of fact, this did not really alarm him very much; it was to the question what he was going to do there and why he was going there that, however much he tried, he could find no reassuring answer. Even if he could somehow or other find a favourable opportunity to say to Nastasya Filippovna: 'Don't ruin yourself by marrying that man, he doesn't love you, he only loves your money, he told me so himself, and Aglaya Yepanchin told me that, too, and I've come to tell you,' it would hardly be the right thing to say from every point of view. There was another unsolved problem, a problem so important that the prince was even afraid to think of it, could not, indeed, dared not, admit its existence, did not know how to formulate it, and blushed and trembled at the very thought of it. But in the end he did go in and ask for Nastasya Filippovna in spite of all his doubts and anxieties.

The flat Nastasya Filippovna occupied was not very large, but it was really magnificently appointed. There had been a period at the beginning of the five years she had lived in Petersburg during which Totsky had not spared any money on her; at the time he had still been counting on her love and had tried to tempt her chiefly by comfort and luxury, knowing very well how easily habits of luxury are acquired and how difficult they are to give up afterwards when luxury gradually becomes a necessity. In this respect Totsky remained true to the good old traditions, without modifying them in any way and having an unbounded faith in the invincible power of sensual influences. Nastasya Filippovna did not spurn luxury, indeed, she loved it, but – and that seemed very strange – she did not succumb to it, just as though she could always have done without it; she even did not hesitate to tell Totsky about it, much to his annoyance. But there was a great deal about Nastasya Filippovna that not only annoyed him, but even made him despise her afterwards. Quite apart from the lack of refinement in the kind of people whom she befriended, and hence showed a tendency to befriend, she showed a number of other rather strange tendencies: there appeared in her a sort of barbarous mixture of two tastes, a capacity for getting used to and being satisfied with things and ways and means whose very existence, one would have thought, no well-bred and refined person would be aware of. Indeed, if, to take an example, Nastasya Filippovna had suddenly betrayed a pretty and refined ignorance of the fact that, for instance, peasant women could not afford to wear the fine cambric petticoats she wore, Mr Totsky would probably be extremely pleased. According to his programme, the whole idea of Nastasya Filippovna's education was from the very beginning conceived with a view to bringing about such results, and he was a great expert in that line, but, alas, the results turned out to be rather disappointing. In spite of that, there had always been, and there still was, something in Nastasya Filippovna that occasionally impressed Totsky himself by its extraordinary and fascinating originality, by a sort of power, which sometimes attracted him even now when all his former designs on Nastasya Filippovna had come to nothing.

The prince was met by a maid (Nastasya Filippovna kept only female servants), who, to his surprise, was not at all startled by his request to announce him to her mistress. She was not in the least perturbed by his dirty boots, his wide-brimmed hat, his cloak, or his look of profound embarrassment. She helped him off with his cloak, asked him to wait in the reception-room, and went at once to announce him.

The company assembled at Nastasya Filippovna's consisted of her usual circle of friends and acquaintances. Indeed, compared with her birthday parties in previous years, there were only a few people. There were present, to begin with, Mr Totsky and General Yepanchin, both of them extremely amiable, though at heart rather apprehensive and anxious – a fact they could not very well disguise – about the promised declaration about Ganya. Besides them, there was, of course, Ganya, who, too, looked very gloomy and very thoughtful and, indeed, extremely 'unamiable'. He stood apart, at a distance, most of the time and did not speak. He had not attempted to bring Varya, but Nastasya Filippovna made no mention of her, though she did remind him of his scene with the prince immediately after greeting him. The general, who had not heard of it, was very interested, however, and Ganya, drily and reservedly, but very frankly, told him what had happened and that he had already gone to offer his apologies to the prince. He concluded by warmly expressing his opinion that it was a complete mystery to him why the prince should have been called an 'idiot' and that he, on the contrary, thought that he certainly had 'all his wits about him'. Nastasya Filippovna listened to this conclusion with great attention, watching Ganya with interest, but the conversation passed immediately to Rogozhin, who had taken so prominent a part in that afternoon's events, and in whom Mr Totsky and General Yepanchin were also highly interested. It seemed that the only person who possessed the latest news about Rogozhin was Ptitsyn, who had been very busy with his affairs almost till nine o'clock that evening. Rogozhin had been most anxious to get hold of a hundred thousand roubles that very day. 'It is true,' Ptitsyn observed, 'he was drunk, but I think he will get his hundred thousand, however difficult they may be to obtain. I am not sure, though, whether he will get them today or whether he will get them all. Many people are trying to raise them for him: Kinder, Trepalov, Biskup. He doesn't care what interest he pays, but, of course,' Ptitsyn concluded, 'he does it all because he's drunk and in the first flush of joy at his good fortune.' All this news was received with interest, though some looked rather gloomy about it; Nastasya Filippovna said nothing, evidently not wishing to express an opinion; Ganya likewise. General Yepanchin was upset by the news almost more than anyone else: the string of pearls he had presented that morning had been accepted with much too cold a civility, and even with a touch of sarcasm. Ferdyshchenko alone of all the guests was in a most festive and merry mood, laughing loudly at times at nothing in particular and that, too, only because he had of his own accord undertaken to play the part of a fool. Totsky himself, who enjoyed the reputation of a witty and elegant raconteur and who on previous occasions had set the tone of the conversation, was evidently out of humour and in a state of bewilderment which was very uncharacteristic of him. The rest of the guests, who were not, however, numerous (a poor old schoolmaster, invited goodness only knows why, a very young and unknown man, who was very shy and silent all the time, a rather sprightly lady of forty, apparently an actress, and an extremely beautiful and gorgeously attired young lady who was quite extraordinarily tongue-tied), were not only unable to add a certain sparkle to the conversation, but sometimes simply did not know what to talk about.

The prince, in these circumstances, arrived at a most opportune moment. The announcement of his arrival caused some surprise and evoked a few strange smiles, especially when it became evident from Nastasya Filippovna's look of astonishment that she had never thought of inviting him. But after her initial surprise, Nastasya Filippovna suddenly looked so pleased that most of her guests at once prepared to welcome the unbidden visitor with mirth and laughter.

'I suppose this is all due to his innocence,' remarked General Yepanchin, 'and anyway to encourage such tendencies is rather dangerous, I think. But I must admit it is not such a bad thing he took it into his head to come at this moment, even though in so original a manner. He may cheer us up, at least if my judgement of him is correct.'

'Particularly,' Ferdyshchenko at once chimed in, 'as he has thrust himself on us.'

'What does that matter?' the general, who hated Ferdyshchenko, asked drily.

'Why, sir,' Ferdyshchenko explained, 'it does matter because, you see, he'll have to pay for admission.'

'Well,' the general, who could still not reconcile himself to the thought of being in the same company and on the same footing as Ferdyshchenko, could not help observing, 'Prince Myshkin isn't Ferdyshchenko, anyway.'

'Please, General, spare Ferdyshchenko,' the latter replied, grinning. 'I'm in a privileged position here.'

'What kind of privileged position, pray?'

'Last time I had the honour of explaining it in detail to the company, but I don't mind repeating it again for your benefit, sir. You see, sir, everyone's so witty, but I am not. As a compensation, I have obtained the permission to speak the truth, for, as everyone knows, the truth is only spoken by people who are not witty. I am, besides, an extremely vindictive man, and that, too, because I'm not witty. I put up meekly with every sort of insult, but only until the person who has insulted me comes to grief; when that happens, I at once remember it and take my revenge. I kick, sir, as Mr Ptitsyn, who of course never kicks anyone, has said about me. Do you know Krylov's fable *The Lion and the Ass,* sir? Well, that's you and me. It was written about us.'

'You seem to be talking a lot of nonsense again, Ferdyshchenko,' the general remarked, flaring up.

'Why, sir, what do you care?' rejoined Ferdyshchenko, who had only been waiting for the chance of making a cutting rejoinder so as to be able to amplify the insult. 'Don't worry, sir, I know my place. If I did say that you and I were the Lion and the Ass out of Krylov's fable, I of course take the part of the Ass. You, sir, are the Lion, as in Krylov's fable – –

> The mighty Lion, the Terror of the Woods,
> With advancing years his strength has lost – –

and I, sir, am the Ass.'

'I agree with your last remark,' the general blurted out incautiously.

All this, of course, was very coarse and deliberately done, but it was generally accepted that Ferdyshchenko was allowed to play the part of the fool.

'Why,' Ferdyshchenko once exclaimed, 'I'm only tolerated and admitted here so that I may talk in this vein. Do you really suppose it's possible to receive a person like me? I quite appreciate that. Do you really think that a person like me can be asked to sit down beside such a perfect gentleman as Mr Totsky? There's only one explanation possible: I'm permitted to do so because it is impossible to imagine such a thing.'

But though coarsely, it was also very acidly put, and sometimes very much to the point, and that was what Nastasya Filippovna seemed to like. Those who had set their hearts on visiting her, had to make up their minds to put up with Ferdyshchenko. Perhaps he hit upon the truth in believing that he was received because from the very first his presence had become intolerable to Totsky. Ganya, for his part, had endured an infinity of torments at his hands, and in that way Ferdyshchenko was able to be very useful to Nastasya Filippovna.

'To begin with, I'm going to make the prince sing a popular song,' concluded Ferdyshchenko, looking to see what Nastasya Filippovna would say.

'I don't think so, Ferdyshchenko,' she remarked drily, 'and please don't get so excited.'

'Oh well, if he is under special protection, I too will be on my best behaviour.'

But Nastasya Filippovna got up without listening to him, and went to meet the prince herself.

'I'm sorry,' she said, appearing suddenly before him, 'that, being in such a hurry to leave this afternoon, I forgot to invite you to my party, and I'm very glad you've now given me the opportunity of thanking you and telling you how much I appreciate your decision to come.'

Saying this, she gazed intently at the prince in an effort to find out what was his motive in coming.

The prince would perhaps have said something in reply to her kind words, but he was so dazzled and fascinated that he could not utter a word. Nastasya Filippovna was pleased to see it. This evening she wore full evening dress, and the impression she created was very striking. She took his arm and led him to her guests. At the door of the drawing-room the prince suddenly stopped and whispered to her hurriedly in great agitation:

'Everything about you is perfection – I mean, even the fact that you're pale and thin – one wouldn't wish to imagine you different – I wanted so much to come and see you – I – I'm sorry – –'

'Don't apologize,' Nastasya Filippovna laughed, 'that would spoil all the strangeness and originality. It's true, then, what they say about your being a strange man. So you think I'm a paragon of perfection, do you?'

'Yes.'

'Well, you may be very good at guessing, but this time you're mistaken. I'll remind you of it to-night.'

She introduced him to her guests, more than half of whom he had met already. Totsky at once murmured a few courteous words. They all seemed to grow more animated. They all started talking and laughing. Nastasya Filippovna made the prince sit down beside her.

'But what's so surprising about the appearance of the prince?' Ferdyshchenko cried louder than anyone. 'It's as plain as a pikestaff. It speaks for itself.'

'It is indeed all too plain and it does speak too much for itself,' Ganya, who had been silent till then, broke in. 'I've been observing the prince almost uninterruptedly to-day, from the very moment he looked at Nastasya Filippovna's portrait for the first time this morning on General Yepanchin's desk. I remember very well thinking at the time of something I'm absolutely sure of now and which, incidentally, the prince confessed to me himself.'

Ganya said all this very seriously and without a trace of facetiousness, even in a sort of dejected tone of voice, which seemed a little strange.

'I've made no confession to you,' replied the prince, blushing. 'I only answered your question.'

'Bravo, bravo!' cried Ferdyshchenko. 'It's sincere, at any rate. Cunning and sincere at the same time!'

They all laughed aloud.

'For goodness sake, don't shout like that, Ferdyshchenko,' Ptitsyn remarked to him in an undertone, in disgust.

'I confess I didn't expect such forwardness from you, Prince,' said General Yepanchin. 'What sort of a person, do you think, would do a thing like this? And I thought you were a philosopher. Oh, these quiet chaps!'

'And to judge from the way the prince blushes at an innocent joke, like an innocent young girl, I conclude that, like an honourable young man, he harbours the most honourable intentions in his heart,' said, or rather mumbled, suddenly and most unexpectedly the seventy-year-old toothless schoolmaster, who had been perfectly silent till then and whom no one expected to utter a word that evening.

They all laughed more than ever. The old man, who probably thought that they were laughing at his witticism, looking at them, began laughing more and more, which brought on so violent an attack of coughing that Nastasya Filippovna, who for some reason was very fond of all such old men, old women, and even mentally defectives, at once began making much of him, kissed him, and ordered some more tea for him. She asked the maid who had brought the tea, to bring her cloak, in which she wrapped herself, and told her to put more logs on the fire. Asked what time it was, the maid replied that it was already half past ten.

'Would you like some champagne, ladies and gentlemen?' Nastasya Filippovna asked suddenly. 'I've got it all ready. Perhaps it will make you more cheerful. Please don't stand upon ceremony.'

The invitation to have champagne, and especially in such naïve terms, seemed very strange from Nastasya Filippovna. They all knew the extraordinary decorum of her previous parties. The party was becoming livelier on the whole, but not in the usual way. The wine, however, was not refused, first, by the general; secondly, by the sprightly lady, the old man, and Ferdyshchenko, and, finally, by the rest. Totsky, too, took his glass, hoping to counterbalance the new tone that was just setting in by giving it as far as possible the character of a charming pleasantry. Ganya alone drank nothing. Nastasya Filippovna also took a glass and declared that she would drink three that evening. But it was very difficult to make any sense of her strange and sometimes very sharp and unexpected outbursts or of her hysterical aimless laughter, alternating suddenly with silent, even sullen, fits of depression. Some of her guests suspected that she was feverish; at last they became aware that she seemed to be expecting something, that she frequently looked at her watch, and was becoming impatient and preoccupied.

'Are you feeling a little feverish?' asked the sprightly lady.

'Not a little, but very much,' replied Nastasya Filippovna. 'That's why I've wrapped myself up in my cloak.'

She looked, as a matter of fact, much paler, and at times she had to suppress a violent shiver.

They all looked alarmed and stirred uneasily in their seats.

'Shouldn't we allow our hostess to retire?' Totsky said, glancing at General Yepanchin.

'Certainly not! I particularly want you to stay. I need your presence specially to-night,' Nastasya Filippovna suddenly declared, significantly and emphatically.

As almost all her guests knew that a very important decision was to be made that evening, her words seemed to be particularly significant. The general and Totsky exchanged glances again, and Ganya made a convulsive movement.

'It wouldn't be a bad idea to have some parlour games,' said the sprightly lady.

'I know an excellent new parlour game,' Ferdyshchenko exclaimed. 'At any rate, one that was only played once, and even then it was not successful.'

'What is it?' asked the sprightly lady.

'One evening a whole crowd of us were at a party – we'd had a few drinks, it is true – and someone suddenly proposed that each one of us should, without rising from the table, tell some incident from his own life, something he himself honestly believed to be the worst of the bad actions he had ever been responsible for in the whole course of his life, but – and this is the point – he had to tell it candidly and he was not to tell lies.'

'A curious idea,' said the general.

'It couldn't be curiouser, sir, but that's why it is so good.'

'A ridiculous idea,' said Totsky, 'but it's not difficult to understand: it's a special form of bragging.'

'Well, perhaps that was exactly what was wanted, sir.'

'Why,' the sprightly lady observed, 'such a parlour game is more likely to make you cry than laugh.'

'The whole thing is utterly absurd and impossible,' declared Ptitsyn.

'But was it successful?' asked Nastasya Filippovna.

'Well, that's the trouble, you see. It was not. It was a dismal failure. Everyone did, in fact, tell something, and many told the truth, and, you know, some of them simply loved telling it, but afterwards everyone was ashamed: it was too much for them! On the whole, however, it was great fun, of its kind, of course.'

'I think it would really be nice,' observed Nastasya Filippovna, suddenly brightening up. 'Do let's try it, ladies and gentlemen. We really need cheering up, don't we? What about everyone agreeing to tell something – well, of this kind, of his own free will, of course? At any rate, it's awfully original. ...'

'A wonderful idea!' Ferdyshchenko exclaimed. 'The ladies are excused, though. The men will begin. We shall cast lots as we did then. Yes, let's. Anyone who doesn't want to, needn't tell anything, of course, but one would have to be specially unobliging not to. Throw the bits of paper with your names into my hat here and let the prince draw them. It's a simple matter – to tell the worst thing you've done in your life – nothing could be easier, gentlemen! You'll see in a minute! Should anyone forget, I'll undertake to remind him.'

The idea was a rather strange one and hardly anyone liked it. Some frowned, others smiled slyly. Some objected, but not much – General Yepanchin, for instance, who did not wish to contradict Nastasya Filippovna and who did not fail to observe how much this strange idea appealed to her, perhaps just because it was strange and almost impossible. Nastasya Filippovna was always irrepressible and inexorable where her own desires were concerned, and she had to have them satisfied, however capricious and useless they might be. And now, too, she seemed to be nervous and hysterical, laughing convulsively, as though in a fit, especially at Totsky's anxious objections. Her dark eyes glittered, two red spots appeared on her cheeks. The dejected and fastidious air of some of her guests perhaps inflamed her desire to have some fun at their expense even more. Perhaps it was the cynicism and the cruelty of the idea that appealed to her particularly. Some were even convinced that she had a special reason for it. However, they agreed in the end. In any case, it was an interesting, and to many of them a very inviting idea. Ferdyshchenko was more excited than anyone.

'But,' the taciturn young man observed timidly, 'what if it's something one cannot possibly tell – in the presence of ladies?'

'Don't tell it, then,' Ferdyshchenko replied. 'As if there aren't enough bad actions without it. Oh, young man, young man!'

'But I don't know which of my actions is the worst,' the sprightly lady interposed.

'Ladies are exempted from the obligation to tell a story,' repeated Ferdyshchenko. 'But only exempted; anything which they feel inspired to tell will be gratefully acknowledged. Men, however, are exempted only if their objections are strong enough.'

'But how can you prove that I shan't tell lies?' asked Ganya. 'And if I do, then the whole idea of the game falls to the ground. And who won't tell lies? I'm sure everyone will.'

'Ah, but don't you see that's what's so fascinating about it! I mean the sort of lie a man will tell. But you, my dear fellow, have no need to be afraid of telling a lie, for anyone knows your worst action, anyway. But just think, gentlemen,' Ferdyshchenko cried with a sort of inspired air, 'just think with what eyes we shall look upon each other to-morrow, for instance, after we've told our stories!'

'But is it really possible?' Totsky asked with dignity. 'Surely, this is not serious, Nastasya Filippovna?'

'If one is afraid of wolves, one doesn't go into a forest,' Nastasya Filippovna observed with a smile.

'But, look here, Ferdyshchenko, you can't make a parlour game out of this sort of thing, can you?' Totsky went on, growing more and more alarmed. 'I assure you such things are never successful. You said yourself it had been unsuccessful once already.'

'Unsuccessful? Why, last time I told them how I stole three roubles. I made no bones about it.'

'I daresay, but surely you couldn't possibly have told it in such a way as to make it sound like the truth. Mr Ivolgin was quite right in pointing out that one false note and the whole point of the story is lost. Truth, in a case like this, is only possible by accident when the man telling the story is in a specially boastful mood of the worst possible taste, which is unthinkable and highly improper here.'

'But what a subtle man you are, Mr Totsky,' cried Ferdyshchenko. 'Why, I'm surprised at you! You realize, of course, ladies and gentlemen, that by his remark that I couldn't tell the story of my theft so as to make it sound true, Mr Totsky implies in the most subtle way that I couldn't possibly have stolen the money (for it is highly improper to have spoken of it in public), though perhaps he, personally, is absolutely certain that Ferdyshchenko is quite capable of having stolen it. But to business, ladies and gentlemen, to business! The lots are collected, and you, Mr Totsky, have put in yours, too, I see, so that no one has refused. Prince, draw, please!'

Without saying a word, the prince put his hand into the hat and drew the first lot – Ferdyshchenko's, the second – Ptitsyn's, the third – General Yepanchin's, the fourth – Totsky's, the fifth – his own, the sixth – Ganya's, and so on. The ladies had not put in their names.

'Oh dear, what awful luck!' cried Ferdyshchenko. 'And I thought the prince would be first and the general second. But, thank goodness, Ptitsyn comes after me, and I shall be rewarded. Well, ladies and gentlemen, I must of course set a good example. But what grieves me most at this moment is that, being an insignificant person, I'm not remarkable in any way. Even my rank in the service is the lowest imaginable. I mean, who cares a rap whether or not Ferdyshchenko has behaved like a cad? And, besides, which is my worst action? It's an *embarras de richesse*. Unless, of course, I'm going to tell you again the same story about the theft, if only to convince Mr Totsky that it is possible to steal without being a thief.'

'You also convince me, Mr Ferdyshchenko, that it really is possible to experience intense enjoyment in telling the story of one's scabrous actions, even if one is not asked about them. However. ... I'm sorry, Mr Ferdyshchenko.'

'Do start, Ferdyshchenko,' Nastasya Filippovna ordered impatiently and irritably. 'You talk too much and never seem to finish.'

They all noticed that after her recent attack of hysterical laughter, she had suddenly become morose, peevish, and irritable; nevertheless she persisted stubbornly and despotically in carrying out her absurd whim. Mr Totsky was terribly upset. He was also angry with General Yepanchin, who sat over his glass of champagne as though nothing were the matter and was perhaps even thinking of telling some story when his turn came.

14

'I'm not witty, madam; that's why I talk too much,' cried Ferdyshchenko, beginning his story. 'Had I been as witty as Mr Totsky or Mr Ptitsyn, I'd have kept silent this evening like Mr Totsky and Mr Ptitsyn. Prince, let me ask you your opinion. I can't help thinking that there are more thieves in the world than non-thieves and that even the most honest man has stolen something once in his life. That's what I think, which, however, does not lead me to the conclusion that all men are thieves, though I must admit that occasionally I'd have liked very much to think so. What do you think?'

'Oh, what a stupid idea,' said Darya Alexeyevna, the sprightly lady, 'and what nonsense it is! It's impossible that everyone should have stolen something. I've never stolen anything!'

'You have never stolen anything, but what will the prince say? He's blushing all over.'

'I think that what you say is true, only you exaggerate a lot,' said the prince, who really was blushing for some reason.

'And what about you, Prince? Haven't you stolen anything?'

'Good Lord, how ridiculous!' the general interceded for the prince. 'What are you talking about, Ferdyshchenko?'

'You're simply ashamed to tell your story when it comes to the point, so you're trying to drag in the prince because you know he can't defend himself,' Darya Alexeyevna snapped out.

'Ferdyshchenko,' Nastasya Filippovna said sharply and irritably, 'either tell your story or shut up and mind your own business. You exhaust my patience.'

'Presently, ma'am, presently. What I mean is that since the prince has confessed – and I maintain that the prince has as good as confessed – what would anyone else – to mention no names – have said if he had even wanted to tell the truth? As for me, ladies and gentlemen, I have not much to tell: it was very simple, stupid, and nasty. But I assure you I'm no thief. I did steal, but I honestly don't know how. It happened two years ago on a Sunday at the country house of Semyon Ivanovich Ishchenko. He had friends dining with him. After dinner the gentlemen remained sitting over their wine. It occurred to me to ask his daughter Maria, a young girl, to play something on the piano. I walked through the corner room and saw on our hostess's work-table a green three-rouble note. She must have taken it out to pay some bill. There was no one in the room – not a soul. I picked up the note and put it in my pocket. I haven't the faintest idea why I did it. Can't understand what came over me. Only I went quickly back and sat down at the table. I sat there waiting in a state of great agitation and talking without stopping. I told lots of funny stories and laughed, and then went and joined the ladies. About half an hour later they discovered that the money was missing and began questioning the maids. The suspicion fell on Darya, one of the maidservants. I showed great interest and sympathy, and I remember that when Darya went all to pieces, I began persuading her to confess, telling her that I was absolutely sure that her mistress would be kind to her if she confessed her guilt. I said it all aloud, so that all could hear. They all stared at the poor girl, and I must say I experienced an extraordinary sensation of pleasure just because I was preaching to her while the note was in my pocket. I spent those three roubles on drinks in a restaurant that evening. I went in and asked for a bottle of Lafitte. Never before had I asked for a bottle of wine like that without ordering anything else. I wanted to get rid of the money as quickly as possible. Neither at the time nor afterwards did I feel any particular compunction. I should certainly not do it again – you can believe me or not, as you please. Well, that's all.'

'Except, of course, that it isn't the worst of your actions,' said Darya Alexeyevna with disgust.

'It's a psychological case, not an action,' remarked Mr Totsky.

'And the maid?' asked Nastasya Filippovna, concealing her feeling of utter disgust.

'The maid, of course, was dismissed next day. It's a strict household.'

'And you let that happen?'

'That's a good one! You didn't expect me to go back and confess, did you?' chuckled Ferdyshchenko, who looked rather surprised at the highly unpleasant impression his story had made on all.

'What a filthy thing to do!' cried Nastasya Filippovna.

'Oh, so you want a fellow to tell you the worst thing he's done and you'd like it to be brilliant, too! The worst actions are always the filthiest, ma'am – we shall hear it presently from Mr Ptitsyn. Why, do you really think it matters if a man is brilliant outside and wants to show off how virtuous he is because he has a carriage of his own? All sorts of people have carriages of their own. But how did they come by them?'

Ferdyshchenko, in short, could not restrain himself, and suddenly became so incensed that he forgot himself and overstepped the mark; his whole face became distorted. Strange as it may seem, it is very likely that he expected quite a different sort of success for his story. These errors of taste and 'special kind of bragging', as Mr Totsky had put it, happened very frequently with Ferdyshchenko and were entirely in character.

Nastasya Filippovna trembled with rage and stared hard at Ferdyshchenko, who at once took fright and relapsed into silence, almost cold with fear: he had gone too far.

'Hadn't we better call it a day?' Mr Totsky asked craftily.

'It's my turn,' said Ptitsyn firmly, 'but I plead my right to exemption, and I shall not tell my story.'

'You don't want to?' Nastasya Filippovna asked.

'I can't, and, anyway, I consider such parlour games quite impossible.'

'General, I believe it's your turn,' Nastasya Filippovna said, addressing him, 'and if you refuse, too, we shall not be able to go on with the game at all, and I shall be sorry, because I was looking forward to telling a certain incident "from my own life" in conclusion. But I only wanted to do that after you and Mr Totsky, for,' she concluded with a laugh, 'I count on you to give me courage.'

'Oh, if you promise to,' the general cried warmly, 'I'm quite ready to tell you the whole story of my life. I confess, though, that while waiting for my turn, I've already got my story ready.'

'And judging from the way you look, sir,' Ferdyshchenko, who had not yet recovered from his confusion, ventured to observe with a sarcastic smile, 'I think I'm right in concluding that the working out of your little story has given you great literary satisfaction.'

Nastasya Filippovna threw a quick glance at the general and she, too, smiled to herself. But it was obvious that her irritation and depression were increasing every moment. Mr Totsky was more than ever alarmed at her promise to tell an incident from her life.

'Like everyone else, ladies and gentlemen,' began the general, 'I have happened to do things in my life which were not exactly nice, but what is so very strange is that I regard the little incident I'm about to relate to you as the most despicable in all my life. And yet almost thirty-five years have passed since it occurred. But I can never remember it without, as it were, experiencing a twinge of regret in my heart. It was, as a matter of fact, an extremely stupid affair: I was at the time only a second lieutenant and led an extremely dreary army life. Well, you know what a second lieutenant is like: alive and kicking and not a penny to bless himself with. I had a batman at the time, Nikifor his name was, who looked after me awfully well: saved, sewed, scrubbed, and cleaned, and even stole anything he could lay his hands on to augment my scanty belongings. He was a most loyal and honest fellow. I was strict, of course, but just. We happened to be stationed in a small town for some time. I was billeted in a suburb at the house of a widow of a retired sub-lieutenant. The old lady must have been eighty, or, at any rate, not very far off. She lived in a tumbledown, wretched little house and was too poor even to keep a servant. The only interesting thing about her was that at one time she had had a very large family and a great many relations; but some of them had died, others had left the town, and others still had forgotten all about her. Her husband she had buried forty-five years before. A niece of hers had lived with her some years previously, a hunchback, as wicked as a witch, I was told, who had once bitten the old lady's finger. But she, too, had died, so that the old lady had been struggling on for three years all alone. I was awfully bored there; besides, the woman was so brainless that one couldn't get anything out of her. Well, one day she stole a cockerel of mine. The whole thing was never really cleared up, but no one else could have done it. We had a quarrel over the cock, and a rather violent one, too, I'm afraid. As it happened, I was transferred, as soon as I put in an application, to other quarters in a suburb at the other end of the town. This time I was billeted on a merchant with a very large family and a quite enormous beard. I remember him distinctly, just as though it had been yesterday. Nikifor and I were very glad to move, but I left the old lady still feeling indignant with her. Three days later, on my return from drill, Nikifor said to me: "We oughtn't to have left your bowl at our old landlady's, sir. I've nothing to serve soup in." I was, naturally, dumbfounded, and I asked him why on earth he had left my bowl behind. Nikifor looked surprised. He told me that our landlady had refused to give him the bowl when we were leaving because I had broken an earthenware pot of hers and that she was keeping my bowl in exchange for her pot. She maintained that I had suggested it myself. Such meanness on her part naturally made me lose my temper. Young officer that I was, it made my blood boil. I jumped up and rushed off to have it out with her. By the time I arrived at the old lady's house I was, as they say, beside myself. I found her sitting all alone in a corner of the passage, as though to get out of the sun, with her cheek leaning on her hand. I at once, you know, told her what I thought of her. Told her off properly. "You so-and-so," and so on, in the true Russian fashion. Suddenly it struck me that there was something funny about her: she sat there staring at me, her eyes popping out of her head, and never uttering a word. She looked at me in such a funny way, and seemed to be swaying to and fro all the time. Well, I calmed down at last, looked closely at her, and asked her if anything was the matter. Not a word in reply. I stood there wondering what to do: the flies were buzzing, the sun was setting, dead silence. Completely taken aback, I walked out of the house. Before I got back home, I was summoned to the major's, then I had to pay a visit to my company, so that I didn't get home till it was quite dark. Nikifor's first words to me were: "Do you know, sir, our old landlady is dead." "When did she die?" "Why, sir, this evening; an hour and a half ago." Which means that she was dying just when I was swearing at her. This, I tell you, was such an awful shock to me that I couldn't get over it. I began, you know, to brood over it, and even dreamed of it at night. I'm not superstitious, but two days later I went to church to her funeral. Well, to cut a long story short, as time goes on I keep brooding over it more and more. Not that it really worries me, but sometimes the whole thing comes back to me and I don't feel so happy. What was it exactly I did wrong? Well, this is as I saw it at last. To begin with, she was a woman – I mean, a human being, a humane being, as they call it nowadays. She had lived to a great age till, at last, she had outlived her time. Years ago she had had children, a husband, a family, relations, and all this round her was, as it were, full of life and activity, and suddenly – nothing, all gone, and she was left alone like – like some fly, labouring under an immemorial curse. At last, God brought her to the end of the road. At sunset, on a quiet summer evening, my old lady, too, passes away and – I suppose, there is some moral in all this – just at that very moment, instead of, as it were, a farewell tear, a desperate young lieutenant, blustering and arms akimbo, sends her to her eternal rest in a choice selection of Russian swear-words, and all for a lost bowl! I am most certainly to blame, and though, because of the length of years and the change in my character, I have long looked upon my action as that of another man, I still am sorry for it. So much so, indeed, that it seems strange to me, particularly as if I am to blame, it is not my fault entirely: for why should she have taken it into her head to die just at that moment? There is an excuse, of course. I mean that my action was in a way psychological, but I could not rest, all the same, till I endowed, fifteen years ago, two beds for ailing old women in an almshouse so as to make it possible for them to spend the few remaining days of their lives well provided for and in decent surroundings. I think of leaving a sufficient sum of money in my will to make this endowment permanent. Well, ladies and gentlemen, that is all. I have, I repeat, perhaps been guilty of many a blameworthy action in my life, but this incident I quite honestly consider the worst action of all my life.'

'Instead of telling us the worst action of your life, sir, you've told us one of your good actions,' Ferdyshchenko said. 'Cheated Ferdyshchenko, that's what you've done, sir.'

'Indeed, General,' Nastasya Filippovna remarked casually, 'I never imagined you had such a good heart. A pity.'

'A pity? Why?' asked the general with a polite laugh, taking a sip of champagne, not without a touch of self-satisfaction.

But it was now Totsky's turn, and he too had prepared himself. They all guessed that, unlike Ptitsyn, he would not refuse to tell his story and, for a number of reasons, they waited for it with particular interest, at the same time throwing furtive glances at Nastasya Filippovna. Totsky began one of his 'charming stories' in a quiet, suave voice, with an air of extraordinary dignity, which was completely in keeping with his stately appearance. (He was, by the way, a good-looking man of stately appearance, tall, a little bald, a little grey, rather stout, with soft, baggy red cheeks, and artificial teeth. He wore loose clothes and exquisite linen. One could not help admiring his plump white hands. On the index finger of his right hand he wore an expensive diamond ring.) All during his story Nastasya Filippovna was gazing intently at the lace frill of her sleeve, pinching it with two fingers of her left hand, and did not even once glance at the speaker.

'What makes my task so much easier,' Totsky began, 'is the fact that I'm absolutely bound to tell you the worst action of my whole life. In such a case there can, of course, be no question of any hesitation: your conscience and the promptings of your heart will immediately suggest to you what to tell. I'm sorry to say that among the many perhaps thoughtless and frivolous actions of my life there is one the memory of which has left all too painful an impression on my mind. It happened about twenty years ago. I was staying at Platon Ordyntsev's country house at the time. He had just been elected marshal of nobility and had come down with his young wife to spend the Christmas holidays in the country. Mrs Ordyntsev had her birthday just then and two dances had been arranged. At that time *La Dame aux Camélias*, the delightful novel of Dumas *fils*, had been in great vogue and had created quite a sensation in high society, a novel which, in my humble opinion, will never go out of fashion or die. All the provincial ladies were in raptures over it, those at least who had read it. The charm of the story, the originality of treatment of the heroine, the enchanting world, described with such subtlety, and, last but not least, all those fascinating details, scattered throughout the book (for instance, the occasions when nosegays of white and pink camelias are to be used in turn) – in short, all these charming bits of information, and the whole of it taken together – produced almost an upheaval. Camelias became extraordinarily fashionable. Everyone wanted them; everyone tried to get them. Now, I ask you, how many camelias do you think one can get in a provincial district when everyone is demanding them for dances, though there were not many dances? Peter Vorokhovskoy, poor fellow, was desperately in love with Mrs Ordyntsev at the time. I honestly don't know if there was anything between them, I mean to say, whether he could possibly have had any ground for hope. The poor fellow was madly anxious to get some camelias for Mrs Ordyntsev by the night of the ball. Countess Sotsky, a Petersburg lady, who was staying with the Governor's wife, and Sophia Bespalov, we knew would most certainly come with bouquets of white camelias. Mrs Ordyntsev, to create an even bigger effect, expressed the wish for red ones. Poor old Platon was nearly driven to distraction by her, but then, after all, he was her husband. He promised faithfully to get her the flowers, and what do you think happened? On the very eve of the dance, Mrs Mytishchev, Mrs Ordyntsev's worst rival in everything – they were at daggers drawn – snapped up the only available red camelias in the district: well, of course, there was a terrible scene – hysterics, fainting fits. Platon was done for. It was obvious that if at that interesting juncture Peter could procure a bouquet from anywhere, his chances would have greatly improved. A woman's gratitude in an emergency like this knows no limits. He rushed about like mad, but, needless to say, it just couldn't be done. Quite unexpectedly, on the eve of the birthday and dance, at eleven o'clock at night, I ran across him at Mrs Zubkov's, one of Mrs Ordyntsev's neighbours. He looked radiant. "What's the matter?" "I've found it! Eureka!" "My dear fellow, you surprise me! Where? How?" "In Yekshaisk (a little town, about fifteen miles away, not in our district). Trepalov, a merchant, lives there with his old wife, an elderly man with an enormous beard, very wealthy, has canaries instead of children. He and his wife have a passion for flowers, and he's got camelias." "But, my dear fellow, it may not be true, and even if it is, he won't give you them." "I'll go down on my knees and grovel at his feet till he gives me them. I won't go away without." "When are you going?" "At dawn tomorrow, at five o'clock." "Well, good luck!" And, you know, I was really glad for him. I went back to the Ordyntsevs'. It was almost two o'clock, and I just couldn't get it out of my head. I was about to go to bed when suddenly – a most brilliant idea! I made my way at once into the kitchen, roused my coachman Savely, thrust fifteen roubles into his hand, and told him to harness my horses in half an hour. Half an hour later my sledge was at the gate. Mrs Ordyntsev, I was told, had migraine, was running a temperature, and was delirious. Well, I got in and was off. Before five o'clock I was at the inn at Yekshaisk. I waited till daybreak, and soon after six o'clock I was at Trepalov's. I told him what had happened and asked him if he had any camelias. "Please, sir, help me, save me! I'll do anything you ask!" He was a tall, grey-haired, stern old man – a terror! "Sorry," he says, "can't do it!" I fell at his feet – flat on the ground. "Good heavens, sir," he cried, "don't do that!" He looked frightened. "But, sir," I cried, "it's a matter of life and death!" "In that case," he said, "take them by all means, and good luck to you!" And I did! A huge bouquet of red camelias – lovely, wonderful camelias! He had a little hot-house full of them. The poor man sighed. I took out a hundred roubles. "No, sir," he said, "you mustn't insult me like that." "Well, in that case, sir," I said, "will you please give it to your local hospital to provide better meals for the patients?" "That's quite a different matter, sir," he said. "That's good, generous, and pleasing in the eyes of the Lord. I'll give it to the hospital in your name and may the Lord bless you." And, you know, I took a liking to the old man, a true Russian born and bred, as it were, *de la vraie souche*. Elated by my success, I drove straight home, but by a round-about way to avoid meeting Peter. As soon as I arrived I sent the flowers up to Mrs Ordyntsev for her to see as soon as she was awake. You can imagine her delight, her gratitude, her tears of gratitude! Platon, so cut up and almost dead the day before, sobbed on my chest. Alas, husbands have all been like that ever since – the invention of marriage! I won't say more except that poor Peter's chances were completely ruined after that episode. At first I thought that when he found out he would kill me, and indeed I prepared myself to meet him, but what actually happened took even me by surprise: he fainted, was delirious by the evening and in a raging fever by the morning; cried like a child and in convulsions. A month later, as soon as he recovered, he volunteered for the Caucasus. A real romance! It all ended by his being killed in the Crimea. His brother, Stepan Vorokhovskoy, was in command of a regiment at the time and distinguished himself. I must say I had a bad conscience about it for many years afterwards: why and for what reason had I dealt him such a blow? It was not as though I had been in love myself at the time. After all, it was a shabby trick to play on him for the sake of a silly flirtation, for it was nothing more. And, who can tell, if I had not snatched those flowers from under his nose, he might have been alive to-day, been happy, successful with women, and it would never have entered his head to go to fight the Turks.'

Totsky fell silent with the same expression of grave dignity with which he began his tale. It was observed that Nastasya Filippovna's eyes flashed rather peculiarly and that even her lips quivered as Totsky finished. Everyone was watching both of them with curiosity.

'Ferdyshchenko has been cheated, disgracefully cheated! Yes, shamelessly cheated!' Ferdyshchenko cried in a tearful voice, realizing that he could and should put in a word.

'And who told you to be such a ninny?' Darya Alexeyevna (an old and faithful friend and accomplice of Totsky's) snapped out almost triumphantly. 'You'd better take a lesson from clever people!'

'You're right, Mr Totsky,' Nastasya Filippovna said in a casual tone of voice, 'it's a most boring parlour game and we'd better finish it quickly. I'll tell you what I promised and let's have a game of cards.'

'But first of all your promised story!' the general cried warmly and approvingly.

'Prince,' Nastasya Filippovna addressed the prince sharply, sitting up rigidly in her chair, 'my old friends here, the general and Mr Totsky, are very anxious for me to get married. Tell me what you think: should I get married or not? I'll do as you say.'

Totsky turned pale and the general was struck dumb. They all stared and craned their necks. Ganya froze in his seat.

'To – to whom?' asked the prince in a sinking voice.

'To Mr Ivolgin,' Nastasya Filippovna went on in the same sharp, firm, and clear voice.

There followed a few seconds of dead silence; the prince seemed to be making a superhuman effort to speak, but could not utter a word, as though a terrible weight lay on his chest.

'N-no – don't!' he whispered at last, and drew his breath with an effort.

'So be it! Mr Ivolgin,' she addressed Ganya, imperiously and with some solemnity, 'you've heard the prince's decision, haven't you? Well, that's my answer, too, and let that be the end of the matter once and for all!'

'Nastasya Filippovna!' Totsky said in a trembling voice.

'Nastasya Filippovna!' the general said in a persuasive but alarmed voice.

They all stirred uneasily in their seats.

'Why, what's the matter, ladies and gentlemen?' she went on, as though scrutinizing her guests with surprise. 'Why are you so upset? Goodness, just look at your faces!'

'But,' Totsky muttered, falteringly, 'remember you made a promise – er – entirely of your own free will and I – I think you could have been a little more considerate. I'm afraid I – I don't know what to say and – er – I'm rather bewildered, but – er – I mean, now – er – at such a moment and – er – before people and – er – to put an end of so important a matter by such – er – a parlour game – er – I mean, a matter affecting the honour and the heart – er – on which – er – depends – –'

'I don't understand you, Mr Totsky. You really don't know what you are saying. First of all, what do you mean by "before people"? Aren't we in the company of excellent and intimate friends? And why "a parlour game"? I really meant to tell my story and I did tell it: isn't it a good one? And why do you say it isn't serious? Isn't it serious? You heard me say to the prince: "As you say, so it shall be". If he had said "yes", I'd have given my consent at once, but he said "no", and I refused. Isn't that serious? Why, my whole life was at stake. Could there be anything more serious?'

'But the prince – why the prince? And, after all, what does the prince mean to you?' the general muttered, almost unable to restrain his indignation that so offensive an authority should be conferred on the prince.

'The prince means a lot to me, for he is the first man I've ever come across in my life in whom I can believe as a true and loyal friend. He believed in me at first sight, and I believed in him.'

'It only remains for me to thank Nastasya Filippovna for the extraordinary delicacy with which she – er – has treated me,' Ganya said at last in a trembling voice and with twisted lips, turning pale. 'I didn't, of course, expect anything else, but – er – the prince – I mean, in this business the prince – –'

'– is after the seventy-five thousand roubles – is that what you were going to say?' Nastasya Filippovna cut him short sharply. 'Don't deny it! You did mean to say that! I'm sorry, Mr Totsky, but I've quite forgotten to add that you can take your seventy-five thousand back and that I want you to know that I'm setting you free for nothing. Enough! It's time you, too, could breathe freely! Nine years and three months! To-morrow I'm starting a new life, and to-day is my birthday and I'm my own mistress for the first time in my life! General, please take back your pearls, too. Give them to your wife – here they are. And to-morrow I shall leave this flat for good. And there won't be any more parties, ladies and gentlemen!'

Having said this, she suddenly got up, as though wishing to go away.

'Nastasya Filippovna! Nastasya Filippovna!' they all cried.

Everyone was excited, everyone got up from his seat; they all surrounded her, they all listened uneasily to her abrupt, feverish, frenzied words. They all felt that something was wrong: no one could make any sense of it, no one could understand anything. At that moment there was a loud and violent ring at the door, exactly as there had been at Ganya's flat that afternoon.

'Ah-h, that puts the finishing touch to the affair! At last! Half past eleven,' cried Nastasya Filippovna. 'Ladies and gentlemen, please be seated! This puts the finishing touch to the whole affair!'

Having said this, she sat down herself. A strange smile trembled on her lips. She sat in silence, in feverish expectation, looking at the door.

'Rogozhin and his hundred thousand – no doubt about it,' Ptitsyn muttered to himself.

15

Katya, the maid, came in, looking very frightened.

'Goodness knows what's going on there, ma'am. About a dozen men have burst in, all of them drunk. They want to see you. They say it's Rogozhin and that you know all about it, ma'am.'

'That's right, Katya. Show them all in at once.'

'Not all of them, ma'am? Why, ma'am, they're such a disreputable lot – they're awful!'

'Yes, let them all in, all of them, Katya; don't be afraid. Let them all come in, or they'll come in without asking your permission. What a row they're making, just like this afternoon. Ladies and gentlemen,' she turned to her guests, 'you're not offended with me for receiving such company in your presence, are you? I'm very sorry and I apologize, but it cannot be helped, and I'd very, very much like you to be witnesses of this last scene, though, of course, you can please yourselves. ...'

Her guests still looked amazed, and they went on whispering to each other and exchanging glances. But it was perfectly plain that all this had been deliberately arranged beforehand and that it was impossible to make Nastasya Filippovna – though she had, no doubt, taken leave of her senses – change her mind. They were all burning with curiosity. Besides, there was nothing anyone had particularly to be alarmed about. There were only two ladies present: Darya Alexeyevna, a very sprightly lady who had seen and been through a great deal in her life and who was not so easily put out, and the beautiful but silent stranger. But the silent stranger could hardly have understood what it was all about, for she was a German lady who had only recently arrived in Russia and who knew not a word of Russian. Besides, she was apparently as stupid as she was beautiful. She was something of a novelty, and it was considered the done thing to invite her to certain parties in a gorgeous dress, and with her hair done up as though for an exhibition, and let her sit there the whole evening like some charming fashion model, in the same way as people borrow a painting, a vase, a statue, or a fire-screen from their friends for their parties. As for the men, Ptitsyn, for instance, was a close friend of Rogozhin's; Ferdyshchenko was in his element, like a fish in water; Ganya, not yet recovered from his shock, had a vague though irresistible feeling that he simply had to stay on his pillory to the bitter end; the old schoolmaster, who had only a dim notion of what was going on, was almost in tears and literally trembling with fear, having noticed how everyone around him, including Nastasya Filippovna, whom he adored like a grandchild, was in a state of great agitation; but he would rather have died than have deserted her at such a moment. As for Totsky, he could not, of course, afford to compromise himself by such adventures, but he was much too interested in the matter, in spite of the crazy turn it was taking. Besides, Nastasya Filippovna had let drop a few remarks at his expense, and he could not possibly have left without having finally cleared the matter up.

He decided to stay to the end without uttering another word, merely as a spectator, which, of course, was all he could do to preserve his dignity. General Yepanchin alone, deeply hurt as he had been by the unceremonious and contumelious return of his present a few moments earlier, might well be still more offended by all these extraordinary eccentricities or, for instance, by the appearance of Rogozhin; besides, a man of his position had already shown sufficient condescension by agreeing to sit down next to Ptitsyn and Ferdyshchenko; but whatever the power of his passion might make him do, could at last be overcome by his feeling of moral obligation, his sense of duty, of his rank, of his importance and his self-respect in general, so that Rogozhin and his company were in any case quite impossible in his presence.

'I'm sorry, General,' Nastasya Filippovna interposed at once as soon as he turned to her with his explanation, 'I had quite forgotten! But you may be sure I had anticipated your protest. If you really feel offended, I won't insist on keeping you against your will, though I'd very much like to have you, especially, beside me at this moment. In any case, I thank you very much for your friendship and flattering attention, but if you are afraid – –'

'Good Lord, madam,' cried the general in an outburst of chivalrous generosity, 'who are you saying this to? Why, I shall stay at your side out of mere devotion for you and so as to be on the spot if there should be any danger. Besides, I must say I'm rather curious to see what's going to happen. I was merely wondering whether they might ruin the carpets and perhaps smash something. ... And – er – I really don't think you ought to see them at all, you know.'

'Rogozhin in person!' announced Ferdyshchenko.

'What do you think, Totsky?' the general managed to whisper to him hurriedly. 'She hasn't gone off her head, has she? I don't mean it metaphorically, but in a strictly medical sense.'

'I've told you she's always been predisposed to it,' Totsky whispered back slyly.

'And she's feverish, too. ...'

Rogozhin's company was composed of almost the same people as in the afternoon. The only additions to it were a dissolute old man, a former editor of some disreputable and scurrilous rag, who was said to have pawned all his false gold teeth and spent the money on drinks, and a retired sub-lieutenant, who was a most determined rival and competitor by trade and calling of the pugilistic gentleman, and who was a complete stranger to Rogozhin's followers. He had been picked up on the sunny side of Nevsky Avenue, where he had been accosting passers-by in the florid style of Marlinsky and begging them for a few coppers under the artful pretext that in his time he used to give away as much as fifteen roubles to those in need. The two rivals at once took up a hostile attitude towards one another. The pugilist felt affronted at the admission of the 'beggar' and, being taciturn by nature, merely growled like a bear from time to time and regarded with the utmost contempt the efforts of the 'beggar', who appeared to be a man of the world and a diplomatist, to make up to him and curry favour with him. When it came to 'business', the sub-lieutenant looked liked getting what he wanted more by resourcefulness and skill than by force and, besides, he was much shorter than the pugilist. Without actually starting an argument, but bragging quite shamelessly, he had already hinted delicately several times at the superiority of English boxing – in short, he showed himself to be an out-and-out Westerner. For his part, the pugilist merely smiled offensively and contemptuously at the word 'boxing', not deigning to enter into an open discussion, but occasionally displaying, silently and as though by chance, a thoroughly native object – a huge fist, sinewy, knotted, covered with reddish down, and it was quite clear that if this pre-eminently native object came into violent contact with anyone, it would leave nothing but a wet mess behind.

None of them, unlike before, was really 'overcome', thanks to the efforts of Rogozhin, who had kept his visit to Nastasya Filippovna in mind all day long. He himself was nearly sober, though rather dazed with the different sensations he had experienced on that hideous day which was so unlike any other day of his life. One thing only he kept constantly in his mind and in his heart every minute and every instant. For this one thing *alone* he had spent the whole time from five o'clock in the afternoon to eleven at night in a state of great misery and anxiety, negotiating with the Kinders and Biskups, who, too, had nearly gone off their heads rushing about like mad on his behalf. And they actually had succeeded in raising a hundred thousand in cash, a sum Nastasya Filippovna had vaguely and ironically hinted at in passing, and at a rate of interest which Biskup himself was too ashamed to speak to Kinder about above a whisper.

As in the afternoon, Rogozhin walked in front of his followers, who advanced behind him rather timidly though fully conscious of their advantages. They were most afraid of Nastasya Filippovna – goodness only knows why. Some of them even thought that they would all be 'kicked downstairs'. Among these, incidentally, was the dandy and lady-killer Zalyozhnev. But the rest, and most of all the pugilist, regarded Nastasya Filippovna, at heart, though never in words, with the utmost contempt, if not with hatred, and had gone to her as though expecting to take her place by storm. But the magnificence of the first two rooms, the articles they had never seen or heard of, the exquisite furniture and pictures, the enormous statue of Venus – all that inspired them with respect and almost with fear. This did not, of course, prevent them, in spite of their fear, from pushing their way into the drawing-room after Rogozhin with insolent curiosity; but when the pugilist, the 'beggar', and some of the others caught sight of General Yepanchin among the guests, they were so taken aback at first that they actually began slowly to retrace their steps to the other room. Lebedev alone was among those who were more cocksure and courageous, and he walked almost side by side with Rogozhin, having grasped the full significance of one million four hundred thousand in ready money and a hundred thousand in cash there in Rogozhin's hands. It must be observed, however, that all of them, not excluding the expert Lebedev, were a little at a loss about the extent and the limits of their powers and were uncertain whether or not they could do anything they pleased now. At certain moments Lebedev was ready to swear that they could, but at other moments he felt the need of reminding himself uneasily, just in case, of several most encouraging and reassuring clauses of the civil law.

The impression Nastasya Filippovna's drawing-room made on Rogozhin was the opposite of that made on all his followers. The moment the curtain over the door was raised and he caught sight of Nastasya Filippovna, everything else ceased to exist for him, as it had that afternoon, and, indeed, much more so than in the afternoon. He turned pale and stopped dead for a moment; it was easy to see that his heart was beating violently. He gazed uneasily and timidly at Nastasya Filippovna for a few seconds, without taking his eyes off her. Then, suddenly, as though taking leave of his senses and almost staggering, he went up to the table; on the way he stumbled against Ptitsyn's chair and trod with his huge dirty boots on the lace trimmings of the magnificent blue dress of the beautiful and silent German lady; he did not notice it and did not apologize. Having reached the table, he put on it the strange object with which he had entered the drawing-room, holding it before him in both hands. It was a large paper parcel, about six inches thick and eight inches long, wrapped firmly and tightly in a copy of *The Stock Exchange News* and tied round and round and twice across with the sort of string used for tying up sugar loaves. Then he stood still without uttering a word and with drooping hands, as though awaiting his sentence. He wore the same clothes as before, except for a brand-new, bright red-and-green silk scarf, fastened with a huge diamond pin in the shape of a beetle, and a big diamond solitaire on a dirty finger of his right hand. Lebedev stopped short three paces from the table; the rest, as already mentioned, were little by little making their way into the drawing-room. Katya and Pasha, Nastasya Filippovna's maids, had also come in to watch with amazement and horror from behind the raised curtain of the door.

'What's this?' asked Nastasya Filippovna, after having scrutinized Rogozhin intently and curiously, indicating the 'object' with her eyes.

'A hundred thousand!' Rogozhin replied almost in a whisper.

'So he's kept his word after all – what a man! Please, sit down, here, on this chair. I'll tell you something afterwards. Who is with you? The same company you had before? Well, let them come in and sit down. They could sit down on the sofa there and on that one over there. And the two arm-chairs there – why, don't they want to?'

And, indeed, some of them were positively overcome with confusion and, withdrawing to the other room, sat down to wait there. But some remained and sat down as they were asked, as far as they could from the table, mostly near the corners of the room, some of them wishing to make themselves as inconspicuous as possible, and others quickly recovering their spirits somewhat as they took their seats further away. Rogozhin, too, sat down on the chair that was indicated to him, but he did not remain sitting long; soon he got up and did not sit down again. Little by little he began to distinguish and scrutinize the guests. Catching sight of Ganya, he smiled spitefully and whispered under his breath: 'Look at him!' He glanced at the general and Totsky without embarrassment and even without any special interest. But when he noticed the prince beside Nastasya Filippovna he was so surprised that he could not take his eyes off him for a long time, as though he were quite unable to explain his presence to himself. He looked as though now and again he really were delirious for several minutes on end. Besides the shocks of that day, he had spent the whole of the previous night in the train and had not slept for almost forty-eight hours.

'This, ladies and gentlemen, is a hundred thousand,' said Nastasya Filippovna, addressing them all with a sort of feverishly impatient defiance. 'Here, in this dirty parcel. This afternoon he screamed like a madman that he'd bring me a hundred thousand to-night, and I've been waiting for him all the time. You see, he made a bid for me: he began with eighteen thousand, then jumped to forty, and after that the hundred thousand here. He has kept his word – I'll say that for him! Goodness, how pale he is! It all happened at Ganya's this afternoon. I went to pay a call on his mother – on my future family, and there his sister shouted in my face: "Won't they turn this shameless creature out?" and she spat in her brother's face. A high-spirited young woman!'

'Nastasya Filippovna!' cried the general reproachfully.

He was beginning to grasp the situation to a certain extent, in his own way.

'Why, what is it, General? Not nice and proper, is it? Don't you think it's time we stopped showing off to one another? If I sat in a box in the French Theatre like the incarnation of some unapproachable dress-circle virtue and shunned – like a wild creature – all those who had been pursuing me for the last five years, looking a picture of proud innocence, it was simply because my foolishness had taken all the life out of me! And now he has come and in your presence put a hundred thousand on the table, and this after my five years of innocence, too, and I'm quite sure he has sledges waiting for me outside. I'm worth a hundred thousand to him! Ganya, darling, I can see you're still angry with me, aren't you? But did you really mean to take me into your family? Me? Rogozhin's slut? What did the prince say just now?'

'I did not say you were Rogozhin's slut – you're not!' the prince managed to say in a trembling voice.

'Nastasya Filippovna, please don't, darling, please don't,' Darya Alexeyevna said suddenly, unable to restrain herself. 'If they've got on your nerves so much, why take any notice of them? And you're not really thinking of going off with a man like that, even if he offers you a hundred thousand, are you? It's true a hundred thousand is not to be sneezed at, but why not take it and send him packing? That's the way to treat them. Oh, if I were you I'd show them all their place. Why take it so seriously?'

Darya Alexeyevna was angry in good earnest. She was a kind-hearted and highly impressionable woman.

'Don't be angry, my dear,' said Nastasya Filippovna, smiling at her. 'I didn't speak to him in anger. I haven't reproached him, have I? I honestly can't understand how I could have been so foolish as to want to enter a decent family. I saw his mother, you know. I kissed her hand. And if I played the fool at your place to-day, Ganya, it was because I quite deliberately wanted to see how far you would go. Well, you did surprise me, you know. I expected a lot, but not that! And how could you really have married me knowing that the general was making me a present of such pearls almost on the eve of our wedding and I was accepting them? And what about Rogozhin? Why, he bid for me in your house in the presence of your mother and sister, and after that you still came here to ask me to marry you and nearly brought your sister with you! Is it really true what Rogozhin said about you? Would you really crawl on all fours to Vassilyevsky Island for three roubles?'

'He would too!' Rogozhin suddenly said quietly, but with an air of the utmost conviction.

'I could understand it if you were starving, but I'm told you're getting a good salary! And in addition to it all, in addition to the disgrace of it, to bring a wife you hate into your house (for you do hate me, I know that)! Yes, now I can very well believe that a man like you would commit a murder for money! For now they're all so obsessed with the lust for gold that they've taken leave of their senses. A mere child, and he's already clamouring to become a money-lender! Or he'll wind some silk thread on his razor to make it fast, and steal behind his best friend and cut his throat like a sheep, as I read recently. Oh, you're a shameless fellow! I'm a shameless creature, but you're much worse! As for the gentleman who told us the story about the flowers, the less said about him the better. ...'

'Is it you, Nastasya Filippovna, is it you?' the general cried, throwing up his hands in genuine distress. 'You, so considerate, with such refined ideas, and now! What language! What expressions!'

'I'm drunk now, General,' Nastasya Filippovna laughed suddenly. 'I want to go and have a good time! To-day's my day, my holiday, my day out! I've been waiting for it a long time. You see this story-teller, Darya Alexeyevna, this *Monsieur aux camélias*, there he sits laughing at us. ...'

'I'm not laughing, Nastasya Filippovna,' Totsky retorted with dignity. 'I'm just listening with the greatest attention.'

'Well, why have I been tormenting him for five years? Why haven't I let him go? Was he worth it? He's no better than he should be. I shouldn't be surprised if he thought that I was to blame for treating him like that. Why, he has given me my education, kept me like a countess, spent thousands, thousands on me, tried to find an honest husband for me in the country, and now dear Ganya here. And what do you think? I haven't lived with him for the last five years, but I have taken his money and thought I was justified! So completely have I lost my head! You say, if I think it's too vile to go with him, take his hundred thousand and send him packing. It's true – it is vile. I could have married long ago, and not a man like Ganya, either, but that also would have been much too vile. And why have I wasted five years of my life just out of spite? You would hardly believe me, but four years ago I did at times wonder whether I shouldn't really marry my Afanasy Totsky. I thought it at the time out of spite: all sorts of ideas came into my head in those days. And I could have made him marry me, you know. He suggested it himself – believe it or not. It's true he was lying; but, then, he is very weak, he can't control himself. But afterwards, thank God, I thought he was not worth such spite. And he became so loathsome to me all at once that even if he had asked me to marry him, I shouldn't have. And to think that I kept this up for five years on end! No, thank you, I'd better walk the streets, for that's where I belong! Either have a good time with Rogozhin or become a washerwoman to-morrow! For, you see, I've nothing of my own. If I go away, I'll let him have it all, leave every rag behind. And who'll take me without anything? Ask Ganya there. Will he? Why, even Ferdyshchenko won't take me!'

'Ferdyshchenko perhaps wouldn't, ma'am,' Ferdyshchenko interrupted. 'I'm a plain man, but the prince will! You sit complaining here, but just have a look at the prince. I've been watching him for some time. ...'

Nastasya Filippovna turned to the prince with curiosity.

'Is it true?' she asked.

'It is,' whispered the prince.

'You'll take me just as I am, without anything?'

'I will, Nastasya Filippovna.'

'Here's something new,' muttered the general. 'I might have expected it.'

The prince bent a mournful, stern, and penetrating gaze on Nastasya Filippovna, who went on scrutinizing him.

'There's another one for you!' she said suddenly, addressing Darya Alexeyevna, 'and he really does it out of the goodness of his heart. I know him. Found a benefactor, I have. Still, perhaps it's true what they say about him, that he isn't *all there*. What are you going to live on if you're really so much in love that you don't mind marrying Rogozhin's slut – you, a prince?'

'I shall be marrying an honest woman, and not Rogozhin's slut,' said the prince.

'Me an honest woman?'

'You.'

'Oh well, you've got that out of – novels! That, my darling Prince, is the sort of thing they believed in the old days. Nowadays the world's grown wiser, and all that's nonsense! And how can you be thinking of marriage when you want a nurse to look after you yourself!'

The prince got up and said in a trembling, timid voice, though at the same time with an air of profound conviction:

'You're quite right, Nastasya Filippovna; I know nothing and I've seen nothing, but I – I think you'll be doing me an honour, and not I you. I'm nothing, but you've suffered and emerged pure out of such a hell, and that is a great deal. What, then, are you ashamed of? And what do you want to go with Rogozhin for? It's a fever. ... You've given back his seventy thousand to Mr Totsky and you say you'll give up everything – everything here. No one here would do that. I – I love you, Nastasya Filippovna. I'm ready to die for you, Nastasya Filippovna. I won't let anyone say a bad word against you, Nastasya Filippovna. ... If we are poor, I shall work, Nastasya Filippovna. ...'

At his last words Ferdyshchenko and Lebedev could be heard sniggering, and even the general cleared his throat with a sort of feeling of great displeasure. Ptitsyn and Totsky could not help smiling, but restrained themselves. The rest just gaped with amazement.

'... But perhaps we shall not be poor, but very rich, Nastasya Filippovna,' the prince went on in the same timid voice. 'I'm afraid I don't know for certain, and I'm sorry I haven't been able to find out anything about it all day. But I received a letter in Switzerland from Moscow, from a certain Mr Salazkin, to say that I might get a very large inheritance. Here's the letter.'

The prince actually took a letter out of his pocket.

'He isn't raving, is he?' muttered the general. 'This is a real madhouse.'

For a moment there was silence.

'Did you say, Prince, the letter was from Salazkin?' asked Ptitsyn. 'He's a very well-known man in his own circle, a well-known solicitor, and if it's really he who wrote to you, you can believe him implicitly. Fortunately, I know his handwriting because I've had business with him recently. If you would let me see the letter, I might be able to tell you something.'

The prince silently held out the letter to him with a shaking hand.

'What's that? What's that?' the general cried, deeply impressed with the news and looking at them all as though he had lost his senses. 'Is it really an inheritance?'

They all fixed their eyes upon Ptitsyn, who was reading the letter. The general curiosity had received a new and powerful impetus. Ferdyshchenko could not keep still; Rogozhin looked on bewildered and kept looking at the prince and Ptitsyn with terrible uneasiness. Darya Alexeyevna seemed unable to bear the suspense much longer. Even Lebedev was unable to restrain himself, came out of his corner, and, craning his neck perilously, began peering over Ptitsyn's shoulder at the letter, with the air of a man who was afraid of getting a sound thrashing there and then for doing so.

16

'It's quite correct,' Ptitsyn announced at last, folding the letter and handing it back to the prince. 'You will receive without any trouble a very large sum of money by the incontestable will of your aunt.'

'Impossible!' cried the general, as though firing off a shot.

They all gaped again.

Ptitsyn explained, addressing himself chiefly to General Yepanchin, that the prince's aunt, whom he had never known personally, had died five months before. She was his mother's eldest sister and the daughter of a Moscow merchant of the third guild by the name of Papushin, who had died bankrupt and in poverty. But Papushin's elder brother, who had also died recently, was a well-known rich merchant. His two sons had both died almost in the same month a year before. The shock of their deaths had affected the old man so much that shortly afterwards he fell ill himself and died. He was a widower and had no direct heirs except the prince's aunt, his niece, a poor woman who had no home of her own. At the time she received the inheritance, she was dying of dropsy, but she had at once taken steps to find the whereabouts of the prince, putting the matter into Salazkin's hands, and had had time to make a will. Neither the prince nor the doctor with whom he lived in Switzerland had apparently thought of waiting for any official notification or of making any inquiries, the prince deciding to set off himself with Salazkin's letter in his pocket.

'I can tell you one thing, though,' concluded Ptitsyn, turning to the prince. 'It's all entirely legal and aboveboard, and everything Salazkin writes to you about the legality and certainty of your case, you can take as so much ready money in your pocket. I congratulate you, Prince. Perhaps you, too, will get a million and a half, and perhaps even more. Papushin was a very rich man.'

'Three cheers for the last surviving Prince Myshkin!' bawled Ferdyshchenko.

'Hurrah!' Lebedev wheezed in a drunken voice.

'And I gave him a loan of twenty-five roubles this morning – the poor fellow, ha, ha, ha! It's fantastic!' cried the general, almost thunderstruck with amazement. 'Well, congratulations, congratulations!' and, rising from his seat, he went up to the prince and embraced him. The others, too, got up from their seats and went up to the prince with their congratulations. Even those who had withdrawn behind the curtain over the door made an appearance in the drawing-room. There was a confused hubbub of talk and exclamations, and there were even demands for champagne: everyone was shoving and bustling about. For a moment they seemed to have forgotten Nastasya Filippovna and that, after all, she was the hostess. But gradually the idea dawned upon them almost at one and the same time that the prince had just made her a proposal of marriage. The whole thing therefore became three times as mad and extraordinary as before. Totsky, profoundly amazed, shrugged his shoulders; he seemed to be the only one to remain sitting, the rest of the company crowding in disorder round the table. They all maintained afterwards that Nastasya Filippovna went mad from that precise moment. She remained sitting and for some time was gazing at everybody with a strange sort of surprised look in her eyes, as though unable to understand and doing her best to grasp what had happened. Then she suddenly turned to the prince and, knitting her brows menacingly, began scrutinizing him intently. But this only lasted a moment. Perhaps it suddenly occurred to her that it was all a joke and a mockery; but the prince's face showed her at once that she was wrong. She pondered, then smiled again vaguely, as though not realizing clearly what she was smiling at.

'Then I really am a princess!' she whispered to herself as though mockingly, and looking up inadvertently at Darya Alexeyevna, she laughed. 'An unexpected ending – I – I did not expect it to end like that. ... But why are you standing, ladies and gentlemen? Please sit down and congratulate me and the prince! I think someone asked for champagne. Ferdyshchenko, please go and tell them to bring it. Katya, Pasha,' she cried, catching sight of her two maids at the door, 'come here. I'm going to be married. Did you hear? To the prince; he has a million and a half – he's Prince Myshkin and he's marrying me!'

'Bless you, darling, it's high time!' cried Darya Alexeyevna, deeply moved by what had happened. 'You mustn't miss a chance like that!'

'Do sit down beside me, Prince,' Nastasya Filippovna went on. 'So. And here they're bringing the champagne. Congratulate us, ladies and gentlemen.'

'Hurrah!' shouted a great number of voices.

Many of them crowded round the champagne, among them almost all Rogozhin's followers. But though they were shouting and, indeed, were ready to shout, many of them, in spite of the strangeness of the circumstances and the surroundings, felt that there had been a change of scene. Others were bewildered and waited mistrustfully. But many whispered to one another that it was a most ordinary affair, that princes married all sorts of women, even girls out of gipsy camps. Rogozhin himself stood and stared, his face screwed up into a fixed and perplexed smile.

'Prince, my dear fellow, pull yourself together!' the general whispered with horror, coming up sideways and pulling the prince by the sleeve.

Nastasya Filippovna noticed it and burst out laughing.

'No, General! I'm a princess myself now. You heard, didn't you? The prince will stand up for me now. Do congratulate me, too, Mr Totsky. I shall now be able to sit down beside your wife everywhere. What do you think? Is it worth while having such a husband? A million and a half, and a prince, and, I'm told, an idiot into the bargain. What could be better? Oh, life is only beginning for me now! You're too late, Rogozhin! Take away your money; I'm marrying the prince and I'm richer than you!'

But Rogozhin had grasped the situation. There was a look of ineffable suffering on his face. He wrung his hands and a groan broke from his breast.

'Give her up!' he shouted to the prince.

The people round them burst out laughing.

'Give her up for a fellow like you?' Darya Alexeyevna cried triumphantly. 'Threw his money down on the table, the oaf did! The prince is marrying her, and you came here to behave like a hooligan!'

'And I'll marry her, too! I'll marry her now, this minute! I'll give her all I have!'

'Well, I never! Listen to the drunken sot from the pub! Why, you ought to be thrown out of here!' Darya Alexeyevna repeated indignantly.

The laughter became louder than ever.

'Do you hear, Prince?' Nastasya Filippovna turned to him. 'That's how this peasant bargains for your bride!'

'He's drunk,' said the prince. 'He loves you very much.'

'And won't you feel ashamed afterwards that your bride almost ran off with Rogozhin?'

'You were in a fever. You still are in a fever. You talk just as though you were delirious.'

'And you won't be ashamed when they tell you afterwards that your wife has been Totsky's mistress?'

'No, I won't. You didn't live with Totsky of your own free will.'

'And you will never reproach me with it?'

'Never.'

'Take care, you can't answer for your whole life!'

'Nastasya Filippovna,' said the prince quietly and as though with compassion, 'I told you just now that I'd consider your consent as an honour and that it was you who were doing me an honour, and not I you. You smiled at those words and I heard them all laughing too. Perhaps I expressed myself funnily and I expect I may have looked funny myself, but I couldn't help feeling that I knew what I was talking about and that I spoke the truth. You were about to ruin yourself just now. You would never have forgiven yourself for it afterwards, for you are not to blame for anything. It's impossible that your life should be utterly ruined. What does it matter that Rogozhin came to you or that Mr Ivolgin tried to deceive you? Why do you keep on harping on it? Few people are capable of doing what you've done. I don't mind saying it to you again. As for your wishing to go off with Rogozhin, you did it when you were too ill to know what you were doing. You're still ill, and you'd better go to bed. You would have become a washerwoman to-morrow – you'd never have stayed with Rogozhin. You're proud, Nastasya Filippovna, but perhaps you're so awfully unhappy that you really think you are yourself to blame. Oh, you must be well looked after, Nastasya Filippovna. I'll look after you. When I saw your portrait this morning, I seemed to have recognized a face I knew well. I felt at once as though you had called me. I – I shall respect you all my life, Nastasya Filippovna,' the prince concluded suddenly, as though recollecting himself, and he blushed as he realized before what sort of people he was saying all this.

Ptitsyn was so overcome by the high moral tone of it all that he bowed his head and stared at the ground. Totsky thought to himself: 'An idiot, but he knows that flattery is the best way of getting what you want: instinct!' The prince also noticed Ganya looking at him from his corner with eyes flashing fire, as though he wished to reduce him to ashes.

'That's a good man!' announced Darya Alexeyevna, deeply touched.

'A cultured man,' the general whispered in an undertone, 'but – doomed!'

Totsky took his hat and prepared to get up, intending to slip away unnoticed. He and the general exchanged glances, deciding to leave together.

'Thank you, Prince,' said Nastasya Filippovna. 'No one has ever spoken to me like this before. They've always been trying to buy me, and no decent man has ever asked me to marry him. Did you hear, sir?' she asked, addressing Totsky. 'What do you make of all the prince said? Why, it's almost indecent, isn't it? Rogozhin, don't be in such a hurry to go. But, I see, you don't intend to go, do you? Perhaps I'll come with you, after all. Where did you mean to take me?'

'To Yekaterinhof,' Lebedev said quickly from his corner, while Rogozhin merely gave a violent start and stared at her as though he could not believe his senses. He looked completely stunned, as though from a violent blow on the head.

'What are you saying, my dear?' cried Darya Alexeyevna in alarm. 'You must be ill. You haven't taken leave of your senses, have you?'

'You didn't really think I'd marry him, did you?' cried Nastasya Filippovna, jumping up from the sofa and bursting out laughing. 'Ruin a babe like that? Why, that's the sort of thing Mr Totsky would do: it's he who's the expert cradle-snatcher! Come along, Rogozhin! Get your money ready! Never mind about wanting to marry me, let's have the money all the same. I may not marry you for all you know. You thought that if you married me you'd keep the money, did you? No fear! I'm a shameless slut myself! I was Totsky's concubine. ... Prince, you ought to marry Aglaya Yepanchin and not Nastasya Filippovna, or else Ferdyshchenko will be pointing the finger of scorn at you! You're not afraid, but I will be afraid of ruining you and of being reproached for it by you afterwards! And as for your saying that I'm doing you an honour, Totsky knows all about that. And you, Ganya darling, have let Aglaya Yepanchin slip through your fingers – do you know that? If you hadn't bargained with her, she'd most certainly have married you! You're all like that: you've only got one choice – to keep company with disreputable or respectable women! Otherwise you will get yourself into an awful muddle. Just look at the general gaping at me with his mouth wide open! ...'

'This is Sodom – Sodom!' the general kept repeating, shrugging his shoulders.

He, too, got up from the sofa; they were all on their feet again. Nastasya Filippovna seemed to be in an absolute frenzy.

'Is it possible?' groaned the prince, wringing his hands.

'Did you think it wasn't? Well, maybe I too am proud, shameless slut though I am! You called me perfection just now – some perfection to go on the streets just to be able to boast of having trampled on a million and a title! What sort of wife should I make you after that? You see, Totsky, I've really flung a million out of the window! How then could you think that I'd be overjoyed to marry darling Ganya for the sake of your seventy-five thousand? You can take back your seventy-five thousand, sir (you didn't go up to a hundred thousand, Rogozhin has outdone you!), and I'm going to console darling Ganya myself. I've got an idea. And now I'm going to have a good time. I'm a street walker, I am! I've spent ten years behind prison bars and now it's my turn to be happy! What are you waiting for, Rogozhin? Come on, let's go!'

'Let's go!' roared Rogozhin, almost beside himself with joy. 'Hey, you there – wine! Ugh! ...'

'Have plenty of wine ready – I feel like drinking. And will there be music?'

'Yes, yes! Don't come near!' Rogozhin bawled in a frenzy, seeing Darya Alexeyevna approaching Nastasya Filippovna. 'She's mine! Everything's mine! My queen! That's the end!'

He was breathless with joy. He kept walking round Nastasya Filippovna, shouting to everybody, 'Don't come near!' His whole company had by now crowded into the drawing-room. Some of them were drinking, others were shouting and laughing. They were all in a most excited and unrestrained state of mind. Ferdyshchenko began trying to attach himself to them. The general and Totsky made another attempt to slip away unobserved. Ganya, too, had his hat in his hand, but he stood still, without uttering a word, as though unable to tear himself away from the scene that unfolded before him.

'Don't come near!' shouted Rogozhin.

'What are you yelling for?' Nastasya Filippovna laughed loudly at him. 'I'm still the mistress here. If I like, I can still kick you out. I haven't taken your money yet – there it is still. Give it to me – the whole bundle! There's a hundred thousand in it, isn't there? Oh, how disgusting! Why, what's the matter, Darya Alexeyevna? You didn't expect me to ruin him, did you?' (She pointed to the prince.) 'It's too soon for him to get married, he needs a nurse himself to look after him. The general will be his nurse – see how he is dancing attendance on him? Look, Prince, your fiancée has taken the money because she's a bad lot, and you wanted to marry her! What are you crying for? Feeling bitter? You should laugh as I do,' went on Nastasya Filippovna, though there were two big tears glistening on her cheeks. 'Put your trust in time – everything will pass! Better change your mind now than later. But why are you all crying? Katya's crying, too! What's the matter, Katya dear? I'm leaving you lots of things – you and Pasha. I've already made all the arrangements. And now good-bye! I made an honest girl like you wait on a depraved woman like me. ... It's better like this, Prince, much better, for you'd have despised me afterwards and we should never have been happy! Don't protest, I don't believe it! And how stupid it would have been! ... No, we'd better part good friends, for, you see, I'm a dreamer myself, and no good would come of it! Haven't I dreamed of you myself? You were quite right, I dreamed of you long ago, when I still lived in the country with him. Five years I lived there all alone. I used to think and dream, think and dream, and always I was imagining someone like you, kind and honest and good and as silly as you, so silly that he would suddenly come and say, "It's not your fault, Nastasya Filippovna, and I adore you!" Yes, I used to spend hours dreaming like that and it nearly drove me crazy. And then that man there would arrive! He used to stay two months a year, dishonour, insult, excite, and deprave me, and then go away, so that I wished a thousand times to drown myself in the pond, but I was a contemptible creature – I had not the courage to do it. ... Well, and now – – Are you ready, Rogozhin?'

'Ready! Don't come near her!'

'Ready!' shouted several voices.

'The sledges are waiting, bells and all!'

Nastasya Filippovna snatched up the bundle of notes.

'Ganya, I've got an idea. I want to reward you, for why should you lose everything? Rogozhin, would he crawl on all fours to Vassilyevsky Island for three roubles?'

'He would too!'

'Well, then, listen, Ganya. I want to see you as you really are for the last time. You've been tormenting me for the last three months. Now it's my turn. You see this bundle of notes? There's a hundred thousand in it. I'm going to throw it now on the fire before all of them – let them all be witnesses! As soon as the fire sets it ablaze, put your hands into the grate, but, mind, take your gloves off first, with your bare hands, and turn up your sleeves, and pull it out of the fire. If you do, the hundred thousand are all yours! You'll only burn your fingers a little, but it's a hundred thousand – think of it! It won't take you long to pull it out. And I'll have a good look at you just as you are when crawling into the fire for my money! All are witnesses that the money will be yours. And if you don't, it'll burn. I won't let anyone touch it. It's my money! I took it for a night with Rogozhin. It is my money, Rogozhin, isn't it?'

'It's yours, my joy! Yours, my queen!'

'Very well, then! Stand back, all of you! I do as I like! Ferdyshchenko, make up the fire!'

'Nastasya Filippovna,' replied Ferdyshchenko, looking stunned, 'I can't do it!'

'Oh-h-h!' cried Nastasya Filippovna, and, seizing the tongs, she raked two smouldering logs together, and as soon as the fire blazed up she threw the bundle of notes on it.

They all gasped loudly; many even crossed themselves.

'She's gone mad – she's gone mad!' they shouted.

'Don't you think we'd – er – we'd better tie her up?' the general whispered to Ptitsyn. 'Or shall we send for – – She's mad, isn't she? Isn't she?'

'N-no, I don't think so,' whispered Ptitsyn, trembling and as white as a sheet, unable to take his eyes off the smouldering bundle of notes. 'Perhaps, she's not as mad as all that.'

'She is mad, isn't she?' the general appealed to Totsky.

'I told you she was a *colourful* woman,' muttered Totsky, who had also gone somewhat pale.

'But, man alive, it's a hundred thousand!'

'Good gracious – good gracious!' people cried on all sides.

They all crowded round the fireplace; they were all pressing forward to see and utter cries of alarm. Some of them even jumped on chairs to look over the heads of those who stood in front of them. Darya Alexeyevna fled to the other room and was whispering something in alarm to Katya and Pasha. The beautiful German woman had run home.

'Madam! Princess! All-powerful one!' Lebedev wailed, crawling on his knees before Nastasya Filippovna and stretching out his arms towards the fireplace. 'A hundred thousand! A hundred thousand! I saw it myself. I saw them wrap it up! Dear, gracious lady, order me to get it out of the fireplace. I'll crawl right into it – I'll put my grey head into the flames! My wife's paralysed, I've thirteen little children – orphans all of them. I buried my father last week – he had starved to death, Nastasya Filippovna!' he wailed, and was about to crawl into the fireplace.

'Back!' cried Nastasya Filippovna, pushing him away. 'Make room all of you! Ganya, what are you standing there for? Don't be ashamed! Go on – it's your chance!'

But Ganya had been through too much that day and evening and he was not prepared for this last and unexpected trial. The crowd parted before him and he remained face to face with Nastasya Filippovna, three paces from her. She was standing close to the fireplace, waiting, her burning eyes fixed intently upon him. Ganya stood silently and meekly before her, in his evening clothes, his gloves and his hat in his hands, with his arms folded, gazing at the fire. An insane smile hovered over his face, white as chalk. It is true he could not take his eyes off the fire and the smouldering bundle of notes, but something new seemed to have risen up in his soul; it was as though he had vowed to endure his ordeal; he did not budge from his place, and after a few moments it became clear to everyone that he would not go after the money, that he had no wish to do so.

'Take care, it'll burn and they'll laugh at you!' Nastasya Filippovna shouted to him. 'Why, you'll hang yourself afterwards – I'm not joking!'

The fire which at first blazed up between the two smouldering brands had died down for a few seconds when the bundle of notes fell and pressed upon it. But a little blue flame still crept from underneath along the corner of the lower log. At last a long, thin tongue of flame licked the bundle and, taking a firm hold, ran upwards along the paper and, suddenly, the whole bundle flared up and a bright flame shot up the chimney. They all gasped.

'Madam!' Lebedev still wailed, trying again to push forward, but Rogozhin dragged him back and pushed him away again.

Rogozhin himself was turned into one motionless stare. He could not tear himself away from Nastasya Filippovna, he fastened his eyes on her, he was in the seventh heaven.

'There's a regular queen for you!' he kept repeating every minute, addressing himself to those who were near him. 'That's the way the likes of us do things!' he kept shouting, beside himself. 'Which of you rogues would think of doing a thing like that – eh?'

The prince looked on, sad and silent.

'I'll put it out with my teeth for just one thousand!' Ferdyshchenko suggested.

'I could do it with my teeth too!' snapped the pugilist from behind in unfeigned despair. 'Damn it, it's burning!' he cried, seeing the flame.

'It's burning – burning!' they all cried in one voice, almost everyone trying to get nearer the fireplace.

'Ganya, don't be a fool! I tell you for the last time!'

'Go on!' roared Ferdyshchenko, rushing up to Ganya in an absolute frenzy and pulling him by the sleeve. 'Go on, you conceited ass! It will burn! Oh, damn the man!'

Ganya pushed Ferdyshchenko violently away, turned round and walked to the door; but before he had time to take two steps, he staggered and crashed to the floor.

'Fainted!' they cried on all sides.

'It will be burnt, madam!' wailed Lebedev.

'It will be burnt for nothing!' they bawled.

'Katya, Pasha, water for him, smelling-salts!' cried Nastasya Filippovna, and seizing the tongs, snatched the money out of the fire.

Nearly the whole of the paper in which the notes had been wrapped was burnt and still smouldering, but it was clear at once that the contents were untouched. The bundle was wrapped round three times in a newspaper and the money was safe. They all heaved a sigh of relief.

'Oh, perhaps just one paltry little thousand has been spoilt, but the rest is safe,' Lebedev said with deep feeling.

'It's all his! The whole bundle is his! Do you hear, ladies and gentlemen?' declared Nastasya Filippovna, laying the bundle near Ganya. 'He didn't do it, after all. Stood his ground! So his vanity is even greater than his lust for money. Never mind, he'll come to. He might have murdered me otherwise – there, he's coming to already. General, Mr Ptitsyn, Darya Alexeyevna, Katya, Pasha, Rogozhin, do you hear? The money is his – Ganya's. I give it to him to do as he likes with as a reward for – well, for anything you please! Tell him that. Let it lie there beside him. Rogozhin, come along! Good-bye, Prince. You're the first human being I've seen! Good-bye, Mr Totsky – *merci!*'

The whole of Rogozhin's gang rushed after Rogozhin and Nastasya Filippovna, shouting and creating an awful din as they passed through the rooms to the front door. In the large drawing-room the maids gave Nastasya Filippovna her fur-coat; the cook Marfa ran in from the kitchen. Nastasya Filippovna kissed them all good-bye.

'You're not leaving us for good, ma'am?' the weeping girls asked, kissing her hands. 'Where will you go? And on your birthday, too! On such a day!'

'I'll go on the streets, Katya. You heard me – that's my proper place, or I'll be a washerwoman! I've had enough of Mr Totsky! Give him my regards, and don't think badly of me. ...'

The prince rushed headlong to the street entrance, where they were all getting into four sledges with bells. The general managed to overtake him on the stairs.

'Good heavens, Prince, be sensible!' he said, catching him by the arm. 'Leave her alone! You see the sort of woman she is! I'm speaking to you as a father. ...'

The prince looked at him, but, without saying a word, broke away and ran downstairs.

At the entrance, from which the sledges had just driven off, the general saw the prince hail a cab, the first that happened to drive past, and shout, 'To Yekaterinhof – follow those sledges!' Then the general's grey stallion drew up and carried him home, full of new hopes and plans, and with the string of pearls, which he had not forgotten to take with him in spite of everything. Among his new plans the alluring figure of Nastasya Filippovna flashed across his mind once or twice. The general sighed.

'A pity! A great pity! A lost woman! A mad woman! Well, it isn't Nastasya Filippovna the prince needs now. ... So after all it's just as well it's turned out as it has.'

The two other guests of Nastasya Filippovna's, who decided to walk part of the way home, delivered themselves of a few highly edifying parting words in a similar vein.

'Do you know, sir,' said Ptitsyn to Totsky, 'this sort of thing, I understand, often happens among the Japanese. A man who's been insulted goes to his adversary and says to him, "You've insulted me, and to pay you back I've come to rip my belly open before your eyes," and, having said that, he really does rip it open before his adversary's eyes and, I daresay, feels highly gratified, as though he had really revenged himself. There are queer types in the world, sir.'

'So you think there's something of the sort here too, do you?' Totsky replied with a smile. 'H'm. You've put it rather cleverly, though, and – er – you've certainly drawn an excellent comparison. But I hope, my dear sir, it hasn't escaped your notice that I did all I could. I can't do the impossible, can I? But you will agree, I hope, that the woman has some excellent qualities – er – some brilliant – er – points. I felt tempted, you know, to call out to her, if, that is, it – er – were at all possible to do so in that bedlam, that she herself was my best reply to all her accusations. Tell me, who would not sometimes be captivated by a woman like that to the point of losing his reason and – er – and all that? Look at that fellow Rogozhin – even he flung a hundred thousand at her feet! No doubt, what happened there to-night was ephemeral, romantic, and improper, but, you must admit, it was colourful and original, too. Dear me, what one might not have made of such a character and with such beauty. But in spite of all my efforts, in spite even of her education – it's all lost! A rough diamond – I've said so a hundred times. ...'

And Mr Totsky fetched a deep sigh.

PART TWO

I

Two days after his strange adventure at Nastasya Filippovna's party, with which we concluded the first part of our story, Prince Myshkin hastened to leave for Moscow to settle the business of his unexpected inheritance. At the time it was said that there were other reasons for his hurried departure; but about this, as well as about the prince's adventures in Moscow and during his absence from Petersburg, we are able to give little information. The prince was away for exactly six months, and even those who had reason to be interested in his fate could find out very little about him during all that time. It is true that certain rumours did reach some of them, though rather infrequently, but they were mostly strange and almost always contradictory. The Yepanchins, of course, took the greatest interest in the prince, though when he went away he had had no time to take leave of them. The general, however, did see him two or three times and they had some serious discussions together. But if Yepanchin saw him, he said nothing about it to his family. Anyway, at first, that is to say, during almost the whole of the first month after the prince's departure, his name was by common consent not mentioned in the Yepanchin household. Mrs Yepanchin alone at the very beginning expressed the opinion that she had been 'cruelly disappointed' in the prince. She added two or three days later rather vaguely and without mentioning the prince's name that 'the chief feature' of her life was her 'continual mistakes' about people. Finally, about a fortnight later, exasperated by something her daughters had done, she summed up the whole situation sententiously in the following words: 'Enough mistakes! We will have no more of them!' In this connexion it is only fair to observe that there was a rather unpleasant atmosphere in the house for some considerable time. There was a feeling of something unsaid, of some depression, tension, and ill-temper in the house; they all wore a frown. The general was busy day and night, engrossed in his business affairs; they had seldom seen him more occupied and active – especially on official business. His wife and daughters hardly ever caught a glimpse of him. As for the Misses Yepanchin, they never of course expressed their opinions aloud. Quite possibly they said very little even among themselves. They were proud and haughty girls, who were sometimes even ashamed to confide their secrets to one another; but they understood each other not only at the first word, but also at the first glance, so that quite often there was no need for them to say much.

One conclusion could have been drawn by an impartial observer, if such a one happened to be on the spot, namely, that judging by the facts mentioned earlier, few as they were, the prince had succeeded in making a considerable impression on the Yepanchin household, though he had only made one appearance there, and that, too, a rather brief one. Perhaps this impression was just the result of simple curiosity, which could be easily explained by some of the prince's eccentric adventures. Be that as it may, the impression remained.

Gradually, even the rumours that had been spread about the town died down. It is true, a story was told of some feeble-minded princeling (no one knew his name for certain) who had suddenly come into an enormous fortune and married a Frenchwoman, a famous can-can dancer from the Château-de-Fleurs in Paris. Others, however, maintained that it was a general who had inherited a fortune and that the man who had married the notorious French can-can dancer was a young Russian merchant, who was immensely rich and who, when drunk at his wedding, burnt in a candle, out of sheer bravado, lottery tickets to the exact value of 700,000 roubles. But all these rumours, too, died down very soon, chiefly as a result of certain circumstances. So, for instance, Rogozhin's entire band, many of whom might have been able to tell something, left in a body, with Rogozhin at the head, for Moscow almost exactly a week after the terrible orgy in the Yekaterinhof pleasure gardens, at which Nastasya Filippovna, too, was present. Someone or other, that is, the very few people who were interested in the affair, learnt, as a result of certain rumours, that the day after the Yekaterinhof orgy Nastasya Filippovna had run off and disappeared, and that, finally, it was found that she had left for Moscow; so that Rogozhin's departure for Moscow, it was believed, was no mere coincidence.

There were also rumours about Gavrila Ivolgin, who, too, was rather notorious in his own circle of friends and acquaintances. But something happened to him which made people quickly lose interest and entirely forget all the unkind stories about him: he fell seriously ill and was unable to go to his office, let alone into society. After a month's illness he recovered, but for some reason resigned his post in the joint-stock company, and his place was taken by another man.

Neither did he make any appearance in General Yepanchin's house, so that the general, too, had to engage another clerk. Ganya's enemies might have concluded that he was so upset by what had happened to him that he was ashamed to go out, but, as a matter of fact, he seemed to be really ill: he sank into a state of morbid depression, he grew thoughtful and irritable. His sister Varya married Ptitsyn that winter. All who knew them attributed the marriage to the fact that Ganya refused to go back to his job and not only ceased supporting his family, but was even in need of assistance himself, and almost of being looked after.

It may be observed in parenthesis that Ganya, too, was never mentioned in the Yepanchin household, as though such a man had never existed in the world, let alone in their house. And yet they learnt (and that very soon) a very remarkable fact about him, namely, that on the fatal night after his unpleasant adventure at Nastasya Filippovna's, Ganya did not go to bed on his return home, but waited with feverish impatience for the prince to come back. The prince, who had gone to Yekaterinhof, returned at six o'clock in the morning. Then Ganya went into his room and put on the table before him the scorched bundle of notes which Nastasya Filippovna had made him a present of when he lay in a faint on the floor. He begged the prince to return the present to Nastasya Filippovna at the first opportunity. When Ganya entered the prince's room he was in a hostile and almost desperate mood, but it seemed that some words were exchanged between them, after which Ganya stayed in the prince's room for two hours, sobbing bitterly all the time. They parted on most friendly terms.

This report, which reached every member of General Yepanchin's family, turned out, as was afterwards confirmed, to be perfectly correct. It is, no doubt, strange that news of that sort should have reached the Yepanchins so quickly; for instance, all that had happened at Nastasya Filippovna's became known at the Yepanchins' almost the next day, and in fairly accurate detail. As for the news about Ganya, it might be assumed that it had been brought by Varya who suddenly began paying visits to the girls, and even became an intimate friend of theirs, much to Mrs Yepanchin's surprise. But though Varya found it necessary for some reason to become such close friends with the Yepanchins, she most certainly would not have talked to them about her brother. For she, too, was rather a proud woman, in her own way, in spite of the fact that she made friends with those who had almost turned her brother out. Though she had been acquainted with the Misses Yepanchin before, she had seen them rarely. Even now she scarcely showed herself in the drawing-room, but went in, or rather slipped in, by the back stairs. Mrs Yepanchin never liked her, neither then nor before, though she had a great respect for her mother. She was surprised and angry, and attributed the friendship with Varya to the caprices and self-will of her daughters, who, she said, thought of nothing else but thwarting her. But Varya went on visiting them for all that, both before and after her marriage.

A month after the prince's departure, Mrs Yepanchin received a letter from old Princess Belokonsky, who had left a fortnight before to stay with her eldest married daughter in Moscow, and this letter produced a marked impression on her. Though she revealed nothing of its contents to her daughters or to her husband, it became evident to the family from many signs that she was somehow particularly excited and even disturbed. She began talking rather strangely to her daughters and all about such extraordinary things; she was clearly anxious to get something off her mind, but for some reason she restrained herself. On the day she received the letter she was very nice to them all, she even kissed Aglaya and Adelaida and apologized to them for something, but what it was they could not make out. She suddenly became indulgent even to her husband, whom she had kept in disgrace for a whole month. Next day, of course, she was terribly angry for her sentimental effusions of the day before and managed to pick a quarrel with all of them before dinner, but towards the evening the weather cleared again. For a whole week, in fact, she continued to be in a fairly serene mood, which had not happened for a long time.

But a week later another letter arrived from Princess Belokonsky, and this time Mrs Yepanchin decided to make a clean breast of it. She declared solemnly that 'the old woman Belokonsky' (she never called the princess anything else when speaking behind her back) gave her very comforting news about that 'eccentric fellow, I mean, the prince, of course'. The old woman had tracked him down in Moscow, made inquiries about him, and found out something very good. The prince had at last been to see her himself, and impressed her tremendously. 'That's quite clear from the fact that she has invited him to visit her every afternoon, from one to two o'clock, and that he goes to see her every day and she has not got tired of him so far,' Mrs Yepanchin concluded, adding the further information that through 'the old woman' the prince had been received in two or three good families. 'It's a good thing that he doesn't sit at home all the time and isn't abashed like a fool.' The girls, who were told all this, could not but notice at once that their mother had for some reason concealed quite a lot of what was in the letter from them. Perhaps they got to know about it from Varya, who could, and of course did, know all Ptitsyn knew about the prince and his stay in Moscow. Ptitsyn, as a matter of fact, was in a position to know more than anyone. But he was an extremely reticent man so far as business matters were concerned, though he did naturally tell Varya about them. Mrs Yepanchin at once disliked Varya more than ever because of it.

But be that as it may, the ice was broken, and it suddenly became possible to speak of the prince aloud. And, besides, it became evident again what an extraordinary impression the prince had left on the Yepanchins and what an exceedingly great interest he had aroused in them. Mrs Yepanchin, indeed, could not help being surprised at the impression made on her daughters by the news from Moscow. And the daughters, too, could not help being surprised at their mother, who had told them solemnly that 'the chief thing in her life' had been her 'continual mistakes' about people, and who was now recommending the prince to the attention of the 'powerful' old Princess Belokonsky in Moscow, a favour it must have taken her a lot of trouble to obtain, for 'the old woman' was notoriously hard to rouse in a case such as this.

As soon as the ice was broken and there was a change in the weather, the general, too, hastened to express his views. It appeared that he had also been greatly interested in the prince. But he merely told them of 'the business aspect of the matter'. It appeared that in the interests of the prince he had made arrangements with two trustworthy and influential persons in Moscow to keep an eye on him and, particularly, on his trustee Salazkin. Everything they had been told about the inheritance, 'that is to say, about the fact of the inheritance', had turned out to be true, but the inheritance itself was not nearly so considerable as had been reported at first. The estate was to some extent in a tangle; there were apparently debts and there were other claimants. The prince, in spite of the sound advice he had received, behaved in a most unbusinesslike manner. 'Of course, may he get what he deserves,' now that 'the ice has been broken', the general was only too glad to say that 'in all sincerity', because, 'though the fellow is *not all there*', he still deserved it. But he had all the same done a lot of stupid things. For instance, when the late merchant's creditors presented their claims, based on doubtful and worthless documents, and some of them, seeing through the prince, had come with no documents at all, what happened? Why, the prince had satisfied nearly all of them, in spite of the representations of his friends that they were all a lot of unimportant people and unreliable creditors who had no legal claims on him. And he had satisfied them simply because it appeared that some of them had really been unfairly treated.

Mrs Yepanchin said that Princess Belokonsky, too, had written something of the sort to her and that it was 'stupid, very stupid – you can't cure a fool,' she added sharply, but it could be seen from her face that she was pleased with what the 'fool' had done. Finally, the general noticed that his wife took an interest in the prince, as though he were her own son, and that she had begun to show particular affection for Aglaya; seeing this, the general assumed a highly business-like air for a time.

All this pleasant atmosphere did not, however, last long. A fortnight later there was again some sudden change. Mrs Yepanchin looked gloomy, and the general, after shrugging his shoulders a few times, again resigned himself to 'icy silence'. What happened was that only a fortnight before he had received some secret information, which, though brief and therefore not altogether clear, was completely reliable. This information was to the effect that Nastasya Filippovna, who had at first disappeared in Moscow and then been found there by Rogozhin, and afterwards had again disappeared and again been found by him, had at last almost promised to marry him. Then, only a fortnight later, the general suddenly received the news that Nastasya Filippovna had run off for the third time almost on the day of her wedding, and this time disappeared somewhere in the provinces, and that Prince Myshkin, too, had in the meantime vanished from Moscow, leaving all his business affairs in the charge of Salazkin. 'Whether he had run away with her or had simply rushed off in search of her is not known, but there's something in it,' the general concluded. Mrs Yepanchin, for her part, had also received some unpleasant news. In the end, two months after the prince's departure, almost every rumour about him had entirely died down, and in the Yepanchin family the 'icy silence' remained definitely unbroken. Varya, however, still visited the girls.

To make an end of all these scraps of news and rumours, one may add that many crucial changes took place in the Yepanchin household towards spring, so that it was not so difficult to forget about the prince, who sent no news of himself and perhaps did not care to do so. During the winter they decided at last to leave for abroad for the summer – Mrs Yepanchin and the daughters, that is. It was, of course, impossible for the general to waste his time on 'frivolous amusements'. This decision was taken as a result of the strong and determined insistence of the young women, who had come to the firm conclusion that their parents did not want to take them abroad because of their constant preoccupation with finding husbands for them and marrying them off. Perhaps their parents, too, had in the end persuaded themselves that husbands could also be found abroad and that a summer's tour abroad would not unsettle anything, but, on the contrary, 'might help things'. Here, by the way, it might be mentioned that the proposed marriage of Totsky and the eldest Miss Yepanchin had not come off and that no formal proposal of marriage had been made. This seemed to have happened somehow of itself, without any long discussions and without any family strife. With the departure of the prince no more had been said about it by either side. This circumstance, too, was partly responsible for the atmosphere of depression in the Yepanchin family, though Mrs Yepanchin had declared at the time that she was so pleased she could have 'crossed herself with both hands'. Although he had been in disgrace and knew that it was his fault entirely, the general sulked for a long time; he was sorry to lose Totsky: 'such a fortune and such a clever chap!' A little later the general learnt that Totsky had been captivated by a French high society woman, a marquise and a *légitimiste*, that they were going to be married and that Totsky would be carried off to Paris, and then to some place in Brittany. 'Oh well,' decided the general, 'the Frenchwoman will be the ruin of him.'

The Yepanchins were making preparations to leave Russia by the summer. Then something suddenly happened which again made them change their plans, and the journey was again postponed, to the great delight of the general and Mrs Yepanchin. A certain Prince Sh. arrived in Petersburg from Moscow, a man well known in society – well known for his excellent qualities. He was one of those men, or rather one of those modern men of action, who are modest and honest, who sincerely and consciously try to be useful, who are always working, and are distinguished by the rare and happy quality of being always able to find work. Without forcing himself on public attention, avoiding the bitter and idle party controversies, and not thrusting himself to the fore, the prince had a most thorough understanding of all that was going on in the world of politics. He had been in the civil service, and had afterwards taken an active part in the work of the rural councils. He was, besides, a useful corresponding member of several Russian learned societies. Together with a friend of his, an engineer, he had collected information and engaged in the preliminary surveys which led to an improved planning of one of the most important of the newly projected railway lines. He was about thirty-five. He belonged to the 'highest society' and was, besides, the owner of a 'good, substantial, and indisputable' fortune, to quote the general, who had met the prince at the office of the count, his superior in the service, in connexion with some rather important business. The prince seemed to take a special interest in Russian 'business men' and never avoided meeting them. It so happened that the prince was also introduced to the general's family and was greatly impressed by Adelaida, the second of the three sisters. Before the spring he proposed to her. Adelaida liked him very much, and so did Mrs Yepanchin. The general was very pleased. The trip abroad was of course put off. The wedding was fixed for the spring.

The trip, though, might still have taken place by the middle or the end of summer, if only in the form of an excursion by Mrs Yepanchin and her two remaining daughters for a month or two as a consolation for the loss of Adelaida. But again something happened. It was at the end of spring (Adelaida's wedding was delayed till the middle of the summer) that Prince Sh. introduced to the Yepanchins a distant relation of his, whom he knew very well, however. This was a certain Yevgeny Pavlovich Radomsky, a young man of twenty-eight, an aide-de-camp of the Emperor, an exceedingly handsome man of 'good family', witty, brilliant, 'modern', 'highly educated', and – quite fabulously wealthy. The general was always careful about the last point. He made inquiries: 'There really seems to be something in it, though, of course, one will have to check it.' This young aide-de-camp with 'a future' was highly recommended by the old Princess Belokonsky from Moscow. There was, however, one rather delicate aspect of his otherwise excellent reputation: he was known to have had several liaisons and, as was credibly asserted, 'conquests' over some unhappy hearts. Having met Aglaya, he became very assiduous in his visits to the Yepanchins. It is true, nothing had been said so far, nor even had any hints been dropped, but it did seem to the parents that there could be no question of any trip abroad that summer. Aglaya herself was perhaps of a different opinion.

All this happened almost before the second appearance on the scene of the hero of our story. By that time, to judge by appearances, poor Prince Myshkin had been completely forgotten in Petersburg. If he had suddenly appeared now among those who had known him, he would have been treated like one who had dropped from the sky. And yet we have still to report one more fact, and so complete our introduction.

After the prince's departure, Kolya Ivolgin at first carried on as before, that is, he went to school, visited his friend Ippolit, looked after the general, and helped Varya in the house, that is to say, ran errands for her. But their lodgers soon disappeared: Ferdyshchenko moved to some other place three days after Nastasya Filippovna's party, and soon every trace of him was lost, so that nothing at all was heard of him; it was said that he was drinking somewhere, but no one could really be sure of it. The prince had gone away to Moscow; there were no more lettings of rooms. Afterwards, when Varya was married, Mrs Ivolgin and Ganya moved with her to Ptitsyn's house in the Izmaylovsky Regiment quarter; as for General Ivolgin, he was almost at the same time overtaken by quite an unexpected misfortune: he was put in the debtors' jail. He was sent there at the instigation of his friend, the captain's widow, for failing to meet the various IOUs to the value of 2,000 roubles which he had given her at various times. All that came as a great shock to him, and the poor general was 'most decidedly the victim of his unbounded faith in human nature'. Having acquired the reassuring habit of signing IOUs and bills of exchange, it never occurred to him that they might have any effect on his life at any time, however remote, thinking always that it didn't *matter*. But it turned out differently. 'How can you trust people after that?' he used to exclaim sorrowfully, sitting over a bottle with his new cronies in the debtors' jail. 'Show your generous confidence in them!' and he went on telling them his stories about the siege of Kars and the soldier who rose from the dead. On the whole, he was perfectly happy. Ptitsyn and Varya used to say that it was the best place for him; Ganya agreed with them entirely. Poor Mrs Ivolgin alone wept bitterly on the quiet (which rather surprised her household) and, though always in poor health, she dragged herself off to visit her husband as often as she could.

But from the time of the general's 'accident', as Kolya put it, and, indeed, ever since his sister's marriage, Kolya had got completely out of hand, so much so that lately he rarely even slept at home. They heard that he had made many new acquaintances and, besides, had become quite well known in the debtors' jail. Mrs Ivolgin could not manage there without him; at home they were no longer even curious to know what he was doing. Varya, who had treated him with such severity before, never bothered him with any questions about his wanderings now; while Ganya, to the amazement of the rest of the family, spoke to him and quite often treated him in a very friendly way, in spite of his recurrent fits of depression; this had never happened before because the twenty-seven-year-old Ganya had naturally never taken any friendly interest in his fifteen-year-old brother. He had treated Kolya callously, had demanded that the family should be severe with him and had constantly threatened to 'box his ears', which drove Kolya to 'the utmost limits of human endurance'. It almost seemed as if Kolya had on occasions become quite indispensable to Ganya. He had been greatly struck by the fact that Ganya had returned the money and for that he was ready to forgive him much.

Three months after the prince's departure the Ivolgin family discovered that Kolya had struck up an acquaintance with the Yepanchins and had been very well received by the young ladies. Varya soon heard of this; Kolya, though, had not been introduced by Varya, but had 'introduced himself'. Gradually the Yepanchins grew very fond of him. At first Mrs Yepanchin was very cross with him, but soon she began to lavish her affection on him 'for his frankness and because he never flattered anyone'. It was quite true that Kolya never flattered anyone: in his relations with them he knew how to assert his absolute independence and make them treat him as an equal, though he did occasionally read books and newspapers to Mrs Yepanchin, but then he always was an obliging boy. Twice, however, he had quarrelled bitterly with Mrs Yepanchin, told her that she was a tyrant and that he would not set his foot in her house again. The first time they quarrelled over 'the woman question' and the second time over the best season of the year for catching siskins. However incredible it might sound, on the third day after their quarrel Mrs Yepanchin sent a note round to him by a servant asking him to come immediately. Kolya did not stand on his dignity and went at once. Aglaya alone for some reason never seemed to like him and treated him in a very haughty manner. It was he, however, who was to give her quite a surprise. One day – it was during the Easter holidays – Kolya, seizing an opportunity when he was alone with her, handed Aglaya a letter, merely saying that he had been asked to give it to her alone. Aglaya gave 'the presumptuous little brat' a withering look, but Kolya went out without waiting to hear what she had to say. She opened the note and read:

> 'Once you honoured me with your confidence. Perhaps you have completely forgotten me now. How is it I am writing to you now? I don't know; but I feel an irresistible desire to remind you of me – you particularly. How many times have I been so much in need of all three of you, but of all three I saw only you. I need you, I need you badly. I have nothing to write to you about myself, nothing to tell you. That is not what I wanted, either. I'd like you to be awfully happy. Are you happy? That was all I wanted to tell you.
>
> Your brother, Pr. L. Myshkin.'

After reading this short and rather incoherent note, Aglaya

suddenly blushed all over and sank into thought. It would be hard to say what she was thinking of. She did ask herself, incidentally, whether she should show the note to anyone. But she felt ashamed, somehow. In the end she threw the letter into the drawer of her table with a strange and ironic smile. Next day she took it out again and put it into a thick and strongly bound volume (she always did this with her papers so that she might find them more quickly if she wanted them). And it was only a week later that she happened to discover what the book was. It was *Don Quixote de la Mancha*. Aglaya burst out laughing – what at, no one knew. Nor is it known whether she showed her acquisition to her sisters.

But when she was reading the letter, she suddenly asked herself why the prince should have chosen as his correspondent that self-opinionated and boastful 'little brat' who – awful thought! – was perhaps his only correspondent in Petersburg. Though with an exceedingly scornful air, she subjected Kolya to a most thorough cross-examination all the same. But the 'little brat' who was always so quick to take offence, took not the slightest notice of her scorn; he explained to her very briefly and rather drily that though he had given the prince his permanent address when he was leaving Petersburg, in case he wanted to write to him, and offered him his services as well, this was the first commission he had received from him and the first letter to him, and to show her that he was speaking the truth, he let her read the letter he had himself received. The letter to Kolya was as follows:

'Dear Kolya,

Be so good as to give the enclosed sealed note to Miss Aglaya Yepanchin. Keep well.

Your loving Pr. L. Myshkin.'

'All the same,' Aglaya said, handing the letter back to Kolya, 'it's ridiculous to trust a silly little boy like you,' and she walked disdainfully away.

This was more than Kolya could bear: he had purposely asked Ganya, without telling him the reason, to let him wear his brand new green scarf for so great an occasion. He was deeply hurt.

2

It was the beginning of June, and for a whole week the weather in Petersburg was particularly fine. The Yepanchins had a luxurious country house in Pavlovsk. Mrs Yepanchin suddenly grew agitated and declared her intention of going there: after only two days of feverish activity they moved to Pavlovsk.

Two or three days after the Yepanchins had left for Pavlovsk, Prince Leo Nikolayevich Myshkin arrived from Moscow by the morning train. No one met him at the station, but as he left the train, the prince suddenly became aware of two strange, burning eyes staring at him from among the crowd of people who came to meet the passengers. When he looked more attentively, he could no longer see anything. Of course he had only imagined that he had seen those eyes, but it left a disagreeable impression. Besides, the prince, as it was, was pensive and sad and seemed to be worried about something.

He took a cab to an hotel not far from Liteyny Avenue. The hotel was not a very good one. The prince took two small, badly furnished, dark rooms; he washed, dressed, asked for nothing, and left hurriedly, as though afraid of being late or not finding someone at home.

If anyone, who had known him on his first arrival in Petersburg six months before, had seen him now, he would have concluded that, if anything, he had changed for the better in appearance. But that was not so. It was only his clothes that were completely different: they were all new, made in Moscow by a good tailor, but even they were not quite right: they were much too fashionable (as clothes made by conscientious but not very talented tailors always are), and, moreover, they were worn by a man who quite obviously took no interest in them, so that anyone who wanted a good laugh would perhaps have found something to smile at if he happened to look intently at the prince. But, then, people will be amused by all sorts of things.

The prince took a cab and drove to the Sands. He soon found the small wooden house he was looking for in one of the streets. To his surprise, it turned out to be a rather attractive-looking house, clean and excellently kept, with a front garden full of flowers. The windows facing the street were open, and he could hear a rather strident voice, talking continuously and almost shouting, just as though someone were reading or even making a speech; from time to time the voice was interrupted by a burst of ringing laughter from several young people. The prince went into the yard, mounted the front steps and asked for Mr Lebedev.

'There he is, sir,' replied the cook who opened the door for him. Her sleeves were rolled up to the elbows, and she pointed to the 'drawing-room'.

The drawing-room had dark-blue wallpaper and was furnished neatly with some pretensions at luxury, that is, with a round table and a sofa, a bronze clock under a glass case, a narrow looking-glass on the wall between the two windows and a small, ancient chandelier with lustres, hanging on a bronze chain from the ceiling. Mr Lebedev himself stood in the middle of the room with his back to the prince. He was in his shirt-sleeves, having discarded his coat because of the summer weather, and, smiting his breast, he mournfully intoned a speech on some subject or other. His audience consisted of a fifteen-year-old boy with a rather cheerful and far from stupid face who held a book in his hands, a young girl of twenty, wearing mourning and holding a baby in her arms, a thirteen-year-old girl, also in mourning, who was laughing loudly with a wide-open mouth and, last but not least, lying on the sofa, a strange-looking young man of twenty, rather handsome, with long, thick black hair, large black eyes, and faint traces of a beard and whiskers on his face. The young man seemed to be frequently interrupting the speechifying Lebedev and arguing with him; and it was this that the rest of the audience was probably laughing at.

'Mr Lebedev, sir – sir! Well, how do you like that? Won't you turn round for a moment? Oh, bother you!'

And the cook gave it up and went away, turning red with anger.

Lebedev turned round and, seeing the prince, stood as though thunderstruck for a few moments, then he rushed up to him with an obsequious smile and stopped dead in his tracks, but not before exclaiming:

'M-most ill-illustrious prince!'

But suddenly, as if still unable to rise to the occasion, he turned round and for no reason at all first pounced on the girl in mourning with the baby in her arms, so that she even recoiled from him in surprise, but leaving her at once, he rushed at the thirteen-year-old girl, who was standing in the doorway of the adjoining room, with the last traces of laughter still trembling on her lips. She was scared by his shout and bolted to the kitchen. Lebedev stamped his feet at her as a further warning, but catching sight of the prince, who looked at him in bewilderment, said in explanation:

'To – er – instil respect, sir, ha, ha, ha!'

'All this is quite unnecessary,' the prince began.

'Wait a moment, sir; I'll be back in a jiffy!'

And Lebedev disappeared quickly from the room. The prince looked with surprise at the girl, the boy, and the young man sprawling on the sofa. They were all laughing. The prince laughed too.

'He's gone to put his frock-coat on,' said the boy.

'I'm awfully sorry,' said the prince, 'I thought – tell me, is he – –'

'Drunk, you think?' a voice called from the sofa. 'Not on your life! Three or four glasses, perhaps – oh, five at most, but with him that's just – moderation!'

The prince turned to the voice from the sofa, but the girl spoke up with a most frank expression on her pretty face.

'He never drinks much in the morning,' she said. 'If you've come to see him on some business, you'd better speak to him now. It's the best time. He's drunk only when he comes back in the evening, though now he usually cries at night and reads us something from the Bible, for, you see, our mother died five weeks ago.'

'I expect he ran away because he did not know how to answer you,' laughed the young man on the sofa. 'I bet you anything you like he's already thinking of cheating you and wondering how to do it.'

'Five weeks – only five weeks,' Lebedev repeated, coming back in his frock-coat, blinking and pulling a handkerchief from his pocket to dry his tears. 'The poor orphans!'

'But why have you put on your tattered old coat?' said the girl. 'Your brand-new coat is hanging behind the door – didn't you see it?'

'Hold your tongue, you busybody! Oh, you!' he cried, stamping his feet at her.

But this time she only laughed.

'Don't try to frighten me. I'm not Tanya. I won't run away. But I daresay you'll waken little Lyuba and send her into convulsions – shouting like that!'

'Don't say that! Touch wood! Touch wood!' Lebedev cried, terribly alarmed of a sudden and, rushing up to the baby asleep in his daughter's arms, he made the sign of the cross over it with a frightened face. 'The Lord save and preserve her! That's my baby daughter, sir,' he turned to the prince, 'my own daughter Lyuba, born in lawful wedlock of my newly deceased wife Yelena, who died in childbirth. And this female dwarf, sir, is my daughter Vera, in mourning. And this – this – oh, this – –'

'Well, go on!' cried the young man. 'Go on, sir, don't look so embarrassed!'

'Sir,' Lebedev cried with a sort of sudden passion, 'have you read in the papers of the murder of the Zhemarin family?'

'I have,' replied the prince with some surprise.

'Well, sir, this is the actual murderer of the Zhemarin family – there he is!'

'What are you saying?' said the prince.

'Metaphorically speaking, of course. He's the future second murderer of the future second Zhemarin family, if there's going to be one. He's getting ready for it.'

They all laughed. It occurred to the prince that Lebedev was perhaps really playing the fool and posturing because, anticipating his questions, he did not know how to answer them and was trying to gain time.

'Conspiring, hatching plots!' cried Lebedev, as though unable to contain himself. 'Now, honestly, sir, can I, have I the right to, recognize such a sharp-tongued fellow, such a strumpet, as it were, and monster as my own nephew, as the only son of my late sister Anisya?'

'Oh, do shut up, you drunkard! Would you believe it, Prince, he's taken it into his head now to start practising law, pleading in the courts, making eloquent speeches, and talking in a high-flown style to his children at home. Made a speech before a county judge five days ago. And who do you think did he undertake to defend? Not the old lady who begged and implored him to take up her case against a scoundrel of a moneylender who had robbed her of five hundred roubles – all she possessed in the world – oh no! It's the moneylender himself he appeared in court for, a certain Seidler, a Jew, because he had promised to give him fifty roubles. ...'

'Fifty roubles if I won the case and only five if I lost it,' Lebedev explained suddenly in quite a different tone of voice, just as though he had never been shouting at all.

'Well, he talked a lot of nonsense, of course, but, after all, things are different now, and they just laughed at him in court. But he was terribly pleased with himself, all the same. You, who are impartial judges, he said, ought to bear in mind that this unhappy old gentleman, deprived of the use of his legs, who earns an honest living by his work, has been robbed of his last crust of bread. Remember the wise words of the lawgiver, Let mercy reign in the courts. And, you know, he keeps repeating his speech to us here every morning, word for word, exactly as he spoke it. It's the fifth time to-day. He was reciting it before your arrival, he is so pleased with it. Full of self-admiration. And he's got someone else to defend. You're Prince

Myshkin, aren't you? Kolya told me about you. He said you were the cleverest man in the world.'

'He's right, he's right!' Lebedev at once put in. 'There isn't anyone cleverer in the world!'

'Well, Uncle, I suppose, is telling a lie. Kolya loves you, but this one here is merely trying to ingratiate himself with you. As for me, I certainly don't intend to flatter you. Make no mistake about that. But, I take it, you're not without commonsense, so won't you judge between him and me? Well' – he addressed his uncle – 'would you like the prince to judge between us? As a matter of fact, Prince, I'm glad you've turned up.'

'I would,' Lebedev cried determinedly, casting an involuntary glance at his audience, which began crowding round him again.

'Why, what is it all about?' said the prince, knitting his brows.

He really did have a headache and, besides, he was getting more and more convinced that Lebedev was deceiving him and was glad to play for time.

'Here's the position. I'm his nephew; he wasn't lying, though he generally is. I haven't finished my course at the university, but I mean to finish it, and I shall insist on doing so, for I have a will of my own. But in the meantime, since I must live somehow or other, I've taken a job on the railways for twenty-five roubles a month. I don't want to deny, moreover, that he has already helped me two or three times. I had twenty roubles and I lost them at cards! Can you believe it, Prince? I was so contemptible, so base that I lost them at cards.'

'To a blackguard – a blackguard who should never have been paid,' cried Lebedev.

'Yes, to a blackguard, but who had to be paid,' the young man went on. 'I'm quite willing to admit that he is a blackguard, and not only because he gave you a beating. He's an army officer, Prince, who has been dismissed the service, a former lieutenant who used to belong to the Rogozhin gang and who teaches boxing. They're roaming about all over the place now that Rogozhin has sent them packing. But the worst of it is that I knew he was a blackguard, a scoundrel, and a petty thief, and yet I sat down to play with him, and when I put down my last rouble (we played "sticks"), I thought to myself, if I lose, I'll go to my uncle and ask him nicely for some money; he won't refuse me. Now, that was a mean trick, a deliberately mean trick!'

'Yes, indeed, that certainly was a deliberately mean trick!' Lebedev repeated.

'Wait a moment; don't crow too soon,' the nephew cried huffily. 'Pleased with yourself, aren't you? I came to him here, Prince, and told him everything. I acted honourably. I did not spare myself. I told him I had behaved disgracefully; everyone here will confirm it. To take up my job on the railway, I simply must get some decent clothes, for I'm walking about in rags. Just look at my boots! I can't possibly appear like that at my job, and if I don't turn up at the proper time, someone else will get the job, and then it's all up with me, for goodness only knows when I shall find another. Now, I'm only asking for fifteen roubles, and I promise never to ask him for money again, and, moreover, I undertake to repay what I owe him to the last penny during the next three months. And I shall keep my promise! I can live on bread and water because I have a will of my own. I shall get seventy-five roubles for the three months. I shall owe him altogether thirty-five roubles, so I shall have enough to pay him back. Let him fix what interest he likes, damn him! Doesn't he know me? Ask him, Prince. Didn't I pay him back before when he lent me money? Why, then, doesn't he want to help me now? He's furious with me because I've paid that lieutenant. There's no other reason! That's the sort of man he is – a dog in the manger!'

'And he won't go away!' cried Lebedev. 'Lives here and won't go away!'

'I've told you I won't go away till you give it me. What are you smiling, at Prince? You don't think I'm right, do you?'

'I'm not smiling, but I don't think you're quite right,' the prince admitted reluctantly.

'Tell me straight that I'm entirely wrong. Don't try to wriggle out of it. Why not *quite* right?'

'If you like, you're entirely wrong.'

'If I like! That's funny. Don't you realize that I'm perfectly well aware that it is unfair to act like this, that the money is his, that it is for him to decide, and that I am merely trying to bully him into giving me the money. But, I'm afraid, Prince, you – er – you don't know life. If you don't teach them a lesson, they'll never mend their ways. They have to be taught a lesson. You see, my conscience is clear. Upon my conscience, he won't lose a penny because of me. I shall repay him with interest. He has got moral satisfaction out of it, too: he has witnessed my humiliation. What more does he want? What's the use of him if he isn't of any use to anybody? Why, what does he do himself? Ask him how he treats other people and how he cheats them. How do you think he bought this house? Why, I bet you anything you like he's already cheated you and is hatching some plan to cheat you again! You smile? You don't believe me?'

'It seems to me this has very little to do with your business,' observed the prince.

'I've been lying on this sofa here for three days now, and you can't imagine the things I've seen!' shouted the young man, without listening. 'Why, he suspects that angel, that young motherless girl, my cousin and his own daughter, and he searches her room for a lover every night. He steals into my room here and looks for something under the sofa. He's gone off his head with suspiciousness. Sees thieves in every corner. Jumps out of his bed every minute at night to see if the windows are properly fastened or if the doors are locked, and to peep into the oven – half a dozen times in the night! Stands up for swindlers in the court, but gets up three times at night to say his prayers – here in the drawing-room – on his knees, banging his forehead on the floor – and who do you think he is praying for? The other night he prayed for the repose of the soul of Countess Du Barry – I heard it with my own ears. Kolya heard it, too. Gone off his head completely.'

'You see – you hear how he reviles me, Prince, don't you?' cried Lebedev, reddening and beside himself in good earnest. 'But he doesn't know that, drunkard, lecher, robber, and villain though I may be, there's one thing that should make up for everything, for I wrapped that sneering fellow in his swaddling clothes when he was a baby, washed him in his bath, and sat up for nights on end without closing my eyes looking after my penniless widowed sister Anisya – I who was as poor as she – when they were both ill, stealing wood from the caretaker downstairs, snapping my fingers to amuse him, on an empty stomach too, and that's the sort of fellow I've reared. Look at him! Laughing at me now! And what business is it of yours if I did cross myself once for the repose of the Du Barry's soul? You see, Prince, three days ago I read her biography for the first time in an encyclopaedia. Do you know what sort of a person the Du Barry was? Tell me, do you?'

'I suppose you're the only man in the world to know it,' the young man muttered sarcastically, though reluctantly.

'She was a countess who, risen from iniquity, ruled liked a queen and whom a great Empress addressed in a letter she wrote in her own hand as *ma cousine*. A cardinal, a papal nuncio, volunteered to put her silk stockings on her bare feet at a *levée du roi* (do you know what a *levée du roi* was?), and, indeed, deemed it an honour – a high and holy personage like that! Do you know that, sir? I can see from your face that you don't. Well, and how did she die? Answer, if you know!'

'Oh, go away! Stop pestering me!'

'This was the way she died. After such great honour, the executioner Samson dragged her, a lady who had ruled the country like an Empress, to the guillotine, innocent as she was, for the amusement of the fisherwomen of Paris, and all the time she did not know what was happening to her – so terrified was she! Seeing that he was bending her neck down under the knife and kicking her from behind – the people laughing all the time – she began screaming: '*Encore un moment, monsieur le bourreau, encore un moment!*' which means, 'Wait one more moment, Mr *bourreau*, just one little moment!' And for that little moment the Lord will perhaps pardon her, for a greater *misère* than that it is impossible to imagine for a human soul. Do you know what the word *misère* means? Well, that's precisely what *misère* is. When I read about that cry of the countess for one little moment, I felt as though my heart had been caught in a vice. And what does it matter to you, miserable worm that you are, that before going to bed I took it into my head to mention her, great sinner that she was, in my prayers? Why, perhaps I mentioned her just because no one has ever crossed himself for her sake or even thought of doing so. I daresay she'll feel happy in the next world to know that there's a sinner like her who has offered up at least one prayer for her on earth. What are you laughing at? You don't believe, atheist. But how do you know? Besides, you told a lie, if you did overhear me: I did not pray for the Du Barry only. What I said was: "Give rest, O Lord, to the soul of the great sinner Du Barry and all like her," and that's something quite different; for there are many such great sinners and living examples of the mutability of fortune, who have gone through great tribulations and who are now in great agony there, moaning and waiting. And I prayed for you too then, and people like you, impudent bullies like you, as you ought to know if you really troubled to listen how I prayed. ...'

'All right, all right; that's enough; pray for whom you like, damn you, and stop shouting like that!' the nephew interrupted, annoyed. 'You see, Prince, he's a well-read chap – didn't you know that?' he added with a sort of awkward grin. 'He's always reading such books and memoirs now.'

'Your uncle, anyway, isn't – er – a heartless man,' the prince observed reluctantly.

He was beginning to feel an intense dislike of the young man.

'For God's sake don't praise him too much! See he's already put his hand on his heart and pursed his lips – his mouth watering for more. I daresay he isn't heartless, but he's a damned scoundrel – that's the trouble. And he drinks, too; has gone all to pieces, like any other man who's been drinking regularly for several years. He's fond of his children, I grant you that. He respected my late aunt. He's fond of me, too, and has left me something in his will. He has, you know.'

'N-nothing! I shall leave you nothing!' cried Lebedev fiercely.

'Listen, Lebedev,' the prince said firmly, turning away from the young man. 'I know from experience that you can be business-like when you choose. I'm afraid I haven't much time and if you – I'm sorry, what's your name and patronymic? I've forgotten.'

'T-timofey.'

'And?'

'Lukyanovich.'

Everyone in the room laughed again.

'A lie!' cried the nephew. 'Couldn't help telling a lie, could you? You see, Prince, he's not called Timofey Lukyanovich at all, but Lukyan Timofeyevich. Why, tell me, did you have to lie? What does it matter to you whether your name is Lukyan or Timofey? And what difference does it make to the prince? He tells lies simply from habit, I assure you.'

'Is it true?' the prince asked impatiently.

'Yes, sir, my name really is Lukyan Timofeyevich,' Lebedev admitted, looking sheepish, humbly dropping his eyes and again putting his hand on his heart.

'But, good heavens, why did you say that?'

'From self-abasement,' murmured Lebedev, lowering his head still more humbly.

'Dear me, what self-abasement is this! If only I knew where to find Kolya now,' said the prince and turned to go away.

'I'll tell you where Kolya is,' the young man volunteered again.

'You mustn't!' Lebedev cried, thrown into violent agitation.

'Kolya spent the night here, but in the morning he went to look for his general, whom you, Prince, have bought out of jail goodness only knows why. The general promised yesterday to come and spend the night here, but he hasn't come. Most probably he spent the night at the hotel "The Scales", which isn't far from here. Kolya is therefore either there or in Pavlovsk at the Yepanchins'. He had the money and he intended to go there yesterday. So he's probably at "The Scales" or in Pavlovsk.'

'In Pavlovsk – in Pavlovsk!' cried Lebedev. 'And we'll go this way, sir, this way, into the garden and – er – have some coffee.'

And Lebedev dragged the prince away by the arm. They went out of the room, crossed the little courtyard, and went through a gate.

There they really found themselves in a very small and very charming little garden, in which all the trees, thanks to the fine weather, were already in leaf. Lebedev made the prince sit down on a green wooden seat before a green table fixed in the ground, and took a seat facing him. A minute later coffee really was served. The prince did not refuse it. Lebedev went on peering eagerly and obsequiously into his eyes.

'I didn't know you had such a big household,' said the prince with the air of a man who was thinking of something quite different.

'Or-orphans,' Lebedev began, wincing, but he stopped short.

The prince was looking absently before him and had, no doubt, forgotten his remark. Another minute passed; Lebedev watched and waited.

'Well?' said the prince, as though coming to. 'Oh yes, you know yourself, of course, what our business is, Lebedev. I've come in answer to your letter. Out with it.'

Lebedev looked embarrassed, was about to say something, but only stuttered: he never uttered a word. The prince waited and then smiled sadly.

'I think I understand you perfectly, Lebedev. You did not expect to see me, did you? You never expected me to come back from the country at your first message, and you only wrote to me to relieve your conscience. Well, I have come. Now, don't try to deceive me, please. Do stop trying to serve two masters. Rogozhin has been here for three weeks. I know everything. Have you succeeded in selling her to him as you did last time? Tell me the truth.'

'The monster found out himself – himself.'

'Don't call him names. He has treated you badly, of course. ...'

'He thrashed me – thrashed me!' Lebedev cried vehemently. 'He set his dog on me in Moscow. Chased me all along the street with his borzoi bitch. A horrible bitch!'

'You take me for a child, Lebedev. Tell me, has she really left him now, in Moscow, I mean?'

'Yes, really, really, and again on the day of their wedding. He was counting the minutes, and she came straight to me in Petersburg. "Save me, Lukyan, protect me, and don't tell the prince. ..." She's more afraid of you than of him, Prince, and there is something very deep here!'

And Lebedev put his finger slyly to his forehead.

'And now you've brought them together again, haven't you?'

'Most illustrious Prince, how could I – how could I prevent it?'

'All right; that's all I wanted to know. I shall find out everything myself. Only, please, tell me where she is now. At his place?'

'Good Lord, no! She still lives by herself. I'm free, she says. And, you know, Prince, she strongly insists on that. I'm still absolutely free, she says! She's still living in the Petersburg suburb at my sister-in-law's, as I wrote to you.'

'Is she there now?'

'Yes, unless she's gone to Pavlovsk, the weather being so fine, and is staying with Darya Alexeyevna at her country cottage. I'm absolutely free, she says. Only yesterday she was boasting to Kolya about her freedom. A bad sign, sir!'

And Lebedev grinned.

'Does Kolya see her often?'

'The boy's thoughtless and unpredictable, but not secretive.'

'Is it long since you saw her?'

'I see her every day, every day.'

'You were there yesterday, then?'

'No, sir. Three days ago.'

'What a pity you've been drinking, Lebedev, or I'd have asked you something.'

'I'm not a bit drunk, not a bit.'

Lebedev stared at him intently.

'Tell me, how did you leave her?'

'On her knees. ...'

'On her knees?'

'I mean, she seemed to be looking for something, just as if she had lost something. She loathes the very thought of her forthcoming marriage and looks upon it as an insult. Of *him* she thinks no more than of an orange peel, or rather more than that, I mean, with fear and trembling. She won't have anyone talk about him, and they only see each other when it is absolutely necessary and – he takes it very much to heart! But she'll have to go through with it! Yes, sir. She's restless, sarcastic, double-faced, short-tempered. ...'

'Double-faced and short-tempered?'

'Short-tempered, for she nearly seized me by the hair last time because of something I said. I was quoting the Apocalypse to her.'

'What do you mean?' the prince asked, thinking that he had misheard him.

'I was reading the Apocalypse. She's a lady with a restless imagination, ha, ha! And I've come to the conclusion, sir, that she likes serious subjects, however irrelevant. Considers it a sign of respect for her. You see, sir, I'm rather good at the interpretation of the Apocalypse, and I have been interpreting it for the last fifteen years. She agreed with me that we've arrived at the time of the third horse, the black one, and of the rider who has a pair of balances in his hand, for everything in our present age is weighed in the scales and everything is settled by agreement, and all people are merely seeking their rights: "A measure of wheat for a penny, and three measures of barley for a penny." And, on top of it, they still want to preserve a free spirit and a pure heart and a sound body and all the gifts of the Lord. But they won't preserve them by seeking their rights alone, and there will therefore follow the pale horse and he whose name was Death, and after whom Hell followed. ... It is this we discuss when we meet, and I'm afraid, sir, it has had a great effect on her.'

'Do you believe it yourself?' asked the prince, casting a strange glance at Lebedev.

'I believe it and interpret it so. For I am poor and naked and an atom in the vortex of men. And who respects Lebedev? Everyone does his best to mock him and everyone all but greets him with a kick. But here, in this interpretation of mine, I'm equal to the greatest in the land. For it's intellect, sir! Intellect! And the great man himself, sir, trembled before me – er – sitting in his arm-chair, as he grasped it with his intellect. Two years ago, sir, just before Easter, his excellency, Nil Alexeyevich, in whose department I served at the time, sent Peter Zakharych specially to summon me from the office to his study and, when left alone with me, asked, "Is it true that you are the expounder of Antichrist?" "I am," I said, without any attempt at concealment, and I expounded and laid it bare before him and did not soften the horror, but deliberately increased it as I unrolled the allegorical scroll before him and computed the figures. At first he smiled, but when I came to the figures and the correspondences, he began trembling and asked me to close the book and go away. He promoted me at Easter, but a week later he gave up his soul to the Lord.'

'You don't mean it, Lebedev, do you?'

'Yes, indeed. Fell out of his carriage after dinner, knocking his head against a post, and gave up the ghost there and then, like a baby, like a dear little baby. Seventy-three years of age he was, according to the civil list. Red face, white hair, sprinkled all over with scent, and always smiling. Yes, sir, always smiling he was, like a baby. It was just then that Peter Zakharych remembered it: "You predicted it," he said.'

The prince began getting up. Lebedev looked surprised and, indeed, flabbergasted that the prince should be getting up so soon.

'You've lost interest in things, I see, sir,' he ventured to observe obsequiously.

'I really don't feel quite well,' replied the prince with a frown. 'My head aches. From the journey, I suppose.'

'What you want is country air, sir,' Lebedev suggested timidly.

The prince stood lost in thought.

'I'm going to the country myself, sir, in another three days. Taking all my family with me. A change of air will do the baby a world of good, and meanwhile I'll have the house done up. We're going to Pavlovsk too.'

'You're going to Pavlovsk too?' asked the prince suddenly. 'Why, does everybody here go to Pavlovsk? And did you say you had a house of your own there?'

'No, sir, not my own. Mr Ptitsyn has let me have one of the houses he's got there. Bought them cheap, he did. You see, sir, the reason why everyone goes to Pavlovsk is because it's so very nice there – high up, green, cheap, fashionable, and musical. However, I shall be occupying only one of the wings. The house itself – –'

'– is let?'

'N-no, sir, not quite.'

'Let it to me,' the prince proposed suddenly.

That seemed to be what Lebedev had been leading up to. The idea had occurred to him three minutes earlier. And yet he had no need of a tenant; indeed, he had already found someone who had told him that he might take the house. Lebedev knew for a fact that it was no longer a question of 'might', but that he was quite certain to take it. But it suddenly occurred to him that it would be much more worth his while letting the house to the prince, taking advantage of the fact that the previous tenant had not clinched the deal. 'A regular clash of contending interests and an entirely new turn of events,' he thought, as the consequences of the prince's offer suddenly dawned on him. He accepted it almost with enthusiasm, and when asked about terms, dismissed the question with a wave of the hands.

'Very well, just as you like. I'll make inquiries. You won't lose anything by it.'

They were both going out of the garden at that moment.

'If you like I – er – I could tell you something very interesting, highly honoured Prince, something that has a direct bearing on the same subject,' murmured Lebedev, so overjoyed that he was almost cutting capers as he walked beside the prince.

The prince stopped.

'Darya Alexeyevna has a house in Pavlovsk too, sir.'

'Oh?'

'And a certain person is a great friend of hers and seemingly intends to visit her frequently in Pavlovsk. With an object.'

'Oh?'

'Aglaya Yepanchin – –'

'Oh, that'll do, Lebedev!' the prince interrupted with a sort of disagreeable sensation, as though he had been touched on a tender spot. 'All that – it's not at all what you think. You'd better tell me when you're moving. The sooner the better, so far as I'm concerned, for I'm staying at an hotel.'

As they talked, they left the garden and, without going into the house, crossed the yard and reached the gate.

'That's all right, then,' Lebedev at last came out with a suggestion. 'You could come straight here from your hotel to-day, sir, and we could all leave for Pavlovsk together the day after to-morrow.'

'I'll see,' said the prince, rapt in thought, and went out of the gate.

Lebedev followed him with his eyes. He was struck by the prince's sudden absent-mindedness. As he went out, he had forgotten even to say good-bye, he did not even nod, which did not square with what Lebedev knew of the prince's courtesy and considerateness.

3

It was nearly twelve o'clock. The prince knew that at the Yepanchins' town house he would find only the general, who might be there attending to his business affairs, though even that was not certain. It occurred to him that the general would quite likely take him to Pavlovsk at once, and he was most anxious to pay one call before that. At the risk of missing General Yepanchin and putting off his trip to Pavlovsk till the next day, the prince decided to go and look for the house which he wished so much to visit.

The visit was, however, risky for him in some respects. He hesitated and could not make up his mind. He knew that the house was in Gorokhovaya Street, not far from Sadovaya Street, and he decided to go there in the hope that by the time he got to the place he would at last have made up his mind.

As he came to the crossroads where the two streets met, he could not help being surprised at his own violent agitation; he never expected his heart to pound so painfully. One house, no doubt because of its peculiar appearance, began to attract his attention from a distance, and the prince remembered afterwards saying to himself: 'That must certainly be the house.' He drew near to verify his conjecture with a feeling of immense curiosity; he felt that for some reason he would be particularly upset if he had guessed right. It was a large, gloomy, three-storied house, of a dirty green colour and of no particular architectural interest. Some, though very few, houses of this kind, built at the end of the last century, are still standing almost unchanged in those streets of Petersburg (where everything changes so quickly). They are built solidly, with thick walls and very few windows; on the ground floor the windows sometimes even have iron bars. The ground floor is mostly occupied by a money-changer's shop. The owner of it, a member of the sect of castrates, usually has a flat upstairs. Without as well as within, the house looks drab and inhospitable, somehow; everything in it seems to be hiding away in some dark corner, and it is difficult to explain why one should get such an impression from the mere exterior of the house. Architectural combinations of lines have, of course, a secret of their own. These houses are inhabited almost exclusively by tradespeople. On approaching the gate and looking up at the inscription on it, the prince read: 'The house of the Hereditary Member of the Order of Citizenship Rogozhin'.

Hesitating no longer, he opened the glass door, which slammed noisily behind him, and began mounting the main staircase to the first floor. It was a dark stone staircase of rough workmanship, and the walls were painted a dull red. He knew that Rogozhin with his mother and brother occupied the whole of the first floor of this gloomy house. The servant who opened the door to the prince asked him in and, without bothering to announce him, led him a long way; they passed through a large drawing-room with walls of 'imitation marble', a parquet floor, and furniture of the 'twenties, coarse and heavy; they passed through a number of tiny rooms, turning again and again round corners, going up two or three steps and going down as many, till at last the servant knocked at a door. The door was opened by Parfyon Rogozhin himself; seeing the prince, he turned so pale and was so stupefied that for a time he seemed to be turned to a stone image, staring with fixed and frightened eyes and his lips twisted into a curious smile of utter bewilderment, as though the prince's visit struck him as something inconceivable and almost miraculous. Though the prince expected something of the kind, he could not help being surprised.

'I'm sorry, Parfyon,' he said at last, looking embarrassed; 'perhaps

I haven't come at the right moment. I can go away, if you like.'

'No, no!' Parfyon cried, recollecting himself. 'Do come in. I'm glad to see you.'

They spoke to each other like two old friends. In Moscow they had met frequently and spent a great deal of time together, and there were moments during their meetings which had left an indelible impression upon their hearts. Now, however, they had not seen each other for three months.

Rogozhin's face was still pale and twitched spasmodically. Though he had invited his visitor in, his extraordinary embarrassment continued. While he led the prince to an arm-chair to make him sit down at the table, the latter happened to turn round to him and was startled by his queer, dull gaze. Something seemed to transfix the prince and at the same time he remembered something sombre and painful that had happened not so long before. Without sitting down, and standing motionless for some time, he looked Rogozhin straight in the eyes, which at the first moment seemed to flash more vindictively. At last Rogozhin smiled, but he still looked lost and a little bewildered.

'What are you staring at me like that for?' he muttered. 'Sit down!'

The prince sat down.

'Parfyon,' he said, 'tell me frankly. Did you know I was coming to Petersburg to-day?'

'I thought you might come and, as you see, I wasn't mistaken,' he added, smiling sardonically. 'But how was I to know you'd come to-day?'

The note of harsh abruptness and the strange irritability of the question surprised the prince even more.

'Even if you'd known I'd come to-day, why be so irritated about it?' the prince asked gently, in confusion.

'But why do you ask?'

'Because when I got out of the train this morning, I saw a pair of eyes that looked at me just as you did a moment ago from behind.'

'Did you? Whose eyes were they?' Rogozhin muttered suspiciously.

The prince thought that he gave a start.

'I don't know. I saw them in a crowd. I think I must have imagined it all. I'm beginning to see things. I'm afraid, old man, I feel almost as I did five years ago when I still used to have my fits.'

'Well,' muttered Rogozhin, 'perhaps you did imagine it. I don't know.'

The affectionate smile on his face did not become him at all at that moment, as though something in that smile was broken and he could not glue it together, however much he tried.

'Well, so you're going abroad again, are you?' he asked, adding suddenly, 'Remember how we travelled in the same carriage from Pskov last autumn – me coming here and you – you wearing that cloak and gaiters – remember?'

And Rogozhin laughed suddenly, this time with a sort of undisguised malice, as though glad that he could give vent to it in some way.

'Are you settled here for good?' asked the prince, examining the study.

'Yes, I'm at home. Where else should I be?'

'It's ages since we met. I've heard things about you which are quite unlike you.'

'Does it matter what people say?' Rogozhin remarked drily.

'But you have got rid of all your gang. You're living in your old home and you're not playing the fool any more. Well, that's all to the good. Is it your house, or does it belong to all of you?'

'The house is my mother's. Her rooms are just across the corridor.'

'And where does your brother live?'

'Simon lives in the wing.'

'Is he married?'

'He's a widower. What do you want to know that for?'

The prince looked at him and made no answer; he sank into thought suddenly and did not seem to have heard the question. Rogozhin did not insist and waited. There was a minute's silence.

'I guessed it was your house a hundred yards off,' said the prince.

'Why?'

'I've no idea. Your house has the appearance of the whole of your family and the whole of your Rogozhin way of life. But if you asked me why I thought so, I shouldn't be able to tell you. It's all nonsense, of course. It frightens me to think that it should bother me so much. You see, before it would never have occurred to me that you lived in such a house, but the moment I saw it, I thought at once, "Why, that's exactly the sort of house he would have!" '

'Did you now?' Rogozhin smiled vaguely, not quite grasping the meaning of the prince's obscure remark. 'This house was built by my grand-dad,' he observed. 'The castrates always lived in it, the Khludyakovs, and they still do.'

'It's so dark here,' the prince said, looking round the study. 'You dwell in darkness,' he added.

It was a large room, lofty, rather dark and cluttered up with furniture of all sorts – mostly with large office desks, bureaux, cupboards, in which ledgers and all sorts of papers were kept. A wide sofa covered in red morocco evidently served Rogozhin for a bed. The prince noticed two or three books on the table at which Rogozhin had made him sit down; one of them, Solovyov's 'History', was open and there was a book-mark in it. A few oil-paintings in tarnished gilt frames hung on the walls. They were dark and grimy and it was difficult to make out what they represented. One full-length portrait attracted the prince's attention: it was of a fifty-year-old man in a very long frock-coat of European cut, with two medals round his neck. He had a very scanty short beard, a yellow, wrinkled face, and a pair of suspicious, secretive and mournful eyes.

'This isn't your father, is it?'

'It's him all right,' Rogozhin replied with an unpleasant grin, as though expecting to hear at once some unceremonious joke at his father's expense.

'He wasn't an Old Believer, was he?'

'No, he went to church, but it's quite true he used to say the old faith was nearer the truth. Had a great respect for the castrates, too, he had. This was his office. Why did you ask whether he was an Old Believer?'

'Will you be married from here?'

'Y-yes,' replied Rogozhin, almost with a start at the unexpected question.

'Will it be soon?'

'You know it don't depend on me, don't you?'

'Parfyon, I'm not your enemy and I don't intend to interfere with you in any way. I tell you this now as I told you once before on a similar occasion. When you were making your arrangements for your wedding in Moscow, I did not interfere with them. You know that. The first time *she* came running to me herself, almost on the day of the wedding, imploring me to 'save' her from you. I'm repeating her own words. Afterwards she ran away from me, too. You found her again and you were going to marry her again, and now I'm told she ran away from you here. Is this true? Lebedev wrote to me about it, and that's why I've come here. And that you've made it up again I learnt for the first time only yesterday in the train from one of your old friends – Zalyozhnev, if you want to know. I came here for a purpose: I wanted to persuade her to go abroad for her health; she's very ill now, mentally and physically, mentally especially, and in my opinion she requires careful nursing. I didn't intend to take her abroad myself. I had in mind to arrange it all without my being with her. I'm telling you the honest truth. If it's really true that you've made it up again, I shan't attempt to see her and I shan't ever come to see you again, either. You know yourself that I'm not deceiving you, because I've always been frank with you. I never concealed what I thought about it from you, and I always said that if she married you, she'd be done for. You, too, would be done for – perhaps more than she. If you were to part again, I should be very happy, but I do not intend to upset your plans or sow dissension between you. Don't worry about it and don't suspect me. Besides, you know perfectly well that I never was your *real* rival, even when she ran away to me. Now you're laughing; I know what you are laughing at. Yes, we lived apart there, in different towns, and you know all that *for a fact*. I explained to you before that I loved her not because I was in love with her, but because I pitied her. I believe this definition of my feelings towards her is exact. You said at the time that you understood what I meant. Is it true? Did you understand me? Don't look at me with such hatred! I've come to set your mind at rest because you, too, are dear to me. I'm very fond of you, Parfyon. And now I'm going and I shall never come again. Good-bye!'

The prince got up.

'Stay with me a little,' Parfyon said softly, without rising from his seat, his head resting on his right hand. 'I've not seen you for a long time.'

The prince sat down. Again both were silent.

'When you're not with me, Leo Nikolayevich, I begin to hate you at once. All during the three months I haven't seen you, I've hated you. Yes, hated you. I felt like poisoning you. That's how I felt. Now you haven't been a quarter of an hour with me, and my hatred's almost gone and you're as dear to me as you ever was. Stay with me a little. ...'

'When I'm with you, you believe me, and when I'm not you stop believing at once and you suspect me again. You're like your father!' replied the prince, smiling in a friendly way and trying to hide his emotion.

'It's your voice I believe when I'm with you. You see, I know it's impossible to regard us as equals, you and me.'

'Why did you add that? And now you're cross again,' said the prince, wondering at Rogozhin.

'Why, old man, nobody asks us our opinion about that,' he replied. 'That's been decided without us. You see, the way we love is different. I mean, everything's different. You say you love her because you pity her. Well, there ain't no such pity for her in me. And, besides, she hates me, too, more than anything. I dream of her every night now: she's always laughing at me with another man. That's how it is, old man. She's going to marry me, but she never gives me a thought, she don't. Just as if she was changing her shoes. You can believe me or not, but I haven't seen her for five days, because I daren't go to see her. She's sure to ask me what I've come for. She's humiliated me enough. ...'

'Humiliated you? Good heavens, what are you saying?'

'As if you don't know! Why, she ran away with you from me on the day of our wedding, as you yourself said just now.'

'But you don't believe yourself that she --'

'Didn't she humiliate me in Moscow with that officer, that Zhemuzhnikov fellow? I know she did, and it was after that she fixed the day of our wedding herself.'

'Impossible!' cried the prince.

'I know it for sure,' Rogozhin declared with conviction. 'Why, don't you think she's that sort? Don't you try to tell me she ain't. That's all nonsense. With you she won't be that sort, and I daresay she'd be horrified at the idea, but with me she's just that and nothing else. It's like that. She treats me like dirt. She pretended to have an affair with Keller, that officer, the boxer, just to make a laughing-stock of me – I know that for sure. Oh, you don't know half the tricks she played on me in Moscow! And the money – the money I spent on her!'

'But how – how can you think of marrying her now? What will it be like afterwards?' the prince asked in horror.

Rogozhin gave the prince a hard, terrible look and said nothing in reply.

'It's five days now since I saw her,' Rogozhin went on after a short pause. 'I'm always afraid she'll kick me out. "I'm my own mistress still," she says. "If I choose, I'll send you about your business and go abroad myself." She told me already that she'd go abroad,' he observed parenthetically, with a peculiar look at the prince. 'Sometimes, it's true, she's just trying to scare me: she always thinks me funny for some reason. But another time she frowns and scowls and never says a word. That's what really scares me. The other day I thought I'd better not go to see her empty-handed like, but I only made her laugh and afterwards she flew into a hell of a temper. She made a present of a shawl I gave her to her maid Katya – a shawl, mind you, such as she never saw the likes of before, though she lived in luxury. As for fixing the date of our wedding, I daren't even mention it. What sort of fiancé is it, I ask you, who's simply terrified to go and see his future bride? So I just sits here, and when I can't bear it no more, I keeps walking past her house stealthily and in secret or hide behind some corner. The other night I kept watch near the gates of her house till daybreak – I fancied something was going on. But she, you see, looked out of the window and saw me. "What would you have done," she says to me, "if you saw me deceiving you?" Well, so I couldn't hold out no longer and I says to her: "You know yourself!" '

'What does she know?'

'How do I know?' Rogozhin laughed angrily. 'In Moscow I couldn't catch her with no one, though I tried hard to. One day I says to her: "You promised to marry me," I says, "and you're about to enter a respectable family, but do you know what sort of a woman you are? You are," I says to her, "such and such a woman!" '

'You told her that?'

'I did.'

'And?'

' "I wouldn't have you for my footman now," she says, "let alone be your wife." "Well," I says, "and I won't leave the house – I'm done for, anyway." "And I," she says, "am going to call in Keller and tell him to kick you out of the house, and he'll do it, too." I rushed at her and beat her black and blue.'

'Impossible!' cried the prince.

'I tell you I did,' Rogozhin said quietly, but with flashing eyes. 'For a day and a half I didn't sleep, nor eat, nor drink, neither. I never left her room, went down on my knees before her, I did. "I shall die," I says, "but I won't go away till you forgive me, and if you tell them to throw me out, I'll go and drown myself, for – what should I be without you now?" She was like a crazy woman the whole of that day: she wept, she threatened to knife me, she called me all sorts of names. She called Zalyozhnev, Keller, Zhemtyuzhnikov, and the rest of them, pointed at me and reviled me. "Let's all go to a show tonight," she says, "and let him stay here if he refuses to go away. I'm not tied to him. And when I'm gone they'll give you some tea, sir, for I expect you must be very hungry to-day." She came back from the theatre alone. "They're a lot of cowards and blackguards," she says. "They're afraid of you, and they tried to frighten me, too. They told me you wouldn't go and you would cut my throat as likely as not. Well, I'll go to my bedroom and won't even lock the door – that's how much I'm afraid of you! I want you to know that and to see it! Have you had your tea?" "No," I says, "and I won't have it." "If your honour had been at stake," she says, " I could have understood it, but, as it is, it doesn't suit you at all." And she did as she said – she never locked the door. In the morning she comes out and – laughs. "Have you gone mad?' she says. "You'll die of hunger if you go on like that." "Forgive me," I says. "I don't want to forgive you," she says. "I won't marry you; I've said so. Have you really been sitting in that chair all night? Haven't you been asleep at all?" "No," I says, "I haven't." "What a clever chap you are! And you won't have breakfast or dinner to-day, either?" "I told you I won't – forgive me!" "Oh, if only you knew," she says, "how it doesn't suit you. It's like putting a saddle on a cow. You're not thinking of frightening me, are you? A lot do I care if you do sit here without eating. You don't frighten me!" She was angry, but not for long. Soon she began railing at me again. And, you know, I couldn't help marvelling at her for having no spite at all. For she's vindictive, and if anyone does her an injury, she won't forget it for a long time. It was then that it occurred to me that she thinks so little of me that she can't even feel much resentment against me! And that's true. "Do you know," she says, "what the Pope of Rome is?" "I've heard!" I says. "You, sir," she says, "haven't studied universal history, have you?" "No," I says, "I haven't studied nothing." "Well," she says, "in that case I'll give you something to read. There was a Pope once, and he got angry with an Emperor, and the Emperor knelt barefoot before his palace for three days until he forgave him. Well, what do you suppose that Emperor was thinking and what vows did he take while kneeling there? But, wait," she says, "I'll read it to you myself." She jumped up and brought a book. "It's poetry," she says, and she read me a poem of how that Emperor vowed during the three days to revenge himself on the Pope. "Why, sir," she says, "don't you like it?" "It's all true," I says, "what you read." "Aha, so you say yourself it's true, so perhaps you, too, are making vows: when I marry her I shall remind her of it all, and then I shall have some fun with her!" "I don't know," I says, "perhaps I'm thinking so." "You don't know?" "I don't," I says, "I've other things to think of now." "What are you thinking of now?" "Well," I says, "when you gets up and walks past me, I'm looking at you and following you with my eyes. When your dress rustles, my heart sinks, and when you goes out of the room, I try to remember every little word you said, and in what voice you said it. And all last night," I says, "I didn't think of nothing, but just listened how you was breathing in your sleep and how you moved about twice. ..." "I shouldn't be surprised," she laughed, "if you didn't think or remember how you beat me!" "Perhaps I do," I says, "I don't know." "And what if I don't forgive you and won't marry you?" "I said I'd drown myself." "I expect you'll kill me before that. ..." She said it and fell to thinking. Then she got angry and went out. An hour later she comes back, looking very gloomy. "I'll marry you, Parfyon," she says, "and not because I'm afraid of you, but because I'm done for anyway. There's no better way, is there? Sit down," she says, "they'll bring you your dinner presently. And," she added, "if I do marry you, I shall be a faithful wife to you. Do not doubt it and do not worry. Before I thought you were a real flunkey." Then she was silent. "Anyway," she says, "you're not a flunkey. But I did think before that you were nothing but a flunkey." It was then she fixed our wedding day, and a week later she ran away from me to Lebedev here. When I came, she says to me: "I'm not giving you up altogether. I just want to wait as long as I like, for I'm still my own mistress. You, too, can wait, if you like." That's the way things are between us now. What do you make of it all, Leo Nikolayevich?'

'What do you make of it yourself?' the prince asked in turn, looking sadly at Rogozhin.

'Me? Why, do you suppose I'm capable of thinking?' Rogozhin blurted out.

He wanted to add something, but stopped short in hopeless despair.

The prince got up again intending to leave.

'I shall not interfere with you all the same,' he said quietly, almost pensively, as though in answer to some secret, inner thought of his own.

'You know what!' Rogozhin cried with sudden animation, his eyes flashing. 'What I can't understand is why you gives in to me like this? Don't you love her at all? Before, at any rate, you used to be in the dumps. I saw it all right. So why have you come here in such a desperate hurry? Out of pity?' (And his face was twisted into a malicious sneer.) 'Ha, ha!'

'You think I'm deceiving you?' asked the prince.

'No, I believe you, only I can't make it out at all. I expect the truth is that your pity is much stronger than my love.'

His face lit up with malice and an uncontrollable desire to speak out at once.

'Well,' the prince smiled, 'your love cannot be distinguished from malice, and when it passes, there's going to be even greater trouble, perhaps. I tell you this, Parfyon. ...'

'Why, you don't think I'll murder her, do you?'

The prince gave a start.

'You'll hate her bitterly for having loved her so much now, for the terrible agony you're going through now. What seems to me so extraordinary is that she should have agreed again to marry you. When I heard of it yesterday, I could hardly believe it, and it made me so unhappy. You see, she's given you up twice already, and she's run away from you on the day of your wedding, and that means that she has a premonition. What can she want with you now? Your money? That's silly. Besides, I expect you must have already squandered quite a lot of it. To get herself a husband? But, then, she could find one besides you. Anyone is better than you, for you really may murder her, and she realizes it perhaps now all too well. That you love her so much? Well, perhaps it's that. I've heard there are women who are looking for just that kind of love – only – –'

The prince paused and pondered.

'Why are you smiling at my dad's portrait again?' asked Rogozhin, who was watching closely every change and fugitive movement on his face.

'Why did I smile? Well, it occurred to me that if this misfortune had not befallen you, if this love hadn't happened, you'd perhaps have become just like your father, and in a very short time, too. You'd have settled down quietly in this house alone with your mute and obedient wife, hardly ever opening your mouth even to utter a stern word, trusting no man and having no need to, and merely making money in gloomy silence. At the most you'd occasionally have praised the old books and taken an interest in the Old Believers' custom of crossing themselves with two fingers, and that, too, only in your old age.'

'You can jeer at me, if you like. She, too, said the same thing, word for word, not long ago when she was looking at that portrait! Funny, the way you two seem to agree about everything now.'

'Why, she hasn't been to see you here, has she?' the prince asked with interest.

'She has. She spent a long time looking at the portrait. Kept asking me about my dad. "You'd have been exactly like him," she says to me at last, laughing. "You've got powerful passions, Parfyon," she says, "such passions as might have landed you in Siberia if you weren't intelligent as well, for," she says, "you've got a lot of intelligence" – believe it or not, but that's exactly what she said, and it was the first time I heard her say such a thing: "You'd have stopped fooling and since you're such an uneducated fellow, you'd have started saving up money, and you'd have settled in this house, like your dad, with those castrates. I daresay," she says, "you'd have been converted to their faith yourself in the end and you'd have grown so fond of your money that you'd have accumulated not two million but perhaps ten million and died of hunger on your bags of gold, for," she says, "with you everything becomes a passion and you drive everything to a point where it grows into a passion." That's exactly what she said, almost word for word. She'd never spoken to me like that before! You see, she always talks a lot of nonsense with me or she keeps jeering at me. And here, too, she began by laughing, but afterwards she grew gloomy. Walked all over the house, she did, examined everything and seemed to be frightened of something. "I'm going to change it all," I says, "have it all redecorated, or I might even buy another house before our wedding." "You mustn't do that," she says; "on no account must you change anything here, for we're going to live like this. I want to live beside your mother," she says, "when I'm your wife." I took her to my mother, and she was very respectful to her, just as if she was her own daughter. My mother has not been quite in her right mind for the last two years (she's an invalid), and after my dad's death she's become quite like a baby and never says a word: she's lost the use of her legs and she sits in her room all day long and she only bows from her chair to everyone she sees. I don't think she'd notice it if she wasn't fed for three days. I took hold of her right hand and, folding her fingers, "Give her your blessing, Mother," I says; "she's going to be my wife." And so she kissed my mother's hand with feeling. "I expect," she says, "your mother's had a great deal of sorrow to bear in her life." She saw this book on the table. "Why," she says, "have you begun to read Russian history?" (It was she who said to me herself in Moscow once: "I wish you'd try to educate yourself. You might at least read Solovyov's *Russian History*. As it is, you don't know anything at all.") "That's good," she says; "go on reading it. I'll write you out a list of the books you ought to read first. Would you like me to?" And never, never before did she talk to me like that, so that I was really surprised: for the first time in my life I breathed freely like a living man.'

'I'm very glad to hear it, Parfyon,' said the prince with genuine feeling. 'Very glad indeed. Who knows? Maybe the Lord will help you to live happily together.'

'That will never be!' cried Rogozhin hotly.

'Listen, Parfyon. Surely, if you love her so much you must want to earn her respect, mustn't you? And if you want to, you must surely hope to do so. A little while ago I said that it seemed strange to me that she should have agreed to marry you. But though I cannot understand it, I'm quite sure there must be a sufficient and sensible reason for it. She's convinced of your love, so she must also be convinced of some of your good qualities. It simply can't be otherwise!

What you told me just now confirms this. You said yourself that she had found it possible to speak to you in a different way from the way in which she had spoken and behaved to you before. You're suspicious and jealous, and that's why you exaggerate everything bad you noticed. I'm sure she doesn't think as badly of you as you say. For if she did, it could only mean that she's deliberately courting death by drowning or the knife by marrying you. Is such a thing possible? Who would deliberately be courting death by drowning or the knife?'

Parfyon listened to the prince's excited speech with a bitter smile. It seemed that nothing in the world could shake his conviction.

'How grimly you look at me now, Parfyon,' cried the prince disconsolately.

'By drowning or the knife!' said Rogozhin at last. 'Ha! Why, she's marrying me just because she knows for certain that I'm going to kill her! Is it possible, Prince, that you haven't yet realized what it's all about?'

'I don't understand you.'

'Well, maybe you really don't understand – ha, ha! No wonder people say you're *not all there*. She's in love with another man – get that into your head! The same as I love her, she loves another man. And do you know who the other man is? It's *you*! You didn't know it, did you?'

'Me!'

'You. She's loved you ever since that evening of her birthday party. Only she thinks she can't marry you because you're too good for her and because she'd ruin your life. Everyone knows, she says, the sort of woman I am. Aye, she keeps on saying that to this day. She told me so straight to my face, she did. She's afraid of disgracing and ruining you, but, you see, I'm different – she can marry me! That's how much she thinks of me – mark that too, please!'

'But why then did she run away from you to me and – from me – –'

'And from you to me! Ha, ha! You can't tell what ideas mightn't enter her head all of a sudden, can you? She seems to be all in a fever now. One moment she screams, "I may as well be dead and marry you – let's have the wedding as soon as possible!" She's in a desperate hurry, she fixes the day, but as soon as the time for the wedding comes near, she gets cold feet or all sorts of new ideas. Goodness only knows what's the matter with her – you've seen it, haven't you? Cries, laughs, shakes with fever. What's so funny about her having run away from you? She ran away from you because she suddenly realized how much she loved you. She hadn't the strength to bear it while she was with you. You said just now that I found her in Moscow. Well, it's not true. It was she who came running to me herself from you. "Fix the day," she says. "I'm ready. Let's have champagne. Let's go to the gypsies!" she screams. Why, if I wasn't there, she'd have thrown herself into the river long ago. It's the truth I'm telling you. She don't drown herself, because I'm perhaps a hundred times worse than the river. It's out of spite she's marrying me – aye, if she marries me, she'll do it *out of spite*.'

'But how can you – how can you – –' cried the prince and stopped short. He looked at Rogozhin with horror.

'Why don't you finish?' Rogozhin asked with a grin. 'If you like, I'll tell you what you're thinking of this minute. How can she marry him now? How is she to be allowed to? Aye, that's what you're thinking.'

'I didn't come here for that, Parfyon. I tell you it wasn't that I had in mind. ...'

'Aye, that's right. You didn't come for that and you never had that in mind, but you certainly have it is mind now, ha, ha! But enough of this! Why are you so upset? Didn't you really know? You surprise me!'

'All this is nothing but jealousy, Parfyon. It's a kind of illness. You're exaggerating it all terribly ...' the prince murmured in great agitation. 'What's the matter?'

'Leave it alone,' said Parfyon, quickly snatching from the prince's hand a knife which he had picked up from the table, and putting it back beside the book where it had lain.

'I seem to have known it when I was coming to Petersburg,' the prince went on. 'I seem to have had a presentiment. I didn't want to come here! I wanted to forget everything here – I wanted to tear it out of my heart! Well, good-bye – but what is the matter with you?'

As he was talking, the prince again absent-mindedly picked up the knife from the table, and again Rogozhin snatched it out of his hands and threw it on the table. It was quite an ordinary knife with a hartshorn handle, not of the folding kind, with a blade of about seven inches long and of a corresponding breadth.

Seeing that the prince had paid particular attention to the fact that the knife had been twice snatched out of his hands, Rogozhin seized it with bad-tempered vexation, put it in the book, and threw the book on to another table.

'Do you cut the pages with it?' asked the prince, but rather absent-mindedly, as though still too preoccupied with his thoughts.

'Yes, the pages. ...'

'It's a garden knife, isn't it?'

'Yes, it's a garden knife. Can't one cut pages with a garden knife?'

'But it's – it's quite new.'

'Well, what of it?' Rogozhin, who was getting more and more exasperated with every word, cried in a kind of frenzy. 'Can't I buy a new knife, if I want to?'

The prince shuddered and looked intently at Rogozhin.

'Good God, how absurd we are!' he laughed suddenly, regaining his self-composure completely. 'I'm sorry, old man. When I've such an awful headache as I have now and – this illness of mine, I – I become so absent-minded and ridiculous. I didn't mean to ask you about this at all – I can't remember what it was. Good-bye.'

'Not that way,' said Rogozhin.

'Sorry, I've forgotten.'

'This way, this way. Come, I'll show you.'

4

They passed through the same rooms that the prince had passed through, Rogozhin walking a little in front and the prince behind him. They went into the big drawing-room. On the walls there were a few pictures, all portraits of bishops and landscapes in which it was impossible to make anything out. Over the door of the next room there hung a picture of a rather curious shape, about five feet wide and no more than ten and a half inches high. It showed our Saviour, who had just been taken from the cross. The prince threw a cursory glance at it as though trying to remember something and was about to pass into the other room without stopping. He felt very depressed and was anxious to get out of this house as soon as possible. But Rogozhin suddenly stopped before the picture.

'All these here pictures,' he said, 'were bought by my dad at auctions for a rouble or two. He liked them. An art dealer examined them all. A lot of rubbish, he said. But this picture here, over the door, also bought for two roubles, isn't rubbish, he said. One fellow offered my dad three hundred and fifty roubles for it, and Ivan Dmitrich Savelyev, a merchant and a great picture-lover, offered as much as four hundred for it, and last week he raised his offer to my brother to five hundred. But I've kept it for myself.'

'Why, it's a copy of a Holbein,' said the prince, who had by then had time to examine the picture, 'and though I'm not much of an expert, I think it's an excellent copy. I saw the picture abroad, and I can't forget it. But – what's the matter?'

Rogozhin suddenly lost interest in the picture and continued on his way. No doubt his absent-mindedness and the peculiar, strangely irritable mood that had come over him so suddenly, might have accounted for this abruptness; but all the same it seemed rather odd to the prince that a conversation, which he had not even started, should have been broken off so suddenly, and that Rogozhin did not even answer him.

'Tell me, Prince, I've long wanted to ask you, do you believe in God?' Rogozhin suddenly broke into speech after walking a few steps.

'How strangely you speak and – look!' the prince observed involuntarily.

'I like looking at that picture,' Rogozhin muttered after a short pause, as though he had again forgotten his question.

'At that picture!' the prince exclaimed, struck by a sudden thought. 'At that picture! Why, some people may lose their faith by looking at that picture!'

'Aye, that also may be lost,' Rogozhin assented unexpectedly.

They had by now reached the front door.

'Why, what are you saying?' the prince cried, stopping suddenly. 'I was only joking, and you are so serious! And why did you ask me whether I believed in God?'

'Oh, for no reason. It just occurred to me. I meant to ask you before. You see, lots of people don't believe nowadays. But, tell me, is it true – you've lived abroad – what a man in his cups told me that in Russia we have more unbelievers than in other countries? He said it was easier for us than for them, because we'd gone further than they.'

Rogozhin smiled sardonically. Having asked his question, he suddenly opened the door and, holding the handle, waited for the prince to go through. The prince looked surprised, but he went out. Rogozhin followed him on to the landing and closed the door behind him. They both stood facing each other as though oblivious of where they were or what they had to do next.

'Well, good-bye,' said the prince, holding out his hand.

'Good-bye,' said Rogozhin, pressing the held-out hand hard, though quite mechanically.

The prince went down a step and turned round.

'As to faith,' he said, smiling (evidently not wishing to leave Rogozhin like that), and, besides, brightening up under the impression of a sudden memory – 'as to faith, I had four different encounters in two days last week. In the morning I was travelling on one of our new railways, and I talked for some hours with a man I met in the train. I had heard a great deal about him before and, incidentally, that he was an atheist. He really is a very learned man, and I was glad of the opportunity of talking to a real scholar. He is, moreover, an exceedingly well-bred person, and he talked to me as though I were his equal in knowledge and ideas. He doesn't believe in God. One thing struck me, though: he didn't seem to be talking about that at all the whole time, and this struck me particularly because before, too, whenever I met unbelievers and however many of their books I read, I could not help feeling that they were not talking or writing about that at all, though they may appear to do so. I told him this at the time, but I'm afraid I did not or could not express myself clearly enough, for he did not understand what I was talking about. The same evening I stopped for the night at a provincial hotel where a murder had been committed the night before, so that everybody was talking about it when I arrived. Two peasants, middle-aged men who had known each other for years – two old friends, in fact – had had tea and engaged a small room in which they were to spend the night. They were not drunk, but one of them noticed that the other was wearing a silver watch on a yellow bead chain, which apparently he had not seen on him before. Now, that man was not a thief. He was, in fact, an honest man and, as peasants go, far from poor. But he liked that watch so much and was so tempted by it that at last he could not restrain himself: he took out his knife, and when his friend turned his back to him, went up cautiously to him from behind, took aim, raised his eyes to heaven, crossed himself and, uttering a silent, agonizing prayer, "O Lord, forgive me for Christ's sake!" – cut his friend's throat at one stroke, like a sheep, and took his watch.'

Rogozhin rocked with laughter. He laughed as though he were in a fit. It was indeed strange to see him laughing like that after the gloomy mood he had been in so recently.

'I like that! Yes, that beats everything!' he cried convulsively, gasping for breath. 'One man don't believe in God at all, and another believes in Him so much that he murders people with a prayer. No, sir, nobody could have invented that! Ha, ha, ha! Yes, that beats everything!'

'In the morning I went for a stroll round the town,' the prince went on as soon as Rogozhin stopped laughing, though his lips were still twitching convulsively and spasmodically. 'There I saw a drunken soldier staggering about the wooden pavement and looking completely bedraggled. He came up to me. "Won't you buy a silver cross, sir? I'll let you have it for twenty copecks. It's a silver one, sir.' I saw a cross on a filthy blue ribbon, which he had evidently just taken off, but it was really made of tin, as one could see at a glance, a very big, octagonal cross of a regular Byzantine pattern. I took out a twenty-copeck piece and gave it to him, and at once put the cross round my neck – and I could see from his face how pleased he was to have cheated a foolish gentleman, and he went off immediately to spend his money on drink – there could be no doubt about that! At the time I was tremendously impressed by all that had come flooding in upon me in Russia. I had not understood anything about Russia before, just as though I had grown up speechless, and had the most fantastic memories of it during my five years abroad. So I walked away, thinking, "I mustn't be too quick to condemn a man who has sold his Christ. Only God knows what is locked away in these weak and drunken hearts." An hour later, on my way back to the hotel, I came upon a peasant woman with a newborn baby. She was quite a young woman, and the baby was about six weeks old. The baby smiled at her for the first time since its birth. I saw her suddenly crossing herself with deep devotion. "What are you doing that for, my dear?" I said. (You see, I was always asking questions just then.) "Well, sir," she said, "just as a mother rejoices seeing her baby's first smile, so does God rejoice every time he beholds from above a sinner kneeling down before Him to say his prayers with all his heart." This was what a simple peasant woman said to me, almost in those words – a thought so profound, so subtle, and so truly religious, in which the whole essence of Christianity is expressed, that is to say, the whole conception of God as our Father and of God's rejoicing in man, like a father rejoicing in his own child – the fundamental idea of Christianity! An ordinary peasant woman! It is true she was a mother – and, who knows, perhaps she was the wife of that soldier. Listen, Parfyon, a few moments ago you asked me a question, and this is my answer: the essence of religious feeling has nothing to do with any reasoning, or any crimes and misdemeanours or atheism; it is something entirely different and it will always be so; it is something our atheists will always overlook, and they will never talk about *that*. But the important thing is that you will notice it most clearly in a Russian heart, and that's the conclusion I've come to! This is one of the chief convictions I have acquired in our Russia. There's work to be done, Parfyon. Believe me, there's work to be done in our Russian world!

Remember how we used to meet and talk in Moscow at one time. ... No, I didn't want to come back here now. And I didn't dream of meeting you like this! Oh, well, it doesn't matter. Good-bye – so long! God be with you!'

He turned and went down the stairs.

'I say,' Parfyon shouted from above when the prince had reached the first half landing, 'that cross, the cross you bought from the soldier, have you got it?'

'Yes, I'm wearing it.'

And the prince stopped again.

'Come up and show me.'

Again something odd! He thought for a moment, went upstairs, and showed him the cross without taking it off.

'Give it me,' said Rogozhin.

'Why? Will you – –'

The prince did not want to part with the cross.

'I'll wear it, and I'll take mine off for you. You wear it.'

'You want to exchange crosses? By all means, Parfyon. If that's what you want, I shall be delighted. We shall be brothers.'

The prince took off his tin cross and Parfyon his gold one, and they made the exchange. Parfyon was silent. The prince noticed with painful surprise that the old mistrust, the old bitter and almost sardonic smile still lingered on the face of his newly-adopted brother; at moments, at any rate, it could be plainly discerned. At last Rogozhin took the prince's hand in silence, and stood for some time as though unable to make up his mind about something; then he suddenly drew him after him, saying in a barely audible voice, 'Come along!' They crossed the landing of the first floor and rang at the door opposite to the one they had come out of. It was presently opened to them. A bent old woman, her head covered with a black kerchief, bowed low to Rogozhin without speaking. Rogozhin quickly asked her something and, without waiting for an answer, led the prince through the rooms. They passed again through several dark rooms of a kind of extraordinarily cold cleanliness, coldly and severely furnished with ancient furniture under clean white covers. Without knocking, Rogozhin led the prince straight into a small room, which looked like a drawing-room and was divided by a polished mahogany partition with two doors at each end, behind which was probably a bedroom. In a corner of the drawing-room, by the stove, a little old woman was sitting in an arm-chair. She did not look very old; indeed, she had a fairly healthy, pleasant, round face, but her hair was quite white, and it could be seen at once that she was in her second childhood. She wore a black woollen dress, with a large black kerchief round her neck and shoulders, and a clean white cap with black ribbons. Her feet were resting on a footstool. Beside her sat another clean old woman, a little older than she, also in mourning and a white cap, probably a poor relation, who was silently knitting a stocking. They both looked as though they never spoke to each other. The first old woman, seeing Rogozhin and the prince, smiled at them and inclined her head affectionately a few times to show that she was pleased.

'Mother,' said Rogozhin, kissing her hand, 'this is a great friend of mine, Prince Leo Nikolayevich Myshkin. I've exchanged crosses with him. He was like a brother to me at one time in Moscow and did a lot for me. Bless him, Mother, just as if it was your own son you was blessing. Wait, do it like this – let me put your fingers right.'

But before Parfyon had time to touch her, the old woman raised her right hand, put three fingers together and devoutly made the sign of the cross three times over the prince. Then she once more nodded her head tenderly and affectionately at him.

'Well, come along,' said Parfyon. 'I only brought you here for that.' And when they came out on the landing again, he added: 'You know, she don't understand a word people say to her, and she didn't understand what I said, either, but she blessed you, which means that she wanted to do so herself. Well, good-bye. It's time you went, and I must go, too.'

And he opened his own door.

'But, good Lord, let me at least embrace you before we part, you funny chap!' cried the prince, looking at him with tender reproach as he was going to embrace him.

But no sooner did Rogozhin raise his arms than he let them fall again. He could not bring himself to do it; he turned away so as not to look at the prince. He did not want to embrace him.

'Never you fear! I may have taken your cross, but I shan't cut your throat for your watch!' he muttered thickly and suddenly broke into a sort of strange laugh.

A moment later his face became completely transformed: he grew terribly pale, his lips trembled, his eyes blazed. He raised his arms, embraced the prince warmly, and said, breathlessly:

'Well, take her, if that's how it is to be! She's yours! I give her to you! Remember Rogozhin!'

And leaving the prince, he went hurriedly in without looking at him, and slammed the door behind him.

5

It was already late – almost half past two – and the prince did not find General Yepanchin at home. Leaving his card, he decided to go to the hotel 'The Scales' and ask for Kolya, and if he were not there, to leave a note for him. At the hotel he was told that Kolya had gone out in the morning, but that before going he left a message that if anyone should ask for him, he should be told that he would be back at three o'clock. But if he were not back by half past three, it would mean that he had gone by train to Pavlovsk to Mrs Yepanchin's, where he would stay to dinner. The prince sat down to wait for him and in the meantime ordered dinner.

Kolya did not turn up at half past three, nor was he back at four. The prince left the hotel and walked on mechanically, without caring where he went. Ther are sometimes quite delightful days at the beginning of summer in Petersburg – bright, hot, and serene. As though on purpose, this was one of those days. The prince wandered about aimlessly for some time. He did not know the town very well. Sometimes he stopped at the crossroads before some houses, or in squares, or on bridges; once he went into a pastry-cook's to rest. Sometimes he began watching the passers-by with great interest, but mostly he noticed neither the passers-by nor where he was going. He was agitated and his nerves were painfully on edge, and at the same time he felt an extraordinary craving for solitude. He wanted to be alone, so as to give himself up entirely and passively to this agonizing feeling of insufferable strain, without seeking to escape it. He loathed the idea of trying to solve the problems that filled his mind and heart to overflowing. 'Am I to blame for everything?' he muttered to himself, hardly realizing what he was saying.

At about six o'clock he found himself on the platform of the Tsarskoye Selo railway station. Solitude had soon become unbearable to him; his heart was seized by a new violent impulse, and for a moment the darkness in which his soul languished was flooded by a bright light. He took a ticket for Pavlovsk and waited impatiently for the train; but there could be no doubt that he was being followed, and this was no longer a delusion, as he had been inclined to think, but a reality. He had almost taken his seat in the train, when he suddenly threw his ticket on the floor and left the station, disturbed and thoughtful. Some time later, in the street, he suddenly seemed instantaneously to have grasped something very strange, something that had long worried him. He suddenly caught himself consciously doing something he had been doing for a long time, but that he had not noticed till that very moment: for several hours now, even while he was at 'The Scales', and perhaps even before he went there, he would from time to time suddenly begin looking about him. He would then forget all about it for as long as half an hour and then suddenly look round uneasily, as if expecting to see someone.

But as soon as he had become aware of this morbid and, till then, quite unconscious impulse which had taken possession of him for so long, he recalled something else that interested him exceedingly. He remembered that at the moment when he became aware that he was looking for something, he was standing on the pavement before a shop window and examining the things in it with great interest. He felt he simply had to find out whether he really had stood just now before that shop window, perhaps five minutes before, or whether he had imagined it all, or got it all mixed up. Did that shop and the things in its window really exist? For he really felt rather ill that day, almost as he used to feel before at the onset of his old illness. He knew that at the time when he was expecting such an attack, he was extraordinarily absent-minded and often mixed up things and people, if he did not look at them with special, concentrated attention. But there was another reason why he was so anxious to find out whether he had been standing in front of that shop; among the goods displayed in the shop window was a thing he had looked at and even thought that it could not cost more than sixty copecks – he remembered that distinctly in spite of his uneasiness and absent-mindedness. If, therefore, the shop existed, the only reason why he stopped in front of it was that object in the window. That object, consequently, had impressed him so much that it had attracted his attention at a time when he was in a state of utter confusion just after he had left the railway station. He walked back, looking almost in anguish to the right, and his heart beat with uneasy impatience. But there was that shop – he had found it at last! He was only about two hundred yards away when he had taken it into his head to go back. And there was the article he had thought cost no more than sixty copecks. 'Of course, sixty copecks; it's not worth more!' he endorsed his former impression and laughed. But it was an hysterical laugh: he felt very miserable. He now clearly remembered that it was just then, while standing in front of that shop window, that he suddenly turned round, as he had done only a short time before when he caught Rogozhin's eyes fixed upon him. Having made sure he was not mistaken (which, by the way, he had been quite sure of before), he left the shop window and walked away from it quickly. He felt that he must think it all over very carefully; it was now clear that he had not just imagined it at the railway station, that something had really happened to him that was most certainly connected with all his former uneasiness. But a sort of overpowering inner loathing again got the better of him: he did not want to think it over and he didn't. He was thinking of something else now.

He was thinking, incidentally, that there was a moment or two in his epileptic condition almost before the fit itself (if it occurred during his waking hours) when suddenly amid the sadness, spiritual darkness and depression, his brain seemed to catch fire at brief moments, and with an extraordinary momentum his vital forces were strained to the utmost all at once. His sensation of being alive and his awareness increased tenfold at those moments which flashed by like lightning. His mind and heart were flooded by a dazzling light. All his agitation, all his doubts and worries, seemed composed in a twinkling, culminating in a great calm, full of serene and harmonious joy and hope, full of understanding and the knowledge of the final cause. But those moments, those flashes of intuition, were merely the presentiment of the last second (never more than a second) which preceded the actual fit. This second was, of course, unendurable. Reflecting about that moment afterwards, when he was well again, he often said to himself that all those gleams and flashes of the highest awareness and, hence, also of 'the highest mode of existence', were nothing but a disease, a departure from the normal condition, and, if so, it was not at all the highest mode of existence, but, on the contrary, must be considered to be the lowest. And yet he arrived at last at the paradoxical conclusion: 'What if it is a disease?' he decided at last. 'What does it matter that it is an abnormal tension, if the result, if the moment of sensation, remembered and analysed in a state of health, turns out to be harmony and beauty brought to their highest point of perfection, and gives a feeling, undivined and undreamt of till then, of completeness, proportion, reconciliation, and an ecstatic and prayerful fusion in the highest synthesis of life?' These vague expressions seemed to him very comprehensible, though rather weak. But that it really was 'beauty and prayer', that it really was 'the highest synthesis of life', he could not doubt, nor even admit the possibility of doubt. For it was not abnormal and fantastic visions he saw at that moment, as under the influence of hashish, opium, or spirits, which debased the reason and distorted the mind. He could reason sanely about it when the attack was over and he was well again. Those moments were merely an intense heightening of awareness – if this condition had to be expressed in one word – of awareness and at the same time of the most direct sensation of one's own existence to the most intense degree. If in that second – that is to say, at the last conscious moment before the fit – he had time to say to himself, consciously and clearly, 'Yes, I could give my whole life for this moment,' then this moment by itself was, of course, worth the whole of life. However, he did not insist on the dialectical part of his argument: stupor, spiritual darkness, idiocy stood before him as the plain consequence of those 'highest moments'. Seriously, of course, he would not have argued the point. There was, no doubt, some flaw in his argument – that is, in his appraisal of that minute – but the reality of the sensation somewhat troubled him all the same. What indeed was he to make of this reality? For that very thing had happened. He *had* had time to say to himself at the particular second that, for the infinite happiness he had felt in it, it might well be worth the whole of his life. 'At that moment,' he once told Rogozhin in Moscow during their meetings there, 'at that moment the extraordinary saying that *there shall be time no longer* becomes, somehow, comprehensible to me. I suppose,' he added, smiling, 'this is the very second in which there was not time enough for the water from the pitcher of the epileptic Mahomet to spill, while he had plenty of time in that very second to behold all the dwellings of Allah.' Oh yes, in Moscow he had met Rogozhin frequently and they had talked not only of this. 'Rogozhin said just now that I had been a brother to him then – to-day was the first time he said it,' the prince thought to himself.

He thought of this sitting on a seat under a tree in the Summer Gardens. It was about seven o'clock. The gardens were deserted; a dark shadow passed over the setting sun for a moment. It was close; it looked like the distant presage of a thunderstorm. There was a certain charm for him in his present contemplative mood. He clung with all his mind and memory to every external object, and he liked that; he seemed to be anxious to forget something, the present, the thing that was uppermost in his mind at that moment, but at the first glance around him he immediately became conscious again of his gloomy thought, from which he wanted to escape so badly. He remembered talking at dinner to the waiter at the restaurant of a recent very strange murder which had created a sensation and had caused a great deal of talk. But he had no sooner remembered it than something peculiar happened to him again.

He was suddenly seized by an intense, irresistible desire, almost a temptation. He got up from his seat and walked straight out of the gardens towards the Petersburg suburb. A short time ago he had asked a passer-by on the Neva Embankment to point out to him the Petersburg suburb across the river. It was pointed out to him, but he had not gone there. Besides, it would have been useless to go there today: he knew that. He had long known the address; he could easily have found the house of Lebedev's relation, but he knew almost for certain that he would not find her at home. 'She has certainly gone to Pavlovsk, or Kolya would have left a message at "The Scales".' So if he was going there now, it was not, of course, because he hoped to see her. Another sombre and tormenting curiosity tempted him now. A new, sudden idea came into his head. ... But for him it was quite enough that he had set off and knew where he was going: a minute later he was again walking along without being aware of his surroundings. The thought of the implications of his 'sudden idea' became all at once repugnant to him and almost impossible. He gazed with painfully strained attention at everything that caught his sight; he looked at the sky, at the Neva. He spoke to a little child he met. Perhaps his epileptic condition was becoming more and more acute. The storm, he felt, was really coming nearer, though slowly. He could already hear the distant thunder. It was getting very close.

For some obscure reason he could not now get out of his head Lebedev's nephew, whom he had seen that morning, just as sometimes one cannot get out of one's head some persistent and stupidly tiresome tune. The strange thing was that he kept thinking of him as the murderer whom Lebedev had mentioned when introducing him to the young man. Yes, he had read about that murderer not so long ago. He had read and heard a lot of such cases since his return to Russia; and he followed them up carefully. And that afternoon he had been very interested in his talk with the waiter about that same murder of the Zhemarins. The waiter agreed with him, he remembered that. He remembered the waiter, too; he was not at all a stupid fellow, reliable and careful, but 'still, goodness knows what sort of fellow he was. It is difficult to make out the new people one meets in a new country.' He did, however, begin to believe passionately in the Russian soul. Oh, during those six months he had been through a great deal – a great deal that was quite new to him, a great deal that he had never suspected, nor heard, nor expected! But a stranger's soul is a dark mystery, and a Russian's soul is a dark mystery – a mystery to many. He had been friends with Rogozhin for a long time, they had been intimate friends, they had been 'like brothers' –

but did he know Rogozhin? But what chaos, confusion, and ugliness there sometimes was in all this! And what a disgusting and conceited pimple that nephew of Lebedev's was! 'But what am I saying?' the prince went on thinking to himself. 'Did he kill those creatures, those six people? I seem to have got it all mixed up – how strange it is! My head seems to be going round and round. ... And what a dear, what a charming face Lebedev's daughter has – the girl standing up with the baby – what an innocent, what an almost child-like expression and what an almost child-like laugh!' It was funny how he had almost forgotten that face and only remembered it just now. Lebedev, who stamped his feet at them, probably adored them all. But what was truer still, what was as certain as that twice two makes four, was that Lebedev adored his nephew, too!

Still, why should he pass so final a judgement upon them, he who had only appeared that day? Why should he pronounce such verdicts? Lebedev had certainly set him a problem that day: had he expected a Lebedev like that? Had he known such a Lebedev before? Lebedev and Du Barry – good heavens! Still, if Rogozhin did kill, he would not kill in such a horrible way. There would not be that chaos there. A weapon made to a previously prepared pattern and six people butchered in a state of absolute delirium! But had Rogozhin ordered a weapon made to a pattern? He had – but was it *certain* that Rogozhin would kill? The prince shuddered suddenly. 'Isn't it criminal, isn't it base of me to assume such a thing with such cynical frankness?' he exclaimed, his face flushing all over with shame. He was amazed, he stood still in the roadway, as though rooted to the spot. He remembered all at once the Pavlovsk station that afternoon and the Nikolayevsk station in the morning, and the question he had asked Rogozhin to his face about the *eyes*, and Rogozhin's cross, which he was wearing now, and the blessing of his mother, to whom Rogozhin had taken him himself, and his last convulsive embrace, Rogozhin's last renunciation on the stairs – and after all that to catch himself looking incessantly for something about him, and that shop, and that article in the shop – how contemptible he was! And after all that he was going now 'with a special purpose', with a special 'sudden idea'! His whole soul was overwhelmed with despair and grief. The prince wanted to turn back to his hotel at once; he did, indeed, turn back and go the other way, but a minute later he stopped, thought it over, and went back again in the first direction.

Why, he was already in the Petersburg suburb, he was near the house; yet he was no longer going there with the same purpose, nor with his 'special idea'! And how could it possibly be! Yes, his illness was coming back, there was no doubt about it; quite probably he would have the fit to-day. All this darkness was because of the impending fit, and the 'idea' too was because of it! Now the darkness was dispersed, the demon banished, he had no more doubts, his heart was full of gladness! And – he had not seen her for so long, he had to see her, and – yes – he would have liked to meet Rogozhin now, he would have taken him by the hand and they would have gone together. ... His heart was pure. Was he Rogozhin's rival? To-morrow he would go to Rogozhin himself and tell him he had seen her. For had he not rushed here, as Rogozhin said that afternoon, just to see her? Perhaps he would find her at home – she might not be in Pavlovsk at all!

Yes, it was necessary to make everything clear now, so that they should be able to read each other's thoughts clearly, so that there should be no more of such sombre and passionate renunciations as Rogozhin's, and let it all be done freely and – joyfully. Was not Rogozhin capable of freedom and happiness? He said that he did not love her like that, that he had no compassion for her, that he had 'no such pity'. It was true that he added afterwards that 'your pity is perhaps stronger than my love' – but he was not quite fair to himself. H'm – Rogozhin poring over a book – wasn't that 'pity' or the beginning of 'pity'? Was not the very presence of that book the best proof that he was fully conscious of his attitude towards *her*? And the story he had told him that afternoon? That was much deeper than just mere infatuation. And did her face merely arouse infatuation? Why, could that face ever arouse any passion now? It aroused suffering, it cast a spell over your whole soul, it – and a poignant agonizing memory suddenly passed through the prince's heart.

Yes, agonizing. He remembered the agony he had gone through when he first began to notice in her symptoms of insanity. Then he had been almost in despair. And how could he have left her when she ran away from him to Rogozhin? He should have run after her himself, and not waited for news of her. But – could it be that Rogozhin had not yet noticed any signs of insanity in her? H'm. ... Rogozhin saw different reasons for everything, passionate reasons! And what insane jealousy! What did he mean by that suggestion of his? (The prince blushed suddenly and something seemed to send a chill through his heart.)

But why, anyway, recall all this? There was madness on both sides. For him, the prince, to love that woman passionately was almost unthinkable. It would be almost equivalent to cruelty, to inhumanity. Yes, yes! Rogozhin was not quite fair to himself; he had a great heart that was capable of suffering and compassion. When he learnt the whole truth, and when he realized what a pitiful creature that unhinged, half-crazy woman was, wouldn't he forgive her all the past, all his agonies? Would he not become her servant, her brother, her friend, her Providence? Compassion would teach even Rogozhin, give a meaning to his life. Compassion was the chief and, perhaps, the only law of all human existence. Oh, how unpardonably and dishonourably he had wronged Rogozhin! No, it was not the Russian soul that was dark mystery, it was his own soul that was plunged in darkness, if he was capable of imagining such a horror. For a few warm and cordial words in Moscow, Rogozhin had called him his brother and he -- But that was sickness and delirium! That would all come right! ... How gloomily Rogozhin had spoken that afternoon about how he was 'losing his faith'. That man must be suffering terribly. He said he liked 'to look at that picture'; it was not that he liked it, but that he felt a need for it. Rogozhin was not just a passionate soul; he was a fighter for all that: he wanted to regain his lost faith by force. He had a tormenting need of it now. ... Yes, to believe in *something*! To believe in *someone*! But how strange that picture of Holbein's was! Ah, here is the street! That must be the house – yes, No. 16, 'The house of Mrs Filissov'. Here! The prince rang and asked for Nastasya Filippovna.

The lady of the house herself answered the door and told him that Nastasya Filippovna had left for Pavlovsk that morning to stay with Darya Alexeyevna, and, she added, 'It is very likely, sir, that she will stay there for several days.' Mrs Filissov was a little sharp-eyed and sharp-faced woman of forty, who looked cunningly and searchingly at the prince. When she asked his name – a question to which she deliberately imparted an air of mystery – the prince refused at first to answer, but immediately came back and asked her earnestly to give his name to Nastasya Filippovna. Mrs Filissov received his earnest request with redoubled attention and with an extraordinary air of secrecy by which she evidently wished to imply, 'Do not worry, sir, I understand.' The prince's name obviously made a tremendous impression on her. The prince looked at her absently, turned round, and went back to his hotel. But he went away, looking quite different from how he looked when he had rung at Mrs Filissov's door. Again an extraordinary change came over him almost in a fraction of a second: he again walked along, looking pale, weak, suffering, and excited; his knees trembled and a vague, forlorn smile hovered over his blue lips: his 'sudden idea' was suddenly confirmed and proved to be correct, and – he believed in his demon again!

Had it not been confirmed? Had it not proved correct? Why, then, that shivering again, that cold sweat, that darkness, and that icy chill in his soul? Was it not because he had again seen those eyes just now? But he had gone out of the Summer Gardens with the sole intention of seeing them! That was what his 'sudden idea' amounted to! He had been extremely anxious to see 'those eyes', so as to be absolutely sure that he would most certainly meet them *there*, at that house. That was a spasmodic wish of his, so why be so crushed and amazed now that he had seen them? As though he had not expected it! Yes, those were the *same* eyes (and there could be no doubt now that they were the same) as those which had flashed fire at him in the crowd this morning when he got out of the Moscow train at the Nikolayevsk station; they were the same (absolutely the same!) he had caught looking at him from behind that afternoon as he was sitting down at Rogozhin's. Rogozhin had denied it: he had asked with a wry, chilling smile, 'Whose eyes were they?' And quite recently, at the station when he was getting into the train to go to Pavlovsk to see Aglaya and suddenly caught sight of those eyes again, for the third time that day, the prince had a strong impulse to go up to Rogozhin and say to him, 'Whose eyes were they?' But he had run out of the station and recovered himself only before the cutler's shop at the moment when he was standing and estimating the cost of a certain article with a hartshorn handle at sixty copecks. A strange and most terrible demon had most certainly taken possession of him and refused to leave him any more. That demon had whispered to him in the Summer Gardens, as he sat lost in thought under a lime-tree, that if Rogozhin had to keep an eye on him and follow him about since early morning, then, having found out that he had not gone to Pavlovsk (which was, of course, fatal news for him), he would most certainly have gone *there*, to the house in the Petersburg suburb, and would most certainly have watched there for him, the prince, who had given his word of honour only that morning that he would not see her and that he had not come to Petersburg for that purpose. And here was the prince rushing off desperately to that house, and what if he did meet Rogozhin there? He had only seen an unhappy man whose state of mind was gloomy, but not difficult to understand. That unhappy man did not even conceal himself now. Yes, that morning Rogozhin had, for some reason, denied it and told a lie, but in the afternoon at the station he took hardly any precautions to conceal himself. It was he, the prince, rather than Rogozhin, who had concealed himself. And now, at the house, he stood on the other side of the street, on the pavement opposite, barely fifty paces away, with his arms folded – waiting. There he was completely in full view and, it seemed, purposely so. He stood there like an accuser and a judge and not as – and not as what?

And why had he, the prince, not gone up to him now himself, but turned away from him, as though he had not noticed anything, though their eyes had met? (Yes, their eyes had met! And they had looked at one another.) Had he not himself a few hours ago wanted to take Rogozhin by the hand and go *there* together with him? Had he not himself wanted to go to him next day and tell him that he had been to see her? Had he not himself renounced his demon, half-way there, when his soul had suddenly been filled with gladness? Or was there really something in Rogozhin – that is, in the whole aspect of the man *that day*, in all his words, movements, actions, looks, taken together – that could justify the prince's forebodings and the outrageous whispered suggestions of his demon? Something that was obvious but that was difficult to analyse and put into words, that was impossible to justify by adequate reasons, but which, in spite of all that difficulty and impossibility, produces an absolutely complete and irresistible impression, which involuntarily becomes a firm conviction.

Conviction of what? (Oh, how the enormity and 'shamefulness' of the conviction, of that 'base foreboding', tortured the prince and how he had blamed himself for it!) 'Tell me, if you dare, of what?' he kept saying to himself, challengingly and reproachfully. 'Formulate it, dare to express the whole of your thought, clearly, precisely, without hesitation! Oh, I am dishonourable!' he kept repeating with indignation and a flush on his face. 'How am I now to look this man in the face all my life? Oh, what a day! God, what a nightmare!'

There was a moment at the end of that long and agonizing walk from the Petersburg suburb when the prince was suddenly overcome by an irresistible desire to go to Rogozhin's at once, wait for him, embrace him with shame, with tears, tell him everything, and end it all at once. But he was already standing at his hotel. ... How he loathed that hotel in the morning, those corridors, the whole building, his room – how he loathed it at first sight! Several times during the day the thought of having to go back there filled him with particular disgust. 'Why do I, like a sick woman, believe in every presentiment to-day?' he thought with exasperated sarcasm, as he stopped at the gate. One occurrence to-day rose before his mind at that moment with great distinctness, but 'coldly', 'dispassionately', not 'like a nightmare'. He suddenly remembered the knife on Rogozhin's table. 'But why on earth shouldn't Rogozhin have as many knives as he likes on his table?' he asked, greatly amazed at himself and, at the same moment, petrified with astonishment, recalled how he had stopped in front of the cutler's shop. 'But what sort of connexion could there be in that?' he cried, and stopped short. A new, unbearable upsurge of shame, almost of despair, held him rooted to the spot at the very entrance to the gates. He stopped dead for a moment. This sometimes happens to people: sudden, unbearable memories, especially if they are accompanied by a feeling of shame, usually make them stop dead for a minute. 'Yes, I'm a man without a heart and a coward!' he repeated gloomily, and abruptly moved on, but only to stop dead again.

The entrance to the gateway, dark at any time, was particularly dark at that moment: the storm-cloud, which had covered the whole sky and blotted out the evening light, burst at the very moment the prince approached the house and the rain came down in torrents. At the time when he moved on abruptly after his momentary halt, he was standing outside the gates in the street. And suddenly, in the semi-darkness, he caught sight of a man inside the gates, close to the stairs. The man seemed to be waiting for something, but quickly sheered off and disappeared. The prince could not see him distinctly and, of course, could not possibly say for certain who it was. Besides, lots of people could have passed through the gates; it was an hotel and people were continually coming and going. But he suddenly felt absolutely and irresistibly convinced that he recognized the man and that it was most certainly Rogozhin. A moment later the prince rushed after him up the stairs. His heart stood still. 'Everything will be decided now!' he said to himself with strange conviction.

The stairs, which the prince ran up from under the gateway, led to the corridors of the ground and first floors, along which were the rooms of the hotel. This staircase, as in all old houses, was of stone. Dark and narrow, it twisted round a thick, stone column. On the first half landing there was a cavity in the column, something like a niche, not more than a yard wide and about eighteen inches deep. But there was enough room for a man to stand there. Dark as it was, the prince, on reaching the landing, immediately noticed that a man was hiding in the niche. The prince suddenly wanted to pass by without looking to the right. He had already taken one step, but could not restrain himself, and turned round.

Those two eyes – *the same two eyes* – suddenly met his own. The man who was hiding in the niche, had also taken a step forward. For a second they stood face to face and almost touching each other. Suddenly the prince seized him by the shoulders, turned him round towards the staircase, nearer to the light: he wanted to see his face clearly.

Rogozhin's eyes glittered and a frenzied smile contorted his face. He raised his right hand and something flashed in it. The prince did not try to stop him. All he remembered was that he seemed to have shouted:

'Parfyon, I don't believe it!'

Then suddenly some gulf seemed to open up before him: a blinding *inner* light flooded his soul. The moment lasted perhaps half a second, yet he clearly and consciously remembered the beginning, the first sound of the dreadful scream, which burst from his chest of its own accord and which he could have done nothing to suppress. Then his consciousness was instantly extinguished and complete darkness set in.

He had an epileptic fit, the first for a long time. It is a well-known fact that epileptic fits, the *epilepsy* itself, come on instantaneously. At that instant the face suddenly becomes horribly distorted, especially the eyes. Spasms and convulsions seize the whole body and the features of the face. A terrible, quite incredible scream, which is unlike anything else, breaks from the chest; in that scream everything human seems suddenly to be obliterated, and it is quite impossible, at least very difficult, for an observer to imagine and to admit that it is the man himself who is screaming. One gets the impression that it is someone inside the man who is screaming. This, at any rate, is how many people describe their impression; the sight of a man in an epileptic fit fills many others with absolute and unbearable horror, which has something mystical about it. It must be assumed that it was this impression of sudden horror, accompanied by all the other terrible impressions of the moment, that paralysed Rogozhin, and so saved the prince from the inevitable blow of the knife with which he had been attacked. Then, before he had time to realize that it was a fit, seeing that the prince had recoiled from him and suddenly fallen backwards down the stairs, knocking the back of his head violently against the stone step, Rogozhin rushed headlong downstairs and, avoiding the prostrate figure and scarcely knowing what he was doing, ran out of the hotel.

Twisting and writhing in violent convulsions, the sick man's body slipped down the steps, of which there were no fewer than fifteen, to the bottom of the staircase. Quite soon, not more than five minutes later, he was discovered and a crowd gathered. A whole pool of blood near his head made the people wonder whether he had hurt himself or whether there had been some foul play. Soon, however, some of them recognized that it was a case of epilepsy; one of the people at the hotel identified the prince as having arrived that morning. The confusion was finally very happily resolved by a fortunate circumstance.

Kolya Ivolgin, who had promised to be back at 'The Scales' at about four o'clock and who had instead gone to Pavlovsk, had on a sudden impulse given up the idea of dining at Mrs Yepanchin's and hurried back to 'The Scales', where he arrived at seven o'clock. Learning from the note the prince had left for him that the latter was in town, he at once went to find him at the address given in the note. Being informed at the hotel that the prince had gone out, he went downstairs to the restaurant and waited for him there, having tea and listening to the organ. Happening to overhear that someone had had a fit, he quite rightly surmised that it must have been the prince and rushed to the spot where he recognized him. The necessary measures were taken at once. The prince was carried to his room; though he had come to, he did not recover full consciousness for a long time. A doctor who had been summoned to examine his injured head, ordered a lotion, and said that there was not the slightest danger of complications from the wound. When, an hour later, the prince began to understand pretty well what was going on around him, Kolya took him in a cab from the hotel to Lebedev's. Lebedev received the patient with bows and extraordinary warmth. For the prince's sake he put forward the date of his going to the country, and three days later they were all in Pavlovsk.

6

Lebedev's country cottage was not large, but it was comfortable and even pretty. The part of it which was to let had been specially decorated. On the rather spacious veranda, at the entrance from the street into the house, a few orange-trees, lemon-trees, and jasmine had been placed in large, green wooden tubs, which in Lebedev's opinion gave the house a most attractive appearance. Some of those trees he had acquired together with the cottage, and he was so charmed with the effect they produced on the veranda that he decided to take advantage of an opportunity to buy, in addition, a number of similar trees in tubs at an auction. When all the trees had at last been brought to the cottage and put in their places, Lebedev had several times that day run down the steps of the veranda into the street and from there admired his property, every time mentally adding to the sum he proposed to ask from his future tenant.

The prince, worn out, depressed, and physically shattered, was very pleased with the cottage. On the day of his arrival in Pavlovsk, that is, three days after his fit – the prince appeared to be almost well again, though inwardly he felt far from well. During those three days he was glad to see everyone around him, he was glad to see Kolya, who hardly left his side, glad to see the Lebedev family (without the nephew who had disappeared somewhere), and glad to see Lebedev himself; he was even pleased to receive a visit from General Ivolgin before he left Petersburg. On the day of his arrival – he arrived in Pavlovsk late in the afternoon – a fairly large number of visitors assembled on the veranda round him: the first to arrive was Ganya, whom the prince scarcely recognized, so changed and so thin had he grown in that time; then Varya and Ptitsyn, who also had a cottage in Pavlovsk, arrived. General Ivolgin practically never left Lebedev's house and, indeed, seemed to have moved to Pavlovsk with him. Lebedev did his best to keep him in his own part of the house and prevent him from going to see the prince; he treated him like a friend, and they had apparently known each other a long time. The prince noticed that during the three days they sometimes had long discussions, quite often shouting and arguing, even, it seemed, about learned subjects, which evidently pleased Lebedev. It almost looked as though Lebedev could not do without him. Ever since their arrival in Pavlovsk, Lebedev had taken the same precautions with his own family as with the general; on the pretext of not disturbing the prince, he would not permit anyone to go to see him, stamping his feet, rushing at his daughters and chasing after them, without making any exception even for Vera and the baby, at the least suspicion that they were going on to the veranda, where the prince was, in spite of the prince's request not to send anyone away.

'In the first place,' he declared at last in reply to the prince's direct question, 'they will lose all respect if allowed too much freedom, and, secondly, it's improper for them. . . .'

'But why not?' the prince appealed to him. 'Really, you're only worrying me with all this supervision and watching over me. I get bored all by myself; I've told you so again and again; and I get even more bored by the way you go on waving your arms about and walking on tiptoe.'

The prince was hinting at the fact that though Lebedev chased everyone away on the pretext that the patient had to be left in peace, he had himself been coming in almost continuously during the last three days, and every time he first opened the door, poked his head in, and examined the room, as though wishing to make sure that the prince was still there and had not run away, and only then, slowly and stealthily, tiptoed to the prince's arm-chair, so that sometimes he quite inadvertently startled his lodger. He kept inquiring constantly if the prince wanted anything, and when the prince began telling him at last to leave him in peace, he turned away obediently and without a word, tiptoed back to the door, waving his arms all the time, as though wishing to imply that he had only just looked in, that he wouldn't say a word, that he had already gone out and wouldn't come in again. And yet ten minutes, or at the most a quarter of an hour, later he would reappear. Kolya aroused in Lebedev a feeling of the deepest mortification and even of outraged resentment simply because he had free access to the prince. He noticed that Lebedev listened at the door to what he and the prince were saying for half an hour at a time, and, of course, he told the prince about it.

'You must regard me as your property since you keep me under lock and key,' the prince protested. 'In the country at least I want it to be different, and I'd like to make it quite clear that I intend to see anyone I like and go anywhere I like.'

'Without a shadow of doubt,' Lebedev replied, waving his arms.

The prince scrutinized him from head to foot.

'And have you brought with you the little safe that used to hang over the head of your bed?'

'No, sir, I haven't.'

'Oh? You didn't leave it there, did you?'

'I couldn't bring it. I should have had to wrench it from the wall. It's firmly fixed – firmly!'

'Well, I suppose you have another one like it here, haven't you?'

'A better one – a much better one. That's why I bought this house.'

'Oh, I see. Who was it you wouldn't admit to see me about an hour ago?'

'Oh, that – that was the general, sir. It's true I didn't let him in to see you. He isn't the right sort of person for you to see. I have a great respect for that man, Prince. He's – er – a great man, sir. You don't believe me? Well, you will see. But all the same, most illustrious Prince, it's much better you did not receive him.'

'And why shouldn't I, pray? And why are you standing on tiptoe now, Lebedev, and why do you always come up to me as though you wanted to whisper a secret in my ear?'

'I'm vile, vile, I feel it,' Lebedev replied unexpectedly, smiting his breast with feeling. 'But won't the general be too hospitable for you?'

'Too hospitable?'

'Yes, sir, hospitable. To begin with, he proposes to come and live with me. I don't mind that, but he's too impetuous. He wants to be treated as a relation at once. I've discussed the question of my relationship with him several times, and it appears that we are connected by marriage. It seems that you are also a sort of nephew of his on your mother's side. If you are his nephew, then I too, most illustrious Prince, am a relation of yours. That wouldn't matter very much – just a little weakness, as you might say – but he has just been assuring me that he had never had fewer than two hundred people sitting down at table every day since he was a subaltern up to the eleventh of June last year. He went even so far as to claim that they never got up from the table, which means, of course, that they had dinner, supper, and tea for fifteen hours out of twenty-four for thirty years on end without a break, and that there was scarcely time to change the tablecloth. As soon as one got up and went, another one came, and on holidays and royal birthdays there were as many as three hundred guests. On the thousandth anniversary of the foundation of Russia he counted as many as seven hundred. Well, sir, that's an obsession, that is. Such – er – stories are a bad sign, a very bad sign, and such dispensers of hospitality, sir, aren't quite safe to receive in one's house. That's why I thought that perhaps a man like that might be a little too hospitable for you and me.'

'But you are on excellent terms with him, aren't you?'

'Oh, we are great friends, and I take it all as a joke. Let us be connexions by marriage – what do I care? The greater the honour. I can see he's a very remarkable man in spite of the two hundred men at dinner and the thousandth anniversary of Russia. I say it in all sincerity, sir. You've been speaking of secrets just now, Prince; I mean, that I come up to you as though wishing to impart some secret. Well, as a matter of fact, there is a secret: a certain person has just let me know that she'd like to have a secret meeting with you.'

'Why secret? Not at all. I'll go and see her myself – to-day even.'

'Not at all, not at all!' Lebedev cried, waving his arms. 'And she isn't afraid of what you think, either. By the way, that monster comes every day to inquire after your health. Did you know that?'

'You call him a monster a little too often. It makes me rather suspicious.'

'There's no need for you to be suspicious at all, sir,' Lebedev reassured him quickly. 'All I wanted to say was that the certain person was not afraid of him, but of something different, something quite different.'

'What is she afraid of? Tell me quickly!' the prince asked impatiently, looking at Lebedev's mysterious contortions.

'Ah, that's the secret.'

And Lebedev grinned.

'Whose secret?'

'Your secret. You forbade me yourself, most illustrious Prince, to speak of it in your presence,' Lebedev murmured and, having thoroughly enjoyed the fact that he had aroused the prince's curiosity to the highest pitch of impatience, he suddenly concluded: 'She's afraid of Miss Aglaya.'

The prince made a wry face and was silent for a minute.

'Quite seriously, Lebedev, I'm going to leave your house,' he said suddenly. 'Where are the Ptitsyns and Mr Ivolgin? Are they at your place? Have you enticed them away, too?'

'They're coming, sir, they're coming. And the general as well. I'll throw open all the doors, and I'll call my daughters in too – everyone, everyone – at once, at once!' Lebedev whispered, looking frightened, waving his arms about and rushing from one door to another.

At that moment, Kolya appeared on the veranda, having come in from the street, and announced that new visitors – Mrs Yepanchin and her three daughters – were following close behind him.

'Shall I ask the Ptitsyns and Mr Ivolgin in or not?' Lebedev, dumbfounded at the news, asked, rushing up to the prince. 'Shall I ask the general in or not?'

'Why not? Let them all come, if they like. I assure you, Lebedev, you've somehow misunderstood me from the very beginning. You seem to be continually wrong. I haven't the slightest reason for hiding and concealing myself from anybody,' the prince laughed.

Looking at him, Lebedev felt it his duty to laugh, too. In spite of his intense excitement, Lebedev was apparently also extremely pleased.

The news brought by Kolya was true. He had come a little in advance of the Yepanchins to announce their arrival, so that the visitors suddenly arrived from two sides – the Yepanchins from the veranda and the Ptitsyns, Ganya, and the general from the inner rooms.

The Yepanchins had only just learnt from Kolya that the prince was ill and that he was in Pavlovsk. Till then, Mrs Yepanchin had been in a state of painful bewilderment. Two days earlier General Yepanchin showed his family the prince's visiting-card, and Mrs Yepanchin was firmly convinced that the prince would follow his card to Pavlovsk and call on them at once. In vain did her daughters assure her that a man who had not written for six months was hardly likely to be in such a hurry to see them and that very likely he had plenty to do in Petersburg without bothering about them – what did they know of his business affairs? Mrs Yepanchin was very angry with them for their remarks and was ready to take a bet that the prince would call next day at the latest, though even that would be 'too late'. That day she had been expecting him all morning; they expected him to dinner, in the evening, and when it grew quite dark Mrs Yepanchin got cross with everything and quarrelled with everybody, without, of course, mentioning the prince as the cause of the quarrel. On the third day no mention of him was made at all. When Aglaya inadvertently blurted out at dinner that their mother was angry because the prince had not come – to which the general at once remarked that it was not his fault – Mrs Yepanchin got up from the table and left the room wrathfully. At last Kolya came in the evening with the latest news and a full description of the prince's adventures as he knew them. As a result, Mrs Yepanchin was triumphant, though Kolya got a severe scolding. 'He hangs about here for days and one can't get rid of him, but now he might at least have let us know, if he didn't think it necessary to honour us with a visit himself.' Kolya was about to get angry with Mrs Yepanchin for saying that 'one can't get rid of him', but he put it off for another time, and if the remark itself had not been so insulting, he might have forgiven it altogether – so pleased was he to see Mrs Yepanchin worried and anxious at the news of the prince's illness. She kept insisting for a long time on the necessity of sending a special messenger to Petersburg to rout out a medical celebrity of the first magnitude and bring him down to Pavlovsk on the first available train. But her daughters dissuaded her; they did not want, however, to be left behind when Mrs Yepanchin got ready at once to go and see the invalid.

'He's on his deathbed,' Mrs Yepanchin kept saying, as she bustled about, 'and we're going to stand on ceremony, are we? Is he a friend of the family or not?'

'We mustn't butt in, either, before we know that he wants to see us,' Aglaya observed.

'Very well, then, don't come. And a good thing, too: if Mr Radomsky comes, there will be no one to receive him.'

After such a retort, Aglaya, of course, immediately set off after them, which, indeed, she intended to do all along. Prince Sh., who had been sitting with Adelaida, at her request at once agreed to escort the ladies. He had been extremely interested before, at the beginning of his acquaintance with the Yepanchins, when he heard them talking about the prince. It appeared that he knew him, that they had met somewhere not so long before, and had spent two weeks in some small provincial town together. That was about three months before. Prince Sh. had indeed told them a great deal about the prince and was generally of a good opinion of him, so that it was with real pleasure that he was now going to call on an old acquaintance. General Yepanchin was not at home that afternoon. Mr Radomsky had not yet arrived, either.

It was no more than a few hundred yards from the Yepanchins' to Lebedev's cottage. Mrs Yepanchin's first disagreeable shock was to find a whole host of visitors at the prince's, not to mention the fact that among them were two or three persons she positively detested; the second shock was of surprise at seeing a fashionably dressed young man, in perfect health and laughing, coming to meet her, instead of the dying man on his deathbed she expected to find. She even stopped in bewilderment, to the intense delight of Kolya, who could of course have explained to her pefectly well before she set off that no one was thinking of dying and that there was no question of a deathbed. But he had not explained in crafty anticipation of Mrs Yepanchin's comic wrath when, as he reckoned, she would certainly be angry at finding the prince, her dear friend, in excellent health. Indeed, Kolya was so tactless as to put his surmise into words and so provoke Mrs Yepanchin in good earnest, for he was always sparring with her, sometimes very acrimoniously, in spite of their affection for one another.

'You wait, my boy, don't be in such a hurry – don't spoil your triumph!' replied Mrs Yepanchin, sitting down in the arm-chair the prince had placed for her.

Lebedev, Ptitsyn, and General Ivolgin hastened to get chairs for the young ladies. The general offered a chair to Aglaya. Lebedev, who offered a chair to Prince Sh., managed to express his profound respect even in the way he bent his back. Varya, as usual, exchanged ecstatic and whispered greetings with the young ladies.

'It's quite true, Prince, that I expected to find you almost in bed. I so exaggerated everything in my fright that – I won't lie about it – I felt terribly put out just now at the sight of your happy face. But I swear it was only for a moment, till I had had time to reflect. I always act and speak more sensibly when I have had time to reflect. I expect you do the same. Actually, I should have been less pleased at the recovery of my own son, if I had one, than I am at yours. And if you don't believe me, so much the worse for you. And this spiteful boy permits himself to play much worse jokes at my expense. He's a protégé of yours, I believe. Well, I warn you that one fine morning I shall deny myself the pleasure of enjoying the honour of his further acquaintance.'

'But what have I done now?' cried Kolya. 'However much I'd have assured you that the prince was almost well again, you wouldn't have believed me because it was much more interesting to imagine him lying on his deathbed.'

'How long are you staying here?' Mrs Yepanchin asked, addressing the prince.

'The whole summer and perhaps longer.'

'You're alone, aren't you? Not married?'

'No, not married.' The prince smiled at the ingenuousness of the insinuation.

'You needn't smile – such things do happen. I was referring to the cottage – why haven't you come and stayed with us? We have a whole wing empty. But just as you like, of course. Are you renting it from him? From that person?' she added in an undertone, nodding at Lebedev. 'What does he go on pulling faces like that for?'

At that moment Vera came out of the inner room on to the veranda, carrying the baby in her arms as usual. Lebedev, who kept fidgeting near the chairs, utterly at a loss what to do with himself and desperately anxious not to go, pounced upon Vera, waving his arms at her in an attempt to chase her away from the veranda and, completely forgetting himself, began stamping his feet.

'Is he mad?' Mrs Yepanchin added suddenly.

'No, he's – –'

'Drunk, perhaps? I must say the company you keep is not particularly nice, is it?' she snapped with a glance at the other visitors. 'What a charming girl, though! Who is she?'

'That's Vera, Mr Lebedev's daughter.'

'Oh! She's very charming. I'd like to know her.'

But Lebedev, hearing Mrs Yepanchin's compliments, was already dragging his daughter forward to introduce her.

'Orphans, poor orphans!' he cried in melting tones as he came up. 'And this orphan child is her sister and my baby daughter Lyubov, born in lawful wedlock, my dear wife Yelena dying six weeks ago in childbirth by the will of God. Yes, ma'am, she's been a mother to my baby, though she's only her sister and no more – no more. . . .'

'And you, sir,' Mrs Yepanchin snapped suddenly in great indignation, 'are no more than a fool, I'm sorry to say. Very well, that'll do. I think you realize it yourself.'

'Perfectly true, ma'am,' Lebedev replied, with a most respectful bow.

'I say, Mr Lebedev, I'm told you're very good at interpreting the Apocalypse. Is it true?' asked Aglaya.

'Quite true, Miss – for the last fifteen years.'

'I've heard about you. I believe there was something about you in the papers, too, wasn't there?'

'No, Miss, that was about another interpreter, another one. He's dead now, I'm sorry to say, and I've taken his place,' Lebedev replied, beside himself with delight.

'Do me a favour and, as we are neighbours, interpret it to me one day soon. I don't understand anything in the Apocalypse.'

'I'm afraid I must warn you, Miss Aglaya, that it's pure charlatanism on his part, believe me,' quickly put in General Ivolgin, who seemed to be on pins and needles and was most anxious to join in the conversation. 'Of course,' he went on, sitting down beside Aglaya, 'a holiday in the country has its own privileges and its own pleasures, and your invitation to this ridiculous amateur for the interpretation of the Apocalypse is a diversion like any other, and, I daresay, a remarkably intelligent diversion at that, but I -- You seem to be looking at me with some surprise, my dear. Allow me to introduce myself – General Ivolgin. I used to carry you in my arms.'

'I'm very pleased to meet you, sir,' Aglaya murmured, trying hard not to burst out laughing. 'I know your wife and daughter.'

Mrs Yepanchin flushed. Something that had been boiling up inside her for a long time suddenly had to come out. She could not bear General Ivolgin, with whom she had been acquainted, though only a long time ago.

'You're lying as usual, sir,' she snapped at him indignantly. 'You never carried her in your arms.'

'You've forgotten, Mother,' Aglaya suddenly came to the general's rescue. 'He really did carry me about in Tver. We were living in Tver then. I was six years old then, I remember. He made me a bow and arrow and taught me to shoot, and I killed a pigeon. You remember we killed a pigeon together, don't you?'

'And he brought me a cardboard helmet and a wooden sword,' cried Adelaida. 'I remember it very well.'

'I remember it, too,' Alexandra said. 'You quarrelled over the wounded pigeon and you were put in a corner. Adelaida stood there wearing her sword and helmet.'

When the general told Aglaya that he had carried her in his arms, he said it without thinking, simply because he was anxious to start a conversation and because he almost always began a conversation with young people like that, if he wanted to make their acquaintance. But this time, as luck would have it, he was speaking the truth and, as luck would have it, he had forgotten it! So that when Aglaya declared that they had shot a pigeon together, his past came back to him in a flash and he remembered it all to the last detail, as very old people not infrequently do remember some detail from their remote past. It is hard to say what there was in that memory to produce so strong an impression on the poor general, who was, as usual, slightly drunk; but he was suddenly extraordinarily moved.

'I remember – I remember everything!' he cried. 'I was only a senior lieutenant then. You were such a little girl – such a pretty little girl. Nina – my wife – Ganya – I – I used to be received in your house then – Ivan Yepanchin – –'

'And you see, sir, what's become of you now!' Mrs Yepanchin broke in. 'So you haven't entirely lost your decent feelings in spite of your drinking habits, if it affects you so much! But you have worried your wife to death, sir. Instead of looking after your children, you've been sitting in a debtors' jail. Go away, sir; go and stand in some corner behind the door and have a good cry. Remember your past innocence and maybe the Lord will forgive you. Go along – go – I'm speaking seriously. Nothing improves a man's character more than remembering his past with a contrite heart.'

But to repeat that she was speaking seriously was unnecessary: the general, like all confirmed drunkards, was very sentimental and, like all drunkards who have come down in the world, could not bear to be reminded of his happy past. He got up and walked meekly to the door, so that Mrs Yepanchin was immediately sorry for him.

'My dear General,' she called after him, 'wait a moment. We all have our faults. When you feel your conscience reproaching you a little less strongly, you can come and see me, and we'll have a talk about the past. I daresay I'm fifty times as great a sinner as you myself. Well, good-bye now,' she added quickly, afraid that he might come back. 'Go along, sir, you've nothing more to do here.'

'You'd better not go after him now,' the prince said, stopping Kolya, who was about to run after his father, 'or he'll lose his temper in a minute and the whole minute will be wasted on him.'

'That's true,' Mrs Yepanchin declared. 'Don't disturb him now. Go and see him in half an hour.'

'That's what comes of telling the truth once in a lifetime,' Lebedev ventured to put in. 'It reduced him to tears.'

'You, too, are a fine fellow, sir, if what I've heard is true,' Mrs Yepanchin at once put him in his place.

The mutual relationship of the visitors who had gathered at the prince's gradually defined itself. The prince was, of course, fully able to appreciate, and he did appreciate, the sympathy shown to him by Mrs Yepanchin and her daughters, and he told them, of course, very frankly that before they called he had intended to pay them a visit that day, in spite of his illness and the late hour. Mrs Yepanchin, glancing at his visitors, replied that he could still do so. Ptitsyn, a very polite man who got on very well with everybody, very soon got up and withdrew to Lebedev's part of the house, and was very anxious to take Lebedev with him. Lebedev promised to join him soon; meantime Varya got into conversation with the Yepanchin girls and remained. She and Ganya were very glad the general had gone; Ganya himself soon followed Ptitsyn out of the room. During the few minutes that he stayed on the veranda with the Yepanchins he had conducted himself very modestly and with dignity, and was not in the least disconcerted by the scornful glances of Mrs Yepanchin, who had twice examined him from top to toe. People who had known him before might really have thought that he had greatly changed. Aglaya was very pleased with it.

'Wasn't it Mr Ivolgin who went out just now?' she asked suddenly in a loud, sharp voice, as she was fond of doing sometimes, interrupting the general conversation by her question and addressing no one in particular.

'Yes,' replied the prince.

'I hardly recognized him. He's changed a lot and – very much for the better.'

'I'm very glad for his sake,' said the prince.

'He's been very ill,' Varya added with lively sympathy.

'How has he changed for the better?' asked Mrs Yepanchin in angry perplexity and almost in alarm. 'Where did you get that idea from? There's nothing better about him. In what way do you think he's better?'

'There's nothing better than the "poor knight"!' Kolya, who had been standing near Mrs Yepanchin's chair, suddenly declared.

'I think so too!' said Prince Sh., and laughed.

'I'm of the same opinion,' Adelaida declared solemnly.

'What "poor knight"?' asked Mrs Yepanchin, looking at those who had just spoken with perplexity and vexation, but seeing that Aglaya flushed, added angrily: 'Some nonsense, I'll be bound. Who is this "poor knight"?'

'It's not the first time – is it – that this guttersnipe, this favourite of yours, has been twisting other people's words!' Aglaya replied with haughty indignation.

In every one of Aglaya's outbursts of anger (and she was often angry) there was, in spite of her unmistakable seriousness and severity, almost always a touch of something so utterly childish, so impatiently schoolgirlish, and so badly disguised, that it was sometimes quite impossible to refrain from laughing, much to the annoyance of Aglaya, who could not understand what people were laughing at and 'how they could, how they dared laugh'. Now, too, her sisters and Prince Sh. laughed, and even the prince smiled, though he, too, blushed for some unknown reason. Kolya roared with laughter and was triumphant. Aglaya got angry in good earnest and looked twice as pretty. Her confusion was very becoming to her, and at that moment she also happened to be annoyed with herself at her own confusion.

'He has twisted many of your words, too,' she added.

'I'm merely going by what you said!' cried Kolya. 'A month ago you were looking through *Don Quixote* and you used those very words about there being nothing better than the "poor knight!" I don't know whom you were talking of: Don Quixote or Mr Radomsky or some other person, but you were talking of someone, and the conversation went on for a long time.'

'You go a little too far with your guesses, young man,' Mrs Yepanchin cut him short with vexation.

'But I'm not the only one, am I?' Kolya went on. 'They were all talking about it and they do so still. Just now Prince Sh. and Miss Adelaida and everyone declared that they were all for the "poor knight", and I believe that were it not for Miss Adelaida, we should have known long ago who this "poor knight" was.'

'What have I done?' laughed Adelaida.

'You refused to draw his portrait, that's what! Miss Aglaya asked you then to draw the portrait of the "poor knight" and told you the whole subject of the picture, which she thought of herself. You remember the subject, don't you? But you refused.'

'But how could I draw it? Whom? According to the subject, I couldn't have drawn his face at all, for --

His face from all was hidden
By the visor of steel he bore.

What was I to draw? A visor?'

'I don't know what you're talking about – what's all this about a visor?' Mrs Yepanchin cried irritably.

She was beginning to have a pretty good idea who was meant by the name (probably agreed upon long ago!) of the "poor knight". But what made her really furious was that the prince, too, looked embarrassed and blushed like a ten-year-old boy.

'Well,' she went on, 'are you going to put an end to this nonsense or not? Will you explain this "poor knight" to me or won't you? Is it such a terrible secret that it's quite beyond your powers to reveal it?'

But they only went on laughing.

'It's simply this,' Prince Sh., who was evidently anxious to drop the subject or change it as soon as possible, intervened on their behalf. 'There's a curious Russian poem about a "poor knight", a fragment without a beginning or an end. A month ago we were all laughing after dinner and trying, as usual, to find a subject for Adelaida's next picture. You know the whole family is always trying to find subjects for Adelaida's pictures. It was then we thought of the "poor knight". Who thought of it first, I can't remember. . . .'

'Miss Aglaya!' cried Kolya.

'Perhaps, I daresay you're right, only I can't remember,' Prince Sh. went on. 'Some of us laughed at the subject and others declared that there could be no better one, but that to depict the "poor knight", we had to find a face for him. We began to think of the faces of all our friends, and not one was suitable. That's as far as we got. That is all. I can't imagine why Master Nicholas should have thought it necessary to bring it up now. What was amusing and appropriate at the time is, I'm afraid, not at all interesting now.'

'Because of some new sort of malicious and offensive foolishness, I'll be bound,' Mrs Yepanchin snapped.

'There's no foolishness about it at all, only the deepest respect,' Aglaya said quite unexpectedly in a grave and earnest voice.

She had succeeded in completely recovering her equanimity and overcoming her confusion. Moreover, it was easy to see from certain signs that she was delighted that the joke had gone so far. This great change in her took place just at the moment when the prince's increasing embarrassment had reached a point where it could no longer be concealed from anyone.

'One moment they're laughing like mad, and another they show their deepest respect! Crazy creatures! Why respect? Tell me at once why should you suddenly and for no reason at all wish to show your deepest respect?'

'Because,' Aglaya continued in the same grave and serious tone of voice in reply to her mother's almost spiteful question, 'because that poem describes a man capable of having an ideal and, secondly, because, having set himself that ideal before him, he believed in it and, having believed in it, he devoted his whole life to it. This does not always happen in this age. The poem doesn't specify exactly what the ideal of the "poor knight" was, but it is evident that it was some bright image, an image of pure beauty, and the love-sick knight even wears a rosary instead of a scarf round his neck. It is true that there is some obscure and unspecified motto there, the letters A.N.B., which he inscribed on his shield – –'

'A.M.D.,' Kolya corrected her.

'And I say A.N.B., and that's what I wanted to say,' Aglaya interrupted with vexation. 'However that may be, it is clear that the poor knight no longer cared who the lady was or what his lady did. It was enough for him that he had chosen her and that he believed in her pure beauty and then worshipped her for ever. That's where his merit lies, for even if she became a thief afterwards, he would still have to believe in her and break a lance for her pure beauty. It seems that the poet wanted to unite in one striking image the whole grand conception of medieval chivalrous and platonic love as it was conceived by some pure and high-minded knight. All that, of course, is just an ideal. But in the "poor knight" that feeling has been brought to the highest degree of asceticism. It must be admitted that to be capable of such a feeling means a great deal, and that such feelings in themselves leave a profound and, from one point of view, highly praiseworthy impression behind, not to mention Don Quixote. The "poor knight" is also a Don Quixote, only serious and not comic. At first I didn't understand him and laughed, but now I love the "poor knight" and, what's more, respect his deeds of valour,' Aglaya concluded, and it was difficult to say whether she was in earnest or laughing.

'Well, he must have been a fool – he and his deeds of valour,' Mrs Yepanchin declared emphatically. 'And you, too, young woman, are talking a lot of nonsense – a whole lecture, if you please! It doesn't become you, if you ask me. It's highly improper, anyway. What poem? Read it. I'm sure you know it. I want to hear that poem at once! I never could stand poetry. I knew it would come to no good. For goodness sake, Prince,' she addressed the prince, 'have patience. It seems you and I have to exercise patience.' She was very vexed.

The prince wanted to say something, but he was still too embarrassed to speak. Aglaya alone, who had taken such liberties in her 'lecture', was not in the least embarrassed, but seemed, indeed, quite pleased. She got up at once, still grave and serious as before, and looking as though she had prepared herself for the recital and was only waiting to be asked, she stepped into the middle of the veranda, and stood facing the prince, who remained sitting in his arm-chair.

Everyone looked at her with some surprise, and almost everyone – Prince Sh., her sisters, and her mother – regarded with an uncomfortable feeling this new prank of hers, which had already gone too far. But it was evident that Aglaya thoroughly enjoyed the affectation with which she was beginning the ceremony of reading the poem. Mrs Yepanchin was on the point of telling her to go back to her place, but at the very moment when Aglaya began to recite the well-known ballad, two new visitors, talking loudly, came in from the street. They were General Yepanchin and a young man. Their entrance caused a slight commotion.

7

The young man who accompanied the general was about twenty-eight, tall and slim, with a handsome and intelligent face, and a pair of large black eyes, full of sparkling wit and irony. Aglaya did not even look round at him, but went on reciting the poem, still gazing pointedly at the prince in an affected manner, and addressing herself to him alone. It was quite obvious to the prince that she was doing it all with some special object. But the new arrivals, at any rate, made his position a little less awkward. Seeing them, he stood up, nodded politely to the general from a distance, signalled to them not to interrupt the recital, and himself managed to retreat behind the arm-chair, and leaning with his left arm on the back of it, he continued to listen to the ballad in a more comfortable and less 'ridiculous' position than before. For her part, Mrs Yepanchin twice motioned peremptorily to the two visitors to stand still. The prince, by the way, was rather interested in his new visitor who accompanied the general. He rightly concluded that he must be Yevgeny Pavlovich Radomsky, of whom he had heard a great deal and thought more than once. He was a little puzzled by his civilian dress; he had understood that Radomsky was an army officer. An ironic smile played on the lips of the new visitor all the time the poem was being recited, as though he, too, had heard something about the 'poor knight'.

'Perhaps it was he who first thought of it,' the prince thought to himself.

But it was quite different with Aglaya. The affectation and pomposity, with which she had begun the recitation, she invested with such earnestness and such an insight into the spirit and meaning of the poem, she spoke every word of it with such understanding and enunciated the lines with such noble simplicity, that by the end of the recitation she not only held the attention of them all, but by her rendering of the lofty spirit of the ballad seemed at least partly to justify the exaggerated and affected gravity with which she had so solemnly stepped into the middle of the veranda. In that gravity one could now only discern her infinite and, perhaps, even naïve respect for what she had undertaken to render. Her eyes shone and a light, barely perceptible tremor of inspiration and ecstasy passed twice over her beautiful face. She recited:

There was a knight, poor and brave,
  Slow of speech and plain,
Sad and pale and lonely,
  But proud and disdainful of gain.

His eyes were shut and blind to all
  But the image in them cast,
His heart was locked and guarded
  To keep his secret fast.

Not a word to woman he spoke,
  No look of soft appeal,
To the grave he'd sworn to take
  His vision true as steel.

Round his neck a rosary,
  No scarf of woman he wore,
His face from all was hidden
  By the visor of steel he bore.

Full of love and duty dear,
  Faithful to his dream,
A.M.D. on his shield he traced
  In his own blood stream.

Crusading knights in Palestine
  Among the rocks so bare,
Into battle wildly dashing,
  Called on their ladies fair.

Lumen coeli, sancta Rosa!
  Wild and fierce he cried,
And struck down, as if by thunder,
  Many Muslims died.

Returning to his distant castle,
There he lived and sighed,
Ever silent, sad, and cheerless,
Of reason bereft, he died.

Recalling it all afterwards, the prince was greatly troubled and worried for a long time by a question to which he could find no answer: how could such a genuine and beautiful feeling be combined with such obvious and malicious mockery? That it was a mockery he had no doubt; he understood that clearly, and with good reason: during her recitation Aglaya did not hesitate to change the letters A.M.D. to N.F.B. That he had not been mistaken or misheard this, he could have no doubt (it was proved afterwards). In any case, Aglaya's substitution of the letters – a joke, of course, though rather an unkind and thoughtless one – was deliberate. They were all talking about (and 'laughing at') the 'poor knight' a month ago. And yet, as far as the prince could remember, Aglaya had pronounced those letters without a trace of jest or sneer and without stressing them in any way to reveal more clearly their hidden meaning. She had uttered them, on the contrary, with such unfailing earnestness, with such innocence and naïve simplicity that anyone might have supposed that those letters were in the ballad and printed in the book. The prince received a painful and unpleasant shock. Mrs Yepanchin, of course, neither understood nor noticed the change of the letters or the insinuation it contained. All General Yepanchin understood was that a poem was being recited. Many of the other listeners understood and were surprised at the audacity of her outburst and the intention behind it, but they said nothing and tried not to show it. But Radomsky (the prince was quite ready to take a bet on it) not only understood it, but also tried to show that he had understood: he smiled much too sarcastically.

'How lovely!' Mrs Yepanchin cried rapturously as soon as the recitation was over. 'Whose poem is it?'

'It's Pushkin's, Mother,' cried Adelaida. 'Really, you make us blush – you ought to be ashamed of yourself!'

'It's a wonder I'm not a greater fool, with daughters like you!' Mrs Yepanchin retorted bitterly. 'Disgraceful! Let me have that poem of Pushkin's as soon as we get home!'

'I don't think we've got a Pushkin.'

'I believe,' Alexandra added, 'there have been two battered volumes lying about somewhere in the house since time immemorial.'

'We must send Fyodor or Alexey to town by the first train to buy one – Fyodor would be best. Aglaya, come here. Give me a kiss, dear.

You recited it beautifully, but,' she added almost in a whisper, 'if your recital was sincere I'm sorry for you. If you did it to make fun of him, I cannot approve of your feelings, so that in any case it would have been better not to have read it at all. Understand? You can go now, madam. I'll speak to you about it another time. I'm afraid we've stayed here too long.'

Meanwhile the prince exchanged greetings with General Yepanchin, and the general introduced Radomsky to him.

'I overtook him on the way here. He was coming from the station. He heard that I was coming here and that all the others were here – –'

'I heard that you, too, were here,' Radomsky interrupted, 'and as I've long ago made up my mind to seek not only your acquaintance but also your friendship, I didn't want to lose time. You aren't well? I've only just heard – –'

'I'm perfectly well and very pleased to meet you,' replied the prince, holding out his hand. 'I've heard a great deal about you and even talked about you with Prince Sh.'

Mutual courtesies were exchanged, both shook hands and gazed intently into each other's eyes. In a moment the conversation became general. The prince noticed (he was noticing everything instantly and eagerly now, but perhaps also what was not there at all) that everyone was greatly astonished to see Radomsky wearing mufti, so much so, indeed, that everything else seemed to have been completely forgotten for a time. One might have supposed that there was something extremely important in this change of dress. Adelaida and Alexandra were questioning Radomsky with perplexed looks, Prince Sh., his relation, with great uneasiness, and the general was speaking almost with agitation. Only Aglaya cast a curious but entirely unperturbed glance at Radomsky, as though wondering whether civilian or military dress suited him best, but a minute later she turned away and did not look at him again. Mrs Yepanchin, too, did not care to ask any questions, though perhaps she also was a little worried. The prince fancied that Radomsky was not in her good books.

'He surprised me, bowled me over,' General Yepanchin kept repeating in answer to all questions. 'I couldn't believe it when I met him a short time ago in Petersburg. And why so suddenly? That's what I'd like to know. He was always saying himself that there was no need to be in such a hurry to give up his career in the army.'

It appeared from the snatches of conversation that Radomsky had long ago announced his forthcoming resignation from the army, but that every time he had spoken of it in so jesting a manner that it had been impossible to take him seriously. Indeed, he always talked in a jesting manner about the most serious matters, so that it was quite impossible to make out whether he meant it or not, especially if he did not want people to be sure.

'Why, I've only retired for a time, for a few months or at most for a year,' laughed Radomsky.

'But there was no need for it at all, at least so far as I know your affairs,' the general cried excitedly.

'And what about visiting my estates? You advised it yourself. Besides, I'd like to go abroad. ...'

But they soon changed the subject; their rather extraordinary and continuing uneasiness, however, seemed excessive all the same, thought the prince, who had been observing it, and he could not help feeling that there was something peculiar about it.

'So the "poor knight" is on the scene again?' asked Radomsky, going up to Aglaya.

To the prince's astonishment, she gave him a puzzled and questioning look as though she wanted him to understand that she could not possibly have ever spoken to him about the 'poor knight' and that she did not even understand his question.

'But it's late, it's too late to send for a copy of Pushkin to town now – it's too late!' Kolya argued with Mrs Yepanchin. 'For the thousandth time – it's too late!'

'Yes, it really is too late to send to town for it now,' Radomsky, who left Aglaya in a hurry, said, coming up to them and breaking into their conversation. 'I expect the shops in Petersburg must be closed – it's past eight,' he added, taking out his watch.

'You've waited so long without missing it, you can wait till tomorrow,' Adelaida put in.

'Besides,' Kolya added, 'it's highly improper for society people to be interested in literature. Ask Mr Radomsky. It's much more becoming to own a yellow landau with red wheels.'

'You've got that out of a book again, Kolya,' observed Adelaida.

'Why,' cried Radomsky, 'everything he says is out of books. He quotes whole sentences out of periodicals. I've long had the pleasure of knowing Master Nicholas's conversation, but this time he isn't talking out of a book. He's quite obviously referring to my yellow landau with red wheels. Only I've already exchanged it. You're too late, I'm afraid.'

The prince listened attentively to what Radomsky was saying. He thought he carried himself excellently, modestly, and jovially, and he was particularly pleased that he talked as man to man and in such a friendly way to Kolya, who was doing his best to provoke him.

'What's this?' Mrs Yepanchin asked, turning to Lebedev's daughter Vera, who was standing before her with some large, almost new, and excellently bound volumes in her hand.

'Pushkin,' said Vera. 'Our Pushkin. Father asked me to present it to you.'

'Did he? Is it possible?' Mrs Yepanchin asked, looking surprised.

'Not as a present, not as a present,' Lebedev cried, jumping out from behind his daughter. 'I shouldn't have presumed, ma'am! At cost price, ma'am! It's our own family Pushkin edited by Annenkov, which you couldn't find anywhere now – for its cost price, ma'am. I'm presenting it to you with reverence, ma'am, wishing to sell it and thereby satisfy the noble impatience of your most noble literary feelings, ma'am.'

'Well, if you will sell it, I'd be greatly obliged to you, sir. I daresay you won't lose anything by it. Only please stop pulling such faces, sir. I've heard about you. I'm told you are very well read. We'll have a talk one day. Will you bring the books yourself?'

'With veneration, ma'am, and – er – respect,' Lebedev grimaced, looking extremely satisfied and snatching the books out of his daughter's hands.

'Well, see you don't lose them on the way. Bring them without respect, for all I care, only, mind,' she added, observing him intently, 'I won't admit you further than the front door, and I do not intend to receive you to-day. You can send your daughter Vera at once, if you wish; I like her very much.'

'Why don't you tell them about those people?' Vera said, addressing her father impatiently. 'If you don't, they'll come in anyway. They are already making a row. I'm sorry, sir,' she turned to the prince, who had already picked up his hat, 'but some people have come to see you. There are four of them. They've been waiting for some time and they're very impatient, but Father won't let them in to you.'

'Who are they?' asked the prince.

'They say they're on business, but they're so angry that if you don't let them in, they're sure to stop you in the street. You'd better have them in, sir, and get rid of them that way. Mr Ivolgin and Mr Ptitsyn are trying to persuade them to go away, but they won't listen.'

'Pavlishchev's son, Pavlishchev's son – he isn't worth it, he isn't worth it!' Lebedev cried, waving his arms about. 'They aren't worth listening to, sir. It isn't proper for you, most illustrious Prince, to disturb yourself on their account. No, sir. They're not worth it....'

'Pavlishchev's son – good Lord!' cried the prince, greatly perturbed. 'I know, but – I – I asked Mr Ivolgin to deal with it. Mr Ivolgin told me just now – –'

But Ganya had already come in from the inner room on to the veranda. Ptitsyn followed him. There was a noise in the next room, and General Ivolgin's voice could be heard trying to shout several others down. Kolya at once rushed off into the next room.

'This is very interesting,' Radomsky observed in a loud voice.

'So he knows about it, does he?' thought the prince.

'What son of Pavlishchev? And – is there a son of Pavlishchev?' General Yepanchin asked in bewilderment, looking at them all with curiosity and noticing with surprise that he was the only one who knew nothing about this affair.

The excitement and expectation were indeed general. The prince was greatly surprised that such an entirely personal affair should have excited their interest so much.

'It would be a very good thing,' Aglaya said in a particularly serious tone of voice, going up to the prince, 'if you could put an end to this business at once *yourself* and let us be your witnesses. They are trying to drag you through the mud, Prince, and you must vindicate yourself triumphantly, and I'm awfully glad for you beforehand.'

'I, too, should like that an end should be put to this odious claim at last,' cried Mrs Yepanchin. 'Let them have it for all they're worth, Prince. Don't spare them! I'm sick of hearing of this affair, and I've been worried to death on your account. Besides, it will be interesting to see what happens. Call them in, and we'll sit down. Aglaya is quite right. You've heard something about it, haven't you, Prince?' she addressed Prince Sh.

'Of course I have, in your house, too,' replied Prince Sh. 'But I'd very much like to have a look at those young people.'

'They are the so-called nihilists, aren't they?'

'No, ma'am,' Lebedev, who was also almost shaking with excitement, interposed, stepping forward, 'they are not exactly nihilists. They are quite different, ma'am, a special sort. My nephew told me that they have gone further than the nihilists. If I may say so, ma'am, you're mistaken in thinking that they will be embarrassed by your presence. No, ma'am, they won't be in the least embarrassed. The nihilists, at least, are sometimes well-informed, even learned people, but these, ma'am, have gone further because they're, above all, business men. This, ma'am, is actually a sort of sequel to nihilism, but not a direct one, but more by hearsay and indirectly. They never publicize themselves in some newspaper article, but directly in action, ma'am. With them, for instance, it is not a question of the senselessness of Pushkin or, for instance, of the necessity of the breaking up of Russia into parts. No, ma'am, if they want anything badly, they claim it as their right not to stop before any obstacle, though they might have to kill a score of people, ma'am, to achieve their aim. No, Prince, I should certainly not advise you – –'

But the prince had already got up to open the door to the visitors.

'You're slandering them, Lebedev,' he said, smiling. 'Your nephew has hurt your feelings very much. Don't believe him, Mrs Yepanchin. I assure you that the Gorskys and Danilovs are exceptions, and these – er – are only mistaken. But I'd rather not see them here – before all of you. I'm sorry, but when they come in, I'll just present them to you and then take them away. Come in, gentlemen!'

He was more worried by another thought that was particularly painful to him. He couldn't help feeling that the whole thing had been prearranged to coincide with that particular time and hour so that it could be discussed in the presence of those witnesses with the idea, perhaps, of disgracing him, and not at all of providing him with an opportunity for a triumph. But he felt very sorry for his 'monstrous and wicked suspiciousness'. He felt he would have died if anyone had known he had such an idea in his mind, and at the moment when his new visitors came in he was quite sincerely ready to believe that, among all those round him, he was morally the lowest of the low.

Five persons entered, four of them new arrivals and the fifth General Ivolgin, who followed them into the room, looking terribly agitated and in a very paroxysm of eloquence. 'This one is most certainly on my side!' the prince thought with a smile. Kolya slipped into the room among them: he was talking heatedly with Ippolit, who was one of the visitors. Ippolit listened and grinned.

The prince made his visitors sit down. They were all very young and hardly grown up at all, so that one could not help being surprised at the occasion that brought them there and the courteous way in which they were treated. General Yepanchin, for instance, who knew and understood nothing of this 'new affair', was outraged at the sight of such young people and would most certainly have made some protest, had he not been stopped by his wife's curious zeal on behalf of the prince's private interests. He remained, however, partly out of curiosity and partly out of the goodness of his heart, hoping to be of some help, or, at any rate, to be of some use by the exercise of his authority; but General Ivolgin's bow to him from a distance roused his indignation again; he frowned and made up his mind to remain absolutely silent.

One of the four visitors, however, was not so very young. He was, in fact, a man of thirty, the 'retired lieutenant' from Rogozhin's band, the pugilist who 'in his time had given fifteen roubles to beggars'. It was easy to see that he had accompanied the rest in the capacity of a faithful friend to make them feel more at ease and, if need be, to lend them his support. Among the others, the first and most prominent place was occupied by the young man who went under the name of 'Pavlishchev's son', though he introduced himself as Antip Burdovsky. He was poorly and slovenly dressed and the sleeves of his dirty coat shone like a mirror; his greasy waistcoat was buttoned up to the neck and showed no trace of a shirt; round his neck he wore a very filthy black silk scarf, twisted into a rope; his hands were unwashed and his face was exceedingly blotchy; he was fair and had, if one may use such an expression, an innocently insolent look. He was thin, of medium height, and about twenty-two years of age. His face showed no trace of irony or introspection; on the contrary, it expressed nothing but a firm and stolid conviction of his own rights and at the same time something in the nature of a curious craving for being and feeling always a martyr. He spoke agitatedly, hurriedly, and stammeringly, as though he were unable to articulate his words and as though he were tongue-tied or even a foreigner, although he was, as a matter of fact, a Russian born and bred.

He was accompanied, first, by Lebedev's nephew, already known to the reader, and, secondly, by Ippolit. Ippolit was a very young man – about seventeen or, perhaps, eighteen – with an intelligent but always irritable expression on his face, on which illness had left its terrible marks. He was as thin as a rake, pale and yellow, with glittering eyes and two hectic spots on his cheeks. He coughed continuously; every word he uttered, almost every breath he took, was accompanied by crepitation. He was obviously in the last stages of consumption. It looked as though he had only two or three more weeks to live. He was very tired and he sank into a chair before anyone else. The others were rather standoffish and almost abashed on entering; they did their best, however, to look important and were obviously afraid of lowering their dignity in some way or other, which was strangely out of keeping with their reputation of spurning all useless worldly trivialities, prejudices, and almost everything on earth except their own interests.

'Antip Burdovsky,' 'Pavlishchev's son' announced himself, hurriedly and stuttering.

'Vladimir Doktorenko,' Lebedev's nephew introduced himself clearly and distinctly, as though proud of the fact that his name was Doktorenko.

'Keller!' muttered the retired lieutenant.

'Ippolit Terentyev,' squeaked the last one in an unexpectedly shrill voice.

They all at last took their seats in a row opposite the prince, they all introduced themselves at once, frowned, and, to keep up their spirits, passed their caps from one hand to another. They were all ready to speak and yet they remained silent, waiting for something with a defiant air, which seemed to say, 'Nonsense, sir, you won't take us in!' One could not help feeling that the moment one of them opened his mouth, all of them would at once start talking together, interrupting and running ahead of each other.

8

'Gentlemen,' began the prince, 'I was not expecting any of you. I have been ill until to-day and I asked Mr Ivolgin to deal with your business' (he turned to Antip Burdovsky) 'a month ago, as I informed you at the time. However, I don't object to a personal explanation, but you must admit that it's hardly the time – I suggest you should go with me to another room, if you will not keep me long. My friends are here now, and believe me – –'

'Your friends – as many as you like, but let me tell you, sir,' Lebedev's nephew interrupted suddenly in a highly sententious tone, though without raising his voice too much, 'let me tell you, sir, that you might have treated us more courteously, and not have kept us waiting for two hours in your servants' hall – –'

'And of course – I too – and it's just like a prince! And this – you are, in fact, behaving like a general, sir! And I'm not your flunkey, sir! And I – I – –' Antip Burdovsky spluttered suddenly with extraordinary excitement, with trembling lips, with a resentful tremor in his voice, drops of saliva flying from his mouth, just as though he had suddenly burst or exploded; but he was at once in such a hurry that after the tenth word it was impossible to understand what he was saying.

'That was just like a prince!' Ippolit screamed in a shrill and cracked voice.

'If this had happened with me,' growled the pugilist, 'I mean, if it had anything to do with me, as an honourable man, then in Burdovsky's place I'd – er – I – –'

'Gentlemen,' the prince repeated again, 'I was only told a minute ago that you were here, I assure you.'

'We're not afraid of your friends, Prince, whoever they may be, because we are within our rights,' Lebedev's nephew declared again.

'But, tell me, sir,' Ippolit squeaked again, but this time in a state of great excitement, 'what right had you to submit Burdovsky's case to the judgement of your friends? For all you know we may not like the judgement of your friends. It's quite clear – isn't it? – what the judgement of your friends will be!'

'But, after all, if you, Mr Burdovsky, don't wish to speak here,' the prince, greatly astonished by such an opening, at last succeeded in interpolating a remark of his own, 'then I suggest we go at once to another room and, I repeat, I only just this minute heard about you. ...'

'But you've no right, you've no right, you've no right! ... Your friends – there!' Burdovsky mumbled suddenly again, glancing wildly and apprehensively round the room, for as he got more excited, he became more and more mistrustful and shy. 'You've no right!'

Having said that, he stopped abruptly just as though he were cut short, and opening wide his bloodshot, short-sighted, and bulging eyes, he stared questioningly at the prince, leaning forward with his whole body. This time the prince was so taken aback that he fell silent himself and also stared at him with bulging eyes and without uttering a word.

'I say,' Mrs Yepanchin addressed the prince suddenly, 'read this at once, this minute, it has a direct bearing on your business.'

She held out a weekly humorous paper to him and pointed to an article with her finger. Just as the new visitors were coming in, Lebedev, wishing to ingratiate himself with Mrs Yepanchin, had sidled up to her and, without uttering a word, had pulled this paper out of his pocket and, holding it up before her, had pointed to a column marked in pencil. What Mrs Yepanchin had time to read had greatly astonished and excited her.

'Would you mind if I didn't read it aloud?' murmured the prince, looking very embarrassed. 'I'd rather read it to myself – later.'

'In that case' – Mrs Yepanchin turned to Kolya, snatching the paper out of his hands before the prince had time to touch it – 'you'd better read it, read it at once, aloud – aloud to all, so that everyone may hear.'

Mrs Yepanchin was a warm-hearted and impulsive lady, so that she sometimes weighed all her anchors suddenly and, without stopping to think, put out to sea regardless of the weather. General Yepanchin stirred uneasily. But while they all stopped involuntarily at first and waited in perplexity, Kolya unfolded the paper and began reading aloud from the place Lebedev rushed up to point out to him.

'*Proletarians and Scions of Nobility, an Episode of Daily and Everyday Robberies! Progress! Reform! Justice!*

'Strange things happen in our so-called Holy Russia, in our age of reforms and private enterprise, an age of national movements with hundreds of millions exported abroad annually, an age of encouragement of industry and paralysis of factory hands, etc., etc., one cannot enumerate everything, ladies and gentlemen, and therefore to business. A strange incident occurred to a scion of our defunct landed gentry (*de profundis!*), one of those scions of nobility, however, whose grandfathers lost all their money at the roulette-tables, whose fathers were forced to serve as subalterns and lieutenants in the army and, as a rule, died while on trial for some innocent error in the handling of public funds, and whose children, like the hero of our story, either grow up as idiots or are caught committing some criminal offence, of which, incidentally, they are acquitted by our juries, with a view to their edification and reformation, or, finally, end up by getting involved in one of those incidents which astonish our public and disgrace our already disgraceful age. Six months ago our scion of nobility, wearing gaiters like a foreigner, and shivering in his unlined cloak, returned in winter to Russia from Switzerland, where he had been under treatment for idiocy (sic!). It must be admitted that he was lucky, so that quite apart from the interesting illness for which he was undergoing treatment in Switzerland (now, who ever heard of being treated for idiocy – can you imagine such a thing?!!!), he may prove the truth of the saying, "Some people have all the luck!" Judge for yourselves: left a baby after the death of his father who, we are told, was a lieutenant and who died while on trial for the misappropriation, at cards, of all his company's funds and quite likely also for ordering an excessive number of strokes of the birch to be given to a subordinate (the good old days, remember, ladies and gentlemen!), our baron was taken and brought up out of charity by a very rich Russian landowner. This Russian landowner – we will call him P. – was in that golden age the owner of four thousand serf souls (serf souls! do you understand such an expression, ladies and gentlemen? I do not. I shall have to look it up in a dictionary: "The legend's fresh, but past belief!"), and was apparently one of those Russian idlers and parasites who spend all their idle lives abroad, in summer at some foreign spa and in winter at the Paris Château-de-fleurs, where they have left enormous sums during their lifetime. Indeed, it can be stated without fear of contradiction that at least one-third of the tax paid in the good old days by the serfs to their owners went into the pockets of the proprietor of the Paris Château-de-fleurs (lucky man!). However that may be, the happy-go-lucky P. brought up our nobleman's orphaned child like a prince, engaged tutors for him, and governesses (pretty ones, no doubt) whom, incidentally, he brought from Paris himself. But the last scion of a noble line was an idiot, the Château-de-fleurs governesses could do nothing about it, and up to his twentieth year our student had not learnt to speak any language, not even Russian. The last circumstance, however, was excusable. Finally, the frantic notion came into the head of the serf-owner P. that the idiot might be taught sense in Switzerland – a fantastic notion which was, however, quite logical: a parasite and property-owner would naturally suppose that he could buy intelligence for money on the market, particularly in Switzerland. Five years were spent in treatment under the care of a certain professor, and thousands were squandered on it: the idiot, of course, did not become intelligent, but we are told that he did without a doubt grow to resemble a human being, more or less, of course. Suddenly P. died of a stroke. He left no will, of course, and, as usual, his affairs were in a frightful mess. There were hundreds of greedy heirs who did not care a fig for any last scions of a noble line undergoing treatment out of charity for congenital idiocy in Switzerland. Though an idiot, our scion of nobility all the same tried to cheat his professor and, it is alleged, managed to be treated without fees for two years by concealing from his doctor the death of his benefactor. But the professor himself was a regular charlatan: alarmed at last at his patient's impecunious condition, and still more at the appetite of this twenty-five-year-old wastrel, he dressed him up in his old gaiters, made him a present of his ragged cloak, and, out of charity, packed him off third-class *nach Russland* – anything to get rid of him in Switzerland. It would seem that luck had turned its back upon our hero. But not a bit of it: fortune which kills off whole provinces with famine, showers her gifts gratis on some insignificant little aristocrat, like the *Cloud* in Krylov's fable that passed over parched fields and emptied itself into the ocean. Almost at the very moment of his arrival in Petersburg from Switzerland, a relation of his mother's died in Moscow (his mother, of course, came from a merchant's family), a childless old bachelor, a typical Russian merchant with a long beard, and an Old Believer, leaving a fortune of several millions in hard cash (if only it were to you and me, dear reader!), and all of it to our scion of nobility, this baron of ours, who had been under treatment in Switzerland for idiocy! Well, of course, it was an entirely different matter now! A whole crowd of friends and acquaintances gathered round our gaitered baron, who was running after a kept woman, a notorious beauty. He even discovered some relations, but most of all he became the cynosure of crowds of young ladies who were desperately anxious to find eligible young men to whom they could be joined in matrimony. And what better husband could they find? An aristocrat, a millionaire, an idiot – all qualifications at once, you could not find such a husband if you were to look for him with a lantern, and you certainly could not get one made to order! ...'

'That – that I – I just can't understand!' exclaimed General Yepanchin, boiling over with indignation.

'Stop it, Kolya!' cried the prince in an imploring voice.

There were outcries on all sides.

'Read it! Read it, I say!' Mrs Yepanchin snapped, evidently restraining herself with a great effort. 'Prince, if you make him stop, we shall quarrel.'

There was nothing to be done about it. Kolya, flushed and excited, went on reading in an agitated voice.

'But while our newly-hatched-out millionaire was, as it were, basking in the sun of his good fortune, something quite unexpected happened. One fine morning a visitor came to see him, calm and stern of countenance, modestly but elegantly attired, and with quite an unmistakable progressive tendency in his views. In courteous, but fair and dignified, terms, he briefly explained the object of his visit. He was a well-known lawyer and he had been instructed by a young man and was appearing on his behalf. This young man was no other than the son of the late P., though he bore a different name. The voluptuous P., having in his youth seduced a girl who was poor but honest, one of his house-serfs who had had a good European education (taking advantage, no doubt, of the old seignorial rights he enjoyed under the old serf régime), and noticing the inevitable but approaching consequence of his liaison, had married her off hastily to a man of irreproachable character, who was engaged in trade and even served in the civil service and who had long been in love with the girl. At first he helped the newly-weds, but very soon her high-minded husband refused to receive any further assistance from him. Some time passed, and P. gradually managed to forget the girl and the son she had borne him, and, as we know, he afterwards died without making any provision for them. Meanwhile his son, who was born in lawful wedlock and grew up under another name, having been adopted by his mother's high-minded husband, who had nevertheless died in the course of time, was left to fend for himself with an ailing, invalid mother who had lost the use of her legs and who lived in one of our remote provinces. He himself earned his living in the capital by unremitting and honest toil, giving lessons in merchants' houses, and in this way kept himself, first at school and later while taking an external course at the university, which he hoped would be useful to him in his subsequent career. But how much can one earn from a Russian merchant for lessons at ten copecks an hour, having, besides, an invalid mother to support who had lost the use of her legs and who did not make his life easier by her death in the remote province? Now the question is what should our scion of nobility have decided in all fairness to do? You, dear reader, no doubt, think he said to himself: "All my life I have enjoyed P.'s munificent gifts; on my education, my governesses, and my treatment for idiocy in Switzerland tens of thousands were squandered; and here I am now with millions to spend while the noble character of P.'s son, who cannot possibly be blamed for the actions of his wanton father who forgot him, is being sapped by giving lessons. What has been spent on me must in all fairness be spent on him. The vast sums that have been spent on me were not really mine. It was just a blind error of fortune; they rightly belonged to P.'s son. They should have been used for his benefit and not for mine, as was done by the fantastic whim of the wanton and forgetful P. If I were an honourable, considerate, and just person, I ought to give his son half of my inheritance, but as I am first of all a prudent man and realize only too well that this is not a legal matter, I shall not give him half of my millions. But it would, at any rate, be too base and shameful on my part (the scion of nobility forgot that it would not be prudent, either), if I do not give back to P.'s son the tens of thousands spent by P. on my idiocy. That would be only right and fair. For what would have become of me if P. had not brought me up and had taken care of his son instead of me?"

'But no, ladies and gentlemen! Our scions of nobility do not reason like that. However eloquently the lawyer, who had undertaken to plead for the young man out of friendship and almost against his will, tried to present his case, however eloquently he pointed out to him the obligations of honour, generosity, justice, and even simple prudence, the Swiss student remained inflexible, and – what do you think? All this would be nothing, but what was really unpardonable and what no interesting illness could excuse, was that this millionaire, who had only just emerged from the gaiters of his professor, was quite incapable of understanding that the young man of honourable character who was ruining his health by giving lessons was not begging for help or asking for charity, but for his rights and for what was due to him, though not legally, and that he was not even asking for it, but his friends were only interceding on his behalf. Flushed by his newly acquired power of grinding the faces of people in the dust by his millions with impunity, our scion of nobility pulled out a fifty-rouble note with a majestic air and sent it to the noble young man by way of an arrogant piece of charity. You don't believe me, ladies and gentlemen? You are affronted, you are outraged, you cannot suppress your cries of indignation? But he did it, nevertheless! Needless to say, the money was at once returned to him, as it were, flung back in his face. How then is this matter to be settled? It cannot be settled in court, and all that remains is publicity! We therefore place these facts before the public and guarantee their authenticity. We are told that one of our most famous humorists has made up a most delightful epigram on the subject which deserves a place not only in the sketches of our provincial manners, but also of those of our capital:

Sweet little Lyova[1] for five years long
In Schneider's[2] cloak was snugly laid,
Right he did not know from wrong,
And silly little games he played.
Home returning in gaiters tight,
He swipes a million from the dead,
Prays in Russian day and night,
And robs poor students of their bread.'

When Kolya finished reading the article, he quickly handed the paper to the prince and, without uttering a word, rushed to a corner, turned his face to the wall, and buried it in his hands. He felt unbearably ashamed, and his boyish sensitivity, unaccustomed as yet to filth, was outraged beyond measure. He felt as though something extraordinary had happened, something that blighted everything, and that he was almost the cause of it merely by the fact that he had read it aloud.

But it seemed that everyone felt something of the same kind.

The girls felt very awkward and ashamed. Mrs Yepanchin was doing her best to control her violent anger and, perhaps, regretted bitterly having interfered in the matter; now she was silent. The prince experienced something that is often experienced by very shy people in similar circumstances: he was so ashamed of the conduct of other people, he was so ashamed for his visitors, that at first he dared not look at them. Ptitsyn, Varya, Ganya, even Lebedev – everybody looked

1. The noble scion's pet name. 2. The Swiss professor's name.

rather embarrassed. What was stranger still, Ippolit and 'Pavlishchev's son' seemed also to be rather surprised; Lebedev's nephew, too, was obviously displeased. Only the pugilist was perfectly calm. He sat twisting his moustache, looking grave, and if his eyes were lowered, it was not from embarrassment, but, on the contrary, from high-principled modesty and quite undisguised triumph. It was quite obvious that he liked the article very much.

'It's outrageous,' General Yepanchin growled in an undertone. 'Just as if fifty lackeys had banded together to compose it.'

'May I ask you, my dear sir,' Ippolit declared, trembling all over, 'how you dare to insult people by such suppositions?'

'This – this – for an honourable man this is – you must admit, General, that, if it's an honourable man, it's insulting!' the pugilist muttered, suddenly starting for some reason, twisting his moustache, and jerking his shoulders and body.

'In the first place, I'm not your "dear sir", and, secondly, I have no intention of offering you any explanations,' General Yepanchin, who had worked himself up into a passion, replied sharply.

He got up and, without saying another word, went to the entrance of the veranda and stood on the top step with his back to the company, highly indignant with Mrs Yepanchin, who even now did not think of stirring from her seat.

'Gentlemen, gentlemen, let me speak at last,' the prince cried in anguish and agitation, 'and do me the favour and let us talk so that we can understand each other. I don't mind the article, gentlemen; it doesn't matter to me whether it's been published or not, except that, gentlemen, there's not a word of truth in it. I'm saying this because you know it yourselves. It's shameful. So that I couldn't help being surprised that any one of you should have written it.'

'I didn't know anything about this article till this moment,' said Ippolit. 'I don't approve of this article.'

'Though I knew it was written,' Lebedev's nephew added, 'I – I too would not have advised its publication because it's premature.'

'I knew,' muttered 'Pavlishchev's son', 'but I have the right – I – –'

'You didn't write it yourself, did you?' asked the prince, looking at Burdovsky with curiosity. 'I can't believe it!'

'One might, however, refuse to recognize your right to put such questions,' Lebedev's nephew interposed.

'I was only surprised that Mr Burdovsky should have – but – what I want to say is that since you've already given the matter publicity, why were you so offended just now when I began talking about it before my friends?'

'At last!' Mrs Yepanchin muttered indignantly.

'And if I may venture to point out, Prince,' cried Lebedev, almost in a fever, unable to contain himself and making his way through the row of chairs, 'if I may venture to point out, sir, you forgot that it was only through your kindness and the unprecedented goodness of your heart that you received them and listened to them, and that they have no right whatever to demand it, particularly as you've already put the matter into Mr Ivolgin's hands, and that, too, you did because of your great goodness, and that now, most illustrious Prince, amidst your chosen friends, you cannot sacrifice their company to these gentlemen, and you could, as it were, throw them out at once – which I, sir, as the master of the house, would do with the greatest pleasure.'

'Quite right!' General Ivolgin thundered suddenly from the back of the room.

'Enough, Lebedev, enough, enough,' began the prince, but a loud outburst of indignation drowned his words.

'No, I'm sorry, Prince, I'm sorry, but now it is not enough!' Lebedev's nephew shouted above the din. 'Now the matter must be clearly and firmly stated because apparently it is not understood. Subtle legal quibbles have been introduced here and it is proposed to kick us out because of these quibbles! But do you really think us such fools, Prince, as not to understand that we have not a leg to stand on so far as the law is concerned, and that if we were to consider our case from the legal point of view, we have not the right to demand a single rouble from you? But we realize very well that if there can be no question here of any legal rights, there is such a thing as human, natural right: the right of common sense and the voice of conscience, and even if that right of ours is not written down in any rotten human code of law, an honourable and honest man – that is to say, a right thinking man – is in duty bound to remain an honourable and honest man even as regards those points which are not written down in codes. That is why we have come here without any fear of being thrown out (as you have threatened to do just now), because, you see, we do not *beg* but *demand*, and as for the impropriety of our visit at such a late hour (though, mind you, we didn't come at a late hour, it was you who kept us waiting in the servants' hall), all I can say is that we've come without fear because we took you to be a man of good sense – that is, a man of conscience and honour. Yes, it is quite true that we did not come cap in hand, we haven't come as your hangers-on and sycophants, but with our heads held high, like free men, and not with any intention of begging, but with a free and proud demand (you hear, not to beg, but to demand – get that clear!). We put a straight question to you, and we do so with dignity: do you consider yourself in the right or in the wrong in the case of Burdovsky? Do you admit that Pavlishchev heaped benefits upon you and perhaps even saved your life? If you do (and you can't very well deny it), then do you intend, or do you find it the right thing to do, having in your turn obtained millions, to compensate Pavlishchev's son, who is in such dire need, though he does bear the name of Burdovsky? Yes or no? If *yes*, or, in other words, if you possess what in your language is called honour and conscience, but what we more appropriately describe by the term of good sense, then satisfy us and the thing is at an end. Satisfy us without requests or thanks from us. Don't expect them from us, for you are doing it not for our sake but for the sake of justice. If, however, you do not want to satisfy us – that is, if your reply is *no* – we'll go away at once and the matter is at an end; but we tell you to your face and in the presence of all your witnesses that you are a man of coarse intelligence and low mentality, that you dare not call yourself in future a man of honour and conscience, that you are trying to buy that right too cheaply. I have finished. I have put the question. Now you can turn us out into the street, if you dare. You can do it, for you have the power. But remember all the same that we demand and don't beg. We demand and do not beg!'

Lebedev's nephew, who had worked himself up into a passion, fell silent.

'We demand, demand, demand; we do not beg!' Burdovsky spluttered, turning red as a lobster.

The words of Lebedev's nephew caused a certain commotion and even a murmur of protest, though everyone among those present, except perhaps Lebedev, who seemed to be in a fever of excitement, was quite obviously anxious not to interfere in the matter. (Strange to say, Lebedev, who was evidently on the prince's side, seemed now to feel a certain glow of family pride after his nephew's speech; at any rate, he looked round at the company with a peculiar air of satisfaction.)

'In my opinion,' the prince began rather quietly, 'in my opinion, Mr Doktorenko, half of what you've just said is quite right. I'm even ready to admit that you're quite right in the greater half of what you've said, and I'd have agreed with you entirely, if you hadn't left something out in your speech. What you've left out, I'm afraid, I'm not able to tell you exactly, but something, of course, is missing from your speech to make it absolutely fair. But to business, gentlemen. Tell me, why did you publish this article? There's not a word in it that isn't libellous, and I cannot help thinking, gentlemen, that what you've done is rather shabby.'

'I say! ...'

'My dear sir! ...'

'This – this – this – –' the excited visitors cried all at once.

'So far as the article is concerned' – Ippolit took up the point shrilly – 'so far as the article is concerned, I've told you already that neither I nor the others approved of it. It was written by him' (he pointed to the pugilist, who sat next to him), 'and I admit it's written indecently, illiterately, and in a style affected by retired army officers like him. He's stupid and, moreover, an adventurer, I agree. I tell him so to his face every day, but he was half in the right, all the same: publicity is the legal right of every man and, therefore, of Burdovsky, too. For his absurdities he must answer himself. As for my protesting in the name of all of us against the presence of your friends, I should like to explain, ladies and gentlemen, that I protested only in order to assert our rights, that, as a matter of fact, we are most anxious to have witnesses, and that shortly before we came here we all four agreed about it. We don't care who your witnesses are, even if they are your friends, and as they cannot but recognize Burdovsky's right (because it can obviously be proved mathematically), it's even better that these witnesses are your friends: the truth will be even more plainly evident.'

'It's quite true,' Lebedev's nephew confirmed. 'We did agree about it.'

'Then why did you begin by raising such a clamour,' the prince asked in surprise, 'if that's what you wanted?'

'And as for the article, Prince,' declared the pugilist, desperately anxious to put in a word of his own and brightening up agreeably (the presence of the ladies, one might suspect, exercised a perceptible and strong influence on him), 'as for the article, I confess I really am the author of it, though my sick friend, whom I'm accustomed to excuse because of his bad health, has just criticized it so severely. But it was I who wrote it, and I published it in the journal of a great friend of mine in the form of a letter to the editor. Only the verses aren't mine, and they really were written by a famous humorist. I only read it to Burdovsky, and not all of it, either, and he immediately gave me his permission to publish it. But you will, I hope, agree that I could have published it without his permission, too. An appeal to public opinion is a noble, universal, and beneficial right. I hope that you, Prince, are sufficiently progressive not to deny that.'

'I'm not going to deny anything, but you must admit that your article – –'

'Is a bit harsh, you were going to say? But, then, it is, as it were, for the public good, you must admit, and after all you don't expect me to overlook such a scandalous case, do you? So much the worse for the guilty, but the public good must come before everything. As for certain inexactitudes – as it were, hyperboles – you will, I hope, also admit that the chief thing is initiative, the chief thing is the motive and the intention. What is important is the beneficent example. Individual cases can be examined afterwards, and, lastly, there's the question of style, the fact that, as it were, it had to be written in a humorous vein, and, finally, everybody, you must admit, writes like that! Ha, ha!'

'No, no, you're wrong, you're absolutely wrong, I assure you, gentlemen,' cried the prince. 'You published an article on the assumption that I would never agree to satisfy Burdovsky, and so you tried to frighten me and get your own back on me in one way or another. But how could you tell? I might have decided to satisfy Burdovsky, mightn't I? I now declare openly in the presence of all these people that I will do so.'

'Spoken like a wise and honourable man!' the pugilist declared.

'Good heavens!' exclaimed Mrs Yepanchin.

'This is intolerable!' muttered the general.

'Please, please, ladies and gentlemen,' the prince besought them, 'let me explain the whole thing. Five weeks ago Chebarov – your authorized representative, Mr Burdovsky – came to see me at Z. You've described him in rather flattering terms in your article, Mr Keller' – the prince turned to the pugilist, laughing suddenly – 'but I'm afraid I didn't like him at all. I realized at once that Chebarov was at the bottom of it and that, to speak frankly, it was he who, taking advantage of your simplicity, Mr Burdovsky, had induced you to start the whole thing.'

'You've no right to say that, sir,' Burdovsky cried agitatedly. 'I – I'm not simple – this is – –'

'You have no right at all to assume anything of the kind,' Lebedev's nephew interposed sententiously.

'This is highly offensive!' Ippolit cried shrilly. 'It's a false, offensive, and irrelevant assumption!'

'I'm sorry, gentlemen, I'm sorry,' the prince apologized hastily. 'Please forgive me. I said it because I thought that it would be best for us to be quite frank with one another. But just as you like, have it your own way. I told Chebarov that, as I was not in Petersburg, I would immediately authorize a friend of mine to deal with the matter and that I would let you, Mr Burdovsky, know about it. I tell you frankly, gentlemen, that the whole thing seemed an absolute swindle to me just because Chebarov was involved in it. Oh, please don't be offended, gentlemen! For God's sake don't be offended!' the prince cried in alarm, noticing again how hurt and resentful Burdovsky looked and how excited and indignant his friends were. 'If I said that the thing was a swindle, it had nothing to do with you personally! You see, I didn't know any of you personally then. I didn't even know your names. I merely judged by Chebarov. I was just speaking generally because – if only you knew how dreadfully I'd been deceived since I came into my inheritance!'

'Prince, you're so naïve!' Lebedev's nephew observed sarcastically.

'A prince *and* a millionaire! You may, for all I know, really be kind-hearted and a bit of a simpleton, but you cannot expect to be an exception to the general rule for all that,' declared Ippolit.

'Possibly, gentlemen, quite possibly,' the prince said hurriedly, 'though I don't know what general rule you're speaking of. But to continue. Please do not get offended for nothing. I swear I haven't the slightest wish to insult you. And really, gentlemen, can't one say a single word in all sincerity without your taking umbrage at once? But, to begin with, what so greatly astonished me was that "Pavlishchev's son" existed and that he was in such a terrible plight, too, as Chebarov explained to me. Pavlishchev was my benefactor and a friend of my father's. (Oh, why did you write such untrue things about my father in your article, Mr Keller? There was no question of any misappropriation of regimental funds, nor of any maltreatment of his subordinates – I'm absolutely sure of that, and how could you bring yourself to write such a calumny?) And what you've written about Pavlishchev is absolutely intolerable. You described that most honourable man as wanton and voluptuous so brazenly and positively, as though you were really speaking the truth, while he was actually the most virtuous man in the world. Indeed, he was a remarkably learned man. He corresponded with a great many distinguished scholars and gave away a great deal of money for the advancement of learning. As for his kind heart and his acts of charity, oh, of course, you were quite right in saying that I was almost an idiot at the time and could not understand anything (though I did speak Russian and could understand it), but, you see, I can fully appreciate everything I remember now. ...'

'Please,' squeaked Ippolit, 'don't you think this is getting a bit too sentimental? We're not little children. You wanted to come straight to the point. Well, it's almost ten o'clock, remember.'

'Very well, gentlemen, very well,' the prince at once agreed. 'After my initial feeling of mistrust I decided that I might have been mistaken and that Pavlishchev might really have had a son. But what surprised me so much was that that son should so lightly, I mean to say, so publicly betray the secret of his birth and, most of all, defame his mother. For even at that time Chebarov was already threatening me with publicity. ...'

'How stupid!' Lebedev's nephew shouted.

'You've no right – you've no right!' Burdovsky exclaimed.

'A son is not responsible for his father's immoral conduct and the mother is not to blame,' Ippolit squeaked warmly.

'All the more reason, surely, for sparing her,' said the prince timidly.

'You're not just naïve, Prince,' Lebedev's nephew smiled spitefully. 'You've perhaps gone a great deal beyond that.'

'And what right had you ...' Ippolit squeaked in a most unnatural voice.

'None whatever!' the prince put in hastily. 'And you're right there, I admit, but I'm afraid I couldn't help it, and I said to myself immediately at the time that I must not allow my personal feelings to influence me in the matter, for if I acknowledge myself that I'm bound to satisfy Mr Burdovsky's demands because of my feelings for Pavlishchev, then I must satisfy them regardless of anything, that is, whether I do or do not respect Mr Burdovsky. I merely referred to it, gentlemen, because it did all the same seem unnatural to me that a son should betray his mother's secret so publicly. In short, that was what chiefly convinced me that Chebarov must be a blackguard and had himself incited Mr Burdovsky by deceit to such a fraud.'

'But this is really intolerable!' cried his visitors, some of whom even jumped up from their seats.

'Gentlemen, but that was exactly why I decided that the unfortunate Mr Burdovsky must be a simple and helpless man who easily falls a victim to rogues, and that therefore it was more than ever my duty to come to his assistance as "Pavlishchev's son", first, by opposing Mr Chebarov, secondly, by my devoted and friendly guidance, and, thirdly, by offering him ten thousand roubles – that is, all that by my reckoning Pavlishchev could have spent on me.'

'What? Only ten thousand?' exclaimed Ippolit.

'I must say, Prince, you're not very good at arithmetic, or else you're too good at it, though you pretend to be a simpleton,' cried Lebedev's nephew.

'I won't accept ten thousand,' said Burdovsky.

'Accept it, Antip!' the pugilist prompted in a quick and audible whisper, bending over the back of Ippolit's chair. 'Accept it, and afterwards we shall see.'

'L-look here, Mr Myshkin,' Ippolit squeaked. 'Please understand that we're not fools, not vulgar fools, as no doubt all your guests think, including these ladies who sneer at us so scornfully, and especially that fine gentleman' – he pointed to Radomsky – 'whom I haven't of course the honour of knowing, but about whom, I believe, I have heard something.'

'Please, please, gentlemen, you've misunderstood me again,' the prince cried, turning to them agitatedly. 'First of all, you, Mr Keller, have described my fortune very inaccurately in your article: I never inherited any millions at all – I've only got perhaps an eighth or a tenth part of what you suppose; secondly, no one spent tens of thousands on me in Switzerland: Schneider received six hundred a year, and that, too, only during the first three years, and Pavlishchev never went to Paris in search of pretty governesses. This again is a calumny. In my opinion the total amount spent on me is much less than ten thousand, but I decided to give ten thousand, and you must admit that, in paying a debt, I could not possibly offer Mr Burdovsky more even if I were very fond of him, and the reason I could not do so is because of a feeling of delicacy, just because I was repaying a debt and not sending him the money out of charity. I fail to see, gentlemen, how you do not understand that! But I intended to make up for all this by my friendship and active interest in the future of the unfortunate Mr Burdovsky, who has obviously been deceived, for, surely, he would not otherwise have agreed to anything so mean as, for instance, the unsavoury publicity about his mother in Mr Keller's article. ... But why are you getting so excited again, gentlemen? If you go on like this, we shall never be able to understand each other! It did turn out as I thought, didn't it? I can see now that I was right all along,' the prince tried to persuade them excitedly, anxious to calm their agitation and failing to notice that he was only increasing it.

'Can you? What can you see?' they demanded almost furiously.

'Why, first of all, I've had time to have a good look at Mr Burdovsky, and I can see now what sort of a man he is. He's an innocent man who is being deceived by everybody. He is a defenceless man, and that's why I must spare him. Secondly, Mr Ivolgin, whom I have authorized to deal with the matter and from whom I did not hear for a long time, because I had been travelling and afterwards was ill in Petersburg for three days, has only an hour ago, at our first meeting, told me that he had got to the bottom of Chebarov's scheme, that he has proofs that Chebarov was exactly the sort of person I thought he was. You see, gentlemen, I know very well that many people think

I'm an idiot, and as I have the reputation of a man who is easily parted from his money, Chebarov, too, thought that he could deceive me easily, and it was on my feelings for Pavlishchev that he counted. But the chief thing – do let me finish what I have to say, gentlemen – the chief thing is that it now appears that Mr Burdovsky isn't Pavlishchev's son at all! Mr Ivolgin has just told me that, and he assures me that he has positive proof of it. Well, what do you think of that? It's quite incredible, isn't it, after all the fuss that has been made! And, mind you, positive proof! I don't believe it myself, I assure you. I'm still doubtful because Mr Ivolgin hasn't had time to give me all the particulars, but that Chebarov is a blackguard there can now be no doubt whatever. He has deceived the unfortunate Mr Burdovsky and all of you, gentlemen, who have come forward so nobly in support of your friend (for he obviously is badly in need of support, I can see that!). He has cheated you all and has involved you all in a criminal attempt to obtain money by false pretences, for, as a matter of fact, it is nothing but a fraudulent swindle!'

'A swindle? Not Pavlishchev's son? What is he talking about?' Exclamations could be heard on all sides.

All Burdovsky's supporters were utterly confounded.

'Of course it's a swindle! For if Mr Burdovsky doesn't turn out to be Pavlishchev's son now, Mr Burdovsky's claim is in that case a pure swindle (I mean, of course, if he knew the truth). But, you see, the whole point is that he's been deceived, and that's why I'm so anxious that his character should be cleared and why I say that he deserves to be pitied for his simplicity and has to have someone to support him; for otherwise he, too, would be a swindler in this affair. Why, I'm absolutely convinced that he doesn't understand anything! I also was in the same state before I went to Switzerland; I also stammered incoherently, tried to express myself and couldn't! I understand it. I'm able to sympathize with him because I'm almost the same as he. I have a right to speak! And, lastly, though there's no such person as Pavlishchev's son, and the whole thing is nothing but a fraudulent hoax, I still do not alter my decision and I'm still prepared to give up ten thousand in memory of Pavlishchev. For even before I heard of Mr Burdovsky, I proposed to spend ten thousand on founding a school in memory of Pavlishchev, but it makes no difference now whether I spend the money on a school or on Mr Burdovsky, for though not Pavlishchev's son, he's almost as good as his son, for he himself has been so wickedly deceived and he sincerely believed himself that he was Pavlishchev's son. Now, listen to what Mr Ivolgin has to say, gentlemen, and let's make an end of it. Don't be angry, don't be excited; please sit down! Mr Ivolgin will explain everything to us now and, I confess, I'm anxious to hear all the particulars myself. He says he's even been to Pskov to see your mother, Mr Burdovsky, who isn't dead at all, as they made you say in that article. ... Sit down, gentlemen, sit down!'

The prince sat down and succeeded in making Burdovsky's friends, who had jumped up from their seats, sit down again. During the last ten or twenty minutes he had been talking loudly and excitedly, with impatient rapidity, completely carried away and trying to make himself heard above the rest, and afterwards, of course, he could not help bitterly regretting some of the words and suppositions that had escaped him. If they had not excited and almost maddened him, he would not have allowed himself so flagrantly and hurriedly to express aloud some of his conjectures and make such unnecessarily frank statements. But no sooner had he sat down than one thing he had said pierced his heart with burning remorse: for, apart from having insulted Burdovsky so publicly by suggesting that he had suffered from the illness for which he himself had been treated in Switzerland, quite apart from that, his offer of ten thousand he had intended to spend on the school had, in his view, been made in a grossly careless manner, as though it had been charity, particularly as he had spoken of it aloud in the presence of strangers. 'I should have waited and offered it him to-morrow in private,' the prince thought at once, 'for now it may not be possible to put it right! Yes I am an idiot, a real idiot!' he decided, feeling ashamed and deeply distressed.

Meanwhile Ganya, who had till that moment held aloof and preserved a stubborn silence, stepped forward at the prince's invitation and, standing at his side, began to give a clear and calm account of the business entrusted to him by the prince. All conversation ceased instantly. Everyone listened with the utmost curiosity, especially every member of Burdovsky's party.

9

'You will not deny, of course,' began Ganya, addressing himself directly to Burdovsky, who listened to him for all he was worth, staring at him with surprise, and obviously in a state of great consternation, 'you will not try, nor, of course, wish to deny seriously that you were born exactly two years after your mother's marriage to Mr

Burdovsky, your father. The date of your birth can be easily proved by documentary evidence, so that the distortion of this fact, so offensive to you and to your mother, in Mr Keller's article can only be explained by Mr Keller's own playful imagination, for Mr Keller, no doubt, thought to strengthen your claim and so promote your interests. Mr Keller says that he read his article to you before publishing it, though not the whole of it – I don't suppose there can be any doubt that he did not read it as far as that particular passage. ...'

'I didn't, as a matter of fact,' the pugilist interrupted, 'but I was given all the facts by a competent person and I – –'

'Excuse me, Mr Keller,' Ganya interrupted him, 'allow me to speak. I assure you your article will be dealt with when its turn comes, and you can offer your explanation then. Now we'd better continue in the proper order. By sheer chance, with the help of my sister, I obtained from an intimate friend of hers, a Mrs Zubkov, a widow and a landowner, a letter Mr Pavlishchev wrote to her from abroad twenty-four years ago. Having made the acquaintance of Mrs Zubkov, I applied, at her suggestion, to the retired Colonel Timofey Vyazovkin, a distant relation of Mr Pavlishchev, who was formerly a great friend of his. I succeeded in obtaining from him two more of Mr Pavlishchev's letters, also written from abroad. From these three letters, from their dates, and from the facts mentioned in them, it can be clearly proved without a shadow of doubt or any possibility of refutation that Pavlishchev had gone abroad (where he stayed for three years without a break) sixteen months before you, Mr Burdovsky, were born. As you know, your mother has never been out of Russia. I do not intend to read those letters at present. It is too late now. I merely want to state that this, at any rate, is a fact. But if you wish, Mr Burdovsky, to fix an appointment with me at my place for tomorrow morning and bring your witnesses (as many as you like) and experts to compare the handwriting, I have no doubt whatever that you cannot but be convinced of the evident truth of this fact. And if that is so, then your whole case falls to the ground and there's nothing more to be said about it.'

Once again there was a general commotion and intense excitement. Burdovsky suddenly got up from his chair.

'If that is so, then I was deceived – deceived, not by Chebarov, but long ago. I don't want experts and I don't want an appointment. I believe you. I refuse – I don't want the ten thousand – good-bye.'

He picked up his cap and pushed back his chair to go out.

'Wait another five minutes, if you can,' Ganya stopped him, quietly and sweetly. 'There are still a few more highly important facts in connexion with this case, which you particularly will find highly interesting. In my opinion, it's absolutely essential that you should know them, and perhaps you, too, will feel better if the whole matter is thoroughly cleared up.'

Burdovsky resumed his seat in silence, lowering his head a little, as though in deep thought. Lebedev's nephew, who had got up to accompany him, also sat down; though he kept his head and was as bold as ever, he, too, seemed to be greatly perplexed. Ippolit was scowling and dejected and appeared to be very surprised. At that moment, however, he had such a violent fit of coughing that his handkerchief was stained with blood. The pugilist looked almost scared.

'Oh, Antip,' he cried bitterly, 'I told you the other day – the day before yesterday – that perhaps you're not Pavlishchev's son at all!'

There was a sound of suppressed laughter. Two or three people laughed louder than the rest.

'The fact you stated just now, Mr Keller,' Ganya was quick to say, 'is extremely valuable. Nevertheless, I think I'm fully entitled to assert, on the most precise evidence, that though Mr Burdovsky, of course, knew very well the date of his birth, he could not possibly have known anything about Pavlishchev's residence abroad, where he spent the greater part of his life, returning to Russia only for short periods. Besides, the very fact of his going abroad at that time is in itself so little remarkable that not only Mr Burdovsky, who was not born at the time, but also those who knew Pavlishchev well could hardly be expected to remember it after twenty years. Of course, to make inquiries now seemed quite impossible, but I must admit that the information I've received was obtained quite by chance and that I could very well not have obtained it at all. So that it was really almost impossible for Mr Burdovsky or even Chebarov to obtain this information, even if it had occurred to them to obtain it. But it may never have occurred to them. ...'

'I'm sorry, Mr Ivolgin,' Ippolit suddenly interrupted him irritably, 'but why all this rigmarole? The whole thing has now been explained, and we agree to accept the main fact, so why drag out this tedious and offensive business? You don't want by any chance – do you – to brag about the clever way in which you conducted your investigation and to show off before us and before the prince what a wonderful investigator, what a fine detective, you are? Or can it really be your intention to excuse and justify Burdovsky by proving that he got mixed up in this business through ignorance? But that's sheer impudence, sir! Burdovsky doesn't want your justifications and apologies – make no mistake about that! He feels hurt, the whole thing is extremely painful to him as it is, he's in an awkward position, and you ought to realize that, you ought to understand it. ...'

'That'll do, Mr Terentyev, that'll do,' Ganya succeeded in interrupting him. 'Calm yourself, don't get excited; you're very ill, aren't you? I sympathize with you. In that case, if you like, I've finished, or rather I shall be compelled to give only a brief account of the facts which, I'm convinced, wouldn't be such a bad thing to know in full detail,' he added, noticing a general movement of impatience. 'I merely wish to point out, and I can prove it, for the information of all who are interested in this case, that your mother, Mr Burdovsky, was treated with such kindness and solicitude by Pavlishchev solely because she happened to be the sister of the serf-girl with whom he had fallen so deeply in love in his early youth that he would have married her, if she had not died suddenly. I have evidence that this intimate fact, which is strictly accurate and true, is very little known and, indeed, has been completely forgotten. I could, furthermore, tell you that your mother, when she was only a girl of ten, was taken by Pavlishchev and brought up as though she were a close relative of his, that he had set apart a considerable dowry for her, and that all this gave rise to highly alarming rumours among Pavlishchev's numerous relations, who feared that he might even marry her. But in the end, at the age of twenty, she married for love (and I can prove it on the most incontestable evidence), Mr Burdovsky, an official of the land-survey department. I've collected a number of most irrefutable facts to show that your father, Mr Burdovsky, who had no business ability whatever, gave up his job in the civil service on receiving your mother's dowry of fifteen thousand roubles and, getting himself involved in all sorts of business enterprises, was cheated, lost his capital, took to drink to drown his troubles, fell ill in consequence, and finally died prematurely eight years after marrying your mother. After that, according to your mother's own testimony, she was left in the direst poverty and would have been utterly lost but for the constant and generous assistance of Pavlishchev, who made her an allowance of six hundred a year. I have, besides, plenty of evidence that he grew very fond of you as a child. From this evidence, and from what I've been told by your mother, it appears that he grew fond of you chiefly because as a child you seemed to be tongue-tied and crippled and were very miserable and unhappy (and Pavlishchev, as I learnt on unimpeachable evidence, had all his life a sort of special tender affection for all who were afflicted and ill-favoured – a fact, in my view, of great importance in our case). Finally, I'm happy to say that during my investigation I've discovered another fact of the utmost importance – namely, that Pavlishchev's great fondness for you (for it was by his efforts that you were admitted to a secondary school where you were taught under special supervision) gradually gave rise to the idea among the members of Pavlishchev's family and his relations that you were his son and that your father had been deceived by his wife. But the important point to remember is that this idea became generally accepted as true only during the last years of Pavlishchev's life, when all his relations became alarmed about his will and when the original facts were forgotten and no inquiries about them were possible. No doubt that idea reached you, too, Mr Burdovsky, and took complete possession of you. Your mother, whose acquaintance I had the honour of making, knew of these rumours, but to this day she does not know (I concealed it from her, too) that you, her son, were also taken in by this rumour. I found your mother, Mr Burdovsky, in Pskov, very ill and extremely poor. She told me with tears of gratitude that, if she is still alive, it is because of you and your support; she expects a great deal of you in the future and believes ardently in your future success. ...'

'That really is quite intolerable!' Lebedev's nephew suddenly declared loudly and impatiently. 'What's all this romantic tale for?'

'Disgusting, indecent!' Ippolit cried excitedly, but Burdovsky noticed nothing and never even stirred.

'What is it for? Why?' Ganya said with slyly simulated surprise, maliciously preparing to sum up his conclusions. 'Well, in the first place, Mr Burdovsky can now be absolutely sure that Pavlishchev was fond of him out of the generosity of his heart and not as a son. That fact alone Mr Burdovsky had to know, for he has just now endorsed and approved Mr Keller's article. I say this because I regard you as an honourable man, Mr Burdovsky. Secondly, it appears that there can be no question here of any robbery or swindling, even so far as Chebarov is concerned. That is rather an important point for me, for just now the prince, in his excitement, asserted that I, too, was of the same opinion about the robbery and swindling in his unhappy affair. On the contrary, there was absolute conviction on all sides, and though, for all I know, Chebarov may really be a great rogue, in this affair he merely showed himself to be an astute lawyer with his eye on the main chance. He hoped to make a lot of money out of it as a lawyer, and his calculation was not only astute and masterly, but also absolutely well founded. He based his hopes on the readiness with which the prince was giving away his money and on his feeling of reverence and respect for the late Pavlishchev and, last but not least, on the prince's well-known chivalrous views about the obligations of honour and conscience. As for Mr Burdovsky, it may even be said that, thanks to certain convictions of his, he was so influenced by Chebarov and his friends that he embarked on this case not out of self-interest at all, but almost as a service to truth, progress, and humanity. Now, after the facts have been made known, it must be clear to everyone that Mr Burdovsky is a man of irreproachable character, in spite of all appearances, and the prince can now offer him all the more expeditiously and readily his friendly assistance and the material help he mentioned just now when he spoke of schools and Pavlishchev.'

'Stop, Mr Ivolgin, stop!' cried the prince in real dismay, but it was too late.

'I've said,' Burdovsky cried irritably, 'I've told you three times already that I don't want any money. I won't accept it – why – I don't want to – I'm off!'

And he nearly rushed out by the veranda. But Lebedev's nephew caught him by the arm and whispered something to him. Burdovsky quickly came back and, taking a large, unsealed envelope out of his pocket, threw it on the table near the prince.

'Here's your money – how dare you? – how dare you? – the money!'

'The two hundred and fifty roubles which you had the impertinence to send him by Chebarov as a charity,' explained Doktorenko.

'The article said fifty!' cried Kolya.

'I'm very sorry!' said the prince, going up to Burdovsky. 'I've done you a great wrong, Burdovsky, but I didn't send it you as a charity, believe me. I am to blame now, too, I'm afraid – I was to blame just now.' (The prince was very upset, he looked worn out and weak, and he spoke incoherently.) 'I spoke of a fraud – but I didn't mean you – I was mistaken. I said that you were suffering from the same – illness as I. But you are not like me, you – give lessons, you support your mother. I said that you have calumniated your mother, but you love her. She says so herself. I didn't know. ... Mr Ivolgin had not told me everything – I'm sorry. I dared to offer you ten thousand, but I was wrong. I shouldn't have done it that way, and now – now it can't be done because you despise me. ...'

'This is a madhouse!' cried Mrs Yepanchin.

'Of course, it's a house of madmen,' Aglaya said sharply, unable to restrain herself.

But her words were drowned in the general uproar. Everyone was talking loudly, everyone was arguing, some were disputing, others laughing. General Yepanchin was highly indignant and, with an air of injured dignity, waited for Mrs Yepanchin. Lebedev's nephew got in the last word.

'Yes, Prince, to do you justice you certainly know how to make use of your – well, illness (to put it politely). You've contrived to offer your friendship and money in such a clever way that no honourable man could possibly accept them under any circumstances. That's either a little too innocent or a little too clever – I expect you know which.'

'I say, gentlemen,' cried Ganya, who had meantime opened the envelope, 'there are only a hundred, and not two hundred and fifty roubles here. I point it out, Prince, so that there should be no misunderstanding.'

'Never mind – never mind!' the prince cried, waving his arms at Ganya.

'No,' Lebedev's nephew at once cottoned on to it, 'it is not "never mind". We regard your "never mind" as an insult, Prince. We do not hide ourselves, we declare openly – yes, there are only one hundred roubles, and not two hundred and fifty there, but isn't it all the same – –'

'No, sir, it isn't all the same,' Ganya managed to put in with an air of naïve perplexity.

'Don't interrupt me, please. We're not such fools as you think, Mr Lawyer,' Lebedev's nephew exclaimed with angry vexation. 'Of course one hundred roubles are not two hundred and fifty, and it isn't all the same, but it's the principle of the thing that matters; it's the initiative that's so important, and the fact that one hundred and fifty roubles are missing is only a detail. The important thing is that Burdovsky does not accept your charity, sir, that he throws it back in your face, and looked at from this point of view it is all the same whether it's a hundred or two hundred and fifty. Burdovsky hasn't accepted your ten thousand, as you've seen. He wouldn't have brought back the hundred roubles if he had been dishonest. The missing hundred and fifty roubles have gone to defray the expenses of Chebarov's journey to see the prince. You may laugh at our stupidity and our inexperience in business, you have, as it is, done your best to make us look ridiculous, but don't dare to say that we are dishonest. These hundred and fifty roubles, sir, we shall all of us return to the prince; we shall return it even if it has to be a rouble at a time. And we shall return it with interest. Burdovsky is poor, Burdovsky has no millions, and Chebarov sent in his bill after his journey. We hoped to win. ... Who would not have done the same in such a case?'

'Who would?' exclaimed Prince Sh.

'I shall go mad here!' cried Mrs Yepanchin.

'This reminds me,' laughed Radomsky, who had been standing there, observing, 'of the celebrated speech made recently by the counsel for the defence who pleaded the poverty of his client as a justification for his having murdered six people in order to rob them. He suddenly wound up his speech with this sort of peroration: "It's quite natural," he said, "that my client, who was so poor, should have thought of murdering six people, for who in his place wouldn't have thought of it?" Or something very funny of the same kind.'

'Enough!' Mrs Yepanchin cried suddenly, almost shaking with anger. 'It's time to put an end to this nonsense!'

She was in a state of terrible excitement; she flung back her head menacingly and looked round at the whole company with flashing eyes and with haughty, fierce, and impatient defiance, hardly distinguishing between friends and foes at that moment. She had reached that point of long-suppressed but, at last, explosive anger when the strongest impulse is to pounce on someone without stopping to think of the consequences. Those who knew Mrs Yepanchin felt at once that something unusual had happened. General Yepanchin told Prince Sh. next day that – 'This sort of thing happens to her, but even with her it rarely assumes such a violent form as yesterday. It happens once in three years or so, but never more often. Never more often!' he added emphatically.

'That'll do,' she cried, turning to her husband, who was offering her his arm. 'Leave me alone. Why are you offering me your arm now? You hadn't enough sense to take me away before, had you? You're my husband, you're the head of the family, you ought to have taken me, fool that I am, by the ear and dragged me out of here if I hadn't obeyed you and gone. You might at least have thought of your daughters! Now we can find the way without you. I've been disgraced enough to last me a whole year. Wait a moment; I've still got to thank the prince! Thank you, Prince, for a delightful entertainment! And to think that I've been sitting here listening to what our younger generation had to say. It's despicable, despicable! This is chaos, infamy, the sort of thing you wouldn't imagine in your wildest dreams! Are there really many like them? Hold your tongue, Aglaya! Hold your tongue, Alexandra! It's none of your business! Don't keep fussing round me, Mr Radomsky; I'm tired of you! So you, my dear man, are asking their forgiveness, are you?' she burst out, addressing the prince again. ' "So sorry to have the impertinence to offer you such a large sum of money. ..." And what are you laughing at, you disgusting little swaggerer?' she pounced suddenly on Lebedev's nephew. ' "We refuse to accept it – we demand, we don't beg!" As though he didn't know this idiot would drag himself off again to them to-morrow and offer them his friendship and large sums of money! You will, won't you? Won't you?'

'I will,' said the prince in a soft and meek voice.

'You hear that?' she turned again to Doktorenko. 'That's what you're counting on, aren't you? The money is as good as in your pocket, so that's why you're swaggering, that's why you're trying to throw dust in our eyes. No, sir, you can find other fools, I can see through you – I can see your game!'

'Mrs Yepanchin!' cried the prince.

'Come away, ma'am; it's high time we went, and let's take the prince with us,' said Prince Sh. with a smile, as calmly as he could.

The girls stood apart, looking almost frightened; the general was frightened in good earnest. They were all rather surprised. Some of them, who were standing furthest away, were grinning stealthily and whispering to one another; Lebedev's face wore an expression of the utmost rapture.

'You'll find infamy and chaos everywhere, madam,' said Lebedev's nephew, looking greatly embarrassed, though.

'But nothing like this, sir! Nothing like the sort of thing you specialize in, sir – nothing like it!' Mrs Yepanchin cried gleefully, as though she were in hysterics. 'Won't you leave me alone?' she shouted to those who tried to persuade her to go home. 'Oh, no, if, as you said yourself, Mr Radomsky, even a counsel for the defence declared in open court that there was nothing more natural for a man than to butcher six people because he happened to be poor, then indeed there's no more hope for the world. Such a thing I've never heard of. Now I understand everything! Why' – she pointed to Burdovsky, who was staring at her in utter bewilderment – 'wouldn't this stutterer murder someone? I bet he would! I daresay he won't take your ten thousand; he won't take it because it's against his conscience, but he'll come back at night and murder you and take it out of your cash-box. He'll take it out with a clear conscience! That's not dishonest to him! That's "an impulse of noble despair", that's "negation", or goodness only knows what. ... Good gracious, everything is upside down with them, everything's topsy-turvy. A girl grows up at home, then suddenly she jumps into a cab in the middle of the street: "Good-bye, Mummie; I've just got married to Karlych or Ivanych or someone!" Do you think that's the right way to behave? Is that the sort of thing one ought to respect? Is that natural? Is that the woman question? This boy here' – she pointed to Kolya – 'was actually arguing the other day that that is what "the woman question" means. Even though your mother's a fool, you ought to treat her like a human being, oughtn't you? Why did you come in tonight with your noses in the air? "Make way there – we are coming!" "Grant us every right, but don't dare to open your mouth before us!" "Show us every respect, even such as one has never heard of, but we shall treat you like dirt!" They are searching for truth, they stand on their rights, but they slandered him right and left in their article, like a lot of heathens. "We do not beg, we demand, and you will get no gratitude from us, for you're doing it for the satisfaction of your own conscience!" What morality! Why, if you won't show any gratitude, the prince is entitled to say to you that he feels no gratitude to Pavlishchev; for Pavlishchev, too, did good for the satisfaction of his conscience. And yet it is on his gratitude to Pavlishchev that you've been counting. He did not borrow any money from you, did he? He doesn't owe you anything. So what have you been counting on, if not on his gratitude? How can you then repudiate it yourself? Madmen! They regard society as inhuman and savage because it casts a slur on the seduced girl. But if you regard society as inhuman, you must admit that the girl feels hurt by the disapprobation of that society. And if she feels hurt, then why do you display her before society in the papers and expect her not to be hurt? Madmen! Conceited creatures! They don't believe in God, they don't believe in Christ! Why, you're so eaten up with vanity and pride that you'll finish up by devouring each other. I make this prophecy to you. And isn't that utter confusion? Isn't that chaos? Isn't that infamy? And after that this shameless fool runs after them and begs their forgiveness. Are there many like you? What are you grinning at? That I have disgraced myself before you? So I have, and there's nothing I can do about it! And don't you dare to grin, you wicked fellow!' she suddenly pounced upon Ippolit. 'He is almost at his last gasp, yet he's corrupting others. You've corrupted this young boy,' she pointed to Kolya again. 'He raves about you, and you teach him atheism. You don't believe in God, but you're not too old to be whipped, sir! Oh, I've had enough of you! So you will go to them to-morrow, Prince?' she asked the prince again, almost out of breath.

'I will.'

'Then I don't want to know you any more!' She turned quickly to go, but suddenly came back. 'And will you go to this atheist too?' She pointed to Ippolit. 'How dare you laugh at me, sir?' she cried in an unnatural sort of voice, and rushed at Ippolit, unable to endure his sarcastic laugh.

'Mrs Yepanchin! Mrs Yepanchin! Mrs Yepanchin!' they all cried at once.

'Mother, this is shameful!' Aglaya cried loudly.

'Don't worry, Miss Aglaya,' Ippolit said calmly, though Mrs Yepanchin had seized him by the arm and was holding it in a tight grip, staring at him intently with frenzied eyes, 'don't worry, your mother will soon realize that one can't strike a dying man. I'm quite ready to explain why I laughed – I shall be very glad of your permission to do so.'

Here he was suddenly seized by a violent fit of coughing, which he was helpless to control for a whole minute.

'He's dying, but he's still making speeches!' exclaimed Mrs Yepanchin, letting go of his arm and looking almost with horror at the blood he wiped from his lips. 'You shouldn't be talking. You ought to go home to bed.'

'I'll do that,' replied Ippolit in a low, hoarse voice and almost in a whisper. 'As soon as I get home, I'll go to bed. I know I shall die in a fortnight. Dr Botkin told me so himself last week. So if you will allow me, I should like to say a few farewell words to you.'

'Goodness, are you out of your mind?' Mrs Yepanchin cried in alarm. 'Nonsense! You have to be looked after. This is not the time for talking! Go along, go to bed!'

'If I go to bed now, I shan't get up again,' smiled Ippolit. 'I meant to go to bed yesterday and not get up again, but I decided to put it off till the day after to-morrow, while I can still stand on my feet, so as to come here with them to-day, but I'm afraid I'm – I'm very tired. ...'

'Sit down, sit down. Why are you standing? Here, sit down on this chair,' Mrs Yepanchin cried solicitously, and placed a chair for him herself.

'Thank you,' Ippolit went on softly, 'and you sit down opposite and we shall have a talk – we shall most certainly have a talk, ma'am; I insist on it now.' He smiled at her again. 'Think, to-day it is the last time I shall be out in the air and among people, and in a fortnight I shall most certainly be under the ground. So this will be a sort of farewell to nature and to men. Though I am not very sentimental, but, you know, I'm very glad that all this happened in Pavlovsk: I can at least take a look at a tree in leaf.'

'You mustn't talk now,' said Mrs Yepanchin, getting more and more alarmed. 'You're in a high fever. A few minutes ago you kept squeaking and squealing, and now you can hardly draw breath. You're panting.'

'I shall be all right in a moment. Why do you want to refuse my last wish? You know, I've been dreaming of meeting you for a long time, Mrs Yepanchin. I've heard such a lot about you from – from Kolya. You see, he's practically the only one who hasn't deserted me. You're an original woman, an eccentric woman – I've seen that for myself now. Do you know that I was a little fond of you even?'

'Good gracious, and I nearly struck him!'

'You were held back by Miss Aglaya. I'm not mistaken, am I? It is your daughter Aglaya, isn't it? She's so beautiful that I immediately recognized her, though I'd never seen her. Let me at least have a look at a beautiful woman for the last time in my life,' Ippolit said with a sort of awkward, wry smile. 'The prince is here, too, and your husband and the whole company. Why do you refuse my last wish?'

'A chair,' cried Mrs Yepanchin, but she seized one herself and sat down facing Ippolit. 'Kolya,' she ordered, 'you'll go with him at once; see him home, and to-morrow I will certainly come myself.'

'If you will allow me, I'd ask the prince for a cup of tea. ... I'm awfully tired. ... Look here, Mrs Yepanchin, I believe you wanted to take the prince home with you to tea. Please stay here; let's spend the time together, and I'm sure the prince will give us all tea. I'm sorry to be giving orders like that, but, you see, I know you: you're kind, and the prince, too, is kind – we're all quite absurdly kind people. ...'

The prince bestirred himself. Lebedev rushed headlong out of the room and Vera ran out after him.

'True enough,' Mrs Yepanchin decided abruptly, 'talk, only quietly and don't get excited. You've made me feel sorry for you. Prince, you don't deserve that I should take tea with you, but so be it. I'm staying, though I'm not apologizing to anybody. Not to anybody! Nonsense! ... Still, I'm sorry if I did scold you. I beg your pardon, but just as you like. I'm not detaining anyone, though.' She turned suddenly to her husband and daughters, looking very angry, as though they had done something to offend her. 'I can find my way home by myself. ...'

But they did not let her finish. They all gathered round her readily. The prince at once begged everyone to stay and have tea and apologized for not having thought of it before. Even the general was so polite as to murmur a few courteous and reassuring words and asked Mrs Yepanchin whether she did not feel a little chilly on the veranda. He nearly asked Ippolit how long he had been at the university, but he thought better of it. Radomsky and Prince Sh. suddenly became extremely amiable and gay, Adelaida and Alexandra looked pleased, though still a little surprised – in short, everyone seemed glad the crisis was over. Aglaya alone frowned and sat down at a distance in silence. The rest of the company remained, too; no one wanted to go, not even General Ivolgin, to whom Lebedev, however, whispered something in passing, probably something not quite pleasant, for the general at once beat a retreat to some faraway corner. The prince also went up to Burdovsky and his friends and invited them to stay, without omitting anybody. They muttered rather stiffly that they would wait for Ippolit, and at once betook themselves to the furthest end of the veranda, where they again sat down side by side. The tea had probably been long prepared by Lebedev himself, for it was brought in at once. It struck eleven.

10

Ippolit moistened his lips with the tea Vera had handed him, put down the cup on the little table, and suddenly, as though feeling embarrassed, looked round almost in confusion.

'Look, Mrs Yepanchin,' he began with a strange sort of haste, 'these cups – these are china cups and, I believe, excellent china. Lebedev keeps them always locked up in the chiffonier under glass. They are never used, of course. He got them as part of his wife's dowry – they usually keep it locked up. But, you see, he has brought them out for us – in your honour, no doubt, so pleased is he. ...'

He was going to add something, but could not find the right words.

'He's feeling embarrassed; I thought so!' Radomsky suddenly whispered in the prince's ear. 'That's dangerous, don't you think? It's the surest sign that he'll do something so eccentric out of spite that even Mrs Yepanchin, I'm afraid, will not put up with it.'

The prince looked interrogatively at him.

'You're not afraid of eccentricity?' added Radomsky. 'You see, I too would like it, as a matter of fact. All I want is that our dear Mrs Yepanchin should be punished, and to-night too. I don't want to leave without seeing it. You're not feeling feverish, are you?'

'Later; don't worry me. Yes, I'm unwell,' the prince replied absent-mindedly and even impatiently.

He had just heard his name mentioned. Ippolit was speaking of him.

'You don't believe it?' Ippolit laughed hysterically. 'That's as it should be, but the prince will believe it at once, and he won't be a bit surprised.'

'Do you hear that, Prince?' said Mrs Yepanchin, turning to him. 'Do you hear?'

They were all laughing. Lebedev kept thrusting himself forward fussily and fidgeting in front of Mrs Yepanchin.

'He says that this hypocrite here – your landlord – corrected the article of that gentleman – the article about you they read this evening.'

The prince looked at Lebedev in surprise.

'Why don't you say something?' cried Mrs Yepanchin, stamping her foot.

'Well,' murmured the prince, still looking steadily at Lebedev, 'I can see he corrected it.'

'Is it true?' Mrs Yepanchin asked, turning quickly to Lebedev.

'Perfectly true, ma'am,' Lebedev replied firmly and unflinchingly, laying his hand on his heart.

'He's actually boasting about it!' Mrs Yepanchin cried, nearly jumping out of her seat.

'I'm vile, vile,' Lebedev muttered, beginning to smite his breast and dropping his head lower and lower.

'What do I care whether you're vile or not? He thinks that by saying he's vile he can get away with it. And aren't you ashamed, Prince, to have anything to do with such contemptible creatures, I ask you again? I shall never forgive you!'

'The prince will forgive me!' Lebedev said with conviction and deep feeling.

'It is simply because as a man of honour, ma'am,' Keller said in a loud, ringing voice, suddenly rushing up to Mrs Yepanchin and addressing himself directly to her, 'it's simply because as a man of honour, ma'am, and not wishing to betray a friend who had compromised himself, that I did not mention the corrections, in spite of the fact that he threatened to kick us down the stairs, as you, ma'am, heard yourself. To put the matter right, I confess, ma'am, that I did really ask him as a competent person for his assistance and paid him six roubles for it, not to correct my style, but simply to supply me with the facts, which were for the most part unknown to me. The gaiters, the appetite at the Swiss professor's, the fifty instead of the two hundred and fifty roubles – in short, he is responsible for all that sequence of events, and he received six roubles for it. But he did not correct my style.'

'I must observe,' Lebedev interrupted him with feverish impatience and in a sort of grovelling voice, while the laughter was growing louder and louder, 'that I only corrected the first half of the article, but as we didn't agree in the middle and quarrelled over one idea, I did not correct the second half, so that everything that is not grammatically correct there (and it is full of grammatical mistakes), I'm not responsible for.'

'That's all he cares about!' cried Mrs Yepanchin.

'May I ask,' Radomsky turned to Keller, 'when the article was corrected?'

'Yesterday morning,' Keller replied. 'We met on the understanding that both of us would keep the secret.'

'That was when he was grovelling before you and assuring you of his devotion! Nice people, I must say! I don't want your Pushkin, and see that your daughter never comes to see me!'

Mrs Yepanchin was on the point of getting up, but suddenly turned irritably to Ippolit, who was laughing.

'You're not thinking of making a laughing-stock of me, my dear sir, are you?'

'God forbid,' Ippolit smiled wrily, 'but I can't help being struck by your extraordinary eccentricity, ma'am. I confess I broached the subject of Lebedev on purpose. I knew what effect it would have on you, and on you alone, because the prince will most certainly forgive him, if indeed he hasn't forgiven him already. He may even have thought of an excuse for him. Haven't you, Prince?'

He was gasping for breath and his strange excitement was increasing with every word he spoke.

'Well?' Mrs Yepanchin cried angrily, surprised by his tone. 'Well?'

'I've heard a lot of the same kind about you – with great delight, I must say, and – and I've learnt to respect you very much,' Ippolit went on.

He was saying one thing, but seemed to imply something quite different by the same words. He spoke with a touch of sarcasm in his voice, but at the same time he was agitated out of all proportion, looked round suspiciously, got muddled, and lost the thread of what he was going to say, so that together with his consumptive appearance and the strangely flashing and seemingly frenzied look in his eyes, he continued involuntarily to attract general attention.

'I should have been surprised, though I do not know anything of the world (I admit it), at your not only remaining in the company of my friends – a scarcely fitting company for you – but also for allowing these – er – young ladies to stay here to listen to such a scandalous affair, though they've read it all in novels already. I don't know, though – because I'm rather confused, but, in any case, who except you, ma'am, would have remained at – at the request of a boy (yes, a boy, I admit it again) to spend the evening with him and – and take an interest in everything and – and so that – that you'd certainly feel ashamed next day (I'm aware, though, that I'm not expressing myself properly). I find this, ma'am, highly commendable and I've the deepest respect for it, particularly as I can see from the face of your husband, the general, how disagreeable it all is to him. ... Ha, ha!' he sniggered, completely muddled, and suddenly began coughing so violently that for about two minutes he could not continue.

'Choked himself!' Mrs Yepanchin observed coldly and harshly, gazing at him with grim curiosity. 'Well, my dear boy, I've had enough of you. It's time we were going.'

'Let me, too, my dear sir, for my part, say,' declared General Yepanchin irritably, his patience completely exhausted, 'that my wife happens to be the guest of the prince, our mutual friend and neighbour, and that, in any case, it isn't for you, young man, to express an opinion about Mrs Yepanchin's actions, nor to refer aloud and in my presence to what is written on my face. No, sir. And,' he went on, getting more and more irritated with every word he uttered, 'if my wife has remained here, it is more from astonishment, sir, than from anything else and from the quite understandable modern interest in such strange young men. I stayed myself just as I sometimes stop in the street when I see something at which one can look as – as – as – –'

'As a curiosity,' prompted Radomsky.

'Quite right,' the general, who had become a little mixed up in his similes, cried delightedly. 'Yes, sir, exactly as a curiosity. But what seems to me most astonishing and distressful, if it is grammatical so to express oneself, is that you, young man, were quite unable to realize that Mrs Yepanchin has stayed with you now because you are ill – if, that is, you really are dying – and that she did it, as it were, out of compassion, because of your pathetic speeches, sir, and that no slur, sir, can attach itself to her name, character, and social position. ... My dear,' concluded the general, whose face had turned crimson, 'if you are going, we'd better say good-bye to our good prince and – –'

'Thank you for the lesson, General,' Ippolit interrupted him gravely and unexpectedly, gazing thoughtfully at him.

'Come along, Mother,' Aglaya cried impatiently and angrily, getting up from her chair. 'How much longer is this to go on?'

'Two more minutes, dear, if you don't mind,' said Mrs Yepanchin, turning with dignity to her husband. 'I think he's in a fever and is simply delirious. I am sure of it from his eyes. He can't be left like that. Could you put him up, Prince, so that he should not have to drag himself to Petersburg to-night? My dear Prince,' she exclaimed, turning for some reason to Prince Sh., 'you're not bored, are you? Come here, Alexandra; put your hair straight, my dear.'

She tidied her hair, which was perfectly tidy already, and kissed her. That was what she had called her for.

'I thought you were capable of enlarging your mind,' said Ippolit, emerging from his reverie. 'Yes, this is what I meant to say,' he exclaimed, looking very pleased, as though suddenly remembering something. 'Burdovsky here sincerely wants to protect his mother, doesn't he? But it turns out that he has disgraced her. The prince here wants to help Burdovsky and in all sincerity offers him his tender friendship and his money, and he is perhaps the only one among us all not to feel an aversion for him, and there they stand facing each other like real enemies. ... Ha, ha, ha! You all hate Burdovsky because in your opinion his behaviour to his mother is not pretty but ungracious. Isn't that so? Isn't it? Isn't it? For all of you are terribly fond of prettiness and gracefulness of external forms, and that's all you care for, isn't it? (I've suspected for a long time that that's all you care for!) Well, I'd like you to know that perhaps not one of you has loved his mother as Burdovsky has! I know that you, Prince, have sent money secretly to Burdovsky's mother through Ganya, and I'll bet' (he laughed hysterically) 'that Burdovsky will now accuse you of indelicacy and disrespect to his mother. I'm sure of that – ha, ha, ha!'

He choked again and went off into a fit of coughing.

'Well, is that all?' Mrs Yepanchin interrupted impatiently, without taking her anxious eyes off him. 'Have you said everything now? Well, go to bed now; you are in a fever. Oh, dear, he is still talking!'

'You're laughing, are you?' Ippolit asked, suddenly addressing Radomsky agitatedly and irritably. 'Why are you laughing at me? I've noticed that you keep on laughing at me!'

Radomsky was really laughing.

'I only wanted to ask you, Mr – er – Ippolit – I'm sorry I've forgotten your name.'

'Mr Terentyev,' said the prince.

'Oh yes, Mr Terentyev. Thank you, Prince; it was mentioned before, but it slipped my mind. I wanted to ask you, Mr Terentyev, if it is true what I've heard – I mean, that you're of the opinion that you have only to talk to the common people for a quarter of an hour out of a window and they will agree with you and follow you without more ado?'

'Quite possibly I did say that,' replied Ippolit, as though trying to remember something. 'Yes, I most certainly did!' he added suddenly, brightening up again and looking hard at Radomsky. 'What about it?'

'Nothing at all. I merely asked as a matter of interest to get everything straight.'

Radomsky fell silent, but Ippolit still kept looking at him in impatient expectation.

'Well, have you finished?' asked Mrs Yepanchin, addressing Radomsky. 'Hurry up and finish, sir, for it's time we went to bed. Or don't you know how to?'

She sounded terribly annoyed.

'I'm sure,' Radomsky went on with a smile, 'I don't mind adding that everything I've heard from your friends, Mr Terentyev, and everything you've said so brilliantly yourself just now boils down, in my opinion, to the theory of the triumph of right over everything and in spite of everything and, indeed, to the exclusion of everything else, even before a proper examination into the nature of right. I'm not mistaken, am I?'

'Of course you are. I don't even understand what you're talking about. Go on.'

There was a murmur of protest in the corner of the veranda, too. Lebedev's nephew muttered something in an undertone.

'I've scarcely anything more to add,' went on Radomsky. 'I only wanted to point out that such a theory leads straight to the conception of the right of might – that is to say, the right of the individual fist and of personal ambition – as indeed has often been the case in world affairs. Did not Proudhon maintain that right is might? In the American civil war many most advanced liberals declared themselves to be on the side of the plantation owners on the ground that Negroes were Negroes and inferior to the white race, and therefore that the right of might was the prerogative of white men.'

'Well?'

'You don't deny, then, the right of might?'

'Go on!'

'You're consistent, after all. I only wanted to point out that from the right of might to the right of tigers and crocodiles, and even to the right of the Danilovs and Gorskys, is but a short step.'

'I don't know. Go on.'

Ippolit was scarcely listening to Radomsky, and if he did say 'well' and 'go on', he apparently did so more from a habit he had acquired long ago in debating than from attention or curiosity.

'Nothing more – that's all.'

'I'm not angry with you, though,' Ippolit concluded quite unexpectedly and, hardly fully conscious of what he was doing, he even held out his hand with a smile.

Radomsky was at first surprised, but he touched the proffered hand gravely, as though accepting forgiveness.

'I can't help expressing,' he said in the same ambiguously respectful tone, 'my gratitude to you for the courtesy with which you've permitted me to speak, for, from my numerous observations, our liberals are never capable of permitting anyone to have an opinion of his own without immediately overwhelming their opponent with abuse or something worse.'

'You're quite right there,' observed General Yepanchin, and, folding his hands behind his back, he retreated with an air of the utmost boredom to the steps of the veranda, where he yawned with vexation.

'Well, that's enough of you, sir,' Mrs Yepanchin suddenly addressed Radomsky. 'I'm sick and tired of you all.'

'It's time to go!' Ippolit said and suddenly got up, looking worried and almost alarmed and gazing round him in perplexity. 'I'm sorry I've detained you. I wanted to tell you everything. I thought that everything – for the last time – it was a delusion....'

It was obvious that he became animated by fits and starts, that he emerged from his state of almost real delirium suddenly, for a few moments, and then, regaining full consciousness, suddenly remembered and talked, mostly in disconnected phrases, which he had perhaps thought out in the long, weary hours of his illness, in bed, during his sleepless nights.

'Well, good-bye!' he suddenly said abruptly. 'You think it's easy for me to say good-bye to you? Ha, ha!' he laughed vexatiously at his own *awkward* question and suddenly, as though angry with himself for not succeeding in saying what he wanted to say, he declared in a loud and exasperated voice, addressing General Yepanchin: 'Sir, I have the honour of inviting you to my funeral, if only you do not deem me unworthy of such an honour and – er – all of you, ladies and gentlemen – after the general! ...'

He laughed again; but this was already the laugh of a madman. Mrs Yepanchin moved towards him in alarm and seized him by the arm. He gazed intently at her with the same laugh, which could not be heard any more, but seemed to have stopped short and frozen on his face.

'Do you know that I came here to see the trees? Those there,' he pointed to the trees in the park. 'That's not absurd, is it? There's nothing absurd in that, is there?' he asked Mrs Yepanchin seriously, and suddenly fell into a reverie; then, a moment later, he raised his head and started searching eagerly for someone among the people on the veranda. He was looking for Radomsky, who was standing not far away, in the same place as before, but he had forgotten it and kept looking round. 'You haven't gone away!' he said, finding him at last. 'You were laughing at me just now for wanting to talk out of the window for a quarter of an hour. ... But do you know I am not yet eighteen: I have lain so long on that pillow and have looked so long out of that window, and thought so much – about everyone – that – – A dead man has no age, you know. I thought that last week when I woke up in the night. ... Do you know what you are afraid of most of all? You're afraid of our sincerity most of all, though you despise us! I thought that, too, lying on my pillow at night. Do you think, madam,' he turned to Mrs Yepanchin, 'that I wanted to laugh at you a few minutes ago? No, I was not laughing at you, I only wanted to say something nice to you. ... Kolya told me that the prince called you a child – that's good. ... Yes – what was it I wanted to say? I wanted to say something more – –' he buried his face in his hands and sank into thought. 'Oh yes! When you were saying good-bye just now, I suddenly thought: Here these people are, and they will never be there again – never! And the trees too – there will be just the brick wall – the red brick wall of Meyer's house – opposite my window – well, tell them all about it – just try and tell them. Here's a beautiful girl – but you're dead – dead – introduce yourself as a dead man, tell her, "A dead man may say anything" – and that Mrs Grundy won't be angry, ha, ha! Aren't you laughing?' He looked at them all mistrustfully. 'You know, I get lots of ideas while lying there on my pillow – I've come to the conclusion that Nature is a very ironic jade. ... You said a few moments ago that I was an atheist, but do you know that this Nature – – Why are you laughing again? You're awfully cruel!' he said suddenly with mournful indignation, gazing at them all. 'I have not corrupted Kolya,' he concluded in quite a different, an earnest and convinced, tone of voice, as though remembering something again....

'No one is laughing at you here, no one, calm yourself!' cried Mrs Yepanchin almost in distress. 'To-morrow you shall see a new doctor. The other one was mistaken. But sit down, please. You can hardly stand on your feet. You're delirious. Oh, what are we to do with him now?' she fussed round him, making him sit down in an arm-chair.

A tear glistened on her cheek.

Ippolit stopped short, looking almost dumbfounded, raised his hand, stretched it out timidly, and touched the tear. He smiled a child-like smile.

'I – –' he burst out happily, 'I – you don't know how I – he, Kolya there – always spoke of you with such enthusiasm – I love his enthusiasm. I've never corrupted him! He's the only one I'm leaving – I'd have liked to leave them all – all of them – but there was no one – no one – I wanted to be a leader of men – I had a right to. ... Oh, I wanted so many things! Now I don't want anything. I don't want to want anything. I vowed that I would not want anything – let them, let them seek the truth without me! Yes, Nature is an ironic jade. Why does she,' he cried suddenly with heat, 'why does she create the best human beings only to make fools of them afterwards? It is she who is responsible for the fact that the only being that is recognized on earth as the acme of perfection – it is she who is responsible for the fact that, having shown him to men, she made him say things which have caused so much blood to be shed that if it had been shed all at once, men would have drowned in it for certain! Oh, it is a good thing that I'm going to die! I, too, would perhaps have uttered some dreadful lie – nature would have contrived it so. ... I have not corrupted anyone. ... I wanted to live for the happiness of all men, for the discovery and the proclamation of truth. I looked out of the window at Meyer's wall and thought of speaking for only a quarter of an hour and convincing everyone – everyone, and now for once in my life I've met – you, if not the others, and what has come of it? Nothing! All that has come of it is that you despise me! Which means that I'm a fool, that I'm not wanted, that it is time for me to go! And I haven't even been clever enough to leave a memory behind me! Not a sound, not a trace, not a single deed! I haven't spread a single truth! Don't laugh at a fool! Forget him! Forget everything – please forget it; don't be so cruel! Do you realize that but for this consumption, I should have killed myself!'

He seemed to wish to say a lot more, but he did not say it, and, falling back into the chair, he buried his face in his hands and burst out crying like a little child.

'Well, what are we going to do with him now?' cried Mrs Yepanchin, and she ran up to him, took his head in her hands, and pressed it tightly to her bosom. He sobbed convulsively. 'There, there, there, don't cry, don't! There, that's enough. You're a good boy. God will forgive you because of your ignorance. There, there, that'll do. Be a man. And, besides, you'll be awfully ashamed afterwards. ...'

'I have at home,' said Ippolit, trying to raise his head, 'I have a brother and sisters at home, poor, innocent little children. *She* will corrupt them! You're a saint, you're a – child yourself – save them! Snatch them away from that woman – she – it's disgraceful. ... Oh, help them, help them! God will reward you a hundredfold for it – for God's sake, for Christ's sake! . . .'

'Won't you tell me what's to be done now?' Mrs Yepanchin cried irritably, addressing her husband. 'Do me the favour and break your majestic silence! If you don't decide something, I shall stay the night here myself. I've had enough of your tyrranical régime!'

Mrs Yepanchin put her question with great feeling and anger, and expected an immediate answer. But in such cases people, even if there are many of them, usually prefer to reply with silence and passive interest, unwilling to accept the responsibility, and then express their views long afterwards. Among those present there were some who were quite ready to sit there till morning without uttering a word; for instance, Varya, who had been sitting the whole evening a little distance away, listening in silence with extraordinary interest, for which she perhaps had her own reasons.

'My opinion, my dear,' the general declared, 'is that, as it were, a trained nurse would be more useful here than excitable people like us, and perhaps a trustworthy, sober person for the night. In any case, we'd better ask the prince and – er – give the patient all the rest he needs immediately. To-morrow we can again discuss what can be done for him.'

'It's twelve o'clock now,' Doktorenko said irritably and angrily, addressing the prince. 'We're going. Is he coming with us or is he staying with you?'

'If you like,' replied the prince, 'you too can stay with him here. There's plenty of room.'

'Sir,' Mr Keller cried enthusiastically, rushing up to the general, 'if you want a reliable man for the night, I'm ready to make a sacrifice for a friend – he's such a wonderful chap! I've long considered him a great man, sir! I admit, sir, that I've rather neglected my education, but if he does criticize me, it's as if he was scattering pearls, sir – pearls!'

The general turned away in despair.

'I shall be very glad if he stays,' the prince said in answer to Mrs Yepanchin's irritable questions. 'Of course, he can't possibly go back.'

'You're not asleep, are you? If you don't want him to stay, I can take him home with me. Good heavens, he can hardly stand on his feet! Are you ill?'

Not finding the prince on his deathbed, Mrs Yepanchin, judging by his appearance, had really greatly exaggerated the satisfactory state of his health, but his recent illness, the painful memories attached to it, the fatigue of this strenuous evening, the incident with 'Pavlishchev's son', and now the incident with Ippolit – all this had so exacerbated the morbid sensitiveness of the prince that he really was in a feverish condition now. Besides, a new sort of worry, almost a fear, could be discerned in his eyes at this moment. He looked apprehensively at Ippolit, as though expecting something more from him.

Suddenly Ippolit got up, dreadfully pale and with an expression of terrible, almost despairing, shame on his distorted face. This was expressed chiefly in his eyes, which stared fearfully and hatefully at the company, and in the forlorn, twisted, and abject smile on his quivering lips. He dropped his eyes at once, and walked slowly, staggering, and still with the same smile, towards Burdovsky and Doktorenko, who were standing near the steps of the veranda: he was going with them.

'That's what I was afraid of!' cried the prince. 'That was bound to happen!'

Ippolit turned round to him with a look of frenzied malice, and every feature of his face seemed to be quivering and speaking.

'Oh, so you were afraid of that, were you? "That was bound to happen", in your opinion, was it? Well, let me tell you that if I hate anyone here – and I hate you all, all of you,' he spluttered in a shrill, hoarse voice, 'I hate you more than anyone and more than anything in the world – you jesuitical, treacly soul, you damned idiot, you philanthropic millionaire, you! I understood and hated you long ago, when I first heard of you; I hated you with all the hatred of my heart. ... It's you who've contrived it all! It is you who've brought on my attack of illness! You have made a dying man ashamed of himself – you, you, you are to blame for my contemptible cowardice! I'd kill you, if I remained alive! I don't want your benefactions, I won't accept anything from anyone – do you hear? – not from anyone! I was delirious and you've no right to triumph! May you be damned, every one of you, for ever and ever.'

At this point he choked completely.

'Ashamed of his tears!' Lebedev whispered to Mrs Yepanchin. 'That was bound to happen! Dear old prince! Saw right through him!'

But Mrs Yepanchin did not deign to look at him. She was standing, drawn up haughtily to her full height, with her head erect, and looked at 'those contemptible creatures' with scornful interest. When Ippolit finished, the general shrugged his shoulders; she looked him up and down angrily, as though demanding an account of his gesture, and at once turned to the prince.

'Thank you very much, Prince, dear eccentric friend of my family, for the pleasant evening you've provided for us all. I expect your heart must be rejoicing now for having succeeded in associating us with your tomfooleries. That's quite enough, dear friend of my family! Thank you for having at last let us get a good idea of yourself, anyway!'

She began putting her cloak straight indignantly, waiting for 'them' to depart. A cab for which Doktorenko had sent Lebedev's schoolboy son a quarter of an hour ago drove up at that moment to take them away. Immediately after his wife, the general put in his word too.

'Really, Prince, I never expected that after – er – after everything, I mean, after – er – all our friendly relations and – er – after all, my wife – –'

'How can you, Father!' cried Adelaida and, walking up quickly to the prince, she gave him her hand.

The prince smiled at her with a forlorn look. Suddenly a hot rapid whisper seemed to scorch his ears.

'If you don't get rid of these disgusting people at once, I shall hate you all my life, all my life!' Aglaya whispered.

She seemed in a sort of frenzy, but she turned away before the prince had time to look at her. Not that he had anyone or anything to get rid of any more: they had managed by this time somehow to get Ippolit into the cab, and it had driven off.

'Well,' Mrs Yepanchin addressed her husband, 'how long do you think this will go on, sir? How long will I have to suffer from these spiteful, odious boys?'

'Why, my dear, I – er – I'm of course, quite ready and – er – the prince – –'

The general, however, did hold out his hand to the prince, but had not time to shake hands with him and ran off after Mrs Yepanchin, who was descending the steps of the veranda noisily and angrily. Adelaida, her fiancé, and Alexandra took leave of the prince with sincere affection. Radomsky did the same, and he alone was in high spirits.

'It happened as I expected,' he whispered with a charming smile. 'I'm only sorry that you, too, poor fellow, have had to suffer for it.'

Aglaya went away without saying good-bye.

But the adventures of that evening were not by any means at an end. Mrs Yepanchin had to put up with another quite unexpected meeting.

Before she had time to descend the steps of the veranda into the street (skirting the park), a magnificent carriage, drawn by two white horses, suddenly dashed by the prince's house. Two gorgeous ladies were sitting in it. But, after driving no more than ten paces past the house, the carriage stopped; one of the ladies turned round quickly, as though she had suddenly caught sight of a friend she wanted to see.

'Is that you, Eugene, darling?' cried a beautiful, ringing voice, which made the prince, and perhaps someone else, start. 'Oh, I'm so glad to have found you at last! I sent a messenger to you in town – two messengers! They've been looking for you all day, darling!'

Mr Radomsky stood on the steps of the veranda, thunderstruck. Mrs Yepanchin, too, stood still, but not transfixed with horror like Radomsky. She looked at the insolent woman with the same proud and cold contempt as she had looked at the 'contemptible creatures' five minutes ago and at once turned her steady gaze on Radomsky.

'I've news for you!' the ringing voice went on. 'Don't worry about Kupfer's IOUs. Rogozhin bought them up for thirty. I persuaded him to. You needn't worry for another three months. As for Biskup and all that rabble, we'll come to a friendly arrangement with them! So, you see, everything's all right! Don't worry, darling! See you tomorrow!'

The carriage drove off and quickly disappeared.

'She must be mad!' cried Radomsky at last, reddening with indignation and looking round him in bewilderment. 'I haven't the faintest idea what she was talking about. What IOUs? Who is she?'

Mrs Yepanchin went on looking at him for a few more seconds; at last she quickly and abruptly walked off towards her country house, followed by the others. Exactly a minute later Radomsky came back to the prince on the veranda in a state of extraordinary excitement.

'Prince, tell me the truth: do you know what it means?'

'I don't know anything about it,' replied the prince, who was himself in a state of extreme and painful nervous excitement.

'You don't?'

'No.'

'I don't, either,' Radomsky laughed suddenly. 'I swear I've had nothing to do with any IOUs. Believe me – on my word of honour! But what's the matter with you? You're going to faint.'

'Oh, no, no! I assure you, no. ...'

II

It was only three days later that the Yepanchins relented. Although, as usual, the prince blamed himself for many things, and quite honestly expected to be punished, he had inwardly been absolutely convinced all the same that Mrs Yepanchin could not be seriously angry with him, but was really more angry with herself. That was why such a long period of disfavour plunged him by the third day into a state of the most gloomy perplexity. There were other circumstances to account for it, and one of them in particular seemed most ominous. In his morbidly suspicious state of mind it had grown progressively during the last three days (and lately the prince blamed himself for two extremes: for his extraordinarily 'senseless and tiresome' trustfulness and at the same time for his 'contemptible and gloomy' suspiciousness). In short, at the end of the third day the incident of the eccentric lady, who had accosted Radomsky from her carriage, assumed frightening and mysterious proportions in his mind. As he saw it, the core of the mystery, quite apart from the other aspects of the affair, was summed up in the painful question: was he responsible for this new 'enormity' or only -- But he refrained from saying who else it could be. As for the letters N.F.B., it was, to his mind, only an innocent prank, a most childish prank, so that it would be shameful and, in one respect, indeed almost dishonourable, to be in the least worried about it.

However, on the day following the disgraceful 'party', for whose scandalous incidents he was chiefly 'responsible', the prince had the pleasure of receiving in the morning a visit from Prince Sh. and Adelaida: they had come *chiefly*, they told him, to inquire after his health. They had just dropped in after a walk in the park together. Adelaida had noticed a tree there, a wonderful spreading old tree with long twisting branches, covered with young green leaves, and with a hollow and a big cleft in it, and she made up her mind that she simply had to draw it! They spoke of practically nothing else during the whole half-hour of their visit. Prince Sh. was nice and charming as usual, asked the prince about his past, and recalled the circumstances of their first meeting, so that hardly anything was said of the events of the previous night. At last Adelaida could not restrain herself and confessed with a laugh that they were there 'unofficially'; but that was all she would say, though it was not difficult to deduce from this 'unofficial' visit that her parents – that is, chiefly Mrs Yepanchin – were particularly ill-disposed towards him. Prince Sh. did not utter one word during their visit about her, or Aglaya, or even General Yepanchin. When they went out to continue their walk, they did not ask the prince to accompany them. There was no hint of asking him to go and see them. So far as that was concerned, Adelaida let drop a rather characteristic remark: telling him of a water-colour she had been doing, she suddenly said that she would very much like him to see it. 'Now, how can we arrange it soon? Wait! I'll send it to you by Kolya, if he comes, or I'll bring it to you myself to-morrow when I go for a walk with the prince,' she solved the problem at last, glad that she had managed to do it so cleverly and so conveniently for everybody.

At last, almost on the point of taking his leave, Prince Sh. seemed suddenly to remember something.

'Oh yes,' he said, 'do you, my dear fellow, happen to know who that person was who shouted to Mr Radomsky last night from the carriage?'

'It was Nastasya Filippovna,' said the prince. 'Haven't you found out yet that it was she? But I don't know who was with her.'

'Yes, I know, I've heard,' Prince Sh. said quickly. 'But what did she mean? I admit it's a complete mystery to me and – to others.'

Prince Sh. was speaking with extreme and evident astonishment.

'She spoke of some bills of Mr Radomsky's,' the prince replied quite simply, 'which Rogozhin had got hold of at her request from some moneylender, and she said that Rogozhin was ready to wait till Radomsky could meet them.'

'I heard it, I heard it, my dear prince; but, you see, that couldn't possibly be true! Radomsky couldn't have given any IOUs to anyone! With a fortune like his? It's true that, being rather improvident, he used to give IOUs before, and, indeed, I used to help him out. But it's quite impossible to give IOUs to a moneylender with his fortune and to be worried about them. And he couldn't be on such familiar and friendly terms with Nastasya Filippovna – that's what's so puzzling about the whole affair! He swears he knows nothing about it and I quite believe him. But what I wanted to ask you, dear Prince, is whether you know anything about it. I mean, has any rumour reached you by some miracle?'

'No, I know nothing and I assure you I had nothing to do with it.'

'Good Lord, Prince, what a funny chap you are! I simply don't know you to-day. Do you really think I could suppose you had anything to do with an affair of that kind? Oh well, I can see you're not quite yourself to-day.'

He embraced and kissed him.

'How do you mean I couldn't have anything to do with an affair of that kind? I'm afraid I can't see that there is any affair "of that kind".'

'No doubt,' Prince Sh. replied rather drily, 'that person wished somehow or other to prevent Radomsky from taking a certain step by making certain people believe that he possessed qualities which he doesn't and couldn't possess.'

The prince looked embarrassed, but he went on looking intently and interrogatively at Prince Sh. But Prince Sh. said nothing more.

'Not simply IOUs?' the prince murmured at last with some impatience. 'Are you sure she didn't mean it literally yesterday?'

'But, look here, can't you see for yourself that there can be nothing in common between Mr Radomsky and – her and Rogozhin of all people? I repeat he's immensely rich. I know that for a fact. And he expects to inherit another fortune from his uncle. Nastasya Filippovna simply – –'

Prince Sh. suddenly fell silent again, evidently because he did not wish to go on talking about Nastasya Filippovna to the prince.

'Then, at any rate, he must have known her, mustn't he?' the prince suddenly asked after a minute's silence.

'Yes, I think so – he's such a frivolous man! Still, if he did know her, it must have been long ago – that is, two or three years ago. You see, he used to know Totsky. But there couldn't be anything of the sort now, and they could never have been on intimate terms. You know yourself that she hasn't been here at all. She hasn't been seen anywhere. I have only noticed her carriage for the last three days, not more.'

'A magnificent carriage!' said Adelaida.

'Yes, the carriage is certainly magnificent.'

Both parted on the most friendly and, one might say, most brotherly terms with the prince.

For our hero, however, this meeting was of most capital importance. No doubt he had suspected a great deal himself since the previous night (and, perhaps, even earlier), but till their visit he could not bring himself to justify his apprehensions. Now he could clearly see that though Prince Sh.'s interpretation of the incident was, of course, incorrect, he was not far from the truth all the same, for he realized that there was some sort of *intrigue* going on. (Perhaps, thought the prince, he understood it all correctly, but not wishing to express an opinion on the matter, purposely put a wrong interpretation on it.)

But there could no longer be any doubt whatever that they had come to see him (Prince Sh. in particular) in the hope that he might be able to shed some light on the affair. If that was so, then they most certainly considered him to have had a hand in the intrigue. Moreover, if that was so, and if it really was important, then *she* must have some dreadful object in view. What could her object be? Oh, it was dreadful! 'And how on earth is one to *stop* her? It is quite impossible to stop her, if she's absolutely convinced that what she's doing is right!' That the prince already knew by experience. 'She is mad! Mad!'

But there were many, many other insoluble problems that morning, all coming at once, and all demanding an immediate solution, so that the prince felt very sad. He was a little diverted by Vera Lebedev, who came in to see him with little Lyuba and, laughing, told him some long story. She was followed by her sister, who stood there with her mouth wide-open, and then by Lebedev's schoolboy son, who assured him that 'the star called Wormwood' in the Apocalypse which fell from heaven upon the fountains of waters was, according to his father's interpretation, the network of railways spread all over Europe. The prince did not believe that Lebedev interpreted it in this way, and they decided to ask him about it at the first favourable opportunity. From Vera Lebedev the prince learnt that Keller had taken up his quarters with them since the day before, and, according to every sign, was not going to leave them for a long time, for he had struck up a friendship with General Ivolgin. He declared, however, that he was staying with them solely in order to complete his education. On the whole, the prince began to like Lebedev's children more and more every day. Kolya had not been there all day: he had gone to Petersburg early in the morning (Lebedev, too, had left very early that morning to attend to some business affairs of his own). But the prince was waiting impatiently for Ganya, who was quite certain to call on him that day.

He arrived at seven o'clock in the evening immediately after dinner. At the first glance at him, it occurred to the prince that that gentleman at any rate must know every detail of last night's affair most thoroughly, and, indeed, how could he not know it with such assistants as Varya and her husband? But the prince's relations with Ganya were somewhat peculiar. The prince had, for instance, authorized him to see to the Burdovsky affair and asked him particularly to do so; but in spite of it, and in spite of something that had happened before, there always were certain things between them which they had apparently agreed not to discuss. Occasionally the prince could not help feeling that Ganya, for his part, perhaps wanted them to be completely and amicably sincere with one another; now, for instance, as soon as he came in, the prince thought Ganya was convinced that at that very moment the time had come for them to break the ice completely. (Ganya was in a hurry, however; his sister was waiting for him at Lebedev's; they were both in a hurry to go somewhere on some business.)

But if Ganya was really expecting a flood of impatient questions, spontaneous communications and friendly confidences, he was, of course, greatly mistaken. During the twenty minutes of his visit the prince was very pensive, almost abstracted. The very idea of any expected questions, or rather of one principal question, which Ganya expected, was preposterous. It was then that Ganya, too, decided to speak with greater reserve. He went on talking and laughing without stopping during the whole of the twenty minutes; he engaged in a light, charming, and rapid conversation without touching on the chief subject.

Ganya, incidentally, told him that Nastasya Filippovna had been only four days in Pavlovsk and was already attracting general attention. She was staying with Darya Alexeyevna in a horrid little house in Matroskaya Street, but her carriage was one of the finest in Pavlovsk. A whole crowd of young and old aspirants for her favour had already gathered round her; her carriage was sometimes escorted by men on horseback. Nastasya Filippovna was as fastidious as ever in the choice of her friends and she only received those she liked. And yet a whole band had already been formed round her, so that she had many people she could rely on in case of need. One of the local holiday-makers had already quarrelled on her account with the girl to whom he was engaged to be married, and one elderly general had all but disowned his son. She often took out driving with her a most charming young girl, who was only just sixteen, a distant relative of Darya Alexeyevna's. This girl sang beautifully, so that their little house attracted general attention in the evenings. Nastasya Filippovna, though, behaved with the utmost propriety, dressed quietly but with extraordinary taste, and all the ladies envied 'her taste, her beauty, and her carriage'.

'Yesterday's eccentric incident,' Ganya declared discreetly, 'was, of course, premeditated and, of course, should not be taken too seriously. To find fault with her about anything, one must either find some appropriate excuse on purpose or spread some discreditable story about her, which, I expect, many people will not be slow to do,' concluded Ganya, expecting that the prince would most certainly ask him why he thought yesterday's incident to have been premeditated and why people would not be slow to do so.

But the prince did not ask it. About Radomsky Ganya talked at some length, but again without being specially asked, which was very strange, considering that he dragged him in without any particular reason. In Ganya's opinion, Radomsky had not known Nastasya Filippovna, and even now he knew her only slightly, for he had been introduced to her by someone four days before, during a walk in the park, and it was very unlikely that he had been at her house even once with the others. As for the IOUs, there might well be something in it, too (Ganya was quite certain about that); Radomsky was, of course, a wealthy man, but the affairs on his estate were far from satisfactory. On this interesting topic Ganya preferred to say no more. Nor did he say anything more about Nastasya Filippovna's extraordinary behaviour of the previous night, except for his earlier cryptic remark.

At last Varya came in to fetch her brother. She stayed a minute, declared (also without being asked) that Radomsky was in Petersburg to-day and would probably be there to-morrow too, and that her husband (Mr Ptitsyn) was also in Petersburg, where she believed he had gone on Radomsky's business, for there really seemed to be something amiss there. Before leaving, she added that Mrs Yepanchin was in a fiendish temper to-day, but, what was most strange, Aglaya had quarrelled with her whole family, not only with her father and mother, but also with her sisters, and that was a bad sign! Having delivered herself (as though in passing) of the last piece of news (which was highly significant to the prince), the brother and sister departed. Ganya did not say a word about the affair of 'Pavlishchev's son', perhaps out of false modesty or out of a desire to 'spare the prince's feelings', but the prince nevertheless thanked him again for the conscientious way in which he had brought the affair to an end.

The prince was very glad to be left alone at last; he went out into the street, crossed the road, and went into the park: he was anxious to think over, and make up his mind about, a certain step he wanted to take. But that 'step' was not one of those one thought over; one did not think it over, but simply made up one's mind about it: he was suddenly overcome by an uncontrollable desire to leave everything here and go back to where he had come from, to some far-away solitary place, and to go away at once without even saying good-bye to anyone. He had a feeling that if he stayed here even a few days longer, he would irrevocably be drawn into this world, and that this world would become his world henceforward. But he did not debate the question with himself even for as long as ten minutes; he decided at once that to run away was 'impossible', that it would be almost cowardice, that he was faced with such problems that now he had no right not to solve them or, at least, not to do all he could to solve them. Absorbed in such thoughts, he returned home, having scarcely been out for a quarter of an hour. He was very unhappy at that moment.

Lebedev was not back home yet, so that towards the evening Keller managed to burst in on the prince; he was not drunk, but overflowing with confidence and confessions. He told the prince, without beating about the bush, that he had come to tell him the whole story of his life and that was why he had stayed behind in Pavlovsk. It was quite impossible to get rid of him: he would not have gone for anything in the world. Keller got ready to talk at great length and not very coherently, but almost as soon as he had begun he skipped to the conclusion and declared that he had so utterly lost 'every vestige of morality' (solely because of his disbelief in the Almighty) that he was even guilty of stealing.

'Can you imagine it?'

'Listen, Keller,' the prince began, 'in your place I shouldn't confess that if I didn't have to, but I expect you're probably making yourself out to be worse than you are on purpose.'

'I'm telling you this – you alone – solely in the interests of my own spiritual development! To no one else – I'll die and carry my secret to the grave. But, Prince, if you knew, if only you knew how hard it is to get any money nowadays! Where is one to get it, I ask you? There's only one answer: "Bring your gold and diamonds as security and we'll give you money." You see, the only thing they want is what I haven't got. How do you like that? Well, in the end I got angry, and after waiting for a little while, I asked: "And what about emeralds for security?" "Yes, sir," he said, "I'll give you money for emeralds as security, too." "Well," I said, "that's fine!" and I put on my hat and walked out. To hell with you, you dirty swine! Yes, sir!'

'But did you have emeralds?'

'Emeralds my foot! Oh, Prince, what a bright, innocent, and, if I may say so, pastoral view you take of life!'

At last the prince felt not so much sorry for him as, somehow, ashamed of him. The thought even occurred to him that one might be able to do something for that man through someone's good influence. His own influence he considered for certain reasons as quite unsuitable – not because of any self-depreciation, but because of his special way of looking at things. Gradually they got to talking, and their conversation became so interesting that they did not want to part. Keller confessed with extraordinary readiness to have been guilty of such actions that it was quite impossible to imagine how a man could talk about them. As a preamble to each story, he assured the prince positively that he was deeply sorry and inwardly 'full of tears', and yet he told it as though he were proud of his action and sometimes so funnily that both he and the prince finished up by laughing like madmen.

'The main thing is,' the prince said at last, 'that you possess such a trusting, child-like nature and are so extraordinarily truthful. Do you realize, I wonder, that by that alone you atone for a great deal?'

'Noble, noble, chivalrously noble – that's me!' Keller assented, deeply moved. 'But you know, Prince, it's all only in dreams and in bravado, so to speak. It never comes to anything actually! Why's that? I just can't understand it.'

'Do not despair. Now, I think, it can be said emphatically that you've given me a full and circumstantial account of your life. At least it seems to me that it's impossible to add anything to what you've told me. Isn't that so?'

'Impossible?' cried Keller, almost pityingly. 'Oh, Prince, how utterly in the Swiss manner, so to speak, you understand human nature.'

'Why, have you really something more to add?' the prince asked, with timid amazement. 'Then what did you expect of me; tell me, please, Keller; and why did you come to me with your confession?'

'Of you? What did I expect? Well, for one thing, it is a pleasure to have a look at so simple-minded a man as you. It is a pleasure to sit down and have a talk with you. At least I know that I'm dealing with a most virtuous person, and, secondly – secondly – –'

He stopped short and looked embarrassed.

'You didn't by any chance want to borrow some money, did you?' the prince prompted him very gravely and simply, almost a little shyly.

Keller gave a violent start; he glanced quickly, with the same look of astonishment, straight into the prince's eyes and banged the table with his fist.

'Well, that's how you stump a fellow completely! Why, Prince, your simplicity and innocence are such as were never heard of in the golden age, and then, all of a sudden, you pierce a fellow through and through, like an arrow, with such profound psychological insight! But, please, Prince, this requires some explanation, for I – I am simply dumbfounded! Of course, the whole object of my visit was to ask you for a loan in the end, but you asked me about the money as though you found nothing reprehensible in it, as though it were the most natural thing in the world.'

'Well – coming from you it was the most natural thing in the world.'

'And you're not shocked?'

'Why should I be?'

'Look here, Prince, I stayed here since yesterday evening, first, out of special respect for the French archbishop Bourdaloue (we kept opening bottles at Lebedev's till three o'clock in the morning), and secondly (and I'm ready to take my oath on every cross in Christendom that I'm speaking the truth and nothing but the truth), and chiefly, I stayed behind because by making a full and heartfelt confession to you I intended, so to speak, to promote my own spiritual development; with that idea I fell asleep at about four o'clock, drenched in tears. Now, will you believe the word of a most honourable man, sir? At the very moment I fell asleep, quite genuinely overflowing with internal and, so to speak, external tears (for, indeed, I was sobbing, I remember that!), a most fiendish thought occurred to me: "And why, after all, shouldn't I ask him to lend me some money – after my confession, of course?" So I prepared my confession like, so to speak, some "spiced sauce laced with tears", so as to pave the way with those tears and, having softened you up, make you fork out one hundred and fifty roubles. Don't you think that was mean?'

'I'm sure it can't possibly be true, but that it's merely a coincidence. Two ideas occurred to you at one and the same time. This happens very often. It always happens to me. Still, I don't think it's a good thing and, you know, Keller, I blame myself most of all for it. You might have been telling me about myself just now. Sometimes, indeed, I couldn't help thinking,' the prince went on very earnestly, truly and deeply interested, 'that everyone is like that, so that I even began patting myself on the back, for it is terribly difficult to fight against these *double* thoughts. I've tried. Goodness only knows how they come and how they arise. And now you call it simply meanness! Now I, too, shall again be afraid of these thoughts. In any case, I'm not your judge. But in my opinion it cannot be called simply meanness. What do you think? You were acting dishonestly so as to wheedle some money out of me? But you swear yourself that your confession was made with quite a different motive, an honourable and not a mercenary one. As for the money, I suppose you want it for going out on a spree, don't you? Which after such a confession is of course a sign of weakness. But, again, how is one to give up drinking at a moment's notice? That's quite impossible, isn't it? Well, then, what's to be done? The best thing is to leave it to your own conscience, don't you think?'

The prince gazed at Keller with great interest. The question of double thoughts apparently occupied his mind for some time.

'Well, after that I simply can't understand why they call you an idiot!' exclaimed Keller.

The prince reddened a little.

'Even the preacher Bourdaloue would not have spared a man, but you did, and you judged me in a human way! To punish myself and to show how touched I am, I won't ask you for a hundred and fifty roubles – just give me twenty-five roubles, and that will be enough! That's all I really want, at least for the next fortnight. I shan't come to you for money before that. I did want to take Agatha out, but she doesn't deserve it. Oh, my dear Prince, God bless you!'

Lebedev came in at last, having only just returned from town, and, noticing the twenty-five-rouble note in Keller's hand, he frowned. But Keller, finding himself in possession of money, was in a great hurry to leave and effaced himself at once. Lebedev immediately began running him down.

'You're unjust,' the prince remarked at last. 'He really was genuinely sorry.'

'But what does it matter whether he was sorry or not? It's just like me yesterday: I'm vile, I'm vile; but it's only words!'

'So that was only words? And I thought – –'

'Well, I will tell you the truth – you only, because you see through a man: words and deeds, truth and falsehood – it's all jumbled up in my mind and quite sincerely, too. I use truth and deeds only as a means to repentance – believe it or not, I swear it, and I use words and lies merely with the infernal (and ever-present) idea of getting the better of a man so as to obtain some advantage even through my tears of repentance! I assure you it is so! I wouldn't tell it to anyone else – he'd laugh or swear. But you, Prince, you will judge in a human way.'

'Well, that's exactly what he said to me just now,' exclaimed the prince. 'And both of you seem to be proud of it! Indeed, you astonish me, but he's more sincere than you, for you've turned it into a regular business. Come, come, Lebedev, that'll do. Don't frown and don't put your hand on your heart. You haven't got anything to tell me, have you? You wouldn't come in for nothing. ...'

Lebedev began pulling faces and wriggling.

'I've been waiting for you all day to ask you a straight question. Tell me the truth for once in your life without beating about the bush. Did you have any part in yesterday's carriage incident or not?'

Lebedev grimaced again, began tittering, rubbing his hands, and at last even sneezing, but still he could not make up his mind to say anything.

'I can see you had.'

'But indirectly, sir, only indirectly! It's the perfect truth I'm telling you. My only part in the business was to let a certain person know in good time that I had such a company in my house and that certain people were present.'

'I know that you sent your son *there*,' exclaimed the prince impatiently. 'He told me so himself to-day. But what is the meaning of this intrigue?'

'It's not my intrigue, not mine,' Lebedev cried, gesticulating wildly. 'Other people are concerned in it, and it's more, as it were, a fantasy than an intrigue.'

'But what is it all about? Explain, for God's sake. Don't you realize that it concerns me directly? Why, they're trying to blacken Mr Radomsky's character!'

'Prince, most illustrious Prince,' Lebedev began wriggling again, 'you won't let me tell you the whole truth. I've tried to tell you the whole truth more than once. You wouldn't let me go on.'

The prince paused and thought it over.

'All right,' he said dejectedly, evidently after a long struggle, 'tell the truth.'

'Miss Aglaya,' Lebedev at once began.

'Shut up – shut up!' the prince cried furiously, reddening with indignation and, perhaps, also with shame. 'The whole thing's impossible – it's all nonsense! You invented it all yourself, or some other madman like you. And don't let me ever hear of it from you again!'

Late in the evening, about eleven o'clock, Kolya arrived with a whole bagful of news. The news was of two kinds: of Petersburg and of Pavlovsk. He rapidly told him the more important Petersburg news (mostly about Ippolit and last night's affair), so as to go over it again later on, and then quickly turned to the Pavlovsk news. He had returned from Petersburg three hours ago and, without going to see the prince, had gone straight to the Yepanchins'. 'What's going on there is just awful!' Of course, the incident with the carriage was in the foreground, but something else must certainly have happened, something he and the prince knew nothing about. 'I didn't, of course, pry, and I didn't want to ask anyone about it. However, they received me well – indeed, much better than I expected – but they never said a word about you, Prince!' The most important and interesting fact was that Aglaya had had a furious quarrel with her parents and sisters over Ganya. The details of the quarrel were unknown to him, except that it was over Ganya ('Can you imagine it?'), and that it was a most violent quarrel, too, so that it was something important. The general had arrived from town late, looking very upset, with Radomsky, who was received very well, and Radomsky himself was remarkably charming and gay. The most important piece of news was that Mrs Yepanchin had quietly asked Varya, who was sitting with the girls, to come and see her, and turned her out of the house once and for all, in the most polite way, though. 'I heard it from Varya herself.' But when Varya had left Mrs Yepanchin to say good-bye to the girls, they knew nothing about her being forbidden the house and that she was saying good-bye to them for the last time.

'But your sister came to see me at seven o'clock,' said the astonished prince.

'She was turned out at eight or a little before,' said Kolya. 'I'm very sorry for Varya, and for Ganya, too. I have no doubt they're always plotting something or other. They can't carry on without it. I never could find out what they were up to, nor do I want to. But I assure you, my dear, kind Prince, that Ganya has a good heart. In many respects, of course, he's a failure, but in many others he has some good points which are worth looking for, and I shall never forgive myself for not understanding him before. ... I don't know if I should go on visiting them now, after the trouble with Varya. It's true that from the very first I took up an independent position, apart from my brother and sister, but I shall have to think it over all the same.'

'I don't think you need to be too sorry for your brother,' the prince remarked. 'If it's gone so far, then Mrs Yepanchin must think him dangerous, and that means it is true that he is still cherishing certain hopes.'

'What hopes?' Kolya exclaimed in amazement. 'You don't think Aglaya – no, that's impossible!'

The prince said nothing.

'You're an awful sceptic, Prince!' Kolya added two minutes later. 'I've noticed that for some time past you've become an extraordinary sceptic. You're beginning to disbelieve everything and imagine all sorts of things. Did I use the word sceptic correctly in this connexion?'

'I think so, though I don't really know myself.'

'But I'll take back the word "sceptic" myself,' Kolya cried

suddenly. 'I've found another explanation! You're not a sceptic, you're jealous! You're fiendishly jealous of Ganya over a certain young lady!'

Having said that, Kolya jumped to his feet and burst out laughing, as perhaps he had never laughed before. Seeing that the prince flushed all over, Kolya laughed more loudly still: he was terribly pleased with the idea that the prince was jealous over Aglaya, but he fell silent at once on noticing that the prince was genuinely distressed. After that, they talked earnestly and anxiously for another hour or an hour and a half.

Next day the prince spent the whole morning in Petersburg on some urgent business. On his way back to Pavlovsk at five o'clock in the afternoon he met General Yepanchin at the railway station. The general quickly seized him by the arm, looked round as though in alarm, and dragged the prince after him into a first-class carriage, so that they might travel together. He was extremely anxious to discuss something important.

'To begin with, dear Prince, don't be angry with me, and if there's been anything on my part, forget it. I should have come to see you yesterday, but I wasn't sure how Mrs Yepanchin would take it. ... At home it's – it's just hell. An inscrutable sphinx seems to have taken up its quarters there, and I just walk about and don't understand anything. So far as you're concerned, I think you're least of all to blame, though, of course, you were the cause of a great many things. You see, Prince, it's nice to be a philanthropist, but not too much so. I daresay you've found it out for yourself already. I like kindness, of course, and I respect my dear wife, but – –'

The general went on for a long time in this vein, but his words were remarkably incoherent. It was evident that he was upset and confused by something that was totally incomprehensible to him.

'I have no doubt whatever,' he expressed himself more clearly at last, 'that you have nothing to do with it, but please don't visit us for some time – I ask you as a friend – till the wind's changed. As for Radomsky,' he cried with extraordinary heat, 'it's all a senseless slander, a most unscrupulous slander! It's a plot – what we have here is an intrigue, a desire to destroy everything and make us quarrel. You see, Prince, let me whisper in your ear: so far not a single word has been exchanged between Radomsky and us – understand? We're not bound in any way, but that word may be spoken, and soon, too, perhaps quite soon! And this is meant to spoil it all! But why – for what reason – I just can't understand! She's a remarkable woman, an eccentric woman, and I'm so afraid of her that I can't sleep at night.

And what a carriage – white horses, why, it's *chic*, it's exactly what in French is called *chic*! Who gave it to her? I tell you frankly, the day before yesterday I – I almost suspected Radomsky. But it seems to be out of the question, and if that is so, what does she want to spoil everything for? That's – that's the problem. To keep Radomsky for herself? But, I tell you again, and I'm ready to take my oath on it, he doesn't know her and the IOU's are a pure invention! And the impudence with which she shouted "darling" to him across the street! It's a plot, I tell you, a plot! It's clear that we must dismiss it with contempt and treat Radomsky with redoubled respect. That's what I told Mrs Yepanchin. And now I'll let you into a secret that concerns me personally: I'm absolutely convinced that she's doing this to revenge herself upon me personally for what happened some months ago – remember? though I've never done anything to her for which I should feel sorry. I blush at the very thought of it. Now she has turned up again, and I had an idea she had disappeared for good. Where's this Rogozhin? Can you tell me? I thought *she* had become Mrs Rogozhin long ago.'

In short, the man was utterly baffled. During the whole of the journey, which lasted for almost an hour, he alone talked, asked questions, answered them himself, pressed the prince's hand, and at any rate convinced him that he never thought of suspecting him of anything. That was important to the prince. He finished by telling him about Radomsky's uncle, the head of some government office in Petersburg. 'Occupies a highly important position, seventy years old, a *bon viveur*, a gourmet, and altogether an old rake – ha, ha! I know he had heard of Nastasya Filippovna and even tried to get her for his mistress. I paid a call on him the other day. He was not receiving, he was unwell, but he's rich, damned rich, a man of great influence and – may he be spared for many more years, but, you see, Radomsky will get all his money. ... Yes, indeed. But all the same I'm afraid. I don't know why, but I'm afraid. There's something in the wind, some trouble flitting about like a bat, and I'm afraid, I'm afraid!'

And three days later, as we have said already, the formal reconciliation between the Yepanchins and the prince took place at last.

12

It was seven o'clock in the evening. The prince was thinking of going out for a stroll in the park. Suddenly Mrs Yepanchin came in alone on to the veranda.

'First of all,' she began, 'don't you run away with the idea that I've come to apologize to you. Nonsense! It was your fault entirely.'

The prince said nothing.

'Was it your fault or not?'

'As much as yours. However, neither you nor I did anything intentionally wrong. The day before yesterday I did think I was to blame, but now I've come to the conclusion that it is not so.'

'So that's your story! Very well. Now, listen and sit down, for I do not intend to stand.'

They both sat down.

'Secondly, not a word about those wicked boys! I'm going to sit and talk to you for ten minutes. I've come to you for some information (and you thought I'd come for goodness only knows what, didn't you?), and if you say a single word about those impertinent boys, I shall get up and go away and never have anything to do with you again.'

'All right,' said the prince.

'Now, tell me, did you two or two and a half months ago, about Easter, send a letter to Aglaya?'

'I d-did.'

'Whatever for? What did you say in the letter? Let me see the letter!'

Mrs Yepanchin's eyes blazed and she almost shook with impatience.

'I haven't got the letter,' said the prince, looking surprised and terribly shy. 'If it still exists and is intact, Aglaya has it.'

'Don't prevaricate! What did you write about?'

'I'm not prevaricating, and I'm not afraid of anything. I see no reason why I shouldn't write. ...'

'Hold your tongue! You can talk afterwards. What was in the letter? Why do you blush?'

The prince thought it over.

'I don't know what you are thinking of, Mrs Yepanchin. I only see that you don't like the idea of the letter very much. You must admit that I could refuse to answer your question, but to show you that there was nothing in the letter I need be afraid of and that I'm not sorry to have written it and am certainly not blushing on account of it' (the prince blushed almost twice as much), 'I'm going to repeat the letter to you, because I think I remember it by heart.'

Having said this, the prince repeated the letter almost word for word as he had written it.

'What a rigmarole! What does all this nonsense mean in your opinion?' Mrs Yepanchin asked sharply, after listening to the letter with great attention.

'I'm afraid I don't quite know myself. All I know is that I meant it sincerely. I had moments of intense life there and of great hopes.'

'What hopes?'

'It's difficult to explain, but not the kind of hopes you have in mind now, perhaps. Hopes – well, in short, hopes of the future and, perhaps, a feeling of joy that I was not a stranger, not a foreigner, *there*. I was suddenly very pleased to be back in my own country. One sunny morning I took up a pen and wrote a letter to her. Why to her, I don't know. Sometimes, you know, one feels like having a friend at one's side, and, I suppose, I was longing for a friend,' the prince added after a short pause.

'You're not in love, are you?'

'N-no. I-I wrote to her as to a sister, I signed myself her brother.'

'I see – on purpose. I understand.'

'I'm awfully sorry, but I find it very hard to answer your questions, Mrs Yepanchin.'

'I know you find it hard, but I don't care whether you find it hard or not. Listen, tell me truthfully as before God: are you lying to me or not?'

'I'm not.'

'Are you telling the truth when you say you are not in love?'

'I think I am.'

'Oh, you "think", do you? Did that guttersnipe give it to her?'

'I asked Nikolay Ivolgin – –'

'A guttersnipe! A guttersnipe!' Mrs Yepanchin interrupted vehemently. 'I don't know anything about Nikolay Ivolgin! A guttersnipe!'

'Nikolay Ivolgin – –'

'A guttersnipe, I tell you!'

'No, not a guttersnipe, but Nikolay Ivolgin,' the prince replied at last firmly, though rather softly.

'All right, my dear man, all right! I won't forget it!'

For a minute she suppressed her agitation and tried to recover her composure.

'And what's the meaning of the "poor knight"?'

'I don't know at all. That was while I was away. Some sort of a joke, I suppose.'

'It's nice to find it out all at once! Only could she really have been interested in you? Why, she herself called you a "little freak" and an "idiot".'

'You needn't have told me that,' the prince remarked reproachfully, but almost in a whisper.

'Don't be angry. She's a headstrong, crazy, spoilt girl – if she ever falls in love with a man, she'll most certainly call him all sorts of names and laugh at him to his face. I was just the same. Only don't, please, run about shouting for joy, my dear man. She isn't yours. I refuse to believe it, and it will never be! I'm saying this so that you may take all the necessary steps now. Listen, swear you're not married to that woman!'

'Good Lord, Mrs Yepanchin, what are you talking about?' The prince nearly jumped out of his chair with astonishment.

'But you nearly did marry her, didn't you?'

'Yes, I nearly did,' the prince whispered and hung his head.

'Well, if so, are you in love with her, then? Have you come here now for *her*? For *that woman*?'

'I have not come here to get married,' replied the prince.

'Is there anything in the world you hold sacred?'

'Yes.'

'Swear that you haven't come to marry *that woman*!'

'I swear by anything you like!'

'I believe you. You may kiss me now. At last I can breathe freely. But remember: Aglaya doesn't love you; take steps in time, for she will never marry you while I'm alive! Do you hear?'

'I hear.'

The prince blushed so much that he could not look Mrs Yepanchin straight in the face.

'Don't you forget it! I've waited for you as for Providence (you were not worth it!). I've cried bitter tears at night – not for you, my dear, don't worry. I have my own sorrow, a different one, and it's always, always the same. But this is why I've been waiting for you with such impatience: I still believe that God Himself has sent you to me as a friend and brother. I have no one to turn to except old Princess Belokonsky, and she, too, has gone away and, besides, she's grown as stupid as a sheep in her old age. Now answer me straight –

yes or no: do you know why *she* shouted from her carriage that night?'

'On my word of honour, I had nothing to do with it and I don't know anything.'

'Very well, I believe you. Now I, too, have other ideas about it, but yesterday morning I still thought that Mr Radomsky was responsible for it all. Yesterday morning and the whole of the day before. Now, of course, I can't help agreeing with them: it is quite obvious that, like a fool, he's been made a laughing-stock for some reason, on account of something (that alone is already suspicious! and not very nice, either!), but – Aglaya will never marry him, I can tell you that! He may be a very excellent man, but that's how it is going to be. I wasn't sure of it myself before, but now my mind is definitely made up: "Lay me in my coffin and bury me first, and then you can marry off my daughter," that's what I told the general to-day. You see that I trust you, don't you?'

'I see and I understand.'

Mrs Yepanchin gazed penetratingly at the prince: she might have been very anxious to find out what an impression her news about Radomsky made on him.

'Do you know anything about Gavrila Ivolgin?'

'You mean – I know quite a lot.'

'Did you know he had been keeping in touch with Aglaya, or didn't you?'

'I had no idea,' the prince replied, looking surprised and even startled. 'Do you say Mr Ivolgin has been keeping in touch with Miss Aglaya? Impossible!'

'Quite lately. It was his sister who had been clearing the way for him all winter. She's been working at it like a rat.'

'I don't believe it,' the prince repeated firmly, after a moment or two of agitated reflection. 'If it had been so, I should have known for certain.'

'Did you expect him to come to you himself with a confession and crying on your bosom? Oh, you simpleton, you simpleton! Everyone is deceiving you like – like – –And aren't you ashamed to trust him? Can't you see that he has cheated you all along?'

'I know very well that he deceives me sometimes,' the prince admitted reluctantly in an undertone, 'and he knows that I know it ...' he added and broke off.

'To know it and to trust him! Now I've heard everything! But, I suppose, that's the sort of thing you would do and there's nothing to be surprised at. Heavens! has there ever been a man like that? Oh dear, oh dear! And do you know that this horrible Ganya and that Varya woman have put her in touch with Nastasya Filippovna?'

'Whom?' cried the prince.

'Aglaya.'

'I don't believe it! It's impossible! With what object?'

He jumped up from his chair.

'I don't believe it, either, though there's some evidence for it. Oh, she's a headstrong girl, a fantastic girl, a crazy girl! A wicked, wicked, wicked girl! I shall go on saying it for a thousand years! They're all like that now, even that silly goose Alexandra, but this one is quite unmanageable. But I don't believe it, all the same! Perhaps because I don't want to believe it,' she added, as though to herself. 'Why haven't you been to see us?' she suddenly turned again to the prince. 'Why haven't you been for the last three days?' she cried impatiently for a second time.

The prince began to tell her his reasons, but she interrupted him again.

'Everyone thinks you're a fool and cheats you. You went to town yesterday, and I'm ready to bet that you went down on your knees begging that scoundrel to accept your ten thousand!'

'Good heavens! no. I never thought of it. I've never seen him and, besides, he's not a scoundrel. I've had a letter from him.'

'Show me the letter!'

The prince took a note out of his brief-case and handed it to Mrs Yepanchin. The note was as follows:

'Dear Sir,

I have, of course, no right whatever in the eyes of the world to possess any pride. In the opinion of the world, I am too insignificant for that. But that is in the opinion of the world and not in yours. I'm entirely convinced, dear sir, that you are perhaps better than other men. I don't agree with Doktorenko and differ from him on this point. I shall never accept a penny from you, but you have helped my mother, and I'm bound to be grateful to you for that, though I regard it as a weakness. In any case, I look upon you differently and thought it my duty to tell you so. And having said this, I wish to state that there can be no further relationship of any sort between us.

Antip Burdovsky.

P.S. The missing two hundred roubles will be repaid to you in the course of time.'

'What utter nonsense!' Mrs Yepanchin declared, flinging back the note. 'It wasn't worth reading. What are you grinning at?'

'Admit that you, too, were glad to read it!'

'Was I? That drivel, corroded with vanity! Why, don't you see they've all gone mad with pride and vanity?'

'Yes, but he has admitted that he was wrong, he has broken with Doktorenko, and the vainer he is the more it must have cost his vanity. Oh, what a baby you are, Mrs Yepanchin!'

'You don't want me to box your ears, do you?'

'Why, of course I don't. For you are glad of the note, but you conceal it. Why are you ashamed of your feelings? You're like that in everything.'

'Don't you dare to show yourself at my house now!' cried Mrs Yepanchin, jumping up from her seat and turning pale with anger. 'Don't let me ever catch sight of you again from now on!'

'In another three days you'll come and ask me to come and see you yourself. ... Well, aren't you ashamed of yourself? These are your best feelings, so why are you ashamed of them? You only torment yourself, you know.'

'I'd rather die than ask you to come and see me! I shall forget your name! I have forgotten it!!'

She rushed away from the prince.

'I've been forbidden to come, as it is, without your telling me!' the prince shouted after her.

'Wha-at? Who has forbidden you?'

She turned round in a flash, as though pricked with a needle; he realized that he had accidentally made a serious slip.

'Who has forbidden you?' cried Mrs Yepanchin furiously.

'Miss Aglaya – –'

'When? Come on, out with it!'

'She sent to say this morning that I must never dare to go and see you again.'

Mrs Yepanchin stood as though turned to stone, but she was thinking hard.

'What did she send? Whom did she send? Through that guttersnipe? By word of mouth?' she cried again suddenly.

'I had a note,' said the prince.

'Where is it? Give it me! At once!'

The prince thought for a moment, but in the end he pulled out of his waistcoat pocket a torn scrap of paper on which was written:

'Prince Leo Nikolayevich, If after all that has happened, you intend to surprise me by a visit to our house, you will not, let me assure you, find me among those who are pleased to see you.

Aglaya Yepanchin.'

Mrs Yepanchin reflected a minute; then she suddenly pounced on the prince, seized him by the arm, and dragged him after her.

'Come along! At once! You'll come at once just to show them! This very minute!' she cried in a paroxysm of extraordinary excitement and impatience.

'But you're exposing me to – –'

'To what? You innocent simpleton! Behaving just as though you weren't a man at all! Well, now I shall see with my own eyes. ...'

'But you might at least let me get my hat!'

'Here's your wretched hat – come along! Can't even choose a hat with taste! She did it – she did it after what had happened – she did it in a temper,' muttered Mrs Yepanchin, dragging the prince after her without for one moment letting go of his arm. 'I took your part this morning. I said aloud that you were a fool not to come and see us – else she wouldn't have written such a silly note! A most improper note. Improper for a well-bred, well-brought-up, clever, clever girl! I don't know though,' she went on, 'perhaps – perhaps – perhaps she was herself annoyed you didn't come, only she didn't realize that one shouldn't write like that to an idiot, for he might take it literally, as he has done. What are you listening to what I'm saying for?' she cried, realizing that she had let the cat out of the bag. 'She needs a clown like you. It's a long time since she's seen one; that's why she's asking for you! And I'm glad, glad that she will make a laughing-stock of you now – glad! You deserve it. And she knows how to – oh, she knows that all right!'

PART THREE

I

People are constantly complaining that we have no practical men; that we have, for instance, hundreds of politicians and hundreds of generals; that one can find as many business managers of all sorts as one wants nowadays, but that we have no practical men. At least everyone is complaining that there are not any to be found. It is even asserted that there is no efficient personnel on some of our railway lines; it is said that it is quite impossible to get a more or less decent administrative staff for a steamship company. You hear of train collisions or of the collapse of a bridge under a train of a newly opened railway; you read of another train almost hibernating in a snowdrift: it was due to arrive in a few hours and it was snowed up for five days. In one place hundreds of tons of goods are lying rotting for two or three months before they are dispatched, and in another it is reported (though it is hardly credible) that a railway administrator – that is, some railway inspector – has administered a punch on the nose to a merchant's clerk, who had been worrying him about the dispatch of his goods, and, indeed, sought to excuse his administrative act on the ground that he had been 'a little short-tempered'. There are, it seems, so many government offices that one's imagination boggles at the mere thought of it; everyone has been in the civil service, everyone is in the civil service, everyone intends to be in the civil service, and, this being so, how is it possible that a decent administrative staff cannot be made up of such excellent material to run some steamship company?

The answer sometimes given to this question is very simple – so simple, indeed, that one finds it difficult to believe such an explanation. It is true, we are told, that everyone in our country is, or has been, in the civil service, and that this has been going on, in accordance with the best German model, for the last two hundred years, from grandfather to grandson, but the trouble is that our civil servants themselves are the most unpractical men in the world, and things have come to such a pass that abstraction and lack of practical knowledge were, till quite recently, considered even by the civil servants themselves as the highest virtues and qualifications. However, we did not really mean to discuss civil servants; we intended to talk only about practical men. There can be no doubt that diffidence and complete absence of personal initiative have always been regarded in our country as the chief and best sign of a practical man – and are so regarded still. But if such an opinion can be regarded as an accusation, we have only ourselves to blame. Lack of originality has from time immemorial been regarded throughout the world as the chief characteristic and the best recommendation of a sensible, business-like, and practical man, and at least ninety-nine per cent of men (and that's putting it at the lowest) always were of that opinion, and only perhaps one man in a hundred looks and always has looked on it differently.

Inventors and men of genius have almost always been regarded as fools at the beginning (and very often at the end) of their careers – that is a platitude too familiar to everyone. If, for instance, for scores of years everyone put his money into a municipal loan bank and invested milliards in it at four per cent, then, needless to say, when the municipal loan banks ceased to exist and everyone had to fall back on his personal initiative, the greater part of these millions could not but be lost in a mad scramble on the Stock Exchange and in the hands of swindlers, and, indeed, this was strictly in accordance with the demands of decency and decorum. Yes, decorum above all. For if a decorous diffidence and a decent lack of originality have till now been generally accepted as the inalienable right of a sensible and respectable man, it would be much too unrespectable and even indecent to change so very suddenly. What fond and devoted mother, for instance, would not be dismayed and sick with apprehension should her son or daughter depart by an inch from the beaten track: 'No, better let him be happy and live in comfort and without originality,' is what every mother thinks as she rocks her child to sleep. And from time immemorial our children's nurses, as they rocked the children to sleep, crooned, and sang: 'You'll be happy, darling, rich and gay, you'll be a general one day!' So that even our nurses regarded the rank of general as the acme of Russian happiness, and so it has always been the most popular national ideal of peaceful and contented bliss. And, to be sure, immediately after passing his examinations and serving thirty-five years in the civil service, who in our country can fail to become a general and amass a considerable sum in a municipal loan bank? It is thus that a Russian achieves almost without effort the status of a sensible and practical man. As a matter of fact, it is only the original man in our country, or, in other words, the man who is never satisfied, who can never become a general. Perhaps this is not altogether true, but, as a rule, it does seem to be true, and our society has been perfectly right in its definition of a practical man. We have, nevertheless, digressed too much; we merely meant to say a few explanatory words about our friends the Yepanchins. The members of the Yepanchin family, or at any rate the more thoughtful of them, were constantly the victims of their common family characteristic, the very opposite of the virtues we have been discussing. Without clearly understanding the fact (for it is difficult to understand it), they sometimes, nevertheless, suspected that everything was not as it should be in their family. In every other family everything was so smooth, while in their family everything was rough; everyone else was keeping to the beaten track, while they were constantly running off it; everyone else was so decorously timid, while they were not. Mrs Yepanchin, it is true, was a little too apprehensive, but theirs was all the same not the decorous worldly timidity for which they longed. Still, it was perhaps only Mrs Yepanchin who was worried: the girls, though they were shrewd and had a sense of humour, were still too young, and though the general did see through things (not without a great effort, however), he only said, 'H'm', when a situation became difficult, and in the end put all his trust in his wife. The responsibility therefore rested entirely on her. Not that this family was, for instance, in any way remarkable for its initiative or stepped off the beaten track from a conscious craving for originality, which, indeed, would have been highly improper. Oh, no! There was nothing of the kind, really – that is, there was no consciously defined aim – and yet in spite of it all the Yepanchin family, though highly respectable in every way, was not quite what every respectable family should be. More recently Mrs Yepanchin was inclined to put the whole blame on herself alone and on her 'unfortunate' character, which only added to her distress. She kept always reproaching herself with being 'a silly, ill-mannered, eccentric old woman' and, being morbidly touchy, she was always worried, she was always at a loss, she could never find a way out of the most ordinary difficulties, and she constantly magnified every misfortune.

Already at the beginning of our story we mentioned the fact that the Yepanchins were highly respected by everybody. Even the general, a man of obscure origin, was received everywhere with respect. Indeed, he deserved respect, first, as a man who was wealthy and 'not to be sneezed at', and, secondly, as an eminently decent, though not particularly intelligent, fellow. But a certain dullness of intellect seems to be almost a pre-requisite if not of every public man, at least of everyone who is seriously set on making money. And, last but not least, the general had excellent manners, was modest, knew when to be silent, and, at the same time, did not suffer anyone to treat him with disrespect – and that not only because of his high rank, but also because he considered himself to be an honest and honourable man. What was even more important – he enjoyed the patronage of a highly influential person. As for Mrs Yepanchin, she was, as has been pointed out already, of good family, though that is not considered of great importance among us, unless there are also good connexions. But she acquired such connexions too, at last; she was respected and, in the end, liked by persons of such consequence that it was only natural that everyone should emulate them in respecting and receiving her. There can be no doubt that her domestic worries were without foundation, that there was little cause for them and that they were absurdly exaggerated; but if you happen to have a wart on your nose or forehead, you cannot help imagining that no one in the world has anything else to do but stare at your wart, laugh at it, and condemn you for it, even though you have discovered America. Nor can there be any doubt that Mrs Yepanchin was really considered 'eccentric' in society, but that did not prevent her from being highly respected: the trouble was that Mrs Yepanchin at last ceased to believe that she was respected. Looking at her daughters, she was worried by the suspicion that she was continually ruining their future prospects, that her character was ridiculous, disgraceful, and unbearable, for which, of course, she incessantly blamed her daughters and her husband, and quarrelled with them for days on end, loving them, at the same time, to distraction and almost with passion.

What worried her most was the suspicion that her daughters were becoming almost as 'eccentric' as she, and that there are not, and ought not to be, girls like them in society. 'They are growing into nihilists, I'm sure of it!' she kept repeating to herself every minute. For the last year, and particularly of late, this melancholy notion had got a firmer and firmer hold on her. 'To begin with, why don't they get married?' she kept asking herself. 'To torment their mother, that's all they live for, and, of course, that's what it is; it's all those new-fangled ideas, it's all that damned woman question! Otherwise would Aglaya have taken it into her head six months ago to cut off her magnificent hair? (Why, I never had hair like that when I was young!) She had the scissors in her hands, and I had to beg her on my bended knees before she changed her mind! Well, I daresay she did it out of spite, to torment her mother, for she's a wicked, wicked girl, headstrong and spoilt, but above all, wicked, wicked, wicked! But did not that fat Alexandra also try to cut off her plaits, and not out of spite, nor caprice, but in all sincerity, like a fool, because Aglaya had persuaded her that without her hair she would sleep better and wouldn't have any headaches? And the countless number of suitors they had had during the last five years! And, really, there were nice fellows among them, some of them, indeed, were remarkably fine men! What are they waiting for? Why don't they get married? Just to provoke their mother – there's no other reason for it! No other reason – none whatever!'

At last her mother's heart, too, was comforted. At any rate one of her daughters, at any rate Adelaida, would at last be settled: 'At least one off my hands!' Mrs Yepanchin would declare whenever she was expected to express an opinion on the subject (she expressed herself much more tenderly when speaking to herself). And how excellently, how nicely the whole thing had been arranged! Even in society it was talked of with respect. A man of good repute and wealth, a prince, a good man, who had, besides, won her daughter's affections. What could be better? But she had always felt less anxious about Adelaida than about her two other daughters, though her artistic leanings sometimes greatly troubled Mrs Yepanchin's perpetually suspicious heart. 'But, thank God, she is of a happy disposition and has plenty of common sense – she'll be all right!' she comforted herself. It was for Aglaya she feared more than for any of them. So far as her eldest daughter was concerned, Mrs Yepanchin did not know herself whether to be anxious about her or not. Sometimes she could not help thinking that the girl had lost her chances – she was twenty-five and would remain an old maid. And such a beautiful girl, too! Mrs Yepanchin even wept for her at night, while Alexandra was sleeping very peacefully. 'But what is wrong with her – is she a nihilist or simply a fool?' That she was no fool even Mrs Yepanchin had no doubt: she had a great respect for Alexandra's opinions and liked to ask her advice. But that she was a bit of 'a silly goose' she did not doubt for a moment: 'She's so imperturbably placid that it is quite impossible to rouse her. Still, even "silly geese" are not placid – oh dear! I can't make them out at all!' Mrs Yepanchin had quite an inexplicable feeling of compassionate sympathy for Alexandra, more, indeed, than for Aglaya, whom she idolized. But her bitter outbursts (in which her maternal solicitude and sympathy mostly found expression), her taunts, and names such as 'silly goose', only amused Alexandra. Things sometimes went so far that the merest trifles made Mrs Yepanchin terribly angry and made her lose her temper. Alexandra, for instance, liked to sleep late and usually had a great many dreams. But her dreams were always remarkable for their extraordinarily trivial and innocent character – the sort of dream one would expect a child of seven to have. And for some reason the very innocence of her dreams used to irritate her mother. Once Alexandra dreamed of nine geese, and this led to a regular quarrel between her and her mother. It would be difficult to explain why. Once, and only once, had she succeeded in dreaming of something that might be said to be original – she dreamed of a monk, who was alone in a dark room into which she was afraid to go. Her dream was at once retailed triumphantly to Mrs Yepanchin by her two laughing sisters, but their mother became angry again and called them all fools. 'H'm! Placid like a fool, and a regular "silly goose", nothing will rouse her, and yet she is sad – she looks quite sad sometimes! What is she unhappy about? What is it?' Sometimes she asked her husband about it and, as usual, waited hysterically and peremptorily for his answer. General Yepanchin hummed and hawed, knit his brows, shrugged his shoulders, and at last, spreading out his hands in a perplexed gesture, gave his opinion: 'She needs a husband!'

'Only God grant he's not like you, sir,' Mrs Yepanchin at last exploded like a bomb. 'Not like you, sir, in his opinions and judgements. Not a coarse fellow like you, sir!'

General Yepanchin promptly made his escape, and Mrs Yepanchin calmed down after her 'explosion'. The same evening, needless to say, she infallibly became particularly attentive, gentle, affectionate, and respectful to her husband, her 'coarse fellow', her kind, dear, and adored Ivan Fyodorovich, for she had been fond of him, and even in love with him, all her life, which General Yepanchin knew very well himself and he respected her greatly for it.

But her chief and constant worry was Aglaya.

'She's just like me,' Mrs Yepanchin used to say to herself. 'The spit and image of me, the headstrong and horrid little vixen! A nihilist, an eccentric, crazy, wicked, wicked, wicked girl! Lord, how unhappy she will be!'

But, as we have said already, her mother's heart had been comforted and mollified for a moment. For a whole month Mrs Yepanchin had a rest from all her worries. Adelaida's approaching marriage made people in society talk of Aglaya, too, and Aglaya carried herself everywhere so beautifully, so composedly, so cleverly, and so triumphantly – a little too proudly, perhaps, but then that suited her so well! She was so affectionate and so gracious to her mother all that month! ('It is true one has to be very, very careful about that

Radomsky, one must find out what sort of a man he is, but, it seems, Aglaya does not favour him much more than the others!') But she had – all the same – suddenly become such a delightful girl – and how beautiful she was, goodness, how beautiful – she grew more beautiful every day! And now – –

And now no sooner had that wretched princeling, that worthless little idiot, made his appearance than everything was in confusion again and everything in the house was topsy-turvy.

What had happened, though?

Nothing would have happened to other people – that was certain. But what made Mrs Yepanchin so different from anybody else was that because of her inherent anxiety, she managed to discover in the combination and confused interplay of the most ordinary things something that sometimes alarmed her till it made her ill, and threw her into a most morbid and inexplicable panic, a panic that for that very reason was so distressing. What must have been her feelings now when, through this confused tangle of absurd and groundless anxieties, she could actually discern something that really seemed important, something that really justified all her anxieties, doubts, and suspicions!

'And how dared they, how dared they send me that beastly anonymous letter about that *creature*, about her being in communication with Aglaya?' thought Mrs Yepanchin all the way home, dragging the prince after her, and at home, when she made him sit down at the round table where the whole family was already gathered. 'How dared they even think of such a thing? Why, I'd die of shame if I believed a word of it or showed the letter to Aglaya! Jeering at us, the Yepanchins! And all, all because of you, sir!' she apostrophized her husband. 'Oh, why didn't we go to Yelagin Island? I said we ought to have gone to Yelagin! I'm sure it's that Varya who wrote the letter, or perhaps – it's all your fault, sir!' she accused her husband again. 'That *creature* played this trick on him just as a reminder of their former relations, to make a fool of him, just as she laughed at him, the fool, before, leading him by the nose, when he was taking her those pearls. ... But, as a matter of fact, we're all in it now – your daughters, too, are in it, sir, young girls, young ladies, young ladies of the best society, marriageable girls; they were there, they were standing there, they heard it all, and they are mixed up in the affair of those horrible boys, too. I hope you're glad of it, for they were there too, and heard it! Oh, I won't forgive him, I'll never forgive this wretched little prince. And why has Aglaya been in hysterics for the last three days? Why has she nearly quarrelled with her sisters, even with Alexandra, whose hands she always used to kiss, as though she were her mother – she had such a respect for her? What secrets had she been concealing from us all for the last three days? What has Gavrila Ivolgin to do with it? Why has she been so ready to sing Gavrila Ivolgin's praises to-day and yesterday? Why has she burst out crying? Why do they mention that damned "poor knight" in the anonymous letter, when she never showed the prince's letter even to her sisters? And why – why, why did I run to him now like a scalded cat and drag him here myself? Dear me, I must be mad to have done it! Talk to a young man about my daughter's secrets and – and about secrets that almost concern him! Oh dear, it's a good thing he's an idiot and – and a friend of the family. Only, could Aglaya have possibly been attracted by such a little freak? Good heavens, what am I talking about? Dear me! We are freaks, all of us – we ought to be put on show under glass – and I first of all – at twopence a peep. I shall never forgive you for this, General, never! And why doesn't she make fun of him now? She promised to, but she doesn't! Look at her, look! Stares at him with wide-open eyes, doesn't say a word, doesn't go away, and she herself told him not to come. ... There he sits, pale as death. And that damned, damned chatterbox Radomsky talks and talks – drawling on and on – doesn't let one get a word in edgeways. I could have found out everything at once, if I could only lead the conversation round to it. ...'

The prince really was rather pale as he sat at the round table and seemed to be at one and the same time in a terrible panic and – at moments – in a state of breath-taking rapture for which he could not account himself. Oh, how he dreaded looking in the direction of the corner from which two familiar black eyes were gazing so intently at him and how, at the same time, his heart almost stopped beating with happiness at the thought that he was sitting among them again and that he would hear her familiar voice – after what she had written to him! 'Good Lord, what will she say now?' He had not uttered one word himself and listened with strained attention to the 'drawling' of Radomsky, who had seldom been in such a happy and excited mood as that evening. The prince listened to him for a long time, but hardly understood a word he said. Except for General Yepanchin, who had not yet returned from Petersburg, they were all there. Prince Sh. was also there. They had apparently been planning to go and listen to the band before tea. The conversation had evidently begun before the prince's arrival. Soon Kolya made his appearance on the veranda from somewhere. 'So he is received here as before,' the prince thought to himself.

The Yepanchins' sumptuous country-house was built in the style of a Swiss chalet and was covered on all sides with exquisite flowering creepers. A small, but lovely, flower-garden surrounded it on all sides. They were all sitting on the veranda, as at the prince's, but the veranda was more spacious and more luxuriously furnished.

The subject of conversation was apparently to the liking of only a few of those present. It appeared to have arisen out of a furious argument and everyone, of course, was anxious to change the subject, but Radomsky seemed to be bent on pursuing it in spite of that, regardless of the impression he was creating; the arrival of the prince apparently stimulated his desire to continue talking. Mrs Yepanchin looked cross, though she did not quite understand what it was all about. Aglaya, who was sitting apart from the rest, almost in a corner, did not go away, but went on listening, obstinately silent.

'I'm sorry,' Radomsky was protesting heatedly, 'but I never said a word against liberalism. Liberalism is not a crime, it is an essential component part of the whole, which would fall to pieces or atrophy without it. Liberalism has the same right to exist as the most right-minded conservatism. What I am attacking is Russian liberalism and, let me repeat again, the only reason why I am attacking it is that a Russian liberal is not a *Russian* liberal, but an *un-Russian* liberal. Show me a Russian liberal and I shall be only too pleased to embrace him in front of you all.'

'Always provided he lets you embrace him,' said Alexandra, who was extremely excited, even her cheeks being redder than usual.

'Look at her now,' thought Mrs Yepanchin to herself. 'All she does is to eat and sleep and you cannot rouse her, and then, suddenly, once a year, she ups and says something so extraordinary that it leaves you speechless.'

Glancing quickly at Alexandra, the prince noticed that she seemed particularly to dislike Radomsky's flippant way of talking about such a serious matter and the fact that, though appearing to be excited, he seemed to be joking.

'I was maintaining just now, a few minutes before your arrival, Prince,' Radomsky went on, 'that so far our liberals have come only from two classes of the population, the old land-owning class (now abolished) and the priestly class. And as those two classes have at last been transformed into regular castes, into something that is entirely separate from the nation, and is getting more and more so from generation to generation, so everything they have done and are doing is entirely not national.'

'What do you mean? Is everything that has been done un-Russian?' Prince Sh. protested.

'Not national – though it's Russian, it isn't national. And our liberals are not Russian, and our conservatives are not Russian, they're all not Russian. You may be sure that the nation does not recognize anything done by the landowners and the graduates of our religious seminaries, neither now nor later.'

'That's fine!' Prince Sh. retorted heatedly. 'How can you maintain such a paradox, if you are serious about it? I cannot allow such absurd statements about the Russian landowner to pass unchallenged – you are a Russian landowner yourself!'

'I'm afraid I didn't speak of the Russian landowner in the sense in which you take it. It's a highly respectable class, if only because I belong to it. Especially now when it has ceased to exist. ...'

'Do you maintain that there is nothing national in our literature, either?' Alexandra interrupted.

'I'm afraid I'm no authority on literature, but in my opinion even Russian literature is not Russian at all, except perhaps Lomonosov, Pushkin, and Gogol.'

'Well, in the first place, that's not so bad, and, secondly, one of them was a peasant and the other two landowners,' Alexandra laughed.

'Quite right, but don't look so pleased about it. Since of all the Russian writers these three have so far been the only ones to say something that was really *theirs*, their very own, something not borrowed from anyone, they have by this very fact at once become national writers. Any Russian who says, writes, or does something of his own, something that is his *by right* and not borrowed, inevitably becomes national, though he may not be able to speak Russian correctly. I regard this as an axiom. But we were not discussing literature. We began talking about socialists, and it is they who set us off arguing. Well, then, I maintain that we haven't a single Russian socialist, and never have had one, because all our socialists have also come out of the ranks of our landowners and seminarists. All our professed, widely advertised socialists, both here and abroad, are nothing more than former liberals from the landed gentry in the days of serfdom. Why are you laughing? Give me their books, give me their doctrines and their memoirs, and, though I'm not a literary critic, I will undertake to write a most convincing critical treatise in which I will prove as clear as daylight that every page of their books, pamphlets, and memoirs has been written, first and foremost, by a former Russian landowner. Their malice, indignation, and wit are all typical of the men of that class (even before Famusov!); their raptures, their tears may be real and sincere, but – they are landowners' tears – landowners' and seminarists' tears. You are laughing again, and you, Prince, are laughing too! You don't agree, either?'

They were, in fact, all laughing, and the prince, too, smiled.

'I can't tell you offhand whether I agree with you or not,' said the prince, suddenly ceasing to smile and starting like a schoolboy caught in the act, 'but I assure you I'm listening to you with the greatest pleasure.'

He was almost gasping for breath as he said it, and a cold sweat broke out on his forehead. These were the first words he had uttered since he sat down at the table. He thought of looking round, but dared not; Radomsky caught his movement and smiled.

'I'll tell you a fact, ladies and gentlemen,' he went on in the same tone of voice as before, that is, with extraordinary vehemence and warmth and, at the same time, almost laughing at his own words, perhaps, 'a fact, an observation, and, I might even say, a discovery which I have the honour of claiming to have made myself and myself alone; at least, I've never read about it or heard of it anywhere before. This fact expresses the whole essence of Russian liberalism of the sort which I'm now discussing. To begin with, what is liberalism, speaking generally, if not an attack (whether a reasonable or mistaken one is another question) on the existing order of things? It is so, isn't it? Well, then, my fact is that Russian liberalism is not an attack on the existing order of things, but an attack on the very essence of things, on the things themselves, and not only on their order, not on the Russian system of government, but on Russia herself. My liberal has gone so far as to deny Russia herself – that is to say, he hates and beats his own mother. Every Russian failure and fiasco excites his laughter and almost delights him. He hates national customs, he hates Russian history, he hates everything. If there is any justification for him, it is perhaps that he doesn't know what he is doing and thinks that his hatred of Russia is the most beneficent kind of liberalism. (Oh, you will often meet among us a liberal who is applauded by everyone and who is, perhaps, actually the most absurd, the most shortsighted and dangerous conservative, and doesn't realize it himself!) This hatred of Russia some of our liberals not so very long ago regarded almost as true love of their country, and they boasted that they knew better than anyone else what the nature of that love should be; but now they have become more outspoken, and are even ashamed of saying that they love their country; they have banished and obliterated the very conception of it as harmful and trivial. This fact is true.

I can vouch for it and – and, after all, it is time one did tell the truth fully, simply, and frankly. But it is also a fact that has never been known anywhere, among any people, since time immemorial, which, of course, may well mean that it is of an accidental nature and may pass away. I freely admit it. For I cannot imagine a liberal anywhere who would hate his own country. How, then, can we explain it all among us? Well, it can be explained by what I have said before, namely, that so far the Russian liberal is only an un-Russian liberal. There can be no other explanation, in my opinion.'

'I take all that you have said as a joke, sir,' Prince Sh. declared earnestly.

'I haven't seen every liberal and cannot judge,' said Alexandra, 'but I must say that I listened to your ideas with indignation. You've taken some individual case and treated it as a universal rule. That's not fair.'

'An individual case? Ah, at last we've got it,' Radomsky cried. 'What do you think, Prince? Is it an individual case or not?'

'I'm afraid,' said the prince, 'I haven't seen or met many – liberals, but I can't help feeling that you may be right to some extent and that the sort of Russian liberalism you are talking about is partly inclined to hate Russia herself, and not only her system of government. Of course, this is only partly true. It – it isn't fair to say that of all liberals.'

He stopped short in confusion. In spite of his excitement, he was deeply interested in the conversation. One of the prince's peculiar characteristics was the extraordinarily naïve attention with which he always listened to anything he was interested in and the naïve answers he gave when he was asked some question. This naïveté, this good faith, unsuspicious of derision or ridicule, seemed to be reflected on his face and even in the way he carried himself. But although Radomsky had for some time addressed him with a peculiar sort of smile, now that he heard his answer he looked at him very gravely, as though he had never expected such an answer from him.

'I see,' he said; 'that's rather strange. Tell me honestly, Prince, did you answer me seriously?'

'Why, didn't you ask me seriously?'

They all laughed.

'Trust him!' said Adelaida. 'Mr Radomsky always pulls everyone's leg! If only you knew the stories he sometimes tells with a straight face!'

'I think this is a very painful subject and we really shouldn't have started discussing it,' said Alexandra sharply. 'We wanted to go for a walk.'

'Well, let's go; it's a lovely evening!' cried Radomsky. 'But to prove to you that this time I was talking absolutely seriously and, above all, to prove it to the prince – you, Prince, interest me greatly, and I swear I'm not such an ass as I must certainly seem to you, though, as a matter of fact, I am rather an ass! – and – er – with your permission, ladies and gentlemen, I'd like to put one more question to the prince, to satisfy my own curiosity, and that will be the end of the matter. This question occurred to me rather appropriately two hours ago (you see, Prince, I, too, think of serious things sometimes). I answered it, but let us see what the prince will say. The phrase "individual case" has been used just now. Now, this phrase is rather significant and one often hears it. Recently everyone was talking and writing about that dreadful murder of six people by that – er – young man and about the strange speech by counsel for the defence, in which he stated that, considering the young man's poverty-stricken condition, it must *naturally* have occurred to him to kill the six people. I'm not quoting him literally, but I think that was the sense of his words or something to that effect. Now, my personal opinion is that in expressing such a strange idea counsel for the defence was absolutely convinced that he was giving voice to the most liberal, most humane, and most progressive sentiment that could possibly be uttered in our time. Well, what do you think? Is this perversion of ideas and convictions, is the very possibility of so wrong-headed and extraordinary a point of view, an individual case or does everybody think the same?'

They all burst out laughing.

'An individual, of course, an individual,' Alexandra and Adelaida laughed.

'And may I remind you again, my dear fellow,' added Prince Sh., 'that your joke is rather stale.'

'What do you think, Prince?' Radomsky asked, paying no attention to the last remark and catching the prince's interested and serious gaze upon him. 'Does it seem to you a general or an individual view? I confess I thought of this question specially for you.'

'No,' the prince said, quietly but firmly, 'it is not an individual view.'

'Good Lord, Prince,' cried Prince Sh. with some annoyance, 'don't you realize that he is trying to catch you out? He's simply laughing and pulling your leg.'

'I thought Mr Radomsky was serious,' the prince said, reddening and lowering his eyes.

'My dear Prince,' Prince Sh. went on, 'do you remember what we were discussing once, about three months ago? We said then that in our newly opened Law Courts one could already point to a great many remarkable and talented counsel! And how many highly remarkable verdicts had been given by the juries! How pleased you were at the time and how pleased I was to see your pleasure. We said that it was something to be proud of. And this absurd defence, this strange argument, is, of course, just an accident, one in a thousand!'

The prince thought it over, but replied with an air of the utmost conviction, though speaking quietly and even, it seemed, timidly:

'All I wanted to say was that the perversion of ideas and conceptions (as Mr Radomsky expressed it) can be met with very often and is, unhappily, a general rule rather than an individual case. Indeed, if this perversion were not such a general rule, there would not be such impossible crimes as these. ...'

'Impossible crimes? But I assure you that just such crimes, and perhaps even more dreadful ones, have existed before, and at all times, and not only in this country, but everywhere, and, in my opinion, will occur again and again for a long time. The only difference is that before they haven't received so much publicity and that people are now talking and writing about them, and that's why it seems that these criminals have only appeared now. That's where you're mistaken, Prince, and your mistake, I assure you, is a very naïve one,' Prince Sh. smiled ironically.

'I know that there were very many crimes before, and just as dreadful. I have visited some of our prisons recently and was successful in making the acquaintance of some criminals and accused persons. There are even more terrible criminals than that one, men who have killed a dozen people and feel no remorse whatever. But there is one thing I did notice: the most hardened and unrepentant criminal still knows that he *is* a criminal – that is, his conscience tells him that he has done wrong, however unrepentant he may be. And every one of them is the same in this. But those Mr Radomsky was talking about don't want even to admit that they are criminals, and think that they had a right to do what they did and – and that they had acted well – I mean, it's almost always like that. That's where, I think, the terrible difference lies. And note, please, that they are all young – I mean, they are of an age when one most easily succumbs to the influence of perverted ideas and is defenceless against them.'

Prince Sh. no longer laughed, and he listened to the prince with a puzzled expression. Alexandra, who had long wanted to say something, said nothing, as though some special thought had made her pause. Radomsky looked at the prince with positive surprise, and this time without a hint of a sneer.

'But why are you surprised at him, my dear sir?' Mrs Yepanchin unexpectedly broke in. 'Did you think he was stupider than you and could not reason as well as you can?'

'No, ma'am, it wasn't that,' said Radomsky; 'but how was it you didn't – I'm sorry, but I have to ask you this – I mean, if you can see and observe it all – please forgive me again – how was it you didn't notice the same perversion of ideas and moral concepts in that strange case – I mean the one that happened the other day – the case of Burdovsky? For it's exactly the same, you know. It seemed to me at the time that you didn't see it at all.'

'And we, my dear sir, saw it all,' Mrs Yepanchin burst out warmly. 'We are sitting here and telling him what clever people we are, and he got a letter from one of them to-day, the principal one, I mean, the pimply one, do you remember, Alexandra? He apologizes to him in his letter, though in his own fashion, and informs him that he has broken with the friend who egged him on at the time – do you remember, Alexandra? – and that he has more faith now in the prince. Well, we haven't received such a letter, so we needn't turn up our noses at him.'

'And Ippolit has also just moved to our house,' cried Kolya.

'Has he?' cried the prince in alarm. 'Is he there already?'

'He arrived just after you left with Mrs Yepanchin. I brought him down from town.'

'Well, I bet you,' Mrs Yepanchin cried angrily, having quite forgotten that she had just been praising the prince – 'I bet you he'd been to see him in his attic yesterday and begged his pardon on his bended knees so that the spiteful little horror should deign to move to his house. Did you go there yesterday? You told me so yourself an hour ago. Did you or didn't you? Did you go down on your knees or not?'

'Of course he didn't,' cried Kolya. 'Quite the contrary: Ippolit took hold of the prince's hand yesterday and kissed it twice. I saw it myself. That's all there was to it. Except that the prince told him that he would feel much better in the country and he immediately agreed to come as soon as he felt better.'

'You shouldn't, Kolya,' the prince murmured, getting up and seizing his hat. 'Why are you telling them this? I – –'

'Where are you off to?' Mrs Yepanchin stopped him.

'Don't worry, Prince,' Kolya went on, quivering with excitement. 'Don't go and don't disturb him. He's asleep after the journey. He's very happy, and you know, Prince, I think it would be much better if you didn't meet him to-day and even put it off till to-morrow, for he might feel embarrassed again. He told me this morning that he hadn't felt so well and so strong for the last six months – he isn't coughing half as much.'

The prince noticed that Aglaya suddenly left her place and came up to the table. He dared not look at her, but he felt with every fibre of his being that she was looking at him at that moment, and perhaps looking at him sternly, and that there was most certainly indignation in her black eyes and that her face was flushed.

'But I cannot help feeling,' Radomsky remarked to Kolya, 'that you shouldn't have brought him down here, if that's the same consumptive boy who burst out crying and invited us to his funeral. He spoke so eloquently about the wall of the house opposite that I'm sure he will feel homesick for that wall.'

'That's quite true: he'll pick a quarrel and have a fight with you and then go back – take my word for it!'

And Mrs Yepanchin drew her work-basket towards her with a dignified air, forgetting that they were all about to go for a walk in the park.

'Yes, I remember he was bragging a lot about that wall,' Radomsky resumed once more. 'He won't be able to die grandiloquently without that wall, and he longs to die grandiloquently.'

'Well, what about it?' murmured the prince. 'If you won't forgive him, he'll die without your forgiveness. ... He's come down here now for the sake of the trees.'

'Oh, so far as I'm concerned, I forgive him for everything. You can tell him that.'

'That's not the point,' the prince replied quietly and, as it were, reluctantly, without raising his eyes, which were still fixed on one spot on the floor. 'The point is that you, too, should be willing to accept forgiveness from him.'

'What have I got to do with him? What wrong have I done him?'

'If you don't see it, then of course – but, I think, you do see it. That night he wanted to give us all – his blessing and to receive your blessing, too. That was all.'

'My dear Prince,' Prince Sh. broke in somewhat apprehensively, exchanging glances with some of the people on the veranda, 'it is not easy to achieve heaven on earth, and you do seem to count on it a little: heaven is a difficult matter, Prince, much more difficult than it seems to your excellent heart. I think we'd better drop the subject, or I'm afraid we shall again be embarrassed and then – –'

'Let's go and listen to the band,' Mrs Yepanchin said sharply, getting up from her place angrily.

The rest of the company followed her example.

2

The prince suddenly went up to Radomsky.

'Please believe me,' he said with strange warmth, seizing his hand, 'that I regard you as the best and most honourable man in the world, in spite of everything – please, do. ...'

Radomsky fell back a step in astonishment. For a moment he restrained himself from bursting out laughing uncontrollably, but on looking closer he noticed that the prince did not seem to be himself, at least he was in a very peculiar state.

'I bet you anything you like,' he cried, 'you didn't mean to say that, and that perhaps you didn't mean to say it to me at all. ... What's the matter? Are you feeling ill?'

'Perhaps you're right – yes, most probably you are right, and it was very clever of you to say that perhaps I didn't mean to come up to you at all!'

Saying this, he smiled a rather strange and even absurd smile, but suddenly, as though working himself up into a passion, he exclaimed:

'Do not remind me of my conduct three days ago! I've been ashamed of it for the last three days. ... I know it was my fault. ...'

'But – but what terrible thing did you do?'

'I can see, Mr Radomsky, that you more than anyone are ashamed of me. You're blushing – that's a sign of a good heart. Oh, I'm going now, don't worry!'

'What's the matter with him?' Mrs Yepanchin asked apprehensively, addressing Kolya. 'Do his fits start like that?'

'Don't mind me, ma'am; I'm not going to have a fit. I shall be going presently. I know that – that I'm an invalid. I've been ill for twenty-four years, from my birth to my twenty-fourth year. You must accept what I have to say now as coming from an invalid. I'm going presently, presently, don't worry. I'm not blushing, for it would be strange to blush because of that, wouldn't it? But my place is not in society. I'm not saying this from vanity. ... I've been thinking it over during the last three days, and I've decided that I must tell you sincerely and honestly about it at the first opportunity. There are certain ideas, certain great ideas, which I mustn't start talking about, because I'm quite sure to make you all laugh. Prince Sh. has just reminded me of it. ... I'm afraid my gestures are not very graceful –

I have no sense of proportion, my words don't express my ideas, and that's degrading to – to my ideas. And that's why I have no right to – besides, I'm so morbidly sensitive – – I mean I – I'm sure that in this house no one would want to hurt my feelings and that I'm loved here more than I deserve, but I know (oh, I know very well) that after twenty years of illness there must be some trace of it left, so that people can't help laughing at me – sometimes – isn't that so?'

He looked round as though expecting a definite answer. They were all looking painfully abashed at this unexpected, morbid and, in any case, quite gratuitous outburst. But this outburst gave rise to a strange incident.

'Why are you saying this here?' Aglaya cried suddenly. 'Why are you saying this to *them*? To them! To them!'

She seemed to be furious with indignation: her eyes blazed. The prince stood mute and speechless before her, and suddenly turned pale.

'There's no one here who is worth such words!' Aglaya burst out. 'No one, no one here is worth your little finger, nor your mind, nor your heart! You're more honest than any of them, better, kinder, cleverer than any of them! There are people here who are not worthy to bend down to pick up the handkerchief you've dropped. Why then are you humbling yourself and making yourself out to be inferior to these people? Why are you all twisted up inside? Why have you no pride?'

'Gracious, how do you like that?' Mrs Yepanchin cried, clasping her hands in a gesture of dismay.

'The poor knight! Hurrah!' cried Kolya, rapturously.

'Do be quiet, Mother!' Aglaya suddenly flew out at Mrs Yepanchin, having reached that pitch of hysteria when nothing matters any more and all obstacles are swept out of one's way. 'How dare they insult me in your house? Why do they all, all of them, torture me? Why have they been pestering me for the last three days because of you, Prince? Nothing in the world will make me marry you! I want you to know that! I shall never marry you! Not for anything in the world. As if one could marry a ridiculous man like you! Have a look at yourself in the glass. Just see what you look like standing there! Why, why do they all tease me and say that I'm going to marry you? You ought to know. You're in the plot with them too!'

'No one has ever teased you – no one!' Adelaida murmured in dismay.

'No one has ever thought of such a thing,' cried Alexandra. 'No one has said a word about it!'

'Who has been teasing her?' Mrs Yepanchin, trembling with anger, turned to everyone in the room. 'When has she been teased? Who could have said such a thing to her? Is she raving?'

'Everyone has been talking about it! Everyone! For the last three days! I shall never, never marry him!'

Having said this, Aglaya burst out sobbing bitterly, buried her face in her handkerchief, and collapsed into a chair.

'But he hasn't even asked – –'

'I haven't asked you, Miss Aglaya,' cried the prince involuntarily.

'Wha-at?' Mrs Yepanchin cried in amazement, indignation and horror. 'What's that?'

She could not believe her ears.

'I mean to say – I mean to say – –' faltered the prince, 'I only wished to explain to Miss Aglaya – I mean, to have the honour of explaining that I never had any intention to – I mean – to have the honour of asking for her hand – at any time. ... I had nothing to do with it, I swear I hadn't, Miss Aglaya! I've never wished to – it – er – it never occurred to me – and I never shall – you'll see for yourself – please, be sure of that! Some wicked person must have maligned me to you! Oh, you needn't worry about it!'

Saying this, he went up to Aglaya. She removed the handkerchief, with which she had covered her face, threw a quick glance at him and his frightened face, and, realizing the meaning of his words, suddenly burst out laughing in his face. Her laughter was so gay and irresistible, so full of fun and mockery, that Adelaida could not restrain herself, especially when she, too, glanced at the prince, and rushing up to her sister, embraced her and burst out into the same sort of irrepressible, gay, schoolgirlish laughter. Looking at them, the prince, too, suddenly began smiling, and kept repeating with a joyful and happy expression:

'Well, thank God, thank God!'

At this point Alexandra could not restrain herself either, and burst into hearty laughter. It seemed as though the three girls would never stop laughing.

'Oh, the mad things!' murmured Mrs Yepanchin. 'First they frighten you to death, and then – –'

But Prince Sh., too, was already laughing, Radomsky was laughing too, Kolya was roaring with laughter and, looking at them all, the prince laughed too.

'Let's go for a walk! Let's go for a walk!' Adelaida cried. 'All of us, and the prince simply must come with us too. There's no need for you to go home, my dear sir! Isn't he a dear, Aglaya? Isn't he, Mother?

And, besides, I simply must kiss him and hug him for – for his explanation to Aglaya just now. May I kiss him, Mother? Aglaya, do let me kiss your prince!' cried the mischievous girl, and she really did rush up to the prince and kissed him on the forehead.

The prince seized her hands and squeezed them so tightly that Adelaida nearly cried out. He gazed at her with infinite joy and suddenly raised her hand to his lips and kissed it three times.

'Do come along,' Aglaya called. 'Prince, you must be my escort. May he, Mother? The man who has refused me? You have refused me for good, haven't you, Prince? Why, that's not the way to offer your arm to a lady! Don't you know how to offer a lady your arm? That's better. Now come along. We'll go on ahead. Would you like us to go on ahead, *tête-à-tête*?'

She chattered away without stopping, still bursting into laughter now and again.

'Thank God! Thank God!' Mrs Yepanchin kept repeating, hardly knowing herself what she was so pleased about.

'Extraordinarily odd people!' thought Prince Sh., perhaps for the hundredth time since he had met them, but – he could not help liking these odd people. As for the prince, he was not sure that he really liked him very much; Prince Sh. appeared to be a little upset and out of humour as they all set off for their walk.

Mr Radomsky seemed to be in the most excellent spirits; all the way to the pleasure gardens he made Alexandra and Adelaida laugh, and they laughed at his jokes a little too readily, so that he was beginning at moments to suspect that they were not listening to him at all. At that thought he suddenly burst out into loud laughter, which sounded very genuine, though he did not explain what he was laughing at (such was the character of the man!). The sisters, who were in a most festive mood, kept looking at Aglaya and the prince, who were walking in front of them; it was quite obvious that their youngest sister had given them something to think about. Prince Sh. still tried to talk about something else to Mrs Yepanchin to take her mind off Aglaya's outburst, and he bored her excruciatingly. She appeared to be distraught, answered absent-mindedly and sometimes did not answer at all. But Aglaya had not by any means done with her mysteries that evening. The last one fell to the lot of the prince alone. When they had walked a hundred yards from the house, Aglaya said in a rapid half-whisper to her obstinately silent escort:

'Please, look to the right.'

The prince looked.

'Have a good look. Do you see that seat in the park – over there where those three large trees are – the greeen seat?'

The prince replied that he did.

'Don't you think it's a lovely spot? I sometimes come and sit there alone very early in the morning, at about seven o'clock, when everybody in the house is still asleep.'

The prince murmured that it was indeed a very lovely spot.

'And now leave me, please. I don't want to walk arm-in-arm with you any more. Or better go on walking arm-in-arm with me, but don't speak to me at all. I'd like to think.'

The warning was, anyway, unnecessary: the prince would most certainly never have uttered a word even without being told not to speak. His heart began pounding violently when she told him about the seat. A minute later he changed his mind and, feeling ashamed of his preposterous idea, dismissed it.

On week-days the public which comes to listen to the band in the Pavlovsk pleasure-gardens, as is generally conceded by everybody, is more 'select' than on Sundays and public holidays, when 'all sorts of people' arrive in large crowds from town. The dresses of the ladies, though not festive, are elegant. To meet at the bandstand is considered to be the correct thing. The orchestra, which perhaps really is the best of our park bands, plays the newest numbers. There is an air of the utmost propriety and decorum, in spite of a certain feeling of informality and even intimacy. Acquaintances, all of them Pavlovsk summer residents, meet to look at one another. Many of them do this with unconcealed pleasure and only go there for that purpose; but there are some, too, who go there only for the music. Breaches of the peace are rare, though, of course, they sometimes do occur even on week-days. But, then, such things are, after all, unavoidable.

On this particular occasion the evening was lovely, and there was quite a large number of people in the pleasure-gardens. All the seats round the bandstand were taken. Our party sat down on chairs not far from the exit, on the left side of the bandstand. The crowd and the music cheered Mrs Yepanchin up a little and diverted the girls; they exchanged glances with some of the people they knew and nodded politely to others; they scrutinized the dresses, noticed some rather quaint points, exchanged a few remarks about them, and smiled ironically. Radomsky, too, bowed frequently to friends. Aglaya and the prince, who were still together, did not fail to attract the attention of several people. Soon several young men went up to exchange greetings with the young ladies and their fond mother; two or three of them remained to talk to them; they were all close friends of

Radomsky's. Among them was a young and very handsome army officer, very gay and very talkative; he hastened to engage Aglaya in conversation and did his best to attract her attention. Aglaya was very gracious to him and chatted and laughed happily. Radomsky asked the prince's permission to introduce him to his friend. The prince hardly understood what was wanted of him, but the introduction took place and both exchanged bows and shook hands. Radomsky's friend asked the prince a question, but the prince either did not answer or mumbled to himself something so strange that the officer stared hard at him, then glanced at Radomsky, realized immediately why the latter had contrived the introduction, smiled faintly and turned to Aglaya again. Radomsky was the only one to notice that Aglaya suddenly coloured at this.

The prince did not even notice that the other men were talking and paying compliments to Aglaya, and occasionally he almost seemed to forget that he was sitting beside her. At times he felt that he would have liked to go away somewhere, to disappear entirely, and he would not have minded going away to some gloomy and deserted spot to be alone with his thoughts if only no one knew where he was. Or, at any rate, to be back home, on the veranda, provided no one else was there, neither Lebedev nor his children; to fling himself on the sofa, bury his face in a cushion, and lie like that for a day and a night and another day. At moments he dreamed of the mountains, and one familiar spot in the mountains in particular, a place he always liked to remember and had been fond of visiting when he was there, from where he could look down on the village, on the faintly gleaming streak of the waterfall below, the white clouds, and the ruins of the ancient castle. Oh, how he wished he could be there now and think of one thing only – oh, all his life of that one thing only – it would have kept him occupied for a thousand years! And let them – let them all forget him entirely here. Oh, that was indeed necessary, and it would have been even better if they had not known him at all and if all this had been just a dream. But was it not all the same whether it was real or a dream? Sometimes he would suddenly begin to look attentively at Aglaya without taking his eyes off her for five minutes at a time, but there was a very strange look in them: he seemed to be looking at her as though she were a mile away or as though it were her portrait and not herself he was looking at.

'Why are you looking at me like that, Prince?' she said suddenly, interrupting her gay talk and laughter with the people around her. 'I'm afraid of you. I have a curious feeling as though you were about to stretch out your hand and touch my face to feel if it was real. He does look like that, Mr Radomsky, doesn't he?'

The prince seemed to listen to her as though he were surprised that she should be talking to him, realized that he was being spoken to, though without altogether grasping what she was saying, and did not reply. Seeing, however, that Aglaya and everyone else were laughing, he suddenly opened his mouth and began laughing himself. The laughter grew louder and the army officer, who was evidently a man with a keen sense of humour, simply spluttered with laughter.

'The idiot!' Aglaya suddenly whispered angrily to herself.

'Good gracious! she can't be in love with a man like that,' Mrs Yepanchin muttered fiercely under her breath. 'She hasn't gone off her head completely, has she?'

'It's only a joke,' Alexandra whispered in her ear. 'It's the same sort of joke as the one about the poor knight – and nothing more! She's merely making a fool of him again in her usual way. Only the joke has gone too far. We must put a stop to it, Mother! A short while ago she was playing a part like an actress in a melodrama and frightened us all out of pure mischief. ...'

'It's a good thing she picked on an idiot like that,' Mrs Yepanchin whispered back.

Her daughter's remark had eased her mind all the same.

The prince, however, heard them call him an idiot and he gave a start, but not because he had been called an idiot. He forgot 'the idiot' at once. He caught sight in the crowd, not far from where he was sitting, of a face, a pale face, with dark, curly hair, and a familiar, very familiar look and smile, but it disappeared the moment he caught sight of it. Very likely he had only imagined it – all that he could remember of it was the wry smile, the eyes, and the smart light-green tie the man was wearing. Nor could the prince decide whether the man had disappeared in the crowd or slipped into the gardens.

But a minute later he suddenly began looking round rapidly and uneasily; the first apparition might be the forerunner of the second. That was almost certain to be so. He could not have overlooked the likelihood of a meeting when they went to the pleasure-gardens. It is true that when he was going there, he did not seem to realize that he was going there – such was his state of mind. Had he been more careful in observing Aglaya, he would have noticed already a quarter of an hour ago that she, too, was looking round uneasily from time to time as though she, too, was looking for someone near her. Now that his uneasiness had become very marked, Aglaya's uneasiness and excitement also increased, and as soon as he looked round, she, too, looked round. The explanation of their agitation followed quickly.

A whole crowd of people, a dozen at least, suddenly appeared from the side entrance near which the prince and the entire Yepanchin party were sitting. Three women walked in front of this crowd, two of them remarkably good-looking, so that there was nothing strange in the fact that they were followed by so many admirers. But there was something peculiar about the women and their admirers, something that made them look different from the rest of the public at the bandstand. Almost everyone noticed them at once, but mostly they tried to pretend that they had not noticed them, and only some of the young men smiled at them and whispered something to one another. Not to see them was quite impossible: they made no pretence at concealing themselves, talking loudly, and laughing. Many of them, it might well have been thought, were drunk, though some of them were wearing smart and elegant clothes; but among them were also men who looked very peculiar, in peculiar clothes, and with peculiarly flushed faces; some of them were army officers, and some were far from young; there were also among them men who were comfortably dressed in wide and well-cut suits, wearing diamond rings and cuff-links, and magnificent pitch-black wigs and side-whiskers, with an imposing, though somewhat fastidious, expression on their faces, who in society are, as a rule, avoided like the plague. In our holiday resorts there are, of course, people who are remarkable for their quite extraordinary respectability and who enjoy a particularly good reputation, but even the most circumspect person cannot always be expected to protect himself against a brick dropping from the house next door. Such a brick was about to drop now on the highly respectable public who had gathered to listen to the music of the band.

To pass from the pleasure-gardens to the bandstand one had to descend three steps. The crowd stopped at the top of these steps; they lacked courage to go down, but one of the women stepped forward; only two of her escorts had the courage to follow her. One was a middle-aged man of rather modest appearance, who looked absolutely respectable, but conveyed the impression of a solitary man – that is, one of those men whom nobody knows and who knows nobody. The other one looked like a tramp of a most disreputable kind. Nobody else followed the eccentric lady; but as she went down the steps she never looked back, as though she did not care a rap whether she was followed or not. She laughed and talked aloud as before; her clothes were expensive and in good taste, but a little too smart, perhaps. She walked to the other side of the bandstand near the road where an open carriage was waiting.

The prince had not seen *her* for over three months. Ever since his arrival in Petersburg he had intended to go and see her; but he was perhaps checked by some secret presentiment. At any rate, he could never imagine what he would feel like when he met her, although he sometimes tried fearfully to imagine it. One thing he did not doubt was that their meeting would be painful. Several times during the last six months he had recalled the first impression made on him by that woman's face when he had seen it only on her portrait; but even the impression her portrait had made on him, he remembered, was rather painful. The month in the provinces, when he had seen her almost every day, had had such a dreadful effect on him that he sometimes tried to wipe even the memory of it from his mind. There was something in the face of that woman that always distressed him: in his talks to Rogozhin, the prince tried to explain this feeling by the feeling of infinite pity he felt for her, and that was quite true – the very sight of her face on the portrait made his heart overflow with agonizing pity; the feeling of compassion and even of torment for this woman never left his heart and it had not left it now. Oh no, it was stronger than ever! But he was dissatisfied with what he had told Rogozhin; and it was only now, at the moment of her sudden appearance, that he realized, intuitively perhaps, what it was he had not told Rogozhin. He had failed to convey his feeling of horror – yes, horror! Now, at that very moment, he was fully aware of it; he was sure, he was absolutely convinced, for reasons of his own, that that woman was mad. If, loving a woman more than anything in the world, or anticipating the possibility of such a love, one were suddenly to see her chained to a wall behind iron bars with a warder standing over her with a stick, such a feeling would be somewhat similar to the feeling the prince had now.

'What's the matter?' Aglaya whispered quickly, glancing at him and pulling ingenuously at his arm.

He turned his head towards her, looked at her, gazed into her black eyes, flashing inexplicably at that moment, and tried to smile at her, but all of a sudden, as though forgetting her instantly, he turned his eyes again to the right and again began watching the extraordinary apparition. Nastasya Filippovna was just then walking past the chairs of the girls. Radomsky went on talking about something very interesting and amusing to Alexandra. He was speaking rapidly and excitedly. The prince remembered that Aglaya suddenly said in a semi-whisper: 'What a – –'

She did not finish; she instantly checked herself and said no more, but that was enough. Nastasya Filippovna, who was walking past without apparently noticing anyone, suddenly turned round in their direction and seemed only now to have become aware of Radomsky.

'Dear me, here he is!' she cried, stopping suddenly. 'I've been looking for him all over the place, and here he sits where I never expected to find him. You see, darling' – she addressed Radomsky – 'I thought you were there – at your uncle's.'

Radomsky flushed, threw a furious look at Nastasya Filippovna, but quickly turned away from her again.

'Why, don't you know? Would you believe it? He does not know yet! He's shot himself. Your uncle shot himself this morning. I heard about it at two o'clock. Why, half the town knows it by now. According to some, three hundred and fifty thousand roubles of public money are missing, according to others, five hundred thousand. And I always counted on his leaving you a fortune! He squandered it all, the dissolute old rake! Well, good-bye, darling, *bonne chance*! But aren't you going there? So that's why you resigned your commission in good time, you cunning old thing! But what am I talking about? You knew it all before, didn't you, darling? I expect you must have known all about it already yesterday. ...'

Though in the impudent way in which she pestered him and in her trumpeting forth of an acquaintanceship and an intimacy which did not exist there was certainly some motive – indeed, there could be no doubt whatever about it now – Radomsky thought at first of entirely ignoring the woman and getting rid of her that way. But Nastasya Filippovna's words struck him like a thunderbolt; hearing of his uncle's death, he grew as white as a sheet and turned round to his informant. At that moment Mrs Yepanchin quickly got up from her seat, made everyone get up after her, and almost ran out of the pleasure-gardens. Only the prince stayed behind for a second, as though undecided what to do, and Radomsky still stood there, unable to recover from his shock. But the Yepanchins had scarcely walked away twenty paces when a hideous scene followed.

The army officer, a close friend of Radomsky's, who had been talking to Aglaya, was highly indignant.

'This shameless creature,' he said almost in a loud voice, 'ought to be horsewhipped. That's the only way of dealing with her sort!' (He seemed to have been in Radomsky's confidence before.)

Nastasya Filippovna immediately turned round to him. Her eyes flashed; she rushed up to a young man who was standing a couple of paces from her and who was a complete stranger, snatched the thin, plaited riding-crop he was holding out of his hands, and struck the army officer with all her might across the face. All this happened in one moment. ... The officer, beside himself, sprang at her. Nastasya

Filippovna's followers were no longer at her side. The respectable middle-aged gentleman had managed to make himself scarce and the tipsy gentleman was standing on one side and was roaring with laughter. A minute later the police would, of course, have appeared on the scene, but in the meantime it might have gone very hard with Nastasya Filippovna, if help had not come in the nick of time: the prince, who had also stopped a couple of paces away, managed to seize the officer's arm from behind. In wresting his hand away, the officer gave him so violent a push in the chest that he was flung back a few paces and fell on a chair. But two men came to Nastasya Filippovna's rescue. The pugilist, the author of the article already known to the reader and a regular member of Rogozhin's former band, stood facing the attacking army officer.

'Keller, retired lieutenant, at your service, sir!' he introduced himself with a swagger. 'If you want a fight, Captain, I shall be glad to take the place of the fair lady. I'm an expert at English boxing. Don't push, Captain. I deeply sympathize with you for the *mortal* insult you've received, but I cannot permit you to raise your hands against a woman in public. But if, as becomes a most honourable gentleman, you'd like a different sort of fight, then – but, I suppose, you see what I mean – er – Captain....'

But the captain had already recollected himself and was not listening to him. At that moment Rogozhin had emerged from the crowd and, seizing Nastasya Filippovna by the arm, led her away with him. Rogozhin looked terribly shaken. He was pale and trembling. As he led Nastasya Filippovna away, he had time to laugh viciously in the officer's face and say with the triumphant look of a shopkeeper in the Arcade:

'Whew! Caught it, didn't you? Your dirty mug's all bloody! Whew!'

Recollecting himself and fully realizing whom he was dealing with, the army officer turned courteously (though covering his face with his handkerchief) to the prince, who had got up from the chair.

'Prince Myshkin, I believe? The gentleman to whom I had the pleasure of being introduced?'

'She's mad! Mad! I assure you!' the prince replied in a trembling voice, for some reason holding out his shaking hands to him.

'I'm afraid your information is better than mine, but I must have your name, sir.'

He nodded and walked away. The police arrived exactly five seconds after the people who had been involved in the scene had gone. However, the incident did not last more than two minutes. A few people in the audience got up and went away; some merely exchanged their seats for others, some were delighted with the disgraceful scene, and some were greatly interested and were discussing it eagerly. In short, the whole thing came to an end in the usual way. The band struck up again. The prince followed the Yepanchins. If he had thought of it and had had time to look to the left after he had been flung into the chair, he might have seen Aglaya, who had stopped about twenty paces from him and watched the scandalous scene, disregarding the calls of her mother and sisters, who had walked on a little ahead. Prince Sh. ran up to her and at last persuaded her to go away quickly. Mrs Yepanchin remembered that Aglaya had come back to them in such a state of excitement that she probably never heard their calls. But exactly two minutes later, as soon as they entered the park, Aglaya said in her usual indifferent and capricious tone of voice:

'I just wanted to see how the farce would end!'

3

The incident at the pleasure-gardens horrified the mother as well as her daughters. Greatly worried and excited, Mrs Yepanchin and her daughters had literally almost run all the way home. In her view, and according to her ideas, so much had happened and had come to light in that incident that, in spite of her dismay and confusion, most definite conclusions were taking shape in her brain. But everyone realized that something peculiar had happened and that, luckily perhaps, a highly important secret was about to be revealed. In spite of Prince Sh.'s former assurances and explanations, Radomsky had now been 'shown up', exposed, found out, and 'publicly unmasked in his relations with that abandoned creature'. So thought Mrs Yepanchin and even her two elder daughters. But all this conclusion did was to increase the mystery. Though among themselves the girls were a little indignant with their mother at her exaggerated alarm and all-too-conspicuous flight, they could not bring themselves to worry her with questions while the excitement lasted. Besides, for some reason they could not help feeling their sister Aglaya perhaps knew more about this affair than the two of them and their mother. Prince Sh., too, looked as black as night and was also very thoughtful and preoccupied. Mrs Yepanchin did not say a word to him all the way, and he apparently never noticed it. Adelaida made an attempt to ask him what uncle they had been talking about just now and what had happened in Petersburg, but he muttered with a very sour expression something very vague in reply about some inquiries and that the whole thing was, of course, utter nonsense. 'There's no doubt about that,' replied Adelaida and asked no more questions. Aglaya, on the other hand, was quite extraordinarily calm, and the only remark she made on the way was that they were walking much too fast. Once she turned round and caught sight of the prince, who was trying to catch up with them. Noticing his efforts to overtake them, she smiled sardonically and never looked round at him again.

At last, almost within sight of their house, they met General Yepanchin, who had only just arrived from Petersburg. He at once inquired after Radomsky. But his wife walked past him sternly, without answering and without even bestowing a glance on him. From the look of Prince Sh. and his daughters he at once guessed that there was serious trouble at home. But quite apart from this, he himself looked extraordinarily perturbed. He at once took Prince Sh.'s arm, stopped him at the front door, and exchanged a few words with him almost in a whisper. From the troubled expression of both of them as they walked on to the veranda afterwards and went up to Mrs Yepanchin's room, it would seem that they had heard some extraordinary news. Soon they all gathered in Mrs Yepanchin's drawing-room upstairs, and only the prince remained on the veranda. He sat in a corner, as though expecting something, though he hardly knew himself what it was; it never occurred to him to go away, in view of the commotion in the house; he seemed to have forgotten the whole world and was ready to go on sitting for two years on end, wherever he might be put. From upstairs he occasionally caught sounds of anxious conversation. He could not have said himself how long he had been sitting there. It was getting late and it grew quite dark. All of a sudden Aglaya came out on the veranda; she looked calm, though she was a little pale. Seeing the prince, whom she evidently did not expect (as she declared afterwards) to meet there, sitting on a chair in the corner, Aglaya smiled, as though in perplexity.

'What are you doing here?' she asked, coming up to him.

The prince muttered something in confusion and jumped up from his chair, but Aglaya at once sat down beside him, and he sat down again. She cast a quick but intent glance at him, then out of the window, as though without thinking of anything in particular, and then looked at him again. 'Perhaps she wants to laugh,' thought the prince, 'but no, for then she would have laughed.'

'Would you like some tea?' she said after a brief silence. 'I will order some.'

'No, thank you – I – I don't know.'

'You don't know? What do you mean? Oh, by the way, look here: if someone challenged you to a duel, what would you do? I wanted to ask you before.'

'But – who – who would – I mean, no one would challenge me to a duel.'

'But if someone did? Would you be awfully frightened?'

'Yes – I – I think I should be very – er – frightened.'

'Do you mean it? Are you a coward, then?'

'N-no, I don't think I am, really. A coward is a man who's afraid and runs away, but a man who is afraid and doesn't run away is not a coward,' the prince said, after a moment's reflection, with a smile.

'And you wouldn't run away?'

'Perhaps not,' he laughed at last at Aglaya's questions.

'I may be a woman, but I shouldn't run away for anything,' she observed, almost in an offended tone. 'But I can see you're laughing at me and giving yourself airs, as usual, to make yourself more interesting. Tell me, do they usually fire at twelve paces? And some at ten? That means that one of them must be killed or wounded, doesn't it?'

'I don't suppose they often hit each other at duels.'

'Not often? But they killed Pushkin.'

'That may have been an accident.'

'It was not an accident. It was a duel to the death, and he was killed.'

'The bullet struck him so low down that Dantès probably aimed higher, at his chest or his head. No one aims so low, so that the bullet must have hit Pushkin by accident, by a mere fluke. I've been told that by people who are experts in that sort of thing.'

'But a soldier I talked to once told me that, according to the army regulations, when spreading out for an attack, they are ordered to fire half way down – that's the expression they use, "half way down". So that, you see, they are ordered to fire not at the chest or the head, but half way down. I asked an officer about it afterwards, and he told me it was quite true.'

'I expect that's because they shoot from a great distance.'

'And can you shoot?'

'I have never fired a shot in my life.'

'Can't you even load a pistol?'

'I'm afraid not. I mean, I know how it is done, but I've never done it myself.'

'Well, in that case you don't know how to, for this sort of thing requires practice. Listen, and please try to remember: first you must buy good gunpowder, not damp (I'm told it must not be damp, but very dry) and very fine. You'd better ask for that sort, and not the sort they use in firing cannons. I'm also told one has to make the bullet oneself somehow. Have you got pistols?'

'No, I haven't and I don't want any,' the prince suddenly laughed.

'Oh, what nonsense! You simply must buy one – a good one, French or English. I'm told they're the best. Then take a thimbleful of powder – or two thimblefuls, perhaps – and charge the pistol. Better put in as much as you can. Then ram in a bit of felt (I'm told it must be felt, for some reason). You can get it easily from a mattress, or doors are sometimes covered with felt. Then, after you've rammed the felt in, put in the bullet, first the felt, then the bullet, or it won't fire. What are you laughing at? I'd like you to practise shooting several times a day so that you should learn how to hit the target. Will you do it?'

The prince laughed. Aglaya stamped her foot with vexation. Her serious air during such a conversation surprised the prince a little. He could not help feeling that he had to find something out, ask about something, anyway, something much more important than how to load a pistol. But everything had faded from his memory, except that she was sitting beside him and he was looking at her, and it made no difference to him at that moment what she talked about.

At last General Yepanchin himself came down from upstairs on to the veranda; he was going out somewhere with a frowning, troubled, and determined expression on his face.

'Oh, Prince, it's you. ... Where are you going now?' he asked, although the prince did not think of stirring from his place. 'Come along, I want to tell you something.'

'Good-bye,' said Aglaya, holding out her hand to the prince.

It was quite dark on the veranda now, and the prince could not make out her face quite clearly at that moment. A minute later, as he and the general were leaving the house, he suddenly flushed crimson and clenched his right hand tightly.

The general, it seemed, was going the same way as he. In spite of the late hour, he was very anxious to discuss something with someone. But meanwhile he suddenly began talking to the prince, rapidly, breathlessly, and rather incoherently, frequently mentioning Mrs Yepanchin's name. If the prince had been able to pay a little more attention at that moment, he would perhaps have realized that, among other things, the general was anxious to find out something from him, too, or rather, to ask him a plain question, but could not bring himself to broach the subject. To his shame, the prince was so absent-minded that at first he heard nothing at all, and when the general stopped before him with some excited question, he had to confess that he did not know what he was talking about.

The general shrugged.

'You're certainly a queer lot, all of you, in every respect,' the general went on. 'I tell you I can't make head or tail of Mrs Yepanchin's ideas and alarms. She's in hysterics, she's crying and declaring that we've been shamed and disgraced. Who? How? Who by? When and why? I'm afraid I am to blame (I admit it), I'm very much to blame, but the attempts at blackmail of that troublesome woman (who is behaving so outrageously into the bargain) could, if the worst came to the worst, be stopped by the police and, indeed, I intend to see someone to-day and take the necessary steps. Everything can be settled quietly, peacefully, in a friendly way, and without scandal. I'm ready to admit, too, that many things may happen in the future and that there's a great deal here that remains unexplained. There's certainly some kind of intrigue here, but if we here don't know anything definite about it, they can't explain it there, either. If I haven't heard, you haven't heard, he hasn't heard, and someone else hasn't heard, then who, I ask you, has heard? How do you suppose it can be explained except that half of it is a delusion and doesn't exist, that it is something like – er – moonshine or – other kinds of spectres.'

'*She* is mad,' murmured the prince, suddenly remembering with pain all that had happened recently.

'If you mean *her*, you've put it in a nutshell. The same idea has occurred to me sometimes, and that's why I've slept so peacefully. But I can see now that the others are more likely to be right, and I don't believe in her insanity. She's a preposterous woman, I grant you that, but, believe me, she is a deep one and far from mad. Her outburst about Kapiton Alexeyevich to-day proves it up to the hilt. So far as she's concerned, there's some jiggery-pokery here – I mean, at least something jesuitical – and it was all done for a special purpose of her own.'

'What Kapiton Alexeyevich?'

'Good Lord, man, you've not been listening at all! I began by telling you about Kapiton Alexeyevich. It's been such a shock to me that even now I'm trembling all over. That's what kept me in town so late. Kapiton Alexeyevich, Eugene Radomsky's uncle – –'

'Well?' cried the prince.

'Shot himself early this morning, at seven o'clock. A highly respected old gentleman, seventy, an epicure and – and, just as she said, a large sum of money is missing, a very considerable sum of money!'

'But how could she – –'

'Have got to know about it? Ha, ha! You see, ever since she appeared here she's been surrounded by a regular suite of her own. You know the sort of people who come to see her now and seek "the honour of her acquaintance", don't you? So she might naturally have heard something this morning from some visitor, for the whole of Petersburg knows it by now, and half of Pavlovsk, too, if not all of it. But what a damned clever remark to make about his uniform, if what I've been told is true – I mean, about Radomsky's resignation from the army at the right moment. What a fiendish hint! No, that's not a sign of madness. I, of course, refuse to believe that Radomsky knew anything about the impending catastrophe – I mean, that it was going to happen on a certain date, at seven o'clock, etc. But he might have expected it to happen. And I and all of us, as a matter of fact, including Prince Sh., thought that he would leave him a fortune! Terrible! terrible! I want you to understand, though, that I'm not accusing Radomsky of anything – please make no mistake about that – but the thing is suspicious all the same. It was a great shock to Prince Sh. It all happened so strangely.'

'But what's so suspicious about Radomsky's behaviour?'

'Nothing! Nothing at all! He behaved in a most honourable way. I wasn't hinting at anything. I don't think his own fortune is in any way affected. But, of course, Mrs Yepanchin won't listen to anything. But it's all these family upheavals, or rather squabbles and worries, or whatever you'd like to call them, that are such a confounded nuisance. You, my dear fellow, are a friend of the family in the true sense of the word, and I don't mind telling you that it appears now – though, mind, it's not at all certain – that about a month ago Radomsky proposed to Aglaya and that apparently he got a definite refusal from her.'

'Impossible!' cried the prince warmly.

'Why, do you know anything abut it? You see, my dear fellow,' went on the general, startled and surprised and stopping dead as though rooted to the spot, 'perhaps I shouldn't have told you that – I'm afraid it slipped out and – er – I really shouldn't, but, you see, I did it because you're – you're such a – er – such a nice fellow. You don't know anything particular about it, do you?'

'I know nothing about – Mr Radomsky,' muttered the prince.

'I don't, either. You see, my dear fellow, all they want is to dig a hole in the ground and bury me in it – yes, sir – and – and it never occurs to them how hard it is on a man and that I can't stand it. There's been such a terrible scene just now! I'm telling you this as if you were my own son. The awful thing about it is that Aglaya seems to be laughing at her mother. About her refusal of Radomsky's proposal a month ago and that she and Radomsky had a rather formal talk about it, we heard from her sisters as a surmise – though a pretty certain surmise. But then she's such an incredibly self-willed and fantastic creature! Great generosity, brilliant qualities of heart and mind – she may quite well possess them all, but at the same time she's capricious and sarcastic and, in short, a fiendish character and full of all sorts of quite fantastic notions to boot. She's just been laughing at her mother to her face, and at her sisters and Prince Sh. And as for me, she never does anything but laugh at me, but then I don't count. I love her, you know; I love her even when she laughs at me, and – I'm damned if that little she-devil doesn't love me specially for it. I mean, she seems to love me more than the others. I bet she's found something to laugh at in you too. I found you talking together after that stormy scene upstairs; she was sitting there with you as if nothing had happened.'

The prince flushed crimson and clenched his right hand, but said nothing.

'My dear, dear fellow,' the general suddenly said warmly and with feeling, 'I and – and Mrs Yepanchin (who, incidentally, has begun abusing you again, and me too on your account, though I'm damned if I know why), we both love you for all that; we love you very sincerely, and respect you, in spite of everything – I mean, in spite of all appearances. But you must admit, my dear boy, you must admit that it was a bit of a puzzle and a shock to us to hear that cold-blooded little she-devil (for she stood before her mother with a look of the deepest contempt for all our questions, and especially for mine; for, damn me, sir, I made a fool of myself and tried to be stern with her, for I'm head of the family, after all, and I made a fool of myself) – well, so that cold-blooded little she-devil suddenly declares with a laugh that that "mad woman" (that's what she said, and, you know, it does seem queer to me that she should agree with you: "Couldn't you have guessed it before?" she says) that that mad woman, she says, "has taken it into her head to marry me off to Prince Leo Nikolayevich at all costs and that's why she's trying to get Mr Radomsky driven out of our house." That's all she said. She refused to give any other explanation. She went on laughing, while we just sat gaping at her. She went out and slammed the door. Then I was told about that scene between you two this afternoon and – and – look here, my dear Prince, you're a sensible fellow, and you're not quick to take offence, I've noticed that about you, but – er, please, don't be angry – you see, she's just laughing at you. Like a child, mind you, and that's why you mustn't be angry with her. But believe me, that's what it certainly is. Don't think there's anything in it – she's simply making fun of you and all of us, because she has nothing better to do. Well, good-bye, my dear fellow. You know what our feelings towards you are, don't you? Our sincere feelings? They're unchangeable – they'll never change, under any circumstances, but – er – I must go that way – good-bye! I've not often been in such a fix (that's the expression, isn't it?) as I am now ... some summer holidays, what?'

Left alone at the cross-roads, the prince looked round, crossed the road quickly, went close up to the lighted window of a house, unfolded a little scrap of paper, which he had been squeezing tightly in his right hand during his conversation with the general, and read it in the faint beam of light:

> 'To-morrow at seven o'clock in the morning I shall be on the green seat in the park waiting for you. I have decided to discuss with you a highly important matter which concerns you directly.
>
> 'P.S. I hope you won't show this note to anyone. Although I'm sorry to be giving you instructions, I think you have to be told and I wrote it blushing with shame for your ridiculous character.
>
> 'P.P.S. It is the same green seat I pointed out to you this afternoon. Shame on you! I felt I had to add this, too.'

The note had been written in a hurry and folded anyhow, most probably before Aglaya came out on the veranda. The prince again clenched the piece of paper tightly in his hand, in indescribable excitement, indistinguishable from terror, and quickly leapt away from the lighted window, like a frightened thief; but as he did so, he collided violently with a gentleman who was standing close behind him.

'I've been following you, Prince,' said the gentleman.

'Is that you, Keller?' cried the prince in surprise.

'I've been looking for you, Prince. I've been waiting for you at the Yepanchins' house. I couldn't, of course, go in. I followed you while you were walking with the general. I'm at your service, Prince. Keller is at your disposal. I'm ready to do anything for you, even to die, if need be.'

'But – why?'

'Well, you know, you're sure to be challenged. That was Lieutenant

Molovtsov. I know him – not personally, of course – and he won't put up with an insult. People like us – I mean Rogozhin and myself – he's of course inclined to look upon as dirt, and perhaps quite rightly, too, so that you're the only one left to answer for what's happened. You'll have to foot the bill, Prince. I hear he's been making inquiries about you, and a friend of his will be sure to call on you to-morrow. For all I know, he may be already waiting for you now. If you do me the honour to choose me for your second, I shall be ready to be degraded to the ranks for you. That's why I've been looking for you, Prince.'

'So you too are talking of a duel!' The prince suddenly burst out laughing, to Keller's great astonishment.

He roared with laughter. Keller, who had been on tenterhooks until he had set his mind at rest by offering to be the prince's second, was almost offended by the prince's hearty laughter.

'But, I say, Prince, you caught him by the arms, you know. That's something no man of honour will put up with, especially in public.'

'And he gave me a push in the chest!' cried the prince, laughing. 'There's nothing for us to fight about. I'll apologize to him, and that's all. But if we have to fight, then fight we will! Let him take a shot at me – I don't mind. Ha, ha! I know how to load a pistol now. You see, I've just been taught how to load a pistol. Do you know how to load a pistol, Keller? First you must buy powder – gunpowder – but it mustn't be damp and it mustn't be as coarse as the sort they fire cannons with. Then you must first put in the powder, get some felt off a door, and shove the bullet in. But not the bullet before the powder, or it won't go off. Do you hear, Keller? Or it won't go off. Ha, ha! Isn't that a marvellous reason, my dear Keller? Oh, Keller, I feel like embracing and kissing you this very minute. Ha, ha, ha! How did you manage to pop up so suddenly before him this afternoon? Come to my house as soon as you can and we will have some champagne. We'll all get drunk! Did you know I had a dozen bottles of champagne in Lebedev's cellar? Lebedev sold me them the other day, the day after I moved into his house. He got them cheap, he said. I took the lot. I'll get the whole company together! You're not going to sleep to-night, are you?'

'Just as on any other night, Prince.'

'Well, pleasant dreams, then, ha, ha!'

The prince crossed the road and disappeared in the park, leaving the somewhat perplexed Keller to wonder what was the matter with him. He had never seen the prince in such a strange mood and, indeed, till that moment he could not have imagined him like that.

'A fever probably, because he's such a nervous chap, and all this has affected him, but of course he won't funk it. It's fellows like him who're never afraid – no, sir!' Keller thought to himself. 'H'm – champagne. Damn it, that's an interesting piece of news. A dozen bottles. Not bad – not bad at all – a well-stocked garrison. I bet Lebedev got the champagne as security from someone. H'm – a very nice fellow that prince – I like that sort of chap. Mustn't waste time, though, and if there is champagne, this is just the right moment for it!'

That the prince behaved as though he were in a fever was, of course, quite true.

He wandered a long time about the dark park and, finally, 'found himself' walking along an avenue. He vaguely remembered having already been in that avenue before and walking thirty or forty times from the seat to a tall, easily discernible old tree, a matter of a hundred yards or so. Even if he had tried, he could not remember what he had been thinking about during the hour at least he must have spent in the park. He did, however, catch himself thinking of something which made him suddenly shake with laughter: he could not help laughing, though there was nothing really to laugh at. It occurred to him that the idea of a duel might not have arisen in Keller's head only and that, consequently, the whole business of the loading of a pistol was perhaps not just an accident. 'Good Lord,' he thought, stopping dead suddenly as another idea dawned on him, 'she came down on the veranda when I was sitting in the corner, and she looked terribly surprised at finding me there and – burst out laughing and – talked about tea; and yet she had that piece of paper in her hand all the time, so that she must have known that I was sitting on the veranda – why then was she so surprised? Ha, ha, ha!'

He snatched the note out of his pocket and kissed it, but stopped at once and fell into thought:

'How odd it is! How odd!' he said a minute later, and there was a note of sadness in his voice. In moments of great joy he always felt sad, he did not know himself why. He looked round intently and was surprised to find himself there. He was very tired, and he went up to the seat and sat down. Everything was very still around. In the pleasure-gardens the music was over. There was probably not a soul in the park; of course, it was at least half past eleven. The night was quiet, warm, and clear – a Petersburg night in early June, but in the thick, shady park, in the avenue where he was sitting, it was almost dark.

If anyone had told him at that moment that he was in love, that he was passionately in love, he would have rejected the idea with surprise, and perhaps even with indignation. And if anyone had added that Aglaya's letter was a love-letter, an appointment for a love assignation, he would have blushed with shame for that man, and perhaps even challenged him to a duel. All this was perfectly sincere, and he never doubted it or admitted the presence of the slightest 'double' thought that this girl could possibly be in love with him or that he could possibly be in love with this girl. He would have been ashamed of such a thought! He would have thought it monstrous that anyone could be in love with him – with 'a man like him'. He could not help feeling that it was just a bit of innocent fun on her part, if there really was something in it; but he was somehow indifferent to the whole idea and thought it only too natural. It was something else that engrossed his thoughts and worried him. He fully believed the remark, dropped in his excitement by the general, about her laughing at everyone, and particularly at him, the prince. He did not feel in the least offended by it; in his view, it was as it should be. All he was concerned about was that he would see her again early to-morrow morning, that he would sit beside her on the green seat and listen to her telling him how to load a pistol and look at her. He wished for nothing more. He had wondered what she wanted to tell him and what was this 'important business' that concerned him directly. But he did not think of it now. Indeed, he did not feel in the least inclined to think of it.

The crunch of quiet footsteps on the sandy path of the avenue made him raise his head. A man, whose face it was hard to distinguish in the dark, came up to the seat and sat down beside him. The prince quickly drew near him, almost touching him, and recognized the pale face of Rogozhin.

'I knew you'd be walking about here somewhere,' Rogozhin muttered through his teeth. 'Didn't take me long to find you.'

It was the first time they had met since their encounter in the corridor of the hotel. Astonished at Rogozhin's sudden appearance, the prince could not collect his thoughts for some time, and a poignant sensation arose again in his heart. Rogozhin evidently understood the impression he had created; but though he was a bit disconcerted at first and spoke with an air of studied jauntiness, the prince soon realized that there was nothing studied about him and that he was not particularly embarrassed, either. If there was a certain awkwardness in his speech and gestures, it was only on the surface; deep down this man was always the same.

'How did you – find me here?' asked the prince in order to say something.

'Heard from Keller (I've just been to your place) that you'd gone to the park. Well, I thought to myself, so that's what it is.'

'What is what?' the prince repeated the words that had escaped him.

Rogozhin smiled, but offered no explanation.

'I got your letter, old man. It's no damn use, you know, and – why should you? And now I've come to you from *her*: she wants to see you badly. She's got something to tell you. Wants to see you to-night.'

'I'll come to-morrow. I'm going home now. Coming with – me?'

'What for? I've told you everything. Good-bye.'

'Are you sure you won't come?' the prince asked gently.

'You're a funny chap and no mistake. Surprised at you, I am.'

Rogozhin smiled venomously.

'What's so funny about me? And why do you hate me so much now?' the prince cried, sadly and warmly. 'You know very well now that all you imagined was not true. However, I had an idea that you still hated me, and do you know why? Because you tried to kill me. That's why you still hate me. I tell you the only Parfyon Rogozhin I remember is the man I exchanged crosses with that day. I wrote to you yesterday to forget all about that horrible nightmare and not to speak to me about it again. Why do you shun me? Why do you hide your hand from me? I tell you I look upon all that happened then simply as a nightmare: I know perfectly well what you had been through that day, just as if it had been myself. The things you imagined never existed and could not exist. Why, then, should there be this hatred between us?'

'You don't know what hatred is!' Rogozhin laughed again in reply to the prince's sudden, heated speech.

He really was shunning him, having moved two steps away from him and hidden his hands.

'It's not right for me to come and see you, old man,' he added slowly and sententiously, in conclusion.

'Do you hate me so much then?'

'I don't like you, old man, so why should I come and see you? Dear me, Prince, you're just like a child: when you want a toy, you must have it at once, but you don't understand things. You're only repeating what you wrote in your letter. Do you think I don't believe you? I believe every word you say, and I know that you've never deceived me and never will deceive me. But I don't like you, all the same. You write that you've forgotten everything, and only remember your brother Rogozhin, with whom you exchanged crosses, and not the Rogozhin who raised his knife against you. But how do you know my feelings?' Rogozhin smiled bitterly again. 'For all you know I've never once been sorry for what I done, and you've already sent me your brotherly forgiveness. Perhaps I was already thinking of something else that evening, and – –'

'Forgotten even to think about that!' the prince interrupted. 'Why, of course! And I bet you went straight to the station, came down here to Pavlovsk and looked for her in the crowd at the bandstand, just as you did to-day. That doesn't surprise me. Why, if you hadn't been in such a state then that you could only think of one thing, you wouldn't perhaps have raised your knife against me. ... As I looked at you that morning, I had a feeling that you were going to do it. Do you know what you were like then? The thought of it occurred to me already when we exchanged crosses. Why did you take me to your mother, then? Did you think that would hold back your hand? I don't think you did. You just felt as I did. We both felt the same. If you hadn't raised your hand against me then (which God averted), what would I have seemed to you *now*? For I did suspect you all the same. The fact is, we were both guilty! (Don't frown! What are you laughing at?) "I was not sorry!" Why, even if you wanted to you couldn't have been sorry, for apart from everything else, you don't like me. And even if I were as innocent in your sight as an angel, you would still not be able to stand me so long as you thought that she loved me and not you. That is, I suppose, what jealousy is like. But do you know what I've thought of this week, Parfyon? I'll tell you. Do you realize that she probably loves you now more than anyone else – so much, indeed, that the more she torments you the more she loves you. She won't tell you that, but one ought to be able to guess it. Why else, after all, is she going to marry you? She will tell you that one day herself. Some women want men to love them like that, and she's that sort of woman. Your love and your character must have impressed her strongly! Do you know that a woman is capable of inflicting unspeakable cruelties and mockeries on a man without once feeling any qualms of consience, because every time she is thinking to herself as she is looking at you: "I'm driving him to distraction now, but I shall make up for it later with my love. ..." '

Rogozhin broke into loud laughter as he listened to the prince.

'But haven't you, Prince, got into the clutches of just such a woman yourself? I've heard something about you – is it true?'

'What – what could you have heard?' the prince started suddenly and stopped short in great confusion.

Rogozhin went on laughing. He had listened to the prince not without interest, and perhaps not without some pleasure; the prince's joyous and burning fervour greatly impressed and encouraged him.

'Aye, I've not only heard of it,' he added. 'I can see for myself now that it's true. Well, when have you talked like this before? Why, this isn't your way of talking at all. If I hadn't heard all about you, I'd never have come here – in the park, at midnight.'

'I don't know what you're talking about, Parfyon.'

'She told me all about you a long time ago, and this afternoon I saw you myself sitting with that girl listening to the band. She swore to me yesterday and to-day that you was head over ears in love with Aglaya Yepanchin. It's all one to me, Prince, and it's none of my business: if you're no longer in love with her, she is still in love with you. You know, of course, that she wants you to marry that girl. She's set her mind on it, ha, ha! She says to me: "I won't marry you without that," she says; "when they've gone to church, we'll go to church." What's behind it I can't understand, and I never could understand: she either loves you as she never loved no one in her life or – but if she loves you, why does she want you to marry another? She says she wants to "see you happy", so she must love you.'

'I've told you and I've written to you that she is not – in her right mind,' said the prince, who had listened to Rogozhin with distress.

'Goodness knows – I daresay you may be wrong about it. She did, though, fix our wedding-day when I brought her home from the gardens this afternoon: "We shall most certainly get married," she says, "in three weeks' time and perhaps much sooner." She took an oath on it, she did. Took off the icon and kissed it. Well, it all depends on you now, Prince, so it seems, ha, ha!'

'That's all madness! What you've said about me now, will never happen – never! I'll come and see the two of you to-morrow.'

'How could she be mad?' Rogozhin observed. 'How could she be sane to everyone and mad to you alone? How could she write letters to her? If she's mad, they'd have noticed it there in her letters.'

'What letters?' the prince asked in dismay.

'She writes to *her*, to the girl, and *she* reads them. Don't you know? Well, you'll find out. She's sure to show them to you herself.'

'I don't believe it!' cried the prince.

'Oh dear, oh dear! I can see, old man, you've walked only a little way along that road. You're only just starting. Wait a bit: you'll be hiring private detectives, you'll be watching day and night, and you'll know every step she takes, if only – –'

'Drop it and never speak of that again!' cried the prince. 'Listen, Parfyon, I was taking a walk before you came and suddenly began laughing – I don't know what there was to laugh about, but, you see, the reason was that I remembered that to-morrow was my birthday. It seems to have come at the right moment. It's almost twelve o'clock now. Come, let's celebrate the occasion! I have some wine; let's drink. Wish for me what I don't know now what to wish for myself, and I want you particularly to wish it for me, and I shall wish all happiness to you. If not, give me back my cross! You didn't send back my cross next day, did you? You've still got it on? You have, haven't you?'

'Yes,' said Rogozhin.

'Well, then, come along. I don't want to meet my new life without you. For my new life has started to-day, hasn't it?'

'Yes, now I can see for myself that it has. I shall tell *her* so. You're not quite yourself, old man!'

4

As he approached his house with Rogozhin, the prince was greatly surprised to see that a large and noisy company was gathered on the veranda, which was brightly lighted. They were all laughing merrily, shouting and even arguing at the top of their voices; they seemed, at the first glance, to be having a rollicking good time. And, to be sure, when he mounted the steps leading to the veranda, he saw that they were all drinking champagne, which they seemed to have been doing for some time, for many of the revellers had managed to become quite agreeably exhilarated. All the guests were known to the prince, but it was strange that they should have come all at once, as if by invitation, though the prince had not invited anyone of them, and he had only himself recollected by chance that it was his birthday.

'You must have told someone you'd treat him to a glass of champagne, so they've all turned up,' Rogozhin muttered, as he came up on the veranda after the prince. 'I know all about that! You've only got to whistle to them – –' he added almost angrily, remembering, no doubt, his own recent past.

They all welcomed the prince with shouts and congratulations, and surrounded him. Some of them were very noisy, others much quieter, but they all hastened to congratulate him, having heard of his birthday, and everyone waited his turn. The presence of certain persons aroused the prince's interest, for instance, Burdovsky's; but the most astonishing thing was that among the whole of this company the prince suddenly noticed Radomsky; he could hardly believe his eyes and, on seeing him, was very nearly frightened.

Meantime Lebedev, flushed and almost ecstatic, ran up to offer explanations; he was very much 'overcome'. From his chatter it appeared that they had all assembled quite naturally and, in fact, by chance. First, towards the evening, Ippolit had arrived and, feeling much better, had expressed the wish to wait for the prince on the veranda. He made himself comfortable on the sofa; then Lebedev had come in to keep him company, and he was followed by all his household – that is, by his daughters and General Ivolgin. Burdovsky had come with Ippolit, having accompanied him. Ganya and Ptitsyn seemed to have dropped in a little later on, passing by, their appearance coinciding with the incident at the pleasure-gardens. Then Keller had arrived, told them about the prince's birthday and asked for champagne. Radomsky had arrived only half an hour ago. Kolya had insisted most firmly on the champagne being served and on having a birthday party. Lebedev had readily brought out the champagne.

'But my own, my own,' he babbled to the prince. 'At my own expense to wish you many happy returns of the day. We shall also have some refreshments, some snacks; my daughter is looking after that. But, Prince, if only you knew what they're discussing. Remember Hamlet's to be or not to be? It's a modern subject, sir, a modern subject! Questions and answers. ... And Mr Terentyev doesn't think of going to bed, sir. He only had a tiny drop of champagne. Just one sip, sir. It won't hurt him. ... Come closer, sir, and settle it! They were all waiting for you. They were only waiting for your ready wit. ...'

The prince noticed the sweet and affectionate glance of Vera Lebedev, who was also trying to get to him through the crowd. Disregarding them all, he held out his hand to her first. She flushed with pleasure and wished him 'many happy returns of the day *from now on*'. Then she rushed back to the kitchen; there she was getting the refreshments ready; but even before the arrival of the prince she had appeared on the veranda as soon as she could spare a minute from her work to listen eagerly to the heated discussions about the most abstract and strange subject she had ever heard of before, which went on without interruption among the somewhat tipsy guests. Her younger sister, who had listened open-mouthed to the discussion, was asleep on a chest in the next room, but the boy, Lebedev's son, was standing beside Kolya and Ippolit and the look on his excited face showed that he was ready to stand there for another ten hours, listening and enjoying himself.

'I have been waiting for you particularly, and I'm awfully glad you've come looking so happy,' said Ippolit when the prince went up to shake hands with him immediately after Vera.

'And how do you know that I am so "happy"?'

'I can see it by your face. Say how-do-you-do to the others, and come and sit here beside us. I've been waiting for you particularly,' he added, emphasizing the fact that he had been waiting.

To the prince's question whether it was not bad for him to be sitting up so late, he replied that he could not help being surprised himself how three days ago he was expecting to die, for he had never felt better in his life than that evening.

Burdovsky jumped up and murmured that he was there by sheer chance, that he had brought Ippolit down from town, and that he was also very glad; that he had written a lot of 'nonsense' in his letter and that now he was 'glad simply to – –' Without finishing the sentence, he shook the prince's hand warmly and sat down again.

Last of all the prince went up to Radomsky, who at once took hold of his arm.

'I've only a couple of words to say to you,' he murmured in an undertone, 'about a highly important matter. Let's leave them for a moment.'

'A couple of words,' another voice whispered in his other ear, and another hand took hold of his arm on the other side.

The prince was surprised to see a terribly dishevelled man with a red, winking, and laughing face, whom he at once recognized as Ferdyshchenko, who had appeared from goodness only knew where.

'Remember Ferdyshchenko?' he asked.

'Where have you sprung from?' cried the prince.

'He'd like to apologize to you!' cried Keller, running up. 'He was hiding. He didn't want to come out to you. He was hiding in that corner. He'd very much like to apologize to you, Prince. He feels guilty.'

'What of? What of, for goodness sake?'

'It was I who met him, Prince. I've just met him and brought him here. He's one of my friends I don't often meet, but he's sorry.'

'I'm very glad, gentlemen. Will you, please, go and sit down with the others; I'll be with you soon.' The prince, anxious to hear what Radomsky had to say, got rid of them at last.

'It is very entertaining here,' Radomsky said, 'and I've quite enjoyed the half-hour I've been waiting for you. But, look here, my dear fellow, I've settled everything with Kurmyshov and I've come to set your mind at rest. You needn't worry. He's taken a very sensible view of the affair, particularly as, in my opinion, it was his fault entirely.'

'What Kurmyshov?'

'Why, the fellow you caught by the arms this afternoon. He was so furious that he wanted to send his seconds to you to-morrow.'

'Good heavens! What nonsense!'

'Of course, it's nonsense, and the whole thing would have come to nothing, but here these people – –'

'Are you sure you haven't come for something else too?'

'Oh, of course I have,' Radomsky laughed. 'You see, my dear Prince, I shall be leaving for Petersburg early to-morrow morning about that unhappy business (I mean, my uncle, of course). Just imagine, it's all true, and everybody knew about it except myself. It was such a shock to me that I hadn't any time to call on them (the Yepanchins). I shan't be able to be there to-morrow, either; for, you see, I shall be in Petersburg. I may not be here for three days – I'm afraid my affairs are rather in a mess just now. Though the whole thing is not so frightfully important, I decided to have a very frank talk with you about something, and without more delay – I mean, before I leave for Petersburg. I propose to stay here, if I may, till your company has gone. I've nowhere else to go, anyway. I'm so upset that I just couldn't go to bed. And – last but not least – though it's shameful and indecent to pursue a man like this, I must be quite frank with you, my dear Prince, and tell you that I've come to ask for your friendship. You're an admirable person – I mean, you don't tell a lie at every turn, and perhaps never, and I want a friend and adviser badly in a certain matter, for I'm really and truly one of the unfortunate ones now. ...'

He laughed again.

'You see,' the prince said after a moment's thought, 'the trouble is that if you're going to wait till they've gone, goodness only knows when that will be. Wouldn't it be better if we went for a walk in the park? I'm sure they'll wait. I'll excuse myself.'

'No, no, don't do that. I have my own reasons. I don't want them to suspect that we have something special to discuss. There are people here who're very interested in our relationship. Don't you know that, Prince? And it would be much better if they saw that we were on the most friendly terms without any special reason for it. Do you understand? They'll be gone in another two hours, and I'll only take up twenty minutes or at most half an hour of your time. ...'

'Why, of course, do stay. I'm very glad to have you here even without any explanations. And I must thank you for your kind words about our friendly relationship. You must excuse me for being absent-minded to-day. You know, I cannot give my full attention at a moment like this.'

'I see, I see,' Radomsky murmured with a faint laugh.

He was ready to laugh at anything that evening.

'What do you see?' asked the prince with a start.

'Why, my dear Prince,' Radomsky said with another laugh, not answering the prince's direct question, 'don't you suspect that I've simply come to cheat you and, in passing, find something out from you?'

'That you've come to find something out I have no doubt at all' – the prince, too, laughed at last – 'and quite possibly you have also decided to deceive me a little. But do you really believe that it will make any difference so far as I'm concerned? And – and – and as I'm absolutely convinced that you're an excellent fellow for all that, we shall perhaps end up by really becoming friends. I like you very much, Mr Radomsky. You – you are a very decent fellow in my opinion.'

'Oh well,' Radomsky concluded, 'it's very nice to have any kind of business dealings with you, anyway. Come, I'll drink a glass to your health. I'm awfully glad I turned to you. I say' – he stopped short suddenly – 'that Mr Ippolit hasn't come to stay with you, has he?'

'Yes, he has.'

'He's not going to die soon, is he?'

'Why?'

'Oh, nothing. I've spent half an hour with him here. ...'

Ippolit had all this time been waiting for the prince, and kept watching him and Radomsky while they had been having their talk apart from the rest. He grew feverishly animated when they came up to the table. He was restless and agitated; beads of perspiration stood out on his forehead. Besides a continuous sort of roving disquiet, his glittering eyes expressed also a sort of vague impatience; his eyes shifted aimlessly from object to object, and from face to face. Though till then he had taken an active part in the noisy general conversation, his animation was clearly feverish; he did not really pay any attention to the conversation itself: his arguments were incoherent, jeering, and carelessly paradoxical; he broke off in the middle of a sentence and did not finish what he had begun with feverish heat a minute before.

The prince learnt with surprise and regret that Ippolit had been allowed to drink two glasses of champagne, and that the half-empty glass before him was the third. But he found it out later; at the present moment he was not very observant.

'Do you know,' cried Ippolit, 'that I'm particularly glad that it's your birthday to-day.'

'Why?'

'You will see. Please sit down. To begin with, because all this – crowd of your friends have come here to-night. I had an idea there'd be a crowd of people. For the first time in my life my expectations have been justified. I'm sorry I didn't know it was your birthday, or I'd have brought you a present. ... Ha, ha! But perhaps I have! How long is it before daylight?'

'It's less than two hours now to sunrise,' observed Ptitsyn, looking at his watch.

'What do you want the sunrise for, when you can read outdoors without it?' someone observed.

'I want it because I must see the rim of the sun – just the rim. Can you drink the health of the sun, Prince? What do you think?'

Ippolit put his question peremptorily, addressing everyone unceremoniously, as though he were giving orders, but he did not seem to be aware of it himself.

'Let's drink to it, if you like. But you must take it easy, Ippolit, mustn't you?'

'Oh, you're always talking about sleep – you are my nurse, Prince! As soon as the sun appears and "resounds in the sky" (who was it said in a poem: "in the sky the sun resounded"? It makes no sense, but it's excellent!), I'll go to bed. Lebedev, the sun is the spring of life, isn't it? What's the meaning of "the waters of life" in the Apocalypse? Have you heard about the "star that is called Wormwood", Prince?'

'I've heard that Lebedev identifies the "star that is called Wormwood" with the network of railways spread all over Europe.'

'No, gentlemen, please; that's impossible!' cried Lebedev, jumping up and waving his arms about, as though wishing to stop the outburst of general laughter. 'Please, gentlemen! With these people – these people are all' – he suddenly turned to the prince – 'you see, on certain points it's like this,' and he brought his fist down twice on the table unceremoniously, which merely intensified the laughter.

Though Lebedev was in his usual 'evening condition', he was on this occasion too excited and exasperated by the long 'learned' discussion that had preceded the arrival of the prince, and in all such cases his attitude towards his opponents was one of infinite and undisguised contempt.

'It isn't that at all, sir. Half an hour ago, Prince, we agreed not to interrupt and not to laugh while anyone was speaking. We agreed that he should be given full freedom to say all he had to say, and let the atheists answer him then, if they liked. We chose the general as our chairman – that's what we did, sir! For what do you suppose would happen otherwise? Why, anyone can be shouted down while expressing some lofty idea, sir, some profound idea, sir!'

'Speak, speak!' shouted several voices. 'No one is interrupting you!'

'Speak, but keep to the point.'

'What is this "star that is called Wormwood"?' someone cried.

'I've no idea!' replied General Ivolgin, resuming his seat as chairman with an important air.

'I like these arguments and disputations awfully, Prince – I mean, intellectual ones, of course,' muttered Keller, fidgeting in his chair impatiently and in a state of absolute rapture. 'Intellectual and political,' he added, turning suddenly and unexpectedly to Radomsky, who was sitting almost next to him. 'You know, I love reading in the papers about the English Parliament. I – I don't mean what they're discussing there (I'm afraid I'm no politician), but the way they talk to each other, the way they behave like politicians: "the noble viscount sitting opposite", "the noble earl who shares my opinion", "my honourable opponent who has astonished Europe by his proposal" – I mean, all those flowery expressions, all this parliamentary procedure of a free people; that's what's so fascinating to a chap like me! It fascinates me, Prince. I've always been an artist at heart. I swear I have, Mr Radomsky.'

'You don't mean to say,' Ganya cried warmly in another corner of the room, 'you don't mean to say – do you – that railways are a curse, that they are the ruin of humanity, that they are a plague that has descended upon the earth to pollute the "waters of life"?'

Ganya was in a particularly exhilarated mood that evening, in a gay and almost triumphant mood, as it seemed to the prince. He was, of course, pulling Lebedev's leg, egging him on, but soon he grew excited himself.

'Not the railways – no, sir!' retorted Lebedev, losing his temper and at the same time enjoying himself immensely. 'The railways will not pollute the waters of life by themselves alone; but the whole thing, sir, is damned, the whole spirit of the last few centuries, taken as a whole, sir, in its scientific and practical application, is perhaps really damned, sir!'

'Is it really damned, or only perhaps?' Radomsky queried. 'You see, in a case like this it is rather important to know which it is.'

'Damned, damned, really damned!' Lebedev asserted vehemently.

'Don't be in such a hurry, Lebedev,' Ptitsyn observed with a smile. 'You're much more good-natured in the morning.'

'But much more outspoken in the evening – much more sincere and more outspoken, sir!' Lebedev cried, turning to him heatedly. 'More simple-minded and more exact, more honest, and more honourable, and though I may expose myself to your attack, I don't care a damn, sir! I challenge you all now, all you atheists: how are you going to save the world and where have you found the right way for it, you men of science, industry, mutual associations, fair wages, and so on? How? By credit? What is credit? What will credit lead you to?'

'You are an inquisitive fellow, aren't you?' observed Radomsky.

'Well, sir, it is my opinion that a man who is not interested in such questions is a good-for-nothing society loafer.'

'At least it leads to solidarity and a balance of interests,' observed Ptitsyn.

'And that is all! That's all! Without admitting any moral reasons except the satisfaction of individual egoism and material necessity! Universal peace, universal happiness – of necessity! Is that, if I may ask, what you mean, my dear sir?'

'But the universal necessity of living, eating, and drinking and the fullest – scientific, of course – recognition that you will never satisfy those necessities without universal association and solidarity of interests, is, I think, a strong enough idea to serve as a basis and as "waters of life" for future generations of mankind,' Ganya observed, excited in good earnest.

'The necessity of eating and drinking or, in other words, the instinct of self-preservation. ...'

'But isn't the instinct of self-preservation enough? Why, the instinct of self-preservation is the normal law of humanity.'

'Who told you that?' Radomsky cried suddenly. 'It's true it is a law, but no more normal than the law of destruction, and perhaps of self-destruction, too. Surely, self-preservation is not the whole normal law of mankind?'

'Aha!' cried Ippolit, turning quickly to Radomsky and scrutinizing him with wild curiosity.

But seeing that Radomsky was laughing, he began laughing himself, nudged Kolya, who was standing beside him, and asked him again what time it was, and even took hold of Kolya's silver watch himself and looked at it eagerly. Then, as though forgetting everything, he stretched himself out on the sofa, put his hands behind his head, and stared at the ceiling; half a minute later he was already sitting at the table again, drawing himself up and listening to the chatter of Lebedev, who was in a state of tremendous excitement.

'A crafty and ironical idea, a pernicious idea!' cried Lebedev, eagerly catching up Radomsky's paradox. 'An idea aimed at provoking opponents to a fight, but a true idea! Because you're an aristocratic scoffer and cavalry officer (though not without brains), you don't realize yourself how profound your idea is – how true it is! Yes, sir. The law of destruction and the law of self-preservation are equally strong in humanity! The devil holds equal dominion over humanity until a date in the far-off future still unknown to us. You're laughing? You don't believe in the devil? Disbelief in the devil is a French idea. It is a flippant idea. Do you know who the devil is? Do you know what his name is? Not knowing even his name, you laugh at his exterior form, following the example of Voltaire, at his hoofs, his tail, and horns, which you have invented yourselves, for the evil spirit is a great and ruthless spirit, but he has not the hoofs and horns you have invented for him. But it isn't a question of him now.'

'How do you know it isn't?' cried Ippolit suddenly, and burst out laughing as though in hysterics.

'A clever and insinuating thought,' Lebedev said approvingly, 'but once again, that's not the question under discussion. Our question is whether the "waters of life" have grown weaker or not with the increase of – –'

'Railways?' cried Kolya.

'Not of railway communications, my young but hot-tempered youth, but of the whole tendency, of which the railways may serve, as it were, as an illustration, as an artistic expression. They hustle, they roar, they rend the air with their noise, they hurry, they say, for the happiness of mankind. "People are getting too noisy and commercial," some recluse of a thinker complains, "there is little spiritual peace." "That may be so," triumphantly answers him another thinker, who is always on the move, "but the rumble of the carts bringing bread to starving humanity is perhaps better than spiritual peace," and he walks away from him conceitedly. But, vile man that I am, I do not believe in the carts that bring bread to humanity! For carts bringing bread to all humanity without a moral basis for that action, may quite deliberately exclude a considerable part of humanity from the enjoyment of what they bring, which has happened already.'

'The carts can quite deliberately exclude?' someone put in.

'Which has happened already,' Lebedev repeated without vouchsafing an answer to the question. 'We've already had Malthus, the friend of humanity. But a friend of humanity whose moral principles are shaky is a destroyer of humanity, to say nothing of his vanity: for you have only to wound the vanity of any one of these innumerable friends of humanity, and he is at once ready to set fire to the world out of a feeling of petty revenge, like any one of us and, to be fair, like myself, the vilest of all, for I will perhaps be the first to supply the fuel and run away myself. But again that's not the point.'

'What is it, then?'

'You make me tired!'

'The point lies in the following anecdote of long ago, for I simply have to tell you this anecdote that happened many centuries ago. In our times and in our country – which, I hope, gentlemen, you love as dearly as I do, for so far as I'm concerned I'm ready to shed my last drop of blood – –'

'Go on, go on!'

'In our country, as well as in the rest of Europe, mankind is regularly visited by terrible famines, and as far as I can remember and as far as it can be calculated, this happens at least once in a quarter of a century or, in other words, once every twenty-five years. I can't vouch for the figures, but comparatively very rarely.'

'Compared with what?'

'With the twelfth century and with those immediately before and after it. For in those days, as writers assert, widespread famines occurred once in two years, or at any rate once in three years, so that in such emergencies people resorted to cannibalism, though they kept it secret. As he was approaching old age, one of these ne'er-do-wells announced, of his own free will and without being forced to, that in the course of his long and starving life he had killed and consumed by himself and in dead secret sixty monks and several lay infants, about six and no more – that is to say, extraordinarily few compared with the number of ecclesiastics he had consumed. Grown-up laymen, it appears, he never attempted to approach with that object.'

'That is impossible!' cried the chairman himself, the general, in almost a hurt voice. 'I often talk and argue with him, gentlemen, and always about such things. But more often than not he talks such nonsense that one gets sick of listening to him – not a shred of truth!'

'Remember the siege of Kars, General, and you, gentlemen, had better know that my story is the naked truth. For my part, I will merely observe that almost every reality, though it has its immutable laws, is almost always incredible and improbable. In fact, the more real it is, the more improbable it sometimes appears to be.'

'But how could he eat sixty monks?' they objected, laughing all round him.

'That he didn't eat them all at once is obvious, but that he had eaten them in the course of fifteen or twenty years is absolutely comprehensible and natural. ...'

'And natural?'

'And natural!' Lebedev parried with pedantic obstinacy. 'Besides, a Catholic monk is by his very nature easily influenced and inquisitive, and it is very easy to entice him into a wood or some secluded spot and then deal with him as aforesaid. But all the same I don't dispute that the number of persons consumed seems excessive to the point of incontinence.'

'It is perhaps quite true, gentlemen,' observed the prince suddenly.

Till then he had listened to the disputants in silence, without attempting to take part in the conversation, often joining heartily in the outbursts of general laughter. It was clear that he was very glad that his party was so noisy and gay; even that they were drinking so much. Perhaps he would not have uttered a word the whole evening, but for some reason he suddenly took it into his head to speak. He spoke in so serious a voice that everyone at once turned to him with interest.

'What I'm driving at, gentlemen, is that in those days such famines were frequent. I have heard about it, too, though I don't know history very well. But apparently it must have been like that. When I found myself among the Swiss mountains I marvelled greatly at the ruins of the old feudal castles built on the slopes of the mountains, on steep precipitous cliffs, at least half a mile high (which means several miles by mountain paths). Everyone knows what a castle is like: it is a whole mountain of stones – a dreadful, impossible task! And, of course, it was built by poor people, the vassals. They had, besides, to pay all sorts of taxes and provide for the priesthood. How could they provide for themselves and till the land? There were not many of them in those days, and hundreds of them probably died of starvation, and they literally may not have had anything to eat. Sometimes I couldn't help wondering how this people had not ceased to exist altogether and how, if any calamity had befallen them, they had managed to overcome it and survive. Lebedev is no doubt right in saying that there were cannibals among them. What I don't understand is why he dragged in monks and what he means by that.'

'No doubt because in the twelfth century one could only eat monks, for monks were the only people who were fat,' Ganya observed.

'A most brilliant and true idea!' cried Lebedev, 'for, indeed, he never laid his hands on laymen. Sixty ecclesiastics and not one layman – a frightful thought, an historical thought, a statistical thought, in fine, and it is out of such facts that history is reconstructed by experts; for it follows with mathematical exactitude that in those days the priesthood lived at least sixty times more happily and contentedly than the rest of mankind. And quite likely it was sixty times as fat as the rest of mankind. ...'

'An exaggeration, a gross exaggeration, Lebedev!' they roared with laughter all round him.

'I agree that it is an historical thought, but what are you driving at?' the prince went on asking. (He spoke so seriously and with such an absence of any desire to laugh or jeer at Lebedev, at whom everyone else was laughing, that among the general tone of the company his tone could not but sound comic; a few minutes later they began laughing at him, too, but he did not notice it.)

'Don't you see he's a lunatic, Prince?' said Radomsky, bending over him. 'I was told here a short time ago that he is obsessed with the idea of being a lawyer and delivering forensic speeches and that he wants to sit for an examination. I am expecting a splendid parody.'

'I'm leading up to a tremendous conclusion,' Lebedev thundered meanwhile. 'But, to begin with, let us examine the psychological and juridical position of the criminal. We see that the criminal or, so to speak, my client, in spite of the impossibility of finding other kinds of food, has several times during his interesting career shown a desire to repent and given up his clerical diet. We see this clearly from the facts: for it is recorded that he did consume five or six infants – a comparatively insignificant number, but remarkable from another point of view. It is obvious that, tormented by terrible remorse (for my client is a religious man and acts according to the dictates of his conscience, which I intend to prove) and desirous of reducing his sin as much as possible, he by way of an experiment changed his monkish diet six times for a lay diet. That he did so by way of experiment is again beyond doubt; for if it were only for the sake of gastronomic variety, the figure six would be too insignificant: why only six and not thirty? (I take half – half of the one and half of the other.) But if it were only an experiment, undertaken out of sheer despair and the fear of sacrilege and of offending the Church, then the figure six becomes all too intelligible; for six experiments for the sake of satisfying one's conscience are quite sufficient, because the experiments might not have come off. And in my opinion an infant is, to begin with, too small – that is to say, not big in size, so that during a given period of time he would need three to five times as many lay infants as ecclesiastics, so that the sin, though lessened on the one hand, would be increased on the other, in quantity, if not quality. In arguing thus, gentlemen, I am of course merely trying to find out what is going on in the heart of a criminal of the twelfth century. So far as I am concerned, as a man of the nineteenth century, I might have reasoned differently, which I should like you to take into consideration so that you need not grin at me, gentlemen; as for you, General, it is most unbecoming to grin at me like that. Secondly, in my personal opinion, an infant is not sufficiently nutritious, and is perhaps too cloying and sweet, so that, without satisfying your appetite, it only leaves you with your qualms of conscience. Now I come to the conclusion, the finish, gentlemen, the finale which contains the solution of one of the greatest problems of that age and of our own! The criminal ends up by going and laying information against himself with the clergy and by giving himself up to the authorities. Now one cannot help asking oneself what tortures awaited him in that age – the wheel, the stake, and the fire! Who induced him to go and inform against himself? Why not simply stop at the figure of sixty and keep the secret till his dying day? Why not simply leave the monks alone and live in penance as a hermit? Or why not, finally, become a monk himself? Well, here is the solution! There must have therefore been something stronger than the stake and even the habits of twenty years! There must have been an idea stronger than any calamity, famine, torture, plague, leprosy, and all that hell which mankind could not have endured without that idea that bound and guided men's hearts and fructified the waters of life! Show me anything resembling that force in our age of lies and railways – I'm sorry, I ought to have said in our age of liners and railways, but I said liars and railways because I'm drunk but just. Now, show me an idea that binds mankind together to-day with half the strength that it had in those centuries. And would you go so far as to say that the waters of life had not weakened and become polluted beneath this "star", under this network in which men are entangled? And don't try to frighten me with your prosperity, your riches, the infrequency of famine, and the rapidity of the means of communication! There is more wealth, but less strength; the binding idea is no more; everything has become soft, everything is flabby, and everyone is flabby. We've all, all, all grown flabby. But enough; that's not the point now. The point, my highly respected Prince, is that we have to see about getting some nice little refreshments ready for your visitors, isn't it?'

Lebedev, who had aroused some of his listeners to positive indignation (it should be noted that the bottles were being opened all the time without interruption), at once pacified all his opponents by the unexpected conclusion of his speech. He called such a conclusion 'a clever legal twist'. Merry laughter rang out again and the visitors brightened up; they all rose from the table to stretch their legs on the veranda. Only Keller was still dissatisfied with Lebedev's speech, and was greatly excited.

'He attacks education, preaches the wild fanaticism of the twelfth century, pulls faces, and not in the simplicity of his soul, either. Where did he get the money to buy himself this house, may I ask?' he said aloud, stopping all and sundry.

'I knew a real interpreter of the Apocalypse,' the general was saying in another corner to other listeners, among them Ptitsyn, whom he had buttonholed, 'the late Grigory Semyonovich Burmistrov, who, as it were, curdled your blood. To begin with, he would put on his spectacles, open up a large ancient tome in a black leather binding. And – well, he had a big grey beard and two medals for his charitable works. He would begin sternly and severely; generals would bow down before him and ladies fainted. And this fellow here ends up with refreshments! It's disgraceful!'

Ptitsyn listened to the general and smiled. He seemed on the point of picking up his hat, but could not apparently make up his mind, or kept forgetting his intention. Ganya had suddenly left off drinking and pushed away his glass before they had got up from the table: a dark shadow seemed to have passed over his face. When they all got up from the table, he went up to Rogozhin and sat down beside him. One might have supposed that they were on the friendliest terms. Rogozhin, who, too, at first had several times been on the point of leaving quietly, was now sitting motionless, with his head bowed, apparently having forgotten that he had intended to go away. He had not drunk a drop of wine all evening and was very thoughtful; only occasionally did he raise his eyes and scrutinize everyone. Now it looked as though he were waiting for something of great importance to happen to him here and had decided not to go away till then.

The prince had drunk two or three glasses and was only feeling a little cheerful. As he rose from the table, he caught Radomsky's eye, remembered the talk they were to have, and smiled affably at him. Radomsky nodded to him, and suddenly pointed to Ippolit, whom he had been observing intently at that moment. Ippolit was asleep, stretched out on the sofa.

'Why, tell me,' he said suddenly with such undisguised vexation and even anger that the prince was surprised, 'why has this wretched boy forced himself upon you? I bet he's up to no good.'

'I've noticed,' said the prince, 'at least it seems to me that you're very interested in him to-day. Am I right?'

'You may as well add that in my present position I have something to worry about myself so that I can't help being surprised at not being able to take my eyes off his detestable face all the evening.'

'He has a handsome face.'

'Look, look!' cried Radomsky, pulling at the prince's arm. 'Look!'

The prince gazed at Radomsky again with surprise.

5

Ippolit, who had suddenly fallen asleep on the sofa at the end of Lebedev's harangue, now as suddenly woke up, just as though someone had jabbed him in the ribs, gave a start, raised himself, looked round, and turned pale; he was gazing round in a sort of terror; but no sooner had the look of horror come into his face than he remembered and realized everything.

'What? Are they going home? Is it over? Is everything over? Has the sun risen?' he kept asking agitatedly, clutching at the prince's hand. 'What time is it? For God's sake what is the time? I have overslept myself. Have I been asleep long?' he added, almost with a look of despair, as though he had missed something on which his whole life at least depended.

'You've been asleep seven or eight minutes,' replied Radomsky.

Ippolit cast an eager look at him and pondered for a few seconds.

'Oh, is that all? So that I – –'

And he drew a long, deep breath of relief, as though casting off a heavy load. He realized at last that nothing 'was over', that the sun had not risen yet, that the guests had got up from the table only for a snack, and that only Lebedev's chatter had come to an end. He smiled, and a hectic flush, in the shape of two bright spots, appeared on his cheeks.

'You seem to have been counting the minutes while I was asleep, Mr Radomsky,' he cried ironically. 'You haven't taken your eyes off me all evening – I have noticed that. Oh, Rogozhin! I've been dreaming about him just now,' he whispered to the prince, frowning and nodding in the direction of Rogozhin, who was sitting at the table. 'Oh, yes,' he went off at a tangent again suddenly, 'where's our orator? Where's Lebedev? So Lebedev has finished, has he? What was he talking about? Is it true, Prince, that you once said that the world would be saved by "beauty"? Gentlemen,' he shouted in a loud voice to all the company, 'the prince says that the world will be saved by beauty! And I maintain that the reason he has such playful ideas is that he is in love. Gentlemen, the prince is in love. I could see that as soon as he came in. Don't blush, Prince, or I shall be sorry for you. What sort of beauty will save the world? Kolya told me that. ... You're a zealous Christian, aren't you? Kolya says you call yourself a Christian.'

The prince looked attentively at him and made no answer.

'You don't answer? You don't by any chance think that I like you, do you?' Ippolit suddenly added, as though the words had escaped him against his will.

'No, I don't think so. I know you don't like me.'

'Do you? Even after yesterday? Wasn't I honest with you yesterday?'

'Yesterday, too, I knew you didn't like me.'

'You mean, because I envy you – envy you? You always thought so, and you think so now, but – but why am I telling you this? I'd like some more champagne – please fill my glass, Keller.'

'You mustn't drink any more, Ippolit. I won't let you.'

And the prince moved the glass away.

'Well, perhaps you're right,' Ippolit at once agreed, as though thinking it over. 'They might say – but what the hell do I care what they say? Am I right? Am I right? Let them say what they damn well like afterwards – isn't that so, Prince? And what does anyone of us care what happens *afterwards*? But I don't think I'm quite awake. What a terrible dream I had. I've only just remembered it. I should hate you to have such dreams, Prince, though perhaps I don't really like you. Still, there's no reason why you should wish a man ill because you don't like him, is there? Why do I keep on asking questions – always asking questions? Give me your hand – let me press it warmly – so. ... You have held out your hand to me, though, haven't you? So you must have known that I would press it sincerely, mustn't you? No, I don't think I will drink any more. What's the time? Don't bother, though; I know what time it is. The hour is at hand! Now is the time. What are they doing there in that corner? Laying the table for refreshments? So this table is free, isn't it? Excellent! Gentlemen, I – but they're not listening – I intend to read an article, Prince. Refreshments are, of course, much more interesting, but – –'

And suddenly, quite unexpectedly, he pulled out of his breast coat pocket a large manuscript, sealed with a large red seal. He put it on the table in front of him.

This unexpected development produced a great effect on the company, which was not prepared for it, or rather which was *prepared*, but not for that. Radomsky even started in his chair; Ganya moved quickly to the table; Rogozhin did the same, but with a sort of peevish annoyance, as though understanding what it was all about. Lebedev, who happened to be near, came up and gazed with his inquisitive little eyes at the manuscript, as though trying to guess what it was about.

'What have you got there?' the prince asked uneasily.

'I shall go to bed as soon as the rim of the sun appears over the horizon, Prince. I've said so. Cross my heart: you'll see!' cried Ippolit. 'But – but do you really think that I cannot bring myself to break the seal?' he added, looking at everyone in turn defiantly, and as though not caring whom he was addressing.

The prince noticed that he was trembling all over.

'None of us ever thought so,' the prince replied for all. 'And why do you suppose that anyone should think so? And what a strange idea to read to us now! What have you got there, Ippolit?'

'What has he got there? What's the matter with him again?' they were asking on all sides.

They all came up to the table, some of them still eating; the manuscript with the red seal drew them all like a magnet.

'I wrote this myself yesterday after I'd given you my word, Prince, that I'd come and stay with you. I spent all day yesterday and all night writing, and I finished it this morning. Early this morning I had a dream. ...'

'Don't you think we'd better leave it till to-morrow?' the prince interrupted timidly.

'To-morrow "there will be time no longer!"' Ippolit laughed hysterically. 'But don't worry. It won't take me more than forty minutes to read – oh, an hour at most. ... And you see how interested they all are. They've all come up, they're all staring at my seal, and if I hadn't sealed my manuscript there would have been no sensation. Ha, ha! There's nothing like a mystery! Shall I break the seal, gentlemen?' he shouted, laughing his strange laugh and gazing at them with glittering eyes. 'A mystery! A mystery! And do you remember, Prince, who it was who proclaimed that "there shall be time no longer"? It was proclaimed by the great and mighty angel in the Apocalypse.'

'Better not read it!' Radomsky suddenly cried, but with an uneasiness so uncharacteristic of him that many people thought it strange.

'Don't read it!' cried the prince, laying his hand on the manuscript.

'Reading? We're eating now!' someone observed.

'An article? For a periodical?' another inquired.

'It won't be boring, will it?' added a third.

'What is it all about?' inquired the rest.

But the prince's frightened gesture seemed to have frightened Ippolit himself.

'So – I'm not to read it?' he whispered to him somewhat apprehensively, with a twisted smile on his blue lips. 'Not read it?' he murmured, gazing at everyone in turn, at all the eyes and faces, and as though again clinging to them all with the same appealing effusiveness. 'You – you're not afraid, are you?' He turned to the prince again.

'What of?' asked the prince, changing countenance more and more.

'Has anyone got a twenty-copeck coin on him?' cried Ippolit, jumping up from his chair suddenly, as though someone had pulled him off it. 'Or any other coin?'

'Here you are!' Lebedev at once offered him it.

The thought flashed through his mind that Ippolit had gone mad.

'Vera,' Ippolit hurriedly invited her to come over to him, 'take it and throw it on the table: heads or tails? Heads – I read it!'

Vera gazed fearfully at the coin, at Ippolit, then at her father, and rather awkwardly throwing back her head, as though in the belief that she must not look at the coin, she tossed it on the table. It came up 'heads'.

'I read it!' whispered Ippolit, as though crushed by the decision of fate; he couldn't have turned paler if a death sentence had been read out to him. 'Still,' he started suddenly, after half a minute's pause, 'what was it? Have I really tossed up just now?' he asked, looking round at everybody with the same appealing frankness. 'Why, it's quite an amazing psychological phenomenon!' he cried suddenly, addressing the prince with genuine astonishment. 'It's – it's quite an incredible phenomenon, Prince,' he repeated, becoming more animated and seeming to recover his wits, 'you must make a note of it, Prince. You must remember it. I believe you're collecting material about capital punishment. ... I've been told, you see, ha, ha! Goodness me, what a senseless absurdity!' he cried, sitting down on the sofa, and, putting his elbows on the table, he clutched at his head. 'Why, it's shameful! But what the hell do I care whether it's shameful or not?' he went on, raising his head at once. 'Gentlemen – gentlemen, I'm going to break the seal,' he declared with a sort of sudden determination. 'But I – I do not force you to listen!'

He unsealed the envelope with hands trembling with excitement, took out several sheets of note-paper covered with small handwriting, put them in front of him, and began to smooth them out.

'What's up? What on earth is it all about? What is he going to read?' some people muttered gloomily; others were silent. But all of them sat down and watched with curiosity. Perhaps they really were expecting something extraordinary. Vera caught hold of her father's chair and was almost in tears with fright; Kolya was almost as frightened as she. Lebedev, who had already sat down, suddenly got up, seized a candle, and put it nearer to Ippolit, so that he might see better.

'Gentlemen, you – you will see presently what this is about,' Ippolit added for some reason, and suddenly began to read: '" My Necessary Explanation. Epigraph: *Après moi le deluge*". ... Damn it!' he exclaimed, as though he had burnt himself. 'Can I seriously have used such a stupid epigraph? Look here, gentlemen, I warn you that the whole thing is most probably the most frightful drivel! I've just jotted down a few random thoughts. ... If you imagine that – er – there's anything mysterious or – er – anything forbidden – I mean – –'

'I wish you'd read it without any preamble,' Ganya interrupted.

'Trying to get out of it,' someone added.

'Too much talk,' Rogozhin, who had been silent till then, put in.

Ippolit looked up at him suddenly and, when their eyes met, Rogozhin grinned at him bitterly and spitefully and slowly brought out the following strange words:

'That's not the way this thing ought to be done, lad, that's not the way. ...'

What Rogozhin meant no one knew, of course, but his words produced a rather strange impression on everyone: a certain idea, which was common to them all, flashed faintly through their minds. On Ippolit these words made a terrible impression: he trembled so violently that the prince held out his hand to support him, and he would most certainly have cried out, if his voice had not suddenly failed him. For a whole minute he could not utter a word and, breathing heavily, stared at Rogozhin. At last, gasping for breath, he ejaculated with a superhuman effort:

'So – it was you – it was you – you?'

'What was me? What did I do?' Rogozhin replied, looking puzzled, but Ippolit, flushing and almost in a frenzy, which suddenly seized him, shouted harshly and vehemently:

'It was *you* who came to see me last week, at night, at two o'clock, on the day I had been to see you in the morning, *you!!* Confess it was you, wasn't it?'

'Last week, at night? Have you really gone off your head, lad?'

The 'lad' was again silent for a minute, putting his forefinger to his forehead as though wondering whether what he suspected could be true; but suddenly a sly and almost gleeful flicker appeared for a moment in his pale smile, which was still distorted with fear.

'It was you!' he repeated at last, almost in a whisper, but with utter conviction. '*You* came to me and sat down silently on a chair in my room, by the window, for a whole hour. For more than an hour. Between one and two o'clock in the morning. Then you got up and went away soon after two. ... It was you, you! Why you tried to frighten me and why you came to torment me I don't know, but it was you!'

And there was a sudden flash of intense hatred in his eyes, though he was still trembling with fear.

'You'll know all about it presently, gentlemen – I – I – listen. ...'

He seized his sheets of paper again, and with desperate haste; they had scattered and got mixed up, and he was trying to put them together; they shook in his hands; he could not put them straight for a long time.

'Gone mad or delirious!' Rogozhin muttered, almost inaudibly.

The reading began at last. For the first five minutes the author of the unexpected *article* was still gasping for breath and he read jerkily and incoherently; but gradually his voice grew firmer and began to express fully the sense of what he was reading. Sometimes he was interrupted by a violent attack of coughing; by the time he reached the second half of the article he was very hoarse, but the extraordinary animation, that grew stronger and stronger as he read, reached an intense pitch towards the end, as did also the painful impression on his audience. Here is the whole of this 'article':

'My Necessary Explanation

"*Après moi le deluge*"

'Yesterday morning the prince came to see me; incidentally, he persuaded me to come and stay with him in the country. I knew that he would most certainly insist on it, and I was sure that he would not hesitate to blurt out to me that in the country I would find it "easier to die among people and trees," as he puts it. But to-day he did not say *die*, but said, "it will be easier to live," which is really pretty much the same thing for a man in my condition. I asked him what he meant by his "trees" he kept harping on, and why he was so keen on my seeing those "trees", and I learnt to my surprise that apparently I said myself that evening that I had come to Pavlovsk to have a look at the trees for the last time. When I told him that it made no difference whether I died under trees or looking out of the window at my brick wall, and that it was not worth making such a fuss about a fortnight, he at once agreed with me; but in his view the green foliage and the fresh air will be sure to bring about some physical change in me, and my excitement and *my dreams* will take a turn for the better, and will perhaps be relieved. I told him again laughingly that he was talking like a materialist. He answered with his smile that he had always been a materialist. As he never tells a lie, his words must mean something. He has a nice smile; I have observed him more closely now. I don't know whether I like him or not now. I have no time now to bother about it. To be quite fair, though, the hatred I felt for him for five months has almost disappeared during the last month. Who knows, maybe I came to Pavlovsk chiefly to see him. But – why did I leave my room then? A man under sentence of death must not leave his corner; and if I hadn't made up my mind definitely now, but had, on the contrary, decided to wait till the last moment, I should not of course have accepted his invitation to move to his place to "die" in Pavlovsk.

'I must hurry up and finish all this "explanation" before to-morrow. So I shall have no time to read it over and correct it; I shall read it over to-morrow, when I am going to read it to the prince and one or two other witnesses I shall probably find there. As there will not be one false word in it, but only the truth, the last and solemn truth, I am already anxious to know what impression it is going to make on me at the hour and the minute when I shall read it over. Incidentally, I should not have written: "the last and solemn truth"; it is not worth telling lies for a fortnight, in any case, because it is not worth while living for a fortnight; this is the best proof that I shall write nothing but the truth. (N.B. Not to forget the thought: am I mad at this moment, or rather at certain moments? I was told positively that during their last phase consumptives sometimes go out of their minds for a time. Must check up on it to-morrow during the reading from the impression made on my audience. Must settle this question with the utmost care; otherwise I cannot start doing anything.)

'I can't help feeling I have just written something terribly stupid; but, as I said, I have no time to correct anything; besides, I promise deliberately not to correct a single line in this manuscript, even though I notice that I am contradicting myself every few lines. For I want to find out during the reading to-morrow whether the logical sequence of my thoughts is correct; whether I shall notice my mistakes, and, consequently, whether what I have thought over in this room during the last six months is true or just pure nonsense.

'If I had had to leave my room, as I am leaving it now, two months ago, and say good-bye to Meyer's wall, I should, I'm sure, have felt sad. But now I do not feel anything, and yet to-morrow I am leaving my room and the wall *for good*! So that my conviction that for one fortnight it is not worth while regretting anything or giving myself up to any sensation, has got the better of my nature and is even now perhaps dictating my feelings. But is this true? Is it true that my nature is entirely vanquished? If I were to be put to torture now, I should certainly scream, and I should not have said that it was not worth while screaming and feeling pain because I have only two more weeks to live.

'But is it true that I have only a fortnight left to live and no more? I told a lie in Pavlovsk that day: Botkin told me nothing and never saw me; but a week ago they brought a student, Kislorod, to see me; by his convictions he is a materialist, an atheist, and a nihilist – that was why I called him in and no one else: I had to have a man who would tell me the naked truth at last without fear or favour. And he did so, and not only readily and without hesitation, but also with obvious pleasure (which, I think, was going a bit too far). He told me frankly that I had only about a month more to live, a little longer perhaps if my circumstances were favourable, but that I might possibly die much sooner. According to him, I might die suddenly, to-morrow for instance: such things had happened, and only the day before yesterday a young woman in Kolomna, who was also consumptive and in a condition similar to mine, was about to go out shopping to the market when she suddenly felt sick, lay down on the sofa, heaved a sigh, and died. All this Kislorod told me with a certain relish, as though he were particularly proud of his lack of feelings and his casualness, and as though he were doing me an honour, that is, by showing me that he, too, takes me to be the same all-denying higher being as himself who, of course, thinks nothing of dying. Anyway, there can be no doubt about it: a month and no more! I am quite sure he is not mistaken.

'I was very much at a loss to know how the prince had guessed the other day that I had "bad dreams". He said *literally* that in Pavlovsk "my excitement and my *dreams*" would change. And why dreams? He's either a doctor or really a man of extraordinary intelligence and able to divine many things. (But there can be no shadow of doubt that, in the final analysis, he is an "idiot".) As luck would have it, I had quite a delightful dream just before he came (I'm having hundreds of them now, though). I fell asleep – I think it was an hour before his arrival – and dreamt that I was in a room (but not my own). The room was larger and loftier than mine, better furnished, lighter, a cupboard, a chest of drawers, a sofa, and my bed – large and wide and covered with a green silk eiderdown. But in the room I noticed a dreadful-looking creature, a sort of monstrosity. It looked like a scorpion, but it was not a scorpion, and more hideous and much more dreadful just because, I think, there are no such creatures in nature, and because it had come to me *deliberately* and that there was some kind of a mystery in that fact. I had a good look at it: it was brown and encased in a shell, a crawling reptile, about seven inches in length, two fingers thick at the head, gradually tapering off to the tail, so that the tip of the tail was no more than one-fifth of an inch thick. About two inches from the head, at an angle of forty-five degrees, two legs grew out of the body, one on each side, about three and a half inches in length, so that, if looked at from above, the animal was in the shape of a trident. I couldn't make out the head, but I saw two feelers, not very long, shaped like two strong needles, and also brown. It had a pair of identical feelers at the end of its tail and at the end of each of its legs, altogether eight feelers. The creature was running about the room very, very swiftly, supporting itself on its legs and its tail, and when it ran, its body and legs wriggled about like little snakes, with extraordinary rapidity, in spite of its shell, and it was very horrible to look at. I was terribly afraid it would sting me; I had been told that it was poisonous, but what worried me most was who could have sent it into my room, what they meant to do to me, and what was the meaning of it all. It kept hiding under the chest of drawers, under the cupboard, and crawled into corners. I sat down on a chair with my legs tucked under me. It ran quickly across the room and disappeared somewhere near my chair. I was peering round in dismay, but as I was sitting with my legs tucked up, I hoped that it would not crawl up the chair. Suddenly I heard behind me, almost on the level with my head, a faint rattling sound; I turned round, and saw that the reptile was crawling up the wall and was already on a level with my head and even touching my hair with its tail, which was twisting and wriggling with incredible rapidity. I jumped up and the creature disappeared. I was afraid to lie down on the bed for fear that it might creep under the pillow. My mother came into the room with some friend of hers. They began trying to catch the reptile, but they were much calmer than I was and were not even afraid of it. But they did not realize how dangerous it was. Suddenly the reptile crawled out again; this time it was crawling very quickly and, it seemed, with some special purpose, across the room towards the door, wriggling slowly, which was more horrible than ever. Then my mother opened the door and called our dog, Norma – a huge, shaggy black Newfoundland bitch; she died five years ago. She rushed into the room and stopped dead over the reptile. The reptile stopped too, though still wriggling and beating a tattoo on the floor with the ends of its tail and legs. If I am not mistaken, animals are incapable of feeling supernatural fear; but at that moment it seemed to me that there was something very unusual and almost supernatural in Norma's terror and that she therefore also felt like me that there was something fatal, some kind of mystery, in that creature. She was moving slowly backwards before the reptile, which was slowly and cautiously crawling towards her; it seemed as though it meant to make a sudden dart and sting her. But notwithstanding her fear, Norma looked very fierce, although she trembled in all her limbs. Suddenly she slowly bared her terrible teeth, opened her huge, red jaws, took careful aim, and suddenly seized the reptile with her teeth. The creature must have darted out of her mouth in order to escape, because Norma caught it once more, this time in the air, and twice got it all into her mouth, still catching it in the air, as though gobbling it up. The shell cracked between her teeth; the tail and legs of the creature, which hung out of the dog's mouth, moved about with terrible rapidity. Suddenly Norma yelped piteously: the reptile had succeeded in stinging her tongue after all. She opened her mouth wide with the pain, whining and yelping, and I saw the horrible creature, though bitten in two, still wriggling in her mouth and out of its half-crushed body a large quantity of a white fluid, similar to the fluid of a crushed black beetle, was oozing out on to her tongue. ... Just then I woke up and the prince came in.'

'Gentlemen,' said Ippolit, looking up from his manuscript suddenly and almost blushing, 'I haven't read this over, but I'm afraid I have really written a great deal of rubbish. This dream – –'

'Is rubbish,' Ganya hastened to chip in.

'I agree there's a lot here that is personal – I mean, about myself. ...'

As he said this, Ippolit looked weary and timid, and he kept wiping the sweat from his forehead with his handkerchief.

'Yes, sir, you're too much interested in yourself,' Lebedev hissed.

'But, let me repeat, gentlemen, I'm not forcing anyone to listen to me. Anyone not interested is free to go.'

'Turns people out – of another man's house,' Rogozhin muttered, almost inaudibly.

'Suppose we all get up and go away?' Ferdyshchenko, who had not had the courage to speak up till then, said suddenly.

Ippolit dropped his eyes and clutched his manuscript; but at the same moment he again raised his head and, his eyes flashing and two red spots coming out on his cheeks again, said, staring at Ferdyshchenko:

'You don't like me at all, do you?'

A few people burst out laughing, though most of them did not laugh. Ippolit flushed dreadfully.

'Ippolit,' said the prince, 'please close your manuscript and give it to me, and go to bed here in my room. To-morrow, too, we can have a talk before bed-time, but on condition that you never open these pages again. Will you do so?'

'How can I?' said Ippolit, looking at him in amazement. 'Gentlemen,' he cried, growing feverishly excited again, 'I'm sorry I behaved so badly. It was very stupid of me. I shall not interrupt the reading again. Anyone who wants to listen, can do so.'

He quickly had a gulp of water from the glass, quickly put his elbows on the table to shield his face from their eyes, and went on reading, obstinately. His shame soon passed off, however.

'The idea (he went on reading) that it is not worth while living for a few weeks began, I think, to take hold of me in good earnest a month ago, when I had only four weeks to live, but it took hold of me completely only three days ago, when I came back from Pavlovsk that evening. The first moment the idea took full and absolute possession of me was on the prince's veranda, at the very instant when I had taken it into my head to make a last trial of life, when I wanted to see people and trees (I grant you I said it myself), when I got excited, insisted on the right of Burdovsky, "my neighbour", and dreamed that they would suddenly spread out their arms and clasp me in their embrace, and beg my forgiveness for something, and I theirs; in short, I ended up like a stupid fool. It was at that time that my "last conviction" flared up in me. Now I can only express my astonishment at how I could have lived for six months without that "conviction"! I knew positively that I had consumption and that it was incurable; I did not deceive myself and I understood my position clearly. But the more clearly I understood it, the more desperately I wanted to live; I clung to life and I wanted to live, come what may. I admit that at the time I might have resented the deaf and blind destiny which had decreed that I should be crushed like a fly and, of course, without knowing why; but why did I not stop at resentment? Why did I actually *begin* to live, knowing that I couldn't possibly begin; why did I try it, knowing that there was nothing more I could try? And yet I could not read through a book, and I gave up reading:

why read, why learn anything for six months? That thought made me more than once fling aside a book.

'Yes, that wall of Meyer's could tell a lot! I have written a lot on it. There is not a stain on that filthy wall that I do not know by heart, that damned wall! And yet it is dearer to me than all the Pavlovsk trees, that is, it would be dearer if it did not matter to me now!

'I can remember now with what avid interest I began at the time to watch *their* life; I had never had such an interest before. Sometimes I used to wait for Kolya with curses and impatience, when I was so ill that I could not leave my room. I got so immersed in all sorts of trivialities and was so interested in all sorts of rumours that I do believe I became a regular gossip. I could not understand, for instance, how people, having so many years of life before them, did not know how to get rich (I don't understand it now, either). I knew one poor man who, I was told afterwards, died of hunger, and, I remember, this made me furious: if it were possible to bring that poor fellow back to life, I believe I should have murdered him. Sometimes I used to feel better for weeks and was able to go out; but the street infuriated me at last to such an extent that I deliberately locked myself up in my room for days, though I could have gone out like everyone else. I could not endure those bustling people, poking their noses into everything, eternally worried, gloomy, and anxious, darting to and fro about me on the pavement. Why their everlastingly mournful looks, their everlasting worry and bustle, their everlasting sullen spite (for they are spiteful, spiteful, spiteful)? Whose fault is it that they are unhappy and do not know how to live, though they have sixty years of life ahead of them? Why did Zarnitsyn let himself die of hunger when he had sixty years of life before him? And everyone shows you his rags, his calloused hands, and screams angrily: "I work like a horse, I labour day and night, and I'm poor, and hungry like a dog! Others never do a stroke of work and are rich!" (The old, old story!) And side by side with them, rushing and scurrying about from morning till night, is some wretched, shrivelled up little beggar, "a gentleman by birth", Ivan Fomich Surikov – he lives in our house on the floor above – always out at elbows and no buttons to his coat, running errands for all sorts of people from morning till night. Talk to him and he'll tell you: "I'm poor, destitute and miserable, my wife died because I had no money to buy her medicine with, and my baby was frozen to death in the winter, my eldest daughter is walking the streets ..." – he's for ever snivelling and complaining! Oh, I've never had any pity for these fools, and I haven't any now – I say this with - pride! Why isn't he a Rothschild? Whose fault is it that he hasn't millions, like Rothschild, that he hasn't bags and bags of gold sovereigns, mountains of them as high as a helter-skelter at a shrovetide fair! He is alive, so everything's in his power! Whose fault is it if he doesn't understand that?

'Oh, now I don't care any more, now I've no time left to be angry; but then, then, I repeat, I literally bit my pillow at night and tore my blanket with rage. Oh, how I used to dream then, how I wished, deliberately wished to be turned out into the street, eighteen years old as I was, barely clothed, barely covered, and left all alone, without a roof over my head, without work, without a crust of bread, without relations, without a single friend in a great city, hungry, beaten (so much the better!), but in good health, and then I would have shown them! ...

'Shown them what?

'Oh, do you really think I don't know how I've humiliated myself as it is by my "Explanation"! Oh, which of you does not think me a feeble little fool who knows nothing of life, forgetting that I am no longer eighteen now, forgetting that to have lived as I did for the last six months means to live to a ripe old age! But let them laugh and say that these are all fairy-tales. As a matter of fact, I have been telling myself fairy-tales. I have filled whole nights with them. I can remember them all now.

'But have I to tell them all over again now – now that the time for fairy-tales has passed even for me? And to whom? I used to amuse myself with them when I realized only too well that I was forbidden even to study Greek grammar, as I once took it into my head to do: "I shall be dead before I get as far as the syntax," I thought at the first page and threw the book under the table. It is still lying there; I've forbidden our maid to pick it up.

'Let those who come across my "Explanation" and have the patience to read it to the end take me for a madman, or even for a schoolboy, or, better still, for a man under sentence of death, who quite naturally believes that everyone except him esteems life far too lightly, is in the habit of wasting it too cheaply and using it too lazily and too unscrupulously, so that none of them is worthy of it! Well, I submit that my readers will be mistaken, and that my conviction has nothing whatever to do with the fact that I am under sentence of death. Ask them, just ask them what they all – every one of them – understand by happiness. Oh, you may be sure that Columbus was happy not when he had discovered America but when he was discovering it; you may be sure that the highest moment of his happiness was, perhaps, exactly three days before his discovery of the New

World, when, in despair, his mutinous crew all but turned their ship round and sailed back to Europe – sailed back! It was not the New World that was important – it might never have existed for all that it mattered. Columbus died without having really seen it and, as a matter of fact, without knowing that he had discovered it. It is life, life that matters, life alone – the continuous and everlasting process of discovering it – and not the discovery itself! But what is the use of talking? I expect that all I am saying now is so much like a string of platitudes that I shall most certainly be taken for a third-form schoolboy handing in an essay on "sunrise", or they will say that I had perhaps something to say but that, try as I might, I could not "make myself clear". Let me add, however, that in every idea of genius or in every new human idea, or, more simply still, in every serious human idea born in anyone's brain, there is something that cannot possibly be conveyed to others, though you wrote volumes about it and spent thirty-five years in explaining your idea; something will always be left that will obstinately refuse to emerge from your head and that will remain with you for ever; and you will die without having conveyed to anyone what is perhaps the most vital point of your idea. But if I too am now unable to convey all that has been tormenting me for the past six months, then at all events you will understand that, having attained my present "last conviction", I have perhaps paid too much for it; it is this I thought it necessary, for certain reasons of my own, to emphasize in my "Explanation".

'However, to continue.

6

'I do not want to tell a lie: reality has been trying to catch me, too, in a trap during the last six months, and sometimes I was so carried away that I forgot about my death sentence, or rather did not care to think of it, and even did some work. By the way, about my position then. When, eight months ago, I became very ill, I threw up all my connexions and dropped all my old friends. As I had always been a rather morose sort of person, my friends easily forgot me; they would, of course, have forgotten me anyway without it. My position at home – that is, "in my family" – was also that of a recluse. Five months ago I shut myself up once and for all and separated myself entirely from the rooms of my family. I was always obeyed and no one dared come into my room, except at a fixed time to tidy it and bring me my dinner. My mother trembled before me and obeyed my orders and did not dare even to whimper when I sometimes made up my mind to let her in. She constantly thrashed the children so that they should not make a noise or disturb me. I must say I often complained of their shouting: how they must love me now! I think I tormented "faithful Kolya", as I called him, a good deal too. Latterly he, too, tormented me: all that is quite natural, for men are created to torment each other. But I noticed that he put up with my irritability as though he had set his mind on humouring the patient. Naturally, that exasperated me; but apparently he took it into his head to imitate the prince in "Christian meekness", which was rather funny. He is a very young and enthusiastic fellow and, of course, imitates everything; but I could not help feeling sometimes that it was high time he had a mind of his own. I am very fond of him. I tormented Surikov, too, who lives on the floor above us and runs errands from morning till night; I was continually telling him that he had no one but himself to blame if he was poor, so that he got frightened in the end and stopped coming to see me. He is a very meek man, the meekest creature imaginable. (N.B. They say meekness is a terrific force; I must ask the prince about it – it is his own expression.) But when, last March, I went upstairs to his flat to see how his baby had, in his own words, been "frozen to death", and accidentally smiled at the corpse of the baby, for I began explaining to Surikov again that he had "no one but himself to blame", this wretched, shrivelled-up little man's lips suddenly quivered and, seizing me by the shoulder with one hand, he showed me the door with the other and said quietly – that is, almost in a whisper: "Get out, sir!" I went out, and I liked it very much; I liked it just then, at the very moment when he was showing me out; but afterwards his words, whenever I remembered them, produced a painful impression on me; I felt a sort of strange and contemptuous pity for him, which I did not want to feel at all. Even at the moment of such an insult (for, you see, I cannot help feeling that I had insulted him, though I never meant to) – even at such a moment this man could not lose his temper! His lips did not tremble from anger, I'm ready to take my oath on that: he seized me by the hand and uttered his magnificent "Get out, sir!" without a trace of anger. There was, indeed, a great deal of dignity in it, which did not suit him at all (so that, to tell the truth, the whole thing was a bit comical), but there was no anger. Perhaps he simply began to despise me suddenly. Since then, once or twice, whenever I've met him on the stairs, he's begun taking off his hat to me, which he never used to do before, but he never stopped as before, but darted past me in confusion. If he did despise me, he despised me in his own way: he despised me meekly. But perhaps he simply took off his hat to me from fear as the son of his creditor, for he always owed money to my mother and could never extricate himself from his debts. Yes, I think that is most likely what it was. I meant to have it out with him and I know for a fact that he would have apologized within ten minutes, but I decided that it was better to leave him alone.

'Just at that time, that is, about the time when Surikov "froze" his baby, about the middle of March, I suddenly felt much better for some reason, and so it went on for a fortnight. I began to go out, mostly at dusk. I was fond of the March evenings, when there was frost in the air and the gas-lamps were lit; sometimes I walked a long way. One evening I was overtaken in the dark by some down-at-heel "gentleman". I did not examine him closely. He was carrying something wrapped up in paper and he wore an old ragged overcoat, which was much too short for him and rather light for the time of year. When he reached a street-lamp, ten yards in front of me, I noticed that something fell out of his pocket. I hastened to pick it up – and in the nick of time, for someone in a long Russian coat rushed up too, but seeing the thing in my hand, he did not stop to argue, glanced at what was in my hand, and darted past me. It was a large old-fashioned morocco wallet, stuffed full; but, somehow, I guessed at the first glance that whatever was in it, it was not money. The man who dropped it was already forty yards ahead of me and very soon was lost in the crowd. I ran after him, shouting, "Hey!" But as all I could shout was "Hey!", he did not turn round. Suddenly he darted through some gateway to the left. When I reached the gateway, which was very dark, there was no one there. The house was of an enormous size, one of those huge buildings which are put up by speculative builders for small tenement flats; some of those houses have as many as a hundred flats. When I ran through the gates, I thought I could see a man walking along the far end of the right-hand corner of the huge yard, though I could scarcely see him in the darkness. When I ran up to the corner, I saw the entrance to the stairs. The staircase was narrow, very filthy, and not lighted at all. But I could hear a man still running up the stairs above me, and I rushed after him, thinking that I would overtake him before they opened the door to him. And so I did. The flights of stairs were very short, but there were lots and lots of them, so that I was terribly out of breath; a door was opened and closed on the fifth story – I guessed that when I was still three flights of stairs below. While I ran up, recovered my breath on the landing and felt for the bell several minutes had passed. The door was opened at last by a peasant woman, who was blowing up the charcoal in the *samovar* in a tiny kitchen; she listened in silence to my questions without, of course, understanding a word of what I was saying, and in silence opened the door of the next room, which was also very small and terribly low, cheaply furnished with the barest essentials and an enormous, wide bed behind a curtain, on which lay "Terentyich" (so the woman called him), who, I thought, was drunk. A candle-end was burning in an iron candlestick on a table and there was a bottle beside it, almost empty. Terentyich muttered something to me without getting up and waved towards another door. The woman went away so that there was nothing for me to do but to open the door. I did so and went into the next room.

'This room was still smaller than the other so that I could hardly turn round in it; the narrow single bed in the corner took up nearly all the space; the rest of the furniture only consisted of three plain chairs, piled up with all sorts of rags, and a plain deal kitchen table in front of an old sofa, covered with American cloth, so that it was almost impossible to pass between the table and the bed. On the table was a lighted tallow candle in the same kind of candlestick as in the other room, and on the bed a tiny baby, who, to judge from its squealing, could not have been more than three weeks old; he was being "changed" – that is, swaddled, by a pale, sickly-looking woman, who seemed to be quite young and who had practically nothing on; she looked as though she had only just got up after her confinement. The baby would not quiet down and kept crying for his mother's emaciated breast. Another child, a three-year-old girl, was asleep on the sofa, covered with what looked like a man's dress-coat. A man in a very shabby coat (he had taken off his overcoat and it was lying on the bed) stood at the table and was unwrapping a blue paper parcel in which were about two pounds of white bread and two little sausages. On the table there was, besides, a teapot with tea in it and a few crusts of black bread. An open trunk and two bundles with some rags stuck out from under the bed.

'The whole place was, in short, in a terrible mess. I could see at the first glance that both of them, the man and the woman, were decent people who had been reduced by poverty to that degrading condition in which disorder at last gets the better of every attempt to cope with it, and even drives people to the bitter necessity of deriving from the daily increasing disorder a sort of bitter and, as it were, vindictive satisfaction.

'When I went in, the man, who had only just entered before me and was unwrapping his parcel of food, was talking rapidly and excitedly. Though his wife had not finished swaddling the baby, she had already started whimpering, for the news he brought was, as usual, bad. The man was about twenty-eight, and his dark, haggard face, with black whiskers and closely shaven chin, looked to me quite handsome and even pleasant; it was morose and with a morose look in the eyes, but with a sort of morbidly self-conscious pride, that could all too easily be hurt. A strange scene took place as I entered.

'There are people who derive great pleasure from their irritable susceptibilities, especially if they are driven to the limit of endurance (which always happens very quickly); at that moment, it seems, they would rather be offended than not. These irritable people are always terribly sorry afterwards, if they are intelligent, of course, and are capable of realizing that they have been ten times as angry as they need have been. The man stared at me for some time in amazement, and his wife in dismay, as though there had been something terribly remarkable in the fact that anyone should come into their room. But all of a sudden he pounced on me almost in a frenzy. I had not had time to murmur a couple of words before he, seeing that I was decently dressed, probably considered himself to be mortally offended at my daring to look into his room so unceremoniously and see the disgraceful surroundings of which he was so ashamed. Of course, he was glad of the opportunity to vent his spite for all his failures on someone. One moment I even thought that he was going to hit me; he turned white like a woman in hysterics and frightened his wife dreadfully.

' "How dare you come in like that, sir? Get out!" he shouted, trembling and scarcely able to articulate his words.

'But suddenly he saw his wallet in my hands.

' "I believe you dropped this," I said as calmly and drily as I could (that was just the right way to talk to him, as a matter of fact).

'He stood before me looking absolutely terrified, and for some time he did not seem to understand anything; then he quickly put his hand to his side-pocket, gaped in terror, and slapped his forehead.

' "Good Lord! Where did you find it? How did it happen?"

'I explained in a few words, and even more drily than before, how I had picked up the wallet, how I had run after him and called out after him and how, finally, thinking that he must be the owner of the wallet, I had groped my way and followed him up the stairs.

' "Good heavens!" he cried, turning to his wife, "all our papers are there and what is left of my instruments – everything's there – oh, my dear sir, do you know what you've done for me? I should have been lost!"

'Meanwhile I had taken hold of the door-handle, intending to go without answering, but I was out of breath myself, and suddenly my excitement brought on such a violent fit of coughing that I could hardly stand on my feet. I saw the man rushing all over the place to find a vacant chair for me, and at last snatching up the rags from one chair, he flung them on the floor, hurriedly offered it to me, and carefully helped me to sit down. But my cough went on without stopping for another three minutes. When I recovered, he was sitting beside me on another chair, from which he probably had also thrown the rags on to the floor, and watching me closely.

' "Are you – ill?" he said in the tone of voice doctors usually employ when talking to a patient. "I – er – I'm a medical man" (he didn't say a doctor), and, as he said it, he pointed to the room, as though protesting against his present position. "I see that you – –"

' "I have t.b.," I said as curtly as possible and got up.

'He, too, jumped up at once.

' "Perhaps you're exaggerating and – er – if you were to take – er – proper measures – –"

'He was utterly confused and did not seem able to collect his wits; he still held the wallet in his left hand.

' "Oh, don't trouble yourself," I interrupted again, grabbing the door-handle, "Dr Botkin examined me last week" (again I dragged in Botkin), "and I'm afraid my case is hopeless. I'm sorry – –"

'I tried again to open the door and leave my embarrassed and grateful doctor, who looked crushed with shame, but my damned cough got hold of me again. Here the doctor insisted that I should sit down again and have a rest. He turned to his wife and, without leaving her place, she said a few grateful and kind words to me. She was very embarrassed as she spoke, so that her thin, pale, yellow cheeks coloured deeply. I remained, but with an air that showed unmistakably that I was very much afraid to intrude on their privacy (which was just the right manner to adopt). The doctor was in a perfect agony of remorse. I could see that.

' "If I – –" he began, breaking off and going off at a tangent every moment, "I – I'm so grateful to you and I – I've treated you abominably – you see – er – I – –" he again pointed to the room, "I'm in an awful mess at the moment – –"

' "Oh," I said, "there's nothing to see – it's the usual thing. I suppose you've lost your job and you've come up here to explain what has happened and find another job."

' "How did you – guess?" he asked with surprise.

' "Oh," I replied with unintentional sarcasm, "I could tell at once. Lots of people come here from the provinces full of hope and run about and live like this."

'He suddenly began to speak with warmth and with trembling lips. He began complaining, telling me his story, and, I confess, I became very interested. I stayed there for nearly an hour. He told me what had happened to him, and, I must say, his story was a very common one. He had been a provincial doctor, had a government post, and then all sorts of intrigues had begun in which even his wife was involved. He was too proud to give in, lost his temper – there was a change in the provincial government which favoured his enemies, who undermined his reputation and lodged complaints against him; he lost his post, got his last savings together, and came to Petersburg to explain what had happened. Of course, he could not get a hearing for a long time, then they answered him by a refusal, then all sorts of promises were held out to him, then he was severely reprimanded, he was told to fill in a form, then they refused to accept it and told him to file a petition – in short, he had been running about from one government department to another for five months, and had spent all his savings. He had pawned his wife's last rags, and meanwhile a new baby had arrived and – "to-day – to-day I received the final refusal to my petition, and I have hardly any bread left – I have nothing – my wife has had a baby. I – I – –"

'He jumped up from his chair and turned away. His wife was crying in a corner, and the baby began squealing again. I took out my notebook and began writing in it. When I had finished and got up, he was standing before me and looking at me with timid curiosity.

' "I've made a note of your name," I said to him, "and, well, all the rest of it: the place where you served, the name of the Governor of the province, dates, and so on. I have a friend, an old schoolfellow of mine, called Bakhmutov, and his uncle is Peter Matveyevich Bakhmutov, a regular state councillor and director – –"

' "Peter Matveyevich Bakhmutov!" cried my medico, almost trembling. "Why, practically everything depends on him!"

'As a matter of fact, everything in my doctor's story and its happy ending, which I was instrumental in bringing about by pure chance, came to pass and was satisfactorily settled just as though it had been purposely arranged, exactly as in a novel. I told those poor people not to try and build any hopes on me, for I was only a poor schoolboy myself (I deliberately pretended to be more insignificant than I am; I finished my studies long ago and am not a schoolboy), and that there was no need for them to know my name, but that I would go at once to Vassilyevsky Island to see my friend Bakhmutov, and as I knew for a fact that his uncle, the regular state councillor, was a bachelor and had no children and simply worshipped his nephew and was passionately fond of him as the last surviving descendant of his family, my friend might be able to do something for them and for me, of course, with the assistance of his uncle.

' "All I want is an interview with his uncle!" cried the doctor, shaking as though in a fever and with flashing eyes. "If only I might be humbly permitted to put my case to him personally!" He actually said: "be humbly permitted."

'After repeating again that the whole thing would probably be a complete flop and come to nothing, I added that if I did not go to see them next morning, it would mean that everything was at an end and they had nothing to expect. They saw me off with bows; they were almost beside themselves. I shall never forget the expression of their faces. I took a cab and drove straight to Vassilyevsky Island.

'At school I was always at daggers drawn with Bakhmutov. We looked upon him as an aristocrat – at least, I called him one. He used to be smartly dressed, arrived at school in his own carriage and pair, was not a bit stuck up, was always a good friend, was always bright and merry, and sometimes even witty, though he was not particularly intelligent, in spite of the fact that he was always top of the form; I, on the other hand, was never top in anything. All his schoolfellows liked him, except me. He had several times tried to make friends with me during those years, but every time I snubbed him, sulkily and irritably. Now I had not seen him for about a year; he was at the university. When at about nine o'clock I entered his room (it was quite a grand entrance: I was announced), he first met me with surprise and far from cordially, but he at once cheered up and, looking at me, suddenly burst out laughing.

' "What on earth has brought you here, Terentyev?" he cried with his customary, sometimes pleasant, sometimes arrogant, but never offensive, familiarity, which I liked so much in him and for which I hated him so much also. "But what's the matter?" he cried in alarm. "You look so ill!"

'A new attack of coughing deprived me of all strength. I sank into a chair and could scarcely recover my breath.

' "Don't worry," I said, "I have t.b. I've come to you with a request."

'He sat down, looking surprised, and I at once told him the doctor's story and explained that, considering his great influence with his uncle, he might be able to do something.

' "I'll do it, I'll certainly do it. I'll see my uncle about it to-morrow, and I'm very glad, and you've told it all so well. But how did it occur to you, Terentyev, to approach me? That's what puzzles me."

' "Well, you see, so much here depends on your uncle and, besides, Bakhmutov, we were always enemies and, since you are an honourable man," I added with irony, "I thought you wouldn't refuse an enemy."

' "Just as Napoleon turned to England!" he cried, roaring with laughter. "I shall do it! I shall do it! I'll go at once, if it's possible!" he added hastily, seeing that I was getting up, gravely and sternly, from my chair.

'And, to be sure, we settled this affair quite unexpectedly and in a most satisfactory manner. Six weeks later our medico was appointed to another post in a different province, his travelling expenses were paid and, in addition, he received some assistance in cash. I suspect that Bakhmutov, who was visiting the doctor almost daily (while I purposely stopped visiting him and received him almost coldly when he called on me) – Bakhmutov, as I suspect, even persuaded the doctor to accept a loan from him. I saw Bakhmutov twice during those six weeks, and I met him for a third time when we saw the doctor off. Bakhmutov gave the doctor a farewell dinner with champagne at his house, at which the doctor's wife was also present, though she soon left to look after the baby. It was at the beginning of May. It was a beautiful evening. The huge disc of the sun was sinking in the bay. Bakhmutov saw me home. We walked across Nikolayevsky bridge; we were both a little drunk. Bakhmutov spoke of his delight at the happy ending of the affair, thanked me for something, explained how happy he felt now after having done a good deed, and assured me that the credit for it was all mine and that many people were wrong in maintaining and preaching that individual acts of charity were of no use. I, too, was very anxious to discuss it.

' "Anyone who attacks an individual act of charity," I began, "attacks human nature and despises the dignity of man. But the organization of 'public charity' and the question of personal liberty are two different questions and are not mutually exclusive. Individual acts of charity will always exist because they are part of man's personal needs, a vital necessity of the direct influence of one personality upon another. There was an old man in Moscow, a 'general' – that is, a regular state councillor – with a German name. He spent all his life visiting prisons and interviewing prisoners; every party of convicts on their way to Siberia knew beforehand that the old 'general' would see them off on Sparrow Hills. He did it all extremely seriously and devoutly; he would arrive, walk down the rows of convicts, who surrounded him, stop before each, interrogating each about his needs, hardly ever lecturing anyone and calling them all his 'darlings'. He gave them money, sent them all sorts of necessary articles – rags to wind round their legs and feet, pieces of linen, and sometimes brought them religious tracts, which he distributed among those who could read in the full conviction that they would read them on the way and that those who could read would read them to those who could not. He rarely asked them about their crimes, but listened if a convict began talking about his. He treated all prisoners alike, making no distinction between them. He talked to them as to brothers, but they themselves in the end began to regard him as a father. If he noticed a woman convict with a child in her arms, he went up to her, fondled the child, and snapped his fingers to make it laugh. He did that for many years, up to the time of his death; things went so far that he was known all over Russia and all over Siberia – by all the convicts, that is. I was told by a man who had been in Siberia that he had seen himself how the most hardened criminals remembered the general, and yet during his visits the general could rarely give more than twenty copecks to each prisoner. It is true that their recollection of him was not particularly warm-hearted nor in any way serious. One or another of the 'unhappy wretches', who had murdered a dozen people or slaughtered six children, solely for his own pleasure (there have been such men, I'm told), would for no reason in the world, and perhaps only once in twenty years, suddenly heave a sigh and say, 'I wonder what the old general is doing now? Is he still alive?' And perhaps he would even smile as he said it – and that is all. How can you tell what seed may have been dropped in his soul for ever by the 'old general' whom he had not forgotten for twenty years? How can you tell, Bakhmutov, what significance this contact of one personality with another will have for the future of one of them? What we are dealing with here is a man's whole life and the innumerable threads which are hidden from us. The best chess-player, the cleverest among them, can only calculate a few moves ahead; a French chess-player, who could calculate ten moves ahead, was written about as a marvel. Well, how many moves have we here and how many of them are unknown to us? In scattering your seed, in offering your 'alms', in doing your good deed, in whatever shape or form, you are giving away part of your personality and absorbing part of another's; you are mutually united to one another and, with a little more effort, you will already be rewarded by knowledge, by the most unexpected discoveries. You will at last most certainly begin to look upon your work as a science; it will absorb all your life and may fill all your life. On the other hand, all your thoughts, all your scattered seeds, which perhaps you have already forgotten, will take root and grow up; the man who received them from you, will pass them on to someone else. And how can you tell what your contribution to the shaping of man's destinies will be? If this knowledge and a whole lifetime of this work at last raises you to such an eminence that you will be able to sow some great seed, to bequeath to the world some great thought, then – –" And so on, I talked a lot during that walk.

' "And to think that a man like you has to die so soon!" cried Bakhmutov with warm reproach against someone.

'At that moment we were standing on the bridge, leaning with our elbows on the balustrade and looking at the Neva.

' "Do you know what has just this minute occurred to me?" I said, bending lower over the balustrade.

' "Not to throw yourself into the river?" cried Bakhmutov, almost in a panic.

'Perhaps he read my thought in my face.

' "No," I said, "for the time being it is only the following reflection: I have only two or three months to live, perhaps four; but when, say, I have only two more months left, and if I should then be terribly anxious to do a good deed, which would require a great deal of work, rushing about and worry, something like the business of our doctor, I'd have to give it up for lack of time and try to find another 'good deed', something on a smaller scale, which would be within my *means* (if I really should be so set on good deeds). You must admit it's an amusing thought."

'Poor Bakhmutov was very worried about me; he took me to my house, and was so tactful that he didn't once try to console me, but was silent almost all the way. As he said good-bye to me, he pressed my hand warmly and asked my permission to call on me. I replied that if he were to come to me as a "comforter" (for even if he never uttered a word he would have come to comfort me, I made that clear to him), he would remind me of death more than ever every time he came. He shrugged, but agreed with me; we parted quite politely, which was more than I expected.

'But that evening and that night was sown the first seed of my "last conviction". I eagerly seized on that *new* idea, eagerly examined it in all its implications, in all its aspects (I did not sleep all night), and the more deeply I considered it, the more I absorbed it, the more frightened I became. At last I was seized by a dreadful panic, which did not leave me during the following days. Sometimes when I thought of this continuous panic of mine, I quickly froze with a new terror: for from this panic I could only conclude that my "last conviction" had taken too firm a hold of me and was bound to lead to a final decision. But I lacked resolution for that decision. Three weeks later it was all over and the resolution came to me, but as a result of an extremely strange circumstance.

'Here in my explanation I note down all these dates and figures. It will make no difference to me, of course, but *now* (and, perhaps, only at this moment) I should like that those who will pass judgement on my action could clearly apprehend the logical chain of conclusions which led up to my "last conviction". I have just written above that the final resolution, which I lacked in order to carry into effect my "last conviction", apparently came to me not as a result of a logical conclusion, but as a result of some curious shock, as a result of a strange circumstance which had nothing to do with anything that had happened so far. Ten days ago Rogozhin dropped in to see me about a certain matter which I do not propose to go into now. I had never seen Rogozhin before, but I had heard a great deal about him. I gave him all the necessary information, and he soon went away, and as he had only come for this information that might have been the end of our acquaintance. But he interested me too much, and all that day I was preoccupied with strange thoughts, so that I decided to go and see him next day, to return his visit. I could see that Rogozhin did not relish my visit and, indeed, he hinted "delicately" that there was no reason why we should continue to know each other; but all the same I spent a very interesting hour, as, no doubt, he did too. The contrast between us was so great, that neither of us, I especially, could help noticing it; I was a man whose days were numbered, and he one who was full of life and vitality, living in the present, without worrying about "last" conclusions, figures, and anything else that had no direct bearing on what – on what – well, on what he was mad on. I hope Mr Rogozhin will forgive me this expression, if only because I am a bad author who doesn't know how to express his idea. Notwithstanding his unfriendliness, I thought he was a man of intelligence and capable of understanding a great deal, though he took little interest in what did not concern him personally. I gave him no hint of my "last conviction", but for some reason I could not help feeling that, while listening to me, he guessed it. He said nothing: he is awfully taciturn. Before leaving, I hinted to him that in spite of all the contrast and all the difference between us, *les extrémités se touchent* (I explained it to him in Russian), so that perhaps he was not as far removed from my "last conviction" as he thought. To that he replied with a very sullen and sour grimace, got up, fetched me my cap himself, pretending that I was going of my own free will, and quite simply showed me out of his gloomy house on the excuse of seeing me off out of politeness. His house made a deep impression on me; it is like a graveyard, but he seems to like it, which is, indeed, understandable; the full and vital life he leads is too full in itself to require any background.

'My visit to Rogozhin exhausted me very much. I had, besides, felt far from well since that morning; in the evening I felt very weak and I lay down on my bed; at times I felt very feverish and occasionally I was delirious. Kolya stayed with me till eleven o'clock. I remember everything he said to me, though, and what we were talking about. But when my eyes closed for a few moments, I seemed to see Surikov, who had apparently received millions of money. He still did not seem to know what to do with it, racked his brains over his bags of gold, trembled with fear that they might be stolen, and at last seemed to have made up his mind to bury them in the ground. In the end I told him that instead of burying such a heap of gold in the ground, he should melt it down into a golden coffin for his "frozen" baby and dig the baby up for the purpose. Surikov appeared to accept my gibe with tears of gratitude, and immediately set about carrying out the plan. I just swore and left him. Kolya assured me when I recovered my senses that I had not slept at all and that I had been talking to him all the time about Surikov. At moments I was in a state of dreadful anguish and confusion, so that Kolya was very uneasy when he left me. When I got up to lock the door after him, I suddenly remembered a picture I had seen at Rogozhin's over the door of one of the gloomiest drawing-rooms of his house. He showed it me himself in passing. I think I stood before it for five minutes. It was not very good as a work of art; but it aroused in me a strange feeling of uneasiness.

'The picture depicted Christ, who has just been taken from the cross. I believe that painters are usually in the habit of depicting Christ, whether on the cross or taken from the cross, as still retaining a shade of extraordinary beauty on his face; that beauty they strive to preserve even in his moments of greatest agony. In Rogozhin's picture there was no trace of beauty. It was a faithful representation of the dead body of a man who has undergone unbearable torments before the crucifixion, been wounded, tortured, beaten by the guards, beaten by the people, when he carried the cross and fell under its weight, and, at last, has suffered the agony of crucifixion, lasting for six hours (according to my calculation, at least). It is true, it is the face of a man who has only *just* been taken from the cross – that is, still retaining a great deal of warmth and life; rigor mortis had not yet set in, so that there is still a look of suffering on the face of the dead man, as though he were still feeling it (that has been well caught by the artist); on the other hand, the face has not been spared in the least; it is nature itself, and, indeed, any man's corpse would look like that after such suffering. I know that the Christian Church laid it down in the first few centuries of its existence that Christ really did suffer and that the Passion was not symbolical. His body on the cross was therefore fully and entirely subject to the laws of nature. In the picture the face is terribly smashed with blows, swollen, covered with terrible, swollen, and bloodstained bruises, the eyes open and squinting; the large, open whites of the eyes have a sort of dead and glassy glint. But, strange to say, as one looks at the dead body of this tortured man, one cannot help asking oneself the peculiar and interesting question: if such a corpse (and it must have been just like that) was seen by all His disciples, by His future chief apostles, by the women who followed Him and stood by the cross, by all who believed in Him and worshipped Him, then how could they possibly have believed, as they looked at the corpse, that that martyr would rise again? Here one cannot help being struck with the idea that if death is so horrible and if the laws of nature are so powerful, then how can they be overcome? How can they be overcome when even He did not conquer them, He who overcame nature during His lifetime and whom nature obeyed, who said *Talitha cumi!* and the damsel arose, who cried, *Lazarus come forth!* and the dead man came forth? Looking at that picture, you get the impression of nature as some enormous, implacable, and dumb beast, or, to put it more correctly, much more correctly, though it may seem strange, as some huge engine of the latest design, which has senselessly seized, cut to pieces, and swallowed up – impassively and unfeelingly – a great and priceless Being, a Being worth the whole of nature and all its laws, worth the entire earth, which was perhaps created solely for the coming of that Being! The picture seems to give expression to the idea of a dark, insolent, and senselessly eternal power, to which everything is subordinated, and this idea is suggested to you unconsciously. The people surrounding the dead man, none of whom is shown in the picture, must have been overwhelmed by a feeling of terrible anguish and dismay on that evening which had shattered all their hopes and almost all their beliefs at one fell blow. They must have parted in a state of the most dreadful terror, though each of them carried away within him a mighty thought which could never be wrested from him. And if, on the eve of the crucifixion, the Master could have seen what He would look like when taken from the cross, would he have mounted the cross and died as he did? This question, too, you can't help asking yourself as you look at the picture.

'All this passed vaguely through my mind by snatches and perhaps while I really was delirious, sometimes even in vivid images, for a whole hour and and a half after Kolya's departure. Can anything appear in a vivid image that has no image? But at times I did imagine that I saw, in a sort of strange and impossible form, that infinite power, that dark, deaf-and-dumb creature. I remember that someone seemed to lead me by the hand, with a lighted candle, and show me some huge and horrible tarantula, assuring me that that was the dark, deaf-and-dumb, and all-powerful creature, and laughing at my indignation. There is always a little light burning at night before the icon in my room, a dim and feeble light, yet one can make everything out and even read under that light. I think it must have been after midnight; I was not asleep at all and I lay with wide-open eyes; suddenly the door of my room opened and in came Rogozhin.

'He came in, closed the door, looked at me in silence, and walked quietly to the chair standing almost under the light of the icon in the corner. I was greatly astonished and looked at him expectantly. Rogozhin leaned against the little table and began to stare at me in silence. So passed two or three minutes, and I remember that I was very much hurt and exasperated by his silence. Why wouldn't he speak? That he should have come so late did, of course, strike me as strange, but I remember that it was not that that surprised me so much. On the contrary, though I had not expressed my idea clearly enough in the morning, I know he understood it; and my idea was of the kind that one might come to talk over once more, however late. I naturally thought that he had come for that. We had parted in the morning on not very friendly terms, and I remember he looked at me once or twice very sarcastically. It was the same sarcastic look that I saw in his eyes now, and it was that which offended me. That it really was Rogozhin and not a phantom or a hallucination I had no doubt whatever at first. Indeed, the idea of doubting it never occurred to me.

'Meanwhile he still went on sitting there and staring at me with the same sarcastic smile. I turned angrily on my bed, leaned with my elbow on the pillow, and made up my mind not to utter a word on purpose, though we spent all the time sitting like that. For some reason I was absolutely determined that he should be the first to break the silence. I think twenty minutes must have passed in this way. Suddenly the idea occurred to me: what if it isn't Rogozhin but just a phantom?

'Neither during my illness nor before it have I ever seen a ghost; but I always felt, even as a boy and even now – that is, quite recently – that if I ever saw a ghost, I should die on the spot, though I don't believe in ghosts. Yet when the thought occurred to me that it was not Rogozhin, but only a ghost, I remember I was not in the least frightened. Not only that, but I was positively angry. Another strange thing was that the answer to the question whether it was Roghozin or a ghost did not seem to interest me or alarm me as much as it should have done; I believe I must have been thinking of something else at the time. What interested me much more, for instance, was why Rogozhin, whom I had seen in the morning in his dressing-gown and slippers, should now be wearing a dress-coat, a white waistcoat, and a white tie. The thought also flashed through my mind that if it was a ghost and I was not afraid of it, then why not get up, go up to him, and make sure? But perhaps I did not dare and was afraid. But no sooner did I think of being afraid than I suddenly felt as though a piece of ice had been passed across my body: a cold shiver ran down my spine and my knees trembled. At that very moment, as though guessing that I was afraid, Rogozhin moved away the hand on which he was leaning, straightened out, and began opening his mouth as though he were going to laugh; he looked straight at me. I was seized with such fury that I longed to rush at him, but as I had vowed not to start talking first, I stayed in bed, particularly as I was still undecided whether it was Rogozhin or not.

'I can't remember for certain how long this went on; neither can I remember whether I lost consciousness from time to time or not. Only, at last, Rogozhin got up and looked at me slowly and intently as he had done on coming in, but he was no longer grinning at me. He went up to the door quietly, almost on tiptoe, opened it, went out, and closed it behind him. I did not get out of bed; I can't remember how long I lay with open eyes, thinking; goodness knows what I was thinking of; I can't remember when I dropped off, either. Next morning I woke up at about ten o'clock when they knocked at my door. I have made it a rule that if I don't open the door myself before ten o'clock and call for tea to be brought to me, our maid should knock on my door. When I opened the door to her, it occurred to me at once that he could not possibly have come in if the door was locked. I made inquiries, and came to the conclusion that the real Rogozhin could not have come in, because all our doors are locked at night.

'It was this curious incident which I have described at such length that was the cause of my making up my mind *definitely*. It was, therefore, not logic, not a logical conviction, but disgust that helped me to arrive at my final decision. It is impossible to go on living when life assumes such grotesque and humiliating forms. That apparition humiliated me. I cannot submit to a dark power which assumes the form of a tarantula. And it was only at dusk, when I felt at last that I had reached the final phase of full determination, that I felt better. But that was only the first phase; for the second one I went to Pavlovsk, but that I have already explained sufficiently.

7

'I had a small pocket pistol; I bought it when I was still a boy, at that ridiculous age when one suddenly gets a liking for stories about duels and hold-ups by bandits; I, too, imagined how I should be challenged to a duel and how nobly I should stand facing the pistol of my adversary. A month ago I examined it and got it ready. In the box where it lay I found two bullets, and in the powder-horn enough powder for three charges. The pistol is quite worthless; it is impossible to aim straight with it and it hits its target no further than at fifteen feet; but of course if you put it close to your temple, it would blow your brains out.

'I decided to die in Pavlovsk at sunrise, in the park so as not to disturb anyone at the house. My "Explanation" would explain everything sufficiently to the police. Those who are keen on psychology and anyone else who likes are at liberty to deduce anything they will from it. I should, however, like my manuscript to be published. I beg the prince to keep one copy for himself and to let Aglaya Yepanchin have another copy. Such is my wish. I bequeath my skeleton to the Medical Academy for the benefit of science.

'I do not recognize any jurisdiction over me and I know that I am now beyond the power of a court of law. Not so long ago I was greatly amused by the thought that if I suddenly took it into my head to kill anyone I liked, or even a dozen people at once, or do something awful – something that is considered the most terrible crime in the world – I should certainly put the court in a quandary with my having only two or three weeks to live, now that every form of torture has been abolished. I should have died most comfortably in their hospital, in warmth, with an attentive doctor, perhaps much more comfortably and warmly than at home. I can't understand why such an idea never occurs to people in my position, even as a joke. But perhaps it does: there are lots of merry fellows even among us.

'But if I do not recognize any jurisdiction over me, I realize of course that I shall be judged when I am a deaf-and-dumb defendant. I do not want to go without leaving a word behind in my defence – a free defence, not an extorted one, not one to justify myself – oh no! I've no one's forgiveness to ask for anything – it's simply because I want to.

'To begin with, there is this strange consideration: by what right and with what motive would anyone take it into his head to impugn my right now to do what I liked with the two or three weeks I have left to live? What business is it of any court of law? Who wants me not only to be sentenced to death, but also to wait, like a good fellow, for the sentence to be carried out at the right time? Does anyone really want it? For morality's sake? I quite understand that if, while full of vigour and in the best of health, I were to take my life which might be "of use to my fellow-men", etc., morality might reproach me in the conventional way for having disposed of my life without asking permission, or for some other reason of its own. But now – now that the date of my death sentence has been fixed? What sort of morality is it that demands not only your life but also the last death-rattle with which you surrender the last atom of your life, listening to the consoling words of the prince whose Christian arguments are bound to come to the happy conclusion that, as a matter of fact, it is much better that you should die? (Christians like him always come to this conclusion: it's their favourite obsession.) And why are they so keen on trotting out their ridiculous "Pavlovsk trees"? To sweeten the last hours of my life? Don't they realize that the more I forget myself and the more I give myself up to this last illusion of life and love, with which they are trying to screen from me Meyer's wall and everything that is so frankly and openly written on it, the more unhappy they make me? What do I want with your nature, your Pavlovsk park, your sunrises and sunsets, your blue skies, and your smug faces, when all that festival, which has no end, has begun by refusing admission to me and me alone? What do I care for all this beauty when every minute, every second I have to – indeed, am forced to – recognize that even that tiny little gnat buzzing in the sunlight beside me now is taking part in this banquet and chorus, knows its place in it, loves it and is happy, and that I alone am an outcast, and have refused to realize it till now only out of cowardice! Oh, I know very well how much the prince and all of them would have liked me, instead of delivering myself of these "insidious and wicked" speeches, to sing, for the sake of decency, and the triumph of morality, the famous classical stanza of Millevoix – –

> *O, puissent voir votre beauté sacrée*
> *Tant d'amis, sourds à mes adieux!*
> *Qu'ils meurent pleins de jours, que leur mort soit pleurée,*
> *Qu'un ami leur ferme les yeux!*

'But believe me, believe me, my dear innocents, that even in these highly edifying lines, in this academic blessing to the world in French verse, there is hidden so much bitterness, so much irreconcilable, self-deluding malice that the poet himself perhaps fell into a trap and took that malice for tears of tender emotion and died in that belief – God rest his soul!

'I'd like you to know that there is a limit to disgrace in the consciousness of one's own worthlessness and powerlessness beyond which a man cannot go, and after which he begins to feel a tremendous satisfaction in his own disgrace. ... Humility, of course, is a great force in that sense, I admit it – though not in the sense in which religion accepts humility as a force.

'Religion! I admit the existence of eternal life, and maybe I always have admitted it. Granted that consciousness, kindled by the will of a higher power, has turned round upon the world and said: "I am!", and granted that it has suddenly been ordered by this higher power to destroy itself because it is for some reason necessary – no explanation is vouchsafed for it – granted all that, I admit it all, but the old, old question still remains: what has my humility to do with it? Can't I simply be devoured without being expected to praise that which has devoured me? Will somebody up there really be offended because I refuse to wait another fortnight? I don't believe it; it is much more likely to suppose that my worthless life, the life of an atom, may simply have been needed for the completion of some universal harmony, for some sort of plus and minus, for the sake of some contrast, etc., just as the lives of millions of creatures are daily required as a sacrifice because without their deaths the world could not exist (though I must say that is not a very generous idea in itself). But granted all that! I agree that otherwise – that is to say, without the continual devouring of one another – it was quite impossible to organize the world; indeed, I am even ready to admit that I understand nothing of that organization. But one thing I do know for certain. If once I have been granted the consciousness of "I am", what does it matter to me that the world has been made with faults and that otherwise it cannot exist? Who will put me on trial after that, and on what charge? Say what you like, but all this is impossible and unjust.

'And yet I never could, try as I might, imagine that there is no future life and no Providence. Most likely they do exist, but we understand nothing about the future life and its laws. But if it is so difficult and even impossible to understand, I could not answer for having failed to comprehend the incomprehensible, could I? It is true they say – and the prince, of course, is with them there – that this is where obedience is needed, that one must obey without reasoning, simply out of moral rectitude, and that I shall most certainly be rewarded in the next world for my meekness. We degrade Providence too much by attributing our ideas to it out of annoyance at being unable to understand it. But again, if it is impossible to understand it, then, I repeat, it is hard to have to answer for what it is not given to man to understand. And if that is so, how am I to be put on trial for not having been able to understand the true will and the laws of Providence? No, we'd better leave religion alone.

'Besides, I've said enough. When I read these lines the sun, I'm sure, will have risen and "resounded in the sky", and its immense and incalculable power will pour forth upon the world. So be it! I shall die gazing straight at the source of power and life, and I shall not want this life! If I had possessed the power not to be born, I should most certainly not have accepted existence upon such ridiculous terms. But I still possess the power to die, though the days I give back are numbered. I'm afraid it is no great power; it is no great rebellion, either.

'A final explanation: I am dying not at all because I have not the strength to endure these three weeks. Oh, I should have had the strength, and if I had a mind to I should have been sufficiently comforted by the mere consciousness of the wrong done to me; but I am not a French poet and I do not want such consolations. Finally, there's the temptation: nature has so limited my activities by its three weeks' sentence that suicide is perhaps the only thing I have still time to begin and end of my own free will. Well, perhaps I want to take advantage of the last possibility of *action*. A protest is sometimes no small matter. ...'

The 'Explanation' was finished; Ippolit stopped at last.

There is, in extreme cases, that final phase of cynical frankness when a nervous person, exasperated and beside himself, is no longer afraid of anything and is prepared for any unseemly scene, and, indeed, glad of it: he falls upon people with a vague, though firm, determination to fling himself from a belfry a minute later and by doing so at once to clear away all the misunderstandings that may exist. An imminent and complete physical exhaustion is usually one of the symptoms of such a state of mind. The extraordinary and almost unnatural tension which had kept Ippolit going until that moment had reached that ultimate phase. This eighteen-year-old boy, worn out by illness, seemed as weak as a trembling leaf torn from a tree. But as soon as he looked round on his audience – for the first time during the last hour – an expression of the most supercilious, most contemptuous, and most offensive disgust appeared in his eyes and in his smile. He was in a hurry with his challenge. But his audience, too, was highly indignant. They were all getting up from the table noisily and without disguising their annoyance. Fatigue, wine, and the nervous strain increased the general disorderliness and, as it were, the sordidness of their impressions, if one may put it like that.

Suddenly Ippolit jumped up from his chair as though he had been pulled out of it by force.

'The sun has risen!' he cried, seeing the gleaming tree-tops and pointing them out to the prince as though it were some miracle. 'It has risen!'

'You didn't think it wouldn't, did you?' observed Ferdyshchenko.

'Another confoundedly hot day,' Ganya muttered, with casual annoyance, stretching and yawning with his hat in his hands. 'I hope this drought won't go on for a whole month! Are we going or not, Ptitsyn?'

Ippolit listened to their remarks with an astonishment almost amounting to stupefaction; suddenly he turned terribly pale and trembled all over.

'Your air of indifference is all too obviously put on with the intention of insulting me,' he said, turning to Ganya and looking straight at him. 'You're a blackguard, sir!'

'That damn well takes the cake,' yelled Ferdyshchenko. 'Letting yourself go like that! What phenomenal weakness!'

'He's simply a fool,' said Ganya.

Ippolit pulled himself together a little.

'I quite understand, gentlemen,' he began, still trembling and his voice failing him at every word, 'that I may deserve your personal resentment and – I'm sorry to have tired you with this nonsense' (he pointed to his manuscript), 'or rather, not to have tired you out completely. ...' (He smiled stupidly.) 'Have I tired you out, Mr Radomsky?' he suddenly turned to Radomsky with the question. 'Have I or haven't I? Tell me?'

'It was a little long-winded, but – –'

'Tell me everything! Don't lie, for once in your life!' Ippolit demanded, trembling.

'Oh, it's absolutely all the same to me! Please leave me alone, I beg you!' Radomsky turned away in disgust.

'Good night, Prince,' said Ptitsyn, going up to the prince.

'But he's going to shoot himself any moment now! Please look at him!' cried Vera and, rushing up to Ippolit in great alarm, she seized him by the arms. 'Why, he said he'd shoot himself at sunrise! Please!'

'He won't shoot himself!' several people, including Ganya, muttered maliciously.

'Take care,' Kolya cried, also grasping Ippolit by the arm. 'Just look at him! Prince! Prince! Please!'

Vera, Kolya, Keller, and Burdovsky crowded round Ippolit; all four of them caught hold of his arms.

'He has the right – he has the right!' muttered Burdovsky, though he, too, looked quite lost.

'I'm sorry, Prince, but what are your orders?' asked Lebedev, walking up to the prince, drunk and insolent with rage.

'What orders?'

'No, sir, I'm sorry, but I'm the master of the house, sir, though I do not wish to treat you with disrespect – I mean, you're master here, but I don't want anything to happen in my own house, sir – – No, sir.'

'He won't shoot himself the boy's just playing the fool!' General Ivolgin unexpectedly cried, indignantly and with confidence.

'Bravo, General!' Ferdyshchenko applauded.

'I know he won't shoot himself, General, my highly honoured General; but all the same, for, you see, I'm master of the house.'

'Look here, Mr Terentyev,' Ptitsyn said suddenly, having said good-bye to the prince and holding out his hand to Ippolit. 'I think you mentioned your skeleton in your manuscript and said that you bequeathed it to the Academy, didn't you? Is it your own skeleton – I mean, your own bones – you're bequeathing?'

'Yes, my own bones. ...'

'I see. I mean, it's so easy to make a mistake, isn't it? I've been told there was such a case – –'

'Why do you tease him?' the prince cried suddenly.

'You've made him cry,' added Ferdyshchenko.

But Ippolit was not crying at all. He was about to move from his place, but the four people, who had crowded round him, at once seized him by the arms. Several people laughed.

'That was what he was leading up to – that people should hold his arms – that was why he read his story,' observed Rogozhin. 'Good-bye, Prince. I've been sitting here a long time. My bones ache.'

'If you really meant to shoot yourself, Terentyev,' laughed Radomsky, 'then in your place I should – after such compliments – make a point of not shooting myself, just to show them.'

'They're dying to see me shoot myself,' Ippolit pitched into him, speaking as though he were attacking someone.

'They are annoyed they won't see it.'

'So you don't think they will see it?'

'I'm not egging you on,' Radomsky said, drawing out his words patronizingly. 'On the contrary, I think it is very likely that you will shoot yourself. But whatever you do, don't lose your temper.'

'It's only now I see how awfully stupid I was to read them my manuscript,' said Ippolit, gazing at Radomsky with such a suddenly appealing look, as though he were asking a close friend for some friendly advice.

'I'm afraid it's a ridiculous situation, but – er – I don't really know what to advise you,' replied Radomsky, smiling.

Ippolit stared at him sternly, without taking his eyes off his face, and uttered no word. It looked as though he were completely abstracted.

'No, sir, I'm sorry, but what a way to talk,' said Lebedev. ' "I shall shoot myself in the park", if you please, "so as not to disturb anyone"! He thinks he won't disturb anyone by going down a few steps into the park.'

'Gentlemen – –' began the prince.

'No, I'm sorry, my dear Prince,' Lebedev went on furiously. 'Since you can see for yourself that it's no joke, and since half of your guests at least are of the same opinion, and are quite sure that after what he has said he has to shoot himself because his honour is at stake, I, as the master of the house, sir, declare in the presence of witnesses that I expect you to assist me.'

'But what are we to do, Lebedev? I'm ready to assist you.'

'I'll tell you what we have to do, sir. To begin with, he must at once give up the pistol he boasted about before us all, with all its appurtenances. If he gives it up, I consent, in view of his state of health, to let him spend the night in this house – under my supervision, of course. But to-morrow he must go anywhere he likes. I'm very sorry, Prince. If he refuses to give up his gun, I shall at once take hold of one of his arms and the general of the other and I shall immediately send for the police. Then, sir, it will be for the police to deal with the matter. Mr Ferdyshchenko, an old friend of mine, will go to fetch them.'

An uproar arose. Lebedev was getting more and more excited; Ferdyshchenko was getting ready to go to the police station; Ganya kept insisting frantically that no one was going to shoot himself. Radomsky was silent.

'Prince, have you ever tried to throw yourself off a belfry?' Ippolit whispered suddenly to him.

'N-no,' replied the prince naïvely.

'You don't imagine I didn't anticipate all this hatred, do you?' Ippolit whispered again, gazing at the prince with flashing eyes, as though he really expected an answer from him.

'Enough!' he shouted suddenly, addressing himself to the whole company. 'It's my fault – more than anyone's! Lebedev, here's the key' (he took out his purse and produced a steel ring with three or four small keys on it). 'This one – the last but one ... Kolya will show you. ... Kolya! Where's Kolya?' he cried, looking at Kolya and not seeing him. 'Oh, here he is – he'll show you. He helped me to pack my bag yesterday morning. Take him, Kolya. In the prince's study – under the table – my bag – open it with this key – at the bottom in a little box – my pistol and powder-horn – he'll show you. But on condition that to-morrow morning when I leave for Petersburg you will give me back my pistol. Do you hear? I'm doing it for the prince, not for you.'

'Ah, that's better!' Lebedev said, snatching up the key and, grinning venomously, he ran into the next room.

Kolya stopped as though wishing to say something, but Lebedev dragged him off after him.

Ippolit looked at the laughing guests. The prince noticed that his teeth were chattering, as though he had a bad chill.

'What blackguards they all are!' Ippolit again whispered to the prince in a frenzy.

Every time he spoke to the prince, he bent over and whispered.

'Leave them alone. You're very weak. ...'

'Presently, presently – I'll go presently.'

Suddenly he embraced the prince.

'I expect you think I must be mad,' he said, looking at him and laughing strangely.

'No, but you – –'

'One moment – be quiet – don't say anything – stand still, I want to look into your eyes. Yes, stand like that; let me look. Let me bid farewell to a human being.'

He stood still, looking at the prince, motionless and in silence, for about ten seconds, very pale, his hair wet with perspiration, clutching rather oddly at the prince with his hand, as though afraid to let go of him.

'Ippolit, Ippolit, what's the matter?' cried the prince.

'One moment – enough – I'm going to lie down. I'll just have one sip to the health of the sun. ... Let me, let me, I want to!'

He quickly snatched a glass from the table, darted away, and in a moment was on the veranda steps. The prince was about to run after him, but it so happened that at that very moment Radomsky held out his hand to him to say good-bye. A second later there was a general outcry on the veranda. It was followed by a minute of great confusion.

This is what had happened.

On reaching the top of the steps leading down from the veranda, Ippolit stopped dead, holding the glass in his left hand and putting his right hand into the right-hand pocket of his coat. Keller asserted afterwards that he had that hand in his right-hand pocket before, while he was talking to the prince and putting his left hand round the prince's shoulders and collar, and, Keller maintained, it was that right hand in the pocket that had aroused his suspicions at first. Be that as it may, a feeling of disquiet made him run after Ippolit. But it was too late. He only saw something flash in Ippolit's right hand, and at the same moment a little pocket pistol was close to his temple. Keller rushed to seize his hand, but at that very moment Ippolit pulled the trigger. There was the sound of a sharp metallic click, but no report followed. When Keller seized Ippolit, the latter collapsed into his arms, as though he were unconscious, and perhaps really imagining that he was killed. The pistol was already in Keller's hand. Ippolit was caught and placed in a chair, and all of them crowded round, shouting and asking questions. They had all heard the click of the trigger and saw a man who was alive, and not even scratched. Ippolit himself sat, not understanding what was going on, staring at them with a senseless expression. Lebedev and Kolya rushed in at that moment.

'A misfire?' they were asking.

'Perhaps it wasn't loaded,' some hazarded a guess.

'It's loaded!' Keller announced, examining the pistol. 'But – –'

'It misfired?'

'There was no firing-cap in it,' Keller announced.

It would be difficult to describe the pitiful scene that followed. At first the general alarm resolved itself in laughter; some of them even roared with laughter, finding a malicious pleasure in the incident. Ippolit sobbed as though he were in hysterics, wrung his hands, rushed up to everyone, even to Ferdyshchenko, clutching him with both hands and swearing that he had the caps on him, a dozen of them, in his waistcoat pocket (he showed them round to everyone), that he had not put one in before because he had been afraid of the gun going off accidentally in his pocket, that he had counted on having plenty of time to put it in at the right moment, but had suddenly forgotten it. He rushed up to the prince and Radomsky, he implored Keller to give him back the pistol, assuring him that he would show them that his 'honour – honour ––' that he was now 'dishonoured for ever....'

He fell unconscious at last. He was carried into the prince's study, and Lebedev, completely sobered, sent at once for a doctor, remaining himself at the sick man's bedside with his son and daughter, Burdovsky, and General Ivolgin. When the unconscious Ippolit had been carried out, Keller took up a position in the middle of the room and announced in a loud voice, so that all could hear, enunciating every word slowly and clearly, with absolute inspiration:

'Gentlemen, if any of you ever express any doubt in my presence that the cap was forgotten intentionally and asserts that the unhappy young man was only pretending to shoot himself, he will have to deal with me.'

But no one answered him. The visitors at last left in a crowd and in haste. Ptitsyn, Ganya, and Rogozhin went away together.

The prince was greatly surprised that Radomsky had changed his mind and was going away without speaking to him.

'Didn't you want to have a talk with me when the others had gone?' he asked him.

'So I did,' said Radomsky, sitting down on a chair suddenly and making the prince sit down beside him, 'but I have changed my mind for the time being. I'm afraid I'm rather upset, and so are you. My thoughts are all confused and, besides, the thing I want to discuss with you is very important to me – and to you, too, for that matter. You see, Prince, I should like for once in my life to do something absolutely honest – I mean something with no ulterior motive – and – well, I can't help thinking that at this moment I'm not quite capable of doing something absolutely honest, and neither are you, perhaps. So that – well – I mean, we'll talk about it later. Perhaps the matter may become much clearer to me and to you, if we wait two or three days, which I propose to spend now in Petersburg.'

Here he began to get up again, so that it seemed strange that he should have sat down at all. The prince imagined, too, that Radomsky was dissatisfied and irritated and regarded him inimically, and that there was something in his eyes that had not been there before.

'By the way, are you going to the patient now?'

'Yes – I am rather apprehensive,' said the prince.

'Don't worry. He'll live another six weeks, I'm sure, and he may even get better here. But I think the best thing you can do is to get rid of him to-morrow.'

'Perhaps I really did provoke him by – er – not saying anything. Perhaps he thought that I too didn't think he'd shoot himself. What do you think?'

'Not a bit. It's because you're so kind that you worry about it. I've heard of it, but I've never seen it actually happen that a man should deliberately shoot himself to gain admiration or out of spite because he was not admired for it. And most of all, I wouldn't have believed in such a frank admission of weakness. Get rid of him to-morrow, all the same.'

'Do you think he'll shoot himself again?'

'No, now he won't shoot himself. But beware of these home-bred Lacenaires of ours. I repeat, crime is all too usual a refuge for mediocre, impatient, and greedy nonentities of that sort.'

'But is he a Lacenaire?'

'At bottom – yes, though their occupations may be different. You'll see if this gentleman isn't capable of butchering a dozen people just to "show off". In fact, exactly as he himself told us in his "explanation". I'm afraid, now, those words of his will give me sleepless nights.'

'I think you're perhaps a little too anxious.'

'You're marvellous, Prince. You don't believe that he is *now* capable of killing a dozen people, do you?'

'I'm afraid to answer you. All this is very strange, but – –'

'Well, as you please, as you please!' Radomsky concluded irritably. 'You're, besides, such a brave person. Only mind you don't find yourself among the dozen.'

'Most likely he won't kill anyone,' said the prince, gazing thoughtfully at Radomsky.

Radomsky laughed spitefully.

'Good-bye! It's time I was off. But did you notice that he bequeathed a copy of his confession to Miss Aglaya?'

'Yes, I did, and – I'm wondering about it.'

'I should, in case of the "dozen", you know.' Radomsky laughed again and went out.

An hour later, about four o'clock, the prince went out into the park. He had tried to go to sleep, but could not, being kept awake by the violent throbbing of his heart. Things had calmed down in the house, and everything, as far as possible, was peaceful. The patient was asleep, and the doctor declared that there was no special danger. Lebedev, Kolya, and Burdovsky were lying down in the patient's room to take turns in looking after him. There was, therefore, nothing to fear.

But the prince's uneasiness increased every minute. He strolled through the park, looking absently around him, and stopped in surprise when he reached the bandstand in the pleasure-gardens and saw a row of empty seats and the music-stands of the orchestra. The place gave him a shock and seemed hideous to him for some reason. He turned back, and following the path along which he had walked the day before with the Yepanchins, came to the green seat where Aglaya had arranged to meet him, sat down on it, and suddenly laughed aloud, which at once made him feel extremely indignant with himself. His feeling of dejection persisted; he longed to go away somewhere. ... He knew not where. A bird was singing in a tree above him and he began looking for it among the leaves; suddenly the bird took wing and flew away, and at the same moment he, for some reason, recalled the 'gnat' in 'the hot sunshine', about which Ippolit had written that 'it knew its place and took part in the general chorus', but he alone was 'an outcast'. This sentence had struck him forcibly at the time; he remembered it now. A long-forgotten memory stirred in his mind, and suddenly it all came back to him clearly.

It had happened in Switzerland during the first year of his cure – during the first months, in fact. At the time he was still like an idiot; he could not even speak properly, and sometimes he could not understand what was required of him. One bright, sunny day he went for a walk in the mountains and walked a long time, tormented by a thought that, try as he might, seemed to be eluding him. Before him was the brilliant sky, below – the lake, and around, the bright horizon, stretching away into infinity. He looked a long time in agony. He remembered now how he had stretched out his arms towards that bright and limitless expanse of blue and had wept. What tormented him was that he was a complete stranger to all this. What banquet was it, what grand everlasting festival, to which he had long felt drawn, always – ever since he was a child, and which he could never join? Every morning the same bright sun rises; every morning there is a rainbow on the waterfall; every evening the highest snowcapped mountain, far, far away, on the very edge of the sky, shows with a purple flame; every 'tiny gnat' buzzing round him in the hot sunshine plays its part in that chorus: it knows its place, it loves it and is happy; every blade of grass grows and is happy! Everything has its path, and everything knows its path; it departs with a song and it comes back with a song; only he knows nothing, understands nothing, neither men nor sounds, a stranger to everything and an outcast. Oh, of course he could not express it at the time in those words, he could not come out with the question; he suffered dumbly, uncomprehendingly; but now it seemed to him that he had said it all at the time, that he had used those very same words, and that Ippolit took that 'gnat' from him, from the words and tears of those days. He was quite sure of that, and for some reason the thought of it set his heart pounding. ...

He dropped off on the seat, but his anxiety did not leave him in his sleep. Just before he fell asleep he remembered that Ippolit would 'kill a dozen people', and he grinned at the absurdity of the idea. A wonderful, bright stillness was all around him, broken only by the rustling of the leaves, which seemed to make everything around even more silent and solitary. He dreamt many dreams; all of them were troubled, and they made him start every moment. At last a woman came to him; he knew her, he knew her agonizingly well; he could always name her and point her out; but, strange to say, she did not seem to have the same face as he had always known, and he felt an agonizing desire not to acknowledge her as the same woman. There was so much remorse and horror in that face that it seemed she was a great criminal and she had just committed a terrible crime. A tear trembled on her pale cheek; she beckoned to him and put her finger to her lips, as though warning him to follow her quietly. His heart stood still; nothing, nothing in the world would make him admit that she was a criminal; but he felt that something terrible was going to happen any moment, something that he would remember all his life. She seemed to wish to show him something – not far off, in the park. He got up to follow her, and suddenly a gay, fresh laugh rang out beside him; he felt someone's hand in his; he seized the hand, pressed it tightly, and woke up. Before him stood Aglaya. She was laughing loudly.

8

Aglaya was laughing, but she was also indignant.

'Asleep! You were asleep!' she cried with disdainful surprise.

'It's you!' murmured the prince, still not quite awake and recognizing her with surprise. 'Why, yes! I was to meet you here – I'm afraid I fell asleep.'

'I saw you.'

'Did no one wake me except you? There was no one here except you, was there? I thought – I thought there was another woman here.'

'There was another woman here?'

At last he was wide awake.

'It was only a dream,' he said pensively. 'Strange that I should have had such a dream at this moment. ... Won't you sit down, please?'

He took her hand and made her sit down on the seat; he sat down beside her and sank into thought. Aglaya did not begin the conversation, but only looked at her companion intently. He, too, kept looking at her, but at times as though he did not see her beside him. She began to blush.

'Oh, yes,' the prince said with a start, 'Ippolit shot himself!'

'When? At your house?' she asked, but without great surprise. 'He was still alive last evening, wasn't he? How could you fall asleep here after all that?' she cried, suddenly becoming animated.

'But he isn't dead. The pistol did not go off.'

At Aglaya's insistent request, the prince had to tell her the whole incident of the previous night in great detail. She kept hurrying him along, though she interrupted him continually with questions, most of them irrelevant. Incidentally, she listened with great interest to what Radomsky had said, and even asked him several times to repeat it.

'Well, that'll do,' she concluded, having heard everything. 'We must be quick. We have only an hour here, till eight o'clock. I simply must be at home at eight o'clock, for they mustn't know I've been here, and I've come on business. I've lots of things to tell you. Only you've completely put me off now. So far as Ippolit is concerned, I think his pistol was bound not to go off – that is just like him. But are you sure that he actually wanted to shoot himself and that he was not trying to deceive you?'

'He was not trying to deceive us.'

'Yes, that's more likely. Did he actually write that you were to give me his confession? Why didn't you bring it?'

'But he isn't dead. I'll ask him for it.'

'Be sure to bring it to me, and you needn't ask him. He'll certainly be very pleased, for I expect he tried to kill himself because he wanted me to read his confession afterwards. Please don't laugh at me, I beg you, because it may very well be true.'

'I'm not laughing, for I'm quite sure myself that it may very well be partly true.'

'You're sure?' Aglaya cried suddenly, in great surprise. 'Do you really think so too?'

She put her questions quickly and spoke rapidly, but seemed at times to be confused and often did not finish her sentences; every moment she seemed in a hurry to warn him about something; she was altogether in a state of extraordinary anxiety, and though she put on a brave and defiant air, it is very likely that she was a little frightened too. She was wearing a very plain ordinary dress, which suited her very well. She often started and blushed; and she was sitting on the edge of the bench. She was very surprised at the prince's confirmation that Ippolit had tried to shoot himself so that she should read his confession.

'Of course,' the prince explained, 'he was anxious that not only you, but all of us should express our admiration for him.'

'Express our admiration? What do you mean?'

'I mean – well, how shall I put it? It is very difficult to put into words. Only I think he was certainly very anxious that we should all crowd round him and tell him that we were very fond of him and respected him, and that we should all beseech him to remain alive. It is very likely, indeed, that he had you in mind most of all, because he mentioned you at such a moment – though, I daresay, he did not know himself that he had you in mind.'

'That I simply can't understand: he had me in mind, and he did not know he had me in mind. And yet I don't know, perhaps I do understand. Do you know that I have thought of poisoning myself about thirty times, even when I was only thirteen, and writing all about it in a letter to my parents, and I also used to imagine how I would lie in my coffin and how everyone would weep over me and blame themselves for having been so cruel to me. ... Why are you smiling again?' she added quickly, frowning. 'What do you think of when you are day-dreaming? I expect you imagine yourself a field-marshal and dream of having defeated Napoleon?'

'Well,' the prince laughed, 'as a matter of fact, I do think of it, especially when I'm falling asleep. Only it's always the Austrians, not Napoleon that I'm defeating.'

'I don't at all feel like joking with you, sir. I'll see Ippolit myself. Please let him know. And I think it's very wrong of you, for it's very callous to think like that and judge a man's soul as you judge Ippolit. You have no tenderness: only truth and that's why you're unfair.'

The prince pondered.

'I don't think you are fair to me,' he said, 'for I don't find anything wrong in his thinking as he does, for we are all inclined to think like that. Besides, he may not have thought it at all, but only felt it – he longed to meet people for the last time and earn their respect and love. Those, you see, are very excellent feelings; only, somehow, it didn't turn out like that – it's his illness and something else! Besides, with some people everything turns out well, and with others as badly as can be. ...'

'I suppose you added that because you were thinking of yourself, didn't you?' Aglaya observed.

'Yes, I was thinking of myself,' replied the prince, not noticing the note of malice in her question.

'All the same I should never have fallen asleep in your place. It seems to me that you have only to sit down somewhere to fall asleep immediately. That's not very nice of you.'

'But I haven't slept all night, and I walked and walked afterwards. I went where they had the music – –'

'What music?'

'Where they were playing yesterday, and then I came here, sat down, thought and thought and fell asleep.'

'Oh, so that's what it was! That does make a difference in your favour. ... And why did you go to the bandstand?'

'I don't know. I just did.'

'Very well, very well – afterwards. You keep interrupting me. What do I care if you did go to the bandstand? What woman was it you were dreaming about?'

'It was – about – you saw her. ...'

'Oh, I understand, I quite understand. You're very much in – – How did you dream of her? What was she like? No, I don't want to know anything,' she snapped with vexation. 'Don't interrupt me. ...'

She waited a little, as though trying to pluck up courage or to overcome her vexation.

'You see, what I've asked you to come here for is this – I want to ask you to be my friend. Why are you staring at me all of a sudden like that?' she added, almost angrily.

The prince really did look at her very intently at that moment, noticing that she was beginning to blush all over again. Whenever that happened, the more she blushed, the more she seemed to be angry with herself, which could be plainly seen in her flashing eyes; ordinarily, a moment later, she would transfer her anger to the person she was talking to, whether he was to blame or not, and begin quarrelling with him. Deeply conscious of her own morbid diffidence and shyness, she usually avoided entering into a conversation and was more silent than her sisters, and sometimes even a little too silent. When, however, she simply had to say something, especially in such delicate circumstances, she began the conversation with an extremely haughty and a seemingly defiant air. She always knew beforehand when she was beginning or was about to begin to blush.

'Maybe you don't wish to accept my proposal?' she asked, looking haughtily at the prince.

'Yes, I do, only it's quite unnecessary – I mean, I never thought it necessary for you to make such a proposal,' said the prince in confusion.

'What did you think then? Why do you suppose I asked you to come here? What's in your mind? But I expect you must be taking me for a little fool, as they all do at home.'

'I didn't know they took you for a fool. I – I don't think you are.'

'You don't? That's very clever of you. You put it very cleverly, I must say.'

'I think that you're perhaps very clever sometimes,' the prince went on. 'Just now you said something very clever. You said in reference to my opinion of Ippolit: "There's nothing but truth here and therefore it's unfair." I shall remember that and think about it.'

Aglaya suddenly flushed with pleasure. All these changes in her mood took place with extreme frankness and extraordinary rapidity. The prince, too, was delighted, and even laughed with pleasure as he looked at her.

'Now listen,' she began again, 'I've been waiting a long time to tell you all this – I've been waiting ever since you wrote me that letter and even before that. Half of it I told you yesterday: I think you're the most honest and truthful man I know – more honest and truthful than anyone, and if people say about you that your mind – I mean, that you sometimes suffer from mental illness, it's unfair. I'm quite sure about it and I've been arguing about it, for although you really are ill mentally (you will not, of course, be angry with me for saying this, for I don't mean it at all derogatively), yet the most essential part of your mind is much better than in any of them. Indeed, it's something they never dreamed of. For there are two sorts of mind – one that is essential and one that isn't. Isn't that so? It is, isn't it?'

'Perhaps it is,' the prince agreed, hardly able to bring out the words, for his heart was trembling and pounding violently.

'I knew you would understand,' she went on gravely. 'Prince Sh. and Mr Radomsky don't understand a thing about these two sorts of mind. Neither does Alexandra. But just imagine: Mother did.'

'You're very like your mother.'

'No? Am I?' she asked with surprise.

'Indeed you are.'

'Thank you,' she said, after a moment's thought. 'I'm very glad I am like Mother. You must respect her very much, then?' she added, without being aware of the ingenuousness of her question.

'Very much indeed, and I'm glad you realized it at once.'

'I'm glad, too, because I've noticed how people – laugh at her sometimes. But, listen, I haven't told you my chief reason for coming here. I've been thinking it over a long time, and at last I've chosen you. I don't want them to laugh at me at home. I don't want to be treated like a little fool. I don't want to be teased. ... I realized it all at once, and I refused Mr Radomsky point blank, because I don't want to be continually being married off! I want – I want – well, I want to run away from home, and I have chosen you to help me.'

'Run away from home?' cried the prince.

'Yes, yes, yes, run away from home!' she cried suddenly, blazing up with extraordinary anger. 'I won't – I won't be made to blush there continually. I don't want to blush before them or before Prince Sh., or before Mr Radomsky, or before anybody, and that's why I have chosen you. I want to talk about everything to you – everything – even about the most important things, whenever I want to; and you, too, must never hide anything from me. With one person at least I want to be able to talk about everything, just as I do to myself. They suddenly began saying that I was waiting for you and that I loved you. That was even before your return, and I never showed them your letter. Now they all talk about it. I want to be brave, and not to be afraid of anything. I don't want to go to their balls. I want to be of some use. I've been wanting to go away for a long time. I've been shut up at home for twenty years, and they are always trying to marry me off. I wanted to run away when I was fourteen, though I was a fool. Now I've got it all worked out, and was just waiting for you to ask you all about going abroad. I have never seen a Gothic cathedral. I want to go to Rome. I want to inspect all the learned institutions. I want to study in Paris. I've been studying and preparing myself all last year, and I have read a great many books. I have read all the forbidden books. Alexandra and Adelaida read any books they like – they're allowed to do it; but I'm not allowed to read all of them. They are always supervising me. I don't want to quarrel with my sisters, but I told my father and mother long ago that I want to change my social position. I've decided to take up teaching, and I've counted on you because you said you liked children. Could we take up teaching together, if not now, then later? We shall be of some use to people in the future, both of us. I don't want to be a general's daughter. Tell me, are you a very learned person?'

'Oh, not at all.'

'A pity, and I thought – what made me think that? But you'll be my guide, all the same, for I have chosen you.'

'That's absurd, Aglaya.'

'I want to – I want to run away from home!' she cried, her eyes flashing again. 'If you don't agree, I'll marry Ganya. I don't want to be looked upon as an abandoned woman at home and be accused of goodness knows what.'

'Are you out of your mind?' cried the prince, almost jumping out of his seat. 'What are you accused of? Who is accusing you?'

'At home, everybody – Mother, my sisters, Father, Prince Sh., even your abominable Kolya! If they don't say it openly, they think it. I told them so to their faces, Mother and Father. Mother was ill the whole day, and next day Alexandra and Father told me that I didn't understand what nonsense I was talking and what words I was saying. So I just told them that I understood everything, all the words, that I'm no longer a little girl, that two years ago I purposely read two Paul de Kock novels to find everything out. Mother almost fainted when she heard me say that.'

A strange thought suddenly flashed through the prince's mind. He looked searchingly at Aglaya and smiled.

He could hardly believe that the same haughty girl who had so proudly and disdainfully read Ganya's letter to him was sitting beside him. He could not understand how so disdainful, stern, and beautiful a girl could be such a child, a child who perhaps really didn't understand *all the words*.

'Have you always lived at home?' he asked. 'I mean, did you never go to a day school or study at a boarding-school?'

'No, I've never been anywhere. I've always sat at home, corked up in a bottle, and I'm to be married straight out of the bottle. What are you smiling at again? I notice that you, too, seem to be laughing at me and are on their side,' she added, frowning menacingly. 'Don't make me angry; I don't know what's the matter with me as it is. ... I'm sure you came here because you thought that I was in love with you and that I had made an assignation with you,' she concluded sharply and irritably.

'I really was afraid of that yesterday,' the prince blurted out good-naturedly (he was rather confused), 'but to-day I'm sure that – –'

'What?' cried Aglaya, and her lower lip began quivering suddenly.

'You were afraid that I – how dare you think that I – goodness, I shouldn't wonder if you thought that I asked you to come here to lay a trap for you so that they might find us here and force you to marry me. ...'

'Aglaya, aren't you ashamed? How could such a sordid idea enter your pure, innocent heart? I bet you don't believe a word of it yourself and – you don't know yourself what you're saying!'

Aglaya sat with her eyes fixed steadily on the ground, as though frightened at what she had said.

'I'm not at all ashamed,' she murmured; 'and how do you know that my heart is innocent? How dared you send me a love-letter that time?'

'A love-letter? My letter – a love-letter? It was a most respectful letter; it came straight from my heart at a most painful moment of my life! I thought of you then as of someone who was very dear to me – I – –'

'All right, all right,' she interrupted him suddenly, no longer in the same tone of voice, but as if she were full of remorse and almost frightened. She even bent over him and, still trying not to look him in the face, almost touched his shoulder, as if to beg him more persuasively not to be angry with her. 'All right,' she added, looking thoroughly ashamed of herself. 'I know I used a very stupid expression. I said it just to – to test you. Take it as though it were never said. I'm sorry if I've offended you. Don't stare at me like that. Turn away, please. You said it was a very sordid idea. I said it on purpose, to hurt you. Sometimes I'm afraid of what I'm going to say myself, but I just can't help myself. You said just now that you wrote that letter at the most painful moment of your life. I know what moment it was,' she said softly, again looking at the ground.

'Oh, if you could know everything!'

'I do know everything!' she cried with renewed agitation. 'You'd been living at that time for a whole month in the same flat with that abominable woman with whom you ran away. ...'

She did not blush, but turned pale as she uttered those words, and suddenly got up, as though not realizing what she was doing, but, recollecting herself, at once sat down; her lips went on quivering for a long time. The silence lasted a whole minute. The prince was dreadfully shocked by the suddenness of her outburst and did not know to what to attribute it.

'I don't love you a bit,' she said suddenly, as though with deadly conviction.

The prince made no answer; again they were silent for a minute.

'I love Ganya,' she said, speaking rapidly, but almost inaudibly, and lowering her head still more.

'That's not true,' the prince said, also almost in a whisper.

'So I'm lying, am I? It is true. I promised to marry him the day before yesterday on this very seat.'

The prince was startled, and thought for a moment:

'That's not true,' he repeated, decisively. 'You've just made it all up.'

'How wonderfully polite you are! Let me tell you, sir, he's turned over a new leaf. He loves me more than his life. He burnt his hand in front of me to show me that he loved me more than his life.'

'Burnt his hand?'

'Yes, his hand. You may believe it or not – I don't care.'

The prince was silent again. Aglaya did not seem to be joking; she was angry.

'Why, did he bring a candle with him, if he did it here? I don't see how he could have done it otherwise. ...'

'Yes, he brought a candle. What's there so incredible about that?'

'A new candle, or one in a candlestick?'

'Well, yes – I mean, no – half a candle – a candle-end – a whole candle – what does it matter? Leave me alone! And he brought matches, too, if you must know. He lighted the candle and he held his finger over it for half an hour. Don't you think it's possible?'

'I saw him last night. There's nothing wrong with his fingers.'

Aglaya suddenly burst out laughing just like a child.

'You know why I told you that lie just now?' she suddenly turned to the prince with child-like trustfulness and her lips still quivering with laughter. 'Because if, when you tell a lie, you skilfully put in something not quite ordinary – something eccentric, I mean, something, you know that very rarely or even never happens – it sounds much more plausible. I've noticed that. Only it didn't come off with me because I didn't know how to do it.'

Suddenly she frowned again, as though recollecting herself.

'If,' she said, turning to the prince and looking gravely and even sadly at him, 'if, when I read you about the "poor knight" that day, I wished to – to express my admiration for you at the same time, I also wished to express my disgust with you for your behaviour and to show you that I knew everything.'

'You're very unfair to me – and to that unhappy woman of whom you spoke in such dreadful terms just now, Aglaya.'

'It is because I know everything – everything – that I spoke like that! I know that six months ago you proposed to her in the presence of everyone. Don't interrupt. You see, I speak without comment. After that she ran off with Rogozhin; then you lived with her in some village or town, and she left you for someone else.' (Aglaya blushed to the roots of her hair.) 'Then she came back again to Rogozhin, who loves her like – like a madman. Then you – also a very clever person – came rushing after her here the moment you heard that she had returned to Petersburg. Yesterday evening you rushed to defend her, and just now you were dreaming of her. ... You see, I know everything. You came to Pavlovsk for her sake, didn't you?'

'Yes, I did,' replied the prince quietly, lowering his head mournfully and pensively and not suspecting with what flashing eyes Aglaya glared at him. 'I came for her sake to find out – I don't believe she'll be happy with Rogozhin, though – in short, I don't know what I could do for her and how I could help her, but I came.'

He gave a start and glanced at Aglaya, who was listening to him with hatred.

'If you came not knowing why,' she said at last, 'you must love her very much.'

'No,' replied the prince – 'no, I don't love her. Oh, if you only knew with what horror I recall the time I spent with her!'

A shudder passed over his whole body as he uttered those words.

'Tell me everything,' said Aglaya.

'There's nothing here you shouldn't know. Why I should want to tell all this to you, and only you, I don't know. Perhaps it is because it was you I really did love very much. That unhappy woman is firmly convinced that she is the most depraved, the most vicious creature in the whole world. Oh, do not hold her up to scorn, do not cast a stone! She has suffered enough already from the consciousness of her undeserved shame! And, good heavens, what has she done to deserve any blame? Oh, she keeps crying every minute in her frenzy that she refuses to admit she has done wrong, that she is the victim of other people, the victim of a libertine and a villain. But whatever she may say to you, I want you to know that she is the first not to believe it and that she believes with all her heart that, on the contrary, she is herself to – to blame. When I tried to dispel that dark obsession of hers she suffered such agonies that my heart will always ache when I remember that dreadful time. I feel as though my heart had been pierced through and through and that my wound would never heal. She ran away from me – do you know why? Simply to prove to me alone that she was a bad woman. But the most dreadful thing is that perhaps she did not realize herself that she wanted to prove it to me alone, but ran away because inwardly she felt that she had to do something disgraceful so as to be able to say to herself at once: "There, you've done something disgraceful again, so you must be a depraved creature!" Oh, perhaps you won't understand this, Aglaya. Do you know that she seems to derive some dreadful, unnatural pleasure from this continual consciousness of shame, a sort of revenge on someone. Sometimes I was successful in making her see the light around her again, but all at once she felt so resentful that she accused me bitterly of putting myself far above her (though such a thought never entered my head), and when I offered to marry her she told me that she did not want condescending sympathy or help from anyone, nor did she want anyone to "raise her up to his level". You saw her yesterday. Do you really think she's happy with that rabble, that it is the sort of society for her? You don't know how well educated she is and the things she can understand! She used to surprise me sometimes!'

'Did you preach such – sermons to her there too?'

'Oh, no,' the prince went on pensively, not noticing the tone of the question. 'I hardly ever spoke. I often wanted to speak, but I really didn't know what to say sometimes. You know, in some cases it is best not to say anything at all. Oh, I loved her, I loved her very much – but later – later – later she guessed everything.'

'What did she guess?'

'That I only pitied her, but that I – I didn't love her any more.'

'How do you know she didn't really fall in love with that – that landowner she went away with?'

'No, she didn't. I know all about it. She only made a fool of him.'

'And she never made a fool of you?'

'N-no. She laughed at me from spite. Oh, then she would reproach me terribly, in anger, and she was miserable herself, too! But – afterwards – oh, don't remind me of it – don't remind me of it!'

He buried his face in his hands.

'And do you know she writes letters to me almost every day?'

'So it's true!' cried the prince in alarm. 'I heard of it, but still didn't want to believe it.'

'Who did you hear it from?' Aglaya asked, starting apprehensively.

'Rogozhin told me yesterday, but not in so many words.'

'Yesterday? Yesterday morning? Before or after the band?'

'After. At night, about twelve o'clock.'

'Oh! Well, if it was Rogozhin. ... And do you know what she writes to me in these letters?'

'I shouldn't be surprised at anything: she's mad.'

'Here are the letters' (Aglaya took three letters in envelopes out of her pocket and threw them down before the prince). 'For a whole week now she's been beseeching, persuading, and coaxing me to marry you. ... She – well, she's clever, though she may be mad, and you're quite right in saying that she's much cleverer than I. She writes she's in love with me and that every day she's trying to get a chance of seeing me even from a distance. She writes that you love me, that she knows it, that she noticed it long ago, and that you used to talk to her about me – there. She wants you to be happy. She's quite sure that only I can make you happy. ... She writes so wildly – so strangely. I haven't shown her letters to anyone. I've been waiting for you. Have you any idea what it can mean? Can't you guess anything?'

'It's madness, it's proof of her madness,' said the prince, and his lips quivered.

'You're not crying, are you?'

'No, Aglaya, I'm not crying,' said the prince, looking at her.

'What am I to do about it? What do you advise me? I can't go on receiving these letters!'

'Oh, leave her alone, I implore you!' cried the prince. 'What can you do in this murky darkness? I'll do all I can to prevent her writing to you again.'

'If so, then you have no heart!' cried Aglaya. 'Don't you see that she isn't in love with me, but that she loves you – you alone! You've had time to notice everything in her, but you have not noticed that! Do you know what this is? What these letters mean? She – do you really think she'll marry Rogozhin, as she writes in her letters? She'd kill herself the day after our wedding!'

The prince gave a start; his heart sank. But he looked in astonishment at Aglaya: it seemed strange to him to realize that this child was a full-grown woman.

'God knows, Aglaya, I'd gladly give my life to restore her peace of mind and to make her happy, but – I cannot love her any more, and she knows it.'

'Then sacrifice yourself! It's the sort of thing that becomes you so well! You're such a great philanthropist. And don't call me "Aglaya". ... A minute ago you also called me simply Aglaya. ... You must, it is your duty to restore her to life. You must go away with her again so as to pacify and soothe her heart. Why, you do love her!'

'I cannot sacrifice myself, though I wanted to once and – perhaps I want to still. But I know *for a fact* that with me she will be ruined, and that's why I am leaving her. I was to have seen her to-day at seven. I don't think I shall go now. In her pride she'll never forgive me for my love – and we shall both perish! This, I suppose, is unnatural, but everything here is unnatural. You say she loves me, but is this love? Can there be such love, after what I've been through? No, it's something else, not love!'

'How pale you've grown!' cried Aglaya, in sudden alarm.

'Oh, it's nothing. I haven't had enough sleep; I'm awfully tired – we really did talk about you then, Aglaya. ...'

'So it's true? You really *could talk to her about me* and – and how could you have fallen in love with me when you had only seen me once?'

'I don't know how. In that murky darkness I dreamed – I seemed to catch a glimpse of a new dawn. I don't know how it was that I thought of you first of all. It was the truth I wrote you then that I didn't know. It was all just a dream – a way of escape from the horror of that time. ... I began to work afterwards. I shouldn't have come back here for three years. ...'

'So you've come back for her sake?'

And there was a faint catch in Aglaya's voice.

'Yes, for her sake.'

For two minutes both of them were sunk in gloomy silence. Aglaya got up from her seat.

'If you say,' she began in an unsteady voice, 'if you yourself believe that that – woman of yours is – is mad, then I have nothing to do with her insane delusions. Please, sir, take these three letters and give them back to her from me! And if she,' Aglaya suddenly screamed, 'if she dares write me a single line again, you can tell her that I shall complain to Father and she'll be put away in an asylum!'

The prince jumped up and looked in dismay at Aglaya's sudden rage, and suddenly a mist seemed to descend before his eyes. ...

'You can't feel like that – it's not true!'

'It's true! True!' screamed Aglaya, almost beside herself.

'What is it? What is true?' a frightened voice near them asked.

Mrs Yepanchin stood before them.

'It's true that I'm going to marry Mr Ivolgin! That I love Mr Ivolgin and I'm going to elope with him to-morrow!' cried Aglaya, turning upon her. 'Do you hear? Is your curiosity satisfied? Are you happy now?'

And she ran off home.

'No, my dear sir, you'd better not go away now,' Mrs Yepanchin stopped the prince. 'Be so good as to come home with me and let me hear what you have to say for yourself. Oh, the things I have to suffer, and I haven't closed my eyes all night, either. ...'

The prince followed her.

9

Arrived home, Mrs Yepanchin stopped in the first room; she could go no further and she sank down on a settee, utterly exhausted, forgetting even to ask the prince to sit down. This was a fairly large drawing-room, with a round table in the middle, an open fireplace, masses of flowers on the chiffoniers near the windows, and a french window leading into the garden opposite the door. Adelaida and Alexandra came in at once and looked interrogatively at the prince and their mother.

In the country the girls usually got up at about nine o'clock. Aglaya alone had taken to getting up a little earlier during the last two or three days and going for a walk in the garden, though never at seven o'clock, but at eight or a little later. Mrs Yepanchin, who had really not slept all night because of her various worries, got up at about eight and, thinking that Aglaya had already got up, went to meet her in the garden. But she did not find her either in the garden or in her bedroom. Thoroughly alarmed, she woke up her two daughters. They found out from the maid that Aglaya had gone out into the park before seven o'clock. The girls smiled at this new whim of their whimsical sister and observed to their mother that Aglaya might well be angry with her if she went to look for her in the park, and that she was most probably sitting with a book on the green seat she had been talking of three days before and about which she nearly quarrelled with Prince Sh. because he did not find anything remarkable about its position. Having found her daughter alone with the prince and hearing her strange words, Mrs Yepanchin was dreadfully alarmed for many reasons; but having now brought the prince back with her, she was sorry to have started the whole thing: 'Why shouldn't Aglaya have met the prince in the park and talked to him even if they had arranged to meet there beforehand?'

'Don't run away with the idea, my dear Prince,' she plucked up courage at last to address him, 'that I've dragged you back here to cross-examine you. After what happened yesterday evening, I might not have been so anxious to see you for a long time.'

She stopped short.

'But all the same you'd very much like to know how I happened to meet Miss Aglaya this morning, wouldn't you?' the prince finished her speech for her very calmly.

'Well, what if I do?' Mrs Yepanchin flared up at once. 'I'm not afraid of speaking plainly. For I'm not offending anyone, and I had no wish to offend anyone.'

'Good heavens, there is no offence in your wanting to know – you are her mother. I met Miss Aglaya this morning at the green seat at seven o'clock at her own invitation yesterday. She let me know by a note yesterday that she had to see me to discuss something important. We met and talked for a whole hour about something that concerns Miss Aglaya alone. That is all.'

'Why, of course, my dear sir, that is all, and I don't doubt it in the least,' Mrs Yepanchin said with dignity.

'Well done, Prince,' said Aglaya, coming into the room suddenly. 'Thank you from the bottom of my heart for thinking me incapable of demeaning myself by telling lies. Are you satisfied, Mother, or do you intend to question us further?'

'You know that so far I have never had any occasion to blush for you, though I daresay you'd have been glad if I had,' Mrs Yepanchin replied pointedly. 'Good-bye, Prince. I'm sorry to have troubled you. You can always count on my unfailing respect.'

The prince at once bowed to Mrs Yepanchin and the three girls and went out without saying a word. Alexandra and Adelaida smiled and whispered something to one another. Mrs Yepanchin looked sternly at them.

'We only smiled because the prince bowed so marvellously, Mother,' Alexandra laughed. 'Sometimes he bows so clumsily, but now he suddenly bowed just like – Mr Radomsky.'

'It is the heart that teaches refinement and dignity, and not a dancing master,' Mrs Yepanchin concluded sententiously, and went straight up to her room without even bestowing a glance on Aglaya.

When the prince got home at about nine o'clock, he found Vera and the maid on the veranda. They were sweeping up and clearing away after the disorder of the night before.

'Thank goodness we've managed to finish before you came,' Vera said joyfully.

'Good morning. I'm afraid I'm feeling a bit dizzy. I didn't sleep well. I'd like to have a nap now.'

'Here on the veranda, as you did yesterday? All right. I'll tell them not to wake you. Father's gone out somewhere.'

The maid went out. Vera was about to follow her, but she came back and went up to the prince, looking worried.

'Prince, have pity on that – poor boy. Don't send him away today.'

'I shan't send him away on any account. Let him stay as long as he likes.'

'He won't do anything now and – don't be harsh with him.'

'Of course not. Why should I?'

'And – please don't laugh at him. That's the main thing.'

'Why, certainly not!'

'It's stupid of me to speak about it to a man like you,' said Vera, colouring. 'You may be tired,' she said, laughing and half turning to go away, 'but your eyes look so nice at this moment – so happy!'

'Not happy, surely?' the prince asked cheerfully and laughed gaily.

But Vera, as simple-minded and unceremonious as a boy, was suddenly embarrassed, coloured more deeply, and, still laughing, went out of the room.

'What a – nice girl!' thought the prince, and immediately forgot all about her. He went over to the corner of the veranda where there stood a settee with a little table in front of it, sat down, buried his face in his hands, and sat like that for about ten minutes; suddenly he put his hand in his side pocket, hurriedly and uneasily, and took out three letters.

But again the door opened and Kolya came in. The prince seemed glad to replace the letters and to put off the moment of reading them.

'Well, what a to-do!' said Kolya, sitting down on the settee and addressing himself straight to the subject, as boys like him always do. 'What do you think of Ippolit now? You don't respect him any longer, do you?'

'Why not? But I'm afraid I'm rather tired, Kolya. Besides, it's not a very cheerful subject to discuss again. ... How is he, though?'

'He's asleep, and he'll sleep for another two hours, I suppose. I understand you didn't sleep at home; you've been in the park and – and it's the excitement – I should think so!'

'How do you know I've been in the park and did not sleep at home?'

'Vera told me just now. She tried to persuade me not to come, but I'm afraid I had to see you – just for a minute. I've been sitting at his bedside for the last two hours. Now it's Kostya Lebedev's turn. Burdovsky has gone. Do lie down, Prince. Good – good day! Only, you know, I am surprised!'

'Of course – all this – –'

'No, Prince, no. I'm surprised at his "Confession". Chiefly that part of it where he speaks of Providence and the future life. There's a ter-rific thought there.'

The prince looked affectionately at Kolya, who had, of course, come in to have a talk about the terrific thought as soon as possible.

'But what is so important is not so much the thought as the whole background! If Voltaire, Rousseau, or Proudhon had written it, I'd have read it and remembered it, but I shouldn't have been struck by it as much as that. But for a man who knows for certain that he had only ten more minutes to live to talk like that – why, it shows pride! It's the highest assertion of personal independence and dignity – why, it's absolute defiance! Yes, sir, it's a gigantic strength of will! And after that to suggest that he deliberately didn't put in the firing cap – why, it's mean and incredible! But, you know, he deceived us last night – threw us off our guard: I never helped him to pack his bag and I never saw the pistol. He packed everything himself, so that for a moment I didn't know what to think. Vera says you're letting him stay here. I swear there's no danger, particularly as we never leave him alone.'

'And who was with him in the night?'

'Kostya Lebedev, Burdovsky, and I. Keller stayed a little while and then went off to sleep in Lebedev's room, because there was no spare bed for him in our room. Ferdyshchenko also slept at Lebedev's. He went off at seven. The general always sleeps at Lebedev's. He too has gone out. ... Lebedev may come to see you presently. He's been looking for you, I don't know why. He asked for you twice. Shall we let him in or not, if you are going to sleep? I'm going to bed too. Oh, by the way, I want to tell you something. I was surprised at the general this morning: Burdovsky woke me soon after six – almost at six, in fact, as it was my turn to look after Ippolit. I went out for a minute and suddenly met the general, who was still so drunk that he didn't recognize me. Stood before me like a post. Then he came to and fairly went for me. Wanted to know how the patient was. He was just coming to find out. I told him, and we talked about all sorts of things. "That's all very well," he said, "but what I really came out for – what I got up for – is to warn you. I have reason to believe that we oughtn't to talk freely in the presence of Ferdyshchenko and – one ought to keep one's mouth shut." Do you follow me, Prince?'

'Really? Still – it's all the same to us.'

'Yes, of course, it's all the same. We're not freemasons! That's why I was so surprised at the general's coming specially to get me out of bed at night to warn me.'

'Ferdyshchenko has left, you say?'

'At seven. He came in to see me on the way – I was sitting at Ippolit's bedside. Said he was going to have a good sleep at Vilkin's –

Vilkin is a friend of his who lives here – a drunkard. Well, I'm off! And here's Mr Lebedev. The prince wants to sleep, sir, right about turn!'

'Just one moment, my dear Prince,' Lebedev said in an undertone, stiffly and in a sort of meaningful tone of voice, bowing with dignity. 'I have come on some business which I believe is rather important.'

He had only just returned home and still held his hat in his hand. He looked worried and quite extraordinarily dignified. The prince asked him to be seated.

'You've inquired twice for me, haven't you? You're not still worried about last night's affair, are you?'

'You mean about that boy, Prince? Oh no, sir. I'm afraid I was a bit confused yesterday, but – er – to-day I do not intend to countermand any of your suggestions in any way.'

'Counter – what did you say?'

'I said countermand, sir. It's a French word, sir, as many other words that have entered into the composition of our language, but I do not defend it in any way.'

'What's up with you this morning, Lebedev? You look so important and dignified and you talk as though you scanned your words,' said the prince, with a smile.

'My dear Nicholas,' Lebedev turned to Kolya, speaking almost with deep feeling, 'in view of the fact that I have to acquaint the prince with some business relating to – er – –'

'Why, of course, it's none of my business! Good-bye, Prince,' said Kolya, withdrawing at once.

'I like the boy for his intelligence,' Lebedev announced, following him out of the room with his eyes. 'A bright boy, though rather tiresome. I'm sorry to say, my dear Prince, I ran into a bit of trouble last night or early this morning – I'm not sure of the exact time.'

'What is it?'

'I have missed four hundred roubles from my coat pocket, my dear Prince. I've been robbed, sir!' Lebedev added with a sour smile.

'You lost four hundred roubles? I'm sorry to hear it.'

'Yes, sir; it's a great loss for a poor man honourably eking out a living by his own exertions.'

'Of course, of course. How did it happen?'

'I'm afraid, sir, it's a result of the drinks I had. I've come to you as to my saviour, my dear Prince. I received the sum of four hundred roubles from one of my debtors at five o'clock yesterday afternoon and came back here by train. I had my wallet in my pocket. When I changed my civil service uniform for my coat, I put the money in the coat pocket with a view to keeping it on my person, intending to lend it that evening to a customer of mine – er – I was expecting my agent to call for it.'

'By the way, Lebedev, is it true that you put an advertisement in the papers that you lend money on gold and silver articles?'

'Through an agent, sir. My name does not appear, nor my address. Possessing only a paltry capital, sir, and in view of the increase of my family, you must admit, sir, that a fair rate of interest – –'

'Quite, quite. I only asked for information. I'm sorry to have interrupted.'

'My agent didn't come. In the meantime the poor boy arrived. I was in a rather – er – elevated condition after dinner. Then your guests, sir, arrived, we drank – er – tea, and I'm afraid I got a bit merry – to my undoing, sir. When that fellow Keller came in rather late and announced your great day and – er – your instructions about the champagne, I, my dear and highly esteemed Prince, having a heart (which, I daresay, sir, you must have noticed already, for I deserve it), having a heart, I will not say a sensitive but a grateful one, and I'm proud of it sir, I – er – owing to the great solemnity of the occasion and in the expectation of congratulating you personally, took it into my head to change my old shabby coat for the civil service uniform I had taken off on my return, which I did, as you, sir, no doubt observed, seeing me the whole evening in my uniform. Changing my coats, I forgot the wallet in my coat pocket. Verily, sir, when God wishes to chastise a man, He deprives him first of all of his reason. And it was only this morning, sir, at half-past seven, on waking up, that I jumped out of bed like a madman and, first thing, grabbed my coat – but the pocket was empty, sir! No trace of my wallet!'

'Dear me, that's unpleasant!'

'Yes, sir, unpleasant is right! You've found the right word for it with true tact,' Lebedev added not without guile.

'But, you know,' said the prince, looking alarmed and pondering, 'that's serious, isn't it?'

'Yes, sir, it is serious – that's another word you've found, sir, to describe – er – –'

'Good Lord, Lebedev, what's there to find? It's not the words that matter. ... You don't suppose you could have dropped the wallet out of your pocket when you were drunk, do you?'

'I could, sir, I could. Everything is possible when one is drunk, as you have so plainly put it, my highly esteemed Prince. But please consider, sir: if, when changing coats, I had dropped my wallet out of my pocket, the dropped article would have been lying there on the floor, wouldn't it? Well, sir, where is it?'

'You didn't put it in a drawer in a table by any chance, did you?'

'I've looked everywhere, sir, turned everything out, though I never hid it anywhere and never opened any drawer, as I distinctly remember.'

'Have you looked in your safe?'

'That's the first thing I did, sir. Looked into it several times this morning, I did, sir. But how could I have put it in the safe, my truly esteemed Prince?'

'I must say, Lebedev, I'm rather worried about it. I expect someone must have found it on the floor.'

'Or picked it out of my pocket! Two alternatives, sir.'

'I'm awfully worried about it, for who could have done it? That's the question.'

'No doubt whatever, sir, that *is* the question. I must say, most illustrious Prince, it's wonderful the way you find the exact words and ideas and hit the nail on the head!'

'No sarcastic remarks, Lebedev, please. This is – –'

'Sarcastic remarks indeed!' cried Lebedev, throwing up his hands.

'All right, all right; I don't mind. It's something else. ... I'm worried about the people. Whom do you suspect?'

'That's a very difficult and – er – complicated question, sir! I can't possibly suspect the maid: she was in the kitchen all the time. Nor any of my children. ...'

'I should think not!'

'So it must have been one of the visitors, sir.'

'But is that possible?'

'Absolutely and utterly impossible, sir, but I'm afraid it must be so. However, I'm quite ready to admit, and indeed I'm convinced, sir, that if it is a case of theft, it was committed not in the evening when we were all together, but at night or even in the morning by someone who spent the night here.'

'Oh dear, oh dear!'

'Burdovsky and Nicholas I naturally exclude. They didn't even go into my room, sir.'

'I should think so! Even if they had gone into your room. Who else spent the night with you?'

'Four, including me, sir. We slept in two adjoining rooms. The general, Keller, Ferdyshchenko, and I, sir. So it must have been one of us four!'

'One of three, you mean. But who?'

'I counted myself in to be fair and correct, but you will admit, Prince, that I couldn't have robbed myself, though such cases have been known. ...'

'Oh, Lebedev, this is so tiresome!' cried the prince impatiently. 'To the point – why do you drag it out so?'

'There are, therefore, three left, sir. Mr Keller, an erratic, drunken fellow and, in certain respects, a liberal – I mean in respect of the pocket, sir; in other respects with chivalrous rather than liberal propensities. He slept at first in the sick man's room, and came over to our room only later in the night on the pretext that he found it hard to sleep on the bare floor.'

'Do you suspect him?'

'I did suspect him, sir. When I jumped out of bed like a madman at about eight o'clock and, discovering the theft, slapped my forehead in despair, I at once wakened the general, who was sleeping the sleep of innocence. Taking into consideration the strange disappearance of Ferdyshchenko, which fact alone aroused our suspicion, we immediately decided to search Keller, who was lying there almost as dead as a door-nail, sir. We searched him thoroughly: not a cent in his pockets, and we couldn't find one pocket without a hole in it, either. His blue, check cotton handkerchief was in a most disgraceful condition, sir. Then we found a love-letter, one love-letter, sir, from some parlourmaid demanding money with threats, and bits of the article you know all about, sir. The general decided that he was innocent. To make quite sure, we woke him up, and that, sir, took some doing, I can tell you. He hardly understood what we were talking about. Opened his mouth wide – a drunken expression – an absurd and innocent, even stupid look on his face – it was not he, sir!'

'Well, I'm awfully glad,' the prince sighed with relief. 'It was for him I was afraid!'

'Afraid? Then you must have had some grounds for it, sir, mustn't you?' asked Lebedev, narrowing his eyes.

'Why, no, not at all,' the prince faltered. 'It was awfully silly of me to say that I was afraid. Do me the favour, Lebedev, don't tell anyone. ...'

'Why, my dear, dear Prince, your words are locked in my heart – deep in my heart! As in a grave, sir!' said Lebedev rapturously, pressing his hat to his heart.

'Very well, very well! So it's Ferdyshchenko? I mean to say, so you suspect Ferdyshchenko?'

'Who else?' said Lebedev quietly, looking hard at the prince.

'Well, yes, of course, who else? But, again, what proof have you?'

'I have proof, sir. First, his disappearance at seven o'clock or even before seven o'clock.'

'I know. Kolya told me he went to him and said that he was going to finish sleeping at – I forget whose house – some friend of his.'

'Vilkin, sir. So Nicholas has spoken to you already, has he?'

'He said nothing about the theft.'

'He doesn't know anything about it, for I've kept it a secret for the time being. So, he went to Vilkin's. Well, sir, it would seem there was nothing unusual about one drunkard going to visit another drunkard like himself, though very early in the morning and without any reason. But here's the first clue: before leaving, he left an address. Now, follow me closely, Prince. The question is, why did he leave an address? Why did he go out of his way expressly to see Kolya and tell him that he was going to finish his night's sleep at Vilkin's? Who is interested in the fact of his leaving and going to Vilkin's? Why announce it? No, sir, that's the cunning part of it, a thief's cunning! For what he meant to say was, "See, I purposely do not cover up my tracks, so what sort of a thief am I? Would a thief have told you where he was going?" An excess of anxiety to divert suspicion and, as it were, to obliterate his footprints in the sand. ... Do you follow me, my dear Prince?'

'I follow your meaning perfectly; but that's not enough, is it?'

'Now, sir, we come to the second clue: the scent turns out to be false and the address given inaccurate. An hour later – that is, at eight o'clock – I was knocking at Vilkin's. He lives here in Fifth Street, and, indeed, I know him. Ferdyshchenko wasn't there. Though I did obtain the information from the maid – deaf as a post, she is, too – that an hour before someone had really been knocking and ringing, and very loudly, too, so that he broke the bell. But the maid wouldn't open the door, not wishing to waken Mr Vilkin, and, perhaps, not wishing to get up herself. That happens, sir.'

'So that is all your evidence. That's not enough.'

'But, Prince, whom else am I to suspect? Consider!' Lebedev concluded sweetly, and there was something sly about his grin.

'You should search your rooms and all the drawers again!' the prince said, looking worried, after thinking it over for a moment.

'I have searched, sir!' Lebedev said, fetching an even sweeter sigh.

'I see! And why, why did you have to change your coat?' cried the prince, banging the table in vexation.

'A question from an old comedy, sir. But, my dear and most benign Prince, you take my misfortune too much to heart. I don't deserve it. I mean, I alone don't deserve it, for I can see that you are suffering for the criminal, too – for worthless Mr Ferdyshchenko!'

'Well, yes, you certainly have worried me,' the prince interrupted him absently, looking displeased. 'So what are you going to do – I mean, if you are so sure it is Ferdyshchenko?'

'But, my dear Prince, who else could it be?' Lebedev wriggled, looking as though butter wouldn't melt in his mouth. 'For you see, sir, there being no one else we can think of, and it being absolutely impossible to suspect anyone else except Ferdyshchenko, it is, as it were, another piece of evidence against Mr Ferdyshchenko – a third piece of evidence! For, once more, who else is there? I couldn't suspect Mr Burdovsky, could I? Ha, ha, ha!'

'What nonsense!' said the prince, almost angrily, turning impatiently on the settee.

'Of course, it's nonsense – ha, ha, ha! And how he made me laugh – the general, I mean! There we were, following the hot scent, to Vilkin's – and, let me tell you, sir, that the general was even more surprised than I was when I woke him up first thing after discovering my loss, so much so that he even changed countenance, turned red and pale, and finally grew so fiercely and righteously indignant that I hardly expected him to be capable of such indignation, sir. A most honourable gentleman! He never stops telling lies, but that's just a weakness of his, for he is a man of the most high-minded sentiments, a man who, though hardly of great intellect, sir, inspires the utmost confidence by his innocence. I believe, my dear Prince, I've told you already that I've not only a weakness but an affection for him. Suddenly he stopped in the middle of the street, flung open his coat and bared his breast: "Search me," he says. "You searched Keller, so why don't you search me? Justice," he says, "demands it!" And his arms and legs were shaking – went white as a sheet, he did, and very stern he looked too. I laughed. "Listen, General," I said, "if anyone else had said that about you, I'd have cut off my head with my own hands, put it on a salver, and carried it myself to anyone who doubted you. Do you see this head?" I'd have said, "Well, I'm ready to vouch with my head for him, and not only that, I'm ready to go through fire and water for him! That's how," I said to him, "I'm ready to vouch for you!" Well, he flung his arms round my neck, there in the middle of the road, burst into tears, and pressed me so tightly to his chest that I nearly choked with coughing. "You are," he said, "the only friend left to me in my misfortune!" Aye, a very sentimental fellow, sir! And, of course, on the way he told me a story, highly relevant to the occasion, of how in his youth he had been suspected of stealing five hundred thousand roubles, but that on the following day he had flung himself into a blazing house and dragged out of the flames the count who had suspected him and his own wife, Mrs Ivolgin, still a spinster at the time. The count had embraced him, and that was how he came to marry Mrs Ivolgin, and next day they found in the smouldering ruins the box with the missing money. It was an iron box of English make with a secret lock, and it had somehow fallen through the floor without anyone noticing it and was only found after the fire. An absolute lie, sir. But when he spoke of Mrs Ivolgin, he began whimpering. A most noble person, Mrs Ivolgin, though she's angry with me.'

'Don't you know her?'

'Well, sir, hardly at all, but I'd like to with all my heart, if only to justify myself to her. She bears a grudge against me, for she thinks I'm encouraging her husband to indulge in drinking. But far from encouraging him, I do my best to break him of his habit. I keep him away from most pernicious company. Besides, sir, he is my friend and, I assure you, sir, I'm not going to let him out of my sight now; why, indeed, where he goes, I go, for it is only by sentiment alone that you can get the better of him. You see, sir, he's stopped visiting his lady-friend, the captain's widow, altogether now, though he longs for her in secret, and sometimes he even moans for her, especially in the morning when he gets up and puts on his boots. I don't know why at that particular time. He has no money, sir – that's the trouble; for he can't possibly go to see her without. He hasn't asked you for money, my dear Prince, has he?'

'No, he hasn't.'

'He's ashamed to. He wanted to. Told me so himself. He'd like to trouble you, but he can't bring himself to, sir, for you lent him some money not long ago, and, moreover, he thinks you wouldn't give him any. He made a clean breast of it to me as his friend.'

'But don't you give him any money?'

'Why, my dear, dear Prince, I'd give him not only money but I'd give my life for him, as it were – but no, sir, I don't want to exaggerate – not my life, but, as it were, a fever, an abscess, or even a cough – why, I'd gladly put up with it for him, provided of course it were absolutely necessary, for I regard him as a great, though utterly ruined, man, sir! Yes, sir. Not only money, sir!'

'So you do give him money?'

'N-no, sir. Money I have never given him, and he knows perfectly well that I won't give him any, but, you see, sir, I do it solely with a view to restraining and reforming him. Now he's insisting on going to

Petersburg with me. For I'm off to Petersburg on Ferdyshchenko's hot trail, because I know for a fact, sir, that he's already there. My general is itching to go, but I suspect, sir, that he'll give me the slip in Petersburg to go and see his lady-friend. Now, I tell you frankly, sir, I shall let him go on purpose, for we have already arranged to go in different directions as soon as we reach Petersburg, this being the most likely way of catching Ferdyshchenko. So I'll let him go and then, like a bolt from the blue, I'll catch him at his lady-friend's – just to put him to shame as a family man and as a man, generally speaking.'

'But don't make a row, Lebedev. For God's sake, don't make a row!' said the prince in an undertone and with great uneasiness.

'Oh no, sir! Just to put him to shame and see what sort of face he makes; for, you see, my dear Prince, one can find out a lot from a man's face, and especially with a man like him! Oh, Prince, great as my own misfortune is, I can't help thinking even at this moment about reforming his morals. I have a great favour to ask you, my dear Prince, and I don't mind admitting that that's really why I came to see you: you know the general's family, and you have even lived in their house. I mean, if only, my dear and most kind Prince, you'd agree to assist me in this matter, just for the sake of the general and his happiness. ...'

Lebedev even put his hands together as though in supplication.

'Well, why not? But how am I to assist you? I assure you that I'm very anxious to understand you, Lebedev.'

'It's simply because I felt sure of that, sir, that I came to you! You could do it through Mrs Ivolgin – I mean, by constantly watching over the general and, as it were, keeping an eye on him in the bosom of his family. Unfortunately, sir, I don't know her. Besides, Nicholas Ivolgin, who worships you with every fibre of his youthful soul, as it were, might be of some assistance, too. ...'

'N-no, we mustn't involve Mrs Ivolgin in this business – God forbid! I'm not sure about Kolya, either. ... But perhaps I don't quite understand you yet, Lebedev.'

'Why, there's nothing to understand here, sir,' cried Lebedev, almost jumping out of his chair. 'Just tenderness and affection – that's all the medicine our patient requires. You do permit me, Prince, to think of him as a sick man, don't you?'

'Indeed, yes; this shows your delicacy and intelligence.'

'I shall explain it to you by an example taken from practice to make it clearer, sir. You see the sort of man he is: his only weakness now is for that captain's widow, and he cannot go to her without money, and it is at her place I intend, for his own good, to catch him in the act to-day; but supposing it were not for his lady-friend, supposing he had committed an actual crime or – well, some dishonourable action (though he's quite incapable of it) – why, even in that case, sir, I say that the only way of influencing him is by magnanimous tenderness, for he is a most sensitive man, sir. Believe me, he won't hold out for five days; he'll let the cat out of the bag himself, burst into tears, and confess everything, and particularly if we act cleverly and honourably, sir, through the supervision of yourself and his family over every move and step he takes. Oh, most benign Prince,' Lebedev said, jumping to his feet, with a sort of inspiration, 'I am not saying it is he. ... I'm ready, as it were, to shed the last drop of blood for him this minute, though you must admit that incontinence, drunkenness, and the widow woman – that all that, taken together – may lead him to anything.'

'I'm, of course, always ready to assist in such a cause,' said the prince, getting up, 'but I must confess, Lebedev, I'm terribly upset. Tell me, you're still – I mean, you said yourself that you suspect Ferdyshchenko.'

'Why, who else? Who else, most sincere Prince?' said Lebedev, smiling sweetly again and putting his hands together ingratiatingly.

The prince frowned and got up.

'You see, Lebedev, a mistake here would be a dreadful thing. That Ferdyshchenko – I shouldn't like to say anything bad about him – but that Ferdyshchenko – I mean, who knows, perhaps it is he! What I mean to say is that perhaps he really is more capable of it than – than anyone else.'

Lebedev pricked up his ears and opened his eyes.

'You see,' went on the prince, frowning more and more and getting more and more muddled, as he paced the room, trying not to look at Lebedev, 'I was given to understand – er – I was told about Ferdyshchenko that he seems to be – besides, the sort of fellow before whom one has to be careful what one says. ... I mean, one must be careful not to say – er – too much – you understand? I'm saying this because perhaps he really is more capable of it than anyone else – I mean, not to make a mistake – that's the chief thing – you understand?'

'And who told you that about Mr Ferdyshchenko?' Lebedev cried eagerly.

'Well, it was whispered to me. Not that I believe it myself, mind you – I'm awfully sorry I had to tell you this. I assure you I don't believe it myself – it's just nonsense. ... Oh dear, it was stupid of me to talk about it!'

'You see, Prince,' said Lebedev, trembling all over, 'this is important – this is very important indeed, now. I mean, not what you told me about Ferdyshchenko, but about how this information reached you.' (Saying this, Lebedev ran up and down the room after the prince, trying to keep pace with him.) 'You see, sir, let me, too, tell you something. This morning the general, when I was going with him to Vilkin's, seething with anger, suddenly began hinting the same thing about Ferdyshchenko, but so incoherently and so vaguely that I simply had to put certain questions to him, and as a result came to the conclusion that the whole thing was just an inspiration of his. Oh, with the best intentions in the world, of course. For, you see, he tells lies simply because he can't control his emotions. Now you see, sir, if he told a lie – and I'm sure he did – how could you have heard about it? For please understand, Prince, that on his part it was just an inspiration of the moment – so who could have told you about it? That's important, sir, and – as it were – –'

'Kolya told me just now, and he was told by his father, whom he met in the hall at six o'clock – or a little later, when he came out for something.'

And the prince told him everything in detail.

'Now, that *is* a clue, sir,' Lebedev said, rubbing his hands and laughing noiselessly. 'That's what I thought! It means that the general interrupted his sleep of innocence at six o'clock to wake his beloved son and tell him of the extreme danger of associating with Mr Ferdyshchenko! What a dangerous fellow Mr Ferdyshchenko must be after that, and how great the general's parental uneasiness must have been, ha, ha, ha!'

'Look here, Lebedev,' said the prince, completely confused, 'look here: act quietly! Don't create a row! I beg you, Lebedev, I implore you. ... In that case I swear I shall assist you, but on condition that not a soul knows about it – not a soul!'

'You may depend on it, most benign, most sincere and most noble Prince,' Lebedev cried with absolute inspiration, 'you may depend on it that all this will be buried in my most generous heart! Gently does it, sir! And together – together! As for me, sir, to the last drop of my blood. ... Most illustrious Prince, I'm vile in soul and spirit, but ask any man, any blackguard even, who he'd rather have dealings with, a blackguard like him or a most magnanimous man like you, openhearted Prince? He'd reply that he'd rather deal with one of the most magnanimous men, and therein, sir, lies the triumph of virtue. Goodbye, my dear Prince. Gently does it – gently does it – and – together!'

10

At last the prince understood why he turned cold every time he touched those three letters and why he had put off reading them till the evening. When, in the morning, he had fallen into a heavy sleep on the settee, still unable to make up his mind to open any of those three envelopes, he again had a bad dream, and again the same 'wicked' woman came to him. She again gazed at him with tears glistening on her long eyelashes, again beckoned to him to follow her, and again he woke up, as before, with an agonizing recollection of her face. He wanted to go to her at once, but he could not; at last, almost in despair, he opened the letters and began to read them.

The letters were also like a bad dream. Sometimes one dreams strange dreams, impossible and grotesque dreams; on waking you remember them distinctly and you are amazed at a strange fact. To begin with, you remember that your reason never deserted you all through the dream, you even remember that you acted with great cunning and logic during all that long, long time when you were surrounded by murderers who tried to deceive you, hid their intentions, treated you amicably, while they had their weapon in readiness and were only waiting for some signal; you remember how cleverly you cheated them in the end and hid from them; then you realize that they are perfectly well aware of your deception and are merely pretending not to know your hiding-place; but you have cheated and hoodwinked them again – you remember all that clearly. But why does your reason at the same time reconcile itself with such obvious absurdities and impossibilities with which, among other things, your dream was crowded? One of your murderers turned into a woman before your very eyes, and from a woman into a cunning and hideous little dwarf, and you accepted it at once as an accomplished fact, almost without the slightest hesitation, and at the very moment when your reason, on the other side, was strained to the utmost, and showed extraordinary power, cunning, shrewdness, and logic? Why, too, when awake and having completely recovered your sense of reality, you feel almost every time, and sometimes with extraordinary vividness, that you have left some unsolved mystery behind with your dream? You smile at the absurdity of your dream, and at the same time you feel that in the intermingling of those absurdities some idea lies hidden, but an idea that is real, something belonging to your true life, something that exists and has always existed in your heart; it is as though something new and prophetic, something you have been expecting, has been told you in your dream; your impression is very vivid: it may be joyful or agonizing, but what it is and what was said to you – all this you can neither understand nor remember.

The reading of those letters produced almost the same effect. But even before he had opened them, the prince felt that the very fact of their existence and their possibility was like a nightmare. How could *she* have brought herself to write to *her*, he kept asking himself as he wandered about alone that evening (sometimes hardly knowing himself where he was going). How could she write about *that*, and how could such an insane, fantastic idea have entered her head? But that fantastic idea had become a reality, and the most amazing thing to him was that, while reading those letters, he almost believed himself in the possibility, and even the justification, of that fantastic idea. Why, of course, it was a dream, a nightmare, insanity; but there was something in it, too, that was poignantly real and tormentingly just, something that justifed the dream, the nightmare, and the insanity. For several hours he seemed to be haunted by what he had read, every minute recalling scraps of it, brooding over them and pondering them. Sometimes he even could not help saying to himself that he had foreseen and known it all along; it even seemed to him that he had read it all before, a long, long time ago, and that everything he had longed for ever since, everything that had tormented him and that he had been afraid of – all that was to be found in those letters he had read long ago.

'When you open this letter [so the first letter began], you will first of all look at the signature. The signature will tell you everything and explain everything, so that I need not justify myself before you and I have nothing to explain to you. If I were in any way your equal, you might be offended by such impertinence. But who am I, and who are you? We are two such extremes, and I am so far beneath you that I couldn't possibly offend you even if I wanted to.

Further, in another place, she wrote:

'Do not consider my words as the morbid raptures of a morbid mind, but for me you are – perfection! I have seen you and I see you every day. I do not judge you; it is not by my reason that I have come to the conclusion that you are perfection; I simply believe in it. But, I'm afraid, I must also plead guilty before you: I love you. And one must not love perfection; one must look on perfection simply as perfection, isn't that so? And yet I am in love with you. Though love makes people equal, do not be afraid. I have never considered you my equal even in my most secret thoughts. I have written: "Do not be afraid"; but can you possibly be afraid? ... I would kiss your footprints, if I could. Oh, I do not put myself on the same footing with you. Look at the signature – quick, look at the signature!'

'I notice, however' [she wrote in another letter], that I associate him with you, and have never asked you whether you love him or not. He fell in love with you after seeing you only once. He spoke of you as of a "light"; those were his own words, I heard him use them. But I knew without words that you were a light for him. I've lived near him for a whole month and I understood that you, too, love him; you and he are one and the same to me.'

'What does it mean?' [she wrote again]. Yesterday I walked past you and you seemed to blush. It can't be true. I must be mistaken. If one were to take you to the filthiest den and show you vice in all its nakedness, you ought not to blush, you cannot possibly resent an insult. You can hate everyone who is vile and base, but not for your own sake, but for the sake of others, for the sake of those whom they wrong. But no one can wrong you. Do you know, I can't help feeling that you even love me. For me you are the same as for him: a bright spirit; an angel cannot hate, cannot help loving. Can one love everyone, all men, all one's neighbours? I have often asked myself that question. Of course not, and, indeed, it would be unnatural. In abstract love of humanity one almost always only loves oneself. But that's impossible for us, and you are a different matter: how could you not love anyone when you cannot compare yourself to anyone, when you are above every insult, every personal resentment? You alone are capable of loving not for yourself, but for the sake of him whom you love. Oh, how bitter it would be for me to discover that you feel shame or anger because of me! For that would be your undoing: you would at once become my equal. ...

'Yesterday, after meeting you, I went home and thought of a subject for a picture. Artists always paint Christ according to the Gospel stories; I would paint Him differently: I would depict Him alone – did not His disciples sometimes leave Him alone? I would have only a little child with Him – the child would be playing beside Him; perhaps he would be telling Him something in his childish language. Christ has been listening to him, but now He is pondering, His hand still resting, forgetfully, unwittingly, on the child's fair little head. He is looking into the distance, at the horizon; a great thought, as great as the universe, dwells in His eyes; His face is sad. The child is silent and is leaning against His knees, resting his cheek on his little hand, and, his head raised, looks intently at Him, pondering, as children sometimes ponder. The sun is setting. ... That is my picture! You are innocent, and in your innocence lies all your perfection. Oh, remember that only! What do you care for my passion for you? You are mine already now, I shall be all my life beside you. ... I shall be dead soon.'

Finally, in her last letter, she wrote:

'For God's sake, don't think anything of me; don't think that I humiliate myself by writing to you like this, or that I am one of those who enjoy humiliating themselves, even out of pride. No, I have my own consolations; but it is hard for me to explain it to you. It would be hard for me even to express it clearly to myself, though it gives me great pain. But I know that I could not humiliate myself even in an access of pride, and I am incapable of self-humiliation from purity of heart. So I do not humiliate myself at all.

'Why do I want to bring you together: for your sake or for mine? For mine, of course, for that would solve all my problems, I told myself that long ago. ... I have heard that your sister Adelaida said of my portrait, when she saw it for the first time, that with such beauty one could turn the world upside down. But I have renounced the world. I expect you must think it funny that I should say so, meeting me covered in lace and diamonds and in the company of drunks and rogues? Don't mind that, for I have almost ceased to exist, and I know that. Goodness only knows what lives in me in my place. I read it every day in two terrible eyes which are constantly staring at me, even when they are no longer before me. Those eyes are now *silent* (they are always silent), but I know their secret. His house is dreary and gloomy, and there is a secret in it. I am sure that he has a razor wrapped round with silk thread hidden in a drawer, like that murderer in Moscow; that man, too, lived in the same house as his mother, and he, too, had wrapped silk thread round his razor to cut a throat with. All the time I was in their house I could not help thinking that somewhere under the floorboards there was a dead man hidden, perhaps by his father, and covered by a piece of American cloth, like the dead man in the Moscow house, and round it in the same way were bottles with Zhdanov fluid. I could even point out the place to you. He is always silent; but I know that he loves me so much that he can't help hating me. Your wedding and mine are to take place at the same time: so I have arranged it with him. I have no secrets from him. I would kill him from fear, but he will kill me first. ... He laughed just now and said that I was raving; he knows I am writing to you.'

And there was much, much more delirious rambling of the same sort in those letters. One of them, the second one, written in a small hand, covered two large sheets of notepaper.

The prince at last left the dark park, in which he had been wandering a long time, just as the day before. The bright, transparent night seemed brighter than usual to him; 'Can it still be so early?' he thought. (He had forgotten to take his watch.) He thought he could hear music somewhere far away. 'In the pleasure-gardens, I suppose,' he thought again. 'Of course, they haven't gone there to-day.' As he thought that, he saw that he was standing close to their house; he knew that he would most certainly find himself there at last, and, with a sinking heart, he went up on to the veranda. There was no one to meet him there. The veranda was deserted. He waited a little and then opened the door into the large drawing-room. 'They never lock this door,' the thought flashed through his mind. But there was no one in the drawing-room, either. It was almost dark. He stopped in the middle of the room in perplexity. Suddenly a door opened and Alexandra came in with a candle in her hand. Seeing the prince, she looked surprised and stopped before him as though wishing to know what he was doing there. She was evidently only passing from one room to another, without thinking of finding anyone there.

'How did you get here?' she said, at last.

'I – I came in.'

'Mother isn't quite well, neither is Aglaya. Adelaida is going to bed. I'm going too. We've spent the whole evening at home by ourselves. Father and Prince Sh. have gone to town.'

'I've come – I've come to you – now. ...'

'Do you know what the time is?'

'N-no.'

'Half past twelve. We always go to bed at about one o'clock.'

'Oh dear, I thought it was – half past nine.'

'Never mind!' she laughed. 'And why didn't you come earlier? You were, perhaps, expected.'

'I – I thought – –' he murmured as he went out.

'Good-bye! I shall make them all laugh to-morrow.'

He walked along the road skirting the park towards his own house. His heart was pounding, his thoughts in a tangle, and everything round him seemed to be like a dream. And suddenly, just as before when he had twice awakened at the same apparition in his dream, the very same apparition again appeared before him. The same woman came out of the park and stood before him, as though expecting him to be there. He gave a start and stopped dead; she seized his hand and squeezed it tightly. 'No, it is not an apparition!'

And so at last she was standing face to face with him for the first time after their parting; she was saying something to him, but he stared at her in silence; his heart overflowed and ached with pain. Oh, he could never forget that meeting with her, and he always remembered it with the same aching pain. She went down on her knees before him, there in the street, like one demented; he recoiled in horror, while she tried to catch his hand to kiss it and, just as recently in his dream, tears glittered on her long eyelashes.

'Get up, get up!' he said in a horrified whisper. 'Get up at once!'

'Are you happy? Happy?' she asked. 'Say only one word to me – are you happy now? To-day – now? With her. What did she say?'

She did not get up and she did not obey him; she questioned him hurriedly and was in a hurry to speak, as though she were pursued.

'I'm going to-morrow as you told me. I shan't – I'm seeing you for the last time – for the last! Now it is absolutely for the last time!'

'Calm yourself,' he cried in despair. 'Get up!'

She scanned his face eagerly, clutching at his hands.

'Good-bye!' she said at last and, getting up, went quickly away from him, almost at a run.

The prince saw that Rogozhin had suddenly appeared at her side, had taken her arm, and was leading her away.

'Wait for me, Prince,' cried Rogozhin. 'I'll be back in five minutes.'

Five minutes later he actually did come back; the prince was waiting for him at the same place.

'I've put her in the carriage,' he said. 'There's been a carriage waiting round the corner since ten o'clock. She knew you would spend the whole evening with the other one. I told her exactly what you wrote to me in your letter to-day. She won't write to the other one again. She has promised, and she'll be leaving to-morrow, as you wish. She wanted to see you for the last time, though you refused to see her. We've been wating for you here, on that seat there, to catch you on your way home.'

'Did she bring you with her of her own accord?'

'Why not?' Rogozhin grinned. 'I saw what I knew already. I suppose you've read the letters?'

'Have you really read them?' asked the prince, amazed at the idea.

'I should think so! She showed me each letter herself. Remember the razor? Ha, ha!'

'She's mad!' cried the prince, wringing his hands.

'Who knows? Perhaps she isn't,' Rogozhin said softly, as though to himself.

The prince did not reply.

'Well, good-bye,' said Rogozhin. 'I'm leaving to-morrow, too. Don't think badly of me. By the way, old man,' he added, turning round quickly, 'why didn't you answer her question? Are you happy or not?'

'No, no, no!' cried the prince with unutterable sorrow.

'I never thought you'd say "yes"!' Rogozhin laughed maliciously, and he went away without looking round.

PART FOUR

I

About a week had passed since the meeting of the two persons of our story on the green bench. One fine morning, about half past ten, Varya Ptitsyn, who had gone out to visit one of her friends, returned home in a state of great and sad dejection.

There are people about whom it is difficult to say something that will at once describe them entirely as they are at their most typical and characteristic; those are the people who are usually called 'ordinary' or 'average', and who actually do represent the average in any sort of society. In their novels and stories writers mostly try to pick out certain social types and represent them imaginatively and artistically – types one rarely comes across in real life in the way they are represented in fiction and which nevertheless are more real than real life. As a type, Gogol's character Podkolyosin is perhaps an exaggeration, but he is not by any means a myth. Think of the thousands of intelligent people who, having learnt from Gogol about Podkolyosin, at once discover that scores of their friends and acquaintances are awfully like Podkolyosin. They knew even before Gogol that their friends were like Podkolyosin; what they did not know was that that was their name. In real life bridegrooms very seldom jump out of windows before their wedding because, apart from anything else, it is rather an inconvenient way of escape; nevertheless, quite a great number of bridegrooms, even worthy and intelligent men, have at the bottom of their hearts been ready to admit on the eve of their weddings that they were Podkolyosins. Nor do all husbands shout at every step, '*Tu l'as voulu, Georges Dandin!*' But, goodness me, how many millions and billions of times has this cry from the heart been repeated by husbands after their honeymoon or – who knows? – even perhaps the day after their wedding.

Therefore, without entering more deeply into the question, we will simply say that in real life the typical characteristics of people seem to be watered down, and that all the Georges Dandins and Podkolyosins actually do exist and are darting and rushing about before us every day, but in a sort of diluted state. Allowing, finally, for the fact that – to be absolutely truthful – Georges Dandin, exactly as Molière has created him, can, though rarely, be met in life, too, we will now conclude our discussion, which is beginning to look like some critical review in a periodical. We have, however, still not answered the question what a novelist is to do with quite 'ordinary', commonplace people and how he is to present them to his readers so as to make them at all interesting. To leave them out of the story altogether is impossible, for ordinary people are nearly always the link in the chain of human affairs; by leaving them out, we shall destroy the verisimilitude of our narrative. To fill novels only with types, or, for the sake of interest, simply with odd and fantastic people, would be unreal and improbable and, perhaps, even uninteresting. In our opinion, a writer ought to try to find interesting and instructive traits of character even among commonplace people. When, for example, the very nature of ordinary people consists entirely of their perpetual and unchangeable ordinariness or, better still, when, in spite of all their strenuous efforts to get out of the rut of ordinariness and routine, they end up all the same by remaining unchangeably and perpetually ordinary and commonplace, then such people acquire a sort of typical character of commonplace people who simply refuse to be what they are and do their utmost to be original and independent without possessing any qualities of independence.

To this category of 'ordinary' or 'commonplace' people belong certain persons of our story who, I must confess, have hitherto not been sufficiently explained to the reader. Such, indeed, are Varya Ptitsyn, her husband, Mr Ptitsyn, and her brother Gavrila Ivolgin.

There is, indeed, nothing more annoying than, for instance, to be rich, of good family, of pleasing appearance, fairly good education, far from stupid, and even kind-hearted, and, at the same time, to possess no talent, no peculiarity, not even any eccentricity, no idea of your own – to be, in fact, exactly 'like everyone else'. To be rich, but not as rich as Rothschild; to be of good family, but one which has never distinguished itself in any way; to be of pleasing appearance, but one which is not expressive of anything in particular; to have a good education, but not to know what to do with it; to be intelligent, but have no ideas of one's own; to possess a kind heart, but without magnanimity, and so on and so forth. There is an enormous number of such people in the world – far more than it appears; like all people, they may be divided into two categories: those of 'limited intelligence' and those who are 'much cleverer'. The first are the happier. For an 'ordinary' man of limited intelligence, for instance, nothing is easier than to imagine himself to be quite an extraordinary and original man and to rejoice in that belief without any misgivings. Some of our young women had only to cut their hair short, put on blue spectacles, and call themselves nihilists, to persuade themselves at once that, having put on their spectacles, they have immediately acquired 'convictions' of their own. Some of our men had only to perceive some faint glimmer of humanitarian feelings in their hearts, to persuade themselves at once that no one felt as they did and that they formed the *avant-garde* of civilization. It was quite enough for someone else to accept without asking any questions an idea he had heard about, or to read a page at random in some book, to imagine at once that it was 'his own idea' and that it was conceived in his own brain. The arrogance of the simple-minded, if one may use such an expression, assumes quite amazing proportions in such cases; all this sounds incredible, yet you come across this sort of thing every moment. This arrogance of the simple-minded, this total absence of doubt in his abilities by a stupid man is excellently portrayed by Gogol in his wonderful character of Lieutenant Pirogov. Pirogov never doubts that he is a genius or, indeed, that he is superior to any genius. He is so certain of it that it never occurs to him to question it; he does not question anything, anyway. The great writer was in the end forced to give him a thrashing to satisfy the outraged feelings of his reader, but, seeing that the great man merely shook himself and, to fortify himself after his severe punishment, treated himself to a cream bun, he just threw up his hands in amazement and left the reader to form his own opinion of his character. I never could quite reconcile myself to the idea that Gogol bestowed so humble a rank on the great Pirogov, for Pirogov was so self-satisfied that nothing could have been easier for him than to imagine himself, as his epaulettes grew thicker and more twisted with years and rise in rank, a great soldier, or rather not imagine it, but to have no doubts whatever about it: he had been made a general, so he must therefore be a great soldier! And how many Pirogovs have there not been among our writers, our men of learning, our propagandists? I say 'have been', but of course we have them still. ...

Gavrila Ivolgin belonged to a different category; he belonged to the category of people who are 'much cleverer', though he was infected from head to foot with the desire of originality. But this category of people, as we observed above, is far less happy than the first. For the trouble is that the clever 'ordinary' man, even if he does imagine himself occasionally (and perhaps all through his life) a man of genius and great originality, nevertheless preserves the worm of doubt in his heart, which sometimes drives the clever man to utter despair. If he does give in, it is only if he has been completely poisoned by vanity driven inwards. However, in either case we have taken an extreme example: in the large majority of cases of this *clever* category of people, things do not turn out so tragically; at most it is a matter of a more or less serious liver complaint in their old age, and that is all. Still, before giving in and resigning themselves to their fate, these people go on playing the fool for a long time, from their early youth to their declining years, and all because of their desire to be original. There are all sorts of strange instances of this: from the desire to be original an honest man is ready to do something base; it also happens that one of these unhappy men, though honest to a fault, kind-hearted, the guardian angel of his family, providing by his labour not only for his own flesh and blood but also for strangers, cannot set his mind at rest all his life. The thought that he has so well fulfilled his duties is no comfort or consolation to him; on the contrary, it is that very thought that exasperates him: 'So this is,' he thinks to himself, 'what I have wasted my life on, what has bound me hand and foot, what has prevented me from discovering gunpowder! But for this I should most certainly have discovered either gunpowder or America, I am not sure which, but I should most certainly have discovered it!' What is so characteristic of such gentry is that they can never be certain what exactly they have to discover or what exactly they have been on the point of discovering all their lives: gunpowder or America? But their agonized longing to discover something would most certainly have sufficed for a Columbus or a Galileo.

Ganya had started on that road, but only just started. He had still many years of playing the fool before him. A profound and continual realization of his own mediocrity and, at the same time, an irresistible desire to convince himself that he was a man of the most independent mind, had rankled in his heart ever since his boyhood. He was a young man of envious and impulsive desires, and he seemed to have been born with overwrought nerves. He mistook the impulsiveness of his desires for strength. In his passionate desire to excel, he was sometimes ready to take the most reckless risks; but as soon as the moment for taking such a risk came, our hero was always too sensible to take it. That drove him to despair. He would perhaps have made up his mind, given the chance, to do something really mean, for the sake of getting what he wanted so badly, but, as though on purpose, as soon as the moment for action came, he always seemed to be too honest to do anything that was too mean. (He was, however, always ready to agree to any petty meanness.) He looked with disgust and loathing on the poverty and downfall of his family. He even treated his mother with haughty disdain, although he knew very well that the character and reputation of his mother had so far been the mainstay of his career too. When he obtained his post as General Yepanchin's secretary, he at once said to himself: 'If I am to act like a rogue, then let me do it thoroughly, so long as I get what I want.' And – he hardly ever did it thoroughly enough. But what gave him the idea that he would have to act like a rogue? At the time he was simply frightened of Aglaya, but he did not give up his idea of marrying her eventually, though he never seriously believed that she would stoop to him. Then, at the time of his affair with Nastasya Filippovna, he suddenly imagined that the key to *everything* was – money. 'If I am to act like a rogue, then let me act like a rogue,' he used to repeat to himself every day with satisfaction, but also with a certain dismay. 'If I have to be a rogue, then let me be a super rogue,' he kept patting himself on the back. 'The ordinary man would be afraid to be one, but I won't!' Having lost Aglaya and crushed by circumstances, he lost courage completely and actually returned to the prince the money which a mad woman had flung at him and which had in turn been given her by a madman. Afterwards he regretted returning the money a thousand times, though he continually bragged about it. He actually cried for three days while the prince was in Petersburg, but during those three days he also had time to come to hate him because the prince seemed to be much too sorry for him, though 'not everybody would have had the pluck' to return so large a sum of money. But the honest admission to himself that his mood of despondency was entirely due to the constant wounds inflicted on his vanity, distressed him terribly. It was only a long time after that he realized what a happy turn his affair with such a strange and innocent girl as Aglaya might have taken. He was eaten up with remorse; he gave up his job, and was plunged into gloom and despondency. He lived with his father and mother at Ptitsyn's house and at his brother-in-law's expense, and he made no effort to disguise his contempt for Ptitsyn, though he listened to his advice at the same time and was sensible enough almost always to ask for it. Ganya was angry with Ptitsyn, for instance, because his brother-in-law was not proposing to become a Rothschild. 'If you are a usurer, then go ahead regardless, squeeze people, coin money out of them, be a man, be a King of the Jews!' Ptitsyn was quiet and modest; he just smiled, but once he found it necessary to have a serious talk with Ganya, and he did it with a certain dignity. He proved to Ganya that he was doing nothing dishonest and that he resented being called a Jew; that it was not his fault if money was so dear; that he was acting honestly and honourably, and that actually he was only an agent in these matters, and that, finally, thanks to his accuracy in business, he had earned an excellent reputation among first-class people and his business was increasing. 'I shall never be a Rothschild, and I don't want to be,' he added, laughing, 'but I shall certainly have a house on Liteyny Avenue and perhaps even two, and that will be as far as I'll go. And who knows,' he added to himself, 'perhaps even three!' – but he never said it aloud, concealing his dream. Nature loves and cherishes such people: it will reward Ptitsyn not with three, but with four houses, and just because he has known since childhood that he would never be a Rothschild. But beyond four houses nature will not go, and this is all Ptitsyn can hope to achieve.

Ganya's sister was quite a different person. She, too, had strong desires, but they were persistent rather than impulsive. She possessed a great deal of common sense in a crisis. It is true, she, too, was one of the 'ordinary' people who dream of being original, but she very soon realized that there was not a bit of originality in her, and was not worried about it too much – who knows? perhaps from a special kind of pride. She took her first practical step with great resolution by marrying Mr Ptitsyn; but when she married him, she never dreamt of saying to herself, 'If I am to act meanly, then let me act meanly, so long as I get what I want,' as Ganya would certainly have said to himself on a similar occasion (and, indeed, nearly said so in her presence, when, as the elder brother, he expressed approval of her decision). Quite the contrary: Varya married after having made absolutely sure that her future husband was a modest, agreeable, and almost educated man who would never do anything really discreditable. Varya did not bother her head about acts of petty meanness, dismissing them as mere trifles. And, indeed, where does one not come across such trifles? She was not looking for the ideal man, was she? Besides, she knew that by marrying she would provide a home for her mother, her father, and her brothers. Seeing that her brother was in trouble, she wanted to help him in spite of their former misunderstandings. Ptitsyn sometimes urged Ganya – in a friendly way, of course – to get himself a job in the Civil Service. 'I know,' he used to say to him jokingly, 'that you despise generals and people of high rank, but let me tell you "they" will all end by being generals. If you live long enough, you will see.' 'What makes them think I despise generals and people of high rank?' Ganya pondered sarcastically to himself. To help her brother, Varya decided to widen her field of action: she ingratiated herself with the Yepanchins, the memories of childhood standing her in good stead, for both she and her brother used to play with the Yepanchin girls as children. We may observe here that if Varya had been pursuing some extraordinary dream in visiting the Yepanchins, she would pehaps have at once relinquished the category of people which she had voluntarily joined; but she was not pursuing a dream: she had a very practical reason for doing so, since she based her calculations upon the peculiar character of the Yepanchin family. As for Aglaya's character, she was never tired of studying it. She set herself the task of bringing her brother and Aglaya together again. Perhaps she really did achieve something; perhaps she made a mistake in building, for instance, too much on her brother and expecting something from him he could possibly never have given. At all events, she acted rather skilfully when visiting the Yepanchins: for weeks she never mentioned her brother's name, she was always very truthful and sincere, and she carried herself very simply, but with dignity. She was never worried by her conscience and she never reproached herself for anything at all. It was this that gave her strength. One thing, though, she did notice about herself, and that was that perhaps she lost her temper too easily, that she, too, had a great deal of pride, if not, indeed, wounded vanity; she became aware of it particularly at certain times, almost every time she went home after a visit to the Yepanchins.

And now, as we have already said, she was on her way home from them in a state of sad dejection. There was a touch of bitter mockery in her distress. Ptitsyn occupied a spacious but rather unattractive wooden house in Pavlovsk. It stood in a dusty street, and it was shortly to become his own property, so that he was already negotiating for its sale. As she was going up the front steps, Varya heard a loud noise upstairs, and she made out the raised voices of her father and her brother. On entering the drawing-room, she saw Ganya pacing up and down, white with fury and almost tearing his hair. She frowned and sank with an exhausted air on the sofa without taking off her hat. Realizing very well that if she kept silent for another minute and failed to ask her brother why he was pacing the room in a temper, he would most certainly be angry with her, Varya brought herself at last to say in the form of a question:

'The same old story?'

'The same old story indeed!' cried Ganya. 'The same! No, not the same, but goodness only knows what is going on now! The old man is going stark raving mad – Mother's howling. Upon my word, Varya, I'm going to kick him out of the house or – I shall go away myself,' he added, probably remembering that he could not very well turn people out of someone else's house.

'You must make allowances,' murmured Varya.

'Allowances? Whatever for? Who for?' Ganya flared up. 'Allowances for his abominations? No, say what you like, but this is impossible! Impossible, impossible, impossible! And what a way to behave! It's all his own fault, but he still struts about! The gate is not big enough for his Lordship – take the fence down! What's the matter? Are you all right?'

'I'm all right,' Varya replied, displeased.

Ganya looked more intently at her.

'Have you been there?' he asked suddenly.

'Yes.'

'Wait a moment, they're shouting again! How disgraceful! And at such a time too.'

'What sort of time? It isn't any special time.'

Ganya looked even more intently at his sister.

'Have you found out anything?' he asked.

'Nothing unexpected, anyway. I found out that it's quite true. My husband was nearer the truth than any of us. It has turned out just as he foretold. Where is he?'

'He's gone out. What has turned out?'

'The prince is formally engaged to her – that's settled. The elder girls told me. Aglaya has given her consent. They don't conceal it any more. You see, till now they made such a mystery of it there. Adelaida's wedding is to be put off again, so that they can have the two weddings on the same day – how romantic! Just like a poem! You'd do better to write a poem on the happy occasion than to walk up and down the room like that. They're expecting Countess Belokonsky this evening – she's arrived just in time – they're going to have visitors. He's to be introduced to the countess, though he has met her already. I suppose their engagement will be announced. They're only afraid he may drop or break something when he comes into the room or else drop down himself. It's just the sort of thing he would do.'

Ganya listened very attentively, but, to his sister's surprise, this astonishing piece of news did not seem to have any striking effect on him.

'Well, that's that,' he said, after a moment's reflection. 'That's the end, then!' he added with a strange sort of smile, throwing a sly glance at his sister's face and still pacing the room, though more slowly.

'It's a good thing you take it so philosophically,' said Varya. 'I'm glad, really.'

'Yes, we can breathe more freely now – at least you can.'

'I think I've done all I could for you without arguing and without worrying you. I never asked you what sort of happiness you looked for with Aglaya.'

'But did I look for – happiness with Aglaya?'

'No, please don't try to be clever about it! Of course you did! Of course, we've had enough of it: we've been made fools of. I confess I never did regard it seriously. I took it up simply on the off chance, relying on her absurd character, and chiefly to please you; it was ten to one it would not come off. Even now I have no idea what you were trying to get out of it.'

'Now I suppose you and your husband will be trying to make me get some job, read me lectures on perseverance and will-power, not being too difficult, and so on. I know it all by heart.' Ganya burst out laughing.

'He's got something new in mind,' thought Varya.

'Well, how are they taking it there – are they pleased – the parents, I mean?' Ganya asked suddenly.

'N-no, I don't think so. However, you can judge for yourself. General Yepanchin is pleased. The mother is uneasy. She always regarded the idea of him as a prospective husband with loathing. Everybody knows that.'

'I don't mean that. It's quite clear he's an impossible and unthinkable bridegroom. I'd like to know what's happening there now. Has she given her formal consent?'

'She hasn't said "no" so far – that's all. But you couldn't expect anything else from her. You know how absurdly shy and bashful she is: she used to hide herself in a cupboard as a child and sit there for two or three hours to avoid coming out to visitors; she grew up a tall and gawky girl, and she's just the same now. You know, I can't help thinking that this time it really is serious, even on *her* part. I'm told she laughs at the prince from morning till night, but that's merely to conceal the fact that she most certainly manages to say something to him secretly every day, for he looks as though he were walking on air. He is radiant with happiness. ... They say he looks awfully funny. It's they who told me all this. I also thought that they were laughing at me to my face – the elder sisters, I mean.'

Ganya began to scowl at last; maybe Varya was deliberately enlarging on the subject to find out what he was really thinking. But again there was shouting upstairs.

'I'll kick him out!' Ganya simply bawled out, as though glad to have something to vent his disappointment on.

'And then he'll go off again disgracing us everywhere, as he did yesterday.'

'What do you mean yesterday?' Ganya cried, terribly alarmed suddenly. 'What happened yesterday? You don't mean to say he – –'

'Oh dear, don't you know?' Varya quickly recollected herself.

'What? Is it really true that he went there?' exclaimed Ganya, flushing with shame and fury. 'But why, you've only just come from there! Did you find anything out? Was the old man there? Was he or wasn't he?'

And Ganya made straight for the door; Varya rushed after him and grabbed him with both hands.

'What are you doing? Where are you going?' she said. 'If you let him out now, he'll do something a hundred times worse, he'll go to everyone. ...'

'What did he do there? What did he say?'

'They couldn't tell me themselves. They couldn't make any sense of it. He only frightened them all. He went to see General Yepanchin – he was out. He demanded to see Mrs Yepanchin. At first he asked her for a job, then he started complaining about us, me and Mr Ptitsyn, and especially of you – he said a lot of things – all sorts of things.'

'You couldn't find out, could you?' Ganya asked, shaking as though in hysterics.

'What could I find out? He scarcely knew himself what he was talking about, and perhaps they did not tell me everything.'

Ganya clasped his head and rushed to the window; Varya sat down at the other window.

'Aglaya is funny,' she remarked suddenly. 'She stopped me and said: "Please give your parents my special and personal regards and I shall most certainly find an opportunity of seeing your father quite soon." Speaking very seriously, too. It was awfully queer. ...'

'She was not sneering, was she?'

'No, not a bit of it, that's why it's so queer.'

'Does she know anything about the old man? What do you think?'

'I've no doubt at all that they know nothing about it in the house. But you've given me an idea: Aglaya perhaps does know. She is the only one who knows, for her sisters, too, were surprised when she asked me to give her regards to father so seriously. And why to him particularly? If she knows, then the prince must have told her!'

'It's not so difficult to guess who told her! A thief! It's the limit! A thief in our family, "the head of the family"!'

'Oh, nonsense!' cried Varya, losing her temper completely. 'A drunken escapade, nothing more. And who invented it all? Lebedev, the prince – they're a pretty pair themselves – wonderfully intelligent! I don't think much of it.'

'The old man is a thief and a drunkard,' Ganya went on bitterly. 'I'm a beggar, my sister's husband's a usurer – something to make Aglaya pine for! Nice, I must say!'

'That sister's husband who is a usurer has to – –'

'Feed me, you mean? Don't be afraid to say it, please.'

'Why are you in such a temper?' said Varya, recollecting herself. 'You don't understand anything. You're just like a schoolboy. You don't think all this will injure you in Aglaya's eyes, do you? You don't know the sort of girl she is. She wouldn't have anything to do with the most eligible young man, but would be delighted to starve in a garret with some student – that's her dream! You never could understand how interesting she would find you if you knew how to put up with our surroundings with pride and fortitude. The prince caught her first, because he was not eager to catch her and, secondly, because everyone regards him as an idiot. The very fact that she's upset her family about him is what appeals to her so much now. Oh, you don't understand anything!'

'Well, we'll see whether I understand or not,' Ganya murmured enigmatically, 'only I shouldn't like her to know about the old man all the same. I thought the prince would keep his mouth shut and not go blabbing about it. He kept Lebedev quiet and he wouldn't tell me everything when I insisted on knowing.'

'So you can see for yourself that everything is already known without him. But what does it matter to you now? What are you hoping for? And even if you had a hope left, that would only make her think of you as a martyr.'

'Oh, she'd be afraid of a public scandal too, in spite of her romantic ideas. Everything up to a point, and everyone up to a point. You're all like that.'

'Aglaya would be afraid?' Varya flared up, looking contemptuously at her brother. 'What a mean little soul you've got! You don't any of you deserve to get anything. She may be an absurd and eccentric girl, but she's a thousand times nobler than any of us.'

'Oh, never mind, never mind, don't be angry!' Ganya murmured again with a self-satisfied air.

'I'm only sorry for Mother,' went on Varya. 'I'm terrified this business about Father may reach her ears. Oh, I'm afraid it will!'

'I'm sure it has,' remarked Ganya.

Varya got up to go upstairs to her mother, but stopped short and looked attentively at her brother.

'Who could have told her?'

'Ippolit, probably. I expect he gave Mother a full account of it as soon as he moved in here. He must have enjoyed it tremendously.'

‘But how does he know? Tell me that, please. The prince and Lebedev decided not to tell anyone. Even Kolya doesn’t know anything.’

‘Ippolit, you mean? He found it out himself. You can’t imagine how clever the beastly fellow is. What a gossip he is! What a nose he has for smelling out anything bad, anything scandalous. You may not believe me, but I’m sure he’s got Aglaya eating out of his hand! And if he hasn’t, he will. Rogozhin, too, has got in touch with him. How the prince doesn’t notice it is beyond me! And how he’d simply love to trip me up now! He looks on me as his personal enemy. I’ve found that out long ago. And for what reason? What will he get out of it? He’s dying, anyway. I can’t understand it! But I’ll get the better of him, mark my words, I’ll trip him up, not he me.’

‘Why then did you get him to come here, if you hate him so much? And is he worth tripping up?’

‘It was you who advised me to get him to come here.’

‘I thought he’d be useful. And do you know that he has now fallen in love with Aglaya himself and has been writing to her? They asked me about it. I’m not sure he has not written to Mrs Yepanchin too.’

‘He’s not dangerous so far as that is concerned,’ said Ganya, with a malicious laugh. ‘Still, if not that, he’s up to something else. Quite likely he is in love with her, for he’s just a boy! But – but I don’t think he’d write anonymous letters to Mrs Yepanchin. He’s such a spiteful, insignificant, conceited mediocrity! I’m convinced, indeed, I’m quite sure he’s represented me as a schemer to her – that’s how he began. I admit that, like a fool, I was rather frank with him. I thought he’d be glad to promote my interests just to revenge himself on the prince. He is such a cunning little beast. Oh, I’ve seen through him now! And he heard about that theft from his mother, the captain’s widow. If the old man did make up his mind to do it, it was only for her sake. Suddenly, for no earthly reason at all, he tells me that the “general” has promised his mother four hundred roubles, and, mind you, for no reason at all, without the slightest ceremony. Of course, I saw it all at once. Stares at me full in the face with a sort of gleeful satisfaction. I suppose he had told Mother, too, for the sole pleasure of breaking her heart. And why doesn’t he die, tell me that! He promised to die in three weeks, and here he’s getting fatter! He isn’t coughing any more. He told me himself last night he hadn’t coughed up any blood for two days.’

‘Get rid of him.’

‘I don’t hate him,’ Ganya said proudly, ‘I despise him. All right, so I do hate him!’ he shouted all of a sudden with quite extraordinary fury. 'And I shall tell him that to his face, even when he lies dying on his bed. I wish you'd read his confession – good Lord, what naïve insolence! He's a second Lieutenant Pirogov, a Nozdryov in a tragedy, and, most of all, an impertinent street urchin! Oh, how I should have enjoyed giving him a thrashing, just to see how surprised he'd be! Now he's trying to revenge himself on everybody because he failed to do it then. But what's this? More shouting! What on earth is going on there? I – I just won't stand it! Ptitsyn,' he shouted to his brother-in-law, who came into the room, 'what's going on there? How long are we going to tolerate it? This is – this is – –'

But the noise was rapidly coming nearer, the door was suddenly flung open, and old Ivolgin, angry, purple in the face, and shaking with rage, also pounced on Ptitsyn. Mrs Ivolgin and Kolya followed the old man into the room, Ippolit bringing up the rear.

2

Ippolit had moved to Ptitsyn's house five days before. This had happened somehow naturally, without any special words and without any disagreement between him and the prince; far from quarrelling, they seemed to all appearances to have parted friends. Ganya, who had been so hostile to him at the prince's birthday party, himself came to see him, though not till three days after, probably impelled by some sudden idea. For some unknown reason, Rogozhin, too, began visiting the invalid. At first the prince thought that it would be better if 'the poor boy' went to live somewhere else. But when leaving, Ippolit said that he was going to stay with Ptitsyn, who was 'so kind as to give him a room of his own' and, as though on purpose, never said that he was going to live with Ganya, though it was Ganya who had insisted on his being received into the house. Ganya had noticed it at the time and – never forgave Ippolit for what he took to be a personal insult.

He was right when he told his sister that Ippolit was getting better. Ippolit was, in fact, feeling a little better than before, which was evident at the first glance. He came into the room without hurry, behind the rest, with an evil and sarcastic smile on his face. Mrs Ivolgin came in looking very frightened. (She had greatly changed during the last six months and looked much thinner; having married off her daughter and moved to her house, she seemed almost to take no further interest in her children's affairs.) Kolya looked worried and a little perplexed; there was a great deal he could not understand in 'the general's madness', as he put it, for he did not, of course, know the real reasons for this latest upset in the house. But he could see that his father was picking quarrels all over the place and at every hour of the day and had suddenly changed so much that he did not seem to be the same man. He was also worried by the fact that the old man had entirely given up drinking for the last three days. He knew that his father had broken and even quarrelled with Lebedev and the prince. Kolya had just come back home with half a pint of vodka he had purchased with his own money.

'Really, Mother,' he had assured Mrs Ivolgin upstairs, 'really, it'd be better to let him drink. For three days he's not touched a drop. He must be feeling awfully miserable. I used to take him drink in prison.'

The general flung the door wide open and stopped dead on the threshold, apparently quivering with indignation.

'Sir,' he shouted in a thunderous voice to Ptitsyn, 'if you have really made up your mind to sacrifice to a milksop and an atheist a venerable old man, your own father, sir, or at least your wife's father – a man, sir, who has done yeoman service for his Emperor – I will never set my foot in your house again, sir, from this very hour. Make your choice, sir! Make your choice this minute: either I or this – this screw, sir. Yes, sir, this screw! The word "screw" escaped me inadvertently, but he is a screw, sir! Because, damme, sir, he probes into my soul with a screw and, sir, without showing any respect – with a screw, sir!'

'Not a corkscrew?' Ippolit put in.

'No, sir, not a corkscrew, for you see a general before you, sir, not a bottle. I have decorations, sir, decorations I received for distinguished service, and you, sir, you haven't a damn thing – not a damn thing. Either he or I, sir! Make up your mind at once, sir, this minute!' he bawled again in a frenzy to Ptitsyn.

Kolya offered him a chair, and he sank into it almost exhausted.

'I think,' murmured Ptitsyn, bewildered, 'you'd better take – er – a nap, sir.'

'He has the face to threaten us!' Ganya said to his sister in an undertone.

'A nap, sir!' cried the general. 'Why, damme, this is an insult. I'm not drunk, sir. I can see,' he went on, getting up again – 'I can see that everybody is against me – everybody, sir, and everything. Very well, I'm going. But let me tell you, sir, let me tell you – –'

He was not allowed to finish; they made him sit down again and began entreating him to be calm. Ganya withdrew to a corner in a rage. Mrs Ivolgin was trembling and weeping.

'What is he complaining of? I haven't done anything to him, have I?' cried Ippolit, grinning.

'Haven't you?' Mrs Ivolgin observed suddenly. 'You, of all people, should be ashamed of torturing an old man. It's – it's so inhuman for someone in your position.'

'First of all, madam, what exactly do you mean by my position? I have a great respect for you, madam, for you in particular, you personally, but – –'

'He's a screw!' shouted the general. 'He bores into my heart and soul! He wants me to believe in atheism! Let me tell you, you whippersnapper, you, that honours were showered on me before ever you were born. And you, sir, you're just an envious little worm, cut in half, a coughing worm, sir, who – who is dying of spite and unbelief. ... And why did Gavrila bring you here? Everyone is against me – from strangers to my own son!'

'Stop acting a tragedy, please!' cried Ganya. 'It would be much better if you didn't disgrace us all over the town!'

'Disgraced you, sir, have I, you puppy – you! Disgraced you? Why, sir, you ought to feel honoured to have me for your father. Dishonoured you, indeed!'

He jumped up, and they could no longer hold him back; but Ganya, too, lost his temper completely.

'I like you talking about honour!' he shouted spitefully.

'What did you say, sir?' the general thundered, turning pale and advancing a step towards him.

'Why,' Ganya suddenly bawled, 'I have only to open my mouth to – –'

He did not finish. The two stood facing each other, stung to the quick, Ganya especially.

'Ganya, what are you saying?' cried Mrs Ivolgin, rushing forward to restrain her son.

'Stop this nonsense – both of you!' Varya snapped indignantly. 'Don't, Mother,' she said, catching hold of her.

'It's only for Mother's sake that I spare him,' Ganya announced tragically.

'Speak, sir!' roared the general in a perfect frenzy. 'Speak on pain of a father's curse – speak!'

'You don't think I'm frightened of your curse, do you? And whose fault is it that you've been walking about like a madman for eight days? Eight days, sir. You see, I've kept count of them. Mind you don't drive me too far. I'll tell everything. ... Why did you drag yourself off to the Yepanchins yesterday? Call yourself an old man, white-haired, the father of a family! A nice father!'

'Shut up, Ganya!' shouted Kolya. 'Shut up, you fool!'

'How have I offended him, I'd like to know,' Ippolit persisted, but still in the same ironical tone of voice. 'Why does he call me a screw? You heard him, didn't you? It's he who wouldn't leave me alone. Came to me and started talking about some Captain Yeropegov. I don't want your company at all, General. I've always avoided it, as you know very well yourself. What do I care for Captain Yeropegov, tell me, sir? I haven't come here for the sake of Captain Yeropegov. I merely expressed the opinion that Captain Yeropegov probably never existed at all. So he kicks up a shindy about it.'

'I'm sure he never existed!' Ganya snapped out.

But the general stood there as though stunned, and kept looking round in a dazed way. He was struck dumb by the extraordinary frankness of his son's remark, and for the first moment was completely at a loss what to say. It was only after Ippolit had burst out laughing in reply to Ganya's remark and shouted, 'There, did you hear? Your own son too says that there never was such a person as Captain Yeropegov,' that the old man muttered, completely bewildered:

'Kapiton Yeropegov, not captain – Kapiton – a retired lieutenant-colonel – Yeropegov – Kapiton – –'

'There was no Kapiton, either!' cried Ganya, thoroughly exasperated.

'Why – why not?' murmured the general, colouring.

'Do stop it,' Ptitsyn and Varya tried to pacify them.

'Shut up, Ganya!' Kolya shouted again.

But their intervention seemed to have restored the general's memory.

'How do you mean, sir? Why didn't he exist?' he shouted menacingly at his son.

'Because he didn't. He didn't exist – that's all. He couldn't have existed! So there! Leave me alone, I tell you.'

'And this is my son – my own flesh and blood, whom I – Lord! Yeropegov – Yeroshka Yeropegov didn't exist at all!'

'There you are! One moment it's Yeroshka and the next – Kapitoshka!' cried Ippolit.

'Kapitoshka, sir, Kapitoshka, not Yeroshka! Kapiton – Kapiton Alexeyevich – retired – married Maria – Maria Petrovna Su – Su – a good friend of mine – comrade in arms – Sutugov – Maria Sutugov – known him as an ensign. Shed my blood for him, sir – threw myself in front of him – killed. No Kapitoshka Yeropegov, indeed! Never existed!'

The general was shouting heatedly, but from the way he shouted it seemed that while talking of one thing, he had in mind quite another. It is true that at any other time he would have put up with something far more insulting than the statement about the complete non-existence of Kapiton Yeropegov. He would have shouted, kicked up a row, lost his temper, but in the end he would have gone upstairs to bed. But now – so extraordinarily unaccountable is the human heart – it turned out that an insult such as the doubt about Yeropegov was the last straw. The old man turned crimson, raised his arms, and shouted:

'I've had enough! My curses – out of this house! Nicholas, fetch my bag – I'm going – away!'

He went out, in a hurry and in a towering rage. Mrs Ivolgin, Kolya, and Ptitsyn rushed after him.

'Look what you have done now!' said Varya to her brother. 'He'll probably drag himself off there again! Oh, the disgrace, the disgrace of it!'

'Well, he shouldn't steal!' cried Ganya, almost choking with anger, and his eyes suddenly lighting on Ippolit, he almost shook with fury. 'And you, sir,' he shouted, 'ought to remember that you're not in your own house and – er – and that you're enjoying our hospitality, and you ought not to exasperate an old man who has obviously gone out of his mind.'

Ippolit, too, seemed to start violently, but he at once controlled himself.

'I'm afraid I cannot quite agree with you that your father has gone out of his mind,' he replied calmly. 'On the contrary, it seems to me that, if anything, he's been saner than ever of late. You don't believe me? Well, you see, he's become so careful, so meticulous, weighing every word, trying to get at the bottom of everything. ... He began talking to me about that Kapiton fellow with an object. Just imagine, he wanted to lead me on to – –'

'What the hell do I care what he wanted to lead you on to!' Ganya shrieked. 'Please don't you try to put anything over on me, sir! If you, too, know the real reason why the old man is in such a state (and you've been so assiduously spying for the last five days that I'm sure you do), you certainly ought not to have irritated the – poor man and worried my mother by exaggerating the affair, because the whole thing is just nonsense, a drunken escapade, nothing more. Nothing has been proved, anyway, and I don't think it's worth a rap. ... But you, sir, have to taunt and spy because you – you are – –'

'A screw,' Ippolit grinned.

'Because you are a rotter, sir. Worried people for half an hour, thinking to frighten them by threatening to shoot yourself with your unloaded pistol with which you made such a damned fool of yourself – you would-be suicide, you bagful of gall on – on two feet. I offered you hospitality, you've put on weight, you've stopped coughing, and that's how you repay me.'

'I'm sorry, but let me point out as briefly as I can that I am in Mrs Ptitsyn's house, and not in yours. You didn't offer me any hospitality and, as a matter of fact, you yourself are enjoying the hospitality of Mr Ptitsyn. Four days ago I asked my mother to find me a couple of rooms in Pavlovsk and to move here herself, for I really do feel better here, though I haven't grown fat at all and I'm still coughing. My mother let me know yesterday evening that the rooms are ready, and, for my part, I hasten to inform you that, after I have thanked your mother and sister for their kindness, I'll move there to-day, as I decided to do last night. I'm sorry to have interrupted you. I believe you wanted to say a lot more.'

'Oh, if that's so – –' Ganya said, quivering.

'If that's so, you will, I'm sure, permit me to sit down,' added Ippolit, calmly sitting down on the chair where the general had been sitting. 'You see, I am ill, after all. Well, I'm ready to listen to you now, particularly as this is the last conversation we shall have together and, indeed, probably our last meeting.'

Ganya suddenly felt ashamed of himself.

'You can be sure I won't demean myself by trying to settle accounts with you,' he said. 'And if you – –'

'You needn't be so much on your high horse with me,' Ippolit interrupted. 'So far as I'm concerned, I made up my mind on the very first day of my arrival here not to forgo the pleasure of telling you exactly what I think of you before we say good-bye to each other. I intend to do so now – after you've had your say, of course.'

'And I ask you to leave the room.'

'I think you'd better speak, or you'll be sorry not to have said all you wanted to say.'

'Don't, Ippolit,' said Varya. 'All this is so awfully humiliating. Please do me the favour, don't say anything more.'

'Well, just to oblige a lady,' laughed Ippolit, getting up. 'By all means, for you, Mrs Ptitsyn, I'm ready to cut it short, but only to cut it short, because some sort of explanation between your brother and myself has become absolutely necessary, and I'd never dream of going away without clearing up all misunderstandings.'

'You're simply a dirty little scandal-monger,' cried Ganya. 'That's why you won't go away without telling us all sorts of slanderous tales.'

'There, you see,' Ippolit observed calmly, 'you simply can't control yourself. You really will be sorry for not speaking out now. Once again, the floor is yours. I can wait.'

Ganya said nothing and looked contemptuously at him.

'You won't speak – want to show me how firm you can be – well, you can please yourself. As for me, I'll be as brief as possible. Two or three times to-day I've been reproached for abusing your hospitality. That's unfair. By inviting me to stay with you, you were trying to trap me. You thought I might want to revenge myself on the prince. You also heard that Aglaya had shown an interest in me and read my confession. Thinking for some reason that I would fall over myself to oblige you, you no doubt hoped that I might assist you. I won't go into more details! Neither do I expect any admissions or confirmations from you. I'm content to leave you to your conscience and that we understand each other perfectly now.'

'But you are making a mountain out of a molehill!' cried Varya.

'I told you he was a scandal-monger and an impertinent little brat,' said Ganya.

'Please, Mrs Ptitsyn, let me go on. The prince, of course, I can neither love nor respect. But he certainly is a very kind person, though a rather – ridiculous one, too. But there is no reason in the world why I should hate him. I never let on to your brother when he tried to incite me against the prince. I hoped, you see, to have a good laugh on him before the end. I knew that your brother would eventually let the cat out of the bag and make a thorough mess of things. And so it happened. I'm quite willing to spare him now, but only out of respect for you, Mrs Ptitsyn. But having explained to you that I'm not so easily taken in, you will, I hope, see why I was so anxious to make a fool of your brother. I want you to know that I did it out of hatred. I admit it freely. Before dying (because I am going to die in spite of having, as you assure me, put on weight) – before dying, I'd like to feel that I shall go to heaven with my mind incomparably more at peace if I succeed in making a fool of at least one representative of that numberless category of people who have persecuted me all my life, whom I hated all my life, and of whom your brother is such a conspicuous example. I hate you, Gavrila Ivolgin, solely because – you may find it a little surprising, perhaps – *solely because* you are the type, the embodiment, the personification, and the height of the most impudent, the most self-satisfied, the most vulgar and nasty mediocrity! A pompous mediocrity, a mediocrity always sure of itself and full of Olympian calm! You are the most ordinary of the ordinary! Not the smallest idea of your own will ever take shape in your head or in your heart. But you are damnably envious; you are firmly convinced that you are the greatest genius on earth, but, in spite of everything, doubt sometimes visits you during your dark moments, and you are filled with malice and envy. Oh, there are still dark clouds on your horizon, they will pass when you become completely stupid, and that's not a long way off. However, you have still a long and chequered road before you, not a very cheerful one, I'm glad to say. To begin with, let me tell you that you will never get a certain person.'

'Really, this is too much!' cried Varya. 'Will you ever finish, you horrid, spiteful little wretch?'

Ganya turned pale, trembled, and said nothing. Ippolit stopped short, looked intently and gleefully at Ganya, turned his gaze upon Varya, grinned, bowed and went out, without adding another word.

Ganya might with justice have complained of his lot and his lack of success. For some time Varya could not bring herself to speak to him, and she did not even look up at him when he strode past her; at last he walked up to the window and stood with his back to her. Varya was thinking of the saying 'it cuts both ways'. Again there was an uproar upstairs.

'Are you going?' asked Ganya, turning round to her suddenly as he heard her get up from her seat. 'Wait a minute. Have a look at this.'

He went up to her and threw on the table a folded piece of paper.

'Good gracious!' cried Varya, clasping her hands.

There were just seven lines in the note:

'Dear Ganya,

Convinced of your friendly feelings towards me, I should like to ask your advice on a matter of great importance to me. I should like to meet you to-morrow morning at precisely seven o'clock at the green seat. It's not far from our house. Your sister Varya, who must accompany you, knows the place well.

A.Y.'

'What is one to make of her after this?' Varya said, spreading out her hands in a gesture of bewilderment.

However little Ganya might have liked to swagger at that moment, he could not help showing his triumph, especially after Ippolit's humiliating predictions. His face beamed with a self-satisfied smile, and, indeed, Varya herself looked radiant with joy.

'And that on the very same day they are going to announce her engagement! What is one to make of her after that?'

'Have you any idea what she wants to talk about to-morrow?' asked Ganya.

'Oh, I shouldn't think that matters. The main thing is that she wants to see you for the first time after six months. Now, listen to me, Ganya: whatever has happened and however it may turn out, remember that *this is important*! It's terribly important! Please don't show off again, don't miss your chance again, and, mind, don't be afraid either. I don't think she could have failed to realize why I've been wasting my time calling on them for the last six months, could she? And would you believe it? She never said a word about it to me to-day! Never a hint! I practically had to smuggle myself into their house, you know. The old woman didn't know I was there, or she'd have thrown me out, I shouldn't wonder. I risked it for your sake, to find out at all costs. ...'

Again there was a noise and shouting upstairs; several people were coming down the stairs.

'We mustn't let it happen for anything in the world now!' Varya exclaimed, frightened and in a flurry. 'There mustn't be a breath of scandal! Go and apologize!'

But the father of the family was already in the street. Kolya was dragging his bag after him. Mrs Ivolgin stood on the top of the front steps, crying. She wanted to run after him, but Ptitsyn held her back.

'You're only making it worse,' he said to her. 'He has nowhere to go to. In half an hour he'll be brought back again. I've already had a word with Kolya about it. Let him play the fool for a bit.'

'Who are you trying to impress?' Ganya shouted from the window. 'Where do you think you're going? You've nowhere to go!'

'Come back, Father!' cried Varya. 'The neighbours can hear!'

The general stopped, turned round, stretched forth his hand, and cried:

'My curse on this house!'

'He would take the theatrical tone!' muttered Ganya, shutting the window with a bang.

The neighbours really were listening. Varya rushed out of the room.

When Varya had gone out, Ganya picked up the note from the table, kissed it, clicked his tongue, and cut a caper round the room.

3

The rowdy scene with the general would at any other time have come to nothing. Before, too, he had indulged in sudden ridiculous scenes of the same kind, though not often, because as a rule he was a very quiet man of an almost good-natured disposition. A hundred times, perhaps, he had made a determined effort to overcome the dissolute habits which had got the better of him in recent years. He would suddenly remember that he was 'the father of a family', and he would make it up with his wife and shed genuine tears. He respected his wife almost to the point of adoration because she had forgiven him so much in silence and even loved him, though he cut such a clownish and degraded figure. But his high-minded struggle against his dissolute mode of life did not usually last long: the general was also, in his way, of too impulsive a nature; he just could not stand the idle life of a penitent in the bosom of his family, and ended up by rebelling against it; he flew into a passion, for which he was perhaps sorry even as he did so, but he could not restrain himself: he quarrelled, began talking pompously and eloquently, demanded to be treated with the greatest and impossible respect, disappeared from the house, and sometimes did not return for a long time. During the last two years he knew very little, and mostly from hearsay, about the circumstances of his family; he had given up discussing them in detail, not feeling the slightest inclination for it.

But this time there was something rather extraordinary in 'the row with the general'; everyone seemed to be afraid to speak of it. The general had made his 'formal' appearance in his family, that is, had come back to his wife, only three days before, but somehow without any show of meekness and penitence, as was customary at his previous 'appearances'. On the contrary, he seemed to be quite extraordinarily irritable. He was loquacious and restless, talked heatedly with everyone he met, taking them by assault, as it were, on subjects so diverse and unexpected that it was quite impossible to find out what he was really worrying about. At moments he was very cheerful, but more often he fell into thought, without knowing himself, however, what he was thinking about. He would suddenly start talking about something – about the Yepanchins, the prince, or Lebedev – and suddenly stopped short and ceased talking altogether, answering all further questions with a vacant smile, without being aware that he had been asked a question or that he was smiling. He had spent the previous night moaning and groaning and had exhausted his poor wife, who had been up all night preparing hot fomentations for him; towards morning he had suddenly fallen asleep, slept for four hours and woken up with a violent and acute attack of hypochondria, which ended in his quarrel with Ippolit and his 'curse upon this house'. It was also noticed that during those three days he was continually subject to violent attacks of self-glorification and was consequently extraordinarily quick to take offence. Kolya, for his part, kept on assuring his mother that all this was the result of his craving for drink and, perhaps, for Lebedev, with whom the general had become quite extraordinarily friendly of late. But three days before he had suddenly quarrelled with Lebedev, and had parted from him in a terrible fury; he seemed to have had some sort of a scene with the prince too. Kolya had asked the prince for an explanation and began at last to suspect that he, too, seemed to want to tell him something. If, as Ganya had thought with good reason, Ippolit and Mrs Ivolgin had had some private conversation, it was strange that this spiteful young man, whom Ganya had called a scandal-monger to his face, had not found the same satisfaction in initiating Kolya into the secret. It was very possible that he was not such a spiteful 'little brat' as Ganya had painted him in his talk with his sister, but was spiteful in a different way; nor was it likely that he had informed Mrs Ivolgin of something he had observed solely for the sake of 'breaking her heart'. Don't let us forget that the motives of human actions are usually infinitely more complex and varied than we are apt to explain them afterwards, and can rarely be defined with certainty. It is sometimes much better for a writer to content himself with a simple narrative of events. This is what we shall do in the rest of our account of the present catastrophe with the general; for, try as we may, we have no choice but to bestow on this secondary character of our tale a little more attention and space than we had originally intended.

These events followed upon each other in the following order:

When Lebedev, after his journey to Petersburg to look for Ferdyshchenko, returned with the general the same day, he told the prince nothing in particular. If the prince had not been too busy and preoccupied with other matters of importance, he would soon have noticed that, far from offering any explanations to him during the following two days, Lebedev seemed to avoid meeting him for some reason. When the prince at last paid attention to this matter, he could not help being surprised that during those two days Lebedev, whenever they happened to run across each other, was in a most radiant state of mind, and almost always in the company of the general. The two friends never parted for a moment. The prince sometimes heard the sound of loud and excited conversation and laughing and cheerful argument coming from upstairs; once, very late at night, he suddenly and quite unexpectedly caught the strains of an army bacchanalian song, and he at once recognized the general's husky bass. But the song was suddenly cut short. Then a highly animated and, from all signs, drunken conversation went on for another hour. As might have been guessed, the two friends, who were having such a gay time, were embracing each other, and one of them finally burst into tears. This was followed by a violent quarrel, which also ceased abruptly soon after. All this time Kolya had somehow been particularly worried. The prince was mostly out all day and sometimes returned very late, and every time he was told that Kolya had been looking and asking for him. But when they met, Kolya had nothing special to tell him except that he was very 'dissatisfied' with the general and his present manner of behaviour: 'They wander about together, get drunk in a pub not far from here, embrace and quarrel in the street, incite each other and can't be parted.' When the prince pointed out to him that the same thing had happened almost every day before, Kolya seemed at a loss what to say to that or how to explain the cause of his present uneasiness.

The morning after the bacchanalian song and quarrel, the general, looking excited and almost distraught, suddenly confronted the prince just as he was leaving the house at about eleven o'clock.

'I've long been looking for a chance of meeting you, my dear Prince, very long,' he muttered, pressing the prince's hand very hard, almost till it hurt. 'Very, very long.'

The prince asked him to be seated.

'No, thank you, I won't sit down; besides, I'm afraid I'm detaining you – another time. I believe I may take this opportunity of congratulating you on – er – the fulfilment of – er – your heart's desire.'

'What heart's desire?'

The prince was embarrassed. It seemed to him, as to many people in his position, that no one saw, guessed, or understood anything.

'Oh, don't worry, sir, don't worry! I shan't hurt your most – er – delicate feelings. I've been through it myself, and I know what it feels like when a stranger – er – pokes his nose into affairs which are no concern of his. I feel it every morning. I have come about another matter: an important – er – matter; a very, very important matter, Prince.'

The prince asked him again to sit down and sat down himself.

'Ah well, for one second, perhaps. ... I've come for advice. I'm afraid, sir, I have no practical aim in life, but as I respect myself and – er – my business ability, in which the Russians, generally speaking, are so deficient, I – er – I'd like to put myself and my wife and children in a position – er – in short, Prince, I'm looking for advice. ...'

The prince expressed warm approval of his intention.

'Well, sir, that's all nonsense,' the general quickly interrupted. 'That's not what I really wanted to say, but something else, something important. I've decided to approach you, my dear sir, as a man in the sincerity of whose reception and the nobility of whose feelings I have complete confidence – as – as – – You're not surprised at my words, Prince?'

The prince was watching his visitor, if not with particular surprise, at all events with extraordinary attention and interest. The old man was a little pale, his lips quivered slightly sometimes, and his hands seemed unable to find a resting-place. He had been sitting for only a few minutes, yet he had twice already managed to get up from his chair suddenly, and as suddenly sit down again, evidently paying no attention to what he was doing. There were a few books on the table; he picked one up, while continuing to talk, glanced at the opened page, and at once shut it and put it back again; then he snatched up another book, which he did not open, and held it all the time in his right hand, constantly waving it about in the air.

'Enough!' he shouted suddenly. 'I can see, sir, that I'm disturbing you!'

'Why, not in the least, sir. On the contrary, I'm listening most attentively, and I'd be glad to know what you have to tell me. ... Please go on.'

'Prince, I'd like to put myself in a position of respect. ... I'd like to respect myself and – er – my rights, sir. ...'

'A man with so noble an ambition is worthy of respect on that account alone.'

The prince delivered himself of this copy-book phrase in the firm conviction that it would have an excellent effect. He felt instinctively that some such spacious but agreeable phrase, used at the right moment, would at once assuage and soothe the mind of such a man, and especially a man in the general's position. In any case, it was necessary to send such a visitor away with a relieved heart, and that was what he must try to do.

The phrase flattered, touched, and pleased the general very much:

he was suddenly deeply moved, instantly changed his tone, and plunged into long and rapturous explanations. But however much he tried and however intently he listened, the prince could not understand a single word. The general talked for ten minutes, heatedly and rapidly, as though too pressed for time to express the thoughts that crowded in his head; towards the end, tears glistened in his eyes. And yet it was only sentences without beginning or end, unexpected words and unexpected ideas, rapidly and unexpectedly bursting forth and stumbling over one another.

'Enough!' he suddenly concluded, getting up. 'You've understood me, and I'm satisfied. A heart such as yours, sir, cannot fail to understand a man who suffers. Prince, you are the ideal of nobility! What are other men beside you? But you are young, and I bless you. All I wanted to ask you was to fix an hour for an important conversation, and that is my chief hope, sir. All I ask for is friendship and sympathy, Prince. I have never been able to cope with the cravings of my heart.'

'But why not now, sir? I'm ready to listen to you.'

'No, Prince, no!' the general interrupted warmly. 'Not now! Now is a vain dream! It is too important – too important! That hour of conversation, sir, will be the hour of final decision. It will be *my* hour, sir, and I wouldn't like to be interrupted at such a sacred moment by anyone coming in, any impudent fellow, and quite likely a fellow so impudent,' he said, suddenly bending down to the prince in a strange, mysterious, and almost frightened whisper, 'a fellow so impudent as to be unworthy to tie your shoe-laces, my dear, dear Prince! Oh, I don't say my shoe-laces. Please note that particularly. I didn't say my shoe-laces; for I have too great a respect for myself not to speak plainly, but you alone are able to understand that by waiving my shoe-laces in such a case, I'm perhaps showing the utmost pride in my dignity. Except you no one will understand it, *he* least of all. *He* understands nothing, Prince. He's quite, quite incapable of understanding! One has to have a heart to understand!'

In the end the prince was almost alarmed and made an appointment to see the general at the same hour next day. The general went out in high spirits, greatly comforted and almost reassured. In the evening, at seven o'clock, the Prince sent to ask Lebedev to come and see him for a moment.

Lebedev made his appearance with quite extraordinary promptitude – 'esteemed it an honour', as he was not slow in announcing on coming in; there was not the faintest trace of a hint that he seemed to have been in hiding for three days and obviously avoided a meeting with the prince. He sat down on the edge of a chair, with smiles and grimaces, with laughing and watchful little eyes, rubbing his hands, and with an air of the most naïve expectation of hearing something, of receiving some news of tremendous importance, news he had been expecting for a long time and which he had guessed long before. The prince winced again; it became clear to him that everyone had suddenly begun expecting something of him, that everyone was looking at him as though wishing to congratulate him upon something, with hidden hints, smiles, and winks. Keller had already been to see him a few times for a moment, and he, too, was evidently wishing to congratulate him: each time he started saying something rapturously and vaguely, but never finished and quickly made himself scarce. (He had been drinking rather heavily somewhere of late, bawling at the top of his voice in some billiard-room.) Even Kolya, in spite of his melancholy, had once or twice also begun talking rather vaguely about something to the prince.

The prince asked Lebedev frankly and somewhat irritably what he thought of General Ivolgin's present condition and why the general was so worried. He told him in a few words of his interview with the general that morning.

'Everyone has his worries, Prince, and – er – especially in our strange and turbulent age – yes, sir,' Lebedev replied rather drily, and fell silent, looking hurt, and with the air of a man who had been disappointed in his expectations.

'What a philosophy!' said the prince, with a laugh.

'Philosophy's necessary, sir. It ought to be particularly necessary in our age, sir – I mean, in its practical application – but it's scorned; that's the trouble. So far as I'm concerned, my dear Prince, though I've had the honour of being trusted with your confidence in a certain matter you know of, but only up to a certain point and no further than the circumstances relating to that point alone. ... I quite understand and I'm not complaining.'

'You're not angry with me, Lebedev, are you?'

'Not at all, my dear and most illustrious Prince, not in the least!' Lebedev cried rapturously, laying his hand on his heart. 'On the contrary, I realized at once that neither by my position in the world, nor by the qualities of my mind and heart, nor by the accumulation of riches, nor by my former behaviour, let alone by my knowledge, am I worthy of your esteemed confidence, so far exceeding my hopes, and that if I can be of service to you, it's only as a slave and a hireling, not otherwise. I'm not angry, sir – I'm merely sad.'

'Come, come, Lebedev!'

'Not otherwise, sir! It's just the same in the present case! Meeting you and watching over you with all my heart and all my thoughts, I said to myself: "I am unworthy to receive any friendly communications from him, but, as his landlord, I may perhaps at the proper time, at some future date, receive the usual notice, or at most, an intimation in view of certain pending and expected changes. ..." '

As he said this, Lebedev fixed his sharp little eyes on the prince, who looked at him in astonishment; he was still hoping to satisfy his curiosity.

'I simply can't understand what you are talking about,' cried the prince, almost angrily. 'And – and you are a most horrible intriguer!' he suddenly burst out laughing with the utmost good humour.

Instantly Lebedev, too, burst out laughing, and his shining eyes at once showed that his expectations were confirmed, and, indeed, redoubled.

'And do you know what I'm going to tell you, Lebedev? Only, please, don't be angry with me, but I'm surprised at your simplicity, and not only yours! You're expecting to hear something from me at this very moment with such simplicity, that I really can't help feeling ashamed and sorry I have nothing to tell you that would satisfy you. But I swear I really have nothing to tell you, however hard you may find it to believe me!'

The prince laughed again.

Lebedev assumed a dignified air. It is true that he was occasionally a little too naïve and tiresome in his curiosity; at the same time, however, he was a rather cunning and slippery customer, and in certain cases a little too craftily silent; the prince almost made an enemy of him by repeatedly rebuffing him. But the prince rebuffed him not because he despised him, but because the subject of his curiosity was a rather delicate one. Only a few days earlier the prince had looked upon certain dreams of his as a crime. Lebedev, on the other hand, regarded the prince's rebuffs as evidence of personal aversion and mistrust and withdrew, cut to the heart and jealous not only of Kolya and Keller, but even of his own daughter Vera. Even at that very moment he could have told the prince a piece of news that was of the utmost interest to him and that he sincerely wished to tell him, but he sank into gloomy silence and did not tell him.

'What can I do for you, my dear Prince, seeing that you have sent for me – er – just now?' he said at last after a short pause.

'It was really about the general,' said the prince with a start, roused from his thoughts, too, 'and – er – that theft you told me about. ...'

'You mean, sir?'

'Oh dear, as if you don't understand me now! Good heavens! Lebedev, why are you always acting some part? The money – the money – the four hundred roubles you lost that day in your wallet and about which you came to tell me in the morning before leaving for Petersburg – do you understand now?'

'Oh, you mean those four hundred roubles,' drawled Lebedev, as though he had only that minute realized what the prince was driving at. 'Thank you, Prince, for your kind solicitude. It is too flattering, indeed, sir, but – er – I have found them – long ago!'

'You have! Well, thank God!'

'A most magnanimous exclamation, if I may say so, sir, for four hundred roubles are no small matter to a poor man who lives by his hard work and who has a large family of motherless children to support. ...'

'But I didn't mean that! Of course I'm glad you found the money,' the prince quickly corrected himself, 'but how – how did you find it?'

'Quite simply, sir. I found it under the chair on which I had flung my coat. My wallet must have slipped out of the pocket on to the floor.'

'Under the chair? It's impossible! You told me yourself that you looked all over the place. How could you have overlooked the most likely place of all?'

'Well, sir, now you're asking! Of course I looked! I do indeed remember looking only too well! Crawled on all fours, felt the place with my hands, moving back the chair, unable to believe my own eyes; but I could see there was nothing there – a bare and empty place, as smooth as the palm of my hand, sir – but I went on looking for it all the same. It's the sort of weakness, sir, a man who is anxious to find something always indulges in whenever he has lost something really valuable and important: he can see there's nothing there, the place is bare, and yet he searches for it a dozen times.'

'Well, I daresay, but how did you find it all the same? I'm afraid I don't understand,' muttered the prince, completely at a loss. 'You say it wasn't there before, that you looked for it there, and then all of a sudden it turned up!'

'Yes, sir, then all of a sudden it turned up.'

The prince gave Lebedev a strange look.

'And the general?' he asked suddenly.

'How do you mean, the general, sir?'

'Good Lord, man, I asked you what did the general say when you found your wallet under the chair? You looked for it together, didn't you?'

'Yes, sir, we did look for it together before. But this time I'm afraid I didn't say anything to him, thinking it better not to tell him that the wallet had been found by me – alone.'

'But – why? And the money? Was it all there?'

'Yes, sir. I opened the wallet. It's all there – to the last rouble.'

'I wish you'd come and told me,' observed the prince thoughtfully.

'I was afraid to disturb you, Prince, in the midst of your personal and, perhaps, immensely important, as it were, preoccupations. Besides, I myself acted as though I had found nothing. I opened the wallet, examined it, then closed it, and put it back under the chair.'

'Whatever for?'

'Oh, just so – out of curiosity, I suppose, sir,' Lebedev suddenly chuckled, rubbing his hands.

'So it is still lying there since the day before yesterday?'

'No, sir. It lay there only for one day. You see, sir, in a way I wanted the general to find it. For if I found it at last, why should not the general notice an object, as it were, under his very nose, protruding from under the chair? I lifted the chair several times, putting it back so that the wallet was in full view, as it were, but the general never seemed to notice it, and so it went on for a whole day. He seems to be very absent-minded nowadays – the general, I mean. One can't make him out at all, sir: talks, tells stories, laughs, simply roars with laughter, in fact, and then all of a sudden he gets terribly angry with me. Don't know why. At last we walked out of the room and I left the door open on purpose. ... Well, sir, he did hesitate a moment, wanted to say something, must have been afraid to leave the wallet with such a large sum of money in a room with an open door, but he suddenly flew into a violent temper and said nothing. Not a word, sir. We had scarcely stepped out into the street when he left me and walked off in a different direction. We only met in the evening in the pub.'

'But in the end you did pick your wallet up from under the chair, didn't you?'

'No, sir. It disappeared from under the chair the same night.'

'So where is it now?'

'Why, sir, it's here.' Lebedev laughed suddenly, rising from the chair and gazing pleasantly at the prince. 'It suddenly turned up here, in the skirt of my coat. Here, have a look, sir. Feel it, please.'

And, to be sure, there was a sort of protuberance in the left skirt of his coat, sticking out conspicuously, and it was only necessary to feel it to realize that it was a leather wallet which had dropped there from a torn pocket.

'Well, sir, I took it out and had a look at it – it's all there. So I put it back, and I've been walking about like that since yesterday morning and carrying it in the skirt of my coat. Knocks against my legs, it does, sir!'

'And you don't take any notice of it?'

'No, sir, I don't take any notice of it, ha, ha! And, just think of it, my dear Prince, though – it's hardly worth drawing your attention to so small a point – my pockets never have any holes in them, and then, all of a sudden, such a huge hole in one night! I examined it most carefully, and it looks to me as though someone had cut it with a penknife. It's hardly believable, is it?'

'And – the general?'

'He was awfully cross with me, for a whole day – yesterday and today. Looked terribly disconcerted about something. ... One moment overflowing with high spirits and quite flatteringly bacchanalian, at another sentimental and shedding tears, and then suddenly flying into such a violent rage that he simply terrifies me – upon my word, he does. After all, sir, I'm not a military man. We were sitting in the pub yesterday, and quite by accident, mind you, the skirt of my coat stuck out right under his nose – as big as a mountain. He kept looking at it out of a corner of his eye, as angry as anything. He hasn't looked me straight in the face for some time now, except when he's very drunk or sentimental. But yesterday he stared so fiercely at me twice that a cold shiver ran down my spine. To-morrow, though, I intend to find my wallet, but before then I'm going to spend another pleasant evening with him.'

'Why are you tormenting him like that?' cried the prince.

'I'm not tormenting him, Prince, I'm not tormenting him,' Lebedev cried warmly. 'I sincerely love and – respect him, sir. And just now, believe it or not, he's dearer to me than ever. Yes, sir, I appreciate him much more now!'

Lebedev said this all so seriously and sincerely that the prince felt thoroughly indignant.

'You love him and you torment him like this! Why, by putting the missing money back under the chair and in your coat, where you could easily find it, by that very fact he shows you plainly that he doesn't want to trick you and good-naturedly asks your forgiveness! Do you hear? Asks your forgiveness! He must therefore be relying on the delicacy of your feelings. He must therefore believe in your friendship for him. And you don't hesitate to humiliate such a man, such a most honest man!'

'Most honest, Prince, most honest!' Lebedev echoed, with flashing eyes. 'And it is only a man like you, most noble Prince, it is only a man like you who is capable of uttering such a true word! That is why I'm so devoted to you – that's why I worship you, rotten as I am with all sorts of vices! That settles it! I'm going to find my wallet now, this minute, and not to-morrow. Here, sir, I take it out before your very eyes. Here it is and here's the money, all untouched. Take it, most noble Prince, take it and keep it till to-morrow. I'll fetch it to-morrow or the day after. And, you know, Prince, the money must have been lying somewhere under a stone in my garden the first night it was missing. What do you think?'

'Now, mind, don't tell him to his face that you've found the wallet. Let him simply see that there is nothing in the skirt of your coat. He'll understand.'

'Are you sure? Wouldn't it be better to tell him that I've found it and pretend that I had never guessed where it was till now?'

'N-no,' said the prince after a moment's reflection. 'No, now it's too late. It's more dangerous. Please, better say nothing about it! And be kind to him, but don't – don't overdo it and – and – you know – –'

'I know, Prince, I know. I mean, I know that I shall probably not carry it out, for I'm afraid in this kind of business one must have a heart like yours. And, besides, he is irritable and too easily carried away. He's recently started treating me sometimes much too disdainfully. One moment he's snivelling and embracing me, and then he starts all of a sudden humiliating me and sneering at me. Well, so I just show him the skirt of my coat on purpose, you understand, ha, ha! Good-bye, Prince, for I can see I'm keeping you and, as it were, interfering with your most interesting feelings. ...'

'But for goodness' sake remember to be as discreet as before!'

'Gently does it, sir, gently does it. ...'

But though the matter was settled, the prince was almost more preoccupied than ever. He awaited with impatience his interview with the general next morning.

4

The interview was fixed for twelve o'clock, but the prince was quite unexpectedly late. On his return home he found the general waiting for him. He saw at once that the general was displeased, and perhaps just because he had been kept waiting. The prince apologized and hastened to sit down; but, somehow, he felt strangely timid as though his visitor was made of porcelain and he was every minute afraid of breaking him. Before he never felt timid with the general, and it had never occurred to him to feel so. Soon the prince realized that he was quite a different man from what he had been the day before: instead of being confused and distraught, he seemed to be quite extraordinarily reserved; one might suppose that this was a man who had finally made up his mind. His composure, however, was more apparent than real. At any rate, the visitor was nonchalantly at his ease, though with reserved dignity. At first, indeed, he treated the prince with a certain air of condescension, as proud but unjustly insulted people sometimes are nonchalantly at their ease. He spoke amiably, but not without a touch of sadness in his voice.

'The book I borrowed the other day,' he said, motioning significantly to the book he had brought which was lying on the table. 'Thank you.'

'Ah, yes. Have you read the story, General? How did you like it? Interesting, isn't it?' said the prince, glad of the opportunity of beginning their conversation with a subject that had nothing to do with their business.

'It's interesting, I suppose, but also crude and, of course, absurd. I shouldn't wonder if it wasn't all a lie.'

The general spoke with great confidence, and even with a drawl.

'Oh, but it's such an artless story of an old soldier who was an eye-witness of the French occupation of Moscow. Some of the things are delightful. Besides, every eye-witness account is precious, whoever the man may be, don't you think so?'

'If I had been the editor, I shouldn't have published it. As for eye-witness accounts in general, people will sooner believe a crude but amusing liar than a man of worth who had seen active service. I know some accounts of the year 1812 which – I've come to a decision, Prince, I'm leaving this house – Mr Lebedev's house. ...'

The general looked significantly at the prince.

'You have your own lodgings in Pavlovsk at – er – at your daughter's. ...' said the prince, at a loss what to say.

He remembered that the general had come for his advice about an important matter on which his fate depended.

'At my wife's, sir. In other words, at home and in my daughter's house.'

'I'm sorry, I – –'

'I'm leaving Lebedev's house, dear Prince, because I've broken with that man. I broke with him last night, and I regret I didn't do it before. I demand to be treated with respect, Prince, and I expect to receive it even from those to whom I give, so to speak, my heart. Prince, I often give my heart to people, and I'm almost always deceived. That man was unworthy of my gift.'

'He's rather unprincipled, I'm afraid,' the prince observed discreetly, 'and he possesses certain qualities which – but amongst them all one cannot but perceive a good heart and a sly and sometimes rather amusing intelligence.'

The refinement of expressions and the respectful tone evidently flattered the general, though he still occasionally looked at the prince with sudden mistrust. But the prince's tone was so natural and sincere that it was impossible to doubt it.

'That he has good qualities,' the general said quickly, 'I was the first to declare when I nearly bestowed my friendship on that individual. But I have no need of his house and his hospitality, having a family of my own. I do not justify my failings. I am intemperate – I've drunk with him, and now perhaps I regret it. But surely, sir, I didn't make friends with him for the sake of the drinks alone, did I? Please forgive the coarseness of candour in an exasperated man, Prince. What appealed to me were, as you say, his qualities. But, damme, sir, if he has the impudence to tell me to my face that as a child he lost his left leg in 1812 and buried it in the Vagankovsk cemetery in Moscow, he's going too far, shows disrespect and is being impertinent.'

'Perhaps it was a joke to make people laugh.'

'I see, sir. An innocent lie to make people laugh may be coarse, but it does not offend the human heart. Some people tell lies just out of friendship – I mean, to please the friends they are talking to; but if, sir, there's the slightest suspicion of disrespect, if by this sort of disrespect your friend perhaps wants to intimate that he's tired of your friendship, then a gentleman, sir, has no choice but to turn away and break off the connexion, thus showing the offender his proper place.'

The general even coloured as he spoke.

'But Lebedev couldn't possibly have been in Moscow in 1812. He's much too young for that. It's ridiculous!'

'That, to begin with. But even assuming that he could have been born then, how could he assure me to my face, sir, that a French chasseur aimed a cannon at him and shot off his leg just for fun; that, moreover, he picked up his leg and took it home with him and afterwards buried it in Vagankovsk cemetery. Why, he actually claims to have erected a monument over it with an inscription on one side: "Here lies the leg of Collegiate Secretary Lebedev", and on the other: "Rest in peace, beloved dust, until the joyful morn", and that, finally, he has a requiem service held regularly for it (which is nothing short of sacrilege) and that he goes to Moscow every time for this occasion. And to prove it, he asks me to go to Moscow with him, where he promises to show me the tomb and even the self-same cannon, captured from the French, in the Kremlin. He assures me it is the eleventh from the gate, a French falconet of an old-fashioned design.'

'And yet he has his own two legs on him for all to see!' laughed the prince. 'I assure you it's just an innocent joke. Please don't be angry, sir.'

'But let me have my own views about that, sir – I mean, about having his legs on him for all to see. This, sir, is not at all as improbable as you think. He tells me he got his leg from Chernosvitov.'

'Oh, I see. I'm told one can dance with a Chernosvitov leg.'

'I'm perfectly aware of that, sir. When Chernosvitov invented his leg, the first thing he did was to run and show it to me. But the Chernosvitov leg was invented much later. Besides, he tells me that during the whole of their married life his late wife did not know that he, her husband, had a wooden leg. "If you," he says to me, "if you were a page of Napoleon's in 1812, you might as well let me bury my leg in Vagankovsk cemetery." '

'But were you – –' the prince began, and paused in embarrassment.

The general, too, seemed to look a little bit embarrassed, but at the same moment he looked at the prince with undisguised disdain and almost with a sneer.

'Go on, Prince,' he drawled very smoothly, 'finish what you were going to say. I don't mind in the least. Tell me everything: admit that the whole idea sounds preposterous to you. I mean, sir, the idea of seeing before you a man in his present degradation and – uselessness, and at the same time, sir, hearing that this man was the eye-witness of great historic events. *He* hasn't been telling you any scandalous tales about me by any chance, has he?'

'No, sir. I haven't heard anything from Lebedev, if it's Lebedev you are talking about.'

'Oh – I thought differently. As a matter of fact, our whole talk yesterday arose in connexion with that strange article in the "Archives". I remarked on its absurdity, and since I've been an eye-witness – you're smiling, Prince, you're looking at my face?'

'N-no, I – –'

'I'm rather young-looking,' the general drawled, 'but I'm older than I look. In 1812 I was ten or eleven. I'm afraid I'm a bit hazy about my age. In the army list my age is less, and I'm sorry to say it's been my weakness all my life to make myself out to be much younger than I am.'

'I assure you, General, that I don't find it at all odd that you should have been in Moscow in 1812 and, of course, you are able to tell us what was going on there – er – as well as anyone else who was there. One of our writers begins his autobiography by the statement that French soldiers fed him with bread when he was a baby in arms in Moscow in 1812.'

'There, you see,' the general expressed his approval condescendingly. 'My own case is rather out of the ordinary, but there's nothing extraordinary about it. Truth, sir, very often seems impossible. A page! It does sound strange, I admit. But the adventure of a ten-year-old boy may perhaps be explained by his age. Had I been fifteen at the time, nothing of the sort would have happened to me, and that's just as it should be, for had I been fifteen I'd have run away from our wooden house in Old Basmanaya Street on the day of Napoleon's entry into Moscow – I'd have run away from my mother, who was too late to leave Moscow and who was trembling with fear. Had I been fifteen, I'd have been afraid, but being only ten, I wasn't afraid of anything and I pushed my way through the crowd to the very entrance of the palace just as Napoleon was dismounting from his horse.'

'You're perfectly right, sir, in remarking that a boy of ten would not be afraid,' the prince assented, flinching and worried by the thought that he might blush at any moment.

'Undoubtedly, sir, and everything happened as simply and naturally as things do happen in life. If a novelist had tried to describe it, he'd have invented a lot of nonsensical and improbable incidents.'

'Oh, that's true!' cried the prince. 'I too, was struck by the same thought quite recently. I know of a genuine case of murder for the sake of a watch – it's in the papers now. If some novelist had invented it, the critics and experts on the life of our peasants would at once have cried out that it was improbable. But when you read it in the newspapers as a fact, you can't help feeling that such facts give you an insight into Russian life. You put it excellently, General,' concluded the prince warmly, terribly glad of having found some excuse for his blushes.

'Did I? Did I?' cried the general, his eyes sparkling with pleasure. 'A little boy, a child, who doesn't realize the danger, makes his way through the crowd to see the splendid pageant, the uniforms, the Emperor's suite and, finally, the great man himself, about whom he had heard people talk so much. For at that time people had talked of nothing else for years on end. The world was full of his name; I had, as it were, sucked it in with my mother's milk. Napoleon, passing within a few feet of me, happened to catch my eye. I was dressed like a gentleman's son – they always dressed me well. I was the only little boy in such a crowd, you must admit that – –'

'No doubt it must have struck him most forcibly and proved to him that not everyone had left Moscow and that there were still some noblemen there with their children.'

'Quite so, quite so! He wanted to win over the *boyars*! When he bent his eagle eye on me, my eyes must have flashed back in response. "*Voilà un garçon bien éveillé! Qui est ton père?*" I answered him at once, almost breathless with excitement: "A general who died fighting for his country." "*Le fils d'un boyard et d'un brave par-dessus le marché! J'aime les boyards. M'aimes tu, petit?*" To this quick question I answered as quickly: "A Russian heart is able to discern a great man even in the enemy of his country!" I mean, as a matter of fact, I don't remember whether I used those very words – I was a child – but the sense of it was the same, I'm sure! Napoleon was amazed, he thought a moment, and then said to his suite: "I like the pride of that child! But if all the Russians think the same as that child, then – –" He did not finish the sentence and went into the palace. I at once mingled with his suite and ran after him. The officers in the suite already made way for me and looked upon me as a favourite. But all that only lasted a moment. ... All I remember was that when he entered the first room, the Emperor stopped before the portrait of the Empress Catherine, looked at it a long time thoughtfully, and at last said: "That was a great woman!" and passed on. In two days everyone in the palace and in the Kremlin knew me and called me "*le petit boyard*". I only went home to sleep. At home they were nearly out of their minds. Two days later Napoleon's page, Baron de Basencour, died, unable to stand the rigours of the campaign. Napoleon remembered me. I was taken and brought to the palace without any explanation; they tried on me the uniform of the dead page, a boy of twelve, and when they had brought me, wearing the uniform, to the Emperor, and he had nodded at me, I was told that I had been deemed worthy of favour and appointed page to his Majesty. I was glad, for I had felt, for a long time, too, a great sympathy for him, and – well – there was, besides, you see, the resplendent uniform, which means a great deal to a child. I was dressed in a dark-green coat with long narrow tails; gold buttons, scarlet facings embroidered with gold braid on the sleeves, a high, stiff, open collar, embroidered with gold, and embroidery on the lapels; white chamois-leather, close-fitting breeches, a white silk waistcoat, silk stockings, and buckled shoes – and whenever the Emperor went riding, if I were one of the suite, I wore high top-boots. Though the position of the French army was far from brilliant and great calamities were already anticipated, the etiquette was kept up as much as possible, and indeed the greater the anticipation of disaster, the more strictly was it kept up.'

'Yes, of course,' murmured the prince, looking terribly embarrassed, 'your memoirs would be – er – extraordinarily interesting.'

The general was, of course, merely repeating what he had already told Lebedev the day before, and he was therefore repeating it fluently, but at this point he again stole a mistrustful glance at the prince.

'My memoirs,' he said with redoubled pride – 'write my memoirs? No, sir, I'm not tempted to do that. If you want to know, my memoirs are already written, but – er – they are lying in my desk. Let them be published when I'm in my grave, let them be published then, and, I have no doubt, be translated into foreign languages, not because of their literary merit – no, sir – but because of the importance of the great historical events of which I was an actual eye-witness, though only a child; all the more so, indeed, for as a child I was able to penetrate into, as it were, the intimacies of the bedchamber of the "great man"! I heard at night the groans of that man who was so "great in misfortune", for he could not feel ashamed to groan and weep in front of a child, though I was already able to realize that the cause of his sufferings was the silence of the Emperor Alexander.'

'Yes, he did write letters with – proposals of peace, didn't he?' the prince assented timidly.

'Well, sir, as a matter of fact, we don't know what kind of proposals he made, but he wrote every day, every hour, one letter after another! He was dreadfully agitated. One night when we were alone, I flung myself weeping on his chest (Oh, I loved him!): "Please, please, beg the Emperor Alexander to forgive you!" I cried to him. You see, I should have said, "Make peace with the Emperor Alexander," but, like a child, I expressed what I thought in a naïve way. "Oh, my child," he replied – he was pacing up and down the room – "Oh, my child," he did not seem to notice at the time that I was only ten, and he loved to talk to me, "Oh, my child, I am ready to kiss the feet of the Emperor Alexander, but for the King of Prussia, the Emperor of Austria – oh, for them I feel nothing but everlasting hatred and – and – but you know nothing of politics!" He seemed suddenly to remember whom he was talking to and fell silent, but his eyes went on flashing long after. Well, sir, if I were to describe all these facts – and I was the eye-witness of the greatest events – were I to publish them now, all those critics, all those vain literary men, all those jealousies, political parties, and – no, sir, not me!'

'You are, of course, absolutely right about the parties, and I agree with you entirely,' the prince remarked quietly, after a brief pause. 'Only the other day I read a book on the Waterloo campaign by Charras. It is evidently a scholarly work and, according to the experts, it is written with profound knowledge. But on every page you can feel how overjoyed the author is at Napoleon's humiliation, and if it were possible to dispute Napoleon's genius in every other campaign, Charras, I'm sure, would be very glad to do so. And in a serious work that isn't good enough, for that's just a party spirit. And – er – were you very busy in your service with – er – the Emperor?'

The general was delighted. The prince's remark, evidently made in all earnestness and simplicity, dispelled the last traces of his mistrust.

'Charras! Oh, it made me so angry! I wrote to him at the time myself, but – er – I'm afraid I don't remember now what I said. ... You ask was I busy in his service? Oh no! I was called a page, but I never took it seriously even then. Besides, Napoleon very soon lost all hope of winning over the Russians, and he would, no doubt, have forgotten all about me, whom he had only taken into his service as a matter of policy, if – if he had not taken a personal liking for me. I can say it boldly now. As for me, I couldn't help feeling drawn to him. I had no special duties. I had sometimes to present myself at the palace and – er – accompany the Emperor on his rides – that was all. I rode a horse fairly well. He went riding before dinner, and his suite was usually composed of Davoust, myself and the Mameluke Roustant – –'

'Constant,' the prince involuntarily corrected him.

'N-no. Constant was no longer there then. He had been sent with a letter to – to the Empress Josephine. But his place was taken by two orderlies and a few Polish Uhlans – well, and that was all, except, of course, for the generals and marshals whom Napoleon took with him to inspect the terrain, the disposition of the troops, and for the sake of consulting them. ... Davoust was nearly always with him. I remember him very well: a huge, stout, cool-headed fellow, wearing spectacles, and with a peculiar expression in his eyes. The Emperor consulted him more often than anyone. He thought very highly of his judgement. I remember they were in consultation for several days. Davoust used to come in the morning and in the evening. They often had arguments with one another. At last Napoleon seemed to agree with him. They were alone in the study. I was the third, but they scarcely noticed me. Suddenly Napoleon's eyes happened to fall on me, and a strange thought flashed in his eyes. "Child," he suddenly said to me, "what do you think? If I adopt the Greek Orthodox faith and set free your slaves, will the Russians come over to me or not?"

"Never!" I cried indignantly. Napoleon was amazed. "In that child's eyes, gleaming with patriotism," he said, "I read the verdict of the entire Russian people! Enough, Davoust! It's all a delusion. Let's hear your other plan."

'But that plan, too, had a great idea in it!' said the prince, his interest evidently aroused. 'So you attribute it to Davoust?'

'Well, at least they discussed it together. Of course, the idea was Napoleon's, the idea of an eagle, but the other plan had also a good idea in it. That was the famous "*conseil du lion*", as Napoleon called that plan of Davoust's. Its idea was to shut himself up in the Kremlin with the whole army, to build barracks, put up fortifications, to place cannons, to kill as many horses as possible and salt their flesh; to get as much corn as possible, by pillage and in other ways, and spend the winter there till spring; and in the spring to fight their way through the Russian lines. Napoleon liked the idea very much. We used to ride round the Kremlin walls every day; he used to show where to knock down walls and where to put up lunettes, ravelins, or a row of block-houses – a look, a quick decision, and it was done! At last everything was settled. Davoust insisted on a final decision. Again they were alone together, with myself as the third. Again Napoleon paced the room with arms folded. I couldn't take my eyes off his face; my heart beat fast. "I'm off!" said Davoust. "Where?" asked Napoleon. "To salt the horses," said Davoust. Napoleon gave a start – his fate was being decided. "My child," he said to me suddenly, "what do you think of our plan?" Of course, he asked me as a man of the greatest intellect will sometimes decide to leave everything to the toss of a coin at the last moment. Instead of replying to Napoleon, I turned to Davoust and said, as though by inspiration, "Get out, General!" The plan was frustrated. Davoust shrugged and, as he went out, whispered "*Bah! Il devient superstitieux!*" And next day the retreat was ordered.'

'All this is most interesting,' said the prince in a very low voice – 'I mean to say,' he hastened to correct himself, 'if it all really was so. ...'

'Oh, Prince,' cried the general, so transported by his story that perhaps he was unable to stop short of the most blatant indiscretions, 'you say, "if it really was so!" But there was more than that, I assure you, much more than that! All these are only paltry political facts. I repeat I was the witness of the great man's tears and groans at night. No one saw that but me. It is true that towards the end he no longer wept, there were no more tears, he only groaned at times; but his face grew more and more overcast. It was as though eternity were already hovering over him with its dark wings. Sometimes, at night, we used to spend hours alone together in silence – the Mameluke Roustant would be snoring in the next room – an awfully heavy sleeper that fellow was. "But," Napoleon used to say about him, "he is loyal to me and my dynasty." Once I was in great distress, and suddenly he noticed tears in my eyes. He looked at me, deeply moved: "You're sorry for me!" he cried. "You, a child, and perhaps another child will be sorry for me, too, my son, *le roi de Rome* – all the rest hate me, all of them, and my brothers will be the first to betray me in misfortune!" I burst out sobbing and flung myself on his chest. Then he, too, broke down. We embraced and our tears mingled. "Write, write a letter to the Empress Josephine!" I sobbed to him. Napoleon started, reflected for a moment, and said to me, "You've reminded me of one other heart that loves me. Thank you, my friend!" He then sat down and wrote the letter to Josephine which was sent off by Constant next day.'

'You did well,' said the prince. 'In the midst of his evil thoughts, you made him have a good feeling.'

'Yes, that's right, Prince, and how beautifully you explain it, as one might expect from a man with your good heart!' cried the general ecstatically and, strange to say, real tears glistened in his eyes. 'Yes, sir, yes, it was a great spectacle! And, you know, I nearly went back to Paris with him and, of course, I should have shared his exile with him on "the tropical prison isle", but, alas, fate separated us! We went our different ways: he to the tropical isle where once at least, in a moment of great sorrow, he perhaps remembered the tears of the poor little boy who had embraced and forgiven him in Moscow; I was sent to the cadet corps where I found nothing but army drill, boorish comrades, and – alas! Everything turned to dust and ashes! "I don't want to take you away from your mother, and I'm not taking you with me," he said to me on the day of the retreat, "but I'd like to do something for you." He was about to mount his horse. "Write something as a souvenir for me in my sister's album," I said, feeling abashed, for he looked very troubled and gloomy. He came back, asked for a pen, and took the album. "How old is your sister?" he asked, his pen poised over the open page. "Three years old," I replied. "*Petite fille alors*." And he wrote quickly in the album:

> "*Ne mentez jamais.*
> *Napoleon, votre ami sincère.*"

Such advice and at a moment like that, think of it, Prince.'

'Yes, it's remarkable.'

'That page in a gold frame under glass hung in the most conspicuous place in my sister's drawing-room till the day of her death – she died in childbirth. Where it is now, I don't know, but, good Lord, it's two o'clock already! I'm sorry I've detained you so long, Prince! It's unpardonable.'

The general got up from his chair.

'Oh, on the contrary,' the prince mumbled, 'you've interested me greatly – yes, indeed, it was very interesting. I'm so grateful to you!'

'Prince,' said the general, again pressing his hand so tightly that it hurt and looking intently at him with flashing eyes, as though recollecting himself suddenly and startled by some sudden idea, 'Prince, you are so good, so simple that I can't help feeling sorry for you sometimes. I am deeply touched when I look at you. Oh, God bless you! May a new life begin for you and blossom forth in – in love. My life is at an end! Oh, forgive me, forgive me!'

He went out quickly, covering his face with his hands. The prince could not doubt the sincerity of his agitation. He realized, too, that the old man had gone away overjoyed by his success; yet he could not help feeling that he belonged to that category of liars who, though they lie passionately and even to self-forgetfulness, still suspect in their most ecstatic moments that they are not believed and, indeed, that they cannot be believed. In his present position the old man might recover his senses, be overwhelmed with shame, suspect the prince of pitying him inordinately and feel insulted. 'Haven't I been guilty of a worse blunder by allowing him to be carried away to such an extent?' the prince asked himself uneasily, and suddenly he could not restrain himself and laughed loudly for several minutes. He began to reproach himself for his laughter, but he realized immediately that he had nothing to reproach himself for, because he was infinitely sorry for the general.

His forebodings proved true. In the evening he received a strange note, brief but firm. The general informed him that he was parting from him for ever, that he respected him and was grateful to him, but that even from him he would not accept 'marks of sympathy, which are derogatory to the dignity of a man who is unhappy as it is'. When the prince heard that the old man had gone back to stay with his wife, he felt almost at ease in his mind on his account. But we have seen already that the general had caused some serious trouble at Mrs Yepanchin's too. Here we cannot go into the details, but we will briefly observe that the upshot of the interview was that the general had frightened Mrs Yepanchin and by his bitter insinuations against Ganya had aroused her indignation. He was shown out in disgrace.

That was why he had spent such a night and such a morning, become completely unhinged and rushed out into the street almost in a state approaching insanity.

Kolya still did not fully realize what was wrong and even hoped to get the better of him by severity.

'Where on earth do you think we can go now, General?' he said. 'You don't want to go to the prince's, you have quarrelled with Lebedev, you have no money, and I never have any. So here we are high and dry in the middle of the road.'

'I'd rather be high and dry than high and low,' muttered the general. 'This – er – pun was a huge success in the – er – officers' mess in – er – forty-two – in one thousand – eight hundred – and – er forty-two – yes, sir! I forget which year. ... Oh, don't remind me – don't remind me! "Where's my youth, where's my freshness?" as – who said that, Kolya?'

'It was Gogol, Father, in Gogol's *Dead Souls*,' Kolya answered, stealing a frightened glance at his father.

'Dead Souls! Oh, yes, dead! When you bury me, write on my gravestone: "Here lies a dead soul!" "Disgrace pursues me!" Who said that, Kolya?'

'I don't know, Father.'

'Yeropegov never existed! Yeroshka Yeropegov! ...' he shouted in a frenzy, stopping for a moment in the street. 'And this is my son, my own flesh and blood! Yeropegov, who took the place of a brother to me for eleven months, for whom I fought a duel ... Prince Vygoretsky, our Captain, said to him over a bottle: "I say, Grisha, where did you get hold of your St Anne's, tell me that?" "I got it on the battlefields of my country; that's where I got it!" I shouted, "Bravo, Grisha!" Well, it ended in a duel, and afterwards he married – Maria Petrovna Su – Sutugin and was killed in action. ... The bullet ricocheted off the cross on my chest and hit him straight in the forehead. "I shall never forget!" he cried, and fell dead on the spot. I – I served my country honourably, Kolya, but disgrace – disgrace pursues me. You and your mother will come to my grave. ... Poor Nina! I used to call her that before, Kolya, a long time ago, in the old days, and she loved me so. ... Nina, Nina! What a mess I've made of your life! For what can you love me, long-suffering soul? Your mother has the soul of an angel, Kolya. Do you hear? Of an angel!'

'I know that, Father. Father, dear Father, let's go home to Mother. She was running after us. Why did you stop here? Just as if you didn't understand. ... Well, what are you crying for?'

Kolya was himself crying and kissing his father's hands.

'You're kissing my hands – my hands!'

'Yes, your hands, yours. What's so strange about that? Well, what are you bawling in the middle of the street for? And you call yourself a general, a soldier! Come along, let's go!'

'God bless you, my dear boy, for being respectful to a poor dishonourable – yes, dishonourable old man, your father – and may you have a son like that – *le roi de Rome.* ... Oh, a curse, a curse on this house!'

'What on earth is going on here?' Kolya suddenly cried angrily. 'What has happened? Why don't you want to go home now? Why have you gone out of your mind?'

'I'll explain – I'll explain it to you – I'll tell you everything. Don't shout – they'll hear you – *le roi de Rome* – oh, I'm sick, I'm miserable – "Nurse, where is thy grave?" Who said that, Kolya?'

'I don't know – I don't know who said that! Let's go home now – now! I'll give Ganya a thrashing if necessary – where are you off to again?'

But the general was dragging him towards the front steps of a house.

'Where are you going? That's not our house!'

The general sat down on the top step, still drawing Kolya towards him by the hand.

'Bend down, bend down!' he muttered. 'I'll tell you everything – disgrace – bend down – your ear – your ear – I'll whisper it in your ear.'

'What is it?' Kolya cried, looking terribly alarmed, but stooping down to the old man.

'*Le roi de Rome,*' whispered the general, also apparently trembling all over.

'What? What do you want with *le roi de Rome*? What?'

'I – I – –' the general began whispering again, clutching more and more firmly at the shoulder of his 'boy', 'I – I – want to tell you everything – Maria – Maria – Su – Sutugin – –'

Kolya tore himself away, seized the general by the shoulders, and looked at him wildly. The old man grew purple, his lips turned blue, rapid convulsions were passing over his face. Suddenly he lurched forward and began to sink slowly into Kolya's arms.

'A stroke!' Kolya screamed, having guessed at last what was the matter.

5

As a matter of fact, Varya, in her conversation with her brother, had somewhat exaggerated the rumours of the prince's proposal of marriage to Aglaya Yepanchin. Perhaps, being a perspicacious woman she had divined what was bound to happen in the near future; perhaps disappointed about her dream (in which she didn't, as a matter of fact, believe herself) which had come to nothing, she, being human, could not deny herself the pleasure of exaggerating the disaster by pouring a little more venom into the heart of her brother, whom, for all that, she loved sincerely and compassionately. In any case, she could not possibly have received such accurate information from her friends the Yepanchins; there were only hints, half-uttered words, silences, and riddles. But perhaps the Yepanchin sisters had deliberately come out with more information than was justified in the circumstances so as to find out themselves something from Varya; it was also possible that they could not deny themselves the feminine pleasure of teasing a friend a little, though they had known each other since childhood: after all that time they surely must have seen through at least a little bit of what she was up to.

On the other hand, the prince, too, though he was absolutely right in assuring Lebedev that there was nothing he could tell him and that nothing special had happened to him, was perhaps also mistaken. Indeed, something rather strange seemed to have happened to all of them: nothing had happened, and yet, at the same time, a great deal had happened. It was this last fact that Varya had guessed with her true feminine instinct.

It is, however, very difficult to explain in an orderly fashion how it came about that everyone at the Yepanchins' suddenly got the identical notion that something of the utmost importance had happened to Aglaya and that her fate was being decided. But as soon as the idea had flashed through the minds of all of them at once, they all at once asserted that they had seen it coming long ago and, indeed, had never been in doubt about it; that it had all been clear ever since the incident of the 'poor knight', and even before that, except that they simply refused to believe in anything so preposterous. That was what the sisters maintained; of course, Mrs Yepanchin, too, had forecast and known it all before everyone else and her heart had been 'aching' for a long time, but – whether she had known it long before or not – now she could not bear the thought of the prince simply because it upset all her calculations. She had been faced with a problem that demanded an immediate solution, and not only was it impossible to solve it, but, try as she might, poor Mrs Yepanchin could not even grasp the problem clearly enough. It was a difficult matter: 'Was the prince a good match or not? Was it all a good thing or not? If not (which was most certain), then why was it not good? And if it was perhaps good (which was also possible), why, again, was it good?' The head of the family himself, General Yepanchin, was first of all, of course, surprised, but afterwards he suddenly confessed that 'by Jove, something of the kind did occur to me vaguely – I'd dismiss it from my mind and then, damn it, back it would come again!' He fell silent at once at the stern look of his wife, but that was in the morning; in the evening, alone with his wife and forced to say something again, he suddenly and with unusual boldness gave voice to a number of surprising opinions: 'After all what is it?' (Silence.) 'Of course, all this is very strange, if true, and I don't dispute it, but – –' (Again silence.) 'On the other hand, if one were to be quite fair, the prince is really a most excellent fellow, and – and – and, after all, the name – it's our family name, all that means we shall be keeping up our family name, as it were, which –er – has come down in the world. I mean, when regarded from the point of view of high society, for, I mean to say, high society – high society is high society, and – er – besides, the prince is not without means – er – though his means are not perhaps very large, he has – er – and – and – and – –' (Prolonged silence and complete collapse.) Having listened patiently to her husband, Mrs Yepanchin lost control of herself completely.

In her opinion, all that had happened was 'unpardonable and even criminal folly, a sort of fantastic nightmare, stupid and absurd!' To begin with, there was the fact that 'the wretched little prince was a sickly idiot', secondly, he was a fool, 'who doesn't know the way of the world and has no place in it'. To whom could he be shown? Where was one to find a decent post for him? A sort of objectionable democrat, had not even got a civil service rank of any sort, and – and – and – what would Princess Belokonsky say? And was it such a husband they had imagined and planned for Aglaya? The last argument was of course the chief one. The mother's heart shuddered at the thought of it, bleeding and weeping, though at the same time something deep inside it stirred and said suddenly to her: 'And why isn't the prince the right sort of man for your daughter?' Well, it was these objections of her own heart that troubled Mrs Yepanchin most.

Aglaya's sisters for some reason liked the idea of the prince. It didn't even strike them as particularly strange – in short, they might very well have suddenly come over to his side entirely. But both of them decided to say nothing. For it had become the accepted rule in the family whenever any argument arose that the more persistent and obstinate Mrs Yepanchin's opposition and objections became on any disputed point, the more surely was it a sign for all of them that she was perhaps already yielding on that point. But Alexandra could not very well keep silent altogether. Having chosen her long ago for her adviser, her mother kept appealing to her now and asking for her opinions and, especially, for her recollections – that is to say, she wanted her to remember how it had happened, why no one had seen it coming, what was the meaning of that horrid 'poor knight', and why was she, Mrs Yepanchin, alone doomed to worry about all of them, to notice and foresee everything, and the rest of them to stand there gaping and doing nothing? And so on and so on. At first Alexandra had been very careful and merely remarked that she thought that her father was not far wrong in thinking that in the eyes of the world the choice of Prince Myshkin as the husband of one of the Yepanchin daughters might seem very satisfactory. Gradually warming up, she even added that the prince was not at all 'a born fool' and never had been, and as for his social position, who could tell whether in a few years' time the social position of a decent man in Russia would depend on his successes in the Civil Service, considered so essential hitherto, or on something else. To all of which her mother at once replied in no uncertain terms that Alexandra was 'a freethinker', and that this was all the result of the hateful 'woman question'. Half an hour later she went off to town, and from there to Kamenny Island to see Princess Belokonsky, who fortunately happened to be in Petersburg at the time, though she was soon due to leave. The princess was Aglaya's god-mother.

The 'old woman' listened to Mrs Yepanchin's feverish and desperate confessions and was not in the least moved by the tears of the harassed mother; she even looked ironically at her. The princess was a terrible despot; she could not bear to be on an equal footing with a friend, not even with an old friend, and she most definitely looked upon Mrs Yepanchin as her protégée, as she had done thirty-five years before, and she could not get reconciled to the impetuosity and independence of her character. She did observe, though, that they all seemed, as usual, to have run much too far ahead and made a mountain out of a molehill; that however carefully she had listened to Mrs Yepanchin, she was not convinced that anything serious had really happened; that it might be better to wait until anything did happen;

that the prince was, in her opinion, a decent young man, though an invalid, and rather eccentric and of little account. The worst thing about him was that he was openly keeping a mistress. Mrs Yepanchin realized very well that the princess was a little cross at the failure of Mr Radomsky, whom she had introduced to them. She returned to Pavlovsk in a greater state of irritation than when she had left, and she at once gave everyone a piece of her mind, chiefly because they had all 'gone off their heads', that it was only in their house that things were done like that. What were they in such a hurry for? What had happened? So far as she could see, nothing had happened! Let them wait till it did! What if General Yepanchin did imagine something? Why make a mountain out of a molehill? And so on and so forth.

It seemed, therefore, that all they had to do was to keep calm, look on coolly, and wait. But, alas, the calm did not last ten minutes. The first blow to coolness was delivered by the news of what had happened during her absence on Kamenny Island. (Mrs Yepanchin's trip to town had taken place the morning after the prince had turned up soon after midnight instead of at nine o'clock.) The sisters replied in great detail to their mother's impatient questions, first, that nothing in particular seemed to have happened during her absence, that the prince had come, that Aglaya had kept him waiting for about half an hour and then at once asked the prince to have a game of chess; that the prince had no idea how to play chess and Aglaya had beaten him at once; that she was in very high spirits and had told the prince that he ought to be ashamed of himself not to know how to play chess and had laughed at him so much that they felt ashamed to look at him. Then she suggested a game of cards, and they played 'fools'. But that had turned out quite the opposite of what they had expected. The prince appeared to be a champion at 'fools', almost – a professor at the game. He played in quite a masterly fashion. However much Aglaya had tried to cheat and change cards and even steal cards from the pack under his very nose, he made a 'fool' of her every time – five times running. Aglaya was furious, and entirely forgot herself; she said such beastly and horrid things to him that he stopped laughing, and he turned white as a sheet when she told him that she wouldn't set foot in the room as long as he was there and that he ought to be ashamed of himself to visit them, and at midnight, too, *after all that had happened*. She then left the room and slammed the door. The prince went away as though from a funeral, in spite of their efforts to console him. Suddenly, a quarter of an hour later, Aglaya had come running down on the veranda in such a hurry that she hadn't time to dry her eyes, which were still wet with tears. She had run downstairs because Kolya had come and brought a hedgehog. They had all begun looking at the hedgehog, and, in reply to their questions, Kolya explained that the hedgehog was not his, and that he was passing their house with a friend of his, Kostya Lebedev, also a schoolboy, whom he had left waiting in the street, as he was too shy to come in because he was carrying a hatchet, that both the hedgehog and the hatchet they had just bought from a peasant they had met. The peasant was selling the hedgehog, and they had given him fifty copecks for it, but the hatchet they had to persuade him to sell because he might just as well 'throw it in', and it was, in fact, a very good hatchet. Then all of a sudden Aglaya had begun pestering Kolya to sell her the hedgehog at once; she got very worked up about it, and even called him 'dear'. Kolya would not agree for a long time, but at last gave way and called in Kostya Lebedev, who came in carrying the hatchet and looked very embarrassed. Then it had suddenly appeared that the hedgehog was not theirs at all, but belonged to a third boy, called Petrov, who had given them money to buy Schlosser's *History* from a fourth boy, who was selling it cheaply because he was in need of money; that they had gone out to buy Schlosser's *History*, but could not resist the temptation and bought the hedgehog so that both the hedgehog and the hatchet really belonged to the third boy, to whom they were now taking them instead of Schlosser's *History*. But Aglaya had kept pestering them so much that at last they made up their minds and sold her the hedgehog. As soon as Aglaya had got the hedgehog, she put it, with Kolya's assistance, into a wicker-basket, covered it with a table napkin, and started begging Kolya to take it straight to the prince for her and ask him to accept it as 'a sign of her most profound respect'. Kolya gladly agreed to her request and promised to take it to the prince, but immediately began pestering her for an explanation. 'What is the meaning of the hedgehog?' he asked, 'and of such a present?' Aglaya replied that it was none of his business. He answered that he was convinced that there was some hidden message in it. Aglaya grew angry and snapped out that he was just a silly little boy. Kolya at once retorted that if he did not respect her as a woman or respect his own convictions, he would have proved it to her at once that he knew what sort of a reply to give to such an insult. However, in the end Kolya had gone off carrying the hedgehog in great delight, and Kostya Lebedev had run off after him. Seeing that Kolya was swinging the basket too violently, Aglaya could not restrain herself and shouted to him from the veranda: 'Please, Kolya, darling, don't drop it!' – just as though she had not been quarrelling with him a few moments earlier. Kolya had stopped and he, too, as though he had not been quarrelling, shouted with the utmost readiness: 'No, I shan't drop him, Miss Aglaya. Don't worry!' and had run off as fast as he could. After that Aglaya had burst into loud laughter and rushed upstairs to her room, highly pleased with herself, and had been in high spirits for the rest of the day.

Mrs Yepanchin was completely stunned by this news. Not that it amounted to anything, but simply because she happened to be in that kind of mood. Her alarm was aroused to quite an acute degree, and chiefly about the hedgehog. What was the meaning of the hedgehog? What was their understanding about it? What mystery lay hidden in it? What sort of sign? What sort of message? Moreover, poor General Yepanchin, who happened to be present at the interrogation, spoilt the whole thing by his reply. In his opinion there was no question of any message here, and the hedgehog was just a hedgehog, and nothing more, except that it was meant, in addition, as a sign of friendship, a desire to bury the hatchet and make it up – in short, just an innocent prank which, in any case, was quite excusable.

We may observe in parenthesis that he had guessed right. The prince, who had returned home ridiculed and banished by Aglaya, sat for half an hour in the blackest despair, when Kolya suddenly appeared with the hedgehog. At once the sky cleared; the prince looked as though he had risen from the dead; he questioned Kolya closely, hung on every word he uttered, asking him the same question over and over again, laughing like a child and again and again pressing the hands of the laughing boy who gazed at him with such bright eyes. It seemed clear that Aglaya forgave him and that he could go and see her again that evening, and that was not only the most important thing for him – it was everything.

'What children we still are, Kolya!' he cried at last ecstatically. 'And – and how lovely it is that we still are children!'

'It simply means that she's in love with you, Prince, and that's all there is to it!' Kolya replied, impressively and with authority.

The prince flushed, but this time he said nothing, and Kolya just laughed and clapped his hands; a minute later the prince, too, laughed, and he spent the rest of the afternoon looking at his watch every five minutes to see how late it was and how much time there was still left till evening.

But her mood got the upper hand of Mrs Yepanchin: she could not bear the suspense any longer and yielded to a momentary fit of hysterics. In spite of the protests of her husband and daughters, she sent at once for Aglaya in order to put a definite question to her and get a definite and straightforward answer. 'To make an end of it once for all, to get it off my mind and not to think of it again! Otherwise,' she declared, 'I shall die before the evening.' And it was only then that they realized the muddle into which they had got. They could get nothing out of Aglaya except feigned surprise, indignation, loud laughter, and sneers at the prince and those who questioned her. Mrs Yepanchin took to her bed, and only came down for tea, when the prince was expected. She waited for the prince in fear and trembling, and when he arrived she nearly had a fit.

The prince, too, came in timidly, almost gropingly, smiling strangely and looking into everyone's eyes, as though questioning them, for again Aglaya was not in the room, which alarmed him at once. There were no other visitors that evening, no one except the members of the family. Prince Sh. was still in Petersburg in connexion with the affairs of Radomsky's uncle. 'Oh, if only he'd been here to say something.' Mrs Yepanchin lamented over his absence. General Yepanchin sat looking extremely preoccupied; the sisters were serious and, as though on purpose, silent. Mrs Yepanchin did not know how to start the conversation. At last she exploded with a vigorous condemnation of the railways and looked defiantly at the prince.

Alas! Aglaya still did not come down and the prince was utterly lost. Barely able to bring out the words and completely put out, he expressed the opinion that it would be an extremely good thing if the railways were put into decent repair, but Adelaida suddenly laughed and the prince was again crushed. It was at that moment that Aglaya came in, calmly and with an air of importance, bowed ceremoniously to the prince, and solemnly took up the most conspicuous position at the round table. She looked questioningly at the prince. They all realized that the moment had arrived when all their perplexities were to be removed.

'Did you get my hedgehog?' she asked firmly and almost crossly.

'I did,' answered the prince, blushing and with a sinking heart.

'Will you kindly explain at once what you think about it? This is necessary for the peace of mind of Mother and the whole family.'

'Look here, Aglaya,' began the general, feeling suddenly rather uneasy.

'This – this is beyond everything!' cried Mrs Yepanchin, who suddenly became alarmed.

'It's not beyond anything at all, Mother,' the daughter at once replied severely. 'I sent the prince a hedgehog to-day, and I want to know his opinion. Well, Prince?'

'What sort of opinion, Miss Aglaya?'

'About the hedgehog.'

'That is – I expect what you want to know is how – er – I received the hedgehog or – er – rather how I look upon this – er – your sending me the – er – the hedgehog – I mean – er – if that's the case, I think that – er – in short – –'

He choked and fell silent.

'I must say you haven't said much,' remarked Aglaya after waiting five seconds. 'Very well, I agree to drop the hedgehog, but I'm glad to be able at last to put an end to all these misunderstandings. I should like to find out once and for all from you personally: are you proposing to me or not?'

'Good gracious!' exclaimed Mrs Yepanchin.

The prince started and drew back; General Yepanchin was dumbfounded; the sisters frowned.

'Don't lie to me, Prince. Tell the truth. It is because of you that I'm persecuted by strange questions. Is there any foundation for these questions? Well?'

'I have not proposed to you, Miss Aglaya,' said the prince, growing suddenly animated, 'but I – I think you know how much I love you and believe in you – even now. ...'

'What I asked you was – do you ask for my hand or not?'

'I do,' the prince answered with a sinking heart.

There was a general and agitated stir in the room.

'I'm sorry, but the whole thing's wrong, my dear fellow,' said General Yepanchin, greatly agitated. 'This – this is quite impossible, if it's like this, Aglaya. ... I'm sorry, Prince, I'm dreadfully sorry, my dear fellow! My dear' – he turned to his wife for help – 'you must try to understand. ...'

'I refuse, I refuse!' cried Mrs Yepanchin, waving her hands.

'Please, Mother, let me speak, for I too must have a say in this matter: the decisive moment of my life has arrived' (Aglaya actually used that expression), 'and I'd like to find out for myself, and, besides, I'm glad it's before everyone. ... Please, Prince, do you mind my asking you if your "intentions are honourable", how do you propose to make me happy?'

'I'm sorry I don't know what answer to give you. ... What – what answer am I supposed to give? And – and is it necessary?'

'You seem to be embarrassed and out of breath. Take your time and pull yourself together. Have a glass of water. Don't bother, though; they'll give you some tea presently.'

'I love you, Aglaya; I love you very much. It's only you I love, and – and, please, don't joke about it. I love you very much.'

'Still, you know, this is a very important matter. We're not children, and we must look at it from a practical point of view. Will you be so good as to tell me now what you are worth?'

'Good Lord, Aglaya, what are you saying?' General Yepanchin muttered in dismay. 'This is not how it's done – no, no!'

'Disgraceful!' Mrs Yepanchin said in a loud whisper.

'She's mad!' Alexandra cried in the same, loud whisper.

'What am I worth?' the prince asked, surprised. 'You mean, money?'

'Exactly.'

'I – I have now one hundred and thirty-five thousand roubles,' murmured the prince, reddening.

'Is that all?' Aglaya cried with loud and frank surprise, without blushing. 'Still, it'll do, I suppose, especially if we try to live economically. Do you intend to join the Civil Service?'

'I was thinking of qualifying as a private tutor.'

'That will be nice. It will, of course, increase our income. You're not thinking of becoming a Court chamberlain, are you?'

'A Court chamberlain? I'm afraid I never thought of it, but – –'

But at this point the two sisters could not restrain themselves and burst out laughing. Adelaida had long observed in Aglaya's twitching face the signs of imminent and irrepressible laughter, which, for the time being, she was doing her utmost to control. Aglaya glared sternly at her laughing sisters, but a second later she, too, could no longer control herself and burst into mad, almost hysterical laughter; at last she jumped up and ran out of the room.

'I knew it was nothing but a joke!' exclaimed Adelaida. 'From the very first – from the hedgehog.'

'No, this I won't allow – I won't!' Mrs Yepanchin burst out angrily and rushed out after Aglaya.

The sisters immediately ran out after her. The prince and the father of the family were left alone in the room.

'This is – this is – could you ever have imagined such a thing, Prince?' cried the general sharply, evidently not knowing himself what he wanted to say. 'No, seriously, seriously, I mean?'

'I see that Miss Aglaya was laughing at me,' the prince replied sadly.

'Wait a minute, my dear fellow. I'll go and see, and you wait here – because – I mean, please can you explain to me how all this has come about and what all this means, viewed, as it were, as a whole? You see, my dear fellow. I'm her father – I mean, I am her father, aren't I? And yet I can't make head or tail of it. So can you perhaps explain it to me?'

'I love Aglaya, sir. She knows it, and I think she has known it a long time.'

The general shrugged.

'Odd – odd – and – er – do you love her very much?'

'Yes, very much.'

'Well, it all seems very odd to me. I mean to say, such a surprise and such a blow that – – You see, my dear boy, it's not your money (though I must say I thought you had much more than that), but – what I'm worried about is my daughter's happiness – I mean – are you capable of making her – er – as it were – happy? And – and – what is it – a joke on her part or is she in earnest? I mean, not on your part, but on hers?'

Alexandra's voice came from behind the door; she was calling her father.

'Wait for me here, my boy, please! Wait a little and think it over; I'll be back presently,' he said hurriedly and rushed off in answer to Alexandra's summons, looking almost scared.

He found his wife and daughter locked in each other's arms and weeping copiously. Those were tears of joy, tender emotion, and reconciliation. Aglaya was kissing her mother's hands, cheeks, and lips; both were clinging ardently to each other.

'Look at the little darling now,' said Mrs Yepanchin to her husband. 'That's what she's really like!'

Aglaya raised her happy, tear-stained, pretty face from her mother's bosom, looked at her father, gave a loud laugh, leapt at him, hugged him tightly, and kissed him several times. Then she rushed back to her mother, buried her face completely in her bosom, so that no one could see it, and immediately started crying again. Mrs Yepanchin covered her with the end of her shawl.

'Well, look what you are doing to us, you cruel girl; for that's what you are, after all that!' she said, but joyfully this time, as though she could suddenly breathe freely again.

'Cruel, yes, cruel!' Aglaya suddenly burst out. 'Worthless! Spoilt! Tell Daddy that. Oh, but he's here! Are you here, Daddy? Do you hear?' she laughed through her tears.

'My darling, my idol!' the general said, kissing her hand and beaming with happiness. (Aglaya did not take her hand away.) 'So you love this – this young man, do you?'

'No, I don't! I can't stand your – young man. I can't stand him!' Aglaya cried, suddenly losing her temper and raising her head. 'And if you dare say that again, Daddy – I tell you seriously – do you hear? – seriously!'

And she was speaking seriously: indeed, she flushed all over and her eyes glittered. Her father held his peace and was alarmed, but Mrs Yepanchin signalled to him behind Aglaya's back and he understood it to mean: 'Don't ask questions.'

'If that is so, darling, then, of course, you shall do as you please. But he's waiting there alone, and we ought to tell him tactfully to go away, oughtn't we?'

The general, in his turn, winked at his wife.

'No, no, that's quite unnecessary, especially if "tactfully"; you'd better go out to him yourselves, and I'll come in afterwards – presently. I want to apologize to this – young man, for I've hurt his feelings.'

'Very much so,' General Yepanchin affirmed gravely.

'Well, if that's so, you'd better stay here, and I'll go first alone. You come in immediately after me – a second later. That'll be better.'

She had already reached the door, but she turned back suddenly.

'Oh, dear, I shall laugh! I shall die of laughing!' she declared mournfully.

But almost at the same moment she turned round and rushed out to the prince.

'Well, what is it all about? What do you make of it?' General Yepanchin said quickly.

'I hate to say it,' Mrs Yepanchin replied as quickly, 'but I think it's clear enough.'

'I think so too. Clear as daylight. She loves him.'

'Not only loves him – she's in love with him!' Alexandra put in. 'And with a man like that!'

'God bless her, if that's how it must be,' Mrs Yepanchin said, crossing herself devoutly.

'Oh well, if it must be, it must be,' the general assented. 'You can't run away from your fate.'

And they all went into the drawing-room, where another surprise awaited them.

Far from laughing as she feared, Aglaya walked up to the prince and said to him almost timidly:

'Please forgive a silly, wicked, spoilt girl' (she took his hand), 'and do believe me when I say that we all respect you very much. And if I dared to make fun of your beautiful and kind-hearted simplicity, forgive me as you would forgive a child for being naughty. I'm sorry I persisted in an absurdity which cannot, of course, have the slightest consequences. ...'

The last words Aglaya uttered with special emphasis.

The father, mother, and sisters reached the drawing-room in time to see and hear all this, and they were all struck by the words: 'an absurdity which cannot have the slightest consequences', and even more by the serious tone with which Aglaya spoke of that absurdity. They all exchanged questioning glances; but the prince had apparently not understood those words and looked radiantly happy.

'Why do you talk like that?' he murmured. 'Why do you – ask forgiveness?'

He even wanted to say that he was unworthy of being asked forgiveness. Who knows, perhaps he did realize the meaning of the words, 'an absurdity which cannot have the slightest consequences', but, being a strange sort of person, he was perhaps glad of those words. There can be no doubt, though, that the very fact that he could come and see Aglaya again as much as he liked and that he was to be allowed to talk to her, sit with her, and walk with her was enough to make him blissfully happy, and, who knows, perhaps he would have been content with that for the rest of his life! (It was just that contentment that Mrs Yepanchin perhaps secretly dreaded; she saw through him; there were many things she secretly dreaded which she could not have put into words herself.)

It is difficult to describe the prince's animation and high spirits that evening. He was so gay that one could not help feeling gay looking at him, as Aglaya's sisters described it afterwards. He never stopped talking, and that had not happened to him since that morning, six months ago, when he had first met the Yepanchins; on his return to Petersburg he was noticeably and deliberately taciturn, and quite recently he inadvertently remarked in the hearing of them all to Prince Sh. that he had to control himself and refrain from talking because he had no right to degrade an idea by putting it into words. He was almost the only one who talked that evening; he told many stories and answered all their questions clearly, gladly, and in detail. But there was nothing even remotely resembling love-making in his words. The ideas he expressed were very serious, and sometimes even abstruse. The prince went so far as to tell them some of his own views, his own private observations, so that it would all have been rather laughable, if it had not been so 'well expressed', as all who heard him agreed afterwards. Though the general liked conversations on serious subjects, both he and Mrs Yepanchin could not help thinking that it was a little too learned, so that towards the end of the evening they even grew melancholy. However, the prince ended up by going so far as to tell a few funny stories, which he was the first to laugh at, so that the others laughed more at his gay laughter than at the stories themselves. As for Aglaya, she hardly spoke the whole evening, but hung on the prince's words, so that she didn't so much listen to him as gaze at him.

'She kept looking at him without taking her eyes off – hanging on every word he said – catching it, catching it!' Mrs Yepanchin said afterwards to her husband. 'But tell her she loves him, and you'll never hear the last of it!'

'Aye, it's fate!' the general shrugged, and kept repeating his favourite phrase a long time.

We may add that, as a business man, there was a great deal in the present situation that he did not like, and he particularly objected to its vagueness; but he made up his mind to say nothing for the time being and just gaze – into Mrs Yepanchin's eyes.

The happy mood of the family did not last long. The very next day Aglaya again quarrelled with the prince, and so it went on without a break for several more days. For hours on end she would make fun of the prince and turned him almost into a clown. It is true that sometimes they would spend an hour or two sitting in the summer-house in the garden, but it was noticed that during that time the prince almost invariably read the newspapers or some book to Aglaya.

'Do you know,' Aglaya said to him once, interrupting his reading of the newspaper, 'I've noticed that you're awfully uneducated. You don't know anything properly; if one turns to you for some information, you never know who it was, in what year it happened, or what treaty it was. You're too pitiful for words.'

'I told you I hadn't much learning,' replied the prince.

'What have you, then, if you haven't got that? How do you expect me to respect you after that? Go on with your reading – no, don't – stop reading!'

And she said again something that evening that struck them all as rather enigmatic. Prince Sh. returned from Petersburg and Aglaya was very nice to him. She asked him many questions about Radomsky. (The prince had not arrived yet.) Suddenly Prince Sh. ventured to drop a hint about 'another approaching change in the family', taking his cue from the few words that escaped Mrs Yepanchin about the likelihood of another postponement of Adelaida's wedding so that the two weddings might take place together. Aglaya flew into such a temper at 'all these stupid suppositions' that they were all taken by surprise; and, incidentally, she dropped the curious remark that she certainly had 'no intention of taking the place of anybody's mistresses'.

These words surprised everybody, but especially her parents. Mrs Yepanchin insisted, at a secret conference with her husband, on his obtaining a definite explanation from the prince about Nastasya Filippovna.

General Yepanchin swore that it was only an 'outburst' which was due to Aglaya's 'shyness'; that had Prince Sh. not mentioned the wedding, there would have been no 'outburst', for Aglaya knew herself, and knew it for a fact, that it was all a slander spread by wicked people, and that Nastasya Filippovna was going to marry Rogozhin, that the prince had nothing at all to do with her, and that he certainly had never been her lover, if the whole truth were to be told.

The prince meanwhile did not seem to be worried about anything and continued to be blissfully happy. Oh, he, too, of course, sometimes noticed a sort of gloomy and impatient expression in Aglaya's eyes, but he put more faith in something else, and the gloom disappeared by itself. Once having put his faith in something, nothing could shake him. Perhaps he was a little too calm; so at least Ippolit thought when he met him by accident in the park.

'Well,' he began, walking up to the prince and stopping him, 'wasn't I right in telling you that night that you were in love?'

The prince held out his hand to him and congratulated him on looking so well. Ippolit seemed rather cheerful himself, as is often the case with consumptives. He had walked up to the prince with the intention of making some sarcastic remark about his looking so happy, but he soon dropped the subject and began talking about himself. He began complaining, and he went on complaining for a long time, and rather incoherently.

'You can't imagine,' he concluded, 'how irritable, petty, selfish, vain, and ordinary they all are there. Would you believe it? They only took me on condition that I should die as soon as possible, and now they are all furious with me because I'm not dying and that, on the contrary, I'm feeling better. A real comedy! I bet you don't believe me!'

The prince did not feel like replying.

'I sometimes think of coming to live with you again,' Ippolit added, casually. 'So I gather you don't believe them capable of inviting a man to stay with them on condition that he is going to die and as soon as possible?'

'I thought they invited you for other reasons.'

'Oho! Why, you're not so simple as people say you are! Now is not the time, or I should have told you something about dear old Ganya and his hopes. They're intriguing against you, Prince, quite pitilessly, too, and – and it's really pitiful to see you so calm about it. But, alas, I don't suppose you can help it!'

'So that's what you're so worried about,' laughed the prince. 'Do you really think I'd be happier if I were less calm?'

'It's much better to be unhappy and *know*, than happy and – be made a fool of. You don't believe you have a rival and – in that quarter, do you?'

'I'm afraid your remark about a rival is a little cynical, Ippolit. I'm sorry I haven't the right to answer you. As for Mr Ivolgin, you must admit that he cannot very well be expected to be calm after all he has lost – if, that is, you have any idea about his affairs at all. It seems to me better to look at it from that point of view. He has plenty of time to change, he has many years of life before him, and life is rich – still – still – –' the prince grew confused suddenly, 'about the intrigues – I'm afraid I don't even know what you are talking about. I think we'd better drop the subject, Ippolit.'

'Yes, let's drop it for the time being. Besides, it would be absurd to expect you not to act honourably. Yes, Prince, you have to touch it with your finger in order not to believe it again, ha, ha! And do you despise me very much now – what do you think?'

'Whatever for? Because you have suffered and are suffering more than us?'

'No, because I'm unworthy of my suffering.'

'He who can suffer more is worthy of suffering more. When Miss Aglaya read your confession, she wanted to see you, but – –'

'She's putting it off – she can't – I understand, I understand ...' Ippolit interrupted, as though anxious to change the subject. 'By the way, I'm told you read all that rigmarole to her yourself – truly, it was written and – done in delirium. And I can't understand how one could be so – I won't say cruel (that would be humiliating) – but so childishly vain and vindictive as to reproach me for that confession and use it as a weapon against me. Don't worry, I'm not referring to you. ...'

'But I'm sorry you repudiate that confession of yours, Ippolit. It is sincere and, you know, even the most absurd parts of it – and there are many of them' (Ippolit made a wry face) – 'are atoned for by suffering, for to admit their authorship was also suffering, and it required a great deal of – courage, too, perhaps. The idea that inspired you had certainly an honourable basis, whatever people may think about it. I see that more clearly as time goes on, I swear I do. I do not judge you. I'm merely saying this just to tell you what I think, and I'm sorry I didn't say it at the time. ...'

Ippolit flushed. For a moment he thought that the prince was pretending and trying to catch him out, but looking more closely into his face, he could not help believing in his sincerity. His face brightened.

'But die I must, for all that!' he said, nearly adding, 'a man like me!' 'And you can't imagine how that Ganya of yours plagues me. One objection he raised was that three or four of those who heard my confession would most likely die before I do. How do you like that? He thinks that's a consolation to me, ha, ha! To begin with, they haven't died yet, but even if they did die, what sort of consolation do you suppose can I get out of that? He judges by himself. However, he's gone further than that. He simply abuses me now. He says that a decent man in my position would die quietly, and that the whole thing was just egoism on my part! How do you like that? No, really, how do you like this sort of egoism on his part? What a refinement, or, better still, what a bovine coarseness of egoism on the part of a fellow like him which he is quite incapable of seeing in himself! Have you ever read, Prince, of the death of a certain Stepan Glebov in the eighteenth century? I happened to read about it yesterday. ...'

'What Stepan Glebov?'

'He was impaled in the reign of Peter the Great.'

'Good heavens, yes, I know! He was fifteen hours on the stake in the frost, in a fur coat, and he died bearing no ill-will towards any man. Yes, of course I've read it. What about it?'

'Why does God grant that kind of death to some people, but not to us? But perhaps you don't think I'm capable of dying like Glebov, or do you?'

'Oh, I do, I do,' the prince said, looking embarrassed. 'All I wanted to say was that you – I mean, not that you would not be like Glebov, but that in those days you – er – would have been more like – –'

'I see, like Osterman and not like Glebov – is that what you were going to say?'

'What Osterman?' asked the prince in surprise.

'Osterman, the diplomat Osterman, Peter's Osterman,' muttered Ippolit, getting rather confused all of a sudden.

For a time they looked puzzled at one another.

'Oh, n-n-no!' the prince suddenly drawled after a short pause. 'I didn't mean to say that. I don't think you would ever have been an – Osterman.'

Ippolit frowned.

'But then, you see,' the prince suddenly resumed, evidently wishing to put things right, 'I'm saying this because men in those days (I assure you I've always been struck by it) were not at all the same people as we are now. They were not at all of the same race as nowadays. Quite honestly, they seem to have been quite a different breed of men. In those days people seem to have been animated by one idea, but now they are much more nervous, more developed, more sensitive – they seem to be animated by two or three ideas at a time – modern man is more diffuse and, I assure you, it is this that prevents him from being such a complete human being as they were in those days. I – I said it only with that idea in my mind, and not – –'

'I understand. You're so very anxious to console me now because you disagreed with me so naïvely, ha, ha! You're a perfect child, Prince. However, I can't help noticing that you are all treating me like a – piece of china. Never mind, never mind; I'm not angry. We had, anyway, a very funny conversation. You are sometimes a perfect child, Prince. But I'd like you to know that I'd perhaps like to be something better than Osterman. It wouldn't be worth while to rise from the dead to be an Osterman. ... However, I can see that I ought to die as soon as possible, or I shall myself – – Leave me – good-bye! All right, tell me, please, what do you think would be the best way for me to die? I mean, so that it should appear most virtuous? Come, tell me!'

'Pass by us and forgive us our happiness,' said the prince in a low voice.

'Ha, ha, ha! I thought so! I certainly thought something of the kind! However, you are – you are – well, well! Men of great eloquence! Good-bye, good-bye!'

6

Varya had also been quite right in what she had told her brother about the evening party at the Yepanchins' at which Princess Belokonsky was to be present: the guests were expected that very evening; but, again, she had put it rather more strongly than was warranted by the occasion. It is true the party had been arranged in rather a hurry and even with some quite unnecessary excitement, but that was because in this family they always did things differently from anyone else. It could all be explained by Mrs Yepanchin's impatience, for she refused 'to be kept in suspense any longer', as well as by the great anxiety of both parents for the happiness of their darling daughter. Besides, Princess Belokonsky was really going away soon, and as her patronage did mean a great deal in high society, and as they hoped that she would be well disposed towards the prince, the parents reckoned that 'the world' would accept Aglaya's fiancé straight from the hands of the all-powerful 'old woman', so that if the match did seem somewhat strange, it would appear much less so under such patronage. The whole trouble was that the parents themselves could not make up their minds whether there was anything strange in the whole of this affair and, if so, how much, or whether there was nothing at all strange about it. The friendly and candid opinion of influential and competent persons was just what was needed at the present moment when, thanks to Aglaya, nothing had been finally settled. In any case, sooner or later the prince would have to be introduced into society, about which he had not the faintest idea. In short, he was to be 'put on show'. However, the party was planned to be a simple one; only a few 'friends of the family' were expected. In addition to Princess Belokonsky, one other lady had been invited, the wife of a rich landowner and high State dignitary. Mr Radomsky was almost the only young man whom they counted on coming; he was to escort Princess Belokonsky.

That Princess Belokonsky would be coming the prince heard almost three days before the party, but that the party was going to be such a formal affair he did not hear until the day before it was to take place. He noticed, of course, the worried looks of the members of the family, and from certain anxious hints they dropped while talking to him he realized that they were afraid of the impression he might make. But for some reason every member of the Yepanchin family without exception had formed the opinion that because of his simplicity he was quite incapable of realizing that they were all so worried about him. That was why when looking at him they were all so troubled. As a matter of fact, he attached scarcely any importance to the approaching event. He was preoccupied with something quite different: Aglaya was becoming every hour more capricious and gloomy – that was what depressed him so much, and when he learned that Radomsky, too, was expected at the party, he was delighted and said that he had long been wishing to see him. For some reason, no one liked these words; Aglaya left the room in a huff, and it was only late at night, at about twelve o'clock, when the prince was on the point of leaving, that she seized an opportunity to say a few words alone with him as she saw him off.

'I wish you would not come and see us all day to-morrow. Come in the evening after those – visitors have arrived. You know that we're expecting visitors, don't you?'

She spoke impatiently and with unwonted sternness: it was the first time she had mentioned the 'party'. She, too, found the idea of the visitors almost unbearable; they all noticed it. She may have greatly wished to pick a quarrel with her parents about it, but her pride and shyness prevented her from mentioning it. The prince realized at once that she, too, was apprehensive about him (and did not want to admit that she was apprehensive), and suddenly he took fright himself.

'Yes, I've been invited,' he said.

She was evidently finding it difficult to go on.

'Can one talk seriously to you about anything – just for once in one's life?' she asked, suddenly getting terribly angry without knowing herself why, but unable to restrain herself.

'You can, and I'm listening – I'm very glad,' murmured the prince.

Aglaya paused for another minute and then began with evident repugnance.

'I did not want to argue with them about it. There are times when you can't make them see sense. I have always thought some of Mother's principles quite revolting. I say nothing about Father; you can't expect anything from him. Mother is, of course, a high-minded person. Just try to suggest anything mean to her and you'll see. But she grovels before that – trash! I'm not talking about the Belokonsky woman: a trashy old woman and a trashy character, but she's clever and she knows how to keep them all under her thumb – at least she's good at that. Oh, the meanness of it! And it's ridiculous, too: we've always been middle-class people, as middle-class as can be – why try to climb into high society? My sisters, too, are out for it. It's Prince Sh. who has got them all confused. Why are you pleased that Mr Radomsky will be coming?'

'Listen, Aglaya,' said the prince. 'It seems to me you're afraid I might perpetrate some howler in – that aristocratic society.'

'Me afraid? For you?' cried Aglaya, flushing crimson. 'Why should I be afraid for you even if you – if you do disgrace yourself utterly? What do I care? And how can you use such expressions? What does "a howler" mean? It's a horrid, vulgar expression.'

'It's a schoolboy's expression.'

'Yes, a schoolboy's expression! A horrid expression! I expect you intend to use such expressions to-morrow evening. Look up some more of them in your dictionary at home; I can imagine the sensation you will cause! It's such a pity you seem to know how to enter a room properly: where did you learn that? Are you sure you'll be able to take a cup of tea and drink it nicely, when everyone is watching to see if you can do it?'

'I think I will.'

'What a pity! I should have had a good laugh at you otherwise. Do at least break the Chinese vase in the drawing-room! It's a very expensive one. Do break it – it's a present, and Mummy will go off her head and burst into tears before everyone – she values it so highly. Wave your arms about, as you always do, knock it down and smash it. Sit near it on purpose.'

'On the contrary, I'll try to sit as far from it as I can. Thank you for warning me.'

'So you are already afraid of waving your arms about, aren't you? I bet you'll start talking on some serious subject, something learned and elevated, won't you? How – nice that will be!'

'I think that would be stupid – if it's not to the point.'

'Listen, once and for all,' cried Aglaya, losing all patience. 'If you start talking about anything like capital punishment, or the economic position of Russia, or about "beauty saving the world", I'll of course be awfully pleased and have a good laugh, but – I warn you in good time: don't let me see you again! Do you hear? I'm serious. This time I am serious!'

She really did utter her threat *seriously*, so that there was even an unusual note in her voice and a strange look in her eyes – something the prince had never noticed before and that did not, of course, sound like a joke.

'Well, now you've made quite sure that I will talk of something "serious" and, perhaps, even break the vase. A moment ago I wasn't afraid of anything, and now I'm afraid of everything. I'm sure to perpetrate a howler.'

'Then don't speak at all. Sit still and don't talk.'

'I'm afraid that's impossible. I'm sure I'll start talking from fear and I'll break the vase from fear. Perhaps I'll fall down on the slippery floor, or something of the sort, for that has happened to me before. I shall dream about it all night. Why did you have to talk to me about it?'

Aglaya looked gloomily at him.

'I tell you what: I'd better not come at all to-morrow. I'll report sick, and that will be the end of it!' he decided at last.

Aglaya stamped her foot, and even turned pale with anger.

'Goodness, have you ever seen anything like it? He won't come when the party has been purposely arranged for him and – oh dear, what a pleasure it is to have anything to do with such – such a fatuous person as you!'

'All right, I'll come, I'll come!' the prince broke in hastily. 'And I promise you faithfully to sit the whole evening without opening my mouth. I'll do that.'

'You'll do well. You just said, "I'll report sick". Where on earth do you get such expressions from? Why will you talk to me like this? You're not trying to provoke me by any chance, are you?'

'I'm sorry. That, too, was a schoolboy expression. I won't do it again. I quite understand that you – you are afraid for me – don't be angry, please, and I'm awfully glad of it. You can't imagine how scared I am now and – and how glad I am of what you've told me. But I swear this panic is not of the slightest importance. It's nonsense. I swear it is, Aglaya. And the joy will remain. I'm awfully glad you're such a child and such a good, kind child! Oh, how splendid you can be, Aglaya!'

Aglaya would of course have lost her temper and, indeed, she was about to lose it, but suddenly a powerful feeling, which she herself never expected, took complete possession of her soul in one instant.

'And you won't reproach me for having been so rude to you just now – ever – afterwards?' she asked suddenly.

'Why, of course not! And why are you flaring up again? Now you're looking gloomy again! You do look very gloomy sometimes, Aglaya. You never looked like that before. I know why it is. ...'

'Shut up! Shut up!'

'No, I'd better say it. I've been wanting to say it a long time. I've said it already, but – that's not enough, because you didn't believe me. Between us two there still stands – one person – –'

'Shut up, shut up, shut up, shut up!' Aglaya interrupted him, suddenly seizing his hand and staring at him almost in horror.

At that moment she was called away. She broke away from him as though greatly relieved and ran off.

The prince was in a fever all night. It was strange that he should have been feverish for several nights. This time, in a half-delirious state, the thought occurred to him: what if he should have a fit tomorrow in the presence of everyone? He had had fits when he was among people before, hadn't he? He turned cold at the thought; all night he imagined himself to be in some strange and extraordinary company, among some strange people. And the extraordinary thing was that he 'started talking'; he knew that he ought not to talk, but he went on talking all the time, and he was trying to talk them into doing something. Radomsky and Ippolit were also among the guests, and they seemed to be on excellent terms.

He awoke at about nine o'clock with a headache, full of confused ideas and strange impressions. For some reason he felt an overwhelming desire to see Rogozhin; to see him and talk a lot to him – he did not know what about himself; then he quite made up his mind to go and see Ippolit. His heart was full of vague forebodings, so much so that though the events of that morning made an extremely strong impression upon him, there seemed something lacking in it, somehow. One of these events concerned his meeting with Lebedev.

Lebedev made his appearance quite early, soon after nine o'clock, and he was almost completely drunk. Though the prince was not particularly observant lately, he could not help noticing that for the last three days – that is, since General Ivolgin had moved out of their house – Lebedev had been behaving very badly. He seemed to have suddenly become extremely greasy and dirty, his tie was askew, and the collar of his coat was torn. In his own part of the house he screamed and raged, and that could be heard across the small courtyard; Vera had once come in in tears and told him something about it. On coming in now, Lebedev began talking rather strangely, smiting his breast and blaming himself for something.

'I've been paid in full for – for my treachery and meanness – I've had my face slapped!' he concluded at last, tragically.

'Your face slapped? Who did it? And so early in the day?'

'Early in the day?' Lebedev said, smiling sarcastically. 'What does the time of day matter – even for physical retribution? But it was a moral – a moral slap I received, not a physical one.'

He suddenly seated himself unceremoniously and began his story. It was very incoherent. The prince made a wry face and was about to go out, but suddenly he was struck by something Lebedev said. He was struck dumb with amazement. Mr Lebedev was telling him strange things.

At first he was apparently talking about some letter. Aglaya's name was mentioned. Then Lebedev began bitterly accusing the prince himself. It could be gathered that he had been offended by the prince. At first, he said, the prince had favoured him with his confidence in his affairs with a certain 'person' (with Nastasya Filippovna); but afterwards he would not have anything to do with him and had dismissed him with ignominy, and so offensively, too, that last time he rudely declined his 'innocent question about the approaching changes in the house'. Lebedev confessed with drunken tears that 'after that I could bear it no more, particularly as I knew a lot – quite a lot – from Rogozhin, from Nastasya Filippovna, from Nastasya Filippovna's friend, from Varya herself, too, and – and even from – from Aglaya Yepanchin – can you imagine it, sir? – through Vera, through my darling daughter Vera, my only child, sir – though, indeed, she is not my only one, for I have three. And who kept informing Mrs Yepanchin by letters and, indeed, in great secret, ha, ha? Who wrote to her about all the goings-on and – and about the movements of the person of Nastasya Filippovna, ha, ha, ha? Who is he, I ask you? Who is this anonymous correspondent?'

'Not you, surely?' cried the prince.

'It's me, sir, me,' the drunkard replied with dignity, 'and to-day, too, at half past eight in the morning, only half an hour ago – no, sir, three-quarters of an hour ago – I informed her ladyship that I have – er – a rather important communication to make to her about a certain – er – affair. I let her know by a letter through one of her maids at the back door. She received me.'

'You've just seen Mrs Yepanchin?' asked the prince, unable to believe his ears.

'I saw her just now and was given a slap in the face – a moral one. Returned me the letter, she did – flung it at me, in fact, unopened – and threw me out neck and crop – morally, of course, not physically – though I must confess it was almost physical, another step and it would have been!'

'What letter did she fling at you unopened?'

'Why, ha, ha, ha! Haven't I told you? I thought I had told you already. ... You see, I had received a certain letter with instructions to hand it over to – –'

'From whom? To whom?'

But it was difficult to understand or make head or tail of some of Lebedev's 'explanations'. The prince, however, did gather that the letter had been handed early in the morning to Vera Lebedev by a maid to be delivered to the person to whom it was addressed – 'just as before – just as before to a certain person and from the same personage (for one of them, sir, I describe as a "personage" and the other only as a "person", as a sign of disparagement, sir, and also to distinguish one from t'other; for there is a great difference between an innocent and well-bred daughter of a general and – er – a kept woman, sir). And so, sir, the letter was from a "personage" whose name begins with the letter "A". ...'

'How is it possible? To Nastasya Filippovna? Nonsense!' cried the prince.

'It is possible, sir, it is. And if not to her, then to Rogozhin, sir; it's all the same, sir, to Rogozhin and – er – even to Mr Terentyev there was a letter once, to be delivered from the personage whose name begins with the letter "A".' Lebedev winked and smiled.

As he often jumped from one subject to another, forgetting what he had begun to say, the prince kept quiet to let him finish his story. But it was still far from clear whether the letters had been transmitted through Lebedev or through Vera. If, as he said himself, he thought that it was all the same whether the letters were addressed to Rogozhin or to Nastasya Filippovna, it seemed more likely that they had not passed through his hands – if, that is, there had been any letters. How this letter had got to him now remained a complete mystery; the most probable explanation was that, somehow or other, he had got it from Vera – stolen it from Vera and taken it to Mrs Yepanchin for some purpose of his own. That was what the prince understood and made out at last.

'You must be mad!' he cried in great agitation.

'Not entirely, my dear Prince, not entirely,' Lebedev replied, not without malice. 'It is true I was going to give it to you, into your own hands, just as a favour, sir, as a favour, but I couldn't help thinking that a favour would be more appreciated there, and so I decided to let her ladyship know everything – since I had informed her once before by an anonymous letter. And when I wrote to her this morning a preliminary note asking her to see me at twenty minutes past eight, I also signed it: "Your secret correspondent", and I was at once admitted, at once, sir, and with the utmost expedition by the back door, to her ladyship the mother. ...'

'Well?'

'Well, sir, as I've told you already, she nearly gave me a beating. I mean, almost, sir, so that one might say she practically did give me a beating. And she flung the letter back into my face. It is true that first she wanted to keep it. I saw it, sir, I noticed it, but she changed her mind and flung it at me. "If," she said, "they entrusted it to a fellow like you to deliver, then deliver it!" Aye, really offended she was. If she wasn't ashamed to say it before me, then it means she was offended. Short-tempered by nature, her ladyship is.'

'And where is the letter now?'

'Why, I've still got it. Here it is, sir!'

And he handed the prince Aglaya's note to Ganya which the latter showed his sister so triumphantly two hours later.

'This letter can't remain with you.'

'It's for you! For you! It's to you I bring it, sir!' Lebedev cried warmly. 'Now I'm yours again, all yours, sir, from head to heart; your servant, sir, after my small act of treachery, sir! Pierce my heart, spare my beard, as Thomas More said – in England, in Great Britain, sir. *Mea culpa, mea culpa,* as the Romish Pope says – I mean, he's the Pope of Rome, but I call him the Romish Pope.'

'This letter must be sent off at once,' said the prince, looking perturbed. 'I'll deliver it.'

'But wouldn't it be better, most gallant Prince, wouldn't it be better to – er – do this, sir!'

Lebedev pulled a strange, unctuous face; he fidgeted violently in his chair, as though he had been suddenly pricked by a needle, and winking craftily, he made some meaningful gestures with his hands.

'What do you mean?' the prince asked sternly.

'Why not open it first, sir?' he whispered ingratiatingly and, as it were, confidentially.

The prince jumped up so furiously that Lebedev took to his heels; but having reached the door, he stopped, waiting for the prince to relent.

'Oh, Lebedev, how could you sink so low as that?' the prince exclaimed sadly.

Lebedev's face brightened.

'I'm vile, vile!' he exclaimed, approaching the prince at once and smiting his breast.

'Why, it's abominable!'

'Yes, sir, it is abominable. That's the right word for it!'

'And what a curious habit you have to – to act in this strange way! Why, you're just a spy! Why did you write the anonymous letter and worry such a – noble and kind-hearted woman? Why, after all, shouldn't Miss Aglaya write to whom she pleases? Did you go there to complain about her to-day? What did you hope to get there? What made you turn informer?'

'I did it solely to gratify my curiosity, sir, and – er – out of a generous impulse to be of service – yes, sir!' muttered Lebedev. 'Now I'm all yours, all yours again! Do anything you like with me!'

'Did you go to see Mrs Yepanchin just as you are now?' the prince inquired with a sort of queasy curiosity.

'No, sir – I was much fresher, sir, and, if I may say so, much more decent. It was only after my humiliation, sir, that I got into this – er – state.'

'All right, leave me now.'

This request had to be repeated a few times, though, before the visitor at last made up his mind to go. But having opened the door, he came back again, tiptoed to the middle of the room, and once more began making signs with his hands to show how to open a letter, he dared not, however, put his advice into words; then he went out with a quiet and sweet smile.

All this had been very painful to hear. It all pointed to one significant fact – namely, that Aglaya was in a state of great anxiety, great uncertainty, and for some reason great mental suffering ('from jealousy', the prince whispered to himself). It was also clear that she was worried by mischief-makers, and it was certainly very odd that she should trust them so much. No doubt in that inexperienced but hot and proud little head all sorts of peculiar plans were brewing, perhaps disastrous and – wild and impossible ones. ... The prince was very alarmed, and in his perplexity did not know what to do. He had to do something to avert a disaster – he felt that. He glanced again at the address on the sealed letter. Oh, he had no doubts nor was he worried on that score, for he trusted her; something else worried him about that letter: he could not trust Ganya. And yet he made up his mind to deliver the letter himself, and he even left the house to do so, but he changed his mind on the way. Almost at the door of Ptitsyn's house he was lucky enough to meet Kolya, and he asked him to deliver the letter into his brother's hands as though it had come straight from Aglaya. Kolya asked no questions and delivered it, so that it never occurred to Ganya that the letter had passed through so many hands. When he returned home, the prince sent for Vera and told her as much as was necessary and set her mind at rest, for she had been looking for the letter all this time and was in tears. She was horrified to learn that her father had carried it off. (The prince had found out from her afterwards that she had run secret errands for Rogozhin and Aglaya more than once; it had never occurred to her that she might be doing a disservice to the prince.)

The prince was at last so upset that when, two hours later, a messenger from Kolya arrived with the news of his father's illness, he could not at first make out what it was all about. But this event restored him, for it greatly distracted his attention. He stayed at Mrs Ivolgin's (where the sick man, of course, had been carried) almost right up to the evening. He was scarcely of any use, but there are people whom one likes for some reason to see beside one in times of distress. Kolya was terribly upset and he cried hysterically, but all the time he had to run errands: he was sent for the doctor and fetched three, he ran to the chemist's, and to the barber's. The general was revived, but he did not regain consciousness; the doctors declared that the patient was, in any case 'dangerously ill'. Varya and Mrs Ivolgin never left the patient's bedside; Ganya was disconcerted and deeply shocked, but he did not go upstairs, and was even afraid to see his father; he was wringing his hands and in the incoherent talk he had with the prince he had managed to express his annoyance that such a misfortune 'would happen' at such a moment! The prince could not help feeling that he understood what kind of a 'moment' Ganya meant. The prince did not find Ippolit at Ptitsyn's. Lebedev, who had slept all day without waking after the morning's 'explanation', arrived late in the afternoon. He was almost sober now, and shed real tears over the sick man, just as though the general were his own brother. He blamed himself aloud, without, however, explaining why, and kept pestering Mrs Ivolgin, assuring her every minute that he, he alone was the cause, and no one but he, that it was 'solely from agreeable curiosity', and that 'the deceased' (as he persisted in calling the still living general) was really 'a man of the greatest genius'. He kept emphasizing the general's 'genius', as though that might be of some extraordinary help at that moment. Seeing his genuine tears, Mrs Ivolgin said to him at last without the faintest suspicion of reproach and, indeed, almost with a note of affection, 'There, there, don't cry – there, God will forgive you!' Lebedev was so amazed at these words, and especially by their tone, that he refused to leave her all the evening (and he spent all the subsequent days, from morning till night, up to the moment of the general's death, in their house). During the day a messenger from Mrs Yepanchin came twice to Mrs Ivolgin to inquire after the general's health. When the prince made his appearance in the Yepanchins' drawing-room at nine o'clock in the evening (all the invited guests were already there), Mrs Yepanchin at once began questioning him about the sick man, with sympathy and in detail, and very gravely replied to Princess Belokonsky's questions who the patient was and who was Mrs Ivolgin. The prince liked that very much. In telling Mrs Yepanchin about the general's condition, the prince himself spoke 'beautifully', as Aglaya's sisters expressed it afterwards: 'modestly, quietly, without any unnecessary words, without gestures, and with dignity; he walked in wonderfully and he was dressed excellently', and not only did he not 'fall down on the slippery floor', as he was afraid he would do the previous night, but seemed to have made a favourable impression all round.

For his part, having sat down and looked round him, he at once noticed that the guests at the party bore no resemblance whatever to the spectres with which Aglaya had frightened him the night before, or to the nightmarish figures he had dreamt of in the night. For the first time in his life he saw a little corner of what was known under the terrible name of 'society'. Following certain inclinations, considerations, and plans of his own, he had long been very eager to break into this charmed circle, and he was therefore very interested in his first impression of it. That first impression of his was quite fascinating. Somehow or other, he at once got the feeling that all those people seemed to have been born to be together, that the Yepanchins were giving no 'party' that evening and had not invited any important guests; that they were just quite 'ordinary people', and that he himself had long been their most devoted friend, who shared their thoughts and had returned to them after a short separation. The charm of elegant manners, simplicity, and apparent candour was almost magical. It could never have occurred to him that all that candour and nobility, wit and lofty personal dignity was perhaps only a magnificent artistic veneer. In spite of their impressive exterior, the majority of the guests were, indeed, rather empty-headed people who, in their smugness, did not realize themselves that much of their excellence was just a veneer, for which they were not responsible, for they acquired it unconsciously and by inheritance. The prince, fascinated by the charm of his first impression, did not as much as suspect that. He saw, for instance, that this old man, this important statesman, who was old enough to be his grandfather, did not hesitate to interrupt his conversation in order to listen to such an inexperienced young man as he, and not only did he listen to him, but he evidently valued his opinion, so gracious and sincerely good-humoured was he with him, and yet they were strangers, who had only met for the first time. Perhaps it was this refinement of courtesy that impressed the prince's eager sensitiveness most. He was perhaps predisposed and biased in favour of so good an impression.

And yet all these people, though, of course, they were 'friends of the family' and of one another, were by no means such great friends of the family or of one another as the prince had supposed they were when he was introduced to them. There were some among them who would never, and not for anything in the world, have admitted that the Yepanchins were in any way their equals. There were people there who absolutely detested one another; the old Princess Belokonsky all her life 'despised' the wife of the 'elderly statesman', who in turn was very far from being fond of Mrs Yepanchin. This 'statesman', who for some reason had been patronizing General Yepanchin and his wife from their youth onwards and who was the most important person present, was considered to be so grand a personage in the general's eyes that he could feel nothing but reverence and awe in his presence, and, indeed, he would have genuinely despised himself if he had considered him in any way his equal, and not an Olympian Jove. There were people there who had not met for several years and who did not feel anything but indifference, if not dislike, for one another, but who greeted each other now as though they had only met the day before in the most friendly and agreeable company. The party was not a large one, however. In addition to Princess Belokonsky and 'the elderly statesman', who really was a man of importance, and his wife, there was, first of all, a very staid army general, a baron or count, with a German name, a man of extraordinary taciturnity, who was reputed to have a wonderful knowledge of the affairs of state, and had almost a reputation of great learning – one of those Olympian administrators who know everything 'except perhaps Russia herself', a man who in the course of five years had delivered himself of one remark that was acknowledged to be 'remarkable for its profundity' and that was quite certain to become a proverb and reach even the most exalted circles; one of those high officials who, after an extremely and even extraordinarily protracted service, usually die after having attained high rank, an excellent position, and amassing an immense fortune, though they have never done anything great and, indeed, have always shown a certain hostility for anything great. This general was General Yepanchin's immediate superior in the service. General Yepanchin, out of the warmth of his grateful heart and even out of a peculiar kind of vanity, regarded him as his benefactor. The general, though, did not by any means consider himself to be General Yepanchin's benefactor; indeed, he treated him with complete unconcern and, though he gladly availed himself of his numerous and manifold services, he would not hesitate to replace him by another official if any considerations, and not by any means the highest, had made it necessary. There was there also an elderly, important-looking gentleman, who was supposed to be a relation of Mrs Yepanchin's, though this was quite untrue; he was a man of high rank and position, wealthy and of aristocratic descent, stout and in good health, a great talker, who even had the reputation of being a discontented person (though, of course, in the most loyal sense of the word), a choleric man (but even this was agreeable in him), with the mannerisms of an English aristocrat and with English tastes (as regards, for instance, underdone roast beef, harness, footmen, etc.). He was a great friend of the 'statesman', whom he amused. Besides, Mrs Yepanchin for some reason cherished the curious idea that this elderly gentleman (a rather frivolous person and said to be a great admirer of the fair sex) might suddenly take it into his head to make Alexandra happy with a proposal of marriage.

This highest and most solid stratum of the assembled guests was followed by a stratum of young people, though these, too, were graced by most exquisite qualities. Besides Prince Sh. and Mr Radomsky, the well-known and most charming Prince N. belonged to this group, once the seducer and vanquisher of female hearts all over Europe, now a man of forty-five, but still of handsome appearance, a wonderful raconteur, a wealthy man, whose affairs, though, were in a rather disordered state, and who, from force of habit, spent most of his time abroad. Last of all, there were people there who seemed to belong to a third special stratum and who by themselves were not part of the 'exclusive set'. The Yepanchins, guided by a feeling of nice discrimination, which they regarded as a rule of social conduct, liked on the rare occasions when they gave an important party to mix the highest society with people belonging to a lower stratum, with selected representatives of the middle classes. The Yepanchins were indeed praised for it and regarded as people of tact who knew their place, and they were proud of such an opinion of themselves. One of the representatives of the middle classes that evening was a colonel of the engineering corps, a serious man, and a very close friend of Prince Sh.'s. He was rather silent in society, though, and wore on the forefinger of his right hand a large and conspicuous solitaire, most probably presented to him. There was present, finally, a literary gentleman, a poet of German origin, but a Russian poet, who, moreover, was perfectly respectable, so that he could be introduced into good society without apprehension. He was of a pleasing, though, for some reason, rather forbidding appearance, about thirty-eight, irreproachably dressed. He belonged to a highly bourgeois, but also highly respectable, German family; he knew how to make the best of every opportunity, fight his way through to important people who could be useful to him, and retain their favour. At one time he had translated into verse some important German poet, knew to whom to dedicate his translation, knew how to boast of his friendship with a famous but dead Russian poet (there is a whole group of writers who are very fond of claiming in print the friendship of great but dead writers), and had been quite recently introduced to the Yepanchins by the wife of the 'elderly statesman'. This lady had the reputation of being a patroness of writers and scholars, and she really was successful in obtaining a pension for one or two writers through persons in high positions, with whom she had influence. And she certainly had influence of a kind. She was a woman of five and forty (a very young wife for so old a man as her husband), who had been a great beauty and still, like many women of forty-five, had a mania for dressing far too smartly; she was not particularly intelligent, and her knowledge of literature was rather dubious. But to patronize literary men was as much a mania with her as to dress smartly. Many original works and translations had been dedicated to her; two or three writers had, with her permission, published letters they had written to her on subjects of the highest importance. ... And it was all this society that the prince took for the real thing, for pure gold without alloy. However, on this particular evening all these people were, as though on purpose, in a most happy frame of mind and extremely pleased with themselves. Every one of them knew that he was doing the Yepanchins a great honour by his presence. But, alas! the prince had no suspicion of such subtleties! He did not suspect, for instance, that the Yepanchins, contemplating such an important step as a decision about their daughter's future, would never have dared not to exhibit him, Prince Leo Nikolayevich Myshkin, to the elderly statesman who was the acknowledged patron of their family. The elderly statesman, too, though he would have received the news of the most dreadful disaster that could have befallen the Yepanchin family with the utmost equanimity, would most certainly have been offended if the Yepanchins had consented to the engagement of their daughter without his advice and, as it were, without his leave. Prince N. – that charming, that indisputably witty, and absolutely straightforward man – was quite firmly convinced that he was something like a sun that had risen that night over the Yepanchin drawing-room. He regarded them as infinitely beneath him, and it was just this artless and generous idea which gave rise to his wonderfully charming ease and friendliness towards the Yepanchins. He knew very well that to delight the company he would have to tell them some story that evening, and he was getting ready for it with positive inspiration. When he heard the story afterwards, the prince felt that he had never heard anything like such brilliant humour and such marvellous gaiety and naïvety, which was almost touching, coming from such a Don Juan as Prince N. And yet had he only realized how old and stale that story was, how it was known by heart, and how sick and tired every drawing-room in town was of it, and that only at the innocent Yepanchins' did it pass for something new, for an impromptu, genuine, and brilliant reminiscence of a splendid and brilliant man! Even the German poet, though he behaved with extraordinary modesty and politeness, felt that he was doing the family an honour by his presence. But the prince never noticed the reverse side of the medal, he did not see what was underneath it all. It was this calamity that Aglaya had not foreseen. She herself looked remarkably beautiful that evening. All the three girls were dressed very becomingly, though not too smartly, and had their hair done with particular care. Aglaya was sitting with Radomsky and talking and joking with him in a most friendly manner. Radomsky seemed to behave much more staidly than he used to, perhaps also out of respect to the state dignitaries. But he had long been known in society; he was no stranger there, though still a young man. He arrived at the Yepanchins' that evening with a crêpe band on his hat, and Princess Belokonsky had complimented him on it: not every man about town would have worn mourning for such an uncle. Mrs Yepanchin, too, was pleased with it, but she seemed on the whole to be somehow a little too preoccupied. The prince noticed that Aglaya looked intently at him twice and he thought she was satisfied with him. Gradually he was beginning to feel very happy. His recent 'fantastic' notions (after his conversation with Lebedev) seemed to him now, when he recalled them again and again, an inconceivable, impossible, and even absurd dream! (And, anyway, his first, though unconscious, impulse and desire all day had been to do everything in his power to disbelieve that dream!) He spoke little and only in answer to questions, and at last was altogether silent; he sat and listened, but was quite obviously enjoying himself immensely. Little by little something like inspiration began piling up within him, ready to flare up at the right moment. ... He began speaking quite by accident, also in reply to a question, and apparently without any special motive.

7

While lost in admiration of Aglaya, as he watched her talking gaily to Prince N. and Radomsky, the middle-aged Anglophile, who was entertaining the 'elderly statesman' and telling him something with great animation in another corner of the room, uttered the name of Nikolai Andreyevich Pavlishchev. The prince turned quickly in their direction and began listening.

They were discussing the new methods of estate management after the recent agrarian reforms and the muddle into which the owners of estates in a certain province had got themselves. The Anglophile's stories must have been rather amusing, because the old man began laughing at last at the ill-tempered vehemence of the speaker. He was explaining smoothly, drawing out his words rather peevishly and dwelling affectionately on the vowels, why he was compelled, as a direct result of the new agrarian reforms, to sell a magnificent estate of his in that province for half its value, though he was not particularly pressed for money, and at the same time keep an estate that had gone to rack and ruin, was losing money and was under litigation, and even to spend some money on it. 'To avoid another law-suit in connexion with the Pavlishchev estate, I ran away from them. Another inheritance or two of the same kind and I shall be ruined. I should have come in for about nine thousand acres of excellent land there, though!'

'This – er – Ivan Petrovich,' General Yepanchin, who had suddenly materialized near the prince, remarked in an undertone, noticing his extraordinary interest in the conversation, 'is a relation of the late Pavlishchev, you know. You've been looking for Pavlishchev's relations, I believe.'

Till then he had been entertaining the general, his superior in the service, but he had observed the prince's quite extraordinary isolation and was beginning to feel uneasy. He was anxious to make him take some part in the conversation and in this way to exhibit him a second time and bring him to the notice of the 'great personages'.

'Prince Leo Nikolayevich was Pavlishchev's protégé after the death of his own parents,' he put in, meeting Ivan Petrovich's eye.

'Very pleased to meet you,' observed Ivan Petrovich. 'Yes, I remember you very well indeed. When General Yepanchin introduced us earlier this evening, I recognized you at once – yes, your face was certainly familiar. You have changed very little, though I only saw you as a child – you were ten or eleven at the time. There's something about your features that brought it all back to me.'

'You saw me as a child?' asked the prince, with a sort of unusual surprise.

'Oh, yes, very long ago,' continued Ivan Petrovich, 'in Zlatoverkhov, where you were living with my cousins. I used to visit Zlatoverkhov very often in those days. Don't you remember me? Ve-ry likely you do not. ... You were then – you – er – had some kind of illness then, so that once, I remember, I was rather struck by your appearance.'

'I don't remember anything!' the prince declared warmly.

A few more words of explanation, very calm on the part of Ivan Petrovich and extraordinarily agitated on the part of the prince, and it appeared that the two ladies, both of them old maids, relations of Pavlishchev, who lived on his Zlatoverkhov estate and by whom the prince had been brought up, were also cousins of Ivan Petrovich's. Ivan Petrovich, like everyone else, could not explain the reasons which induced Pavlishchev to take so much trouble over his adopted child, the little prince. 'As a matter of fact,' he said, 'I don't think I was particularly interested in it at the time!' But all the same he seemed to have an excellent memory, for he even remembered how strict his elder cousin, Marfa Nikitishna, had been with the little boy, 'so that on one occasion I even had words with her on your account about her system of education. Why, birching, birching a sick child all the time – you must admit that's a little – –' He also remembered how tender, on the other hand, his younger cousin, Natalya Nikitishna, had been to the poor child. 'Both of them,' he went on to explain, 'are now in — province, where Pavlishchev left them a very nice little property, but I don't know whether they're still alive. Marfa Nikitishna, I believe, wanted to go into a convent. Though, there again I'm not sure. Perhaps it was someone else. ... Yes, I heard that about a doctor's wife the other day. ...'

The prince listened to this with eyes shining with emotion and delight. He declared with extraordinary warmth that he, for his part, would never forgive himself for not having seized an opportunity during the six months he had been travelling in the central provinces to find and visit the old ladies. He had intended to go every day, but was always prevented by circumstances. But now he had quite made up his mind – yes, certainly – even if he had to go to — province. 'So you really know Natalya Nikitishna? What a splendid, what a saintly woman! But Marfa Nikitishna, too – I'm sorry, but I think you're mistaken about Marfa Nikitishna! She was strict but – you couldn't blame her for losing patience with – with such an idiot as I was then (hee, hee!). I was an utter idiot, you know – you will hardly believe it (ha, ha!). But then – but then you saw me at that time and – – How is it I don't remember you, tell me, please? So you are – why, good heavens! so you really are a relation of Pavlishchev's?'

'I as-sure you I am,' Ivan Petrovich smiled, scrutinizing the prince.

'Oh, please, please, I didn't say that because I – er – doubted it – and after all, it's impossible to doubt it, isn't it? (Ha, ha!) I mean, there's not a shadow of doubt, is there? (Ha, ha!) I merely said it because the late Mr Pavlishchev was such a splendid man! A most magnanimous man, I assure you!'

The prince was not so much out of breath as 'overflowing with the milk of human kindness' as Adelaida expressed it next morning to her fiancé Prince Sh.

'Why, bless my soul,' Ivan Petrovich laughed, 'can't I be a relation of a mag-nanimous man even?'

'Dear me,' cried the prince, looking embarrassed, talking rapidly and getting more and more excited. 'I'm afraid I – I've said something stupid again, but – that's as it should be because I – I – I – but again that's nothing to do with it! And what do I, tell me please, what do I amount to beside such interests – such – er – vast interests! And by comparison with such a most magnanimous man, because he was, I assure you, a most magnanimous man! Don't you think so?'

The prince was absolutely trembling all over. Why he got suddenly so excited, why he got himself into such a state of emotional rapture for no apparent reason and, it seemed, out of all proportion to the subject of the conversation, it would be difficult to say. He just happened to be in such a mood, and at that moment he almost felt the warmest and liveliest gratitude to someone for something, perhaps even to Ivan Petrovich and, indeed, almost to every person in the room. He was 'drunk with happiness'. Ivan Petrovich began at last to stare at him more intently; the 'statesman' too was staring at him fixedly. Princess Belokonsky glared at him angrily and tightened her lips. Prince N., Radomsky, Prince Sh., the girls, all broke off their conversation and listened. Aglaya appeared to be frightened. As for Mrs Yepanchin, she simply lost her nerve. They, too, were odd creatures, the daughters and their mother: it was they who had proposed and decided that it would be better for the prince to be silent all the evening; yet when they saw him sitting all alone and perfectly happy, they had at once become terribly anxious. Alexandra had been on the point of going up to him and discreetly taking him across the room to join their company – that is, Prince N.'s group, near Princess Belokonsky. And now that the prince had begun talking himself, they grew even more anxious.

'I agree with you that he was a most excellent man,' Ivan Petrovich said impressively, but no longer smiling. 'Yes – yes, to be sure, he was an excellent man! Excellent and worthy,' he added after a short pause. 'Worthy, I might say, of every respect,' he added even more impressively after a third pause, 'and ... and I must say it's nice to see you – er ––'

'Wasn't it this same Pavlishchev who was involved in a curious story – er – with the abbé – er – with the abbé – I'm afraid I've forgotten which abbé, only I remember everybody talking about it at the time,' the 'statesman' said, as though trying to remember.

'With the Abbé Goureau, a Jesuit,' Ivan Petrovich reminded him. 'Yes, sir, that's the sort of people our most excellent and worthy men are! For, after all, he was a man of good birth and fortune, a Court chamberlain, and if he'd gone on serving his country –– But he preferred to give up the service and everything else and go over to Roman Catholicism and become a Jesuit, and quite openly, too, almost with a sort of fanaticism. I suppose it was just as well that he died – yes. Everybody said so at the time.'

The prince was beside himself.

'Pavlishchev – Pavlishchev converted to Catholicism? Impossible!' he cried in horror.

'Well, you know, "impossible" is rather putting it a little too strongly,' Ivan Petrovich mumbled solemnly. 'Don't you think so, my dear Prince? However, you have such a high opinion of the deceased who – er – really was a most kind-hearted man which, I think, chiefly accounts for the success of that cunning old fox Goureau. But you'd better ask me – me, sir, how much trouble and worry I had over this affair afterwards – and particularly with that fellow Goureau! Imagine it,' he suddenly addressed the old man, 'they actually tried to put in a claim under the will and I had to resort to – er – the strongest measures to – er – to bring them to their senses, for – er – they are past-masters at this sort of thing! Won-der-fully clever rogues! But, thank goodness, it all happened in Moscow – I went straight to the count and – er – we brought them to their senses. ...'

'You don't know how you've shocked and upset me!' cried the prince.

'I'm sorry, but, as a matter of fact, it's all strictly speaking nonsense and it would have come to nothing in the end, as such things always do. I'm sure of that. Last summer,' he again turned to the little old man, 'Countess K., I'm told, also entered some Catholic convent abroad. Our people are, somehow, unable to put up a fight once they get into the clutches of those – cunning old rascals – especially abroad.'

'It's all because of our – er weariness, I think,' the little old man mumbled authoritatively. 'And, well, their way of preaching, too, is – er – very elegant and – all their own. And – er – they know how to put the fear of God into people. They tried to frighten me too, I assure you, in Vienna in 1832, but I stood up to them and ran away, ha, ha! I really did run away from them.'

'I heard, my dear sir,' Princess Belokonsky put in suddenly, 'that you gave up your post in Vienna and ran away to Paris with the beautiful Countess Levitsky, and not from a Jesuit priest.'

'Well, yes, ma'am, but it was from the Jesuit all the same, it was from the Jesuit!' the little old man cried, laughing at the pleasant memory. 'You seem to be very religious, which is so rare with our young men nowadays,' he addressed the prince amiably.

The prince was listening open-mouthed, still too shocked to say anything. The old man was apparently anxious to get to know the prince more intimately. He became very interested in him for some reason.

'Pavlishchev was a man of great intellect and a true Christian,' the prince said suddenly. 'How could he possibly submit to a faith that is – unchristian? Catholicism,' he added suddenly with flashing eyes and looking round as though appealing to them all with his eyes, 'Catholicism is the same as an unchristian religion!'

'Well, that is going a bit too far,' muttered the old man, and he looked with surprise at General Yepanchin.

'How do you mean Catholicism is an unchristian religion?' Ivan Petrovich asked, turning round in his chair. 'What kind of a religion is it, then?'

'It is an unchristian religion, in the first place!' the prince resumed in great agitation and with excessive sharpness. 'That's in the first place, and, secondly, Roman Catholicism is even worse than atheism – that's my opinion. Yes, that's my opinion! Atheism merely preaches a negation, but Catholicism goes further: it preaches a distorted Christ, a Christ calumniated and defamed by it, the opposite of Christ! It preaches Antichrist – I swear it does, I assure you it does! This is my personal opinion, an opinion I've held for a long time, and it has worried me a lot myself. ... Roman Catholicism believes that the Church cannot exist on earth without universal temporal power, and cries: *Non possumus!* In my opinion, Roman Catholicism isn't even a religion, but most decidedly a continuation of the Holy Roman Empire, and everything in it is subordinated to that idea, beginning with faith. The Pope seized the earth, an earthly throne and took up the sword; and since then everything has gone on in the same way, except that they've added lies, fraud, deceit, fanaticism, superstition, wickedness. They have trifled with the most sacred, truthful, innocent, ardent feelings of the people, have bartered it all for money, for base temporal power. And isn't this the teaching of Antichrist? Isn't it clear that atheism had to come from them? And it did come from them, from Roman Catholicism itself! Atheism originated first of all with them: how could they believe in themselves? It gained ground because of abhorrence of them; it is the child of their lies and their spiritual impotence! Atheism! In our country it is only the upper classes who do not believe, as Mr Radomsky so splendidly put it the other day, for they have lost their roots. But in Europe vast numbers of the common people are beginning to lose their faith – at first from darkness and lies, and now from fanaticism, hatred of the Church and Christianity!'

The prince paused to take breath. He had been talking terribly fast. He was pale and breathless. They all exchanged glances; but the little old man at last burst out laughing openly. Prince N. took out his lorgnette and kept staring at the prince for some time. The little

German poet crawled out of his corner and edged his way nearer to the table, with an evil smile on his face.

'You do ex-agger-ate a lot, you know,' drawled Ivan Petrovich in a somewhat bored tone and as though he were rather ashamed of something. 'There are representatives of the Catholic Church who are worthy of all respect and ex-tremely virtuous. ...'

'I am not saying anything about individual representatives of the Church. I am speaking of Roman Catholicism in its essence. I am speaking of Rome. Can a church disappear entirely? I never said that!'

'Agreed, but all that's not new and even – irrelevant and – er – belongs to the domain of theology. ...'

'No, sir, no! It isn't only a question of theology. I assure you it isn't. It concerns us more closely than you think. That's our whole mistake that we are still unable to see that it is not exclusively a theological question. For socialism, too, is the child of Catholicism and the intrinsic Catholic nature! It, too, like its brother atheism, was begotten of despair, in opposition to Catholicism as a moral force, in order to replace the lost moral power of religion, to quench the spiritual thirst of parched humanity, and save it not by Christ, but also by violence! This, too, is freedom through violence. This, too, is union through the sword and blood. "Don't dare to believe in God! Don't dare to have property! Don't dare to have a personality of your own! *Fraternité ou la mort!* Two million heads!" By their works ye shall know them – as it is written. And don't think that all this is so innocent and without danger to us. Oh, we must organize our resistance, and do it now – now! It is necessary that our Christ should shine forth in opposition to the ideas of the West, our Christ, whom we have preserved and they have never known! Not by slavishly swallowing the bait the Jesuits spread for us, but by carrying our Russian civilization to them, we must now stand before them. And don't let it be said among us that their preaching is elegant, as someone has said just now. ...'

'But please, please,' cried Ivan Petrovich, becoming dreadfully worried, looking round the room and even beginning to be frightened, 'all your ideas are of course praiseworthy and highly patriotic, but all this is terribly exaggerated and – er – I think we'd better drop the subject.'

'No, sir, it isn't an exaggeration, but rather an understatement. Yes, sir, an understatement, because I'm not able to express myself properly, but – –'

'Plea-se!'

The prince fell silent. He sat upright and motionless in his chair, looking fiercely at Ivan Petrovich.

'It seems to me,' the little old man remarked gently and without losing his composure, 'that what happened to your benefactor has been too great a shock to you. You're over-excited because of your – solitary life, perhaps. If you were to live more among people, society, I hope, would welcome you as a remarkable young man and, of course, you'd become much less excitable and you'd realize that all this is much simpler and – in my opinion – such – rare cases occur partly because we are surfeited and partly – because we are bored. ...'

'Yes, yes, you're quite right,' cried the prince. 'A splendid idea! Yes, from boredom, from our boredom, and not from surfeit – on the contrary, from thirst, not from surfeit – that's where you're wrong! And not only from thirst, but from fever, from burning thirst! And – and don't think this is so slight a matter that we can just laugh at it. I'm sorry, but one must be able to foresee the consequences. As soon as we Russians reach the shore, as soon as we are sure it is the shore, we are so glad of it that we lose all sense of proportion. Why is that? I can see you are surprised at Pavlishchev. You attribute everything to his madness or goodness, but you're wrong! It is not only we who are surprised at our passionate intensity in such cases, but the whole of Europe. If a Russian is converted to Catholicism, he is sure to become a Jesuit, and a rabid one at that; if he becomes an atheist, he is sure to demand the extirpation of belief in God by force – that is, by the sword! Why is all this? Why such fury all of a sudden? Don't you know? Because he has found his motherland at last, the motherland he has missed here, and he feels happy; he has found the shore, the land, and he rushes to kiss it! It is not from vanity alone, it is not from bad, vain feelings that Russians become atheists and Jesuits, but from spiritual agony, from spiritual thirst, from a yearning for higher ideals, for the firm shore, for the mother country in which they have ceased to believe because they have never even known it! And it is so easy for a Russian to become an atheist, much easier than for anyone else in the whole world! And Russians do not simply become atheists, but actually *believe* in atheism, as though it were a new religion, without noticing that they believe in a negation. Such is our thirst! "He who has no firm ground beneath his feet, has no God, either." That's not my saying. It's the saying of one of our merchants, an Old Believer, whom I met on my travels. It is true he didn't put it that way. He said: "He who has renounced his native land has also renounced his God." To think that some of our most educated men have even turned flagellants! But, then, in what way are flagellants worse than nihilists, Jesuits, or atheists? They may even be more profound! But that's what their anguish has brought them to! Show the thirsting and parched companions of Columbus the shores of the "New World", show a Russian the Russian "World", let him find the gold, the treasure hidden from him in the bowels of the earth! Show him the renaissance of the whole of mankind in the future, and, perhaps, its resurrection by Russian thought alone, by the Russian God and Christ, and you will see into what a mighty, truthful, wise, and gentle giant he will grow before the eyes of the astonished world, astonished and frightened, for all they expect from us is the sword, the sword and violence, for, judging us by themselves, they cannot even imagine us free from barbarism. And that has always been so till now, and the more it goes on like that, the more it will be so! And – –'

But here something happened that cut short the orator's speech in a most unexpected manner.

All this delirious tirade, all this onrush of passionate and agitated words and disjointed ecstatic ideas, which seemed to be jostling each other and tumbling over each other in confusion, all this betokened something perilous, something peculiar in the mental condition of the young man who had worked himself up into a passion so suddenly and apparently for no reason at all. Of the people in the drawing-room all who knew the prince marvelled apprehensively (and some of them with shame) at his outburst, which was so out of keeping with his habitual and, indeed, timid restraint, with his rare and singular tact, and his instinctive feeling for true decorum. They could not understand how it happened. The news of Pavlishchev could not possibly have been the cause of it. The ladies looked upon him as on one who had taken leave of his senses, and Princess Belokonsky admitted afterwards that in another minute she would have 'run for her life'. The old gentlemen were at first almost taken aback with amazement. The general, General Yepanchin's superior, looked sternly and with displeasure from his place. The colonel of engineers sat perfectly motionless. The little German even turned pale, but he went on smiling his insincere smile and looking at the others to see how they were taking it. However, all this and the whole 'scandalous incident' might have been brought to an end in the most ordinary and natural way, perhaps, in another minute; General Yepanchin, who was greatly astonished, but who had regained his composure before anyone else, had tried to stop the prince several times already and, having failed, he was now making his way towards him with the intention of taking firm and resolute action. Another minute and, had it been necessary, he would perhaps have made up his mind to lead the prince out of the room in a very friendly way on the pretext of his being ill, which perhaps was quite true and which General Yepanchin fully believed himself. ... But things took quite a different turn.

At the very beginning, as soon as the prince entered the drawing-room, he sat down as far as possible from the Chinese vase about which Aglaya had frightened him so much. It seems incredible, but after what Aglaya had told him the night before, he was obsessed by a sort of unshaken conviction, a sort of curious and absurd presentiment that he would most certainly break the vase, and that next day, too, however much he kept away from it and however hard he tried to avoid the disaster! But so it was. In the course of the evening other strong but bright impressions began to take possession of him; we have spoken of that already. He forgot his presentiment. When he had heard Pavlishchev's name mentioned and General Yepanchin led him up to Ivan Petrovich and introduced him for the second time, he had changed his seat and sat down in the arm-chair next to the large and beautiful Chinese vase, which stood on a pedestal almost at his elbow and a little behind him.

As he uttered his last words he suddenly got up from his seat, unthinkingly waved his arm and, somehow, moved his shoulder and – there was a general gasp of horror! The vase swayed, at first as though uncertain whether to fall on the head of one of the elderly gentlemen, but suddenly lurched in the other direction, towards the little German, who jumped out of the way in terror, and crashed on the floor. The crash, the gasp of horror, the precious fragments scattered on the carpet, the dismay, the astonishment – oh, it's difficult and, indeed, almost unnecessary to describe what the prince felt at that moment! But we simply must mention a queer sensation that came over him at that very moment and that suddenly emerged clearly out of the throng of all the other confused and terrible sensations: what struck him most was not the shame, the disgrace, the fear, the suddenness of it all, but the fact that the prophecy had come true! What was so breathtaking about this idea he could not explain to himself; he only felt that he was struck to the heart and he stood still in almost mystic terror. Another moment and everything seemed to expand before him: instead of horror – light and gladness and ecstasy; his breath began to fail him and – but the moment had passed. Thank God, it wasn't *that*! He drew a deep breath and looked round.

For a long time he did not seem to understand the bustling activity that was going on around him, or rather he understood it perfectly and saw everything, but stood there just as though he were some other man who took no part in anything and who, like the invisible man in the fairy-tale, had made his way into the room and was watching people he did not know but whom he found interesting. He saw them picking up the broken pieces of china, he heard them talking rapidly to each other, he saw Aglaya, pale and looking strangely at him, very strangely: there was no hatred in her eyes, not a trace of anger; she looked at him with a frightened, but also with such an affectionate expression and at the others with such flashing eyes that his heart suddenly ached with sweet pain. At last he saw with strange amazement that they had all sat down again and were, indeed, laughing just as though nothing had happened! Another minute and their laughter grew louder: they were now laughing at him, at his dumb stupefaction, but their laughter was friendly and gay; many of them spoke to him, and they spoke so kindly, and most of all Mrs Yepanchin: she was talking laughingly to him and saying something very, very kind. Suddenly he became aware that General Yepanchin was patting him on the back in a very friendly way; Ivan Petrovich, too, was laughing; but the little old man was most agreeable and most sympathetic of all; he took the prince by the hand and, pressing it gently and patting it lightly with his other hand, urged him to pull himself together, just as though he were a frightened little boy, which pleased the prince very much, and at last made him sit down beside him. The prince gazed into his face with pleasure and still somehow found it difficult to speak – his breath failed him: he liked the old man's face so much.

'I say,' he murmured at last, 'do you really forgive me? And you, too – Mrs Yepanchin?'

The laughter grew louder. Tears came into the prince's eyes. He could not believe it, and he was enchanted.

'Of course, the vase was very beautiful,' began Ivan Petrovich, 'I can remember it here for the last fifteen years – yes, fifteen – –'

'Well, what does it matter?' Mrs Yepanchin said in a loud voice. 'A man, too, has to come to an end, and all this bother about a clay pot! You're not really so terribly alarmed about it, are you?' she added rather apprehensively, addressing the prince. 'It doesn't matter a bit. Really, my dear boy, you frighten me.'

'And do you forgive me for *everything* – for everything, besides the vase?' asked the prince, getting up from his seat.

But the old man at once drew him back again by the hand. He was unwilling to let him go.

'*C'est très curieux et c'est très sérieux!*' he whispered across the table to Ivan Petrovich, though rather loudly, so that the prince may have heard it.

'So I haven't offended any of you? You can't imagine how happy this makes me! But that's as it should be. How could I have offended anyone here? I should be offending you again if I thought so.'

'Calm yourself, my dear fellow; you're again exaggerating. You have nothing to thank us for. It's an excellent feeling, but I'm afraid exaggerated.'

'I'm not thanking you – I'm only – admiring you. I'm happy looking at you. Perhaps what I'm saying is silly, but I have to say it, I have to explain – if only out of respect for myself.'

Everything about him was abrupt, confused, and feverish; possibly the words he uttered were often not those he wished to say. His eyes seemed to be asking for permission to speak. They fell on Princess Belokonsky.

'Never mind, my dear sir; go on, go on; only don't get out of breath,' she observed. 'You started just now by being short of breath and look what you've done. But don't be afraid to speak. These people here have seen stranger sights than you. You won't surprise them. And however clever you are, you've managed to break the vase and given us all a fright.'

The prince listened to her with a smile.

'It was you, sir,' he suddenly addressed the little old man – 'it was you, wasn't it, who saved the student Podkumov and the civil servant Shvabrin from exile to Siberia three months ago?'

The old man even blushed a little and murmured that he must try and calm himself.

'And wasn't it you, sir,' he turned at once to Ivan Petrovich, 'who, I've heard, distributed timber among your peasants when their village burnt down, although they were already free and had given you a lot of trouble?'

'Well,' murmured Ivan Petrovich, looking very pleased, all the same, 'that's an ex-agger-ation.'

This time, however, he was quite right about it's being an exaggeration; the rumour that had reached the prince was untrue.

'And did not you, Princess,' he suddenly addressed Princess Belokonsky with a bright smile, 'receive me six months ago in Moscow just as though I had been your own son because of a letter of introduction from Mrs Yepanchin, and, just as though I really was your own son, gave me a piece of advice which I shall never forget? Do you remember?'

'Gracious me, what a fuss you make!' cried Princess Belokonsky, with annoyance. 'You're a good fellow, but you're absurd: someone gives you twopence and you thank him as though he had saved your life. You think it's nice, but let me tell you, it is disgusting.'

She was on the point of getting angry with him in good earnest, but suddenly burst out laughing, and this time it was good-natured laughter. Mrs Yepanchin's face also brightened; General Yepanchin, too, beamed.

'I told you the prince was a man – er – a man – in short – er – if only he wouldn't get so breathless, as the princess observed – –' the general murmured in joyful rapture, repeating Princess Belokonsky's words, which had struck him.

Aglaya alone appeared to be sad; but her face was still flushed, perhaps, with indignation.

'He really is very charming,' the little old man murmured again to Ivan Petrovich.

'I came in here with anguish in my heart,' went on the prince, with ever-mounting agitation, speaking more and more rapidly, more strangely and animatedly. 'I – I was afraid of you, I was also afraid of myself. Of myself most of all. On my way back to Petersburg I decided that I must see our foremost men, men in high places, men belonging to our oldest families, to which I belong myself, men among whom I am the foremost by birth myself. For now I am sitting among princes like myself, am I not? I wanted to get to know you, and that was necessary – very, very necessary! I have always heard a great deal more evil than good about you – about the pettiness and exclusiveness of your interests, your backwardness, your inadequate education, your absurd habits – oh, so much is being written and talked about you! I came here to-day full of curiosity, fear, and confusion. I had to see for myself and form my own opinion as to whether the whole of this upper crust of Russian society is really worthless, has outlived its time, has exhausted itself by existing too long, and is only fit to die, but not without a petty and envious struggle with the men of – the future, obstructing them and not noticing that it is dying itself. I never quite believed in it before, for we really never had an upper class in Russia, except perhaps the courtiers, by uniform or by – accident, and now it has disappeared completely – isn't it so? Isn't it?'

'No, it isn't so at all,' Ivan Petrovich laughed sarcastically.

'Dear me, he's off again!' Princess Belokonsky could not forbear saying.

'*Laissez – le dire!*' the little old man warned them again in a low voice. 'He's trembling all over.'

The prince was absolutely beside himself.

'And what do I see? I see people who are charming, good-natured, and intelligent; I see a venerable old man who listens to a boy like me and is kind to him; I see people who can understand and forgive, Russian people, and kind-hearted, almost as kind-hearted and friendly as those I met abroad, almost as good as those. You can imagine what a delightful surprise it has been to me! Oh, let me tell you this! I have heard a lot, and I myself believed that everything in society was just outward manners, nothing but antiquated form, that there was nothing *real* in it, but I can see for myself now that among us it cannot possibly be so. It may be so somewhere else, but not here. Surely, you cannot all be Jesuits and frauds? I have just been listening to Prince N. – wasn't that good-natured but inspired humour? Wasn't that true good nature? Could such words fall from the lips of a man who is – dead, a man whose heart and talents are dried up? Could dead men treat me as you have treated me? Isn't that – material for the future, for hope? Could such men fail to understand and be behind the times?'

'I beg you again, my dear fellow, do be calm,' the 'statesman' remarked with a smile. 'We'll talk about it another time, and I shall be delighted to.'

Ivan Petrovich grunted and turned round in his chair; General Yepanchin stirred uneasily; his superior was talking to the old statesman's wife, without taking the slightest notice of the prince; but the statesman's wife kept listening and glancing at him.

'No, sir, I think I'd better speak, you know,' the prince went on, with a new feverish impetus, addressing himself to the little old man with a special sort of trustful and even confidential air. 'Yesterday Miss Aglaya told me not to talk, and she even mentioned the subjects that I shouldn't talk about. She knows how absurd I am when discussing them! I'm nearly twenty-seven, but I know I'm just a child. I have no right to express an opinion. I've always said so. I've talked frankly only with Rogozhin in Moscow. ... We read Pushkin together – all his works. He did not know anything. Didn't know even the name of Pushkin. I'm always afraid of discrediting the thought or the *chief idea* by my absurd manner. My gestures are all wrong. They are always contrary to what I am saying, and that provokes laughter and debases the idea. I have no sense of proportion, either, and that's the main thing – yes, that's the most important thing. ... I know that it's much better for me to sit still and say nothing. When I persist in keeping quiet, I appear to be quite a sensible fellow, and, besides, it gives me time to reflect. But now it's better that I should speak. I began to speak because you looked so nicely at me. You have such a nice face! I promised Miss Aglaya yesterday that I'd keep quiet all the evening.'

'*Vraiment?*' smiled the old man.

'But there are moments when I cannot help thinking that I'm wrong in thinking that: sincerity is more important than absurd gestures, don't you think so?'

'Sometimes.'

'I want to explain everything, everything, everything! Oh, yes! You think I'm a utopian? An ideologist? Oh, no. I assure you all my ideas are so simple. You don't believe me? You are smiling? I'm sometimes despicable, because I lose my faith. Just now, as I was coming here, I was thinking: "How on earth shall I talk to them? How shall I start so that they may understand at least something?" Oh, how I was afraid, but I was more afraid for you. Awfully, awfully! And yet how could I be afraid? Was it not shameful to be afraid? What does it matter if there are thousands of backward and wicked people to one progressive man? You see, the reason why I am so happy now is that there aren't thousands of them at all, but that it's all promising material! Nor ought we to be so dreadfully upset because we're absurd, ought we? It's quite true that we are absurd and frivolous, that we have bad habits, that we are bored, that we don't know how to look at anything or understand anything. We are all like that, all of us, you and I and everybody! You're not offended because I'm telling you to your face that you are absurd, are you? And if that's so, aren't you promising material? You know, in my opinion, it's sometimes quite a good thing to be absurd. Indeed, it's much better; it makes it so much easier to forgive each other and to humble ourselves. One can't start straight with perfection! To attain perfection, one must first of all be able not to understand many things. For if we understand things too quickly, we may perhaps fail to understand them well enough. I'm telling you this, you who have been able to understand so much already and – have failed to understand so much. Now I'm no longer afraid for you: you're not angry with a boy like me for saying such things to you, are you? Of course not! Oh, you will be able to forget and forgive those who have offended you and those who have done nothing to offend you. For it is more difficult to forgive those who have done nothing to offend you just because they have *not* offended you and because your complaint is, therefore, without foundation: that's what I expected of men of a high order of intelligence, that's what I was so anxious to tell them as I came here, and I'm afraid did not know how to. ... You're laughing, Ivan Petrovich? You think that I was afraid for the *others*, that I am *their* advocate, a democrat, an upholder of equality?' he laughed hysterically (he kept interrupting his speech every minute by short, rapturous bursts of laughter). 'I am afraid for you, for all of you, and for all of us. For I am a prince of ancient lineage myself, and I am sitting among princes. I am saying this to save you all, so as to prevent our class from vanishing for nothing into utter darkness, without realizing anything, abusing everything and losing everything. Why should we vanish and give up our position to others, when we might remain in the front rank and be the leaders of men? Let us stay in the front rank and be leaders. Let us be servants in order to be leaders.'

He began trying to get up from his chair, but the little old man still kept him back, though looking at him with growing uneasiness.

'Listen,' the prince went on. 'I know that it's no good talking, that it's much better to set an example, much better simply to start – I've started already and – and can one really be unhappy? Oh, what do my grief and my troubles matter, if I have the power to be happy? You know, I can't understand how one can pass by a tree and not be happy at the sight of it! To talk to a man and not be happy in loving him? Oh, it's only that I'm not able to put it into words, but – but think how many beautiful things there are at every step, things even the most wretched man cannot but find beautiful! Look at a child, look at God's sunset, look at the grass, how it grows, look at the eyes that gaze at you and love you. ...'

He had been standing talking for some time. The little old man was looking at him in alarm. Mrs Yepanchin cried out, 'Oh, my God!' having before anyone else guessed what was amiss, and threw up her hands in dismay. Aglaya ran up to him quickly, and was just in time to catch him in her arms, and with horror and a face distorted with pain heard the wild shriek of 'the spirit that stunned and cast down' the unhappy man. The sick man lay on the carpet. Someone hastened to place a cushion under his head.

No one had expected this. A quarter of an hour later Prince N., Radomsky, and the little old man tried to revive the party, but half an hour later they were all gone.

They expressed their regrets and sympathy and some of them gave their views of the prince. Ivan Petrovich declared, among other things, that 'the young man was a sla-vo-phile, or something of the kind, but that this was not dangerous'. The little old man did not express any opinion. It is true that afterwards, two or three days later, they were all a little cross. Ivan Petrovich was even offended, but not much. General Yepanchin's superior in the service was for some time rather cold to him. The 'patron' of their family, the elderly statesman, too, mumbled something by way of admonition to the father of the family, observing, incidentally, in rather flattering terms that he was very much interested indeed in Aglaya's future. He was, in fact, a rather kind man; but one of the reasons for his interest in the prince at the party was the prince's old affair with Nastasya Filippovna; he had heard something about it and he was greatly interested and had even intended to ask a few questions about it.

Before leaving the party, Princess Belokonsky said to Mrs Yepanchin:

'Well, my dear, he's good and bad, but if you want to know my opinion, he's more bad than good. You can see for yourself the sort of man he is – a sick man!'

Mrs Yepanchin's final decision was that the prince was 'impossible' as a fiancé, and that night she vowed that never while she lived would he become her Aglaya's husband. She got up next morning determined to stick to her decision. But that very morning at lunch at one o'clock she contradicted herself in a most extraordinary way.

In reply to a very guarded question put to her by her sisters, Aglaya suddenly said coldly but haughtily, just as though she wished to put an end to such questions in future:

'I have never given him any promise, and I've never in my life regarded him as my fiancé. He's the same sort of stranger to me as anyone else.'

Mrs Yepanchin suddenly flared up.

'That I did not expect from you,' she said with chagrin. 'He's an impossible husband for you, I know, and thank God that it all turned out for the best, but I did not expect to hear such words from you! I expected to hear something quite different from you. I'd have turned everyone out last night and kept him – that's the sort of man I think he is!'

Here she suddenly stopped short, frightened of what she had just said herself. But if only she knew how unfair she had been to her daughter at that moment! Everything had been settled in Aglaya's mind; she, too, was waiting for the hour that would decide everything; and every hint, every careless touch, cut into her heart like a knife.

8

For the prince, too, that morning began with painful forebodings; they could be explained by the bad state of his health, but his melancholy was too indefinable, and that was what made it so much more agonizing for him. It is true he was faced with clear-cut, painful, and humiliating facts, but his melancholy went beyond everything he remembered or thought about; he realized that he would not be able to set his mind at rest by himself. Little by little he came to the firm conclusion that something special and decisive would happen to him that very day. His fit of the night before had been a slight one. Except for his feeling of depression, a certain heaviness in his head, and a pain in his limbs, he felt no particular ill effects. His brain worked quite normally, though his heart was heavy. He got up rather late and at once clearly remembered all that had happened the previous evening; he also remembered, though not so clearly, that half an hour after his fit he had been taken home. He learnt that the Yepanchins had already sent someone to inquire after his health. At half past eleven they sent someone again; that pleased him. Vera Lebedev was among the first to come to see how he was and to look after him. The moment she saw him, she suddenly began crying, but when the prince at once reassured her, she burst out laughing. He was immediately struck by the strong compassion that girl felt for him; he seized her hand and kissed it. Vera blushed.

'Oh, don't do that, please don't!' she cried in dismay, snatching her hand away quickly.

She soon went away, looking strangely embarrassed. She managed to tell him, incidentally, that her father had rushed off at daybreak to 'the deceased', as he referred to the general, to find out whether he had died in the night, and that she had heard it said that he was expected to die quite soon. At about twelve o'clock Lebedev himself returned home and went straight to see the prince, 'just for a minute or two to inquire after his precious health', etc., and also 'to have a drop or two'. He did nothing but moan and groan, and the prince soon let him go, but he did try to find out from the prince about his fit of the previous night, though it was quite obvious that he knew all the details about it already. After him Kolya rushed in, also for a minute or two. Kolya really was in a great hurry and looked very upset and distressed. He began by asking the prince, frankly and insistently, for an explanation of all that they had been concealing from him, adding that he had found out almost everything the day before. He was deeply shocked.

With all the possible sympathy he was capable of, the prince told him the whole story exactly as it had happened, without concealing a single fact, and the poor boy was struck as by a thunderbolt. He could not utter a word, and wept in silence. The prince felt that it was one of those impressions that remain for ever and form a turning point in the life of a boy in his teens. He hastened to give him his view of the affair, adding that, in his opinion, the old man's approaching death was perhaps due to the horror he had felt at his action, and that not everyone was capable of such a feeling. Kolya's eyes flashed as he listened to the prince.

'Ganya, Varya, and Ptitsyn are a worthless lot! I'm not going to quarrel with them, but I shall have nothing to do with them in future! Oh, Prince, I've been through a lot since yesterday, and this will be a lesson to me! I consider it my duty now to provide for my mother, too, though she is well provided for at Varya's, but that's not the same thing. ...'

He jumped to his feet, remembering that he was expected, inquired hastily after the prince's health, and, having received an answer, added quickly:

'Are you sure there isn't something else? I heard yesterday – I have no right to, of course, but if you ever want a faithful servant for anything, he's before you now. It seems to me neither of us is very happy – isn't that so? But – I am not asking you to tell me anything. ...'

He went away, and the prince pondered still more deeply; everyone was prophesying disaster, everyone had already come to some conclusion, everyone was looking at him as though they knew something he didn't know; Lebedev was trying to get some information out of him, Kolya was openly hinting at something, and Vera was crying. At last he dismissed it all in vexation: 'It's my damned morbid suspiciousness,' he thought. His face brightened when, soon after one o'clock, he saw the Yepanchins, who came to visit him 'for a minute'. They really did come only for a minute. Getting up from lunch, Mrs Yepanchin declared that they would all go for a walk together. The announcement was made in the form of an order, abruptly, drily, and without explanations. They all went out – that is to say, the mother, the girls and Prince Sh. Mrs Yepanchin at once went in the opposite direction from their daily walks. They all realized what she had in mind, and they all kept silent, afraid to irritate their mother, and, as though wishing to escape from reproaches and objections, she walked in front of them all, without looking back. At last Adelaida observed that, if they were going for a walk, there was no need to rush like that, and that, anyway, it was impossible to keep up with their mother.

'I say,' Mrs Yepanchin suddenly turned round to them, 'we're just passing his home. Whatever Aglaya may think, and whatever may happen afterwards, he is no stranger to us, and now he is ill and unhappy into the bargain. I, at any rate, will go in and see how he is.

If you care to come with me, you can; if not, you can go on. No one is preventing you.'

They all went in, of course. The prince, as was to be expected, apologized again for breaking the vase and for making a disgraceful scene.

'Oh, never mind that,' replied Mrs Yepanchin. 'I'm not sorry for the vase, I'm sorry for you. So you realize yourself now that there was a disgraceful scene. That's, I suppose, what "the morning after" means. But that doesn't matter either, for everyone can see now that it's useless to blame you. Well, good-bye. If you're feeling strong enough, take a walk and then have some sleep – that's my advice. And if you feel like it, come and see us as usual. I want you to know, once and for all, that whatever happens, whatever may come, you'll always remain a friend of our family – a friend of mine, anyway. I can, at any rate, answer for myself. ...'

They all took up the challenge and confirmed their mother's sentiments. They went away, but in this good-natured eagerness to say something kind and heartening there was hidden a great deal that was cruel, which Mrs Yepanchin did not realize at the time. In her invitation 'to come and see us as usual' and in her words 'a friend of mine, anyway' there was again an ominous hint of what he might expect to happen. The prince tried to recollect what Aglaya had looked like. It is true she had given him a wonderful smile both when she came in and when she went out, but she had not said a word even when the others had all assured him of their friendship, though she did look at him intently twice. Her face was paler than usual, as though she had slept badly that night. The prince decided that he would certainly go and see them again in the evening 'as usual', and he looked feverishly at his watch. Vera came in exactly three minutes after the Yepanchins had gone.

'Miss Aglaya has just given me a message for you in secret, Prince.'

The prince trembled all over.

'A note?'

'No, sir, a message. And she had hardly time even for that. She asks you very much not to go out to-day for a single moment till seven o'clock in the evening or even till nine. I'm afraid I'm not quite sure which.'

'But what – what for? What does it mean?'

'I'm afraid I don't know at all. All she said was that I mustn't forget to tell you.'

'Did she say you mustn't forget?'

'No, sir, she didn't say that in so many words. She had hardly time to turn round and give me the message, but, luckily, I rushed up to her myself. I could see from her face that she meant it. She looked at me in a way that made my heart stop beating.'

A few more questions and the prince, though he had learned nothing more, became more agitated than ever. Left by himself, he lay down on the sofa and began to think again. 'Perhaps they're expecting a visitor till nine o'clock and she's afraid I might do something silly again in the presence of visitors,' he thought at last, and again began waiting impatiently for the evening and looking at his watch. But the solution of the mystery came long before the evening, and also in the form of a new visit, a solution in the form of a new, agonizing mystery: exactly half an hour after the Yepanchins' departure Ippolit came into his room, looking so worn out and exhausted that, without uttering a word, he literally collapsed, as though in a dead faint, in an arm-chair and at once broke into a dreadful fit of coughing. He coughed till the blood came. His eyes glittered and hectic flushes burnt on his cheeks. The prince murmured something to him, but he did not reply, and for a long time kept waving the prince away. At last he recovered.

'I'm going,' he managed to bring out at last in a hoarse voice.

'I'll see you home, if you like,' said the prince, getting up, and stopped short, remembering that he had been forbidden to leave the house.

Ippolit laughed.

'I'm not going away from you,' he went on, gasping for breath and with short bursts of coughing. 'On the contrary, I've thought it necessary to come to see you, and on business too – I shouldn't have troubled you otherwise. I'm going *there*, and this time, I think, it's in earnest. I'm done for! I haven't come for sympathy, believe me. ... I lay down at ten o'clock this morning with the intention of not getting up again till the time came *to go*, but changed my mind and got up again to come to you – so you see, I had to.'

'I'm sorry to see you so ill. You'd better have sent for me, instead of troubling to come.'

'Well, that's all right, then. You've said you're sorry, and that ought to be sufficient to satisfy the demands of good manners. Oh, I forgot. How are you yourself?'

'I'm all right. I'm afraid last night I – I wasn't quite – er – –'

'I know, I know. The Chinese vase caught it all right! I'm sorry I wasn't there! I've come on business. First, I had the pleasure of seeing Ganya and Aglaya this morning – they met at the green seat. It's quite amazing how stupid a man can look. I said as much to

Aglaya after Ganya had gone – but you don't seem to be surprised at anything, Prince,' he added, gazing mistrustfully at the prince's calm face. 'Not to be surprised at anything, they say, is a sign of great intelligence. In my opinion, it might as well be a sign of great stupidity. I'm sorry, I didn't mean you. ... I'm very unfortunate to-day in my expressions, I'm afraid.'

'I knew yesterday that Mr Ivolgin – –' The prince stopped short, looking embarrassed, though Ippolit was annoyed at his not being surprised.

'You knew! That's news! But perhaps you'd better not tell me. You were not a witness of their rendezvous to-day, were you?'

'You saw I wasn't there if you were there yourself.'

'Oh, but you may have been sitting behind some bush. Still, I am glad, for your sake, of course, for I was beginning to think that Ganya was – the favourite!'

'I beg you not to speak to me about it, Ippolit, and in such terms.'

'Particularly as you know everything already.'

'You're mistaken. I know scarcely anything, and Miss Aglaya knows for certain that I know nothing. I didn't even know anything about this meeting. You say there's been a meeting? All right, then let's leave it at that.'

'What do you mean? You knew and you didn't know. You say "all right" and "let's leave it at that". Oh, no, don't be so trustful! Especially if you don't know anything. You're so trustful because you don't know anything. And do you know what those two – the brother and sister – are counting on? You don't suspect anything, do you? All right, all right, I'll drop it,' he added, noticing the prince's impatient gesture. 'But I've come on some private business of my own, and it's this I – I'd like to have a talk to you about. Damn it all, a chap can't even die without all sorts of explanations. It's awful how much explaining I have to do. Do you care to hear?'

'Go on, I'm listening.'

'Oh dear, I'm afraid I've changed my mind again. I'll start with Ganya, all the same. You won't believe me, I know, but I too had an appointment at the green seat this morning. I don't want to tell a lie, though: I insisted on the appointment. I asked for it, promised to reveal a secret. I don't know whether I came a little too early (I think I did actually), but no sooner had I taken my place beside Aglaya than I saw Ganya and Varya approaching us arm in arm, just as though they were out for a walk. I believe both were greatly astonished to see me. They certainly didn't expect it, and they looked very embarrassed indeed. Aglaya flushed and, believe it or not, was rather put out. I don't know whether it was because I was there or simply because she caught sight of Mr Ivolgin – for he is such a handsome fellow, you know – but she flushed all over and settled the business in less than a minute – and very funny it was, too: she got up, answered Mr Ivolgin's bow and Mrs Ptitsyn's ingratiating smile, and suddenly blurted out: "I've asked you to come here because I want to tell you myself how much I appreciate your sincere and friendly feelings and that, if I ever am in need of them, believe me – –" Here she bowed and the two of them went away – I don't know whether looking like fools or triumphantly. Dear old Ganya, of course, must have felt like a fool. He couldn't make anything of it and turned as red as a lobster (what a wonderful expression he has sometimes!), but Mrs Ptitsyn, I think, did understand that they had better make themselves scarce, and that that was quite enough from Miss Yepanchin, and she dragged her brother away. She's cleverer than he and, I'm sure, she's triumphant now. I came to have a talk with Aglaya about arranging an appointment with Nastasya Filippovna.'

'With Nastasya Filippovna?'

'Oho! I believe you're losing your sangfroid and beginning to show some surprise. I'm very glad you're beginning to look like a human being at last. I'm going to amuse you for that. That's what comes of doing a good turn to fine young gentlemen and high-minded young ladies: I got a slap in the face from her to-day!'

'A – moral one?' the prince could not help asking.

'Yes – not a physical one. I don't think anyone would raise a hand against a chap like me. Not even a woman would strike me now – even dear old Ganya wouldn't! Though for one moment yesterday I thought that he would pounce on me. ... I bet you I know what you are thinking of now. You're thinking: "I agree he mustn't be thrashed, but he could be smothered with a pillow or with a wet rag in his sleep – indeed, he ought to be!" It's written all over your face that that's what you're thinking at this moment.'

'I've never thought of such a thing!' the prince said with disgust.

'I don't know. I dreamt last night that I was smothered with a wet rag by – er – a certain fellow – oh well, I might as well tell you who it was – Rogozhin! What do you think? Is it possible to smother a man with a wet rag?'

'I don't know.'

'I've heard it is possible. All right, let's drop it. Well, but tell me why am I a scandalmonger? Why did she call me a scandalmonger today? And, mind you, she did it after she'd heard all I had to tell her, and she even asked me to repeat certain things. ... But that's just like a woman! It was for her sake that I got into touch with Rogozhin – such an interesting chap! And it is in her own interests that I've arranged a personal interview with Nastasya Filippovna for her. Was it, I wonder, because I hurt her feelings by hinting that she was glad of Nastasya Filippovna's "leavings"? But, then, I kept telling her that in her own interests. I don't deny that I wrote her two letters in that strain and to-day the third – our meeting. This morning I – I began by telling her that it was humiliating for her – and, besides, the word "leavings" wasn't mine at all, but someone else's. At least, everyone was saying so at Ganya's – and she confirmed it herself. So why on earth should she accuse me of being a scandalmonger? I see, I see – you're very amused as you look at me now, and I bet you're applying those silly lines to me – –

> Perchance her love with a farewell smile
> Will the joyless sunset of my life beguile –

Ha, ha, ha!' He broke suddenly into an hysterical laugh, ending in a fit of coughing. 'Observe, please,' he gasped out through his coughing, 'what a fine fellow dear old Ganya is: speaks of "leavings", but what would he like to do himself now?'

The prince did not say anything for a long time; he was too horrified to speak.

'Did you mention a meeting with Nastasya Filippovna?' he murmured at last.

'Dear me, don't you really know that there's going to be a meeting between Aglaya and Nastasya Filippovna to-day? Why, Nastasya Filippovna has been specially summoned from Petersburg, through Rogozhin, at the invitation of Aglaya and by my efforts, and she is now staying with Rogozhin not very far from you, at Darya Alexeyevna's – a lady of very questionable reputation, a friend of hers, and it is to her house of questionable reputation that Aglaya is to go to-day for a friendly chat with Nastasya Filippovna and for the solution of various problems. They want to study arithmetic. Didn't you know? Honestly?'

'It's incredible!'

'Oh, all right, so it is incredible. Still, how are you to know about it? It's enough for a fly to buzz past for everyone to know about it – that's the kind of glorious place this is! But I've warned you, and you may be grateful to me. Well, good-bye – till we meet in the next world, I suppose. And another thing – though I've behaved disgracefully to you, for – why should I lose what's mine by right, tell me, please? For your sake? I've dedicated my "Confession" to her (you didn't know that, did you?). And if you knew how she received it! Ha, ha! But I didn't behave disgracefully towards her – I haven't wronged her in any way. It is she who disgraced and cheated me. ... However, I don't think I've wronged you in any way, either. If I did talk about "leavings" there and said something more of the same kind, I'm now telling you the day and hour and the place of their meeting, and I'm letting you into the whole game – out of spite, of course, not out of magnanimity. Good-bye – I'm sorry I'm as garrulous as a stammerer or as a consumptive. Mind, take all the necessary measures, and that as soon as possible – if you deserve to be called a man, that is. The meeting is to take place this evening – that's certain!'

Ippolit walked to the door, but the prince called to him and he stopped in the doorway.

'So according to you, Miss Aglaya will be going herself to see Nastasya Filippovna to-day?' he asked, red spots appearing again on his cheeks and forehead.

'I don't know for certain, but I expect so,' replied Ippolit, half turning to the prince. 'It can't possibly be otherwise. You don't expect Nastasya Filippovna to go to her, do you? And they wouldn't meet at dear old Ganya's – there's a man almost dead there. How do you like the general, eh?'

'That alone makes it impossible!' the prince cried. 'How could she leave the house, even if she wanted to? You don't know the – the customs of that household: she couldn't leave her home alone to go to see Nastasya Filippovna. It's nonsense!'

'You see, Prince, no one ever leaves his house by jumping out of a window, but if the house is on fire, the finest gentleman and the finest lady will jump out of a window. If needs must, there's no choice, and our young lady will go to see Nastasya Filippovna. And don't they let them go anywhere, your young ladies?'

'No, I didn't mean that – –'

'Well, if you didn't mean that, then all she has to do is to walk down the front steps and walk off, and she needn't even go back home again. There are cases when one may sometimes burn one's boats and not go back home again: life does not consist only of luncheons, dinners, and Princes Sh. I believe you take Aglaya for a young lady or some schoolgirl. I've already told her that, and I think she agreed with me. Wait till seven or eight o'clock. ... If I were in your place I'd send someone there to keep watch so as to be on the spot when she comes down the steps. You could send Kolya. He'd be delighted to act as a spy – as your spy, I mean – you may be sure of that, because, you see, everything's relative, ha, ha!'

Ippolit went out. The prince had no need to ask anyone to spy for him, even if he had been capable of doing such a thing. Aglaya's order that he should stay at home was almost explained now: she might want to come and fetch him. Perhaps, indeed, she did not want him to turn up there, and had therefore asked him to stay at home. That might be so, too. His head was spinning; the whole room was going round and round. He lay down on the sofa and closed his eyes.

Whatever it was, the matter was to be decided at last – finally. No, the prince did not take Aglaya for a young lady or a schoolgirl: he felt now that he had dreaded it for a long time, and that he had dreaded something of this kind. But what did she want to see her for? A cold shiver passed over the prince's whole body; he was in a fever again.

No, he did not take her for a child! He had been horrified by some of the looks she had given him of late, by some of her words. Sometimes he could not help feeling that she was trying to force herself too much, that she was putting too big a restraint on herself, and he remembered how alarmed that had made him. It is true he had been trying not to think of it during the last few days, he had driven away his painful thoughts, but what lay hidden in that soul of hers? This question had worried him a long time, though he had faith in that soul. And now all that had to be settled and brought to light to-day. An awful thought! And again – 'that woman'! Why did it always seem to him that that woman would make an appearance at the very last moment and snap his life in two like a rotten thread? That he had always had that feeling he was ready to swear to, though he was almost semi-delirious. If he had tried to forget *her* lately, it was solely because he was afraid of her. Well? Did he love that woman or did he hate her? He never asked himself that question to-day; his conscience was clear so far as that was concerned: he knew whom he loved. ... He was not so much afraid of the meeting of the two, or of the strangeness, or of the cause of that meeting, unknown to him, or of the outcome of it, whatever it might be – it was Nastasya Filippovna herself he was afraid of. He remembered afterwards, a few days later, that almost all through those feverish hours he could see her eyes, her glance, and he could hear her words – strange words, though he did not retain many of them in his memory after those feverish and anguished hours had passed. He scarcely remembered, for instance, that Vera had brought him his dinner and that he ate it. He did not remember whether he had slept after dinner or not. All he knew was that he began to give himself a clear account of everything that evening only from the moment Aglaya had suddenly stepped on to the veranda and he had jumped up from the sofa and walked to the middle of the room to meet her: it was a quarter past seven. Aglaya was quite alone. She was simply and, as it seemed, hastily dressed, wearing a light cloak. Her face was pale, as it had been that morning, and her eyes glittered with a bright, dry light. He had never seen such an expression in her eyes before. She scrutinized him attentively.

'You're quite ready,' she observed quietly and seemingly very calmly. 'Dressed and your hat in your hand. So you have been warned, and I know by whom – Ippolit?'

'Yes, he told me,' murmured the prince, more dead than alive.

'Let's go, then: you know that you must escort me there. You're strong enough, I suppose, to go out.'

'Yes, I am but – but is it possible?'

He broke off at once and could not utter another word. This was his only attempt to stop the mad girl, and after that he followed her like a slave. However confused his thoughts were, he realized very well that she would go *there* without him and that he had therefore to follow her in any case. He guessed the strength of her determination; he was not the man to check this wild impulse. They walked along in silence, hardly exchanging a word the whole way. He only noticed that she knew the way well, and when he wanted to make a detour because the road there was more deserted, and suggested this to her, she listened to him with strained attention and said abruptly: 'It's all the same!' When they had almost reached Darya Alexeyevna's house (a big old wooden house), a gorgeously dressed woman and a young girl were just coming down the front steps; both of them got into a magnificent carriage, which was waiting for them at the steps, laughing and talking loudly, not once even glancing at them, and drove away without appearing to notice them. As soon as the carriage had driven off, the door of the house opened a second time, and Rogozhin, who had been waiting for them, let the prince and Aglaya in and closed the door behind them.

'There's no one in the house except the four of us,' he observed aloud and looked strangely at the prince.

Nastasya Filippovna was waiting for them in the first room they went into. She too was dressed very simply and all in black. She got up to meet them, but she did not smile and didn't even offer her hand to the prince.

Her intent and restless eyes were fixed impatiently on Aglaya. Both sat down at a little distance from each other, Aglaya on the sofa in the corner of the room and Nastasya Filippovna at the window. The prince and Rogozhin did not sit down, nor were they asked to sit down. The prince looked in bewilderment and as though in pain at Rogozhin, but Rogozhin merely smiled as before. The silence continued for a few more moments.

At last a sort of ominous expression passed over Nastasya Filippovna's face; there was an obstinate, hard, and almost hateful look in her eyes, which were fixed steadily on Aglaya. Aglaya was visibly embarrassed, but she showed no signs of fear. As she came into the room, she threw a quick glance at her rival, but for the time being she sat with downcast eyes, as though sunk in meditation. Once or twice, as though by accident, she threw a glance round the room; there was a distinct expression of disgust on her face, as though she were afraid of contamination in this place. She arranged her dress mechanically, and even changed her place uneasily once, moving to the corner of the sofa. She was probably unconscious of her own movements; but their unconsciousness made them still more insulting. At last she looked firmly straight into Nastasya Filippovna's eyes and instantly read all the suppressed bitterness and anger that smouldered in her rival's look. Woman understood woman; Aglaya sighed.

'You know, of course, why I asked to see you,' Aglaya brought herself to say at last, but in a very low voice, and even pausing once or twice in this short sentence.

'No, I know nothing,' Nastasya Filippovna replied drily and abruptly.

Aglaya blushed. Perhaps it suddenly struck her as very strange and incredible that she should be sitting here with that woman, in the house of 'that woman', and be waiting anxiously for her reply. At the first sounds of Nastasya Filippovna's voice a sort of shudder passed over her whole body. 'That woman', of course, noticed it all very well.

'You understand everything,' Aglaya almost whispered, her eyes fixed sullenly on the floor, 'but – but you purposely pretend not to understand.'

'Why should I do that?' Nastasya Filippovna asked with a faint smile.

'You want to take advantage of my position – I mean, that I am in your house,' Aglaya went on, absurdly and awkwardly.

'You're responsible for your position, not I!' Nastasya Filippovna flushed suddenly. 'I didn't invite you to come here. It's you who asked me to see you, and I still have no idea why.'

Aglaya raised her head haughtily.

'Hold your tongue, madam. I haven't come to fight you with this weapon of yours. ...'

'Oh, so you've come "to fight" me, then? You know I imagined you were – cleverer than that.'

Both looked at one another without disguising their malice any longer. One of them was the woman who had only recently been writing such letters to the other. And all of this had vanished into thin air at their first meeting and at their first words. But, then, why not? At this moment not one of the four people in the room seemed to think it strange. The prince, who the day before would not have believed it possible to see it even in a dream, now stood, looked and listened as though he had foreseen it long ago. The most fantastic dream became suddenly transformed into the most vivid and sharply defined reality. One of these women so despised the other one at that moment, and was so anxious to tell her so (perhaps she had only come for that purpose, as Rogozhin said next day), that however fantastical the other one was, with her disordered mind and sick soul, she would not have been able to stand up against the malevolent purely feminine contempt of her rival, whatever her original intentions might have been. The prince was certain that Nastasya Filippovna would not mention her letters herself; he could see from her flashing eyes how sorry she was now to have written them; and he would have given half his life that Aglaya should not mention them now, either.

But Aglaya seemed suddenly to pull herself together and instantly to regain her composure.

'I'm afraid you misunderstood me,' she said. 'I haven't come to – to quarrel with you, though I don't like you. I – I have come to speak to you as – one human being to another. When I asked to see you, I had already decided what I was going to say to you, and I won't run away from my decision now, even if you don't understand me at all. That will be the worse for you, and not for me. I wanted to reply to what you have written to me, and to reply in person, because this seemed to me the more convenient way. Please listen to my reply to all your letters: I felt sorry for Prince Leo Nikolayevich on the very first day I made his acquaintance and when afterwards I heard what happened at your party. I felt sorry for him because he was such a simple-minded man and in his simplicity he believed that he could be happy with – with a woman of – of such a character. What I feared for him, actually happened: you couldn't possibly be in love with him, you tortured him and jilted him. You could not have been in love with him because you're too proud – no, not proud, I'm sorry – but because you are vain – no not that, either – because you're selfish – because your self-love amounts to – to madness, and your letters to me prove it. You couldn't be in love with a man as simple as he is, and, I daresay, you despised him in your heart and laughed at him. All you are able to love is your dishonour and the constant thought that you have been dishonoured and humiliated. If your dishonour were less, or if it had not existed at all, you'd be more unhappy than you are. ...' (It was with a feeling of great delight that Aglaya uttered those words, which fell all too glibly from her lips and which she had long thought out and prepared – thought out at a time when she had never dreamt of the present meeting; she watched with malignant eyes their effect on Nastasya Filippovna's face, distorted with agitation.) 'You remember,' she went on, 'he wrote me a letter then. He told me that you knew about that letter. You did read it, didn't you? From that letter I understood everything, and I understood it correctly. He has since confirmed it to me himself – I mean, all I'm telling you now, word for word. After that letter I waited. I guessed that you were sure to come here, for without Petersburg you can't exist: you're still much too young and too good-looking for the provinces. ... But those are not my words, either,' she added, blushing terribly, and from that moment the colour never left her cheeks to the very end of her speech. 'When I met the prince again, I felt awfully pained and hurt on his account. Don't laugh. If you laugh, you're not worthy to understand that. ...'

'You can see that I'm not laughing,' Nastasya Filippovna said sadly and sternly.

'I don't mind, though; you can laugh as much as you like. When I began questioning him myself, he told me that he had long ceased to love you, that even the memory of you was painful to him, but that he was sorry for you and that every time he thought of you he felt as though his heart were "pierced for ever". I must also tell you that never in my life have I met a man like him for noble simplicity of mind and for boundless trustfulness. I realized after what he had told me that anyone who wished could deceive him, and that whoever deceived him, he would forgive afterwards, and that is why I fell in love with him. ...'

Aglaya paused for a moment, as though dumbfounded, as though she could not believe herself that she could have uttered those words; but almost at the same instant her eyes shone with infinite pride; she did not seem to care any more if 'that woman' burst out laughing at the confession that had escaped her.

'I've told you everything and, I suppose, you know now what I want of you.'

'Perhaps I do, but tell me yourself,' Nastasya Filippovna replied softly.

Aglaya's face flushed with anger.

'I wanted to find out from you,' she said firmly and slowly, 'what right you have to interfere with his feelings for me? By what right you dared to send me letters? By what right do you continually tell him and me that you love him, after leaving him yourself and – and running away from him in such an insulting and – and shameful way?'

'I never told him or you that I loved him,' Nastasya Filippovna brought out with an effort, 'and – and you're quite right – I did run away from him,' she added, almost inaudibly.

'What do you mean you never told him or me?' cried Aglaya. 'And what about your letters? Who asked you to be our matchmaker and to persuade me to marry him? Wasn't that telling us? Why are you forcing yourself upon us? At first I thought that, on the contrary, you wanted to make me loathe and detest him by your meddling in our affairs so that I might give him up, and it was only afterwards that I realized what you were up to: you simply imagined that you were making a great sacrifice by putting on all those airs and graces of yours. ... How could you have loved him, if you love your vanity so much? Why didn't you simply go away from here instead of writing me those ridiculous letters? Why don't you now marry the generous man who loves you so much and who has done you the honour of offering you his hand? Oh, that's plain enough, isn't it? If you married Rogozhin you wouldn't have any grievance left, would you? Why, you'd have too much honour done you! Mr Radomsky said about you that you had read too much poetry and that you were "much too educated for – your position", that you were a bookish woman, and that you've never done a stroke of work in your life. Add to that your vanity, and there's a true explanation of your motives. ...'

'And have you done a stroke of work in your life?'

They had reached this unexpected development much too rapidly, much too crudely, unexpected because on her way to Pavlovsk Nastasya Filippovna still dreamed of achieving something, though, of course, she expected things to turn out badly rather than well; Aglaya, on the other hand, was absolutely carried away instantaneously by her emotion, just as though she were falling over a precipice, and she could not restrain herself from the dreadful delight of revenge. Indeed, Nastasya Filippovna felt strange to see Aglaya like this; she looked at her as though she could not believe her own eyes, and was decidedly at a loss for the first moment. Whether she was a woman who had read too much poetry, as Radomsky had suggested, or simply mad, as the prince was convinced, this woman, at any rate – though her behaviour was sometimes arrogant and cynical – was really far more shy, tender, and trustful than one might have supposed her to be. It is true, there was a great deal that was bookish, romantic, self-centred, and fantastic, but there was also a great deal too that was strong and profound in her. ... The prince understood that; and there was a look of great suffering in his face. Aglaya noticed it, and trembled with hatred.

'How dare you speak to me like this?' she said with indescribable haughtiness in reply to Nastasya Filippovna's remark.

'You must have misunderstood me,' said Nastasya Filippovna in surprise. 'How have I spoken to you?'

'If you wanted to be an honest woman, why didn't you give up your seducer Totsky simply – without any theatrical scenes?' said Aglaya suddenly, without rhyme or reason.

'What do you know of my position that you dare to judge me?' asked Nastasya Filippovna, with a start and turning terribly pale.

'I know that you didn't go to work, but went away with a wealthy man like Rogozhin in order to pose as a fallen angel. I am not surprised that Totsky tried to shoot himself to escape from a fallen angel!'

'Don't!' Nastasya Filippovna said with disgust and as though deeply hurt. 'You have understood about as much as – Darya Alexeyevna's parlour-maid who sued her fiancé for breach of promise recently. She'd have understood better than you. ...'

'I expect she's an honest girl who works for her living. Why do you speak with such contempt of a parlour-maid?'

'I don't speak with contempt of work, but of you when you speak of work.'

'If you'd wanted to be an honest woman, you'd have taken in washing.'

Both got up and were looking with white faces at one another.

'Aglaya, stop it!' the prince cried, in great distress. 'This isn't fair!'

Rogozhin was no longer smiling, but listened with compressed lips and folded arms.

'Just look at her,' said Nastasya Filippovna, shaking with anger, 'look at this young lady! And I took her for an angel! Have you come to me without your governess, Miss Yepanchin? And do you want me – do you want me to tell you frankly – without mincing words, why you came to see me? You were afraid – that's why you came!'

'Afraid of you?' asked Aglaya, beside herself with naïve and arrogant amazement that this woman should dare to talk to her like that.

'Yes, of me, of course! You are afraid of me, or you wouldn't have decided to come and see me. If you are afraid of a person, you don't despise him. And to think that I've respected you up to this very moment! And shall I tell you why you are afraid of me and what you are so concerned about now? You wanted to make quite sure yourself whether he loved me more than you or not, because you're awfully jealous – –'

'He has told me already that he hates you!' Aglaya could just bring herself to murmur.

'Perhaps, perhaps I'm not worthy of him, only – I think you're lying! He can't hate me, and he could not have said so! I'm quite ready to forgive you, though – in view of your position – only I did think better of you. I thought you were more intelligent and much prettier even – I did, indeed! Well, take your treasure – there he is – he's looking at you – he's too stunned to talk – take him – take him, but on one condition: get out of here at once! This minute!'

She sank into an arm-chair and burst into tears. But suddenly something new blazed up in her eyes; she looked steadily and intently at Aglaya and got up from her seat.

'But if you like I shall order him – or-der him at once – do you hear? – I have only to order him and he'll leave you – leave you at once and stay with me for good and marry me, and you'll run back home alone. Do you want me to? Do you want me to?' she shouted like a mad woman, perhaps not believing herself that she could utter such words.

Aglaya rushed to the door in terror, but stopped dead in the doorway, as though rooted to the spot, and listened.

'If you like I'll turn Rogozhin out – shall I? You thought I was going to marry Rogozhin to please you, did you? Well, I'll call out now, in your presence – "Rogozhin, get out!" and I'll say to the prince, "Remember your promise?" Heavens, why have I so humiliated myself before them? Didn't you, Prince, tell me yourself that you would never leave me, that you would follow me whatever happened to me, that you loved me, that you forgave me everything and that you res – res ––Yes, you said that too! And it was only to set you free that I ran away from you, but now I don't want to! Why did she treat me as though I were some loose woman? Am I a loose woman? Ask Rogozhin – he'll tell you! Will you, now that she has disgraced me, and before you, too – will you turn away from me also, and walk away arm-in-arm with her? Damn you, then, damn you; for you were the only one I believed in. Get out, Rogozhin; you're not wanted here!' she cried, almost unconscious of what she was saying, forcing the words out with difficulty, with a distorted face and parched lips, evidently not believing a single word of her boastful speech, but at the same time wishing to prolong the scene, if only for a second, and so deceive herself. Her outburst was so violent that it might have killed her – at least, the prince thought so. 'There he is – look!' she cried at last to Aglaya, pointing to the prince. 'If he won't come up to me now, if he won't take me and give you up, then you can have him. I'll let you have him. I don't want him!'

Both she and Aglaya stood still, as though in expectation of the prince's decision, and both of them looked at him, as though they had gone out of their minds. But he did not perhaps even realize the whole force of that challenge; indeed, he most certainly did not. He only saw before him the distracted, frenzied face which, as he had once said to Aglaya, 'pierced his heart for ever'. He could bear it no longer, and he turned imploringly and reproachfully to Aglaya, pointing to Nastasya Filippovna: 'How could you? She's so – unhappy!'

But that was all he had time to say, struck dumb by Aglaya's terrible look. There was so much suffering in that look and, at the same time, so much hatred, too, that he threw up his hands in despair, uttered a cry, and rushed after her. But it was too late. She could not endure even the brief moment of his hesitation, covered her face with her hands, cried, 'Oh, my God!' and ran out of the room, followed by Rogozhin, who went out to unbolt the front door for her.

The prince, too, ran, but in the doorway he was clasped by a pair of hands. The distracted, distorted face of Nastasya Filippovna was staring at him, and her lips, which had turned blue, moved, asking:

'After her? After her?'

She fell unconscious in his arms. He raised her, carried her into the room, laid her in an arm-chair, and stood over her, not knowing what to do. There was a glass of water on the table. Rogozhin, coming back into the room, snatched it up and sprinkled some water on her face. She opened her eyes and for a minute did not know what had happened. But suddenly she looked round, gave a start, and rushed up to the prince.

'Mine! mine!' she cried. 'So the proud young lady has gone, has she? Ha, ha, ha!' she laughed hysterically. 'Ha, ha, ha! I was giving him up to that young lady! Why? Why? I was mad! Get out, Rogozhin! Ha, ha, ha!'

Rogozhin looked intently at them and, without uttering a word, picked up his hat and went out. Ten minutes later the prince was sitting beside Nastasya Filippovna, gazing at her steadily and stroking her head and face with both hands, as though she were a little child. He laughed when she laughed and was ready to cry when she cried.

He never said a word, but listened intently to her abrupt, rapturous, and incoherent babble, hardly understanding anything, but smiling gently; and the moment he thought that she was again beginning to fret or weep, to reproach or to complain, he immediately began stroking her head again and passing his hands tenderly over her cheeks, comforting and soothing her like a child.

9

A fortnight had passed since the events described in the last chapter, and the position of the characters of our story had changed so much that we find it extremely difficult to continue without certain explanations. Yet we feel that we have to confine ourselves to a bare statement of facts, if possible, without any special explanations, and for a very simple reason: because we ourselves find it difficult in many instances to explain what took place. Such a statement on our part must appear very strange and obscure to the reader: how can we describe something of which we have no clear idea and no personal opinion? To avoid putting ourselves in a still falser position, we had better try to explain what we have in mind by an example, and perhaps the gentle reader will understand the nature of our difficulty, particularly as this example will not be a digression, but, on the contrary, a direct continuation of our story.

Two weeks later – that is to say, at the beginning of July, and during those two weeks – the story of our hero and, particularly, the last event in that story, is turned into a strange, extremely entertaining, almost incredible and, at the same time, glaring scandal, which gradually spread through all the streets adjoining Lebedev's, Ptitsyn's, Darya Alexeyevna's, and the Yepanchins' country houses or, to put it more briefly, through the whole town, and even its environs. Almost all the inhabitants of the town – the natives, the holiday-makers, the day trippers who come to the concerts – began telling each other the same story, in a thousand versions: about how a certain prince, after making a scandalous scene in a well-known and most respectable household and jilting a young girl of the family, to whom he was already engaged, fell in love with a notorious woman of easy virtue, had broken off with his old friends and, regardless of everything, regardless of threats and regardless of public indignation, was going to marry this woman of ill repute within the next few days in Pavlovsk, openly, in public, with his head erect and looking everyone straight in the face. The story was so richly embellished with scandalous details, so many well-known and eminent people were involved in it, and so many fantastic and enigmatic twists were given to it, while, on the other hand, it was presented with such incontrovertible and convincing facts, that the general interest and gossip were, of course, very pardonable. The most subtle, clever, and, at the same time, plausible interpretation of this event was left to a few serious-minded scandalmongers, belonging to the category of sensible people, who in any class of society are always in a hurry to explain any occurrence to their friends and neighbours, and regard this as their vocation, and quite often their consolation in life. According to their interpretation, a young man of a good family, a prince, who was almost wealthy, a born fool, but a democrat who had gone crazy over the modern nihilism, revealed by Mr Turgenev, who could hardly speak a word of Russian, had fallen in love with a daughter of General Yepanchin and had got so far as to be received in the house as the girl's fiancé. But like that French divinity student who, according to a recently published story, had purposely allowed himself to be consecrated as priest, had gone through all the rites, genuflexions, kissings, vows, etc., only to declare publicly in a letter to his bishop next day that, not believing in God, he considered it dishonourable to deceive the people and be kept by them for nothing, and had therefore resigned his living and sent his letter for publication in the Liberal press – like that atheist, the prince, too, had played some sort of trick. It was alleged that he had purposely waited for the great occasion of the engagement party at the house of his fiancée's parents, at which he had been presented to a large number of eminent people, to declare his views aloud in the presence of everyone, to heap abuse on the distinguished statesman, to break off his engagement publicly and in a most offensive manner, and, in resisting the servants who were turning him out of the house, had broken a magnificent Chinese vase. It was further added, as an illustration of modern manners, that the fatuous young man was really in love with his fiancée, the general's daughter, but had broken with her simply for nihilistic reasons and for the sake of the ensuing public scandal, so that he might enjoy the satisfaction of marrying a fallen woman before the whole world, and so prove that in his view there were neither fallen nor virtuous women, but only women who were free to do as they liked; that he did not believe in the old conventional division, but only in the 'woman question'. That, last but not least, in his eyes a 'fallen' woman was, indeed, superior to a woman who had not 'fallen'. This explanation seemed very plausible and was accepted by the majority of the summer residents, especially as it seemed to be borne out by the daily happenings. It is true that a great many things still remained unexplained: it was said that the poor girl was so much in love with her fiancé or, as some preferred to describe him, her 'seducer', that on the day after he broke with her she had come running to him when he was sitting with his mistress; others claimed, on the contrary, that he had purposely lured her into the house of his mistress, solely out of his nihilistic ideas – that is, with the intention of disgracing and humiliating her. Be that as it may, the interest in the event grew every day, particularly as there seemed to be no doubt whatever that the scandalous wedding would actually take place.

Now, if we were asked for an explanation – not of the nihilistic aspects of this business, oh no! – but simply how far the forthcoming marriage satisfied the prince's actual desires, what those desires were at the moment, how our hero's state of mind was to be defined at present, and so on and so forth, we should, we admit, be hard put to it for an answer. All we know is that the marriage had been actually arranged and that the prince himself had authorized Lebedev, Keller, and a friend of Lebedev's, who had been introduced to the prince for that very purpose, to take over all the necessary arrangements, both religious and domestic; that he had told them not to spare any money, that Nastasya Filippovna had insisted that the wedding should take place as soon as possible, that Keller was to be the prince's best man, at his own earnest request, that Burdovsky, who had accepted the appointment with enthusiasm, was to give away the bride, and that the wedding day had been fixed for the beginning of July. But besides these highly precise circumstances, a number of other facts are known to us, which we are completely at a loss to account for just because they flatly contradict the foregoing. We have a strong suspicion that, having authorized Lebedev and the others to take over all the arrangements, the prince almost forgot the very same day that he had a master of ceremonies, a best man, and a wedding, and that if he had been in such a hurry to entrust the arrangements to others, he did so solely because he did not want to think of it himself and, indeed, was anxious to forget all about it. What was he thinking of in that case himself? What did he wish to remember? What was it he was after? Neither is there any doubt that there was no question of any coercion (on the part of Nastasya Filippovna, for instance), that Nastasya Filippovna really desired the wedding to take place as soon as possible, and that it was she, and not the prince, who had thought of the wedding; but the prince gave his consent freely, indeed, rather absent-mindedly, just as if he had been asked for some quite ordinary thing. We possess many such strange facts, but they do not in the least explain, but, in our opinion, merely make any interpretation of the affair more difficult, however many of them are brought forward. But let us give another example.

Thus, we know for a fact that during that fortnight the prince spent whole days and evenings with Nastasya Filippovna; that she took him with her for walks and to listen to the music of the band; that he went for rides with her every day in her carriage; that he began to be worried about her if an hour passed without his seeing her, which, of course, meant that, to all appearances, he truly loved her; that he listened for hours on end to whatever she might be saying with a quiet and gentle smile, scarcely uttering a word himself. But we also know that during those days he suddenly called several times, in fact, many times, on the Yepanchins, without concealing it from Nastasya Filippovna, which nearly drove her to despair. We know that, while they remained in Pavlovsk, the Yepanchins did not receive him, and time and again refused to permit him to see Aglaya; that he went away without saying a word and went to see them again next day, as though completely forgetting their refusal the day before, and, of course, was refused again. We know, too, that an hour after Aglaya had run out of Nastasya Filippovna's house, and perhaps even less than an hour, the prince was already at the Yepanchins', confident, of course, of finding Aglaya there, and that his appearance at the Yepanchins' had caused great confusion and dismay in the household, because Aglaya had not yet come back and it was only from him they had first learnt that she had gone to Nastasya Filippovna's with him. It was said that Mrs Yepanchin, her daughters, and Prince Sh. had treated the prince with great harshness and hostility and that it was on that occasion that they had told him, in the strongest possible terms, that they no longer desired his friendship and acquaintance, especially when Varya suddenly arrived and told Mrs Yepanchin that Aglaya had been at her house for over an hour in a dreadful state and seemed loath to return home. This last piece of news shocked Mrs Yepanchin most of all, and it was perfectly true: on leaving Nastasya Filippovna's, Aglaya would certainly rather have died than have faced her people, and had therefore gone straight to Mrs Ivolgin's. For her part, Varya considered it her duty at once to inform Mrs Yepanchin of all this. The mother and her daughters immediately rushed off to Mrs Ivolgin's, and they were followed by the father of the family himself, who had just arrived home. Undeterred by his expulsion and the severe words, the prince dragged himself after them, but, at

Varya's express orders, he was not permitted to see Aglaya. The end of it was that when Aglaya saw her mother and sisters weeping over her and not reproaching her in the least, she flew into their arms and at once returned home with them. It was said, though the rumour could not well be checked, that Ganya was very unlucky on this occasion, too. That, finding himself alone with Aglaya, while Varya had run off to Mrs Yepanchin's, he thought it the right moment to make a declaration of his love and that, as she listened to him, Aglaya, in spite of her anguish and tears, suddenly burst out laughing and suddenly put a strange question to him. Would he, she asked, to prove how much he loved her, burn his finger on a lighted candle? Ganya, it was said, taken aback by her proposal, and at a loss what to say, had looked so flabbergasted that Aglaya had burst out laughing at him, as though she were in hysterics, and had run upstairs from him to Mrs Ivolgin, where her parents found her. This story reached the prince through Ippolit next day. Ippolit, who was bedridden now, sent for the prince on purpose to tell him the story. How this rumour had reached Ippolit we do not know, but when the prince heard about the candle and the finger he laughed so much that even Ippolit was surprised; then he suddenly began to tremble and burst into tears. During those days he was altogether in a state of great uneasiness and extraordinarily vague but agonizing confusion. Ippolit bluntly declared that he was out of his mind; but it was quite impossible to be absolutely certain about that just then.

In presenting all these facts and refusing to explain them, we do not at all want to justify our hero in the eyes of our readers. Moreover, we are quite ready to share the indignation he aroused even among his friends. Even Vera Lebedev was indignant with him for some time; even Kolya was indignant; Keller, too, was indignant up to the moment he was chosen as best man, not to mention Lebedev who even began to intrigue against the prince, and that, too, from indignation which was quite genuine. But of that later. Generally speaking, we are in complete sympathy with some strong and psychologically profound remarks which Mr Radomsky frankly and unceremoniously made to the prince on the sixth or seventh day after the incident at Nastasya Filippovna's. We must, incidentally, observe that not only the Yepanchins, but also everyone who directly or indirectly had any connexion with the Yepanchin family, found it necessary to break off all relations with the prince. Prince Sh., for instance, even turned away on meeting the prince, and did not return his bow. But Mr Radomsky was not afraid to compromise himself by going to see the prince, in spite of the fact that he was again visiting the

Yepanchins every day and was received with undisguisedly increased cordiality. He came to see the prince the next day after all the Yepanchins had left Pavlovsk. When he entered, he knew already all the current rumours and, indeed, he might have assisted in spreading them himself. The prince was very glad to see him, and at once began talking about the Yepanchins; such an artless and frank beginning put Mr Radomsky completely at his ease, so that, without more ado, he went straight to the point.

The prince did not know that the Yepanchins had left; he was startled and turned pale; but a minute later he shook his head, looking embarrassed and pensive, and admitted that 'it was bound to happen'; then he quickly inquired where they had gone to.

Meanwhile Radomsky was watching him closely, and all this – that is, the rapidity of his questions, their simplicity, his embarrassment, and, at the same time, his strange sort of frankness, his restlessness and his excitement – all this rather surprised him. However, he gave the prince all the information he wanted very courteously and in full detail, for there was a great deal the prince did not know, and Radomsky was the first person to bring him news from the Yepanchins'. He confirmed that Aglaya had really been ill, that she had been running a high temperature and had not slept for three nights; that she was much better now and out of danger, but still in a nervous and hysterical state. 'It is a good thing that there is peace in the house,' he said. 'They are trying not to make any allusions to the past, even among themselves, not only in Aglaya's presence. The parents have already agreed to go abroad in the autumn, directly after Adelaida's wedding, and Aglaya has received the preliminary announcement of the projected trip in silence.' He, Radomsky, would probably also go abroad. Even Prince Sh. would perhaps be ready to follow them with Adelaida in two months' time, if business permitted. General Yepanchin, however, would remain. They had now gone to Kolmino, their estate, fifteen miles out of Petersburg, where they had a large country house. Princess Belokonsky had not yet gone to Moscow and seemed, indeed, to be staying in Pavlovsk on purpose. Mrs Yepanchin had strongly insisted that they could not possibly stay on in Pavlovsk after what had happened; he, Radomsky, had written to her every day about the rumours that were going round the town. They did not find it possible as yet to move to their country house on Yelagin Island.

'And, come to think of it, you must admit that they could hardly have stood it much longer,' added Radomsky. 'Particularly as they knew everything that was going on in your house here, Prince, and after your daily visits *there*, in spite of their refusing to see you. ...'

'Yes, yes, yes,' the prince nodded again, 'you're quite right. I wanted to see Miss Aglaya. ...'

'But, good Lord, my dear Prince,' Radomsky suddenly cried, animatedly and sorrowfully, 'how could you have – er – let it all happen? Of course, of course, it must all have been so unexpected and – and I quite see that you must have lost your head – and – and, besides, you couldn't have stopped the mad girl – that was not in your power! But, my dear fellow, you ought to have realized how much and how seriously that girl – er – cared for you. She did not want to share you with another woman, and how could you – er – how could you throw away and smash to pieces a treasure like that!'

'Yes, yes,' the prince said again, in terrible distress, 'you're right. Yes, I'm to blame. And, you know, she alone – Aglaya alone – looked upon Nastasya Filippovna like that. No one else ever looked upon her like that.'

'But, don't you see, that's what makes it so shocking – I mean, that there was nothing serious in it!' cried Radomsky, positively carried away. 'I'm sorry, Prince, but I – I have been thinking about it. I've thought it all over very carefully, Prince. I know all that happened before, I know all that happened six months ago, and – all that was not serious! All that was just an idea you got into your head, just your imagination, a fantasy, a delusion, and it was only the frightened jealousy of a wholly inexperienced girl who could have taken it for anything serious!'

At this point Radomsky, regardless of the prince's feelings, gave full vent to his indignation. Clearly and sensibly and, we repeat, with quite extraordinary psychological insight, he unfolded before the prince the whole story of the latter's personal relationship with Nastasya Filippovna. Radomsky had always been a fluent speaker, but now he rose to positive eloquence.

'From the very beginning,' he declared, 'both of you began with a lie, and what begins with a lie must end with a lie – that is a law of nature. I don't agree – indeed, I feel positively indignant – when someone – oh, whoever it is – calls you an idiot. You're much too intelligent to be called that. But you must admit you're also so strange that you are not like other people. I have come to the conclusion that the fundamental cause of all that's happened is due to your, as it were, inherent inexperience (mark that word, Prince: inherent), as well as to your extraordinary simplicity; furthermore, to your phenomenal lack of a sense of proportion (which you have several times admitted yourself), and, finally, to the enormously great mass of intellectual convictions which you, with that extraordinary honesty of yours, have hitherto taken for true, natural, spontaneous, and sincere convictions. You must admit, Prince, that in your relations with Nastasya Filippovna there was from the very beginning something *conventionally-democratic* (to put it succinctly), some fascination, as it were, of the "woman question" (to put it even more succinctly). You see, I know every detail of that strange and scandalous scene at Nastasya Filippovna's when Rogozhin brought his money. If you like, I'll analyse you thoroughly; I'll show you yourself as in a looking-glass. I know so exactly how it all happened and why it all turned out as it did! You, a youth, longed for your country in Switzerland; you were anxious to go back to Russia as to an unknown country, a promised land. You had read many books about Russia – excellent books, perhaps, but harmful for you. You came here in the first flush of eagerness for action and, as it were, flung yourself into action! And then, on the very first day of your arrival, the sad and heart-rending story of a badly used woman is told to you – you, a knight-errant, a virgin – and about a woman! The very same day you saw the woman, you were bewitched by her beauty, her fantastic, demonic beauty (you see, I admit that she is beautiful). Add to this your nerves, your epilepsy, our Petersburg thaw, which is so shattering to the nerves; add to this the whole of that day, in an unknown and to you almost fantastic town, a day of meetings and scenes, a day of unexpected acquaintances, a day of the most unexpected reality, a day of three beautiful Yepanchin girls, and, among them, Aglaya; add to this your fatigue, your tremendous excitement; add to this Nastasya Filippovna's drawing-room, the atmosphere of that drawing-room – and what could you have expected of yourself at that moment – what do you think?'

'Yes, yes, yes, yes.' The prince shook his head, beginning to blush. 'Yes, that's almost exactly how it was. And, you know, I really had scarcely slept at all the night before in the train, or the night before that, and I didn't feel well at all. ...'

'Yes, of course, that's what I'm driving at!' Radomsky went on, excitedly. 'It's quite clear that, carried away by your enthusiasm, as it were, you pounced on the chance of publicly proclaiming your generous idea that, as a prince of ancient lineage and as a clean-living man, you did not consider a woman dishonoured who had fallen from virtue not through any fault of her own, but through the fault of a disgusting aristocratic libertine. Why, good Lord, it's quite understandable! But, my dear Prince, that's not the point. The point is whether your feeling was true, whether it was a genuine feeling, a natural feeling, or whether it was nothing but intellectual enthusiasm. What do you think? The woman taken in adultery – the same kind of woman – was forgiven, but she was not told that she had done well and that she was deserving of honour and respect, was she? Didn't your commonsense tell you three months later what the true position was? Granted she is innocent now – I won't insist on that point, for I don't want to – but could all her adventures justify such intolerable, diabolical pride, such arrogant, such rapacious egoism? I'm sorry, Prince. I'm afraid I've been carried away, but – –'

'Yes,' the prince again murmured, 'it may be so. Perhaps you're right. She really is very fretful, and you're right, of course, but – –'

'She deserves to be pitied? Is that what you were going to say, my dear, kind-hearted fellow? But how could you, out of pity and for her satisfaction, put to shame another high-minded and pure girl, humiliate her in those disdainful and hateful eyes? Where will your pity lead you next? Why, an exaggeration like that is – is quite incredible! And how could you so humiliate a girl you are in love with before her rival, throw her over for another before the very eyes of that other woman after – after you had yourself made her an honourable proposal of marriage – and you did propose to her, you know – you did so in the presence of her parents and her sisters! Do you think you're an honourable man after that, Prince, may I ask? And – and did you not deceive that divine girl by telling her that you loved her?'

'Yes, yes, you're right,' said the prince in great anguish. 'Oh, I do feel that I'm to blame!'

'But is that enough?' cried Radomsky indignantly. 'Is it enough just to cry "Oh, I'm to blame!" You are to blame, and yet you persist! And where was your heart then, your "Christian" heart? You saw her face at that moment, didn't you? Was *she* suffering less than *your other* woman – the woman who has come between you? How could you have seen it and let it happen? How could you?'

'But – but I – I didn't – –' murmured the unhappy prince.

'You didn't?'

'No, of course I didn't. I don't understand even now how it all happened. I – I ran after Aglaya, and Nastasya Filippovna fainted. And since then they won't let me see Aglaya.'

'That's no excuse! You should have run after Aglaya, even if the other woman did faint!'

'Yes, yes, I should have – but, you see, she would have died! She would have killed herself – you don't know her – and – and, anyhow, I should have told Aglaya everything afterwards and – you see, my dear fellow, I can see that you don't know everything. Tell me, why don't they let me see Aglaya? I'd have explained everything to her. You see, neither of them talked about the things that mattered at the time – no, not at all about the things that really mattered, and that's why it all happened like that. I'm afraid I can't explain it to you, but I might have been able to explain it to Aglaya. ... Oh dear, oh dear! You speak of her face at that moment when she ran out – oh dear, I remember it! Let's go – let's go!' he cried, jumping up from his seat and suddenly dragging Radomsky by the arm.

'Where?'

'Let's go to Aglaya – let's go at once!'

'But I told you she wasn't in Pavlovsk now, and why go to her?'

'She'll understand, she'll understand!' muttered the prince, clasping his hands imploringly. 'She'll understand that it isn't *that* at all – that it's something quite, quite different!'

'Something quite different? But you're going to marry that woman, aren't you? You still persist, don't you? Are you going to be married or not?'

'Yes, I am – of course I am!'

'Then why isn't it "that"?'

'Oh no, it isn't, it isn't! It makes no difference whether I'm going to be married or not! That doesn't matter!'

'Doesn't it? It's not such a trifling matter, is it? You're marrying a woman you love to make her happy, and Aglaya sees that and knows it! So how can you say it makes no difference?'

'Happy? Oh, no! I'm just getting married to her – that's all. She wants me to. And what does it matter if I do get married? – I – but it doesn't really matter – not a bit. Only, you see, she would most certainly have died. I can see now that her proposed marriage to Rogozhin was madness! Now I understand everything I didn't understand before, and – well, you see, when they stood there facing each other, I couldn't bear to see Nastasya Filippovna's face. You don't know, my dear fellow,' he went on, lowering his voice mysteriously, 'I've never told anyone about it – never – not even Aglaya, but I can't bear to see Nastasya Filippovna's face. ... It was true what you said just now about that party at Nastasya Filippovna's, but there was one thing there you've missed because you don't know it: I looked at *her face*! That morning even – I mean, when I looked at her portrait, I could not bear it. ... Vera Lebedev, for instance, has quite different eyes. I,' he added with extraordinary terror, 'I am afraid of her face!'

'Afraid?'

'Yes – she is mad!' he whispered, turning pale.

'Are you sure?' asked Radomsky with great interest.

'Yes, I am. I'm sure of it now – now, during the last five days, I've found it out for certain!'

'Then, for heaven's sake, Prince, what are you doing?' Radomsky cried in dismay. 'So you're marrying her out of a sort of fear? I simply can't understand it! You're not even in love with her, perhaps?'

'Oh no, I love her with all my soul! Why, she's just a – a child, an absolute child! Oh, you know nothing!'

'And at the same time you swore to Aglaya that you loved her?'

'Oh, yes, yes!'

'But how can that be? You mean you want to love both of them?'

'Oh yes, yes!'

'Good Lord, Prince, what are you saying? Do come to your senses!'

'Without Aglaya I – I must see her – I must! I – I shall soon die in my sleep. I thought I was going to die in my sleep last night. Oh, if Aglaya only knew – if only she knew everything – I mean, absolutely everything! For, you see, here one must know everything – that's most important! Why is it we can never know *everything* about another person, when we ought to, when that other person is to blame! ... But I'm afraid I don't know what I'm saying – I'm all muddled. You've shocked me terribly. ... And, surely, her face now doesn't look as it did when she ran out of the room, does it? Oh, yes, I'm to blame all right! Most likely it is all my fault! I don't quite know how – but it's all my fault. ... There's something here I can't explain to you – I can't find the right words, but – but Aglaya will understand! Oh, I always believed that she would understand!'

'No, Prince, she won't understand! Aglaya loved like a woman, like a human being, and not like – a disembodied spirit! Do you know what I think, my poor Prince? Most likely you've never loved either of them!'

'I don't know – perhaps, perhaps. You're right about many things – you're very clever, my dear fellow. Oh, my head's beginning to ache again. Let's go to her – for God's sake – for God's sake!'

'But I'm telling you she isn't in Pavlovsk, she's in Kolmino.'

'Let's go to Kolmino. Let's go at once!'

'That is im-poss-ible!' Radomsky drawled, getting up.

'Listen, I'll write her a letter. Take it to her!'

'No, Prince, no! Spare me such commissions – I can't!'

They parted. Radomsky went away with strange convictions: in his opinion, too, the prince was not entirely in his right mind. And what was the meaning of the *face* he was so afraid of and loved so much?

And yet perhaps he might really die without Aglaya, so that Aglaya would never find out how much he loved her! Ha, ha! And how can one love two persons at once? With two different kinds of love? That was interesting – the poor idiot! And what would become of him now?

10

The prince did not, however, die before his wedding, either when awake or 'in his sleep', as he predicted to Radomsky. Perhaps he really did not sleep well and had bad dreams; but during the daytime, in the company of people, he seemed kind and even contented, except that sometimes he was very thoughtful, but that was only when he was alone. The wedding was hurried on; it was fixed for a week after Radomsky's visit. In view of such haste, even the prince's best friends, if he had any, must have despaired of their efforts to 'save' the poor, deluded fellow. There were rumours that General Yepanchin and Mrs Yepanchin were partly responsible for Radomsky's visit. But even if the two of them, out of the infinite goodness of their hearts, had wished to save the wretched madman from the abyss, they had, of course, to confine themselves to this feeble effort; neither their position nor, perhaps, their warm sympathy for the prince (which was natural enough) permitted any more serious efforts on their part. We have mentioned already that even those who were in the closest proximity to the prince had turned against him. Vera Lebedev, though, confined herself to crying when by herself and spending most of her time in her part of the house and looking in upon the prince less frequently than before. Kolya was at this time occupied with his father's funeral; the old man died of a second stroke eight days after the first. The prince showed great concern in the family's bereavement and for the first few days spent several hours a day at Mrs Ivolgin's; he was present at the funeral and at the service in the church. It was noticed by many that the people in the church could not help whispering to one another at his arrival and departure: the same thing happened in the streets and in the park; every time he passed or drove by people began to talk about him, mentioned his name, pointed at him, and Nastasya Filippovna's name could be heard, too. People looked out for her at the funeral, but she was not there. Neither was the captain's widow at the funeral, Lebedev having succeeded in preventing her going in time. The funeral service made a strong and painful impression on the prince; he whispered to Lebedev in the church, in answer to some question, that it was the first time he had been present at an Orthodox funeral service, and that he had only a vague memory of being present at a funeral service at a village church as a little boy.

'Yes, sir, it doesn't seem to be the same man in the coffin whom we chose to be our chairman only recently – remember, sir?' Lebedev whispered to the prince. 'Who are you looking for, sir?'

'Oh, nothing – I thought – –'

'Not Rogozhin?'

'Is he here?'

'Yes, sir, in the church.'

'Oh, so that's why I thought I caught sight of his eyes,' the prince murmured in confusion. 'But what is he – why is he here? Was he invited?'

'Why no, sir. They never thought of inviting him. They don't know him at all. But then everyone is free to come if he likes. Why are you so surprised? I often meet him now. I've seen him at least four times this week here in Pavlovsk.'

'I haven't seen him once – since that time,' murmured the prince.

As Nastasya Filippovna had not once mentioned to him meeting Rogozhin since 'that day', the prince concluded now that Rogozhin was for some reason purposely keeping out of his sight. The whole of that day he was lost in thought; Nastasya Filippovna, on the other hand, was unusually cheerful all day and in the evening.

Kolya, who had made it up with the prince before his father's death, suggested that he should ask Keller and Burdovsky to be his best men, since the matter was urgent and a decision could no longer be postponed. He vouched for Keller's good behaviour, adding that he might be of 'some use'; as for Burdovsky, there was no need to be apprehensive about him, as he was a quiet and modest fellow. Mrs Ivolgin and Lebedev repeatedly pointed out to the prince that if he had made up his mind to go through with the wedding, there was no reason why it should be held in Pavlovsk at the height of the season and so publicly. Would it not be better to have a quiet wedding in Petersburg, or even at the house? The prince knew perfectly well what they were afraid of, but he replied briefly and simply that it was Nastasya Filippovna's express wish.

Next day Keller, already informed that he was to be the best man, came to see the prince. Before entering, he stopped in the doorway, as soon as he caught sight of the prince, raised his right hand, as though taking an oath, and cried:

'Haven't had a drop!'

Then he went up to the prince, shook both his hands warmly, and declared that when he first heard of the wedding he was against it, which, indeed, he had announced at billards, and for no other reason than that he had hoped and, with the impatience of a true friend, had waited every day, to see him married to no less a person than the Princess de Rohan, or, at least, de Chabot; but now he could see that the prince's way of thinking was ten times more noble than that of all the rest of them put together! For what he wanted was not pomp, nor riches, nor even honour, but only – the truth! The sympathies of exalted persons were well known, and the prince was too exalted by his education not to be an exalted person, generally speaking! 'But the dirty scum and all sorts of riff-raff are of a different opinion: in the town, in the houses, in the assemblies, in the summer cottages, at the bandstand, in the pubs and billiard-rooms they are talking and shouting of nothing but the coming event. I've heard it said that they are planning to organize a *charivari* and kick up a row under your windows, and on the wedding night, too! If you should need the pistol of an honest man, Prince, I'm quite ready to challenge half a dozen of these ruffians and exchange honourable shots with them before you rise on the morning after your wedding night!' He also advised the prince to get a fire-engine ready in the courtyard to disperse the large crowds who, eager for free drinks, might invade the house on coming out of the church. But Lebedev would not hear of it. 'If we get the fire-engine,' he said, 'they'll pull the house down.'

'That fellow Lebedev,' Keller said, 'is intriguing against you, Prince. I'm damned if he isn't! They want to certify you and put you under the supervision of the court, and everything that belongs to you, your money and your freedom, the two things that distinguish every one of us from a quadruped! Yes, sir, I've heard it for a fact. It's the truth I'm telling you!'

The prince recalled that he, too, had heard something of the kind, but of course he had paid no attention to it. Now, too, he just laughed and forgot it at once. Lebedev really had been very busy for some time; the plans of this man were always conceived, as it were, on the spur of the moment, becoming more and more complicated, branching out, and getting further and further away from their starting point as he got more and more excited about them; that was why he had so little success in life. When, almost on the wedding day, he came to the prince to confess his guilt (for it was his regular habit to come with a confession to the people against whom he had been intriguing, especially if his intrigue had not succeeded), he declared that he was born a Talleyrand and for some unknown reason always remained a Lebedev. He then proceeded to disclose his whole game, which interested the prince extremely. According to him, he had begun by looking for the assistance of highly placed persons on whose support he could rely in case of need, and had been to see General Yepanchin. The general was taken aback, wished 'the young man' well, but declared that however much he'd like 'to save' him, it would not be 'seemly' for him to act in this matter. Mrs Yepanchin would not see him or listen to him; Mr Radomsky and Prince Sh. simply waved him away. But he, Lebedev, did not lose heart, and sought the advice of a very shrewd lawyer, a very worthy old gentleman, a great friend of his, almost his benefactor, in fact; in his opinion, the thing could be easily arranged provided he had competent witnesses to testify that the prince was not in the full possession of his faculties and, in fact, was undoubtedly insane, and, above all, provided he obtained the support of influential persons in this matter. Lebedev did not lose heart even then, and one day he even brought a doctor, who was spending the summer in Pavlovsk, to see the prince – also a worthy old gentleman with a St Anne ribbon – to reconnoitre the terrain, as it were, get acquainted with the prince, not officially but, as it were, in a friendly way, and let him know what his conclusion was. The prince remembered the doctor's visit; he remembered that Lebedev had kept telling him the day before that he looked ill, and when the prince would not hear of calling in a doctor, he suddenly appeared with the doctor, under the pretext that they had both just come from Mr Terentyev, who was very ill, and that the doctor had something to tell the prince about the sick man. The prince thanked Lebedev and received the doctor very affably. They at once began talking about Ippolit; the doctor asked the prince to tell him all about Ippolit's attempted suicide, and the prince absolutely fascinated him by his account and his explanation of the incident. They then began talking about the Petersburg climate, the prince's illness, Switzerland, and Schneider. The prince interested the doctor so much by his exposition of Schneider's system and his stories that he stayed two hours with him, smoking the prince's excellent cigars; Lebedev, for his part, regaled them with a most delicious liqueur which was brought in by Vera, the doctor, a married man, paying the girl such extravagant compliments that he aroused her intense indignation. They parted friends. After leaving the prince, the doctor told Lebedev that if such people were to be put under restraint there would be no one left to keep an eye on them. In reply to Lebedev's tragic account of the forthcoming marriage, the doctor shook his head slyly and knowingly and, at last, remarked that quite apart from the fact that 'there's no telling whom a man may not marry', the ravishing creature in question, so at least he had heard, besides her incomparable beauty, which alone might be sufficient to account for the infatuation of a wealthy man, possessed a great deal of money, which she had obtained from Totsky and Rogozhin, pearls and diamonds, shawls and furniture, so that the dear prince's choice, far from being a sign of any, as it were, peculiarly glaring foolishness, showed the shrewd and calculating intelligence of a man of the world and, therefore, led to an opposite conclusion, which, indeed, was highly favourable to the prince. Lebedev, too, was rather struck by this point of view – and he stuck to it. 'And now,' he added to the prince, 'now you will see nothing from me but loyalty and readiness to shed my blood for you – that's what I've come to tell you.'

Ippolit, too, helped to distract the prince during those last few days; he sent for him rather frequently. His family lived in a little house not far away. The little children, Ippolit's brother and sister, were at any rate glad to be in the country because they could escape from their sick brother into the garden; his poor mother, however, was always at his beck and call and was entirely at his mercy; the prince had to intervene and make peace between them every day. Ippolit kept calling him his 'nurse' and at the same time dared not deny himself the pleasure of despising him for his part of peacemaker. He was very cross with Kolya for scarcely visiting him recently, spending his time at first with his dying father and afterwards with his widowed mother. At last he made the prince's approaching marriage to Nastasya Filippovna the particular butt of his gibes and finished up by offending the prince and, finally, making him lose his temper completely; the prince stopped visiting him. Two days later, the captain's widow came to see the prince in the morning and begged him tearfully to come and see them as otherwise '*he* will devour me alive'. She added that Ippolit wished to disclose a great secret to him. The prince went. Ippolit wanted to make it up, he burst into tears and afterwards, of course, grew more spiteful than ever, but was afraid to give vent to his spite. He was very ill and there could be no more doubt that he would die very soon. He had no secrets to disclose, except for his earnest appeals, delivered in a voice gasping, as it were, with emotion (probably put on), 'to beware of Rogozhin': 'He's the sort of man who will never give up what he thinks belongs to him. He's no match for you or me, Prince. If he wants something, he won't stop at anything to get it. ...' and so on and so forth. The prince began questioning him in detail, trying to get at some facts; but there were no facts except Ippolit's personal impressions and feelings. To his intense gratification, Ippolit ended up by at last scaring the prince thoroughly. At first the prince refused to answer some of his rather singular questions and only smiled at his advice 'to run away, abroad, if necessary. There are Russian priests everywhere,' Ippolit went on, 'and you can get married anywhere you like.' But, finally, Ippolit concluded with the following reflection: 'All I'm concerned about is Aglaya: Rogozhin knows how much you love her; a love for a love; you've taken Nastasya Filippovna from him, so he will kill Aglaya, for though she is no longer yours now, it would be a great blow to you, wouldn't it?' He achieved what he had set out to do: the prince left him in great distress.

These warnings about Rogozhin came the day before the wedding. The same evening, for the last time before the wedding, the prince saw Nastasya Filippovna; but Nastasya Filippovna was not able to set his mind at rest; on the contrary, during the last day or two she was making him feel more and more ill at ease. Before – that is, a few days earlier – she did all she could to cheer him up. She was terribly afraid of his melancholy looks, and even tried singing to him: most of all she tried to tell him any amusing story she could think of. The prince almost always pretended to be hugely amused, and sometimes he really did laugh at the brilliant wit and vivacity with which she sometimes told her stories when she was in the right mood, as she often was. Seeing how amused the prince was, seeing the impression she made on him, she was delighted and began to feel proud of herself. But now her melancholy and her pensiveness increased with almost every hour. His opinion of Nastasya Filippovna was firmly fixed, otherwise, of course, everything about her would have appeared enigmatic and incomprehensible to him now. But he genuinely believed that she still had a chance to become a different woman. He had quite truthfully told Radomsky that he loved her truly and sincerely, and in his love for her there really was a sort of attraction to some sick pathetic child whom it was difficult and even impossible to leave to its own devices. He did not explain to anyone his feelings for her and, indeed, did not like to talk about it, unless it was quite impossible to avoid the subject; when alone with Nastasya Filippovna they never spoke of their 'feelings', just as though they had agreed not to do so. Everyone could take part in their happy and lively conversation. Darya Alexeyevna used to say afterwards that every time she looked at them she could not help being delighted and overjoyed.

But it was this opinion of Nastasya Filippovna's mental condition that saved him to some extent from all sorts of other perplexities. Now she was quite different from the woman he had known three months before. Now, for instance, he no longer wondered why she had run away from marrying him then, with tears, with curses and reproaches, and was now insisting herself on marrying him as quickly as possible. 'So it seems,' thought the prince, 'that she is no longer afraid, as she used to be then, that her marriage to me would be my ruin.' Such a rapidly restored confidence in herself could not, in his opinion, be natural to her. Nor could this confidence be due only to her hatred of Aglaya: Nastasya Filippovna was capable of feeling more deeply than that. Surely, it could not come from her fear of what would happen to her if she married Rogozhin? In short, all these reasons together with others might have contributed to it; but what was most evident to him was what he had been suspecting for a long time, and that her poor, sick mind had broken down under the strain. Though all this did in a way save him from misunderstandings, it could not give him any rest nor any peace of mind all that time. Occasionally he did seem to try not to think of anything; he certainly appeared to regard his marriage as some unimportant formality; he set too little store by his own future. As for any objections and discussions, such as his discussion with Radomsky, he was quite unable, and felt absolutely incompetent to answer them, and that was why he did his best to avoid any discussions of that kind.

He did observe, though, that Nastasya Filippovna understood and knew very well what Aglaya meant to him. She merely said nothing, but he saw her 'face' when she sometimes found him, at the very beginning, setting out to go to the Yepanchins. When the Yepanchins had gone she was simply radiant with joy. Unobservant and unsuspecting as he was, he had begun to be worried by the thought that Nastasya Filippovna might decide to make some scene in public to drive Aglaya out of Pavlovsk. It was to some extent Nastasya Filippovna, of course, who kept up the uproar and the commotion among the Pavlovsk residents in order to annoy her rival about the wedding. As it was difficult to meet the Yepanchins, Nastasya Filippovna had, on one occasion, got him to accompany her on a drive round the town and ordered the coachman to drive past the windows of their house. That was a dreadful surprise for the prince; he realized what was happening when, as usual, it was too late, and when the carriage was already driving past the windows. He said nothing, but he was ill for two days afterwards; Nastasya Filippovna did not repeat the experiment. During the last few days before the wedding she was beginning to brood a great deal; she usually finished up by getting the better of her melancholy and becoming cheerful again, but, somehow, more quietly, not so noisily, not so happily cheerful as she had been not so long ago. The prince redoubled his attention. It struck him as curious that she never spoke to him of Rogozhin. Only once, five days before the wedding, a message was suddenly brought to him from Darya Alexeyevna asking him to come immediately, as Nastasya Filippovna was feeling very queer. He found her in a state bordering on complete madness: she kept screaming, shivering, shouting that Rogozhin was hiding in the garden, in their house, that she had seen him just now, that he would kill her in the night – cut her throat! She would not calm down all day. But the same evening, when the prince paid a short call on Ippolit, the captain's widow, who had just returned from town, where she had gone on some business of her own, told him that Rogozhin had been to see her at her flat that day and had questioned her about Pavlovsk. In answer to the prince's question, she said that Rogozhin had called on her almost at the same hour when he was supposed to have been seen by Nastasya Filippovna in her garden. The whole thing was, therefore, a simple case of delusion; Nastasya Filippovna later went to the captain's widow herself, and after questioning her in greater detail, was completely comforted and relieved.

On the day before the wedding, the prince left Nastasya Filippovna in a state of great excitement; her finery for next day's ceremony had arrived from a dressmaker's in Petersburg – the wedding-dress, the bridal veil, and so on. The prince never expected her to be so excited about her dresses; he kept praising everything, and his praises made her happier than ever. But she made a slip: she told him that she had heard that the townspeople were indignant and that some young rowdies were actually organizing some sort of *charivari* with music and almost with verses composed for the occasion, and that this was being done practically with the approval of the rest of Pavlovsk society. And so it was now that she was even more anxious than ever to hold up her head and dazzle them all by the taste and richness of her wedding attire. 'Let them shout, let them boo, if they dare!' Her eyes flashed at the very thought of it. She had one more secret dream, but she did not speak of it: she hoped that Aglaya, or at least someone sent by her, would also be in the crowd, incognito, in the church, and would see it all, and she was secretly preparing herself for it. She parted from the prince, still preoccupied with these thoughts, at about eleven o'clock at night; but before it had struck midnight, a messenger came running to the prince from Darya Alexeyevna with a request 'to come immediately, she is very bad'. The prince found his bride shut up in her bedroom, in tears, in despair, in hysterics; for a long time she could hear nothing that was said to her through the closed door. At last she opened the door, let only the prince in, locked the door after him, and fell on her knees before him. (So, at any rate, Darya Alexeyevna, who had managed to catch sight of something, reported afterwards.)

'What am I doing? What am I doing? What am I doing to you?' she cried, embracing his legs convulsively.

The prince spent a whole hour with her; we don't know what they talked about. Darya Alexeyevna said that they had parted an hour later reconciled and happy. The prince sent again to inquire after her that night; but Nastasya Filippovna was asleep. In the morning, before she awoke, two more messengers arrived from the prince at Darya Alexeyevna's, and it was the third messenger who was instructed to tell the prince that Nastasya Filippovna was surrounded by a whole crowd of dressmakers and hairdressers from Petersburg, that there was not a trace of her breakdown of the night before, that she was busy as only a beautiful woman like her could be busy with her dressing on the morning of her wedding, and that at that very moment an important conference was in progress as to which of her diamonds she should wear and how she was to wear them. The prince was completely reassured.

The whole of the following account was given by people who were present at this wedding, and it appears to be correct.

The wedding was fixed for eight o'clock in the evening; Nastasya Filippovna was ready at seven. Already since six o'clock crowds of onlookers had begun to gather round Lebedev's house and, especially, round Darya Alexeyevna's; by seven o'clock the church, too, began to fill. Vera Lebedev and Kolya were terribly anxious on the prince's account. But they had a great deal to do in the house: they were busy with the arrangements for the reception of the wedding guests in the prince's rooms. There was going to be no big reception after the wedding. In addition to the people who were taking part in the wedding ceremony, Lebedev had invited the Ptitsyns, Ganya, the doctor with the St Anne order, and Darya Alexeyevna. When the prince asked Lebedev why he had invited the doctor, whom he hardly knew, Lebedev replied self-complacently: 'He's been decorated, sir – a very respectable old gentleman, sir – it'll make a good impression!' – and the prince was amused. Keller and Burdovsky looked very correct in evening dress and gloves; Keller, though, still caused the prince and those who had put their trust in him some alarm by his unconcealed hankerings for battle, and he glared in a very hostile manner at the onlookers who were gathering round the house. At last, at half past seven, the prince left for the church in a carriage. We may, incidentally, observe that the prince himself was loath to omit any of the recognized customs and traditions of such an occasion; everything was done publicly, openly, and 'according to the rules'. In the church, having somehow or other made his way through the crowd, who kept up a barrage of whisperings and exclamations, the prince, escorted by Keller, who cast menacing glances to right and left, disappeared for a time behind the altar gates. Keller went off to fetch the bride, and in front of Darya Alexeyevna's house he found a crowd which was not only twice or three times as large as at the prince's, but perhaps also three times as free and easy. As he went up the front steps, he was greeted by such exclamations that he could no longer restrain himself and was about to address the crowd in appropriate language, but was luckily stopped by Burdovsky and Darya Alexeyevna, who ran out to meet him. They got hold of him and dragged him into the house by force. Keller was irritated and in a hurry. Nastasya Filippovna got up, cast another glance at the looking-glass, observed with 'a wry smile', as Keller related afterwards, that she was 'as white as a corpse', bowed reverently before the icon, and went out of the house. A hubbub of voices greeted her appearance. It is true that at first there was laughter, applause, and almost hisses, but a moment later other voices were heard:

'What a beauty!' some people in the crowd exclaimed.

'She's not the first, and she won't be the last!'

'Marriage makes everything right, you fools!'

'You won't find such a beauty anywhere,' those who stood in front of the crowd shouted. 'Hurrah!'

'A princess!' shouted some clerk. 'For such a princess I'd sell my soul! "One night of love and my life I'll gladly give"!' he sang.

Nastasya Filippovna was really as white as a sheet when she came out, but her large black eyes blazed like burning coals upon the crowd. The crowd recoiled at her look; indignation was transformed into exultant cries. The door of the carriage was already opened, Keller had already offered his arm to the bride, when suddenly she uttered a cry, and rushed straight from the front steps into the crowd. All who accompanied her were stupefied with amazement. The crowd parted before her, and Rogozhin suddenly appeared five or six paces from the steps. It was his eyes in the crowd that Nastasya Filippovna had caught. She rushed up to him, like one demented, and seized both his hands.

'Save me! Take me away! Anywhere you like – now!'

Rogozhin seized her in his arms and almost carried her to the carriage. Then, in a flash, he pulled out a hundred-rouble note from his purse and held it out to the driver.

'To the station, and if you catch the train there's another hundred for you!'

And he leapt into the carriage after Nastasya Filippovna and closed the door. The coachman did not hesitate for a moment, and whipped up his horse. Keller afterwards put the blame on the unexpectedness of it all.

'Another second and I'd have known what to do – I wouldn't have let it happen!' he explained afterwards, describing the incident. In fact, he and Burdovsky hailed another carriage that appeared to be driving past at the time, but on the way to the station he changed his mind because, as he said, 'It is too late, anyway. You won't bring her back by force!'

'And the prince wouldn't like it, either,' decided Burdovsky, who was thoroughly upset.

Rogozhin and Nastasya Filippovna reached the station in time. As he got out of the carriage and was on the point of stepping into the train, Rogozhin had time to stop a girl, who was wearing an old but decent dark cloak and a silk kerchief on her head.

'Like fifty roubles for your cloak?' he asked, holding out the money to the girl.

Before she had time to express her surprise or realize what was happening, he had thrust the fifty-rouble note into her hand, relieved her of her cloak and kerchief and thrown them over Nastasya Filippovna's head and shoulders. Her magnificent dress was too conspicuous and would have attracted the attention of the passengers in the train, and it was only afterwards that the girl realized why her old and worthless rags had been bought at so much profit to herself.

The news of what had happened reached the church with extraordinary rapidity and provoked an excited hubbub of voices. When Keller was making his way through the crowd to the prince, a great number of people whom he did not know rushed up to question him. People were talking loudly to each other, shaking their heads, even laughing; no one left the church; everyone was waiting to see how the bridegroom would take the news. He turned pale, but took the news quietly, murmuring in a hardly audible voice: 'I was afraid of it, and yet I didn't think it would happen ...' and after a short pause he added, 'Still – in her condition – it might have been expected.' Such a comment even Keller described afterwards as 'a piece of unexampled philosophy'. The prince left the church, to all appearances, calm and cheerful, so at any rate many people noticed and said afterwards. He seemed to be very anxious to get home as soon as possible and be left alone; but that they would not let him do. Some of the invited guests followed him into the room, including Mr Ptitsyn, Ganya, and the doctor, who did not seem inclined to go home, either. Besides, the whole house was literally besieged by idle crowds. While he was still on the veranda, the prince heard Keller and Lebedev start a fierce altercation with a number of highly respectable-looking people who were complete strangers and who insisted on entering the veranda. The prince went up to the disputants, asked what was the matter and, courteously pushing aside Lebedev and Keller, tactfully addressed a stout, grey-haired gentleman, who was standing on the steps at the head of a few other men who wished to come in, and invited him politely to honour him with his visit. The gentleman was covered with confusion, but came in all the same, followed by two more people. About seven or eight people elbowed their way through the crowd and came in, too, trying to look as free and unconcerned as possible; but there were no more volunteers, and people in the crowd soon began criticizing those who had pushed their way in. Those who had come in were asked to sit down, and a conversation sprang up and tea was served. All this was done very modestly and decorously, to the considerable astonishment of the intruders. A few attempts were, of course, made to enliven the conversation and turn it to the 'most burning' topic of the day; a few indiscreet questions were asked and a few 'pointed' remarks made. The prince answered everyone with such simplicity and cordiality and, at the same time, with so much dignity and so much confidence in the decency of his guests, that the indiscreet questions petered out by themselves. Gradually the conversation became almost serious. One gentleman, apropos of some remark made by one of the speakers, vowed with intense indignation that he would not sell his estate, whatever happened, but would wait and see and, indeed, was sure that things would in the end turn to his advantage and that 'enterprise is better than money – and there, my dear sir, you have my system, if you like to know'. As he was addressing the prince, the prince praised him warmly, though Lebedev whispered in his ear that the particular gentleman had neither house nor home and never had had any estate of any kind. Almost an hour passed, tea was finished, and after tea the guests felt too ashamed to stay longer. The doctor and the grey-haired gentleman shook hands warmly with the prince and, indeed, they all took leave warmly and noisily. Good wishes were expressed and several remarks were dropped to the effect that it was 'no use crying over spilt milk' and that 'perhaps it is all for the best', and so on. Attempts were made, it is true, to ask for champagne, but they were restrained by the older guests. When all were gone, Keller bent over to Lebedev and said, 'You and I would have made a row, started a fight, disgraced ourselves, and dragged in the police, but he made some new friends and – what friends! I know them!' Lebedev, who was quite 'overcome', sighed and said, ' "Thou hast hid these things from the wise and prudent, and hast revealed them unto babes", I said so about him before, but now I'll add that the Lord has preserved the babe himself and has saved him from the abyss, He and all His saints.'

At last, about half past ten, the prince was left alone. His head was aching. Kolya was the last to go, and he helped him to change into his everyday clothes. They parted warmly. Kolya did not speak about what had happened, but promised to come early next day. It was he who testified afterwards that at their last parting the prince had not told him anything of what he was going to do, so that he concealed his intentions even from him. Soon there was almost no one left in the whole house: Burdovsky had gone off to Ippolit's, Keller and Lebedev had also gone off somewhere. Vera Lebedev alone remained for some time in the prince's rooms, hurriedly putting everything in its usual order. Before going, she looked into the prince's room. He was sitting at the table, with his elbows propped up on it and his head buried in his hands. She went up softly to him and touched him on the shoulder; the prince looked at her in perplexity and almost for a minute seemed to be trying to remember something; then, having remembered and realized what had happened, he suddenly grew extremely agitated. All he did, however, was to beseech Vera very earnestly to knock at his door at seven o'clock next morning, in time for the first train to town. Vera promised; the prince began begging her earnestly not to say anything about it to anyone. She again promised and, at last, when she opened the door to go out, the prince stopped her for the third time, took her hands, kissed them, and then kissed her on the forehead, and, with a sort of 'peculiar' expression, said to her, 'Till to-morrow!' So, at any rate, Vera said afterwards. She went away in great anxiety about him. She felt a little more cheerful in the morning when, soon after seven o'clock, she knocked, as agreed, at his door and told him that the train would be leaving for Petersburg in a quarter of an hour; it seemed to her that when he answered the door he looked quite cheerful, and had even smiled at her. He had hardly undressed that night, but he had slept. He told her he thought he might return in the evening. It would appear, therefore, that he had thought it possible and necessary to tell her alone at that moment that he was going to town.

11

An hour later he was already in Petersburg, and at about ten o'clock he was ringing at Rogozhin's door. He went in at the main entrance, and for a long time no one answered. At last the door of the flat of Rogozhin's mother was opened and a pleasant-looking old maid-servant appeared.

'Mr Rogozhin is not at home, sir,' she announced from the door. 'Whom do you want?'

'Parfyon Rogozhin.'

'He's not at home, sir.'

The maid was examining the prince with intense curiosity.

'Would you tell me at least if he spent the night at home? And – did he come back alone yesterday?'

The maid kept looking at him, but did not reply.

'Wasn't – er – Nastasya Filippovna with him – yesterday, I mean, here, yesterday evening?'

'May I ask you, sir, who you may be yourself?'

'Prince Leo Nikolayevich Myshkin – we are very good friends.'

'I'm sorry, sir, but he's not at home.'

The maid dropped her eyes.

'And Nastasya Filippovna?'

'I don't know anything about that, sir.'

'Wait a moment! When will he be back?'

'I don't know that either, sir.'

The door was closed.

The prince decided to come back in an hour's time. Looking into the yard, he saw the caretaker.

'Is Mr Parfyon Rogozhin at home?'

'Yes, sir.'

'Why was I told just now that he wasn't at home?'

'Did his man tell you that, sir?'

'No, his mother's servant. I rang at Mr Rogozhin's door, but there was no answer.'

'Well, sir, perhaps he's gone out,' the caretaker decided. 'You see, sir, he doesn't say. Sometimes he takes the key with him and his flat is locked up for three days maybe.'

'Are you sure he was at home yesterday?'

'Yes, sir, he was. Sometimes, though, he uses the main entrance and I don't see him.'

'Was Nastasya Filippovna with him last night?'

'I'm afraid I can't tell you that, sir. She doesn't come here often. I think I'd have known it if she had come.'

The prince went out, and for some time walked up and down the pavement deep in thought. The windows of the rooms occupied by Rogozhin were all closed; the windows of his mother's flat were almost all open; it was a hot, sunny day, and the prince crossed over to the pavement on the other side of the street and stopped once more to have a look at the windows; they were not only closed, but almost everywhere the white curtains were drawn.

He stood there for a moment and – strange to say – it suddenly seemed to him that the corner of one curtain was lifted and for a moment he caught sight of Rogozhin's face, but no sooner did he catch sight of it than it disappeared. He waited a little longer and decided to go back and ring again, but he changed his mind and put it off for one hour. 'Who knows? perhaps I just imagined it. ...'

What he was most anxious to do at the moment was to get as quickly as possible to the flat Nastasya Filippovna had recently occupied. He knew that, having at his request left Pavlovsk three weeks before, she had gone to live with an old friend of hers, the widow of a schoolmaster, a highly respectable lady with a family of her own, who almost made her living by letting well-furnished rooms near the Izmaylovsky Barracks. It was very likely that, on going back to Pavlovsk, Nastasya Filippovna had kept on her rooms; it was at least very probable that she had spent the night at her old flat, where Rogozhin, of course, had brought her that evening. The prince took a cab. On the way it occurred to him that he should have gone there before, because it was most improbable that she would have gone straight to Rogozhin's at night. He remembered, too, the caretaker's words that Nastasya Filippovna did not go there often; for if she did not usually go there often, there was no reason why she should have stayed at Rogozhin's now. Cheering himself with such comforting reflections, the prince arrived at the Izmaylovsky Barracks at last more dead than alive.

To his great amazement, no one at the widow's place had heard of Nastasya Filippovna either that day or the day before, but they all ran out to have a look at him as at some strange beast. The whole of the widow's numerous family – all her eight girls from seven to fifteen – rushed out after their mother and surrounded him, staring at him with gaping mouths. They were followed by a lean and sallow aunt in a black kerchief, and, finally, by their grandmother, an old lady in spectacles. The widow asked him to go in and take a seat, which he did. He at once realized that they knew very well who he was, and that they were perfectly well aware that his wedding should have taken place yesterday and were dying to ask him about the wedding and about the extraordinary fact that he was inquiring after the woman who should at that moment have been with him in Pavlovsk, but that they were too polite to ask him. He satisfied their curiosity about the wedding in a few words, but their cries of surprise and their consternation were so genuine that he was obliged to tell them almost everything else – in a brief outline, of course. At last, the council of the sage and agitated ladies decided that he must first of all knock up Rogozhin and get the whole truth out of him. If he was not at home (which he must find out for certain), or if he refused to say anything, he should go to the Semyonovsky Barracks and see a German lady, a friend of Nastasya Filippovna's, who lived with her mother: perhaps in her excitement and her anxiety to conceal herself Nastasya Filippovna had spent the night with them. The prince got up completely crushed; they said afterwards that he looked terribly pale; indeed, his legs were almost giving way under him. At last, through the terrible babble of their voices, he made out that they were trying to persuade him to act with them and were asking for his address in town. As he had no address, they advised him to stop at some hotel. After a moment's thought, the prince gave them the address of the hotel where he had stayed before and where five weeks earlier he had had his epileptic fit. Then he set off again to Rogozhin's. This time he not only got no answer from Rogozhin's, but none even from his mother's flat. The prince went down to look for the caretaker and found him with some difficulty in the yard; the caretaker was busy and hardly answered him – hardly looked at him, in fact. He did, however, declare most emphatically that Rogozhin had gone out very early in the morning, had gone to Pavlovsk and would not be back home that day.

'I'll wait. Perhaps he'll be back in the evening?'

'He may not be back for a whole week, sir. I'm sure I don't know, sir.'

'So he did spend the night here, didn't he?'

'Yes, sir, he did and all.'

All this was suspicious and highly unsatisfactory. The caretaker might very likely have received fresh instructions in the interval: before he had been quite talkative, and now he simply turned his back on him. But the prince decided to call again in about two hours and even to keep watch on the house, if necessary; now there was still the hope that he might find Nastasya Filippovna at the German lady's house, and he set off in a cab for the Semyonovsky Barracks.

But at the German lady's they did not even understand what he wanted. From certain words she let slip, he was, indeed, able to gather that about a fortnight before the beautiful German woman had had a violent quarrel with Nastasya Filippovna, so that she had not heard anything of her all that time and was doing her best to make him understand that she was not even interested to hear from her 'even if she had married all the princes in the world'. The prince made haste to get out. It occurred to him, incidentally, that she might have gone to Moscow, as she had done before, and Rogozhin, no doubt, had gone after her, or with her. 'At least, let me find some trace of her!' He remembered, however, that he had to stop at a hotel, and he hurried off to Liteyny Avenue. There he was given a room at once. The waiter asked him if he would like to have a meal; he replied absent-mindedly that he would and, recollecting himself, was furious with himself because the meal had delayed him for half an hour, and it was only afterwards that he realized he need not have had the meal that was served him. He was overcome by a strange sensation in that dark and stuffy corridor, a sensation that was trying painfully to take the form of a thought; but he could not get hold of that tantalizing thought. He left the hotel, at last, completely distraught; his head was spinning round and round, but – where was he to go now? He rushed off to Rogozhin's again.

Rogozhin had not come back; no one answered the door; he rang at Mrs Rogozhin's; the door was opened and he was again told that Rogozhin was not at home and might not be back for three days. What worried the prince was that, as before, the maid-servant had looked at him with such intense curiosity. This time he could not find the caretaker at all. He crossed over, as before, to the opposite pavement, looked up at the windows and walked up and down in the stifling heat for half an hour, or perhaps more; this time nothing stirred; the windows were not open, the white curtains were motionless. He came to the conclusion that before he had most certainly imagined it all; that, indeed, the windows were so grimy and had evidently not been cleaned for a long time so that even if someone had been looking through them, it would have been very difficult to make anything out. Relieved by this reflection, he drove back to the schoolmaster's widow at the Izmaylovsky Barracks.

There they were already expecting him. The widow had been to three or four places, and even to Rogozhin's: not a trace of Nastasya Filippovna! The prince listened in silence, went into the room, sat down on the sofa, and began staring at them as though unable to understand what they were talking about. It was strange: one moment he was keenly observant and the next suddenly quite incredibly absent-minded. The whole family afterwards declared that he was a 'surprisingly' strange person that day so that 'quite possibly all the symptoms were there already'. At last he got up and asked to be shown Nastasya Filippovna's rooms. They were two large, light, lofty rooms, very decently furnished and, no doubt, let at a high rent. The ladies declared afterwards that the prince examined every object in the rooms, saw on a little table an open library book, the French novel *Madame Bovary*, turned down the corner of the open page, asked permission to take it with him, and, without listening to their objections that it was a library book, put it in his pocket. He then sat down at the open window and, catching sight of a card-table with chalk marks, asked who played cards. They told him that Nastasya Filippovna used to play every evening with Rogozhin at 'fools', 'preference', 'millers', 'whist', or 'your own trumps' – at all the games, and that they had started playing cards only recently after her return from Pavlovsk to Petersburg because Nastasya Filippovna was always complaining that she was bored and that Rogozhin never uttered a word all evening and did not know how to talk about anything, and she often cried; and the next evening Rogozhin suddenly took a pack of cards out of his pocket; Nastasya Filippovna had laughed and they began playing. The prince asked where the cards were they had been playing with, but they could not find them; Rogozhin always used to bring the cards in his pocket himself, a new pack every time, and took it away with him again.

The ladies advised him to go and see Rogozhin again, and this time knock at the door more loudly, but to wait till the evening before going there: 'Perhaps he will be there'. The widow herself volunteered to go down to Pavlovsk before the evening and have a talk to Darya Alexeyevna: perhaps she might know something. They asked the prince to call again at ten o'clock, in any case to make plans for the next day. In spite of their words of comfort and the hopes they held out to him, the prince gave way to black despair. He reached his hotel in a state of indescribable anguish. The dusty and stifling Petersburg summer crushed him as in a vice; he was jostled by grim-looking or drunken men, stared aimlessly at the faces of passers-by, and perhaps walked much further than was necessary; it was almost evening when he went into his room at the hotel. He decided to rest a little and then go back to Rogozhin's, as he had been advised; he sat down on the sofa, leaned both his elbows on the table, and sank into thought.

Goodness only knows how long he sat there and what he thought. He was afraid of many things and he felt painfully and agonizingly that he was terribly afraid. He suddenly thought of Vera Lebedev; then it occurred to him that perhaps Lebedev knew something about it, and if he didn't, he could find out much more quickly and easily than he could. Then he remembered Ippolit and that Rogozhin used to visit Ippolit. Then he recalled Rogozhin himself, as he had seen him recently at the funeral service, then in the park, then – suddenly here in the corridor when he had hidden in a corner and had been waiting for him with a knife. He could now remember his eyes – the eyes that glared at him then in the darkness. He gave a start: the thought that had so tantalizingly escaped him a few hours before suddenly came into his head.

It was partly that Rogozhin, if he were in Petersburg, and even though he were hiding for a time, would eventually end up by coming to see him, the prince, with good or with evil intention, quite likely as he had done before. At all events, if Rogozhin wanted to see him for some reason or other, he would come here, again to this corridor. Rogozhin did not know his address, so he might very well assume that the prince would put up at the same hotel as before; at least, he would try to look for him there – if he needed him very badly. And who knows? perhaps he would need him very badly indeed.

So he reflected, and the idea seemed for some reason quite plausible to him. If he had tried to follow up his idea, he would most certainly not have been able to say why, for instance, he should become so indispensable to Rogozhin and why it was quite impossible that they should not meet again. But the thought was an oppressive one: 'If he is happy,' the prince went on reflecting, 'he won't come. He'd be more likely to come if he was unhappy. And he is quite certainly unhappy.'

Of course, with such a conviction, he ought to have waited for Rogozhin at home, in his hotel room; but he seemed not to be able to endure his new idea, and he jumped up, snatched up his hat, and ran out of his room. In the corridor it was almost dark already. 'What if he suddenly came out of that corner now and stopped me at the stairs?' it flashed through his mind as he reached the familiar spot.

But no one came out. He went down to the gateway, walked out on the pavement, marvelled at the dense crowds of people, who had flocked into the streets at sunset (as always in Petersburg during the long summer vacation), and walked on in the direction of Gorokhovaya Street. Within about fifty yards of the hotel, at the first cross-roads, someone in the crowd suddenly touched his elbow and said in his ear in an undertone:

'Leo Nikolayevich, come along with me, old man; I want you.'

It was Rogozhin.

Oddly enough, the prince was so overjoyed that he suddenly began telling him rapidly, almost swallowing his words, how he had been expecting to see him just now in the corridor at the hotel.

'I was there,' Rogozhin unexpectedly replied. 'Come on.'

The prince was surprised at his answer, but that was at least two minutes later, when he had taken it in properly. Having taken it in, he got frightened and began looking attentively at Rogozhin, who was walking almost half a yard in front of him, looking straight ahead, without glancing at the passers-by and making way for them with mechanical care.

'Why, then, didn't you ask for me if – if you were at the hotel?' the prince asked suddenly.

Rogozhin stopped, looked at him, thought it over, and, as though he did not understand the question, said:

'Look here, old man, you go on straight there – to the house – you know, don't you? And I'll walk on the other side. And see that we keep together.'

Saying this, he crossed the road to the other pavement, looked round to see whether the prince was walking on and, seeing that he was standing still, looking open-eyed at him, he waved his hand in the direction of Gorokhovaya Street, and walked on, turning every moment to look at the prince and waving to him to follow. He was evidently relieved to see that the prince understood him and did not cross over to the other side to join him. It occurred to the prince that Rogozhin was anxious to look out for someone whom he did not want to miss on the way and that was why he had crossed over to the other side. 'But why didn't he tell me then whom he has to look out for?' So they walked for about five hundred yards, and then the prince began trembling, for some reason; Rogozhin kept glancing back at him, though not so often. The prince could not hold out any longer, and he beckoned to him to come across. Rogozhin at once crossed the road to him.

'Nastasya Filippovna isn't at your house, is she?'

'She is.'

'And it was you – wasn't it – who looked at me from behind the curtain this morning?'

'Yes. ...'

'But how could you – –'

The prince did not know what more to ask, nor how to finish his question. Besides, his heart was throbbing so violently that he found it difficult to speak. Rogozhin, too, was silent and looked at him as before – that is to say, as though dreamily.

'Well, I'd better go,' he said suddenly, preparing to cross the street again, 'and you just follow me. ... We mustn't be seen together in the street – it's better so – on opposite sides – you'll see.'

When, at last, they turned on the opposite sides of the street into Gorokhovaya Street, and began to approach Rogozhin's house, the prince's feet began to give way under him again, so that he scarcely found it possible to walk. It was already about ten o'clock in the evening. The windows of Mrs Rogozhin's flat were open as before, and the windows of Rogozhin's rooms were closed, and the white curtains seemed even more conspicuous. The prince approached the house from the opposite pavement; Rogozhin, from his side of the pavement, was already walking up the front steps and he was waving to him. The prince crossed over to him and joined him at the front door.

'Even the caretaker don't know now that I've come back,' he whispered with a cunning and almost self-satisfied smile. 'I told him I was going to Pavlovsk, and I told them that at my mother's too. We'll go in, and no one will hear.'

He had the key in his hand. As he was walking up the stairs, he turned round and shook his finger warningly to the prince to go up more quietly, then he unlocked the door of his flat, let the prince in, walked in after him cautiously, locked the door behind him, and put the key in his pocket.

'Come on,' he said in a whisper.

Ever since they had met on the pavement in Liteyny Avenue he had been speaking in a whisper. In spite of his outward composure, he was inwardly in a state of great agitation. When they went into the big drawing-room and almost reached the door of his study, he walked up to the window and beckoned mysteriously to the prince.

'You see, when you rang this morning, I guessed at once that it was you and no one else. I went up to the door very quietly – on tiptoe – and I heard you talking to my mother's maid. And, you see, I gave her strict orders early this morning that if you or anyone from you, or anyone at all, was to knock at my door, she was under no circumstances to say that I was in, particularly if you was to come yourself and ask for me. I gave her your name. And afterwards when you went out, I thought to myself, "What if he was standing there outside the door waiting or keeping watch in the street?" So I went up to this here window, turned back the curtain, and there you was looking straight at me. ... That's how it happened.'

'But – where is – Nastasya Filippovna?' the prince brought out breathlessly.

'She's – here,' Rogozhin said slowly, as though pausing for a fraction of a second with his answer.

'Where?'

Rogozhin raised his eyes at the prince and looked intently at him.

'Come on.'

He was still talking in a whisper, and without hurrying, slowly and, as before, with the same queer, dreamy expression. Even while he told him about the curtain, he seemed to wish to tell him something else, in spite of the glibness with which he spoke.

They went into the study. Since the prince had been there, there had been a certain change in the room: a green damask curtain was stretched right across the whole length of the room; it could be drawn aside at either end, dividing the study from the alcove, where stood Rogozhin's bed. The heavy curtain was drawn at both ends. But it was very dark in the room; the summer 'white' Petersburg nights were beginning to get darker, and if it were not for the full moon, it would have been difficult to make out anything in Rogozhin's dark rooms with the drawn curtains. It is true, they could still see each other's faces, though not very distinctly. Rogozhin's face was pale, as usual; he stared intently and fixedly at the prince with his glittering eyes.

'Why don't you light a candle?' asked the prince.

'No, I don't think so,' replied Rogozhin and, taking hold of the prince's hand, he made him sit down on a chair; he sat down opposite, pulling up his chair, so that their knees were almost touching. There was a little round table between them, a little to one side. 'Sit down, let's sit here for a bit,' he said, as though trying to persuade the prince to stay where he was. They were silent for a minute or so. 'I knew you'd be staying at that hotel,' he began, as people sometimes do begin talking about some irrelevant subject which has no relation to the main point. 'As soon as I got to the corridor, I thought to myself, I thought, I expect he's probably sitting waiting for me now, as I'm waiting for him at this moment. Have you been to see the teacher's widow?'

'I have.' The prince could hardly bring out the words, so violently was his heart throbbing.

'I thought of that too. There'll be talk, I thought – and then I thought I'd better bring him here for the night so that we may spend the night together like. ...'

'Rogozhin, where is Nastasya Filippovna?' the prince suddenly whispered, getting up and trembling in every limb.

Rogozhin got up too.

'There,' he whispered, motioning towards the curtain.

'Asleep?' whispered the prince.

Again Rogozhin looked intently at him as before.

'I suppose you'd better come and see! Only, mind – oh well, come along!'

He lifted the curtain, stopped, and turned to the prince again.

'Come in,' he said, nodding towards the curtain and inviting the prince to go in first.

The prince went in.

'It is dark here,' he said.

'You can see!' muttered Rogozhin.

'I can just see – the bed.'

'Go nearer,' Rogozhin suggested softly.

The prince took a step nearer, then another, and stopped dead. He stood still, staring for a minute or two; neither of them uttered a word while standing by the bed; the prince's heart beat so violently that it seemed it could be heard in the room, in the dead silence of the room. But his eyes had already got used to the dark, and he could make out the whole bed; someone lay asleep on it in an absolutely motionless sleep; not the faintest movement could be heard, not the faintest breath. The sleeper was covered, from head to foot, with a white sheet, but the limbs were, somehow, only faintly visible; only from the raised outlines was it possible to make out that a human being was lying there stretched out full length. All around, in disorder, on the bed, at the foot of the bed, on the arm-chair beside the bed, even on the floor, clothes were scattered – a rich white silk dress, flowers, ribbons. On the little table at the head of the bed diamonds, which had been taken off and thrown down, lay glittering. At the foot of the bed some sort of lace lay in a crumpled heap, and on the white lace, protruding from under the sheet, the tip of a bare foot could be made out: it seemed as though it were carved out of marble, and it was dreadfully still. The prince looked, and he felt that the longer he looked the more still and death-like the room became. Suddenly a fly, awakened from its sleep, started buzzing, and after flying over the bed, settled at the head of it. The prince gave a start.

'Let's go back,' Rogozhin said, touching his arm.

They went back and sat down on the same chairs, again facing each other. The prince was trembling more and more violently, and he did not take his questioning eyes off Rogozhin's face.

'I notice you're trembling, old man,' Rogozhin said at last, 'almost as much as you do when you're having your fits – remember? You had one in Moscow. Or just as you did it once before your fit. Can't think what I'm going to do with you now. ...'

The prince listened, straining every nerve to understand, and still questioning him with his eyes.

'Was it you?' he brought out at last, motioning towards the curtain.

'Yes – me,' whispered Rogozhin, and lowered his eyes.

They were silent for about five minutes.

'For, you see,' Rogozhin suddenly went on, as though he had never stopped speaking, 'if you was to become ill now, have a fit and start screaming, someone might hear you in the street or in the yard and guess that people are spending the night in the flat. They'll start knocking and – come in – because, you see, they all think I'm not at home. I haven't lighted a candle because they might guess from the street or the yard. For, you see, when I'm out I takes the keys with me, and nobody comes in here to tidy up when I'm not here for three or four days. Them's my orders. I mean, to make sure they don't know we're spending the night here. ...'

'Wait,' said the prince. 'I asked the caretaker and your mother's maid this morning whether Nastasya Filippovna hadn't stayed the night here. So they must know, I suppose.'

'I know you asked them. I told the maid that Nastasya Filippovna came here yesterday and went away to Pavlovsk the same evening and that she only stayed ten minutes here. They don't know she stayed the night here – no one knows. I came in with her very quietly last night, just as I did with you. I thought on the way here she'd never come in, but – not a bit of it! She whispered, walked in on tiptoe, gathered up her skirts round her, held them in her hands – not to make a noise – put her finger to her lips at me on the stairs – it was you she was afraid of. She was scared to death on the train, and it was she who suggested staying the night here. I first thought of taking her to her lodgings at the widow's – but Lord, no! "He'll find me there in the morning," she says, "but you'll hide me and to-morrow we'll go off to Moscow by the first train." She wanted to go to Oryol. And when she went to bed, she kept saying we'd go to Oryol.'

'Wait, what are you going to do now, Parfyon? What do you want to do?'

'Well, you see, I'm not sure what to do about you. You're trembling all the time. We'll stay the night here – together. There's no bed except that one there – so I thought we might take the pillows from the two sofas and I'll make up a bed here, near the curtains, for you and me – see? – so that we can be together. For if they comes in and starts looking round or searching, they'll see her at once and take her away. They'll start questioning me, and I'll say it was me what done it, and they'll take me away at once. So let her lie there now beside us, beside you and me. ...'

'Yes, yes!' the prince assented warmly.

'So we won't confess and won't let them take her away.'

'No, not for anything in the world,' the prince decided. 'No, no, no!'

'Aye, so I'd decided not to give her up on no account, lad, and to no one! We'll spend the night quietly here. I left the house for only one hour to-day, in the morning; all the rest of the time I stayed with her. And then I went to fetch you in the evening. The only thing I'm afraid of is that it's so close and that there's going to be a smell. Can you notice a smell or not?'

'Perhaps I can – I don't know. There's sure to be a smell to-morrow morning.'

'I've covered her with American cloth – good American cloth – and a sheet on top of that, and I put four uncorked bottles of Zhdanov disinfectant there. They are there now.'

'Just as they did there – in Moscow?'

'For, you see, old man, it's the smell. And you know the way she is – lying there. ... Have a look in the morning, when it's light. What's the matter? Can't you get up at all?' Rogozhin asked with apprehensive surprise, noticing that the prince was trembling and unable to get up.

'My legs won't move,' murmured the prince. 'It's from fear, I know – when the fear goes I'll get up.'

'Wait till I've made the bed – and then you can lie down – and I'll lie down beside you – and we'll listen – for, you see, lad, I don't know everything yet; I'm telling you this in good time, so you should know about it in good time.'

Muttering these obscure words, Rogozhin began making up the bed. It was clear that he had thought of the bed perhaps even that morning. The night before he had lain down on the sofa. But there was no room for two on the sofa, and he had made up his mind that they should lie side by side, and that was why he now dragged, with a great effort, cushions of all shapes and sizes across the whole room from the two sofas and placed them near the curtain. Somehow or other he managed to make up the bed; he then went up to the prince, took him tenderly and rapturously by the arm, raised him up, and led him to the bed; but it seemed that the prince could walk by himself; so that his 'fear' was passing off; and yet he was still trembling.

'For, you see, old man,' Rogozhin suddenly began, after laying the prince down on the left and best cushion and himself stretching out on the right, without undressing and with his hands clasped behind his head, 'it's hot now and, you know, there's sure to be a smell. ... I'm afraid to open the windows, but Mother has flower-pots with lots of flowers, and they smell so beautifully. I thought of fetching them in, but that old woman of mother's might have guessed something – she's such a nosey-parker.'

'She is that,' the prince agreed.

'We could buy some, of course – put bouquets and flowers all round her, eh? Only, you see, old man, I can't help thinking it'll make us so unhappy to see her covered in flowers!'

'Listen,' said the prince, as though he were all muddled, as though he were trying to think what he was going to ask and forgetting it at once, 'listen, tell me: what did you kill her with? The knife? The same one?'

'Aye, the same.'

'Wait a minute! I want to ask you something else, Parfyon. I shall have to ask you lots of questions about – about everything – but you'd better tell me first – first of all – so that I may know – did you mean to kill her before my wedding, before she entered the church – at the church door, with the knife? Did you or didn't you?'

'I don't know whether I did or didn't,' Rogozhin replied drily, as though a little surprised at the question and not quite understanding it.

'You did not take the knife with you to Pavlovsk, did you?'

'No, I did not. I can tell you this about the knife, old man,' he added after a pause. 'I took it out of a locked drawer this morning – because it all happened in the morning: at about four o'clock. I had kept it in a book all the time – and – and – and there's something else that was funny: you see, the knife only went in three or four inches – just under the left breast – and no more than half a tablespoonful of blood came out on her chemise – not a drop more.'

'That – that – that – –' the prince sat up suddenly in intense agitation, 'that – that I know – I've read about it – it's called internal haemorrhage. ... Sometimes there's not even one drop – if the blow goes straight to the heart. ...'

'Hark, do you hear?' Rogozhin interrupted him suddenly, sitting up in terror on the cushions. 'Do you hear?'

'No!' the prince replied, as quickly and fearfully, looking at Rogozhin.

'Footsteps! You hear? In the drawing-room. ...'

They both began to listen.

'I hear,' the prince whispered firmly.

'Footsteps?'

'Yes.'

'Shall we shut the door or not?'

'Yes, let's.'

They closed the door, and they both lay down again. For a long time neither spoke.

'Oh yes!' the prince suddenly cried in the same rapid and agitated whisper, sitting up on the bed, as though he had again caught hold of a thought and was dreadfully afraid of losing it again. 'I meant to ask you for – for those cards – those cards! I'm told you used to play cards with her. ...'

'I did,' said Rogozhin after a short pause.

'Where are – the cards?'

'Here they are,' said Rogozhin after a still longer pause, 'here. ...'

He pulled out an old pack of cards, wrapped up in a bit of paper, and held it out to the prince. The prince took it, but as though not knowing what to do with it. A new sad and desolate feeling weighed heavily on his heart; he suddenly realized that at that moment, and for some time past, he had been saying not what he had been meaning to say and had been doing what he should not have been doing; and now the cards, which he held in his hands and which he had been so pleased to have, would be of no use – of no use at all now. He got up and threw up his hands in dismay. Rogozhin lay motionless, and did not seem to see or hear his movement; but his eyes glittered brightly in the dark and were wide open and staring fixedly. The prince sat down on a chair and began looking at him with terror. Half an hour passed; suddenly Rogozhin uttered a loud and abrupt scream and began laughing at the top of his voice, as though forgetting that he had to talk in a whisper.

'The officer – that officer – remember how she hit that officer with the crop – remember? Ha, ha, ha! And the subaltern – the subaltern that rushed up too. ...'

The prince jumped up from his chair in new terror. When Rogozhin grew quiet (and he grew quiet suddenly), the prince bent over him gently, sat down beside him, and began looking at him closely with a violently beating heart, breathing heavily. Rogozhin did not turn his head to him, and indeed seemed to have forgotten all about him. The prince looked and waited; time was passing, it began to get light. Now and again Rogozhin began to mutter suddenly, loudly, harshly, and incoherently; he began uttering little screams and laughing; then the prince stretched out his trembling hand and gently touched his head and his hair, stroking them and stroking his cheeks – he could do nothing more! He began trembling again himself, and again his legs suddenly seemed to give way under him. Quite a new sort of sensation was oppressing his heart with infinite anguish. Meanwhile it had grown quite light; at last, he lay down on the cushion, as though in utter exhaustion and despair, and pressed his face against Rogozhin's pale and motionless face; tears flowed from his eyes on Rogozhin's cheeks, but perhaps he no longer noticed his own tears and knew nothing about them. ...

At any rate, when, many hours later, the door was opened and people came in, they found the murderer completely unconscious and in a raging fever. The prince was sitting motionless beside him on the cushions, and every time the sick man burst out screaming or began rambling, he hastened to pass his trembling hand gently over his hair and cheeks, as though caressing and soothing him. But he no longer understood the questions he was asked, and did not recognize the people who had come into the room and surrounded him. And if Schneider himself had come from Switzerland now to have a look at his former pupil and patient, remembering the condition in which the prince had sometimes been during the first year of his treatment in Switzerland, he would have given him up with a despairing wave of a hand and would have said, as he did then: 'An idiot!'

12

CONCLUSION

On her arrival in Pavlovsk, the schoolmaster's widow went straight to see Darya Alexeyevna, who had been greatly upset by the events of the previous day, and telling her all she knew, frightened her out of her wits. The two ladies immediately decided to get in touch with

Lebedev, who was also greatly agitated, as a friend of his lodger and as his landlord. Vera Lebedev told them all she knew. By Lebedev's advice, they decided that all three of them should go to Petersburg in order to avert, as quickly as possible, 'what might quite well happen'. So it was that about eleven o'clock next morning Rogozhin's flat was opened in the presence of the police, Lebedev, the ladies, and Semyon Rogozhin, who lived in a wing of the house. The successful result of the search was largely due to the evidence of the caretaker, who declared that he had seen Rogozhin on the previous evening going in at the front door with a friend in what looked like a very surreptitious manner. After this the police did not hesitate to break down the door, there being no answer to their repeated ringing.

Rogozhin survived the two months of inflammation of the brain, and when he recovered – his judicial examination and his trial. He gave straightforward, exact, and entirely satisfactory evidence on every point, as a result of which the case against the prince was quashed at the very outset. During his trial Rogozhin did not attempt to speak. He did not contradict his eloquent and clever counsel, who proved clearly and logically that the crime was a result of the brain fever, which had set in long before the crime was committed, as a consequence of the great distress of the accused. He added nothing on his own account to confirm that opinion and, as during the police investigation, clearly and concisely admitted and recalled all the minutest details of the crime. He was sentenced, in view of the extenuating circumstances, to fifteen years' hard labour in Siberia, and heard his sentence grimly, silently, and 'dreamily'. His vast fortune, with the exception of a comparatively speaking small portion of it, squandered during the first few months of debauchery, went to his brother Semyon, to the latter's great satisfaction. Rogozhin's old mother is still living, and seems at times to remember her favourite son Parfyon, but not very clearly: God spared her mind and heart from the realization of the terrible calamity that had befallen her sorrow-stricken house.

Lebedev, Keller, Ganya, Ptitsyn, and the many other characters of our story are carrying on as before, have changed little, and we have almost nothing to tell about them. Ippolit died in a state of terrible agitation, and a little earlier than he had expected, a fortnight after Nastasya Filippovna's death. Kolya was greatly shocked by what had happened; and he grew more deeply attached to his mother than ever. Mrs Ivolgin is worried about his being too thoughtful for his years; he will very likely grow up into a very practical man of affairs. Incidentally, it was partly due to his efforts that the future of the prince was satisfactorily arranged: he had long before picked out, among all the people he had known of late, Mr Radomsky as a highly reliable person; he was the first to go to him and acquaint him with all the details he knew of the recent events and of the present condition of the prince. He was not mistaken: Radomsky took a most warm interest in the fate of the unhappy 'idiot' and, as a result of his efforts and solicitude, the prince again found himself in Schneider's Swiss clinic. Radomsky, who had gone abroad with the intention of spending a long time in Europe and openly refers to himself as 'an utterly superfluous man in Russia', visits his sick friend at Schneider's clinic quite often – at least once every few months; but Schneider frowns and shakes his head; he hints at a complete breakdown of his patient's mental faculties; he does not say definitely that his patient's illness is incurable, but he does go so far as to suggest the most unhappy possibilities. Radomsky takes it very much to heart – and he has a heart, which he has amply proved by receiving letters from Kolya, and even answering them occasionally. But, besides this, another curious trait of his character has come to light and, as it is a good trait, we hasten to mention it: after every visit to Schneider's clinic, Radomsky, in addition to writing to Kolya, sends another letter to someone in Petersburg in which he gives the fullest and most sympathetic particulars of the prince's condition at that moment. Besides the most respectful expression of devotion, those letters sometimes (and more and more frequently) contain a number of outspoken statements of his views, conceptions and feelings – in short, something that is beginning to look like an expression of friendly and intimate feelings. This person who is in correspondence with him (though their letters are not particularly frequent), and who has won so much attention and respect from him, is Vera Lebedev. We have never been able to find out exactly how such a relationship could have arisen between them; it arose, of course, as a result of the misfortune that had overtaken the prince, when Vera Lebedev was so grief-stricken that she fell ill; but we do not know how they actually became acquainted and grew to be friends. We have mentioned these letters chiefly because some of them contained news of the Yepanchins, and particularly of Aglaya Yepanchin. Radomsky wrote of her, in a rather cryptic letter from Paris, that, after a brief and extraordinary attachment to an *émigré* Polish Count, she had suddenly married him against the wishes of her parents, who had only given their consent at last because the affair might have ended in a terrible scandal. Then, after almost six months' silence, Radomsky informed his correspondent, again in a long and most circumstantial letter, that during his last visit to Schneider's clinic he had met there the whole Yepanchin family (except, of course, General Yepanchin, whose business affairs kept him in Petersburg) and Prince Sh. It was a strange reunion; they all greeted Radomsky with a sort of rapturous delight; Adelaida and Alexandra even expressed their gratitude to him for his 'angelic solicitude for the unhappy prince'. Mrs Yepanchin wept bitterly when she saw the prince in his sick and humiliating condition. Evidently all was forgiven him. Prince Sh. delivered himself of a few happy and intelligent truisms. Radomsky could not help feeling that he and Adelaida had not yet become intimate friends; but it seemed inevitable that in future Adelaida's impulsive nature would submit voluntarily and whole-heartedly to Prince Sh.'s intellect and experience. Besides, the lessons learnt by her family, and particularly Aglaya's affair with the *émigré* count, had made a deep impression on her. Everything the family had dreaded in giving Aglaya to this count, had come to pass within six months, with the addition of such surprising developments as they had never dreamed of. It turned out that the count was not a count at all, and if he really were an *émigré*, it was because of some dark and dubious affair in the past. He had fascinated Aglaya by the extraordinary nobility of his soul, lacerated by his sufferings for his native land, and he fascinated her so much that even before she married him she became a member of some committee abroad for the restoration of Poland, and, furthermore, had found herself in a Catholic confessional of some famous priest, who gained an ascendancy over her mind to quite a fanatical degree. The vast fortune of the count, of which he had given Mrs Yepanchin and Prince Sh. almost incontrovertible evidence, proved to be non-existent. Moreover, within six months of the wedding, the count and his friend, the famous priest, had managed to engineer a violent quarrel between Aglaya and her family, so that they had not seen her for some months. ... In short, there was a great deal to talk about, but Mrs Yepanchin, her daughters, and even Prince Sh. had been so shocked by all this 'terror' that they were afraid even to mention certain things in their conversations with Radomsky, though they knew very well that he was perfectly aware of Aglaya's latest obsessions. Poor Mrs Yepanchin was longing to be back in Russia and, according to Radomsky, she criticized everything she saw abroad bitterly and quite unfairly: 'They don't know how to bake decent bread anywhere and they freeze in their cellars like mice in winter,' she said. 'At least,' she added, pointing agitatedly to the prince, who had not shown the least sign of recognizing her – 'at least I have had a good Russian cry over this poor fellow. We've had enough of being carried away by our enthusiasms. It's high time we grew sensible. And all this, all this life abroad, and all this Europe of yours is just a delusion, and all of us abroad are a delusion. Mark my words, you'll see it for yourself!' she concluded almost angrily as she took leave of Radomsky.

BY THE SAME AUTHOR

Crime and Punishment

When Dostoyevsky began, in 1865, to write the novel that was to bring him international recognition he was as embarrassed with debts as the hero he created. Raskolnikov, an impoverished student, decides to murder a stupid and grasping old woman for gain. After the murder he is unable to tolerate his growing sense of guilt. This universal theme is one which had preoccupied the author during his own imprisonment in Siberia.

The Brothers Karamazov

Dostoyevsky completed *The Brothers Karamazov*, the culmination of his work, in 1880 shortly before his death. This profound story of parricide and fraternal jealousy involves the questions of anarchism, atheism and the existence of God.

The Devils

This political drama, the most controversial of his masterpieces, has been both hailed as a grim prophecy of the Russian Revolution and denounced as the work of a reactionary. It is a penetrating commentary on men and affairs as well as a work of tragic intensity in which the recesses of the mind and the dark passions of men are probed.

Also published

THE GAMBLER; BOBOK; A NASTY STORY
THE HOUSE OF THE DEAD
NETOCHKA NEZVANOVA
NOTES FROM UNDERGROUND and THE DOUBLE